Disney · PIXAR

COCO

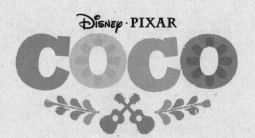

ALSO FROM JOE BOOKS

Disney • Pixar Comics Treasury

Disney • Pixar Inside Out Cinestory Comic

Disney Big Hero 6 Cinestory Comic

Disney Gravity Falls Cinestory Comic Volume One

Disney Gravity Falls Cinestory Comic Volume Two

Disney Gravity Falls Cinestory Comic Volume Three

Disney • Pixar The Good Dinosaur Cinestory Comic

Disney • Pixar Finding Nemo Cinestory Comic

Disney • Pixar Finding Dory Cinestory Comic

Disney • Pixar Cars Comics Treasury

Disney • Pixar Cars Cinestory Comic

Disney • Pixar Cars 3 Cinestory Comic

DISNEY · PIXAR

CINESTORY COMIC

JOE BOOKS LTD

Disney • Pixar Coco Cinestory Comic
Copyright © 2017 Disney Enterprises, Inc. and Pixar.
All rights reserved.

Published simultaneously in the United States and Canada by Joe Books Ltd,
489 College Street, Suite 203, Toronto, ON M6G 1A5.

www.joebooks.com

First Joe Books edition: November 2017

ISBN: 978-1-77275-491-9

Design: Sayre Street Books

Library and Archives Canada Cataloguing in Publication
information is available upon request.

For information regarding the CPSIA on this printed material,
call: (203) 595-3636 and provide reference #RICH 767319.

1 3 5 7 9 10 8 6 4 2

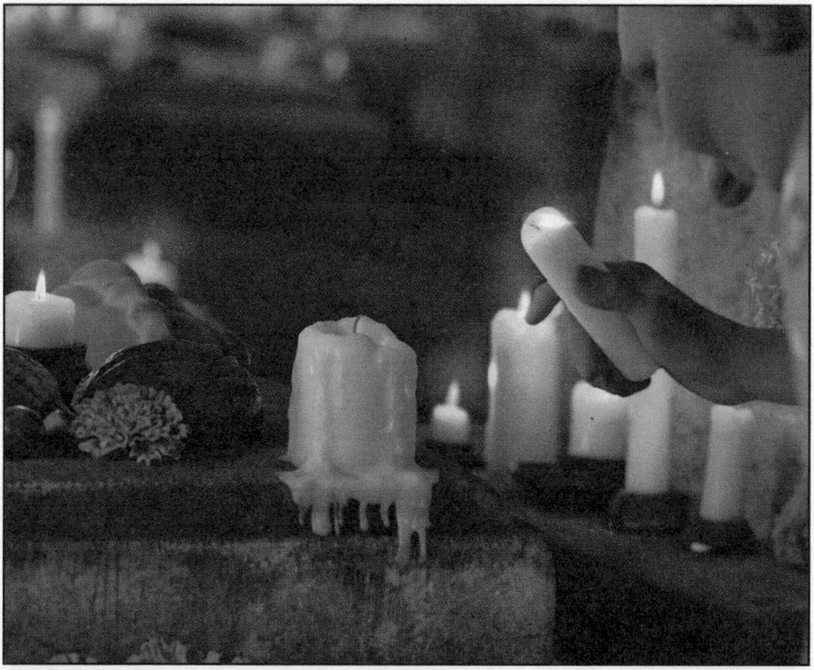

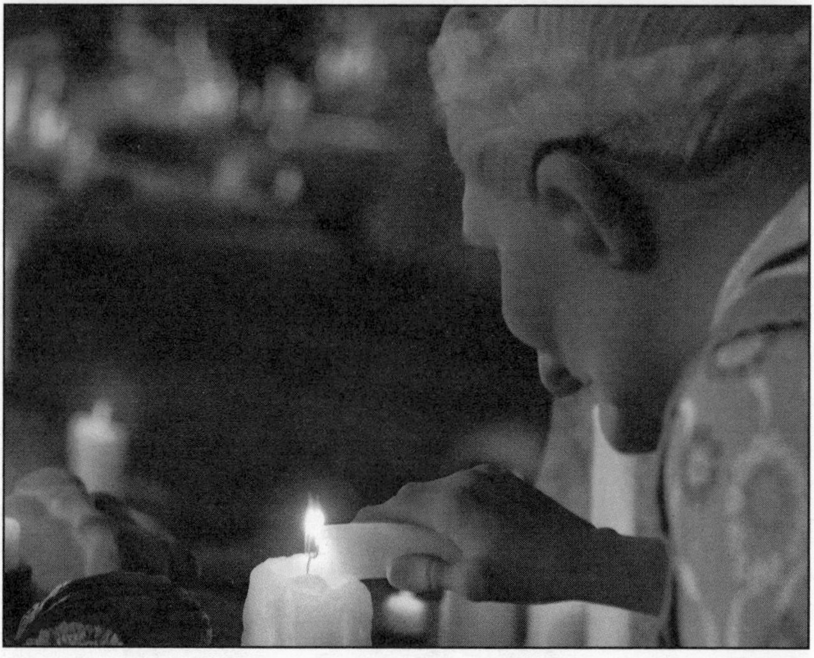

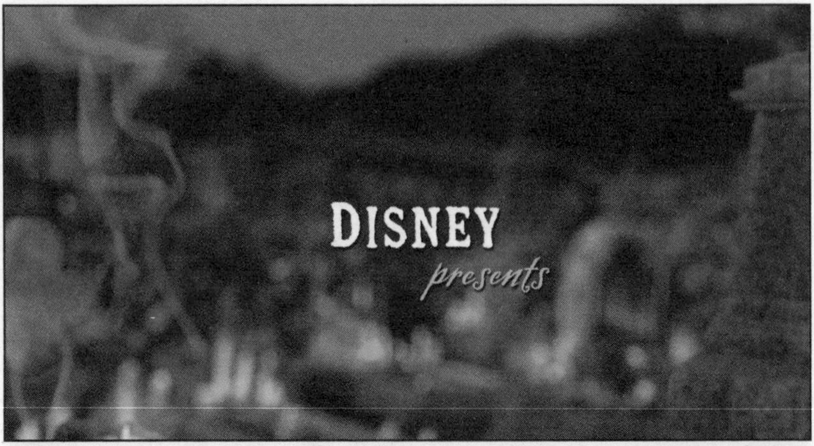
DISNEY
presents

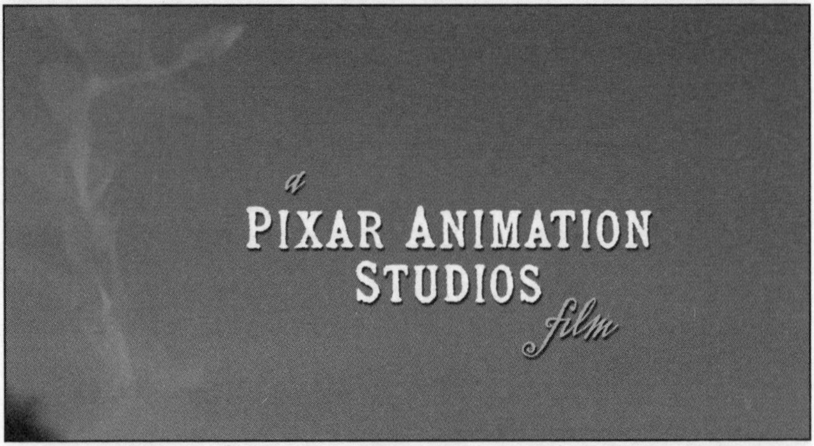
a
PIXAR ANIMATION
STUDIOS
film

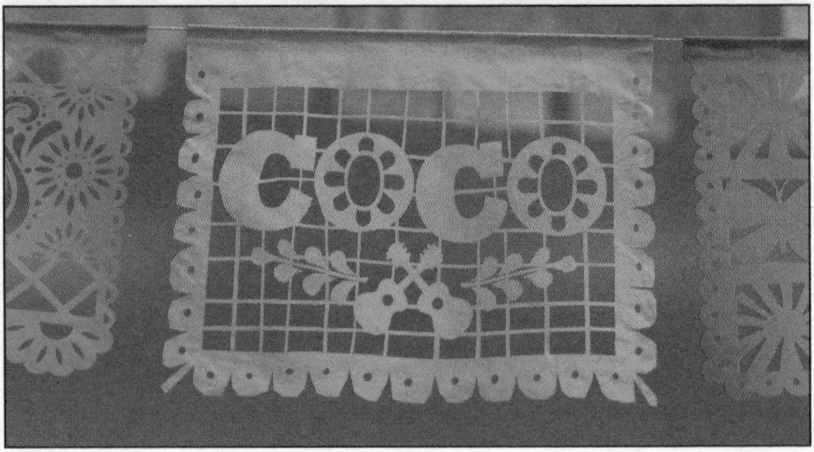
COCO

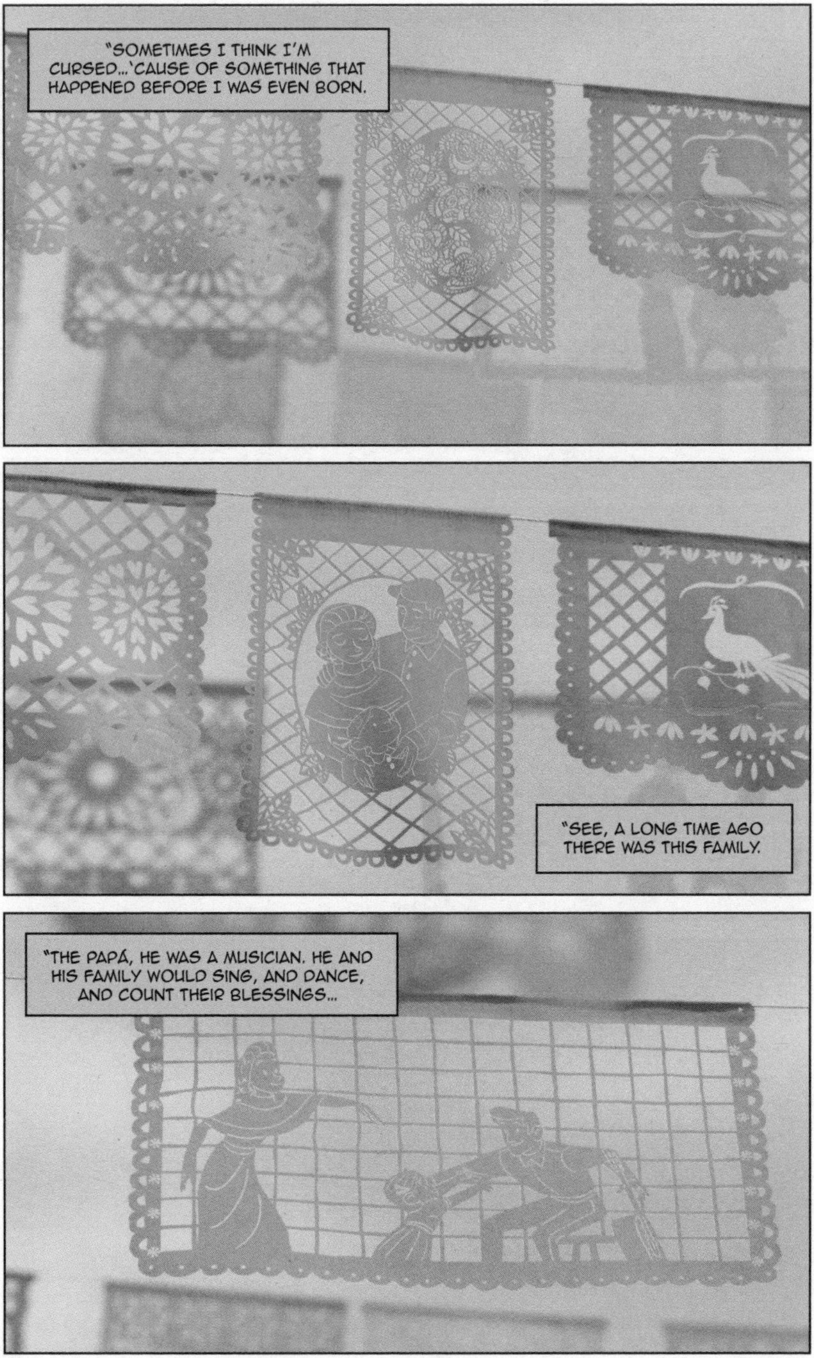
"SOMETIMES I THINK I'M CURSED...'CAUSE OF SOMETHING THAT HAPPENED BEFORE I WAS EVEN BORN.
"SEE, A LONG TIME AGO THERE WAS THIS FAMILY.
"THE PAPÁ, HE WAS A MUSICIAN. HE AND HIS FAMILY WOULD SING, AND DANCE, AND COUNT THEIR BLESSINGS...

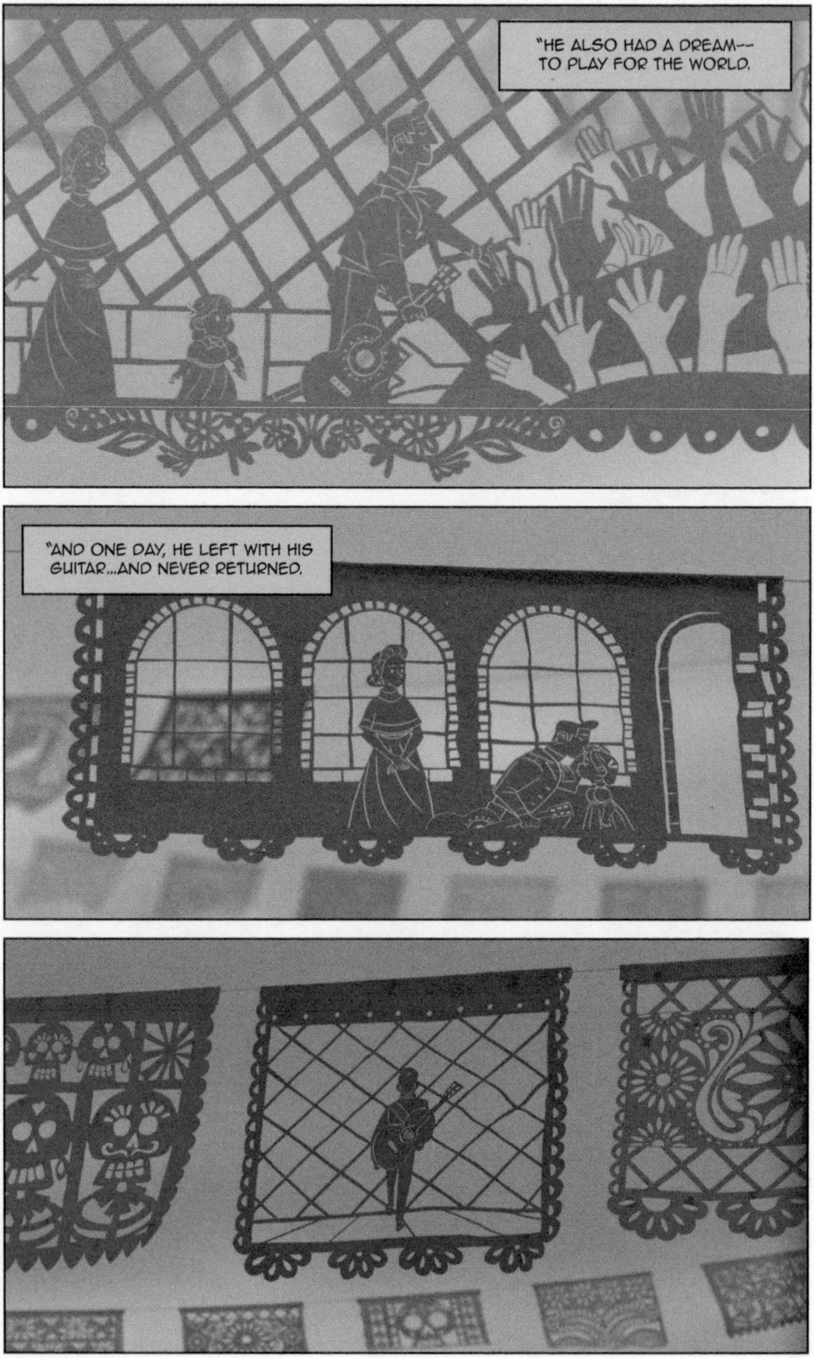
"HE ALSO HAD A DREAM--
TO PLAY FOR THE WORLD.
"AND ONE DAY, HE LEFT WITH HIS
GUITAR...AND NEVER RETURNED.

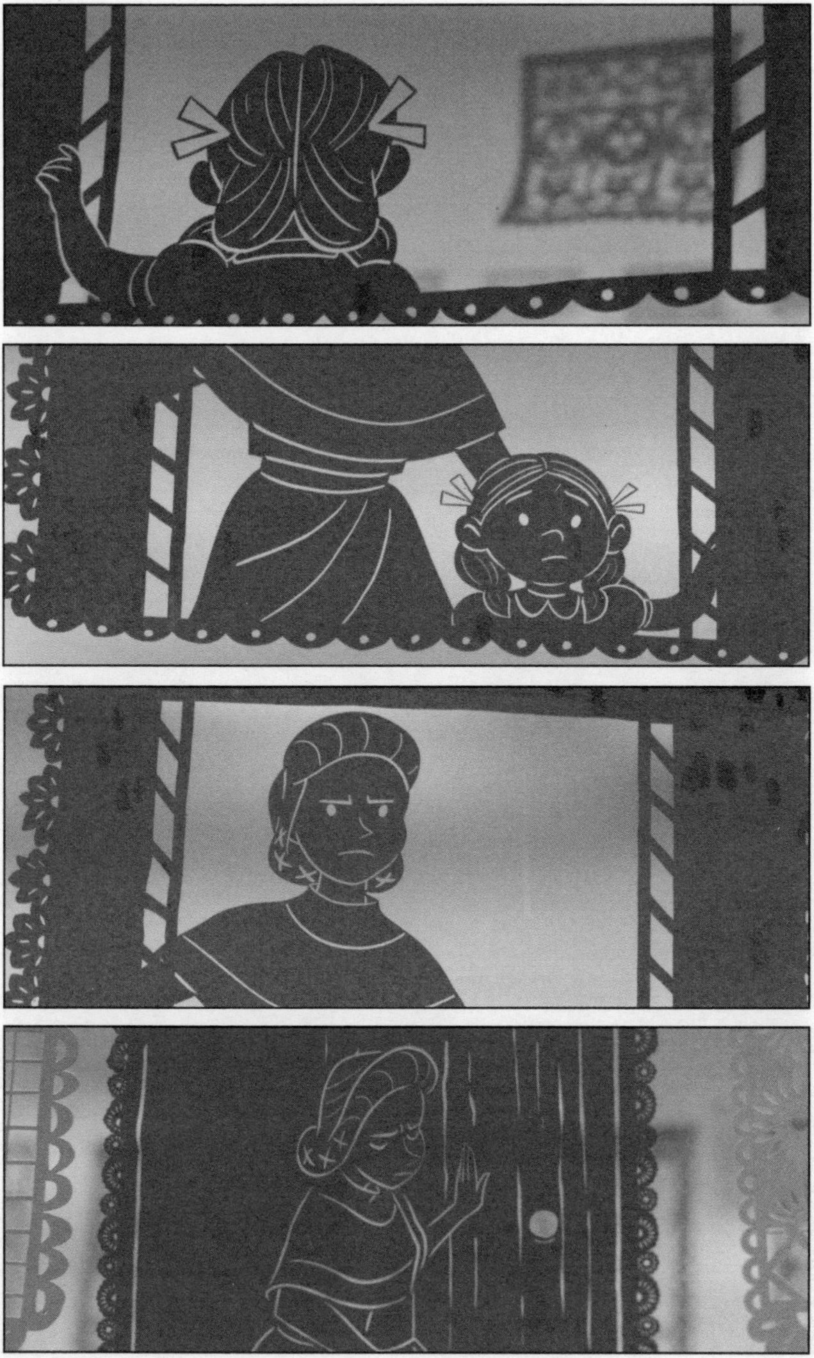

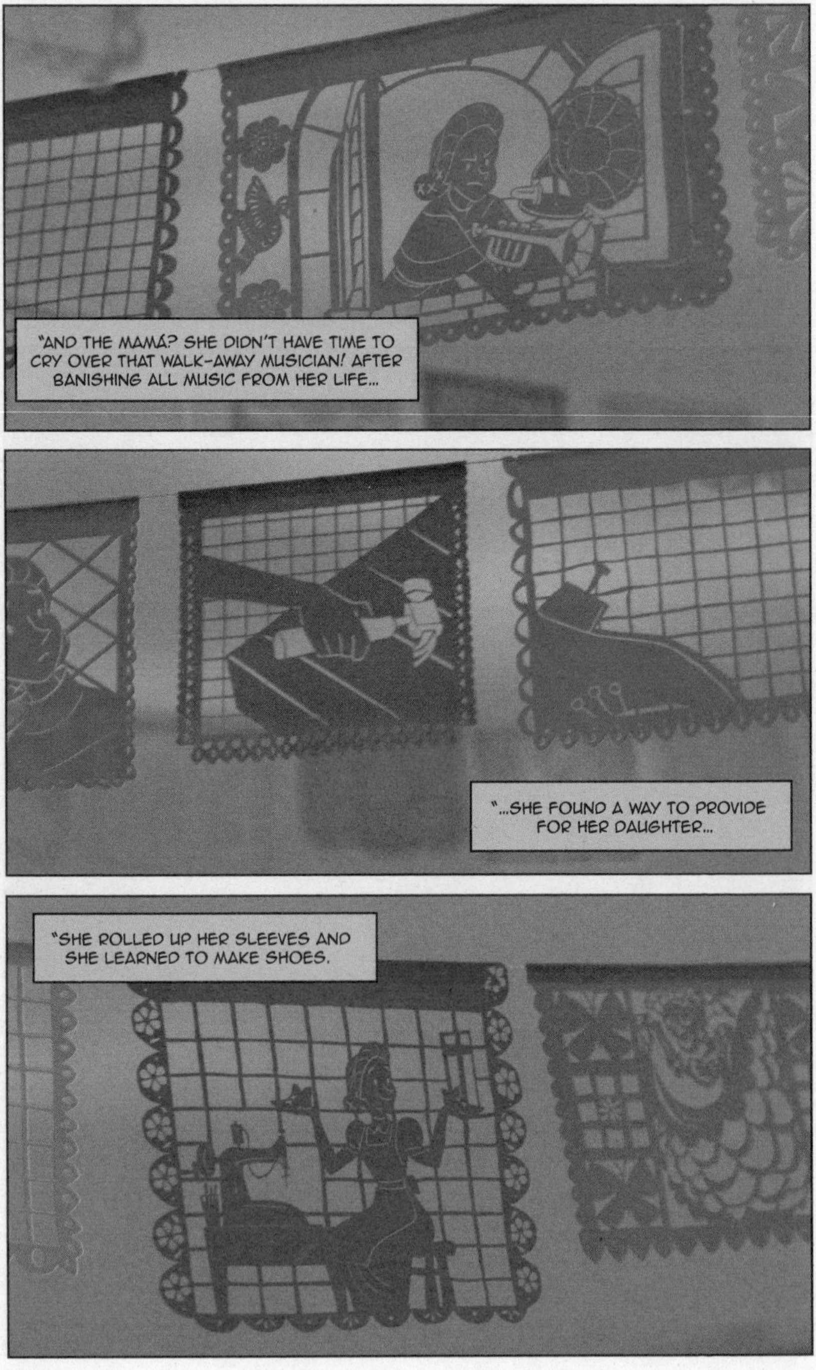
"AND THE MAMÁ? SHE DIDN'T HAVE TIME TO CRY OVER THAT WALK-AWAY MUSICIAN! AFTER BANISHING ALL MUSIC FROM HER LIFE...
"...SHE FOUND A WAY TO PROVIDE FOR HER DAUGHTER...
"SHE ROLLED UP HER SLEEVES AND SHE LEARNED TO MAKE SHOES.

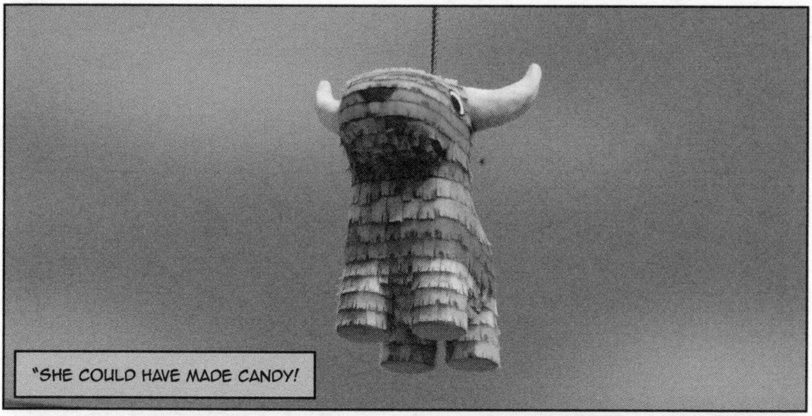
"SHE COULD HAVE MADE CANDY!

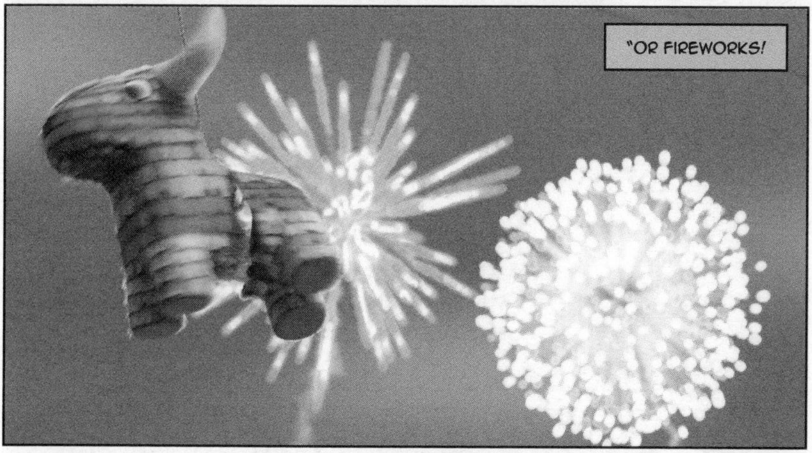
"OR FIREWORKS!

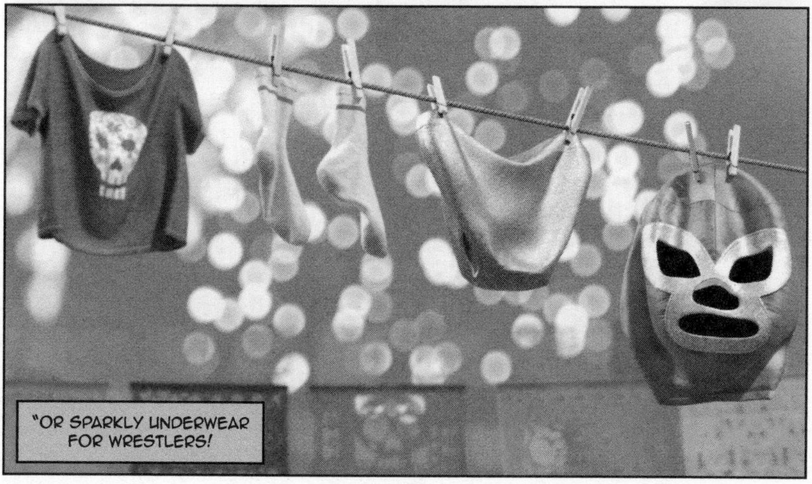
"OR SPARKLY UNDERWEAR
FOR WRESTLERS!

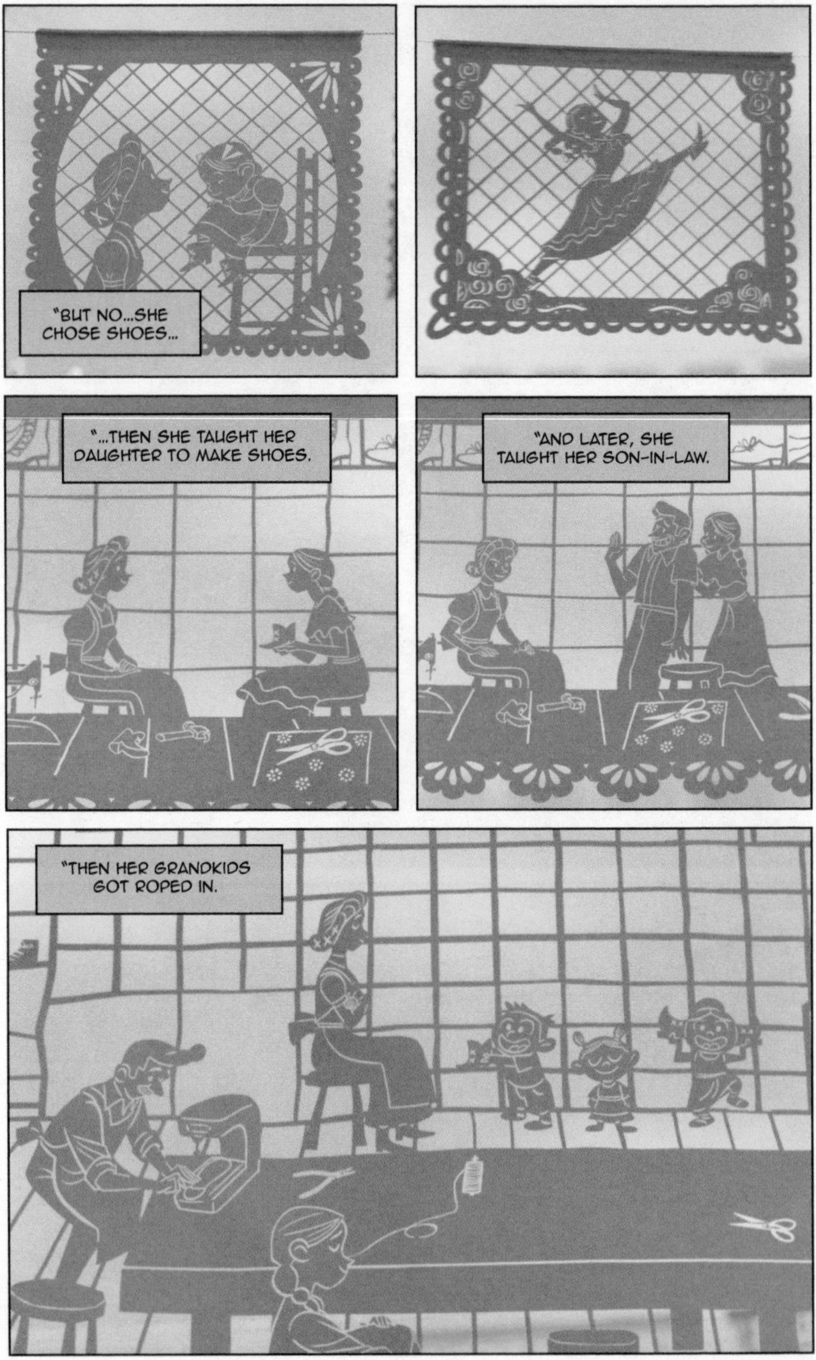
"BUT NO...SHE CHOSE SHOES...
"...THEN SHE TAUGHT HER DAUGHTER TO MAKE SHOES.
"AND LATER, SHE TAUGHT HER SON-IN-LAW.
"THEN HER GRANDKIDS GOT ROPED IN.

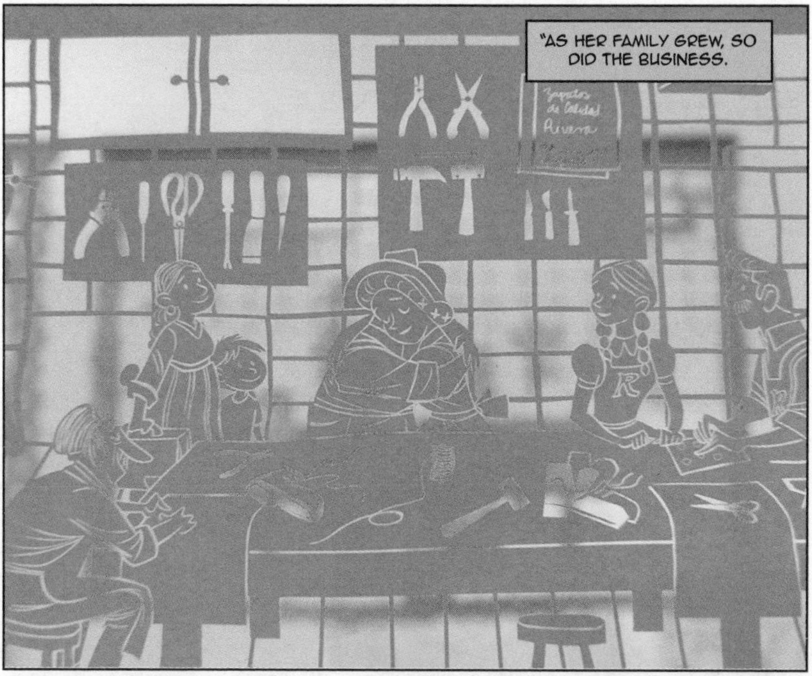
"AS HER FAMILY GREW, SO DID THE BUSINESS.
Zapatos de Calidad Rivera

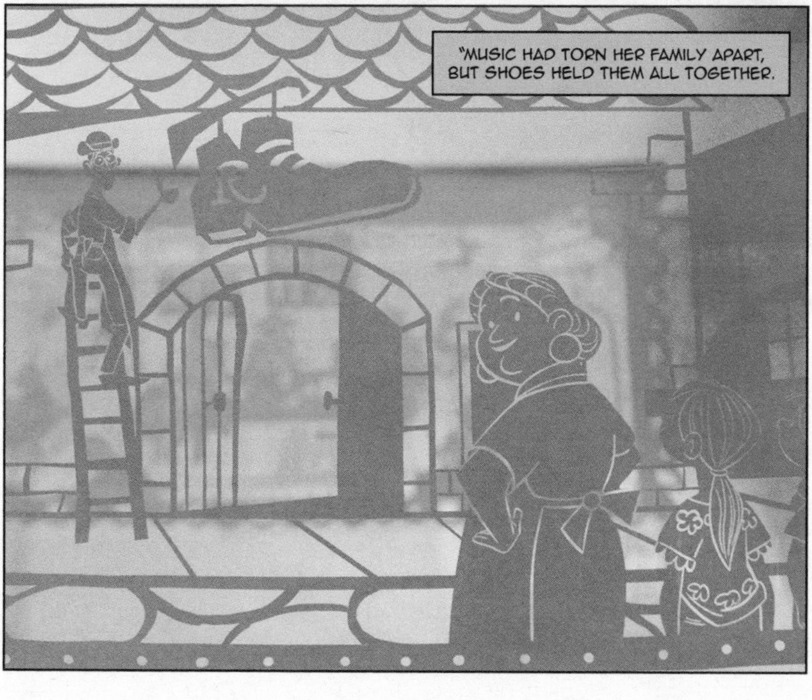
"MUSIC HAD TORN HER FAMILY APART, BUT SHOES HELD THEM ALL TOGETHER.

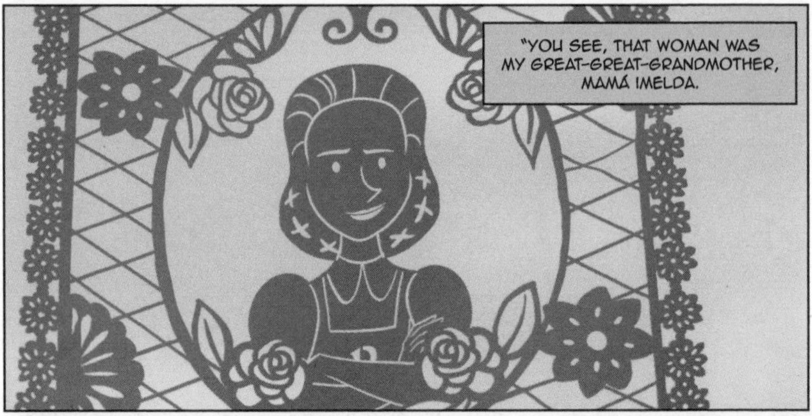
"YOU SEE, THAT WOMAN WAS MY GREAT-GREAT-GRANDMOTHER, MAMÁ IMELDA.

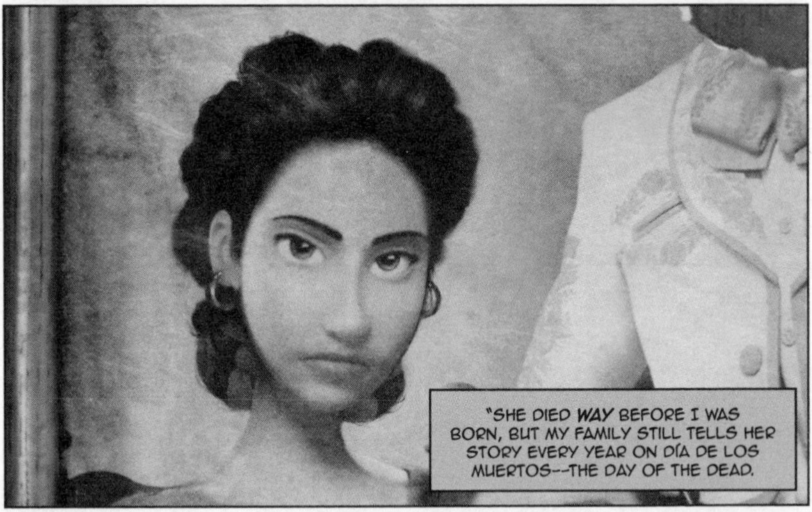
"SHE DIED *WAY* BEFORE I WAS BORN, BUT MY FAMILY STILL TELLS HER STORY EVERY YEAR ON DÍA DE LOS MUERTOS--THE DAY OF THE DEAD.

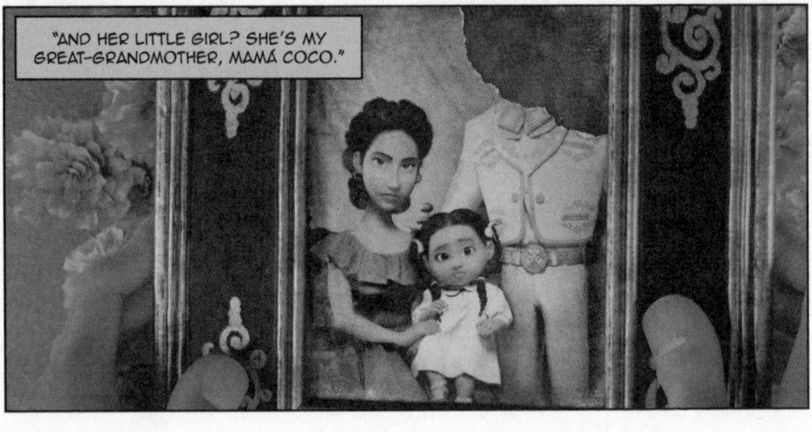
"AND HER LITTLE GIRL? SHE'S MY GREAT-GRANDMOTHER, MAMÁ COCO."

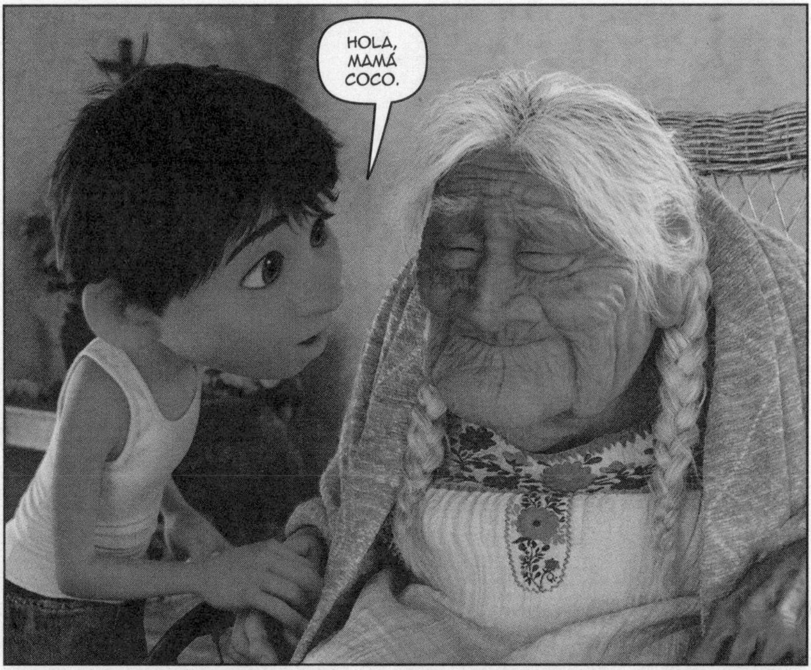
HOLA, MAMÁ COCO.

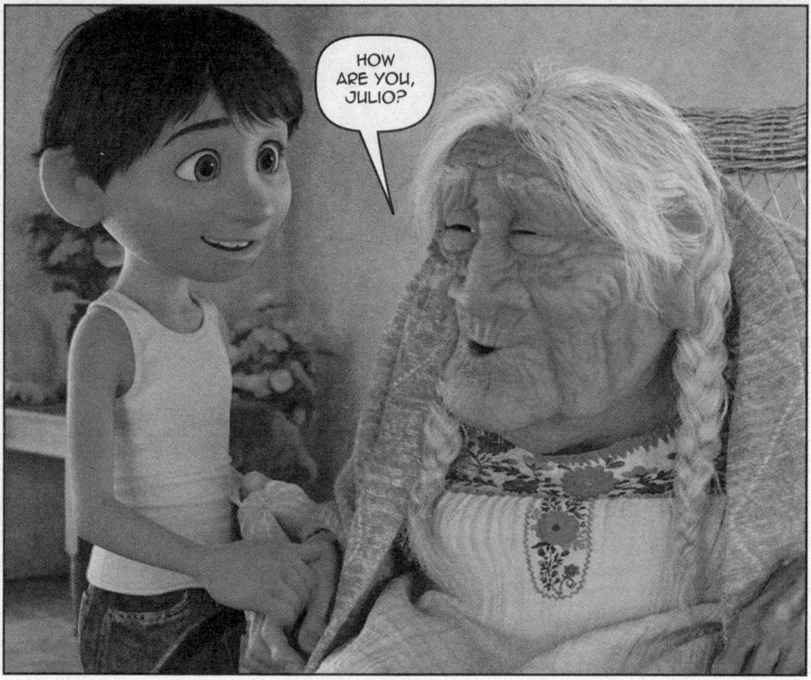
HOW ARE YOU, JULIO?

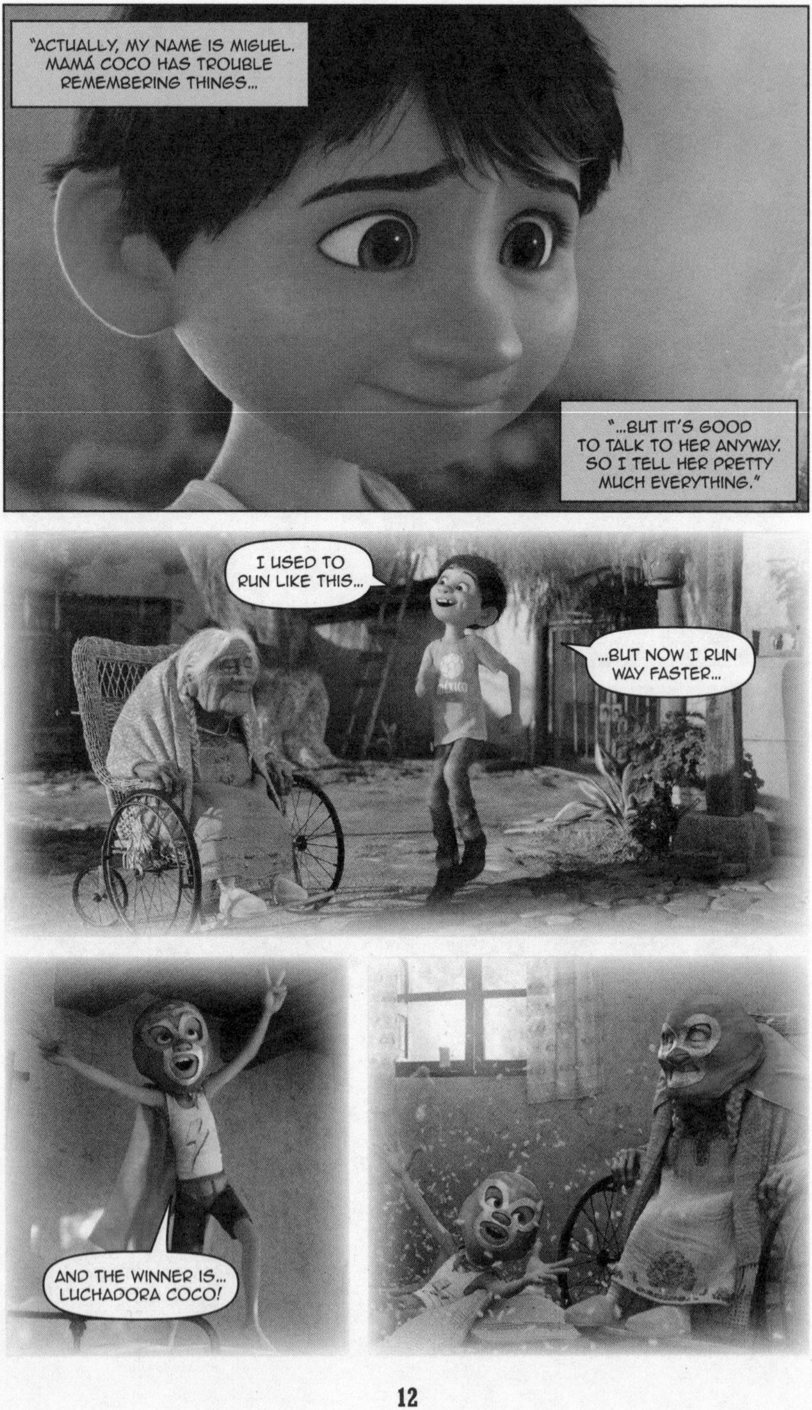
"ACTUALLY, MY NAME IS MIGUEL. MAMÁ COCO HAS TROUBLE REMEMBERING THINGS...
"...BUT IT'S GOOD TO TALK TO HER ANYWAY. SO I TELL HER PRETTY MUCH EVERYTHING."
I USED TO RUN LIKE THIS...
...BUT NOW I RUN WAY FASTER...
AND THE WINNER IS... LUCHADORA COCO!

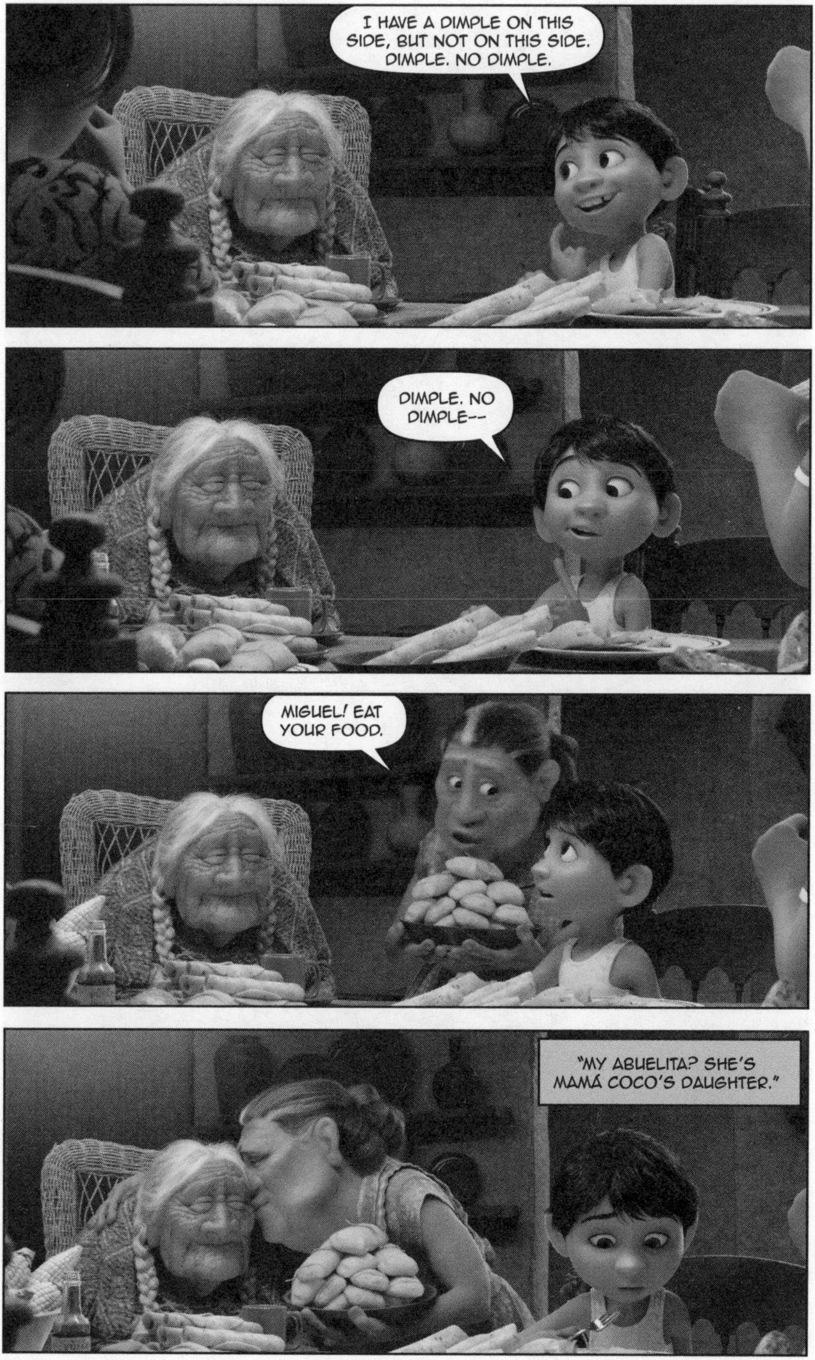
I HAVE A DIMPLE ON THIS SIDE, BUT NOT ON THIS SIDE. DIMPLE. NO DIMPLE.
DIMPLE. NO DIMPLE--
MIGUEL! EAT YOUR FOOD.
"MY ABUELITA? SHE'S MAMÁ COCO'S DAUGHTER."

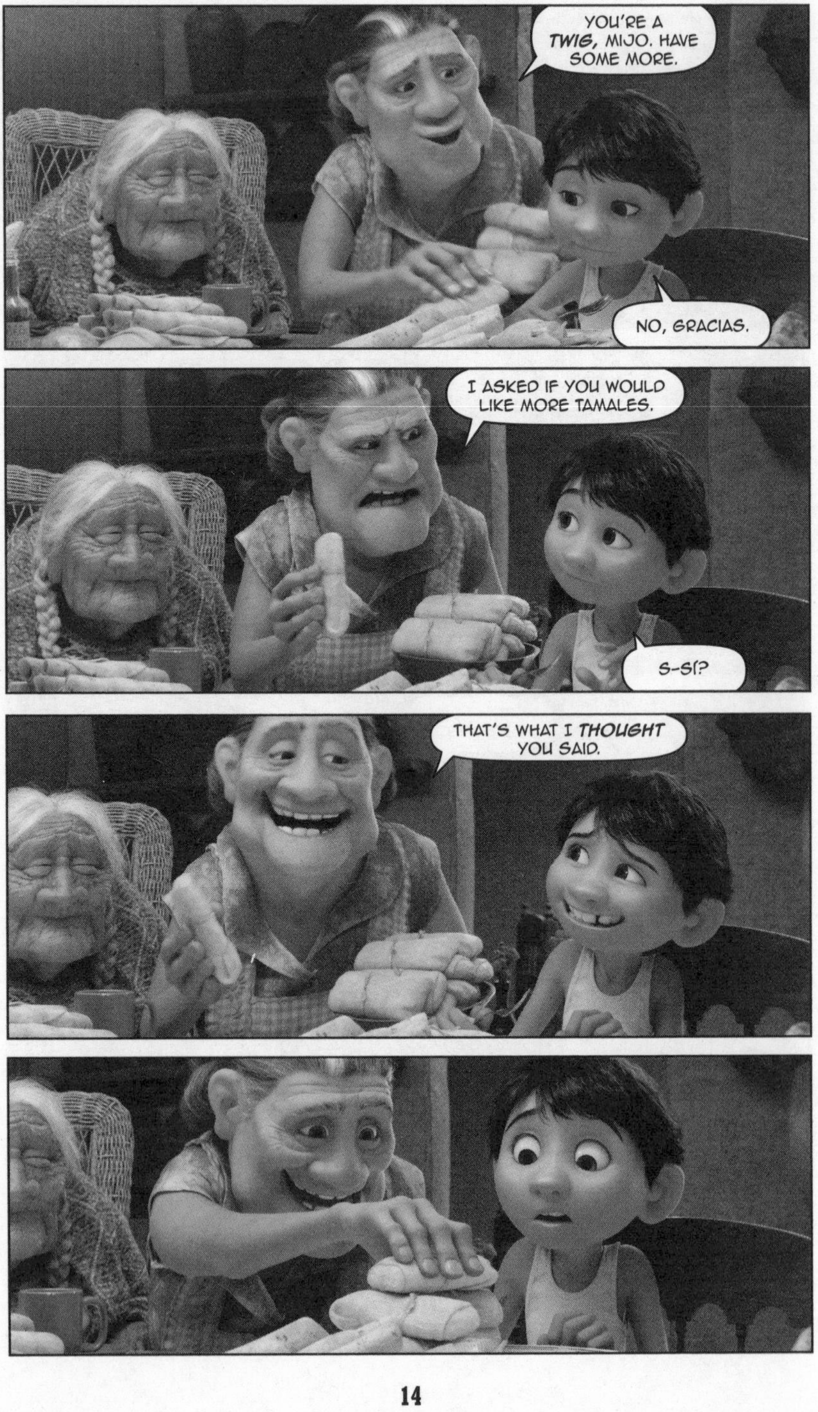
YOU'RE A *TWIG,* MIJO. HAVE SOME MORE.
NO, GRACIAS.
I ASKED IF YOU WOULD LIKE MORE TAMALES.
S-SÍ?
THAT'S WHAT I *THOUGHT* YOU SAID.

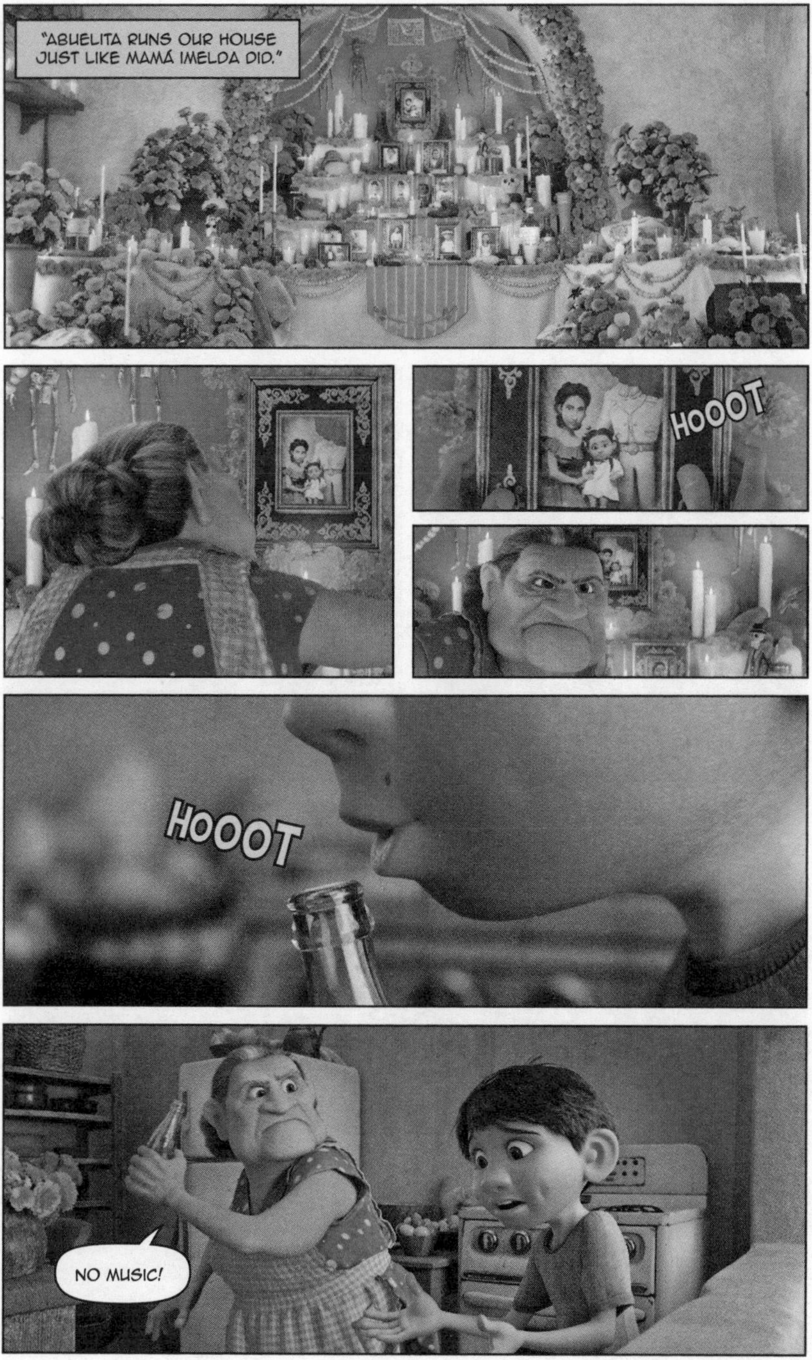
"ABUELITA RUNS OUR HOUSE JUST LIKE MAMÁ IMELDA DID."
HOOOT
HOOOT
NO MUSIC!

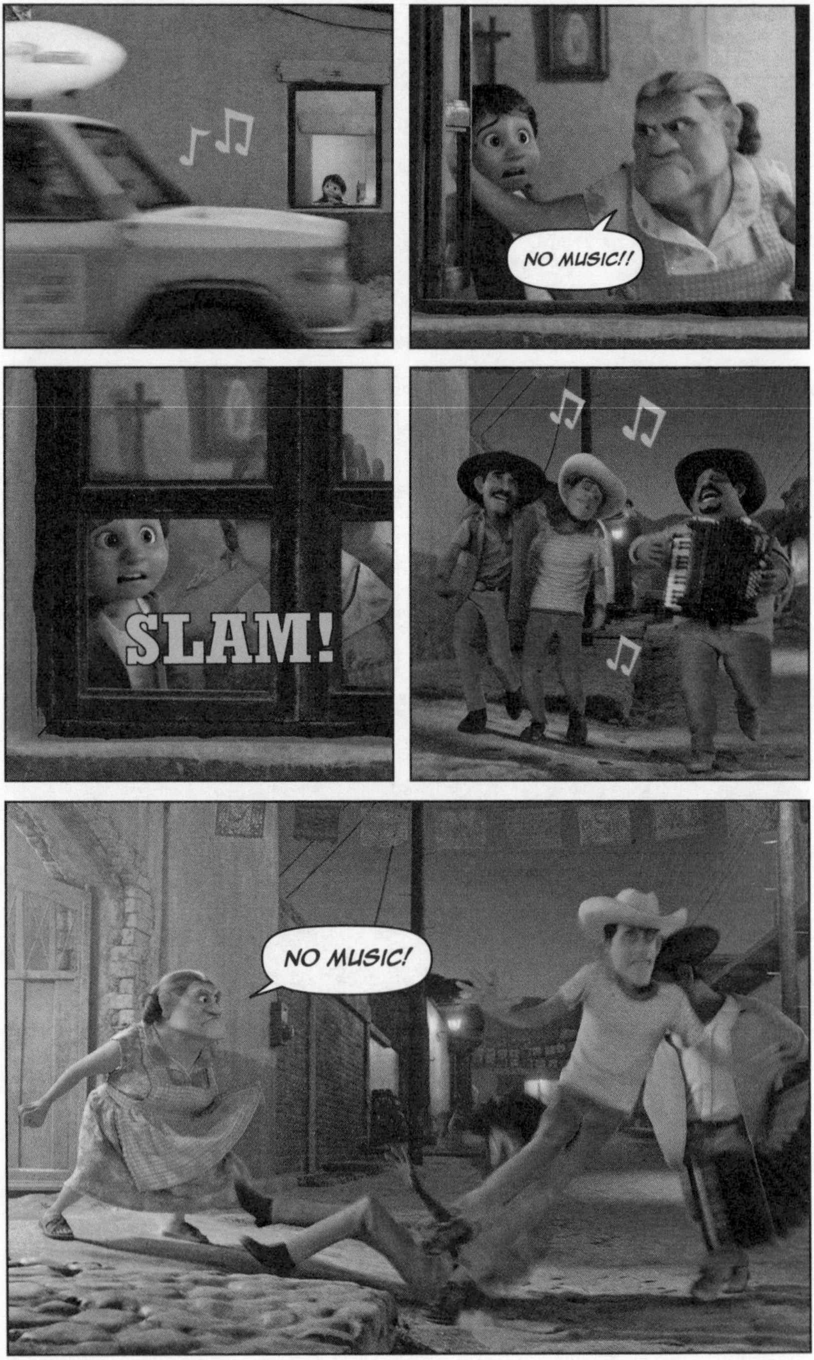
NO MUSIC!!
SLAM!
NO MUSIC!

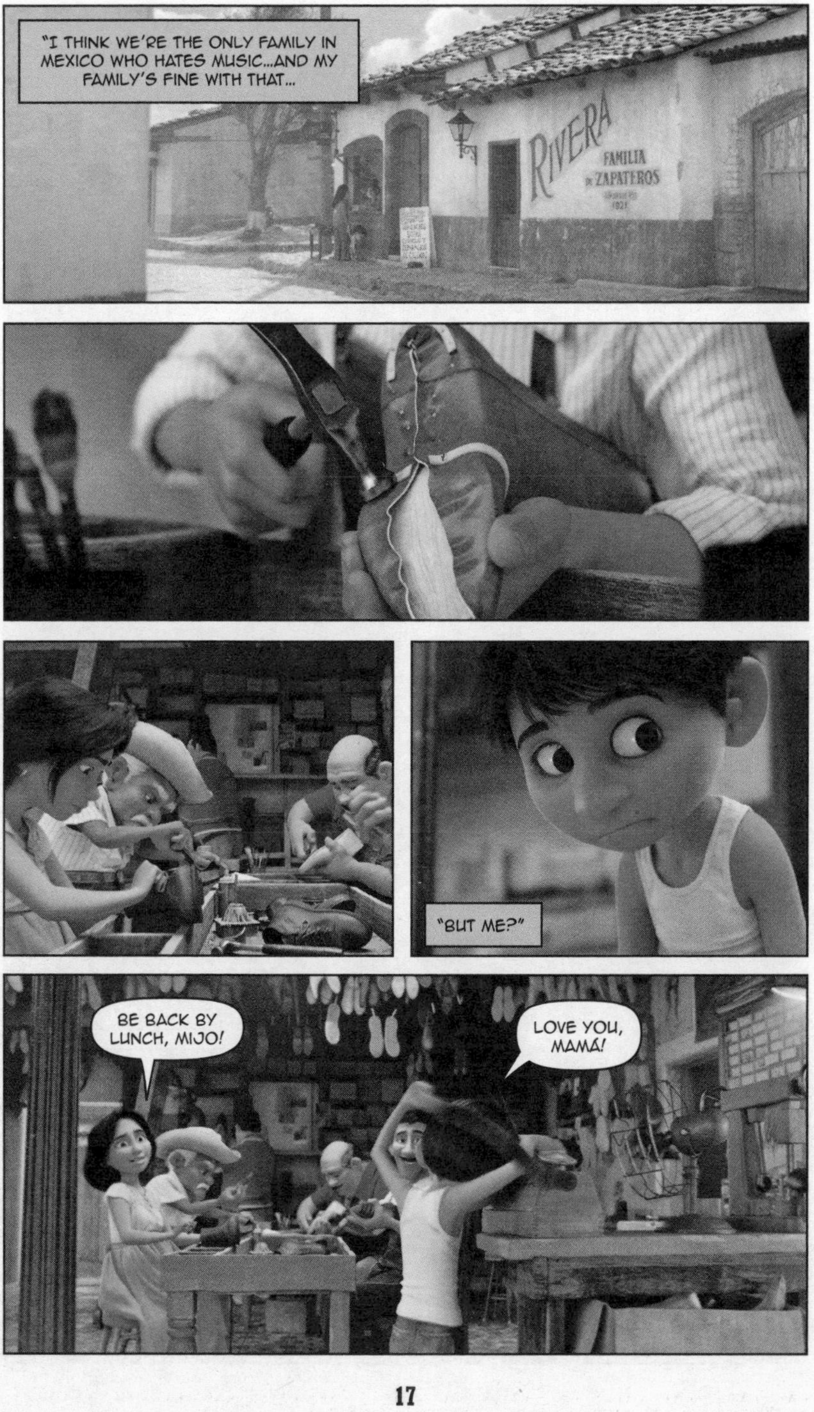
"I THINK WE'RE THE ONLY FAMILY IN MEXICO WHO HATES MUSIC...AND MY FAMILY'S FINE WITH THAT...
RIVERA
FAMILIA
DE ZAPATEROS
"BUT ME?"
BE BACK BY LUNCH, MIJO!
LOVE YOU, MAMÁ!

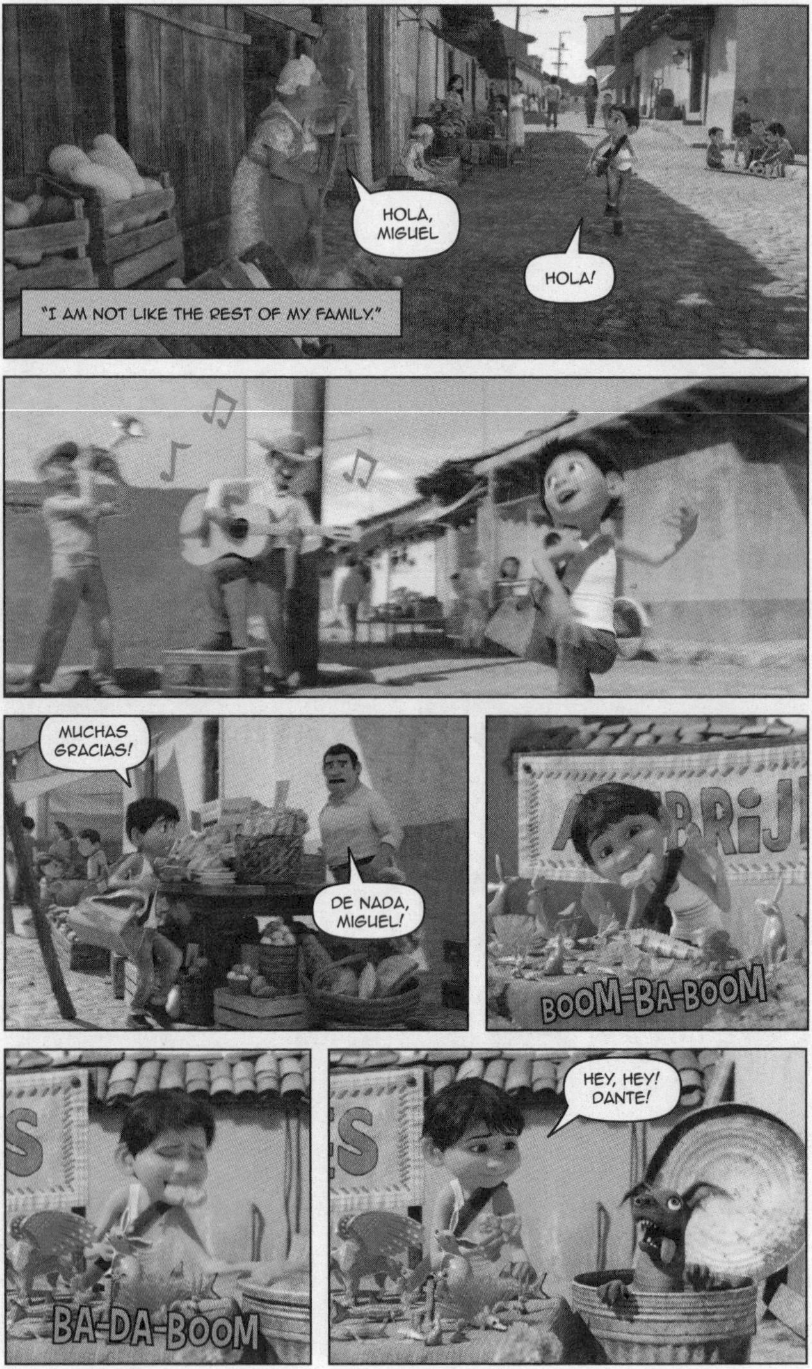
HOLA, MIGUEL
HOLA!
"I AM NOT LIKE THE REST OF MY FAMILY."
MUCHAS GRACIAS!
DE NADA, MIGUEL!
BOOM-BA-BOOM
BA-DA-BOOM
HEY, HEY! DANTE!

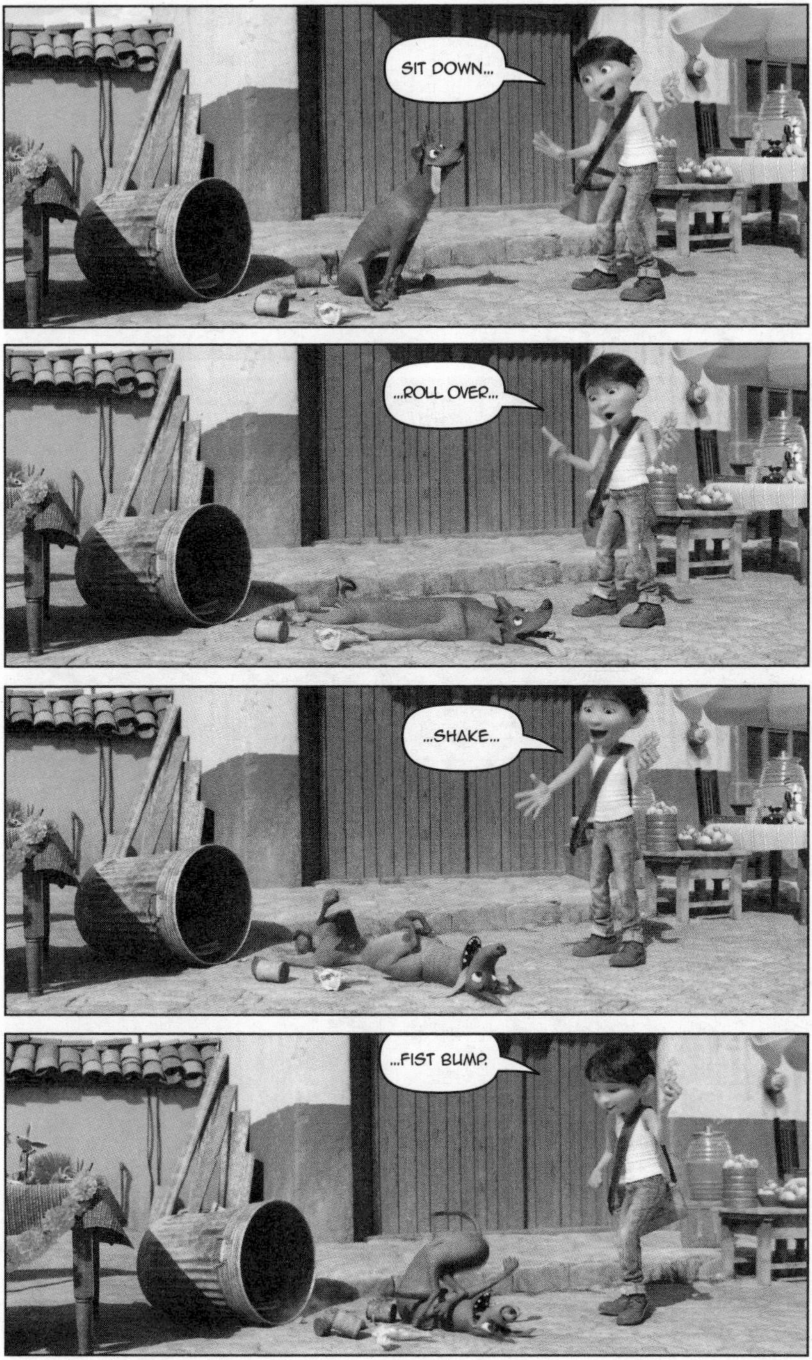
SIT DOWN...
...ROLL OVER...
...SHAKE...
...FIST BUMP.

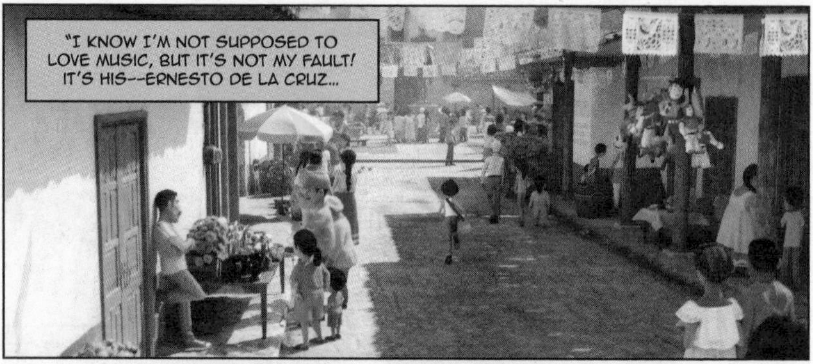
"I KNOW I'M NOT SUPPOSED TO LOVE MUSIC, BUT IT'S NOT MY FAULT! IT'S HIS--ERNESTO DE LA CRUZ...

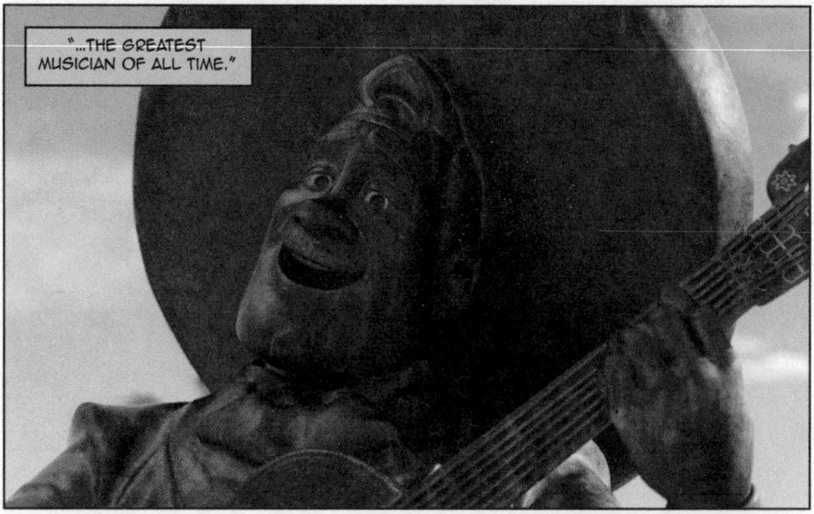
"...THE GREATEST MUSICIAN OF ALL TIME."

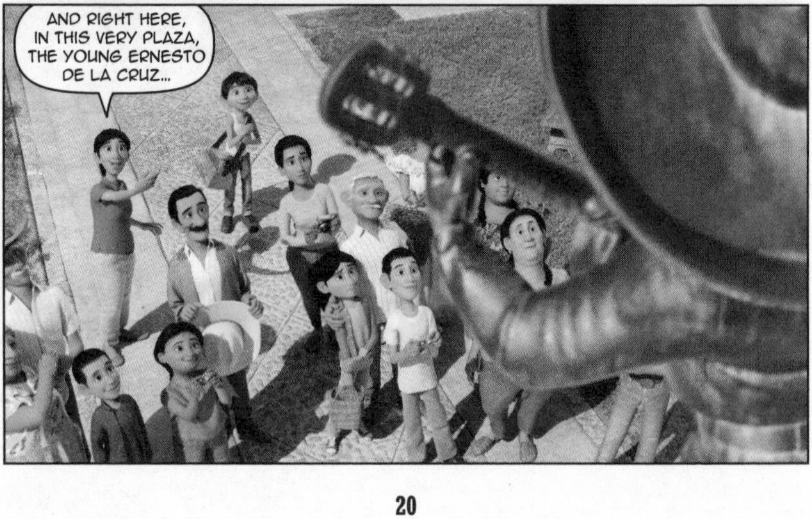
AND RIGHT HERE, IN THIS VERY PLAZA, THE YOUNG ERNESTO DE LA CRUZ...

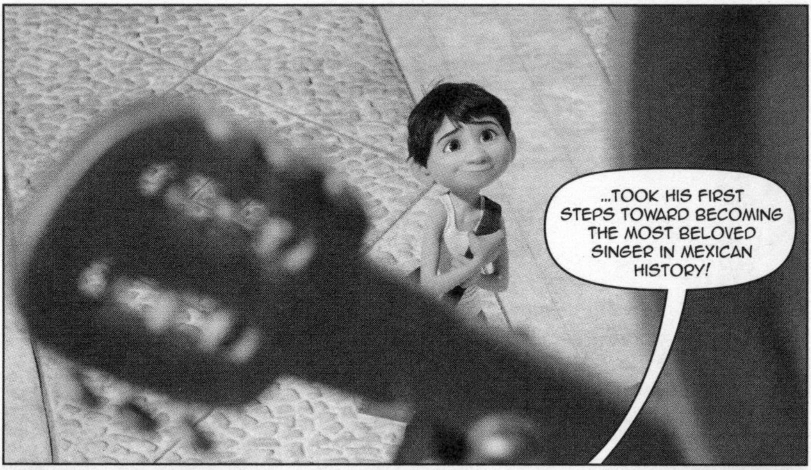
...TOOK HIS FIRST STEPS TOWARD BECOMING THE MOST BELOVED SINGER IN MEXICAN HISTORY!

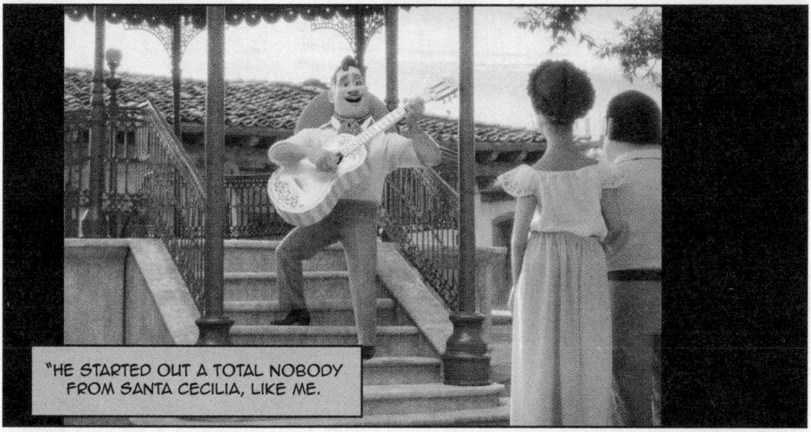
"HE STARTED OUT A TOTAL NOBODY FROM SANTA CECILIA, LIKE ME.

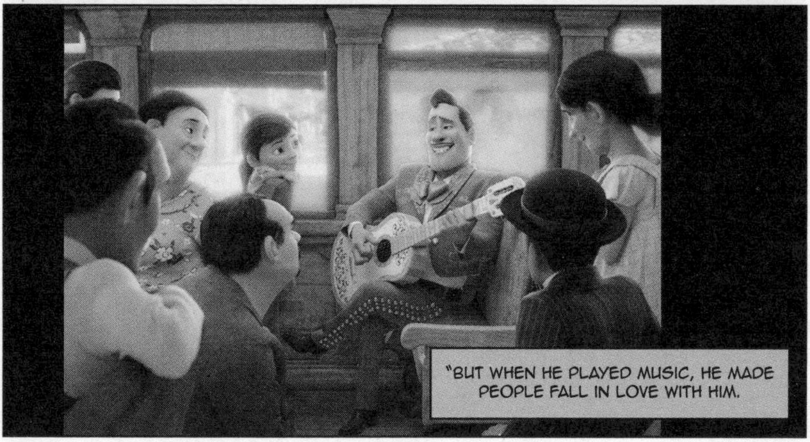
"BUT WHEN HE PLAYED MUSIC, HE MADE PEOPLE FALL IN LOVE WITH HIM.

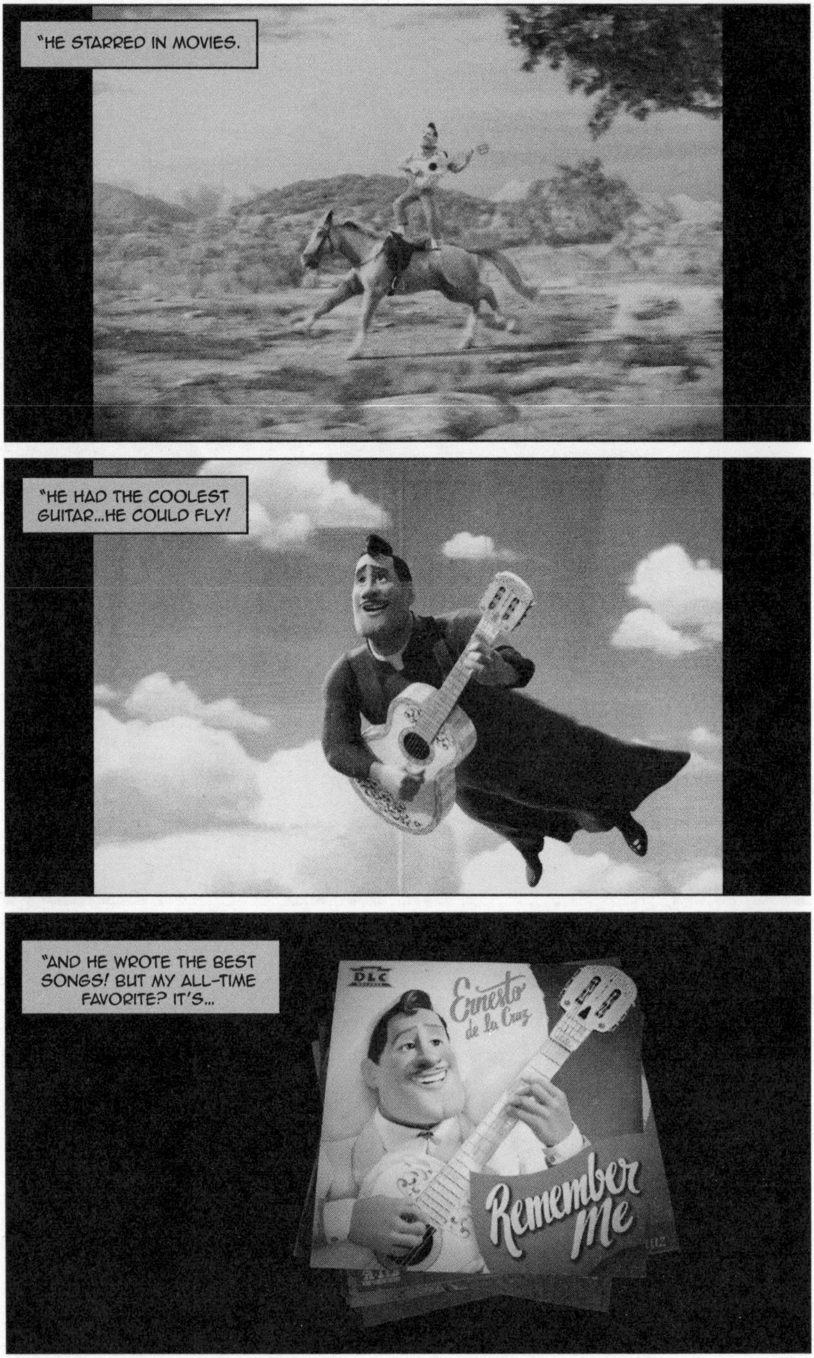
"HE STARRED IN MOVIES.
"HE HAD THE COOLEST GUITAR...HE COULD FLY!
"AND HE WROTE THE BEST SONGS! BUT MY ALL-TIME FAVORITE? IT'S...
DLC
Ernesto de la Cruz
Remember Me

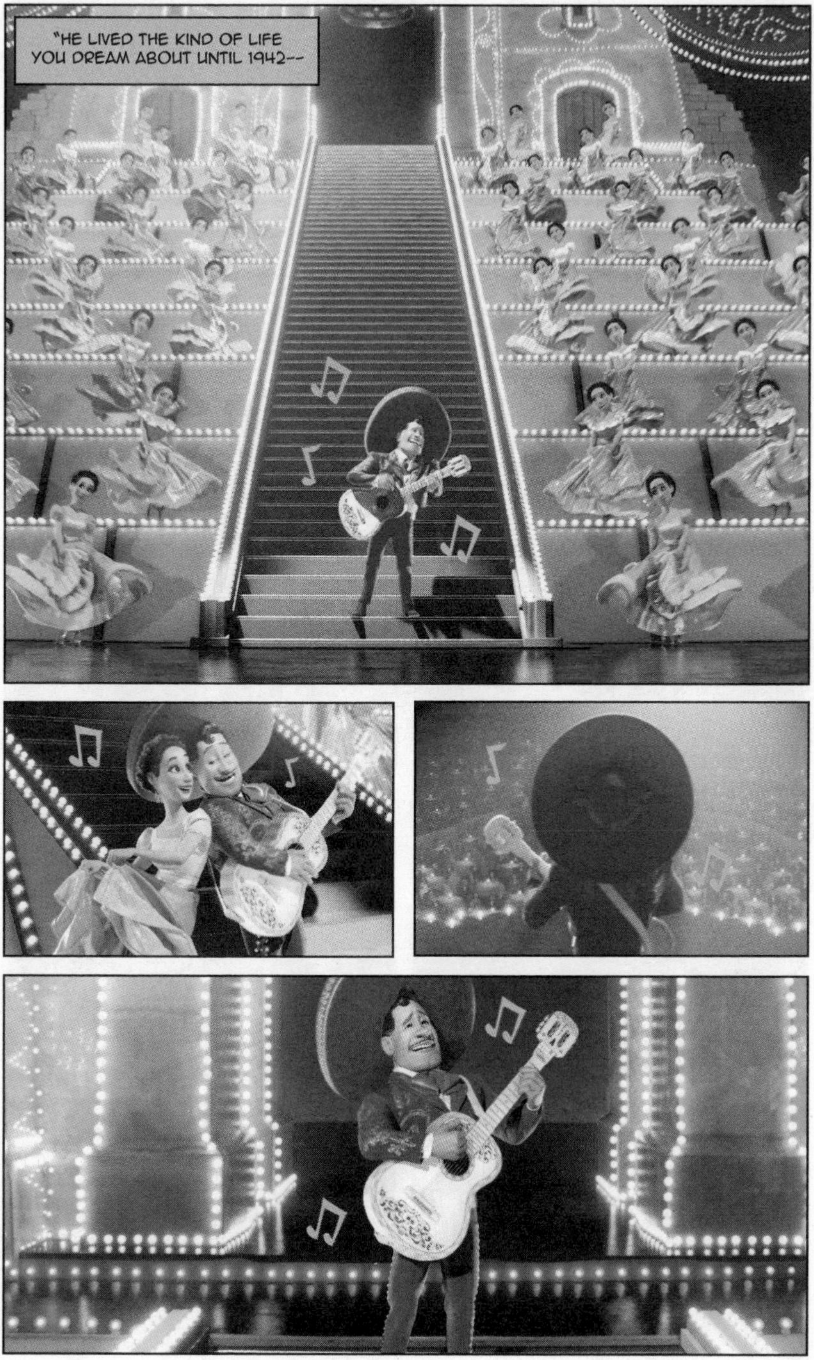
"HE LIVED THE KIND OF LIFE YOU DREAM ABOUT UNTIL 1942--

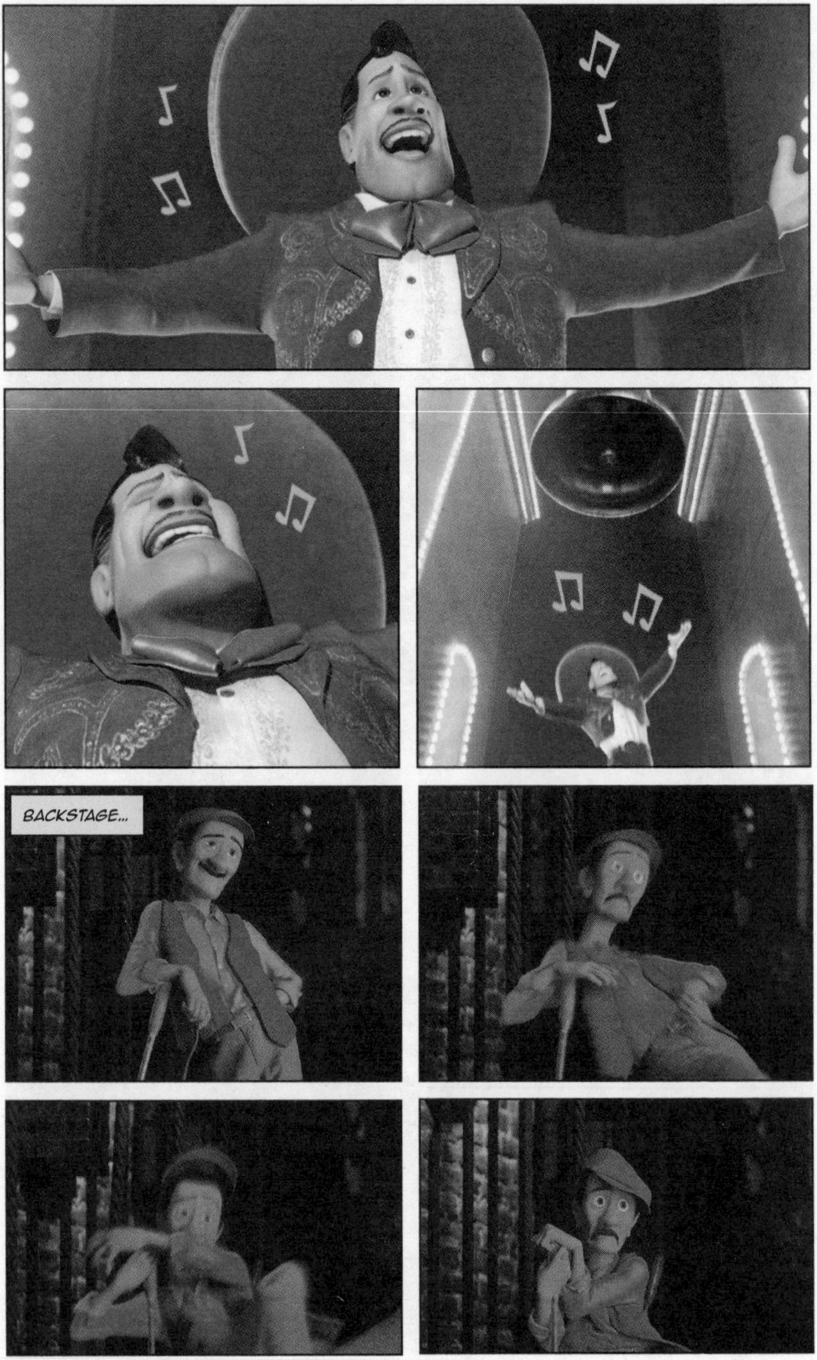
BACKSTAGE...

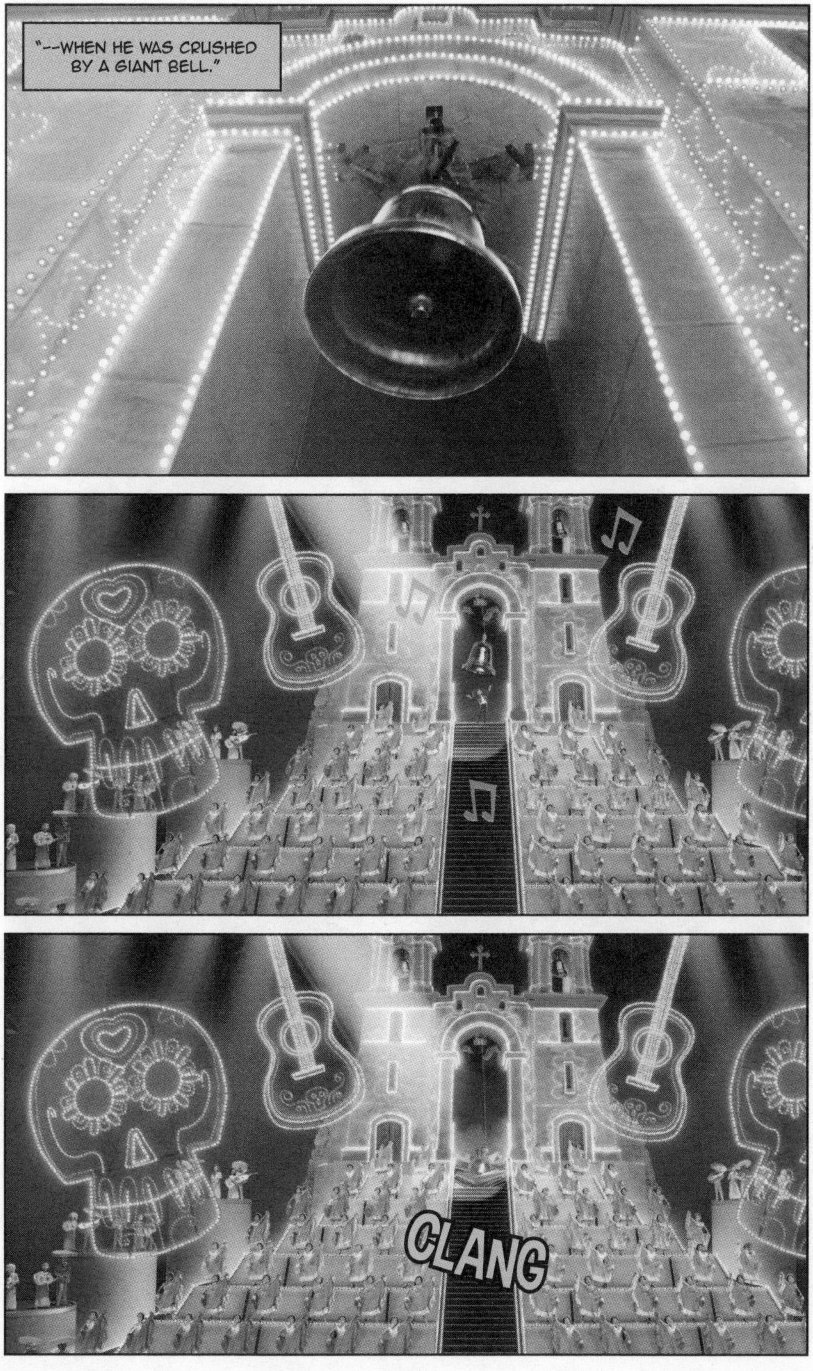
"--WHEN HE WAS CRUSHED BY A GIANT BELL."
CLANG

"I WANNA BE JUST LIKE HIM.

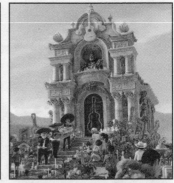

"SOMETIMES, I LOOK AT DE LA CRUZ AND I GET THIS FEELING...LIKE WE'RE CONNECTED SOMEHOW. LIKE, IF *HE* COULD PLAY MUSIC, MAYBE SOMEDAY I COULD TOO..."

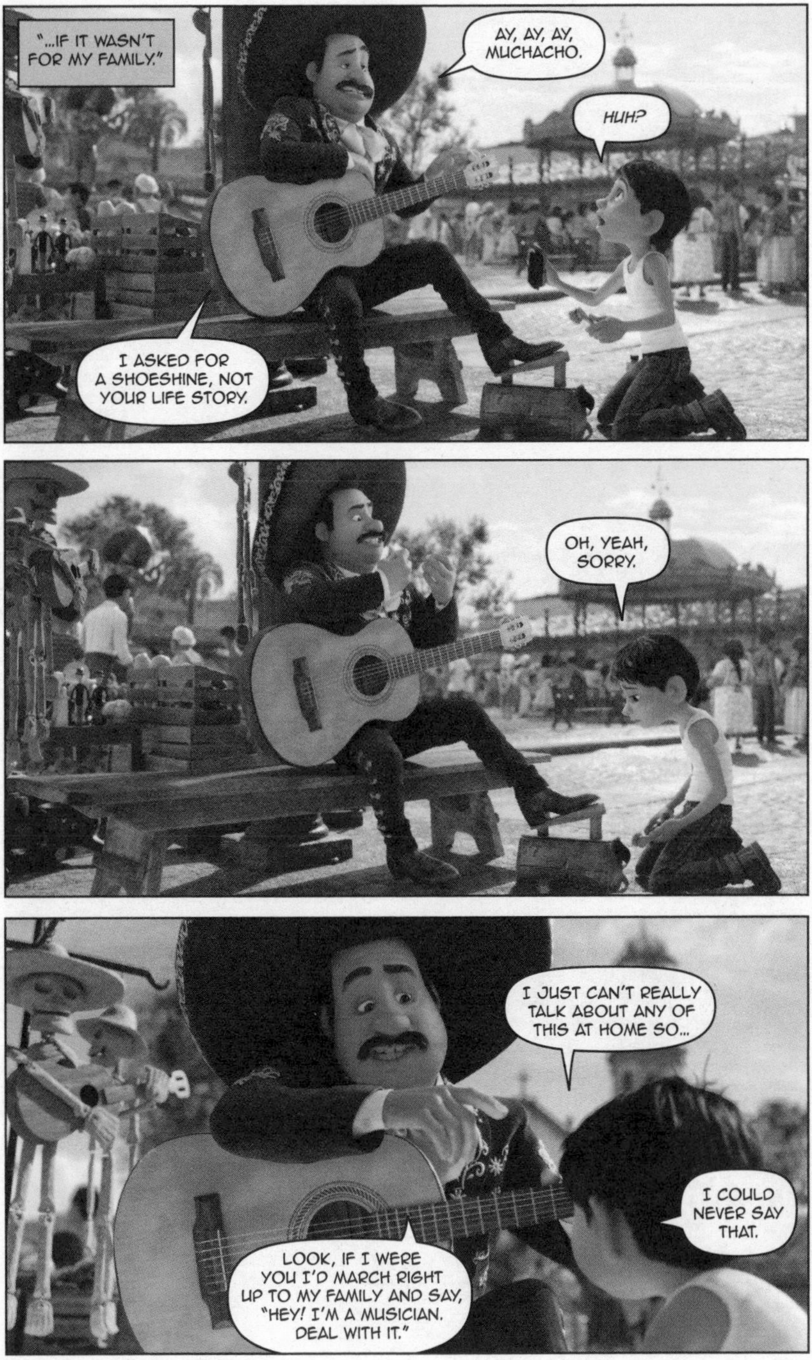
"...IF IT WASN'T FOR MY FAMILY."
AY, AY, AY, MUCHACHO.
HUH?
I ASKED FOR A SHOESHINE, NOT YOUR LIFE STORY.
OH, YEAH, SORRY.
I JUST CAN'T REALLY TALK ABOUT ANY OF THIS AT HOME SO...
LOOK, IF I WERE YOU I'D MARCH RIGHT UP TO MY FAMILY AND SAY, "HEY! I'M A MUSICIAN. DEAL WITH IT."
I COULD NEVER SAY THAT.

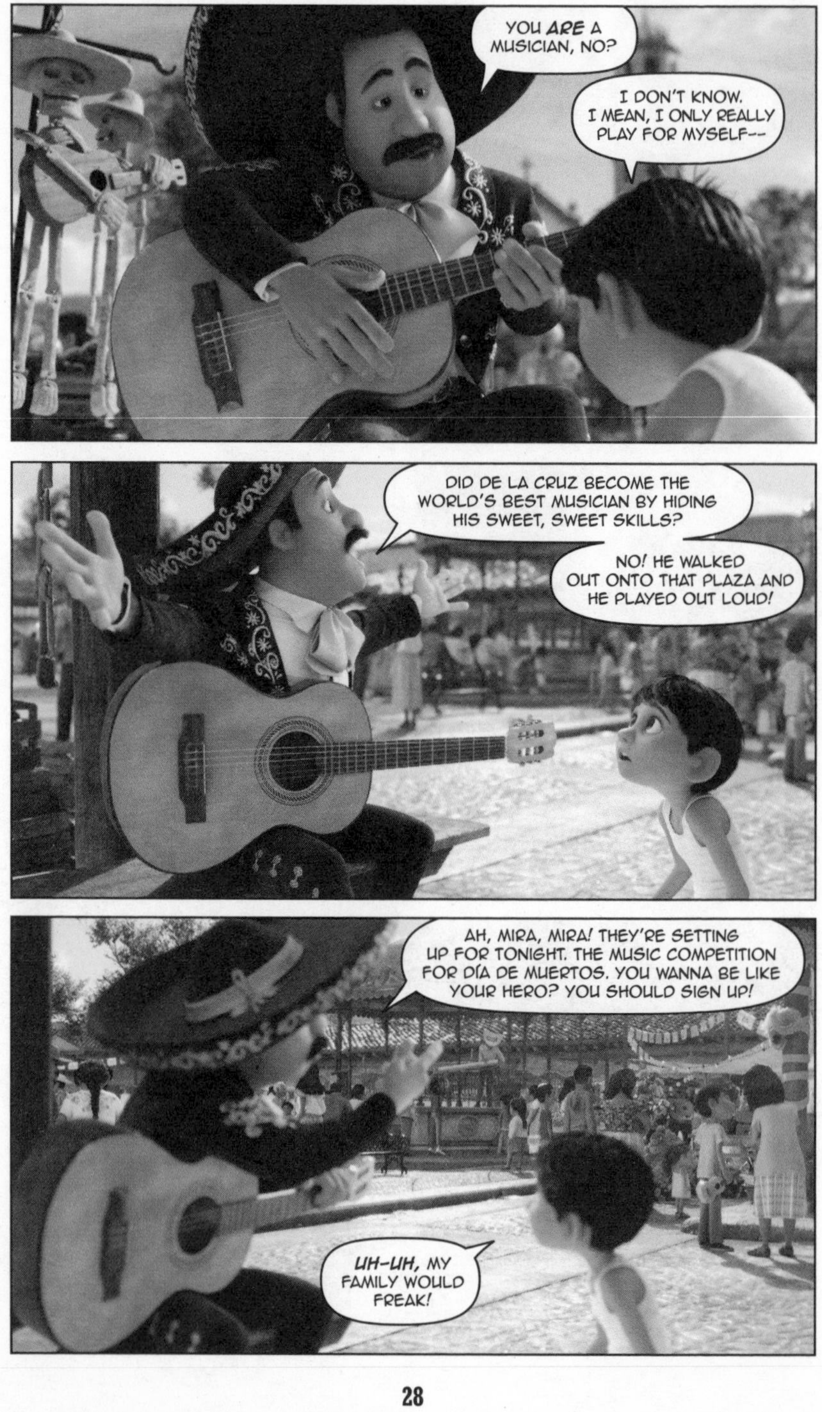
YOU *ARE* A MUSICIAN, NO?
I DON'T KNOW. I MEAN, I ONLY REALLY PLAY FOR MYSELF--
DID DE LA CRUZ BECOME THE WORLD'S BEST MUSICIAN BY HIDING HIS SWEET, SWEET SKILLS?
NO! HE WALKED OUT ONTO THAT PLAZA AND HE PLAYED OUT LOUD!
AH, MIRA, MIRA! THEY'RE SETTING UP FOR TONIGHT. THE MUSIC COMPETITION FOR DÍA DE MUERTOS. YOU WANNA BE LIKE YOUR HERO? YOU SHOULD SIGN UP!
UH-UH, MY FAMILY WOULD FREAK!

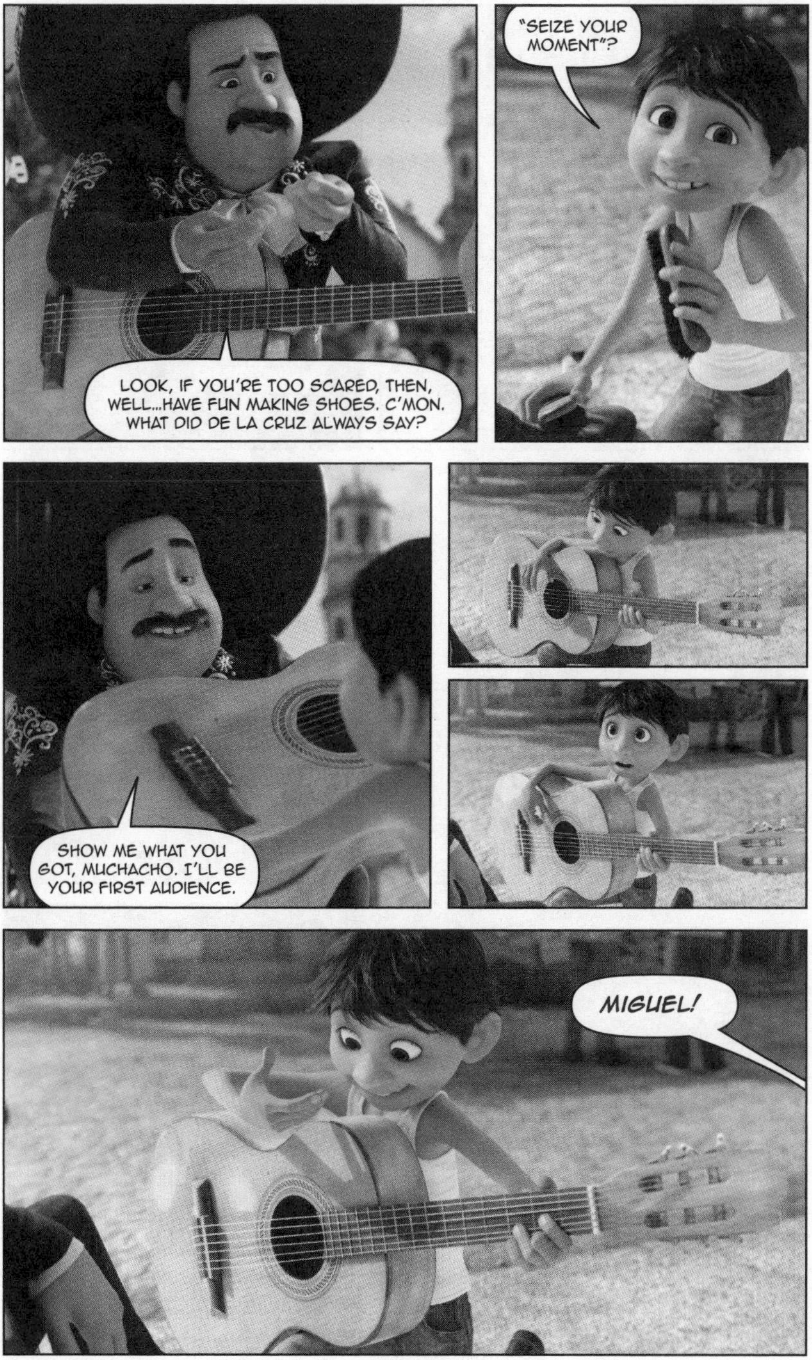
LOOK, IF YOU'RE TOO SCARED, THEN, WELL...HAVE FUN MAKING SHOES. C'MON. WHAT DID DE LA CRUZ ALWAYS SAY?
"SEIZE YOUR MOMENT"?
SHOW ME WHAT YOU GOT, MUCHACHO. I'LL BE YOUR FIRST AUDIENCE.
MIGUEL!

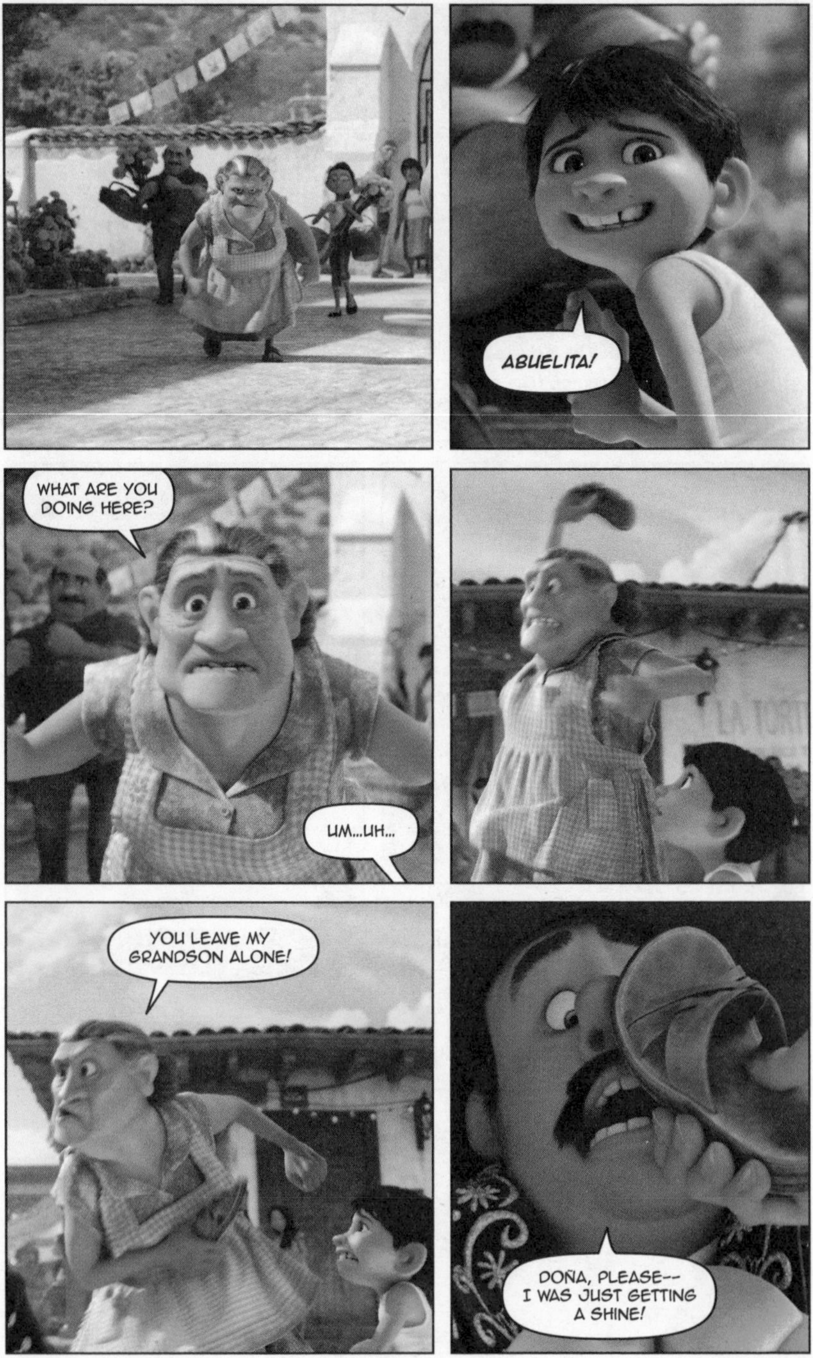
ABUELITA!
WHAT ARE YOU DOING HERE?
UM...UH...
YOU LEAVE MY GRANDSON ALONE!
DOÑA, PLEASE-- I WAS JUST GETTING A SHINE!

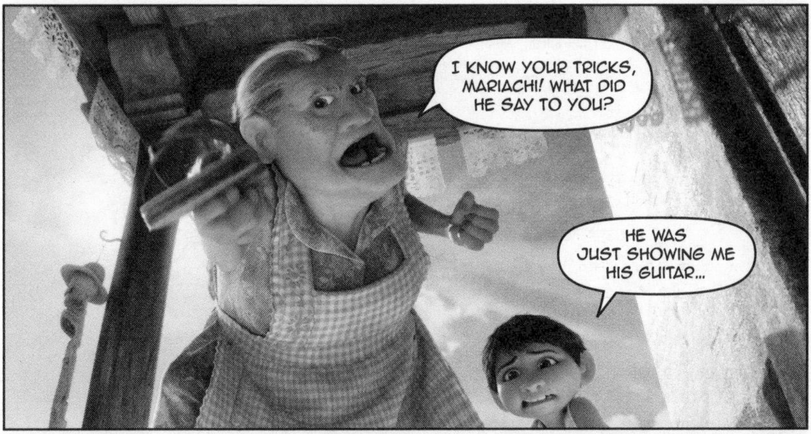
I KNOW YOUR TRICKS, MARIACHI! WHAT DID HE SAY TO YOU?
HE WAS JUST SHOWING ME HIS GUITAR...

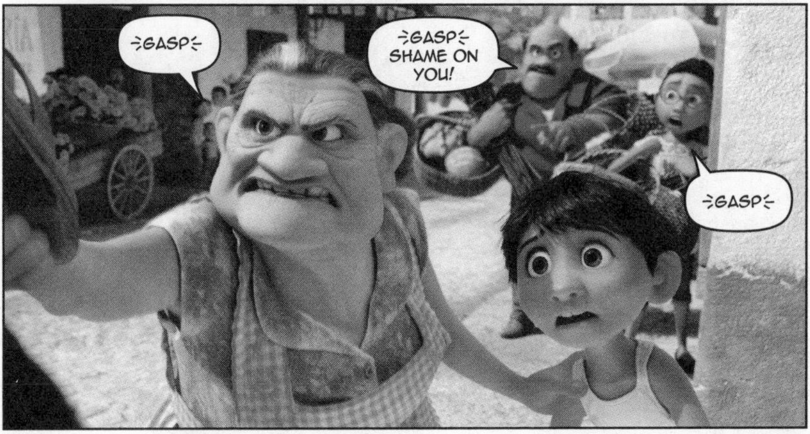
GASP
GASP SHAME ON YOU!
GASP

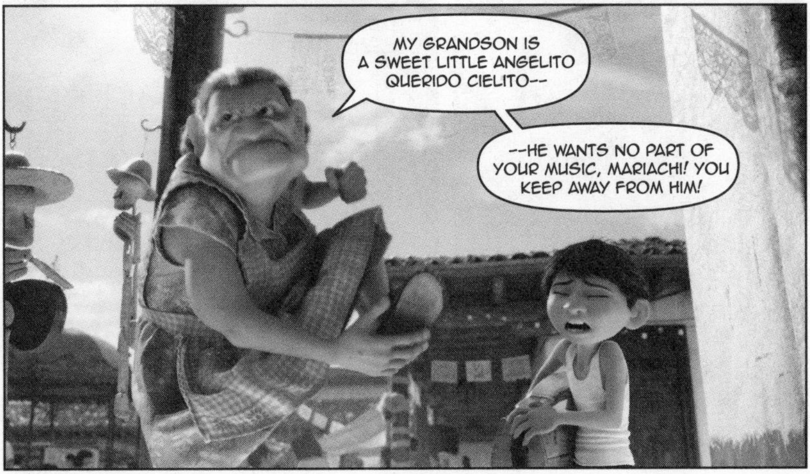
MY GRANDSON IS A SWEET LITTLE ANGELITO QUERIDO CIELITO--
--HE WANTS NO PART OF YOUR MUSIC, MARIACHI! YOU KEEP AWAY FROM HIM!

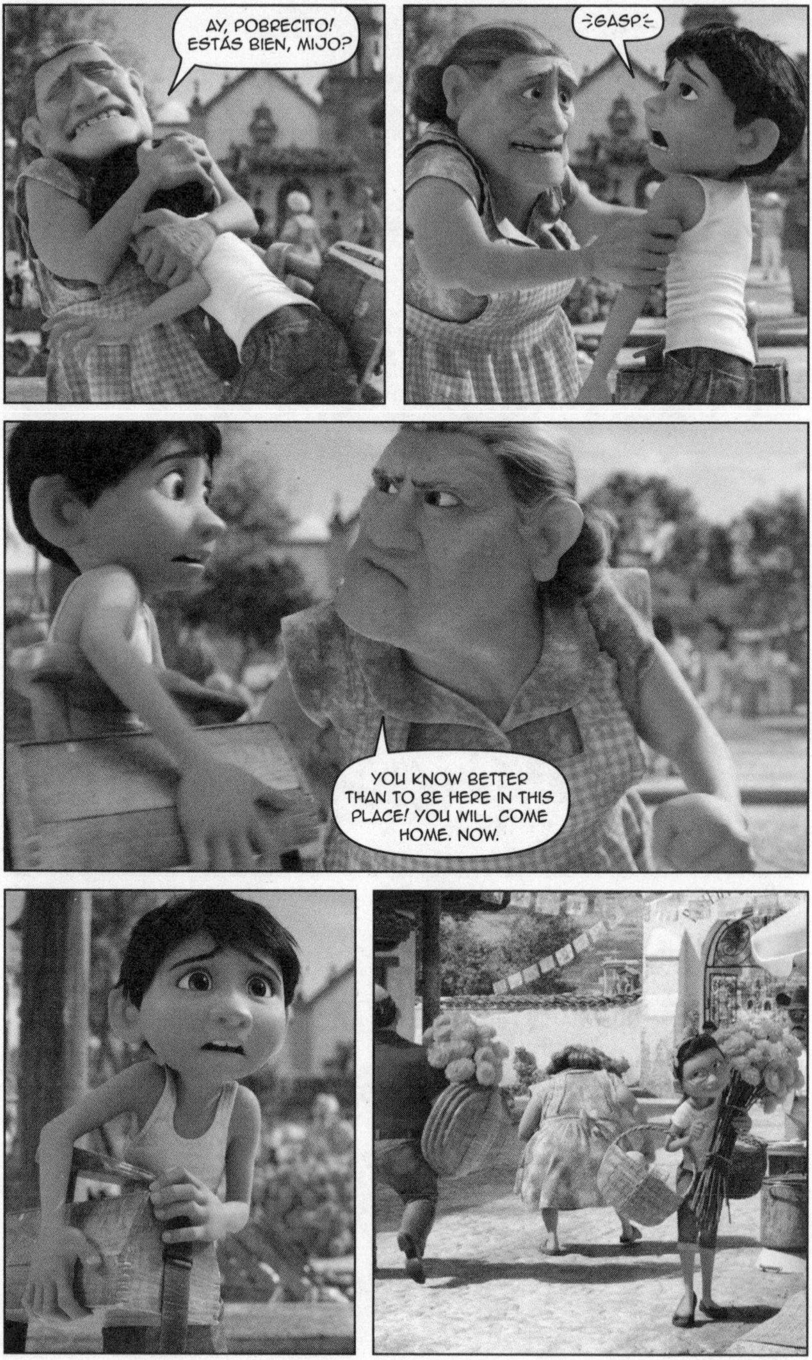
AY, POBRECITO! ESTÁS BIEN, MIJO?
GASP
YOU KNOW BETTER THAN TO BE HERE IN THIS PLACE! YOU WILL COME HOME. NOW.

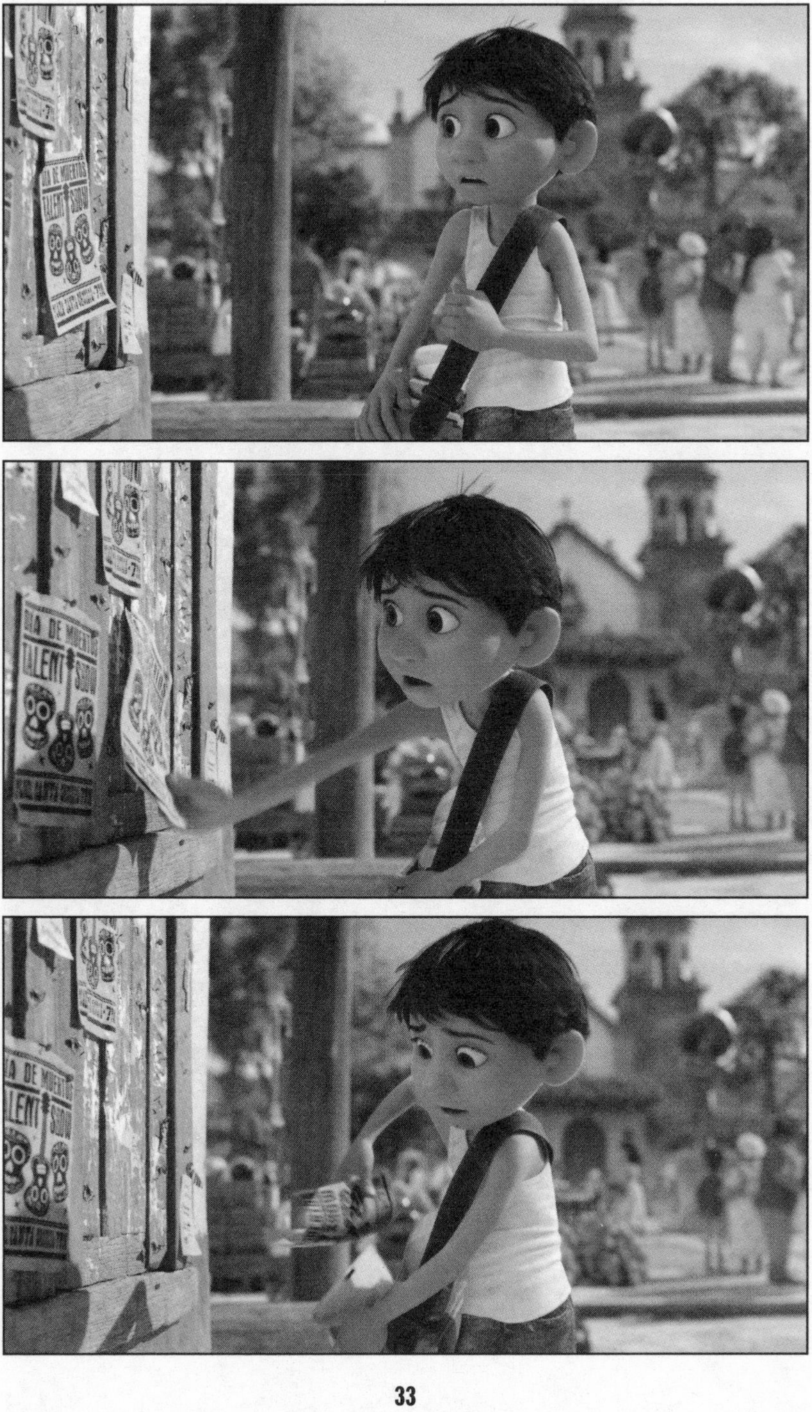
DIA DE MUERTOS
TALENT SHOW

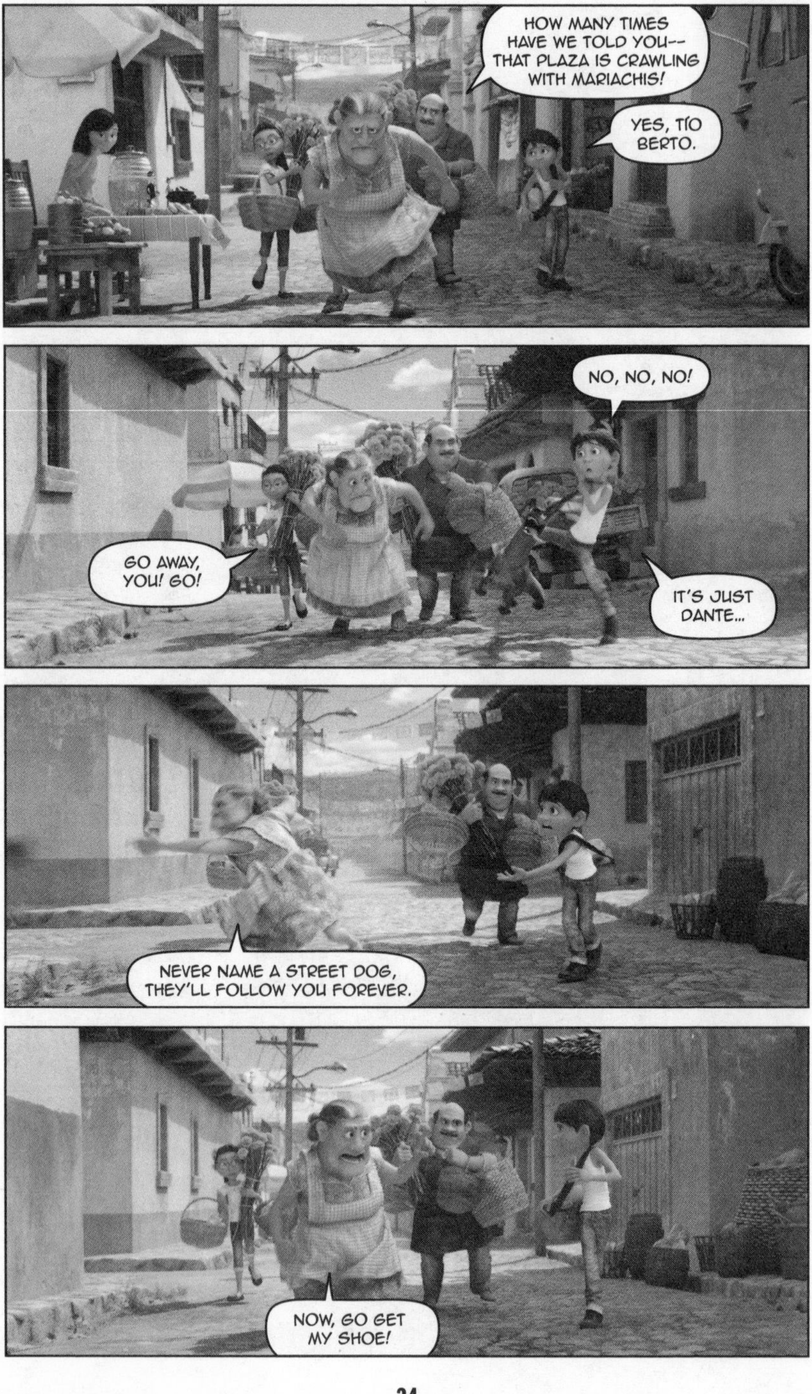
HOW MANY TIMES HAVE WE TOLD YOU-- THAT PLAZA IS CRAWLING WITH MARIACHIS!
YES, TÍO BERTO.
NO, NO, NO!
GO AWAY, YOU! GO!
IT'S JUST DANTE...
NEVER NAME A STREET DOG, THEY'LL FOLLOW YOU FOREVER.
NOW, GO GET MY SHOE!

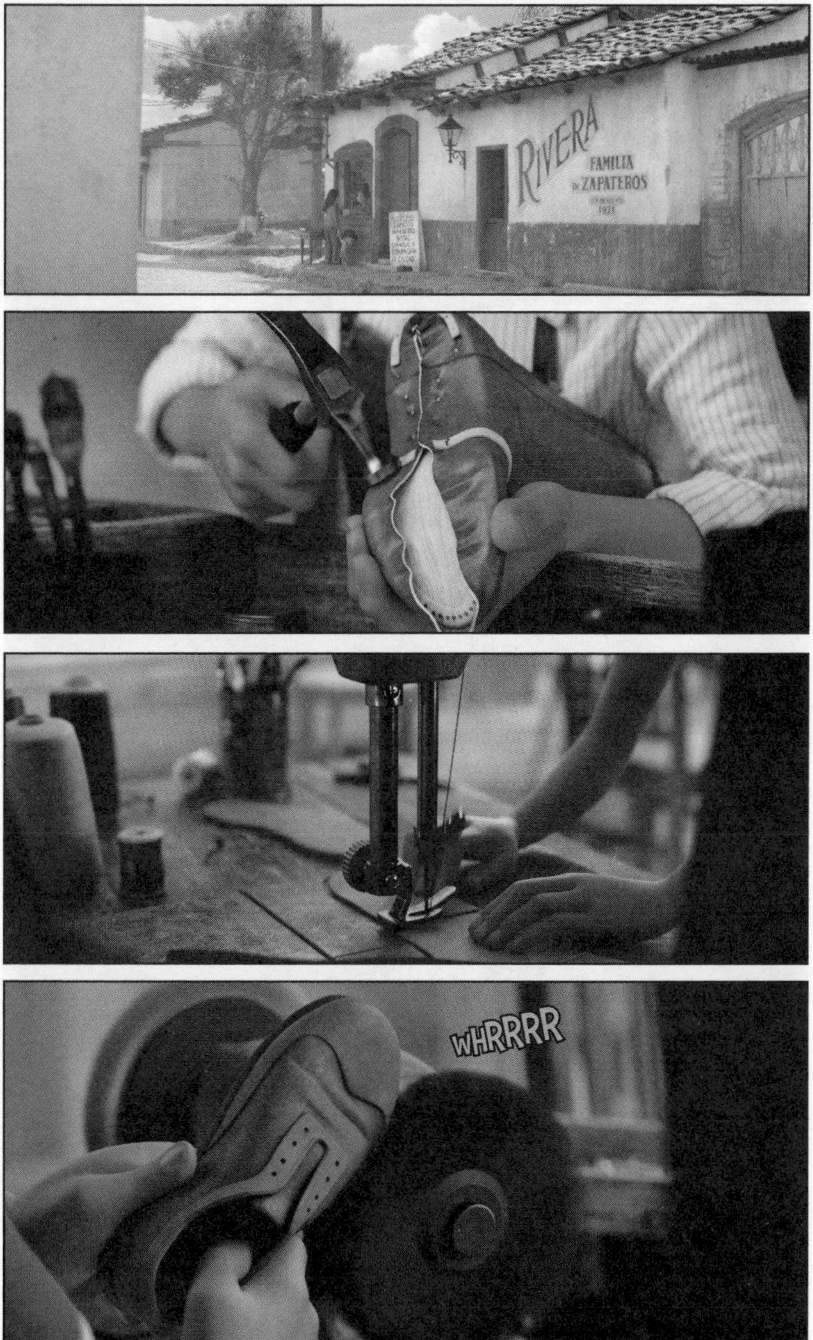
RIVERA
FAMILIA
ZAPATEROS
WHRRRR

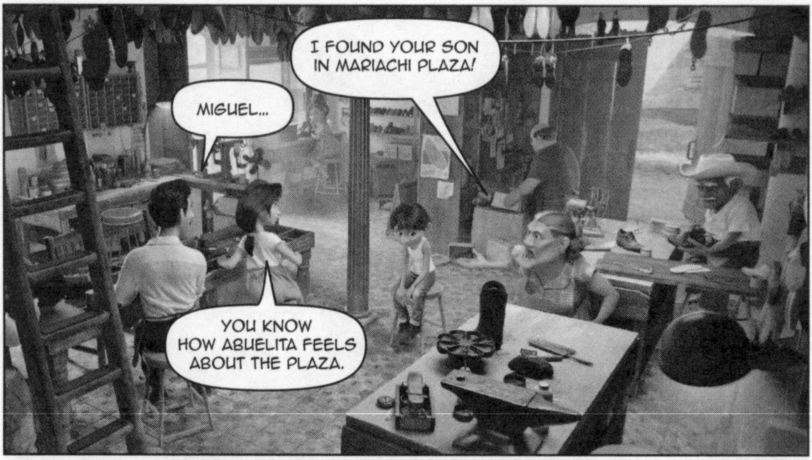
I FOUND YOUR SON IN MARIACHI PLAZA!
MIGUEL...
YOU KNOW HOW ABUELITA FEELS ABOUT THE PLAZA.

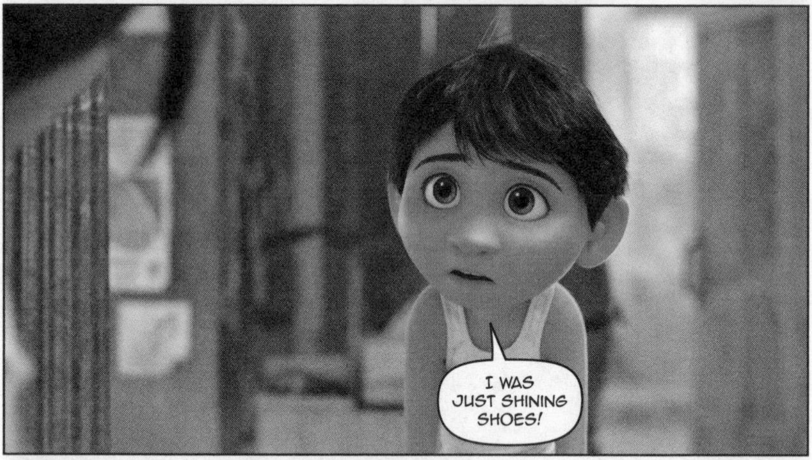
I WAS JUST SHINING SHOES!

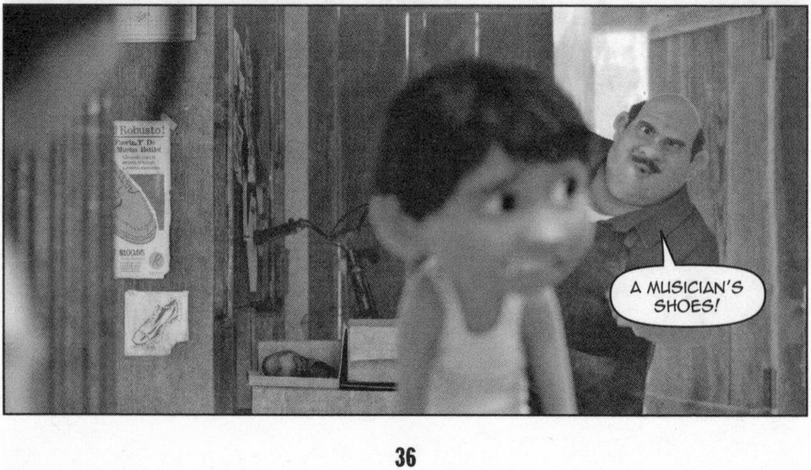
Robusto!
A MUSICIAN'S SHOES!

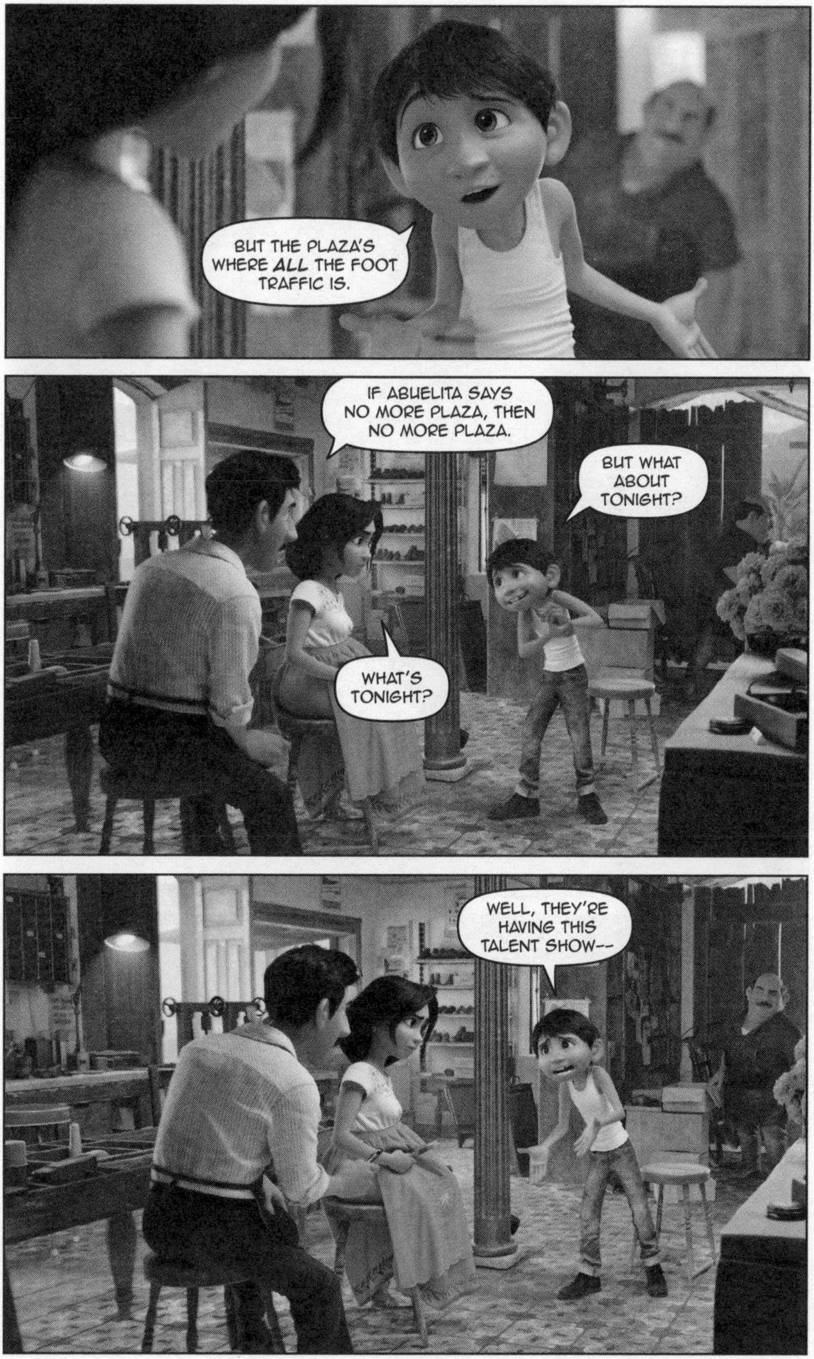
BUT THE PLAZA'S WHERE *ALL* THE FOOT TRAFFIC IS.
IF ABUELITA SAYS NO MORE PLAZA, THEN NO MORE PLAZA.
BUT WHAT ABOUT TONIGHT?
WHAT'S TONIGHT?
WELL, THEY'RE HAVING THIS TALENT SHOW--

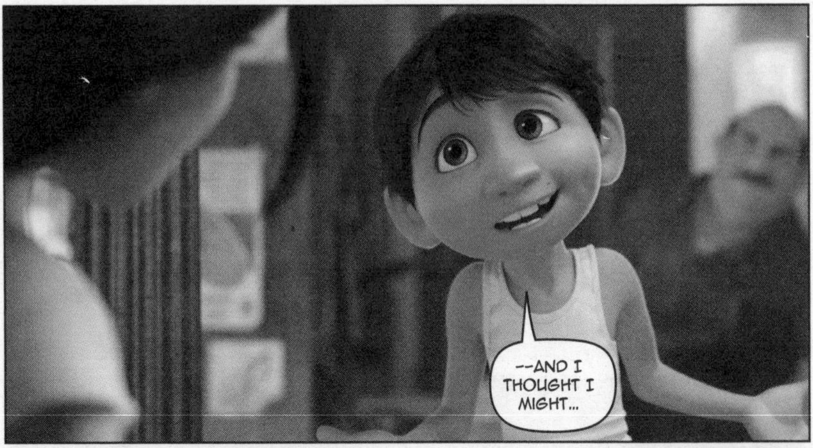
--AND I THOUGHT I MIGHT...

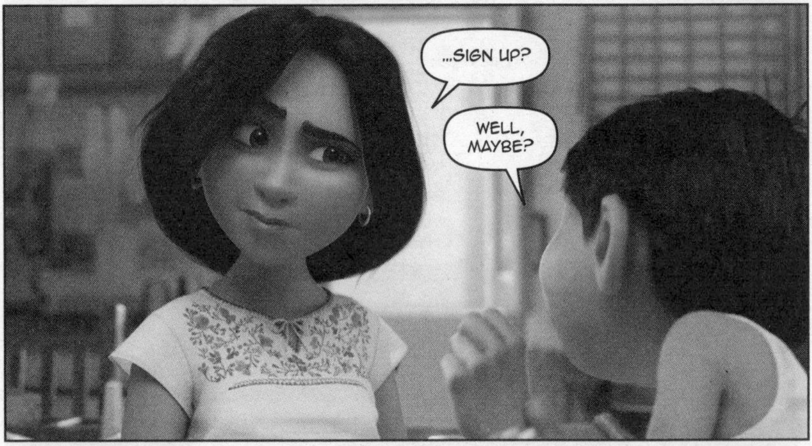
...SIGN UP?
WELL, MAYBE?

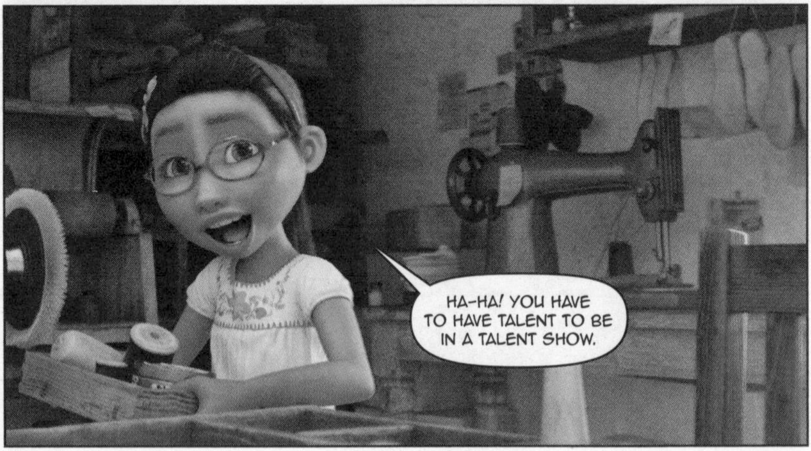
HA-HA! YOU HAVE TO HAVE TALENT TO BE IN A TALENT SHOW.

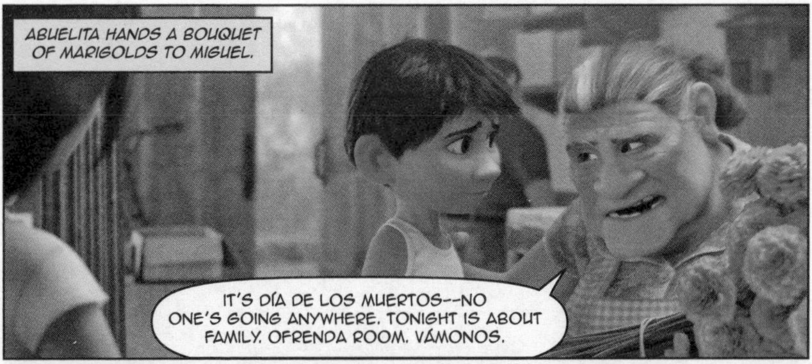
ABUELITA HANDS A BOUQUET OF MARIGOLDS TO MIGUEL.
IT'S DÍA DE LOS MUERTOS--NO ONE'S GOING ANYWHERE. TONIGHT IS ABOUT FAMILY. OFRENDA ROOM. VÁMONOS.

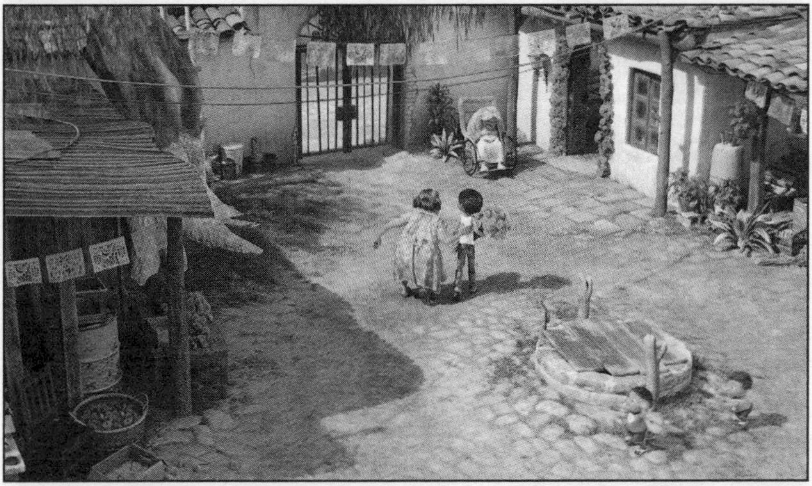

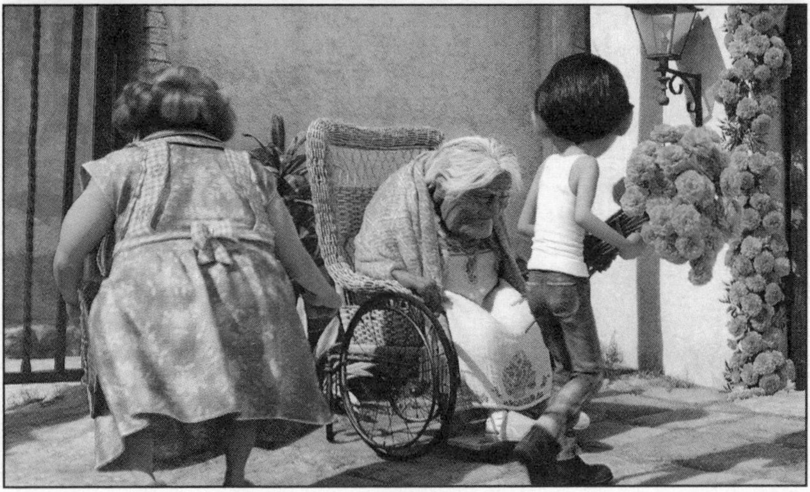

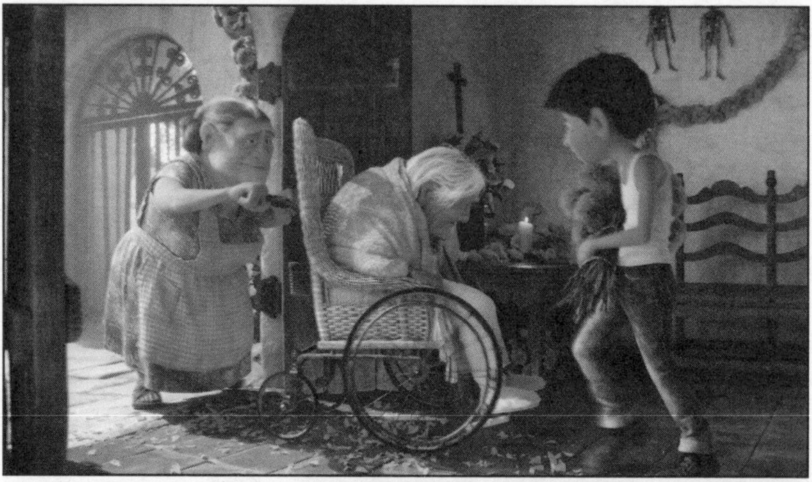

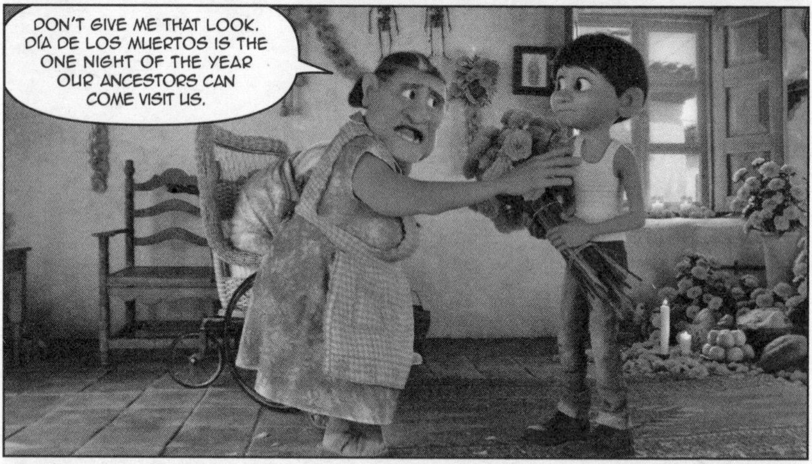
DON'T GIVE ME THAT LOOK. DÍA DE LOS MUERTOS IS THE ONE NIGHT OF THE YEAR OUR ANCESTORS CAN COME VISIT US.

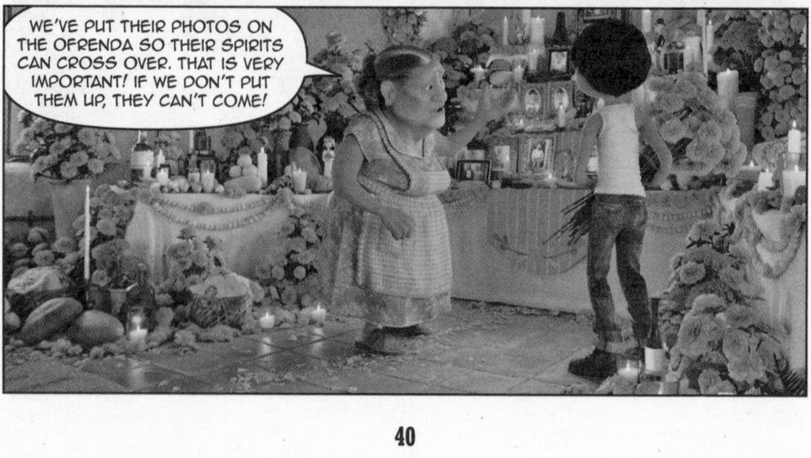
WE'VE PUT THEIR PHOTOS ON THE OFRENDA SO THEIR SPIRITS CAN CROSS OVER. THAT IS VERY IMPORTANT! IF WE DON'T PUT THEM UP, THEY CAN'T COME!

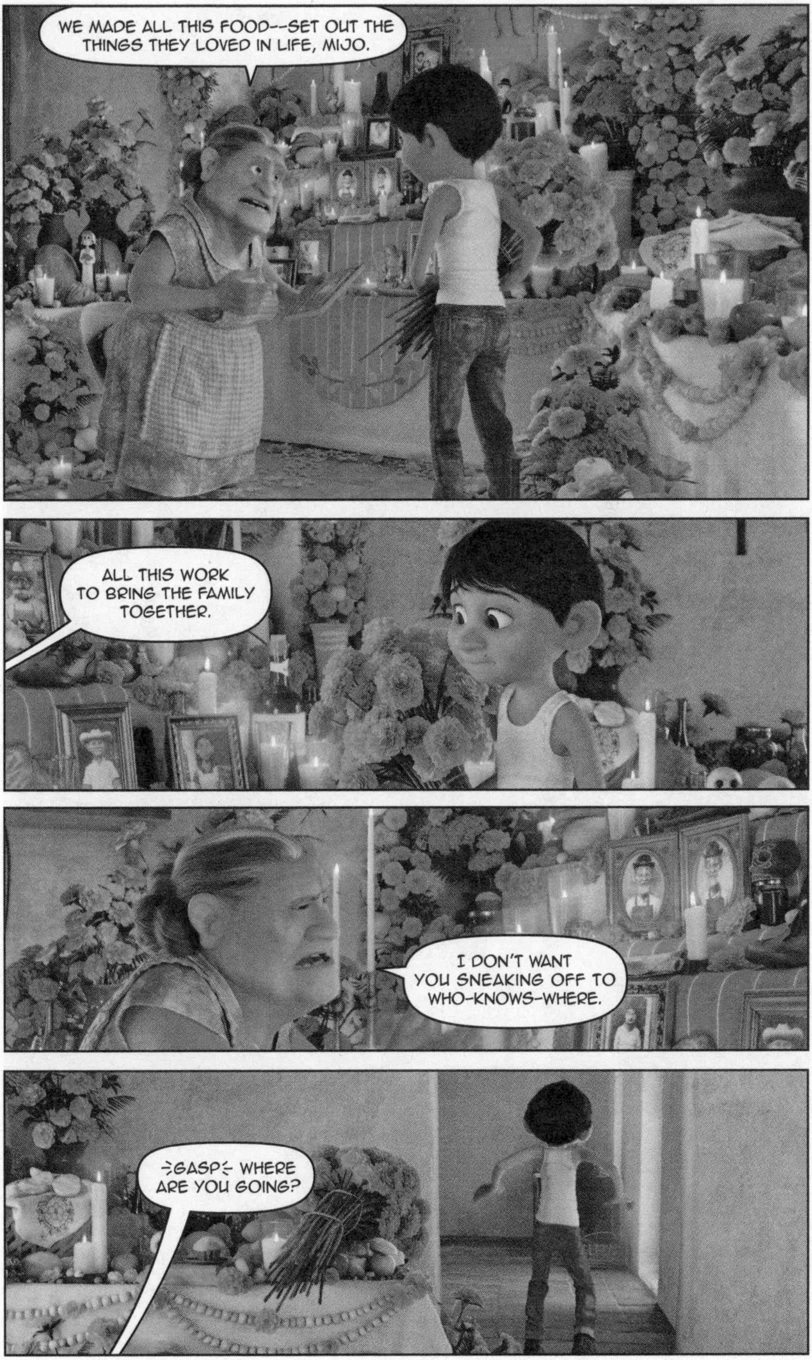
WE MADE ALL THIS FOOD--SET OUT THE THINGS THEY LOVED IN LIFE, MIJO.
ALL THIS WORK TO BRING THE FAMILY TOGETHER.
I DON'T WANT YOU SNEAKING OFF TO WHO-KNOWS-WHERE.
-GASP- WHERE ARE YOU GOING?

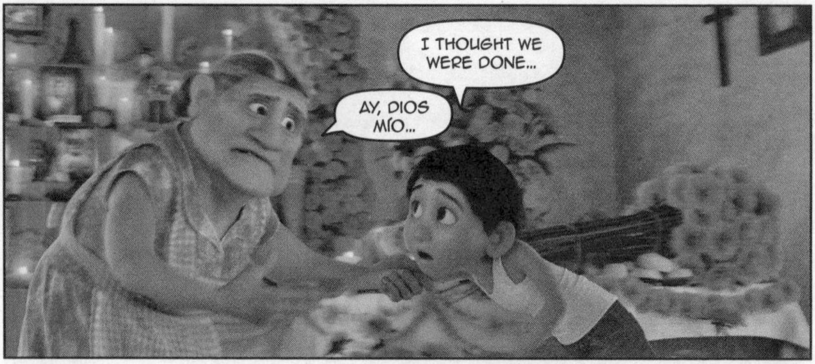
I THOUGHT WE WERE DONE...
AY, DIOS MÍO...

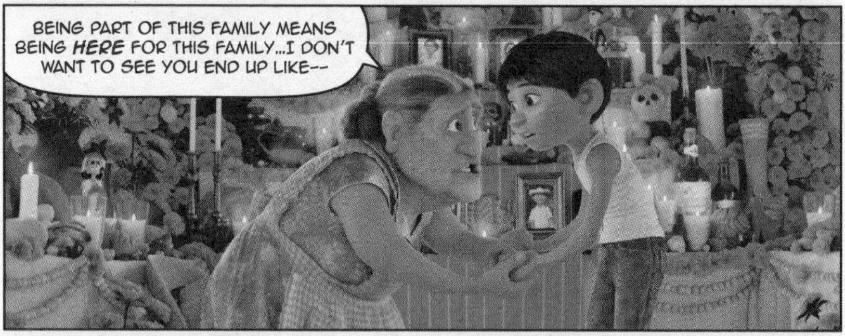
BEING PART OF THIS FAMILY MEANS BEING HERE FOR THIS FAMILY...I DON'T WANT TO SEE YOU END UP LIKE--

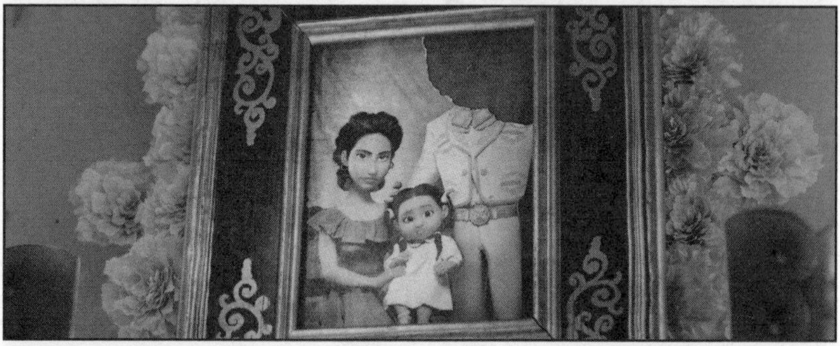

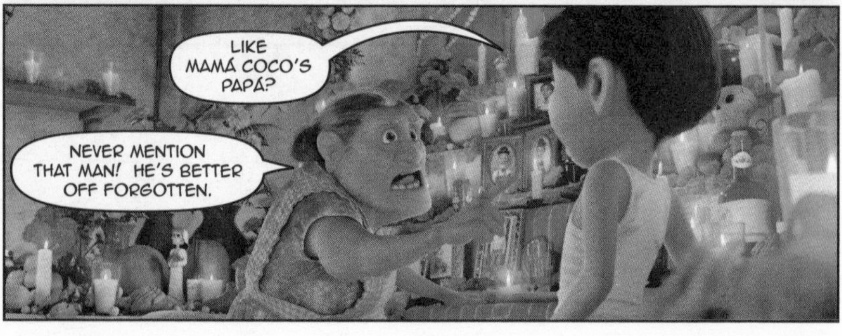
LIKE MAMÁ COCO'S PAPÁ?
NEVER MENTION THAT MAN! HE'S BETTER OFF FORGOTTEN.

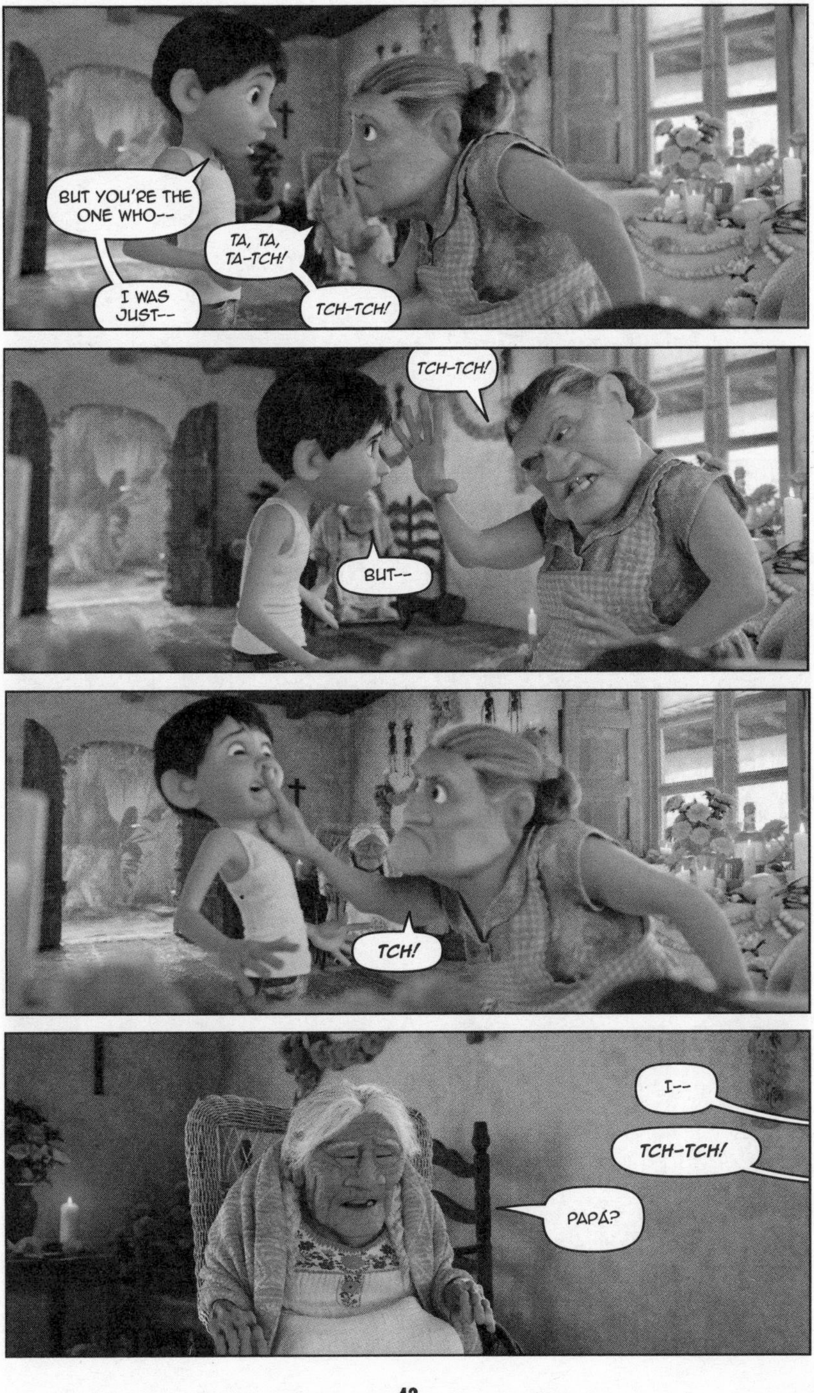
BUT YOU'RE THE ONE WHO--
I WAS JUST--
TA, TA, TA-TCH!
TCH-TCH!
TCH-TCH!
BUT--
TCH!
I--
TCH-TCH!
PAPÁ?

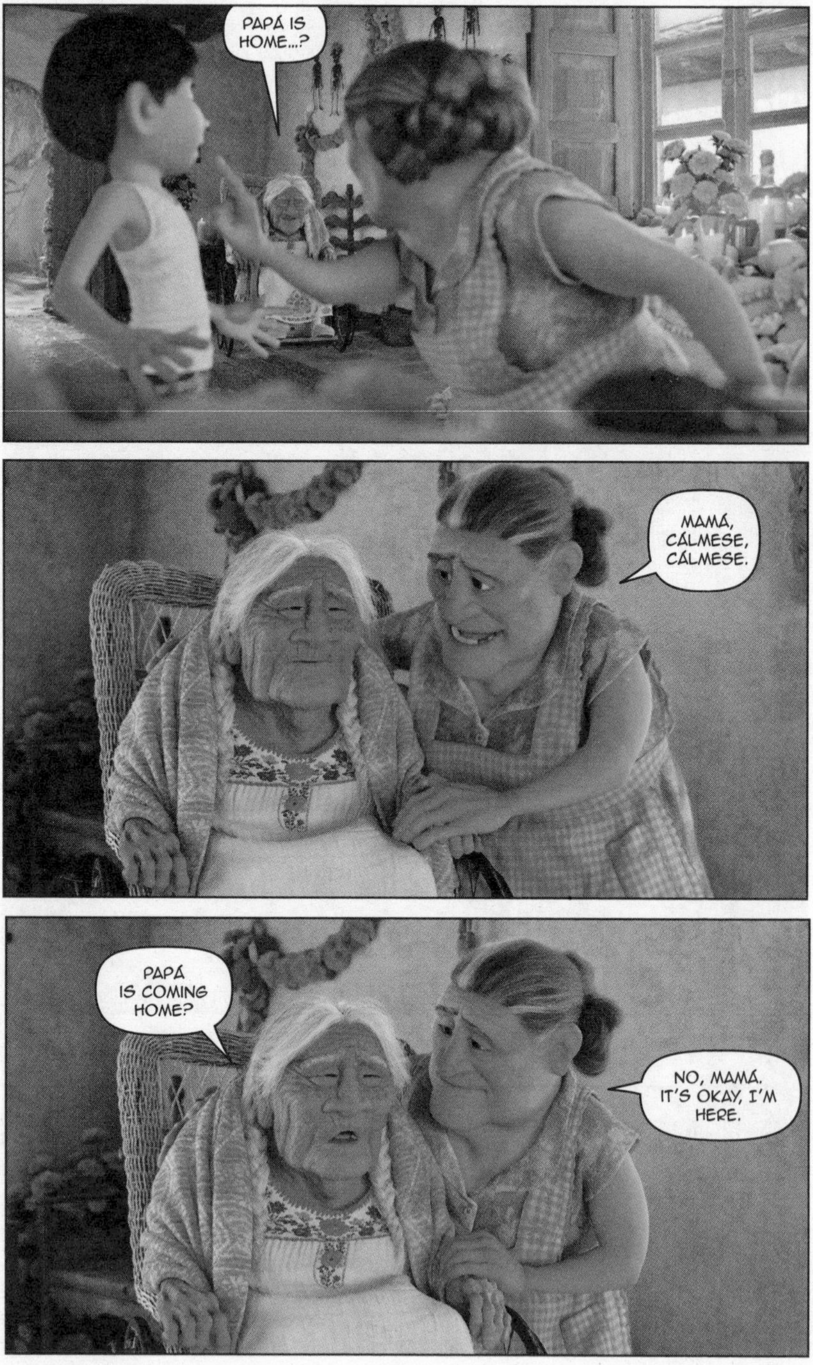
PAPÁ IS HOME...?
MAMÁ, CÁLMESE, CÁLMESE.
PAPÁ IS COMING HOME?
NO, MAMÁ. IT'S OKAY, I'M HERE.

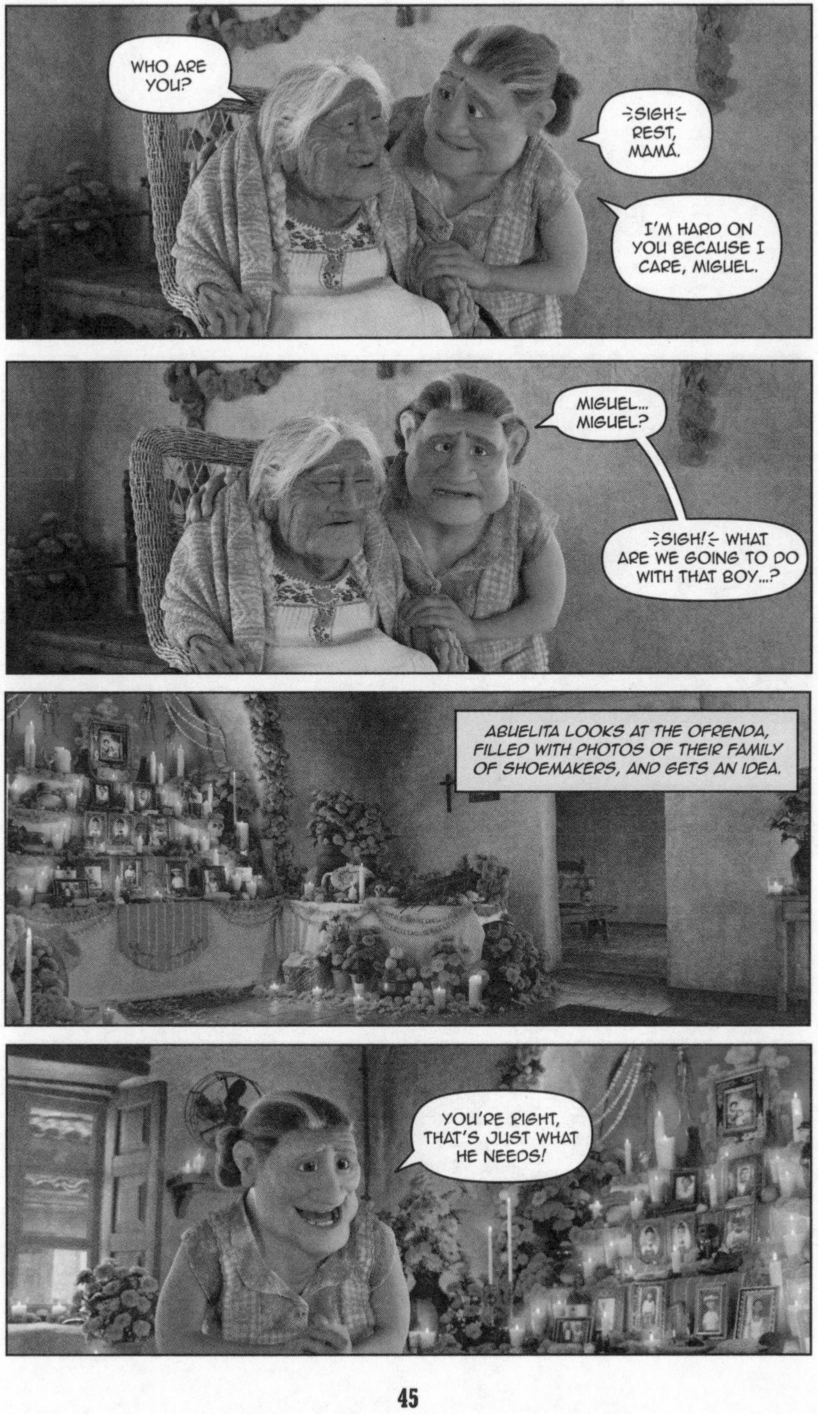
WHO ARE YOU?
SIGH REST, MAMÁ.
I'M HARD ON YOU BECAUSE I CARE, MIGUEL.
MIGUEL... MIGUEL?
SIGH! WHAT ARE WE GOING TO DO WITH THAT BOY...?
ABUELITA LOOKS AT THE OFRENDA, FILLED WITH PHOTOS OF THEIR FAMILY OF SHOEMAKERS, AND GETS AN IDEA.
YOU'RE RIGHT, THAT'S JUST WHAT HE NEEDS!

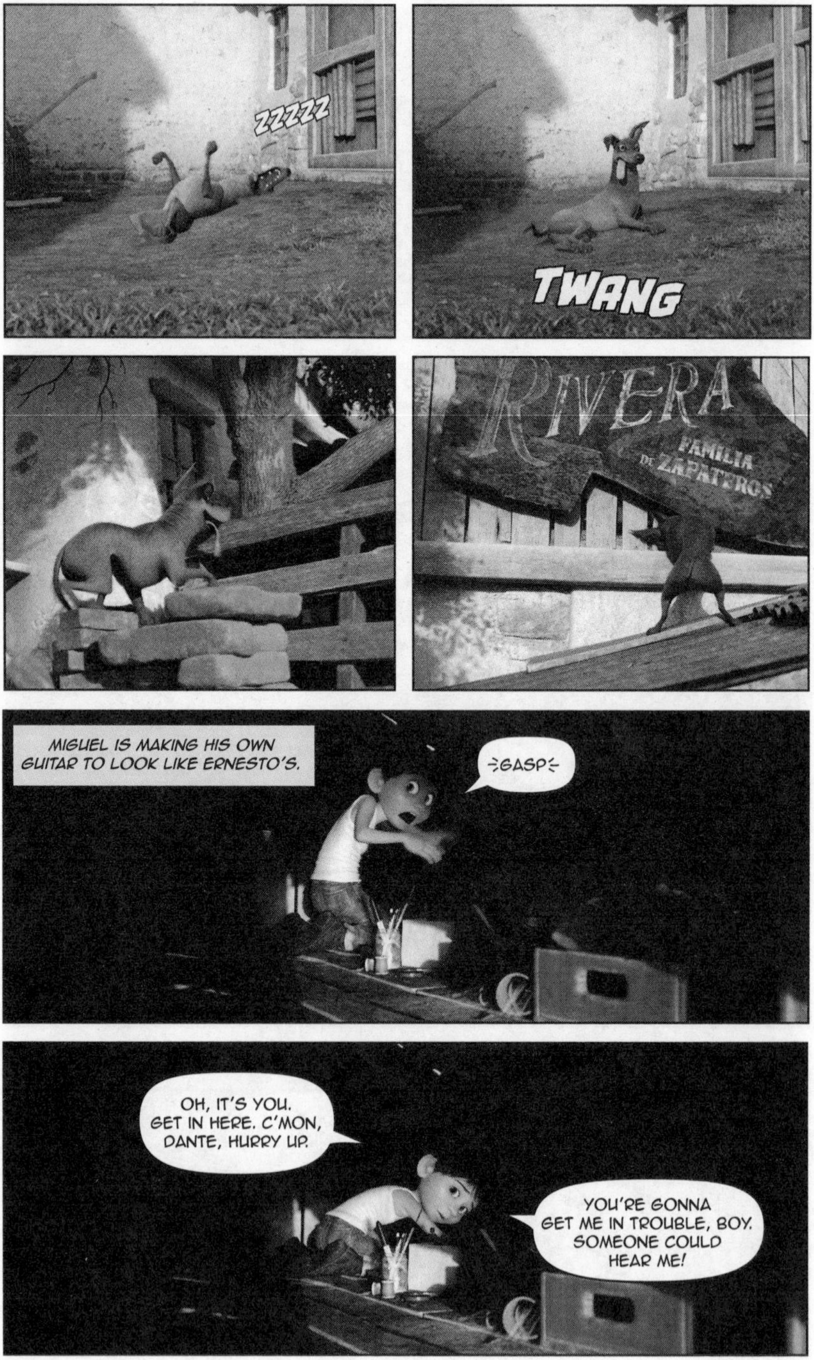
ZZZZZ
TWANG
RIVERA
FAMILIA
MIGUEL IS MAKING HIS OWN GUITAR TO LOOK LIKE ERNESTO'S.
GASP
OH, IT'S YOU. GET IN HERE. C'MON, DANTE, HURRY UP.
YOU'RE GONNA GET ME IN TROUBLE, BOY. SOMEONE COULD HEAR ME!

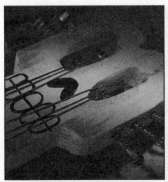

I WISH SOMEONE WANTED TO HEAR ME... OTHER THAN YOU...

PERFÉCTO!

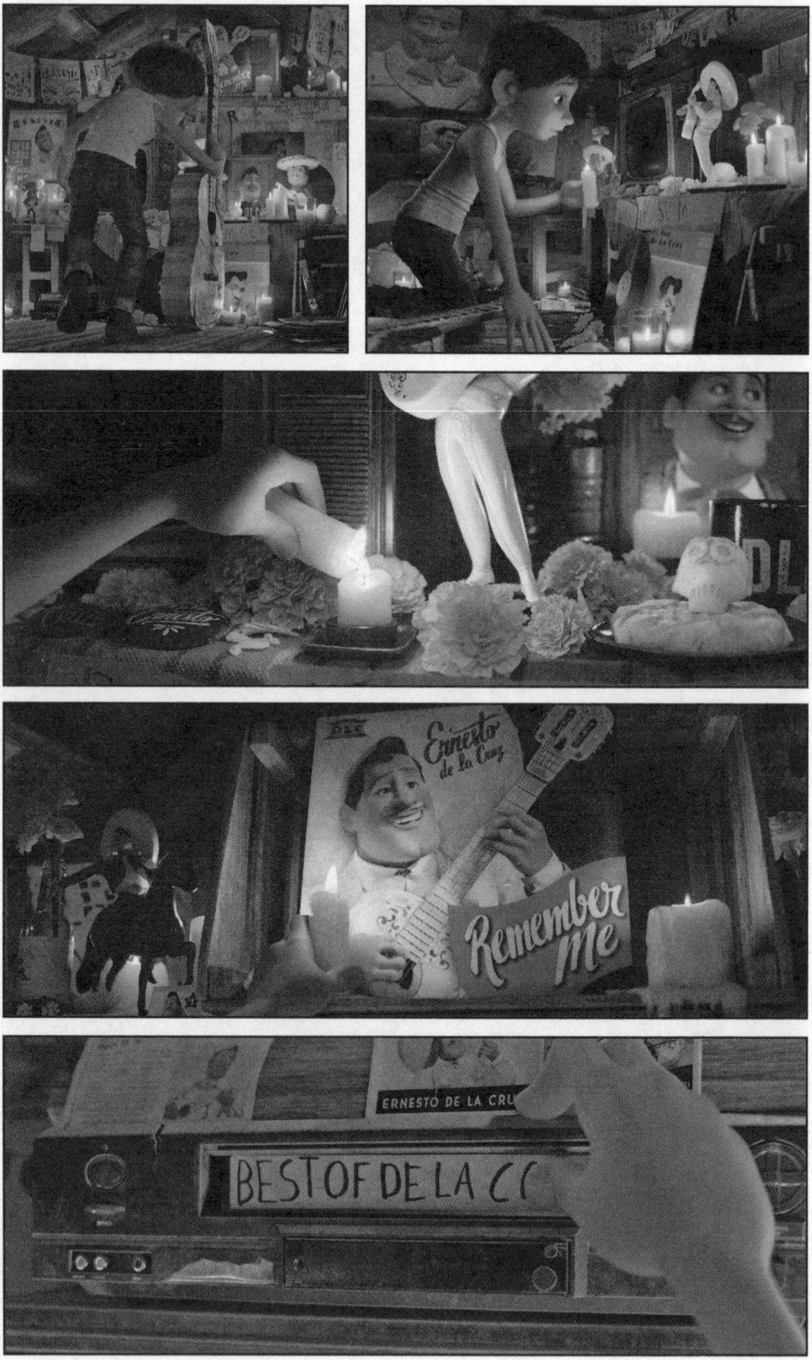

Ernesto de la Cruz
Remember Me
ERNESTO DE LA CRU
BEST OF DE LA C

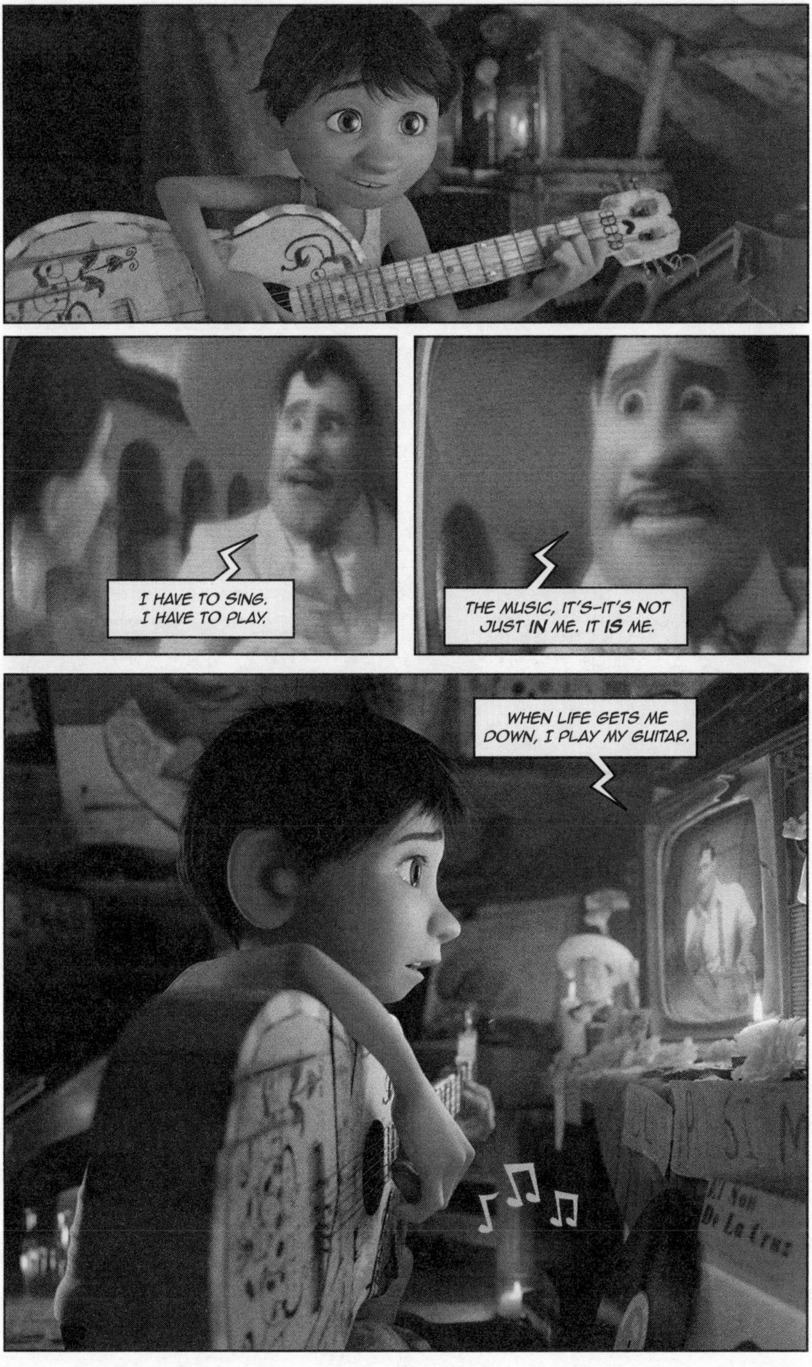
I HAVE TO SING. I HAVE TO PLAY.
THE MUSIC, IT'S–IT'S NOT JUST IN ME. IT IS ME.
WHEN LIFE GETS ME DOWN, I PLAY MY GUITAR.

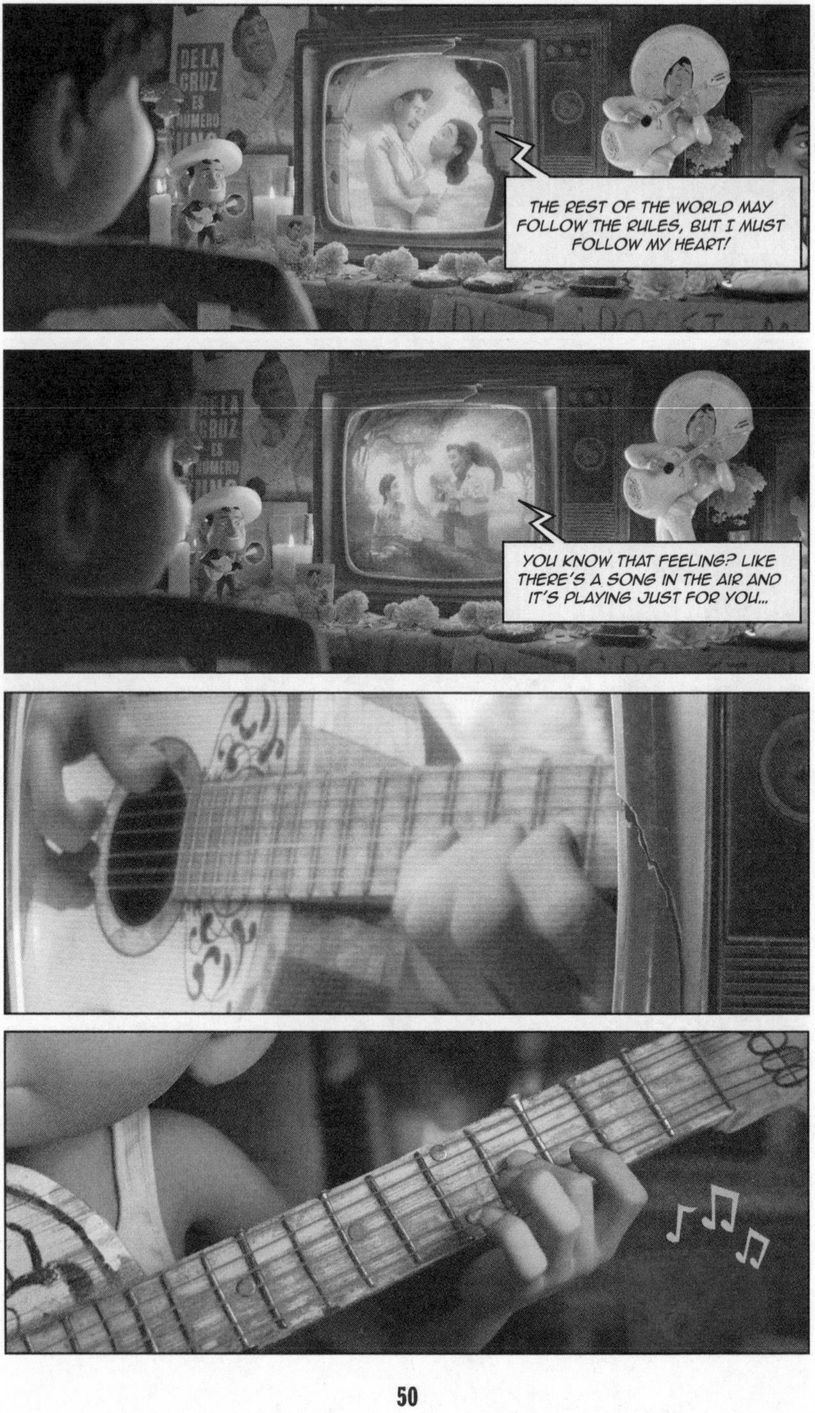
THE REST OF THE WORLD MAY FOLLOW THE RULES, BUT I MUST FOLLOW MY HEART!
YOU KNOW THAT FEELING? LIKE THERE'S A SONG IN THE AIR AND IT'S PLAYING JUST FOR YOU...

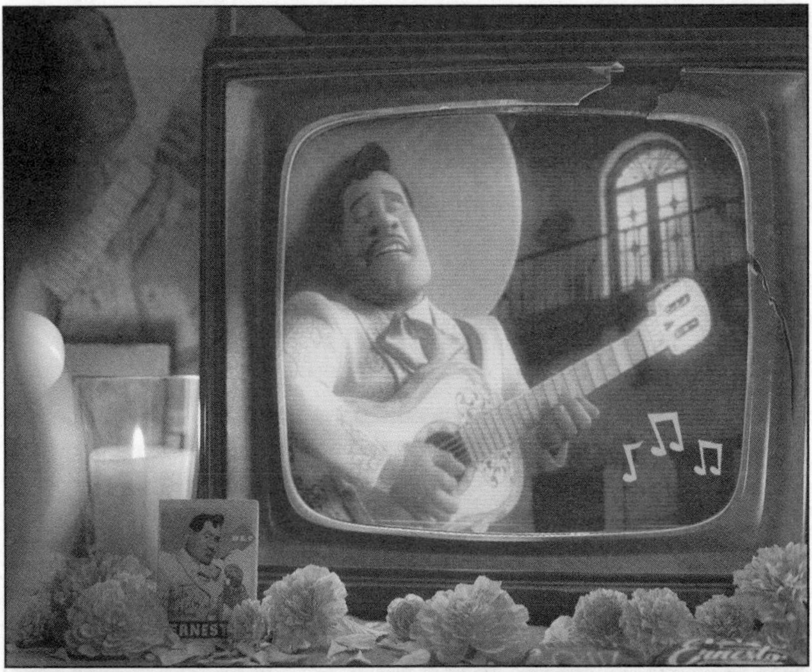

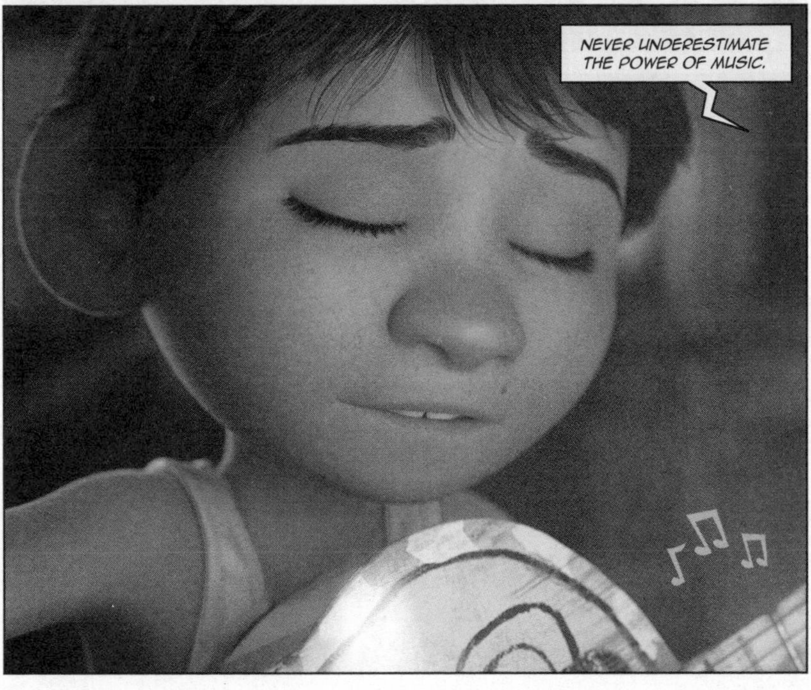
NEVER UNDERESTIMATE THE POWER OF MUSIC.

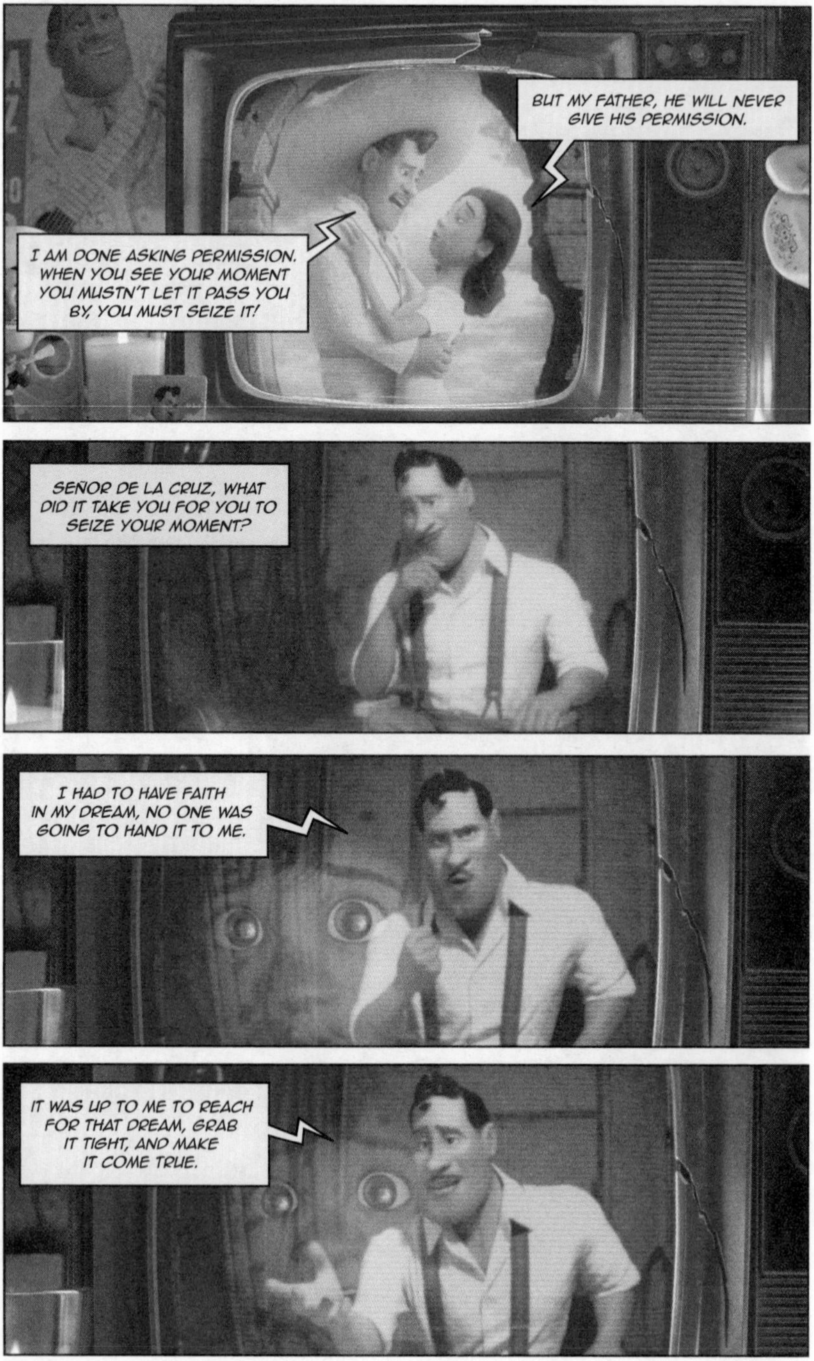
BUT MY FATHER, HE WILL NEVER GIVE HIS PERMISSION.
I AM DONE ASKING PERMISSION. WHEN YOU SEE YOUR MOMENT YOU MUSTN'T LET IT PASS YOU BY, YOU MUST SEIZE IT!
SEÑOR DE LA CRUZ, WHAT DID IT TAKE YOU FOR YOU TO SEIZE YOUR MOMENT?
I HAD TO HAVE FAITH IN MY DREAM, NO ONE WAS GOING TO HAND IT TO ME.
IT WAS UP TO ME TO REACH FOR THAT DREAM, GRAB IT TIGHT, AND MAKE IT COME TRUE.

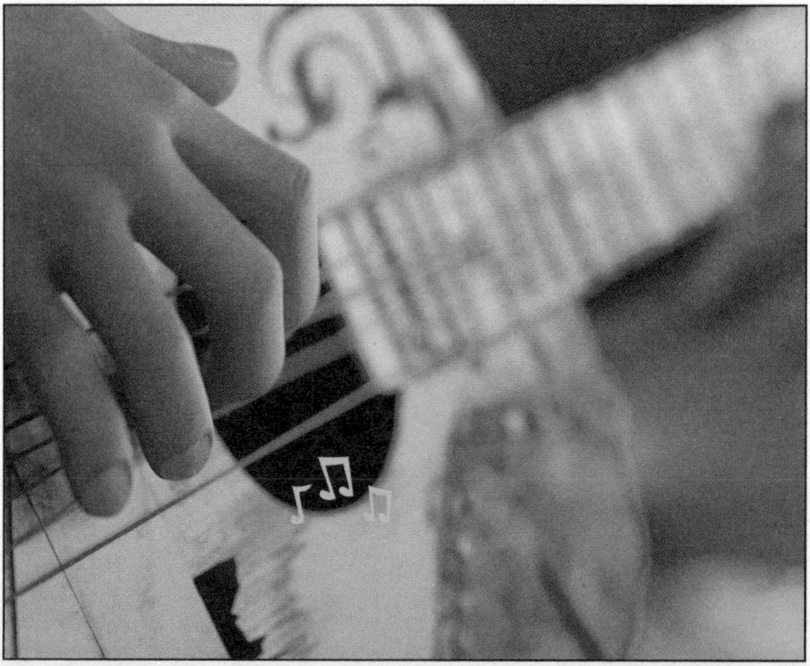

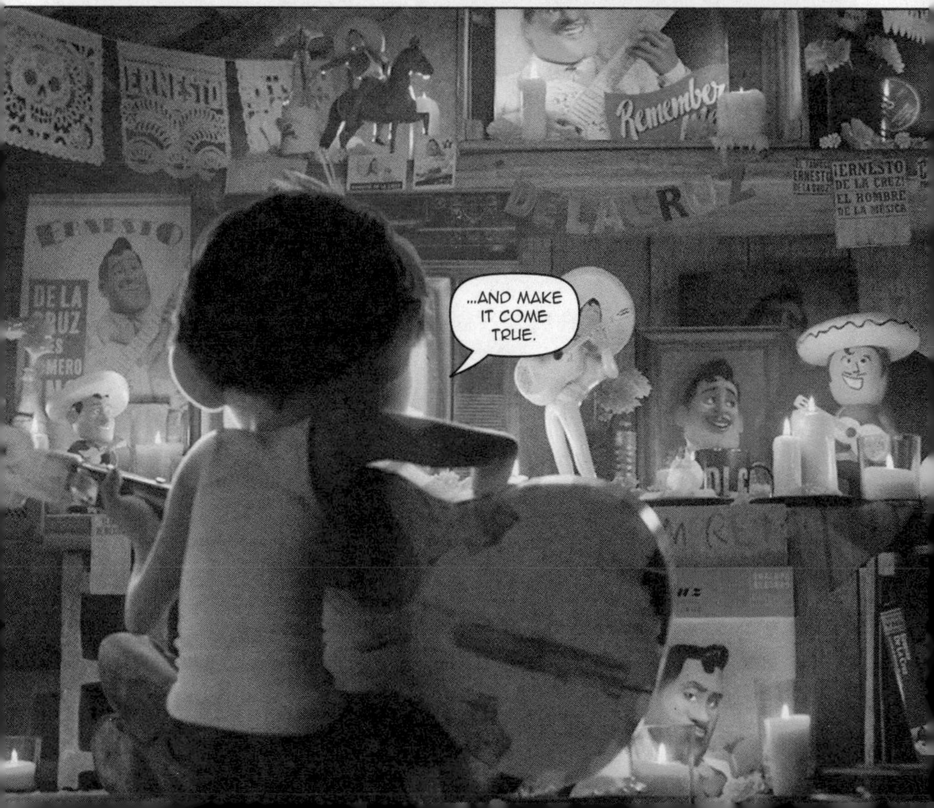
ERNESTO
Remember
...AND MAKE IT COME TRUE.

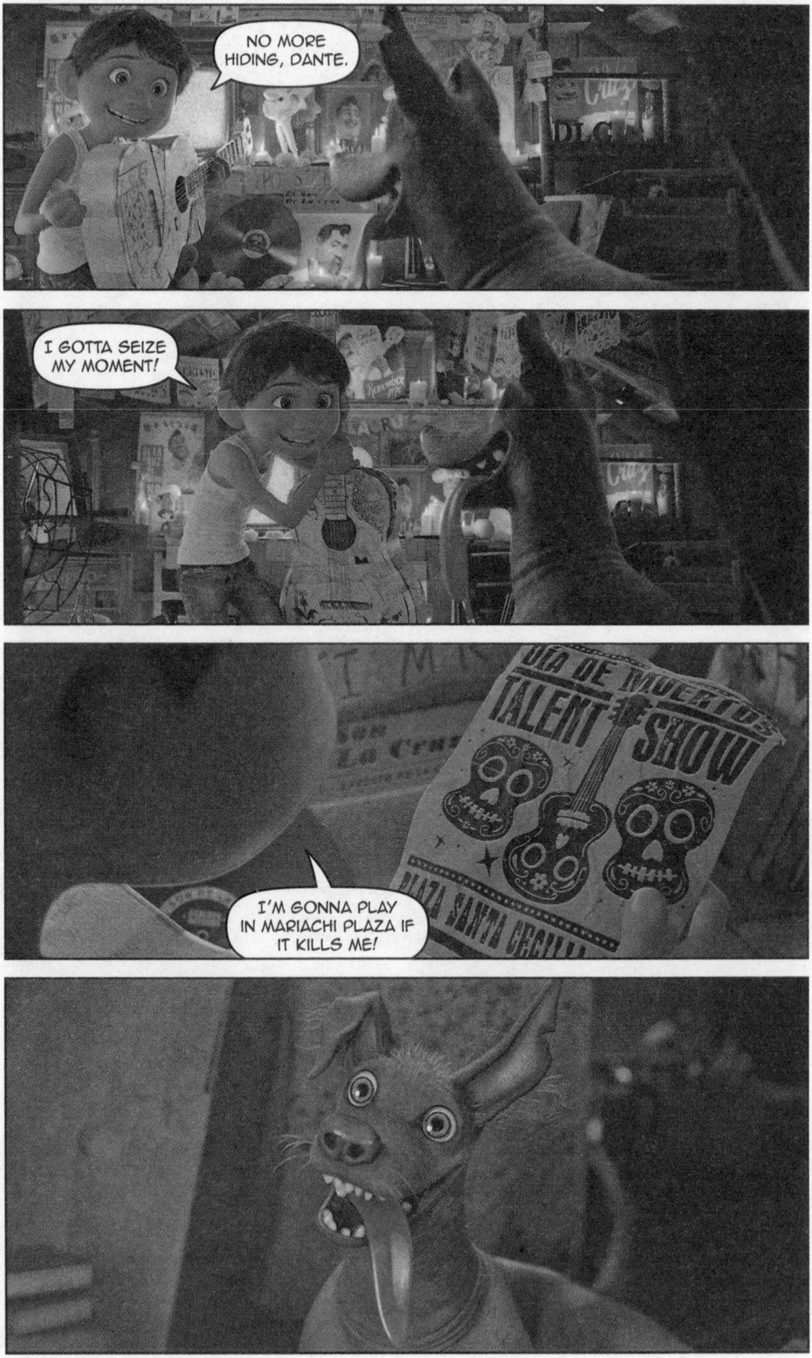
NO MORE HIDING, DANTE.
I GOTTA SEIZE MY MOMENT!
TALENT SHOW
I'M GONNA PLAY IN MARIACHI PLAZA IF IT KILLS ME!

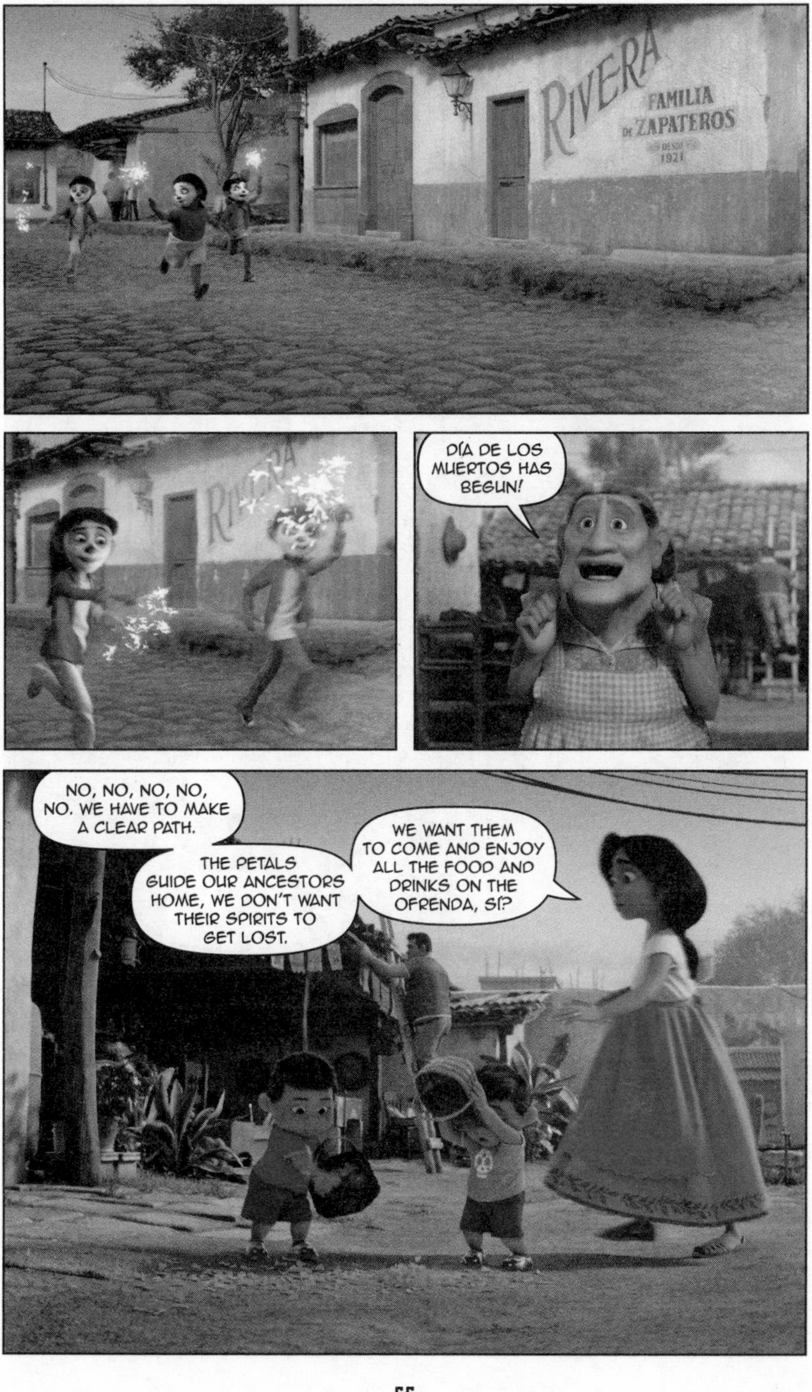
RIVERA
FAMILIA
DE ZAPATEROS
DESDE
1921
DÍA DE LOS MUERTOS HAS BEGUN!
NO, NO, NO, NO, NO. WE HAVE TO MAKE A CLEAR PATH.
THE PETALS GUIDE OUR ANCESTORS HOME, WE DON'T WANT THEIR SPIRITS TO GET LOST.
WE WANT THEM TO COME AND ENJOY ALL THE FOOD AND DRINKS ON THE OFRENDA, SÍ?

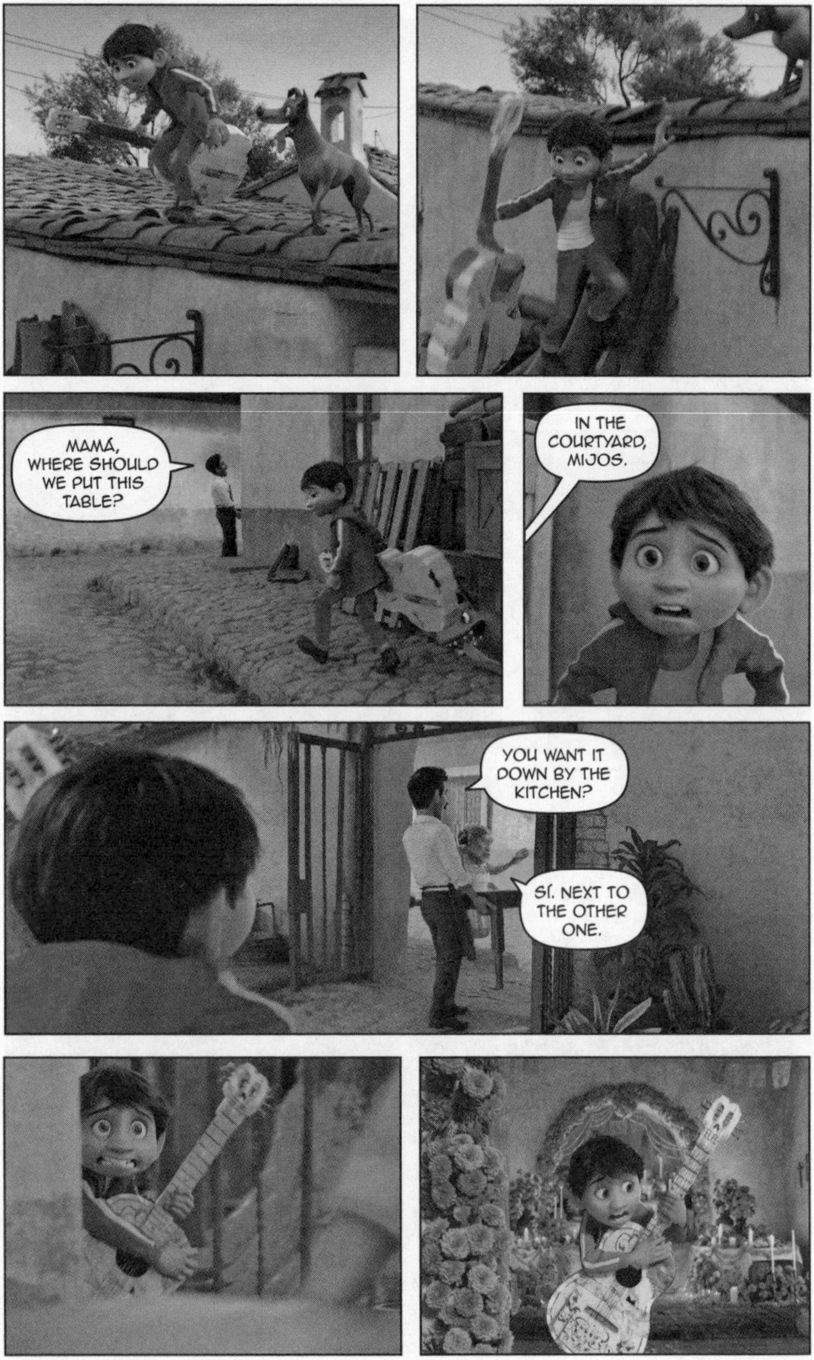
MAMÁ, WHERE SHOULD WE PUT THIS TABLE?
IN THE COURTYARD, MIJOS.
YOU WANT IT DOWN BY THE KITCHEN?
SÍ. NEXT TO THE OTHER ONE.

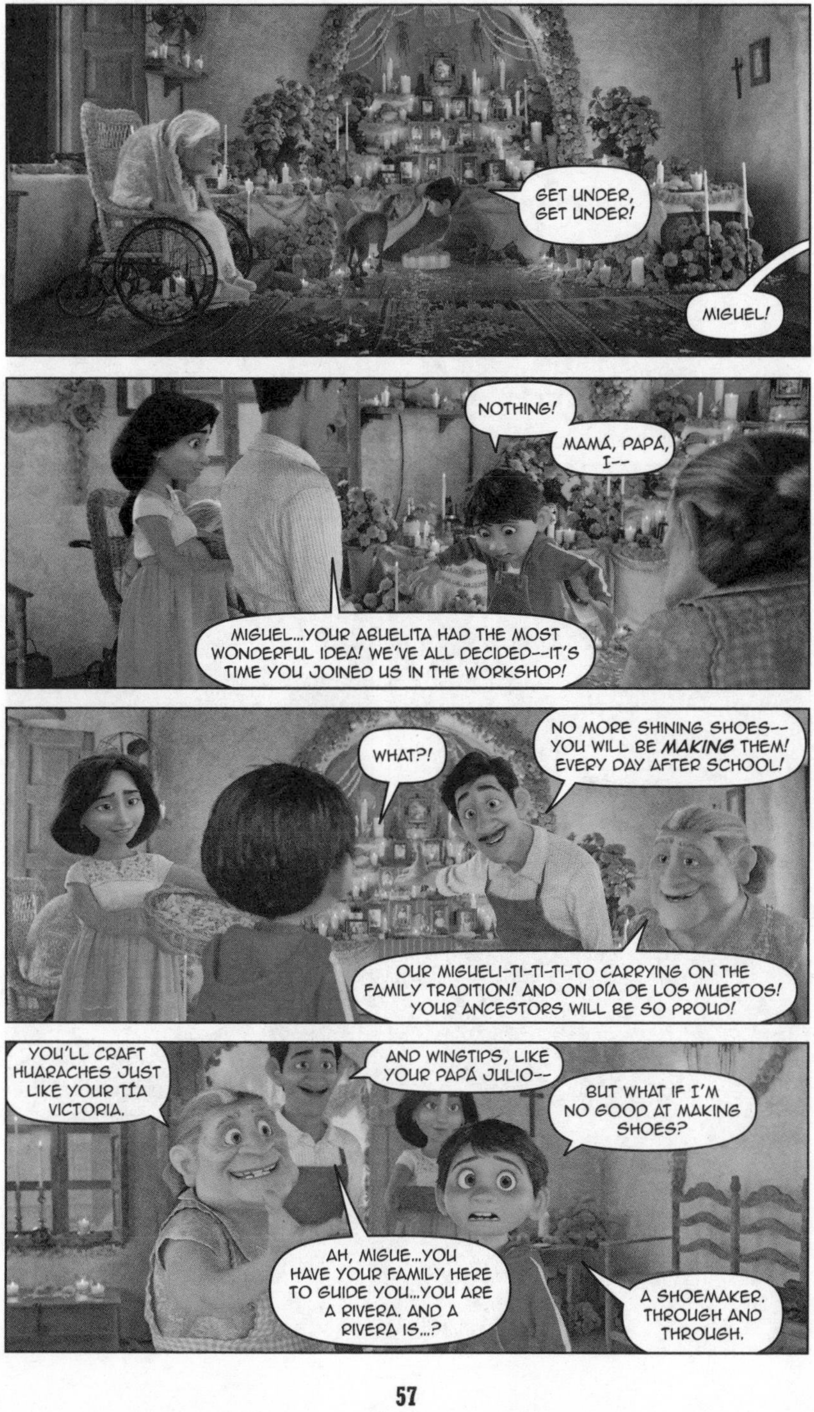
GET UNDER, GET UNDER!
MIGUEL!
NOTHING!
MAMÁ, PAPÁ, I--
MIGUEL...YOUR ABUELITA HAD THE MOST WONDERFUL IDEA! WE'VE ALL DECIDED--IT'S TIME YOU JOINED US IN THE WORKSHOP!
WHAT?!
NO MORE SHINING SHOES--YOU WILL BE *MAKING* THEM! EVERY DAY AFTER SCHOOL!
OUR MIGUELI-TI-TI-TI-TO CARRYING ON THE FAMILY TRADITION! AND ON DÍA DE LOS MUERTOS! YOUR ANCESTORS WILL BE SO PROUD!
YOU'LL CRAFT HUARACHES JUST LIKE YOUR TÍA VICTORIA.
AND WINGTIPS, LIKE YOUR PAPÁ JULIO--
BUT WHAT IF I'M NO GOOD AT MAKING SHOES?
AH, MIGUE...YOU HAVE YOUR FAMILY HERE TO GUIDE YOU...YOU ARE A RIVERA. AND A RIVERA IS...?
A SHOEMAKER. THROUGH AND THROUGH.

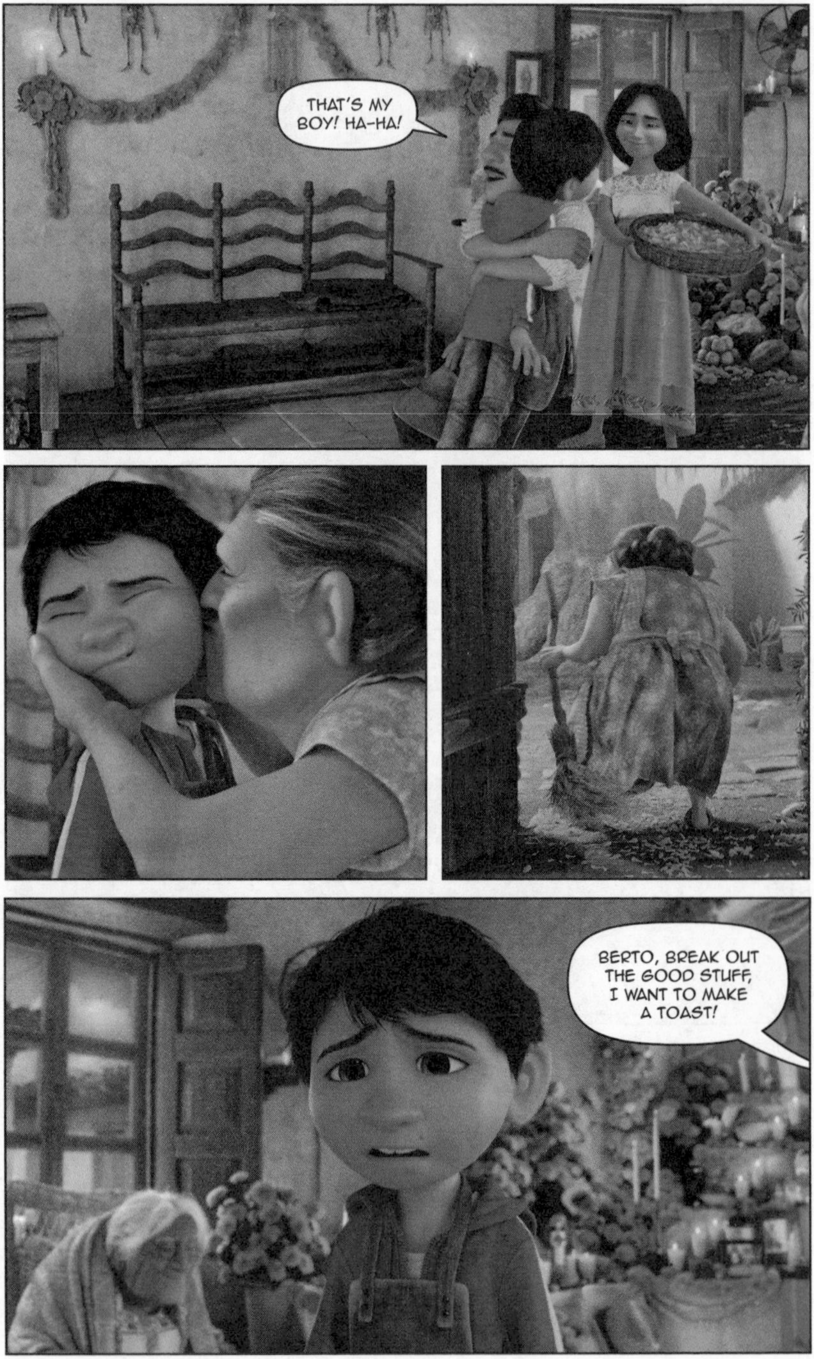
THAT'S MY BOY! HA-HA!
BERTO, BREAK OUT THE GOOD STUFF, I WANT TO MAKE A TOAST!

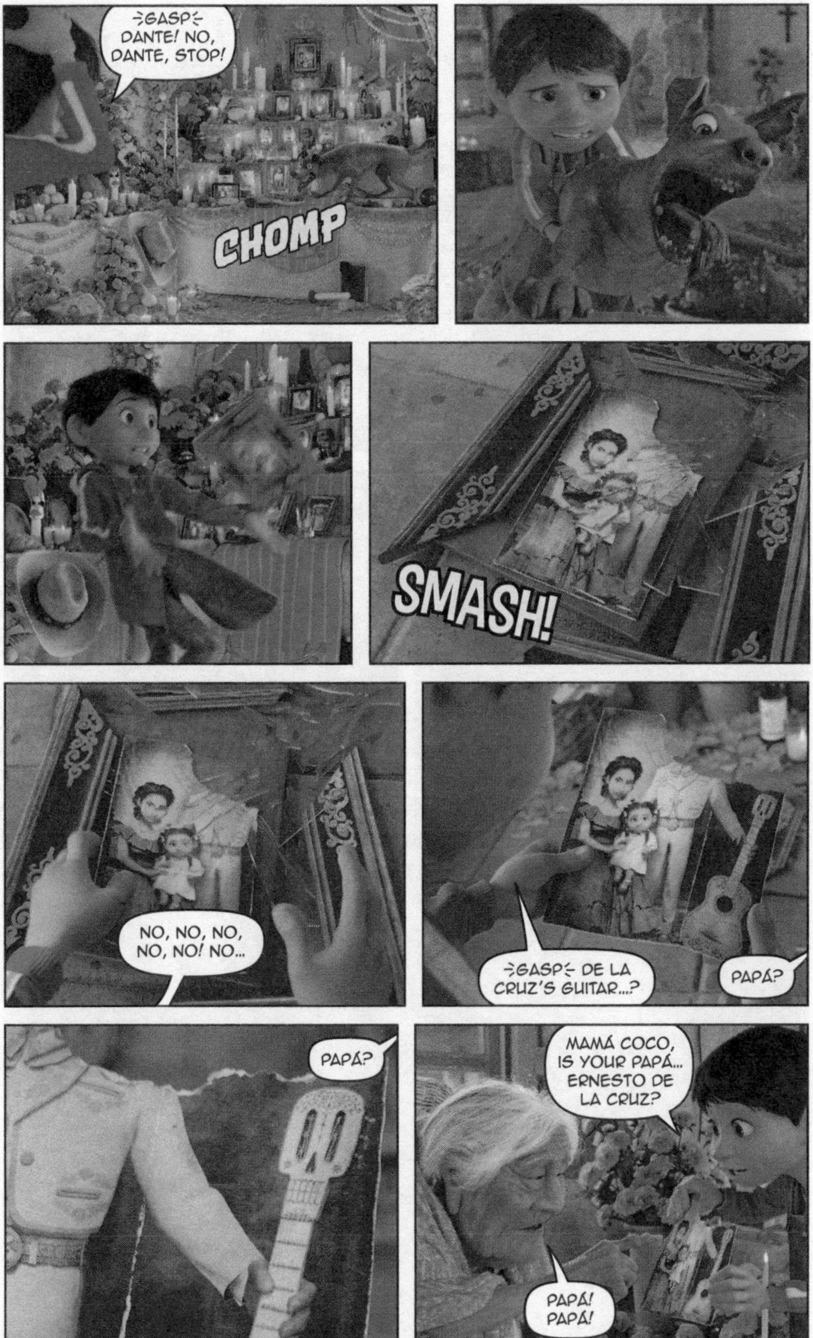

⸗GASP⸗ DANTE! NO, DANTE, STOP!
CHOMP
SMASH!
NO, NO, NO, NO, NO! NO...
⸗GASP⸗ DE LA CRUZ'S GUITAR...?
PAPÁ?
PAPÁ?
MAMÁ COCO, IS YOUR PAPÁ... ERNESTO DE LA CRUZ?
PAPÁ! PAPÁ!

BACK AT MIGUEL'S SECRET OFRENDA...
Remember Me
LACRUZ
HA-HA!
Ernesto de la Cruz

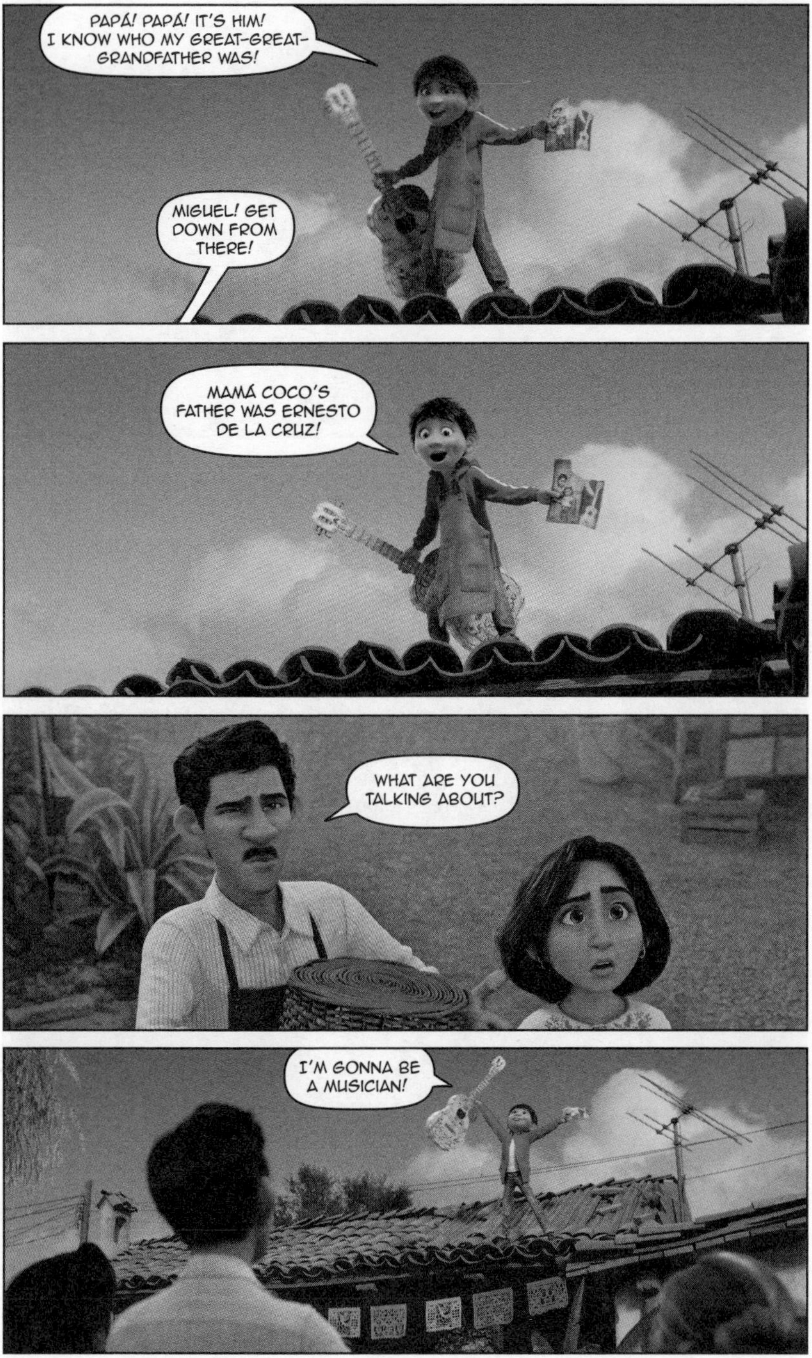
PAPÁ! PAPÁ! IT'S HIM! I KNOW WHO MY GREAT-GREAT-GRANDFATHER WAS!
MIGUEL! GET DOWN FROM THERE!
MAMÁ COCO'S FATHER WAS ERNESTO DE LA CRUZ!
WHAT ARE YOU TALKING ABOUT?
I'M GONNA BE A MUSICIAN!

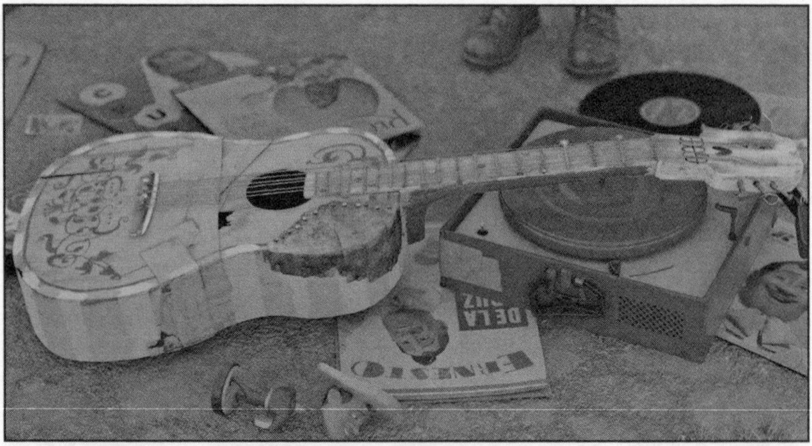

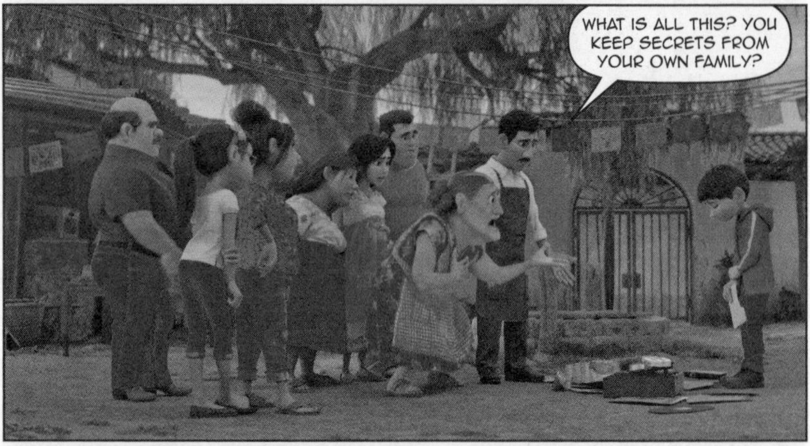
WHAT IS ALL THIS? YOU KEEP SECRETS FROM YOUR OWN FAMILY?

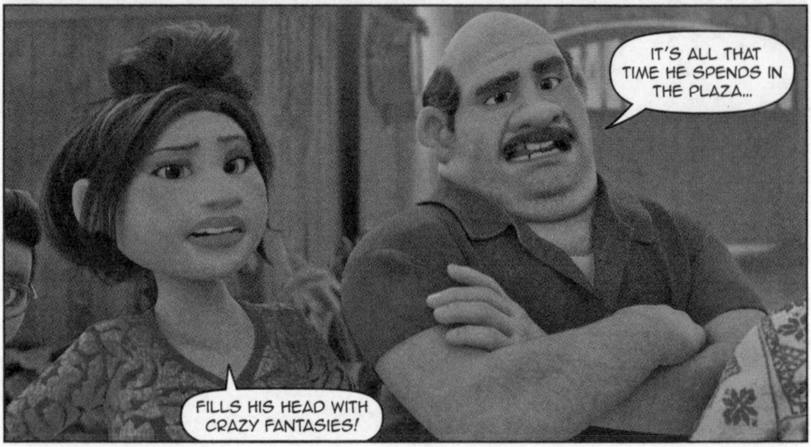
IT'S ALL THAT TIME HE SPENDS IN THE PLAZA...
FILLS HIS HEAD WITH CRAZY FANTASIES!

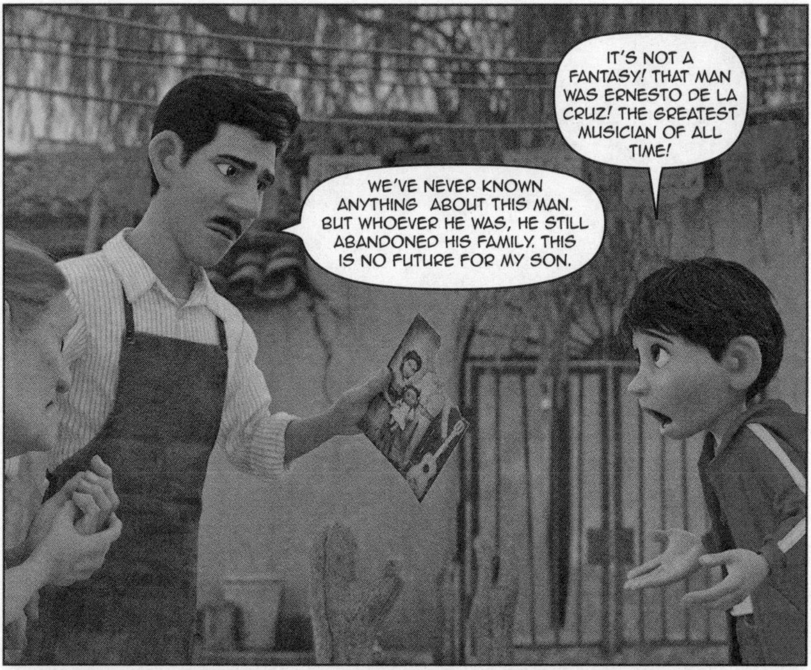
IT'S NOT A FANTASY! THAT MAN WAS ERNESTO DE LA CRUZ! THE GREATEST MUSICIAN OF ALL TIME!
WE'VE NEVER KNOWN ANYTHING ABOUT THIS MAN. BUT WHOEVER HE WAS, HE STILL ABANDONED HIS FAMILY. THIS IS NO FUTURE FOR MY SON.

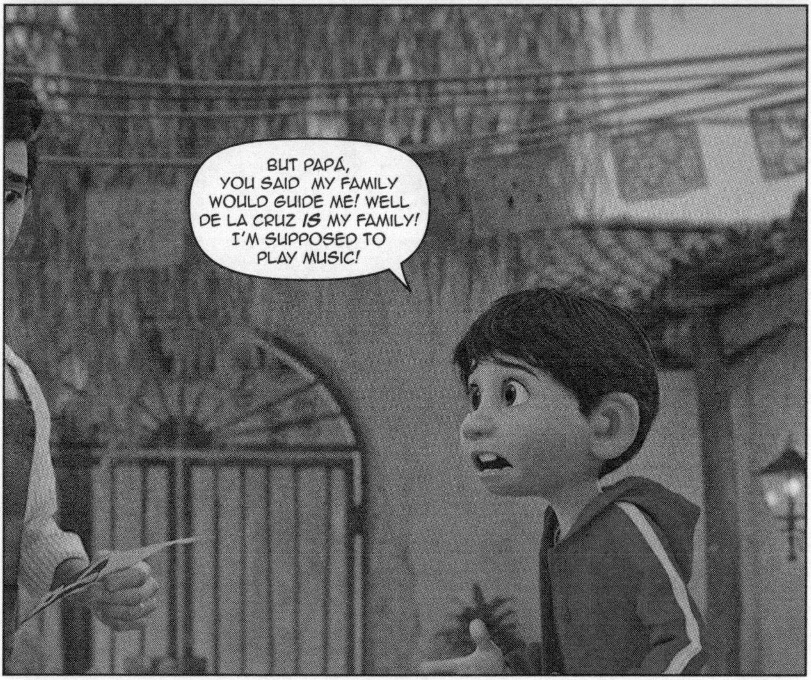
BUT PAPÁ, YOU SAID MY FAMILY WOULD GUIDE ME! WELL DE LA CRUZ *IS* MY FAMILY! I'M SUPPOSED TO PLAY MUSIC!

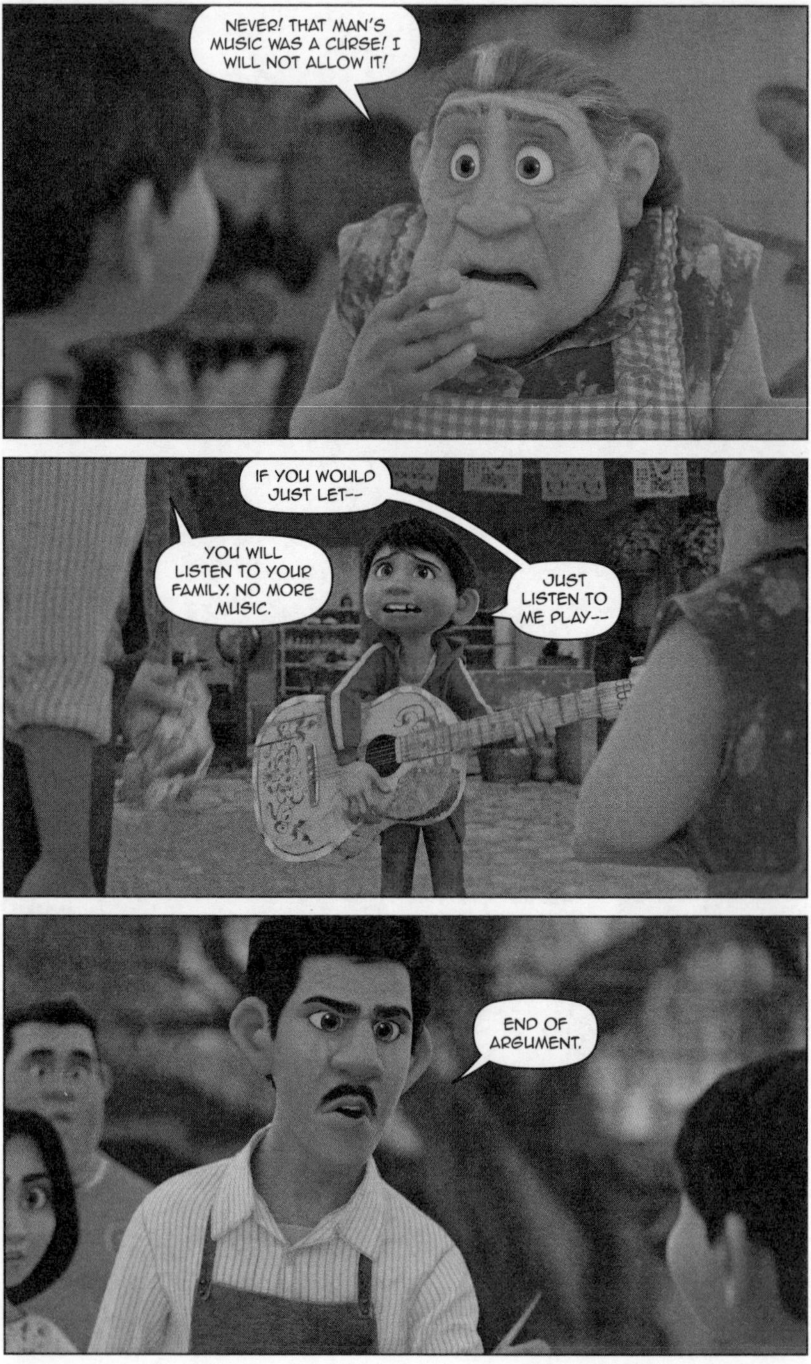
NEVER! THAT MAN'S MUSIC WAS A CURSE! I WILL NOT ALLOW IT!
IF YOU WOULD JUST LET--
YOU WILL LISTEN TO YOUR FAMILY. NO MORE MUSIC.
JUST LISTEN TO ME PLAY--
END OF ARGUMENT.

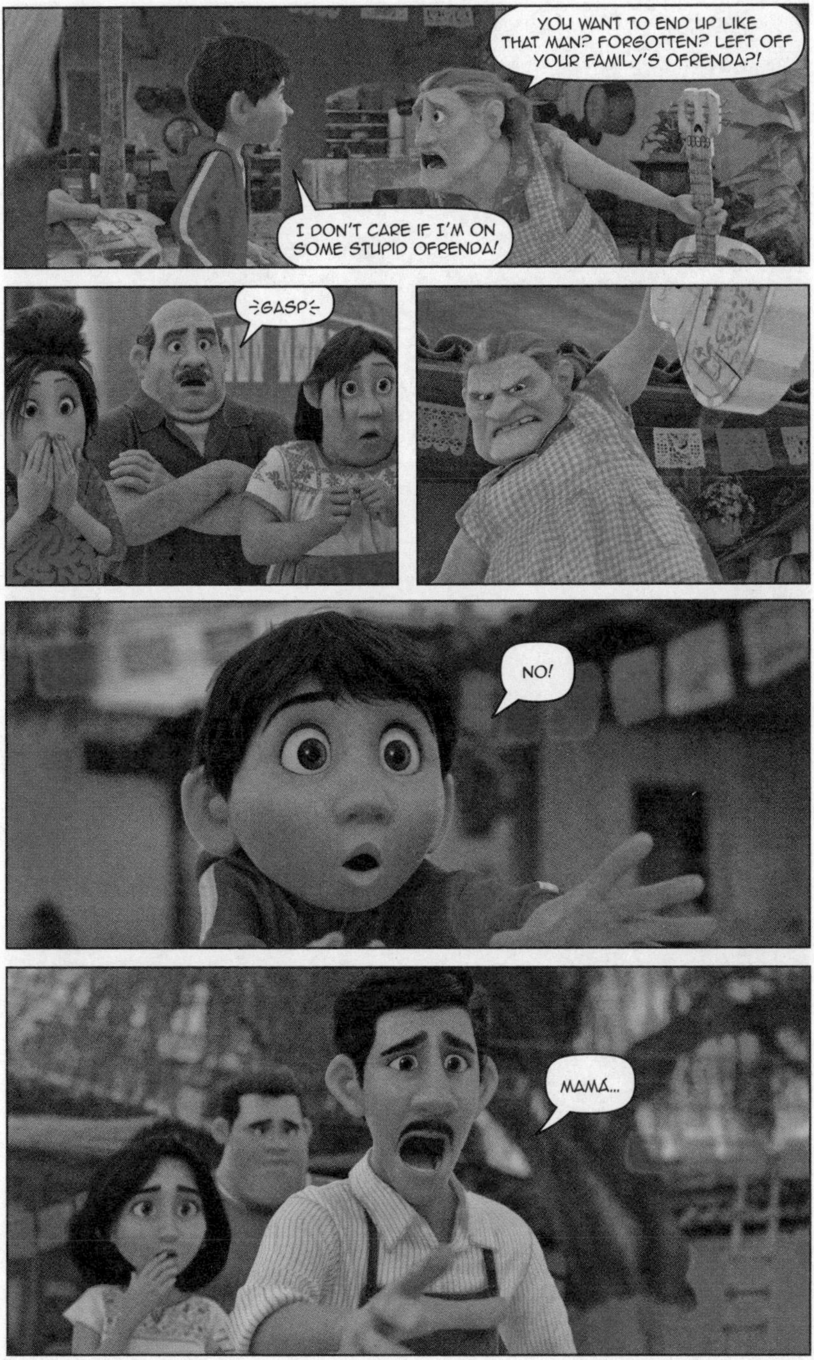
YOU WANT TO END UP LIKE THAT MAN? FORGOTTEN? LEFT OFF YOUR FAMILY'S OFRENDA?!
I DON'T CARE IF I'M ON SOME STUPID OFRENDA!
GASP
NO!
MAMÁ...

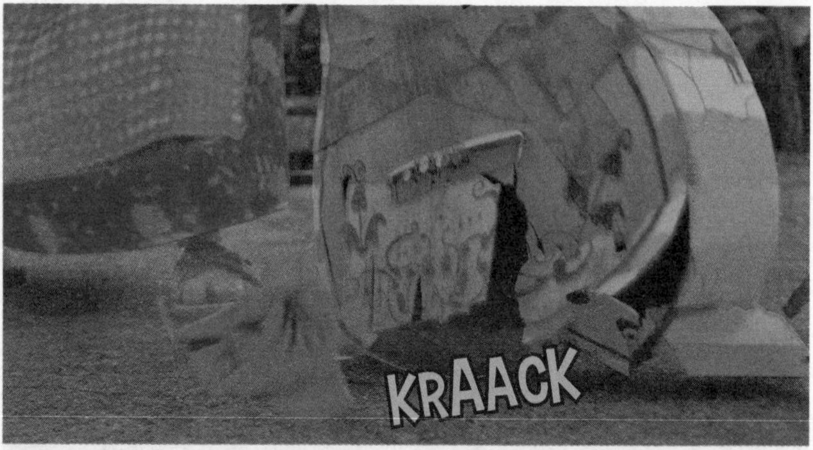
KRAACK

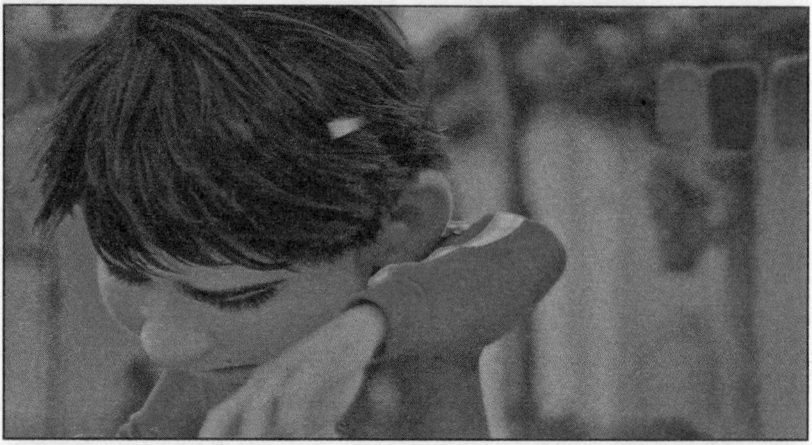

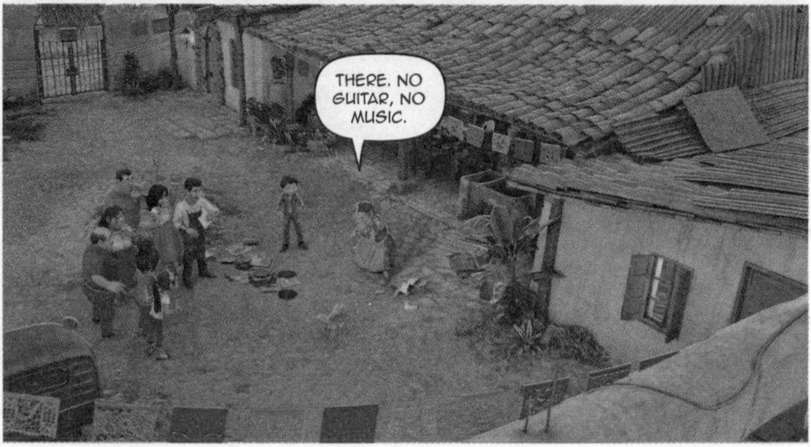
THERE. NO GUITAR, NO MUSIC.

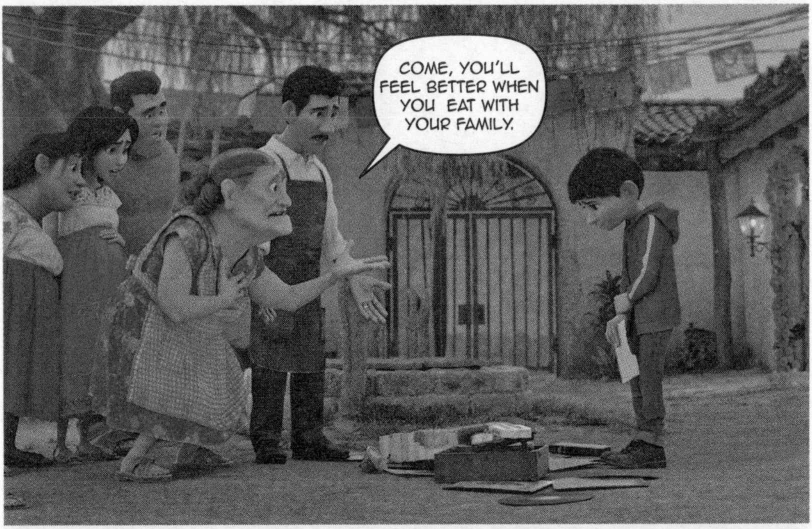
COME, YOU'LL FEEL BETTER WHEN YOU EAT WITH YOUR FAMILY.

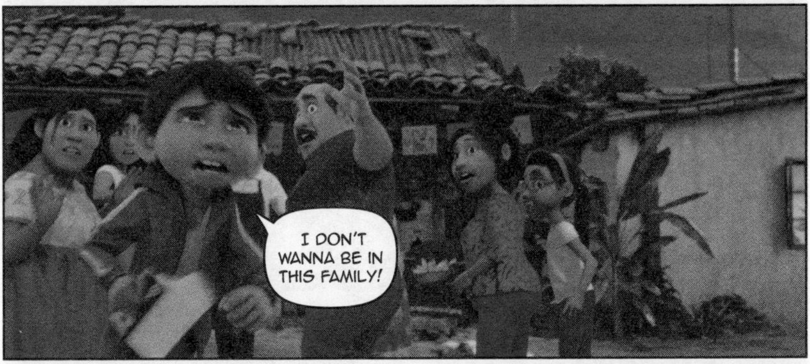
I DON'T WANNA BE IN THIS FAMILY!

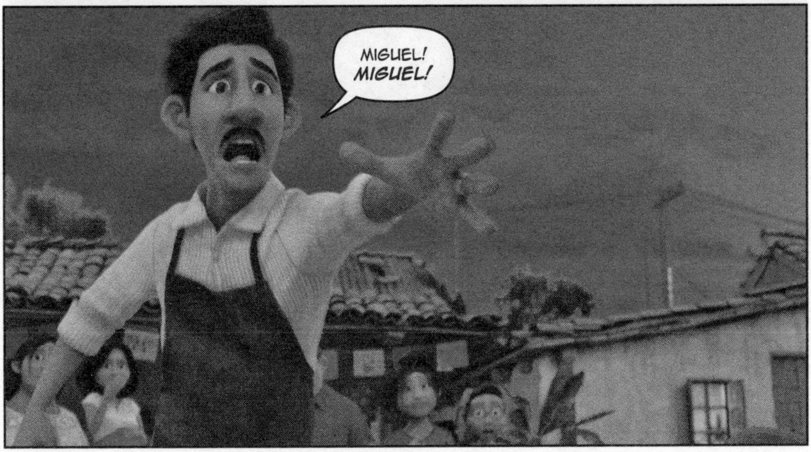
MIGUEL! MIGUEL!

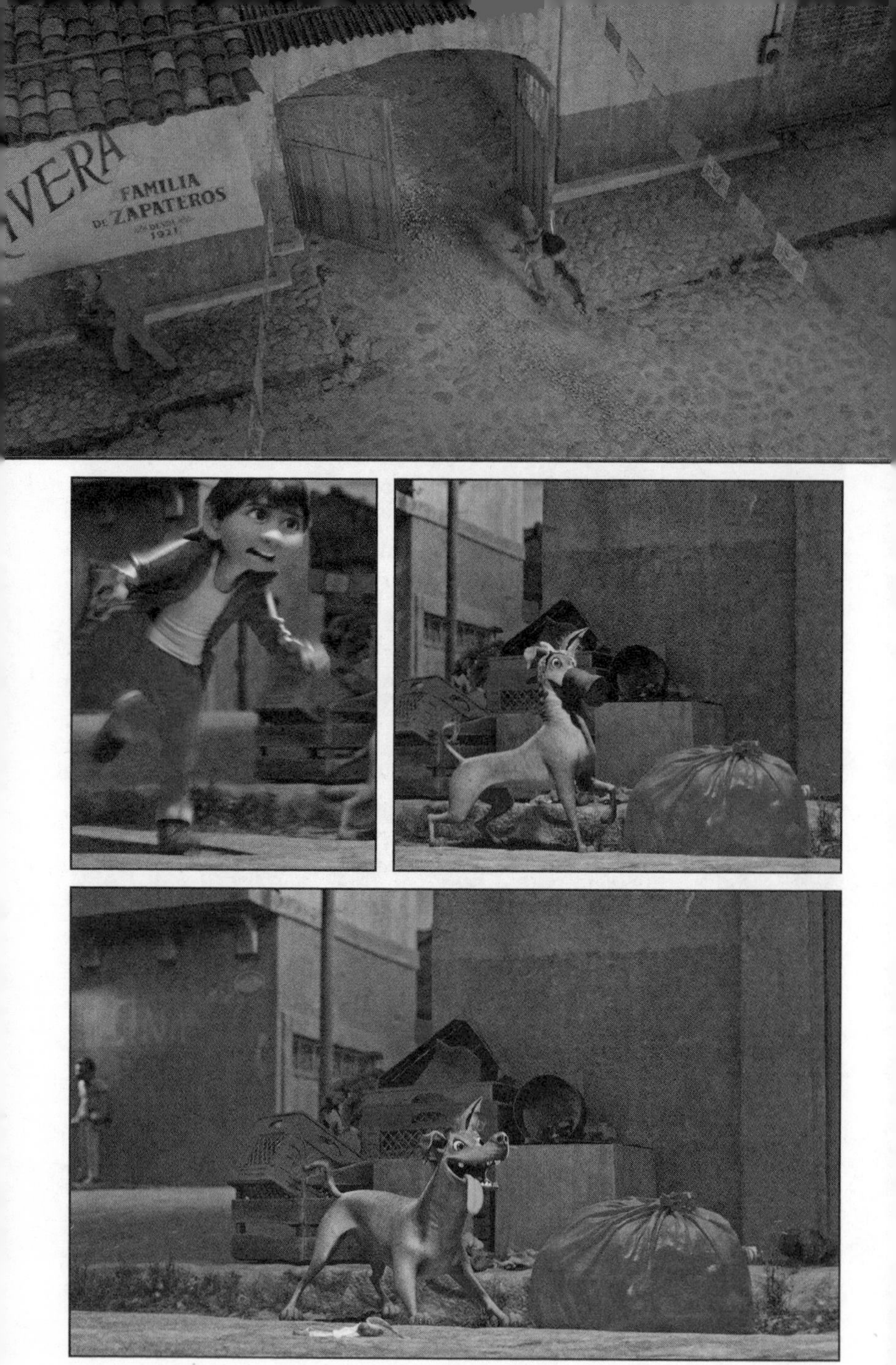
VERA
FAMILIA
DE ZAPATEROS
1921

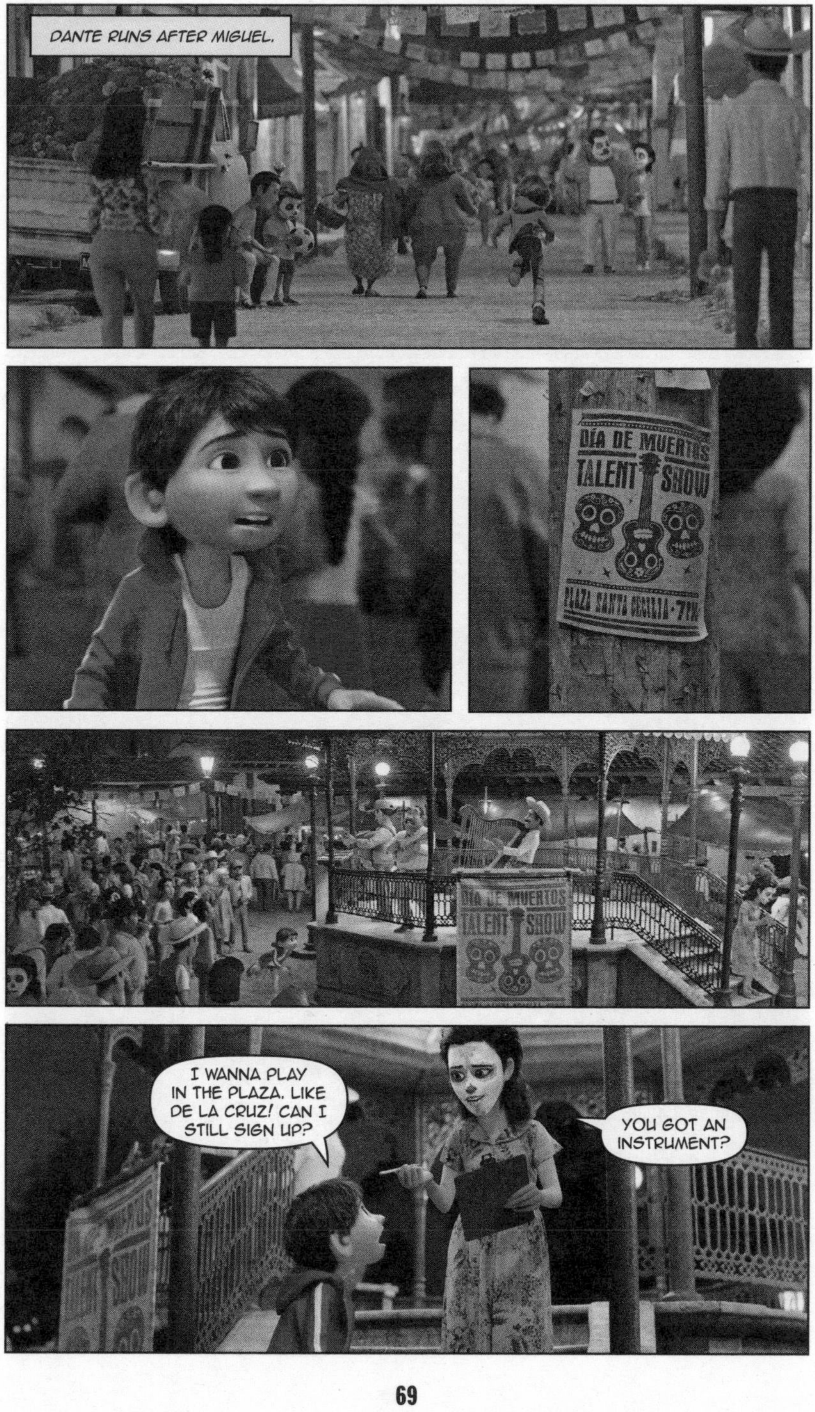
DANTE RUNS AFTER MIGUEL.
DÍA DE MUERTOS TALENT SHOW
PLAZA SANTA CECILIA · 7PM
I WANNA PLAY IN THE PLAZA, LIKE DE LA CRUZ! CAN I STILL SIGN UP?
YOU GOT AN INSTRUMENT?

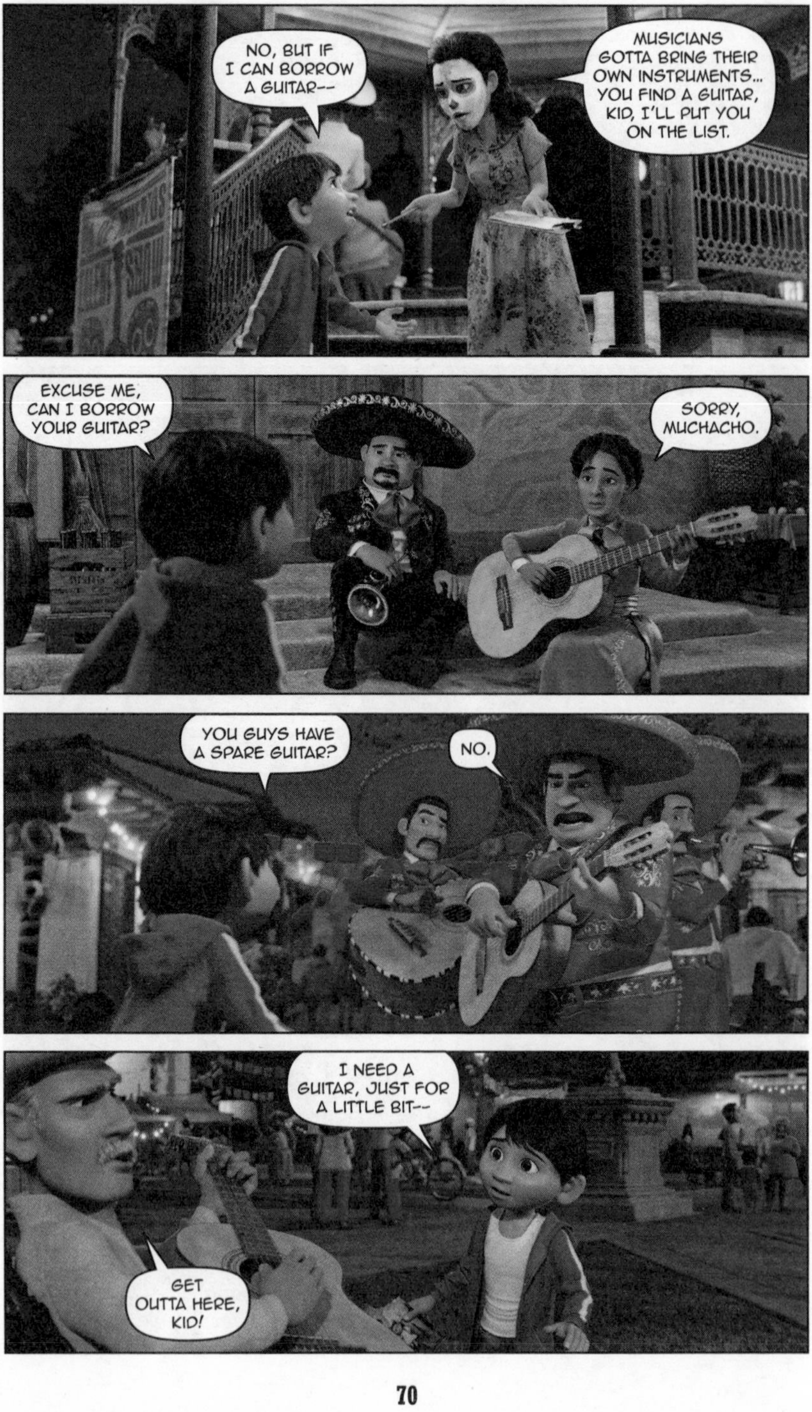
NO, BUT IF I CAN BORROW A GUITAR--
MUSICIANS GOTTA BRING THEIR OWN INSTRUMENTS... YOU FIND A GUITAR, KID, I'LL PUT YOU ON THE LIST.
EXCUSE ME, CAN I BORROW YOUR GUITAR?
SORRY, MUCHACHO.
YOU GUYS HAVE A SPARE GUITAR?
NO.
I NEED A GUITAR, JUST FOR A LITTLE BIT--
GET OUTTA HERE, KID!

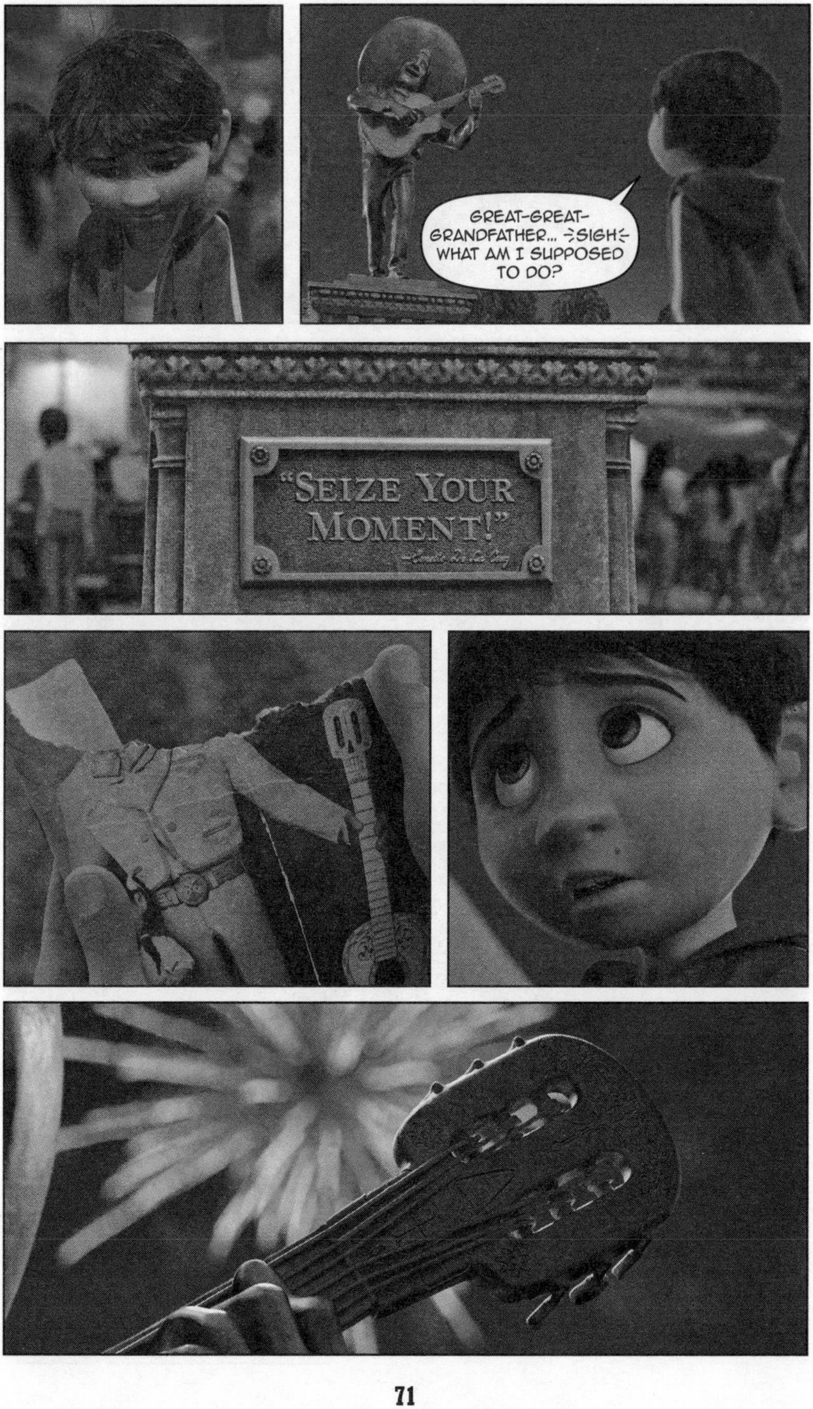
GREAT-GREAT-GRANDFATHER... SIGH WHAT AM I SUPPOSED TO DO?
"SEIZE YOUR MOMENT!"

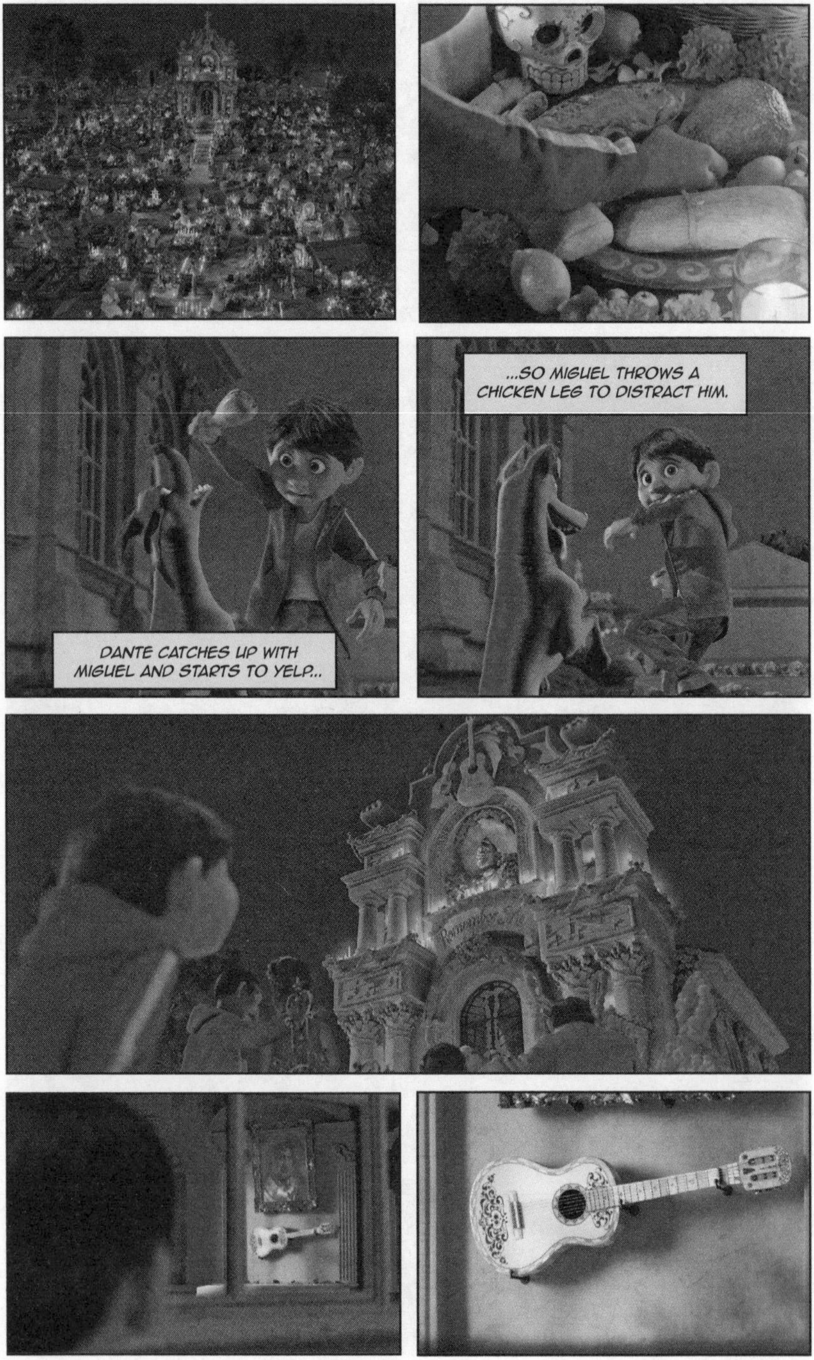
DANTE CATCHES UP WITH MIGUEL AND STARTS TO YELP...
...SO MIGUEL THROWS A CHICKEN LEG TO DISTRACT HIM.

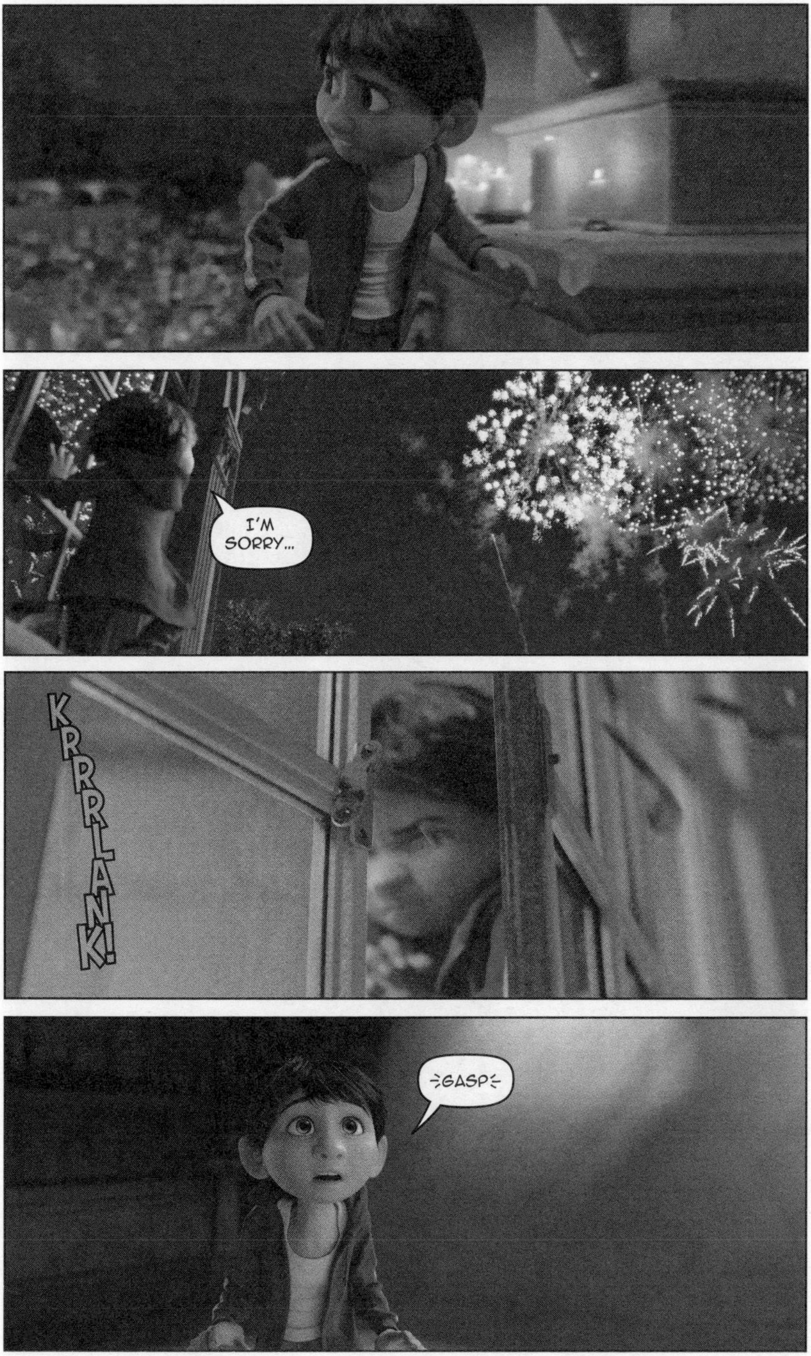
I'M SORRY...
KRRRLANK!
GASP

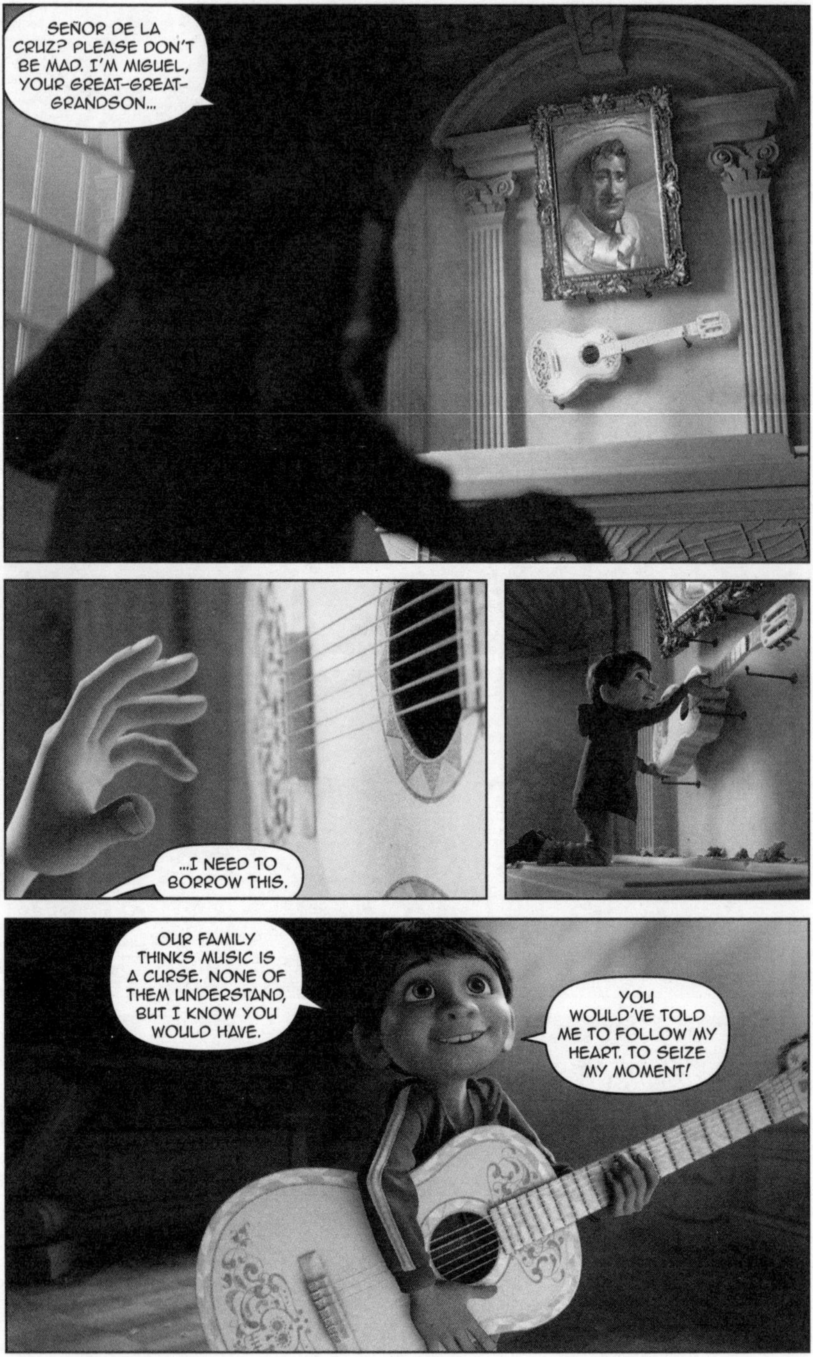
SEÑOR DE LA CRUZ? PLEASE DON'T BE MAD. I'M MIGUEL, YOUR GREAT-GREAT-GRANDSON...
...I NEED TO BORROW THIS.
OUR FAMILY THINKS MUSIC IS A CURSE. NONE OF THEM UNDERSTAND, BUT I KNOW YOU WOULD HAVE.
YOU WOULD'VE TOLD ME TO FOLLOW MY HEART. TO SEIZE MY MOMENT!

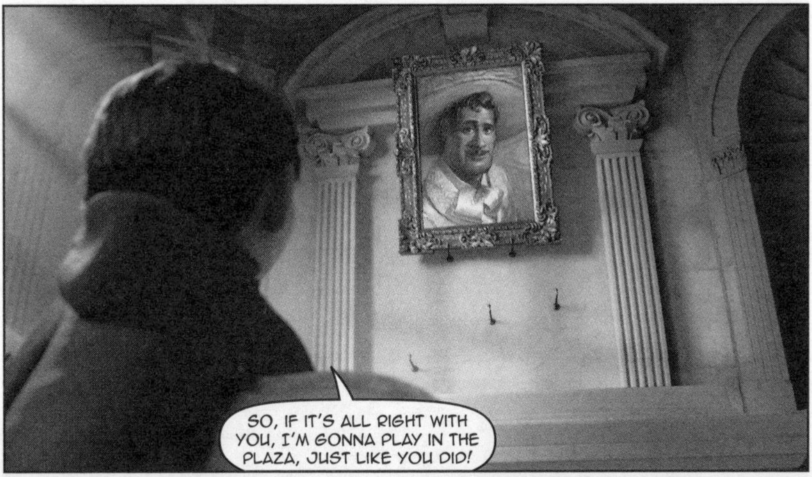
SO, IF IT'S ALL RIGHT WITH YOU, I'M GONNA PLAY IN THE PLAZA, JUST LIKE YOU DID!

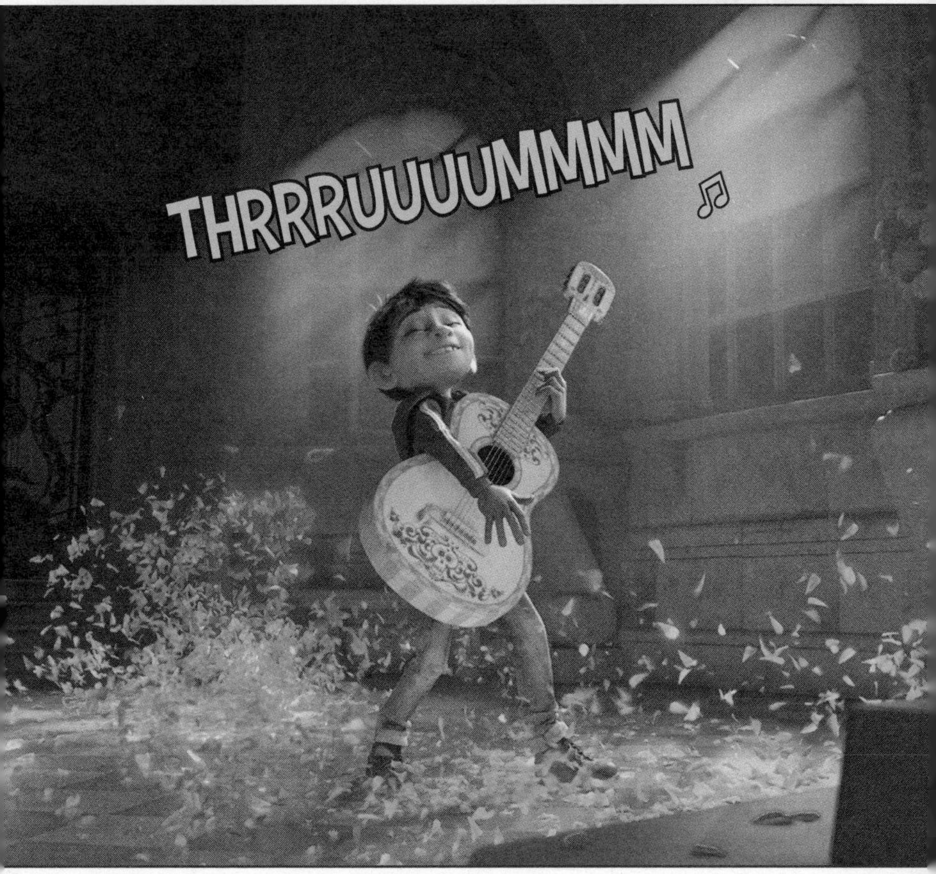
THRRRUUUUMMMMM

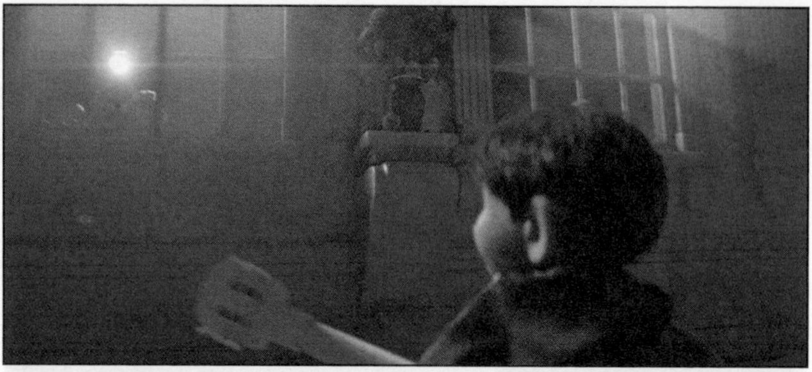

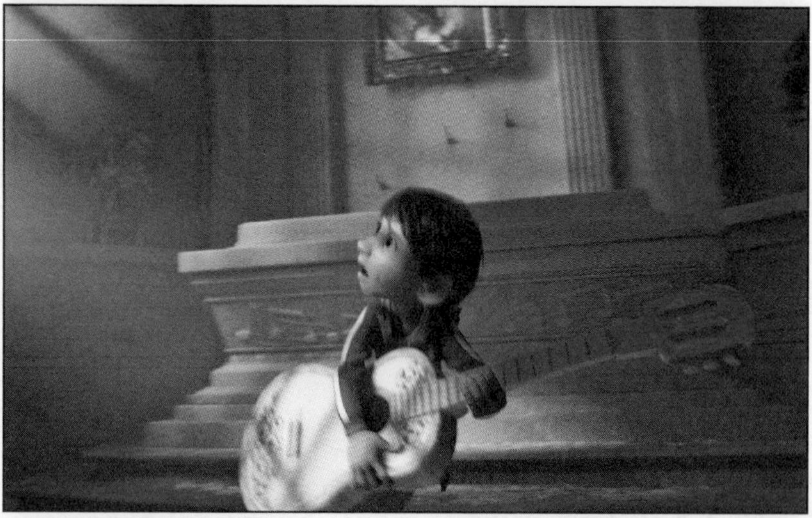

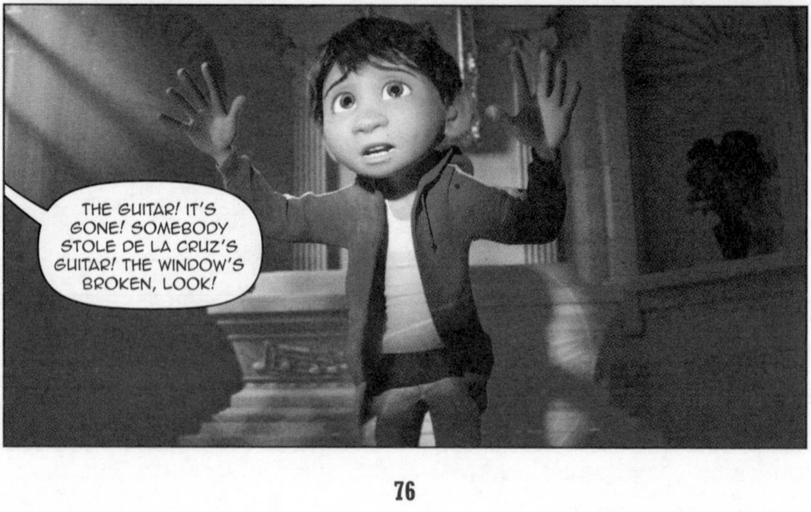
THE GUITAR! IT'S GONE! SOMEBODY STOLE DE LA CRUZ'S GUITAR! THE WINDOW'S BROKEN, LOOK!

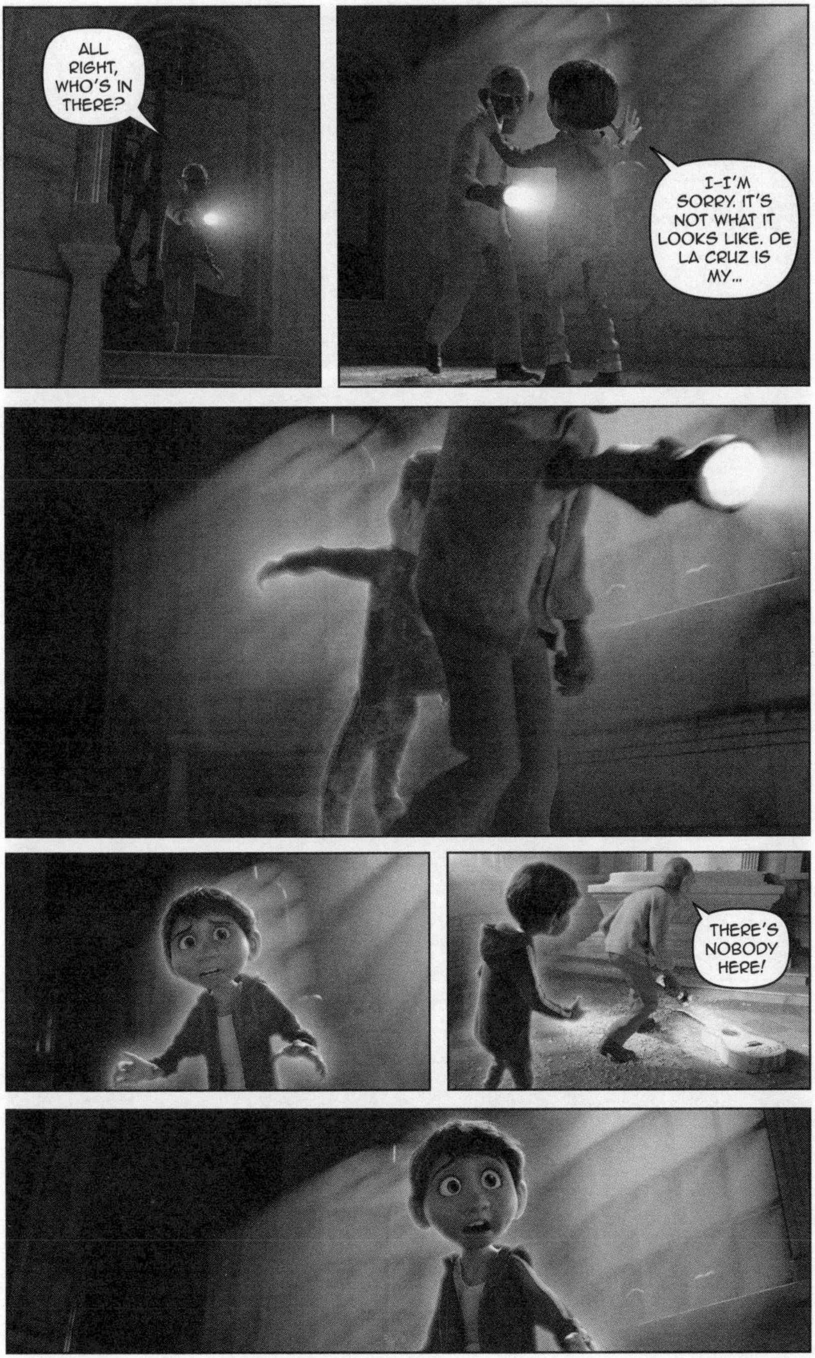
ALL RIGHT, WHO'S IN THERE?
I-I'M SORRY. IT'S NOT WHAT IT LOOKS LIKE. DE LA CRUZ IS MY...
THERE'S NOBODY HERE!

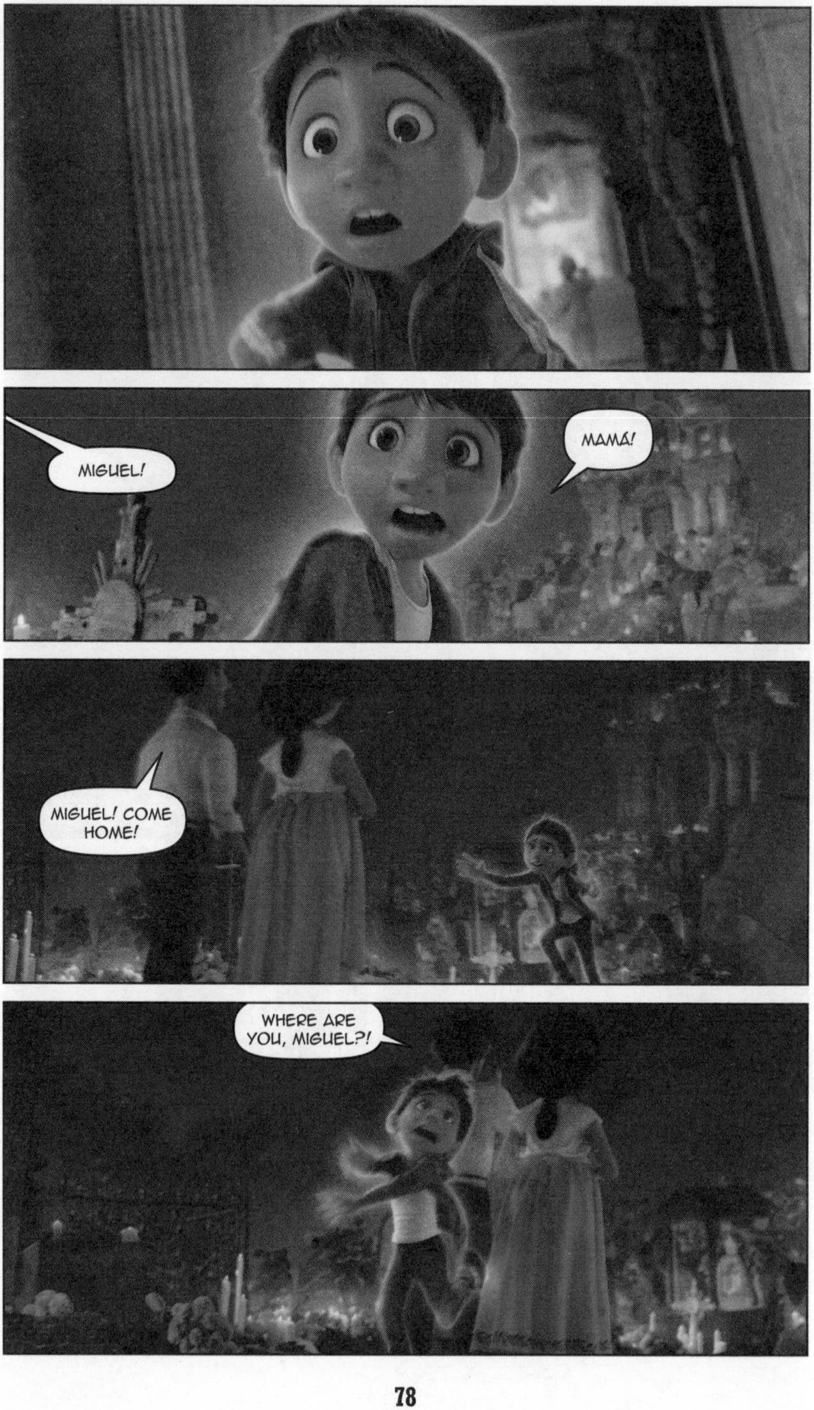
MIGUEL!
MAMÁ!
MIGUEL! COME HOME!
WHERE ARE YOU, MIGUEL?!

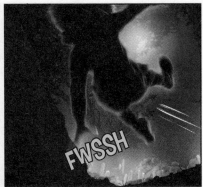

FWSSH

DIOS MÍO!
LITTLE BOY, ARE
YOU OKAY? HERE,
LET ME HELP
YOU.

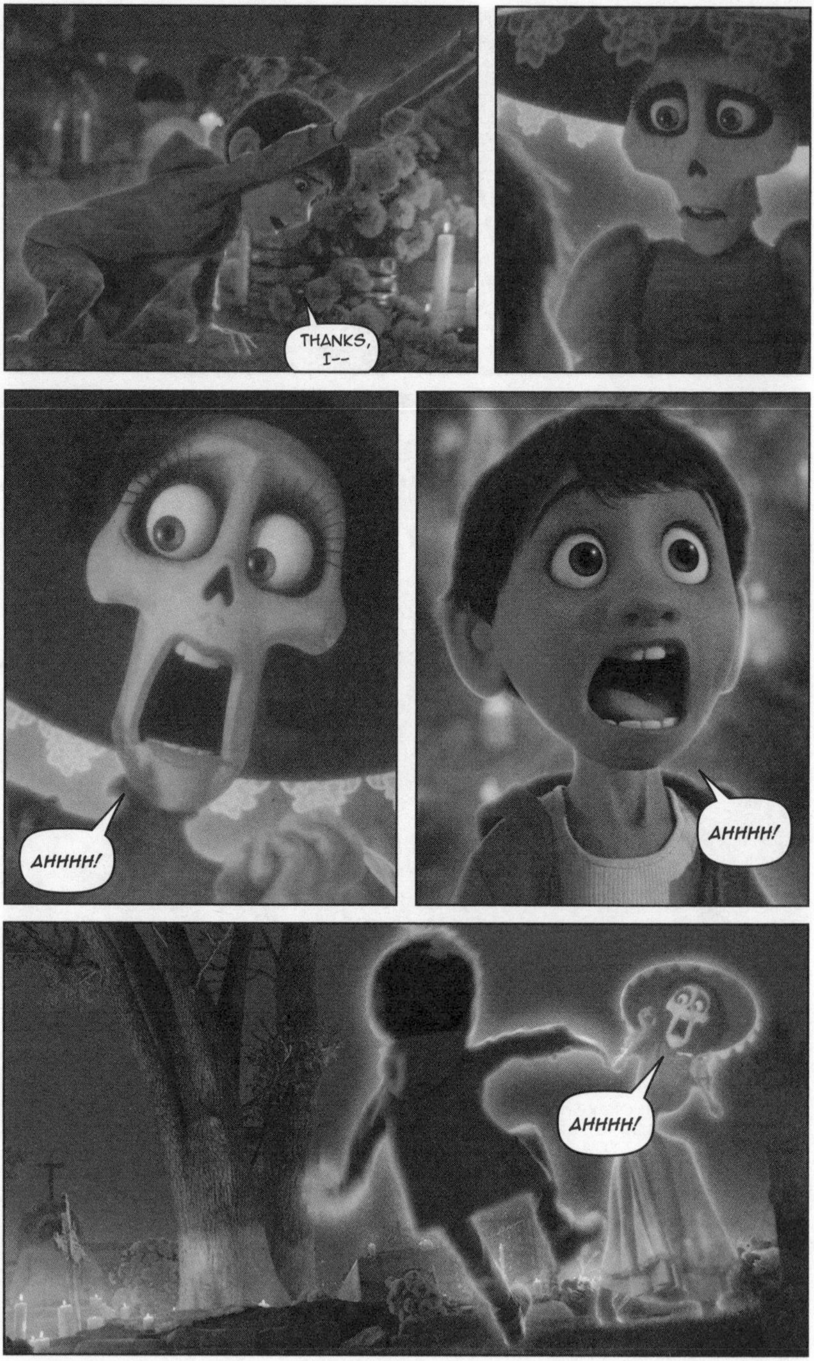
THANKS, I--
AHHHH!
AHHHH!
AHHHH!

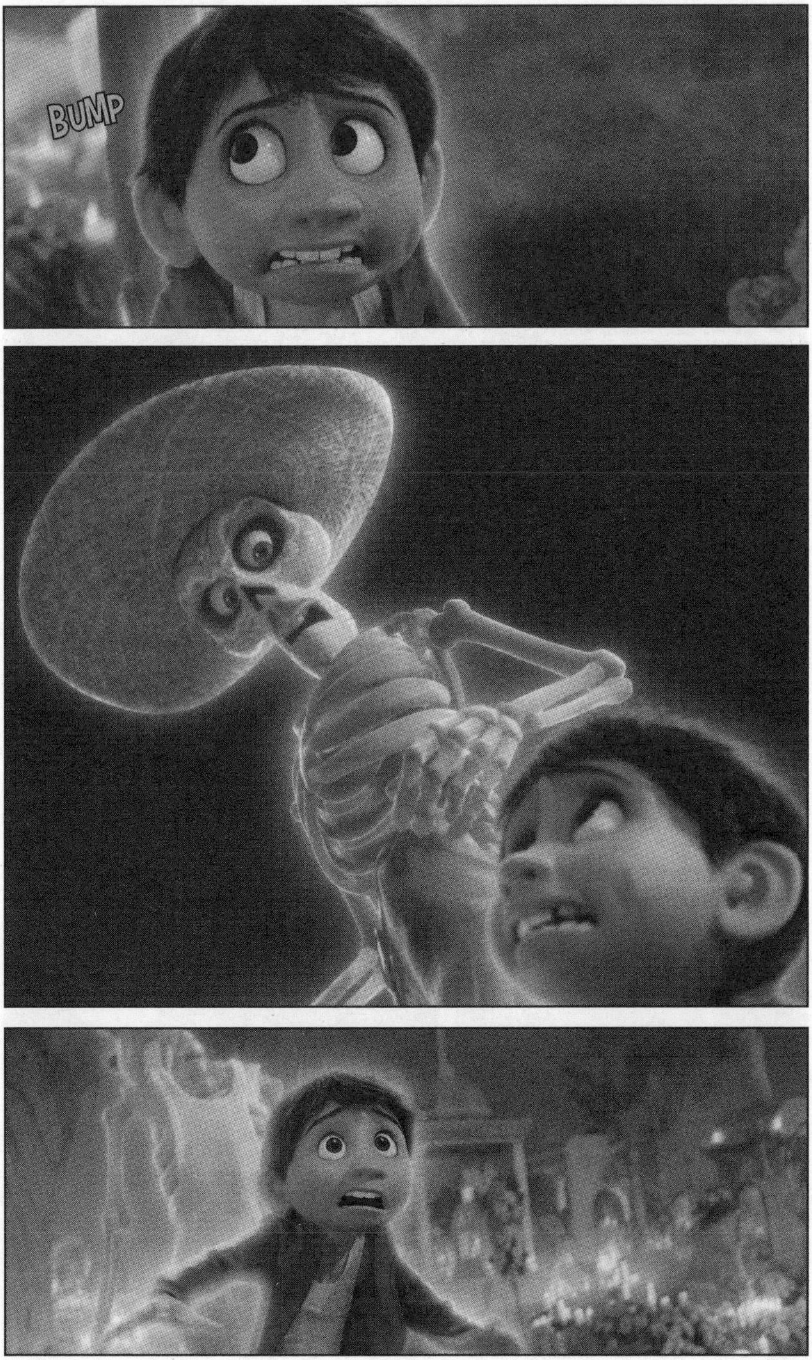
BUMP

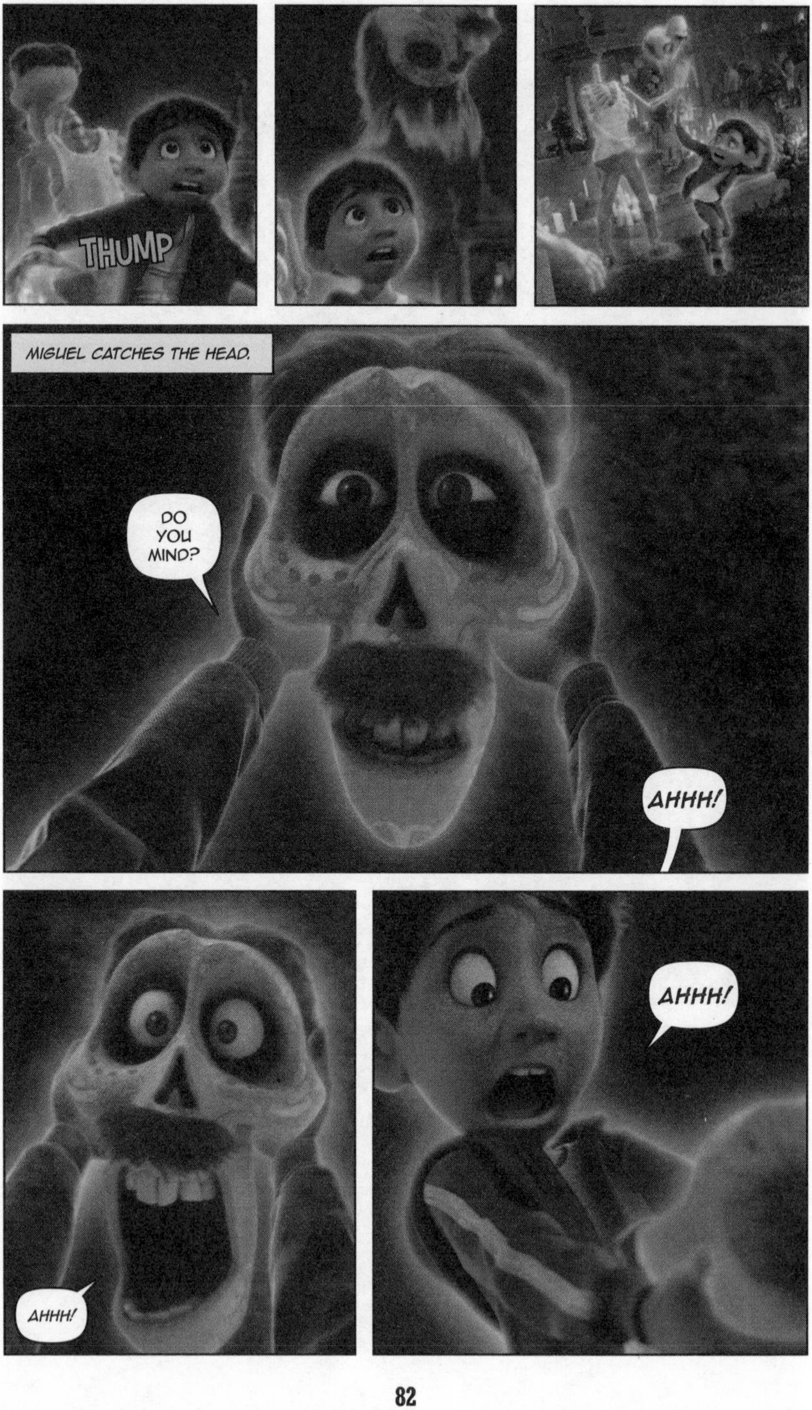
THUMP
MIGUEL CATCHES THE HEAD.
DO YOU MIND?
AHHH!
AHHH!
AHHH!

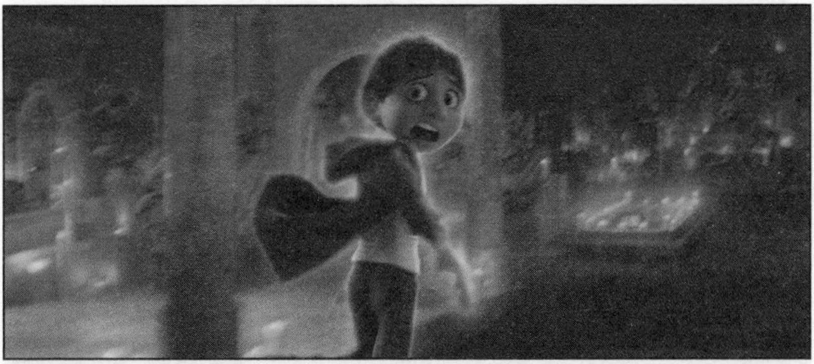

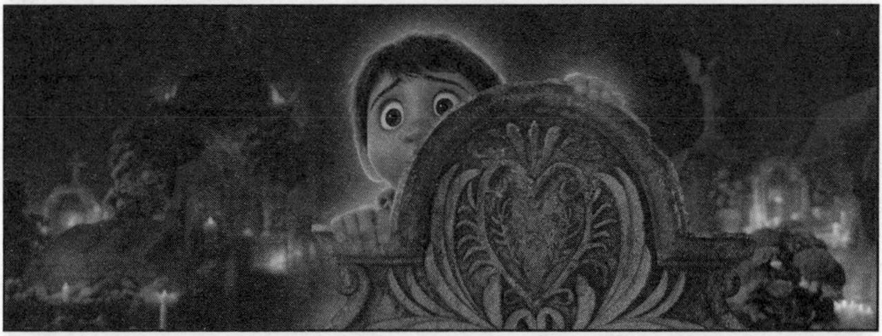

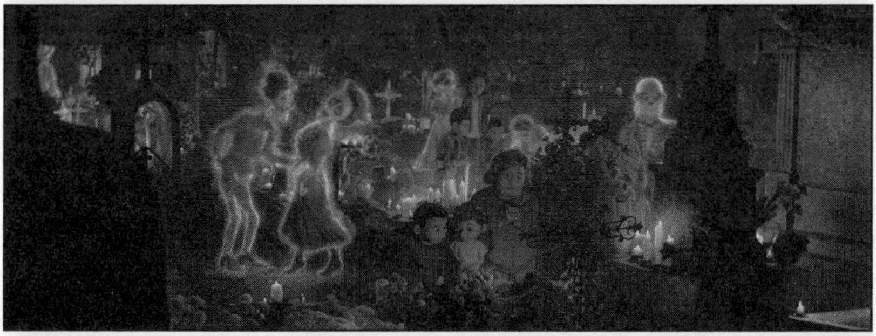

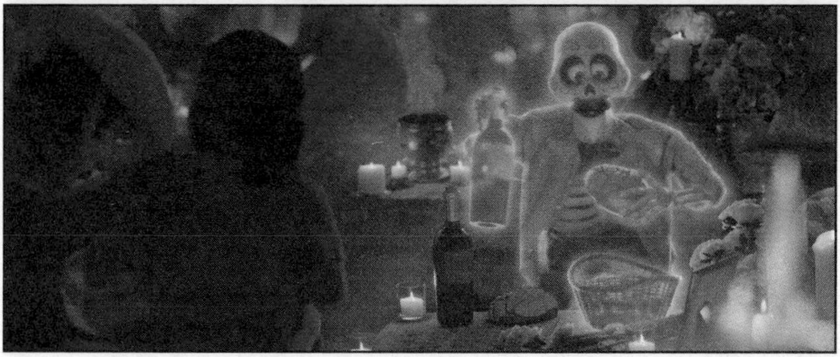

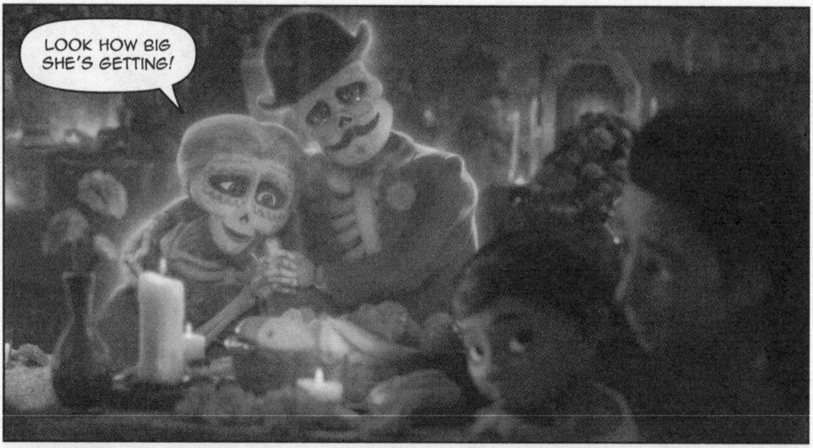
LOOK HOW BIG SHE'S GETTING!

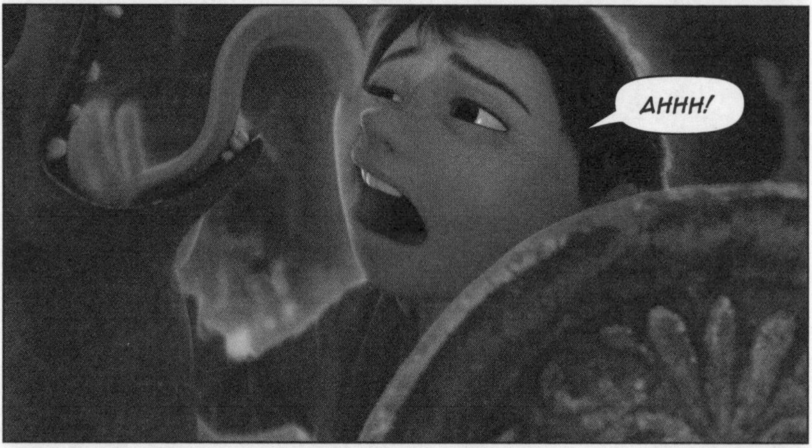
AHHH!

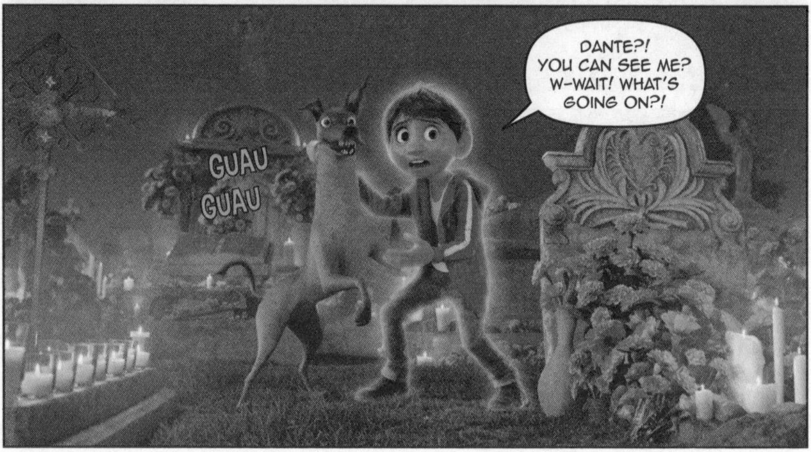
GUAU GUAU
DANTE?! YOU CAN SEE ME? W-WAIT! WHAT'S GOING ON?!

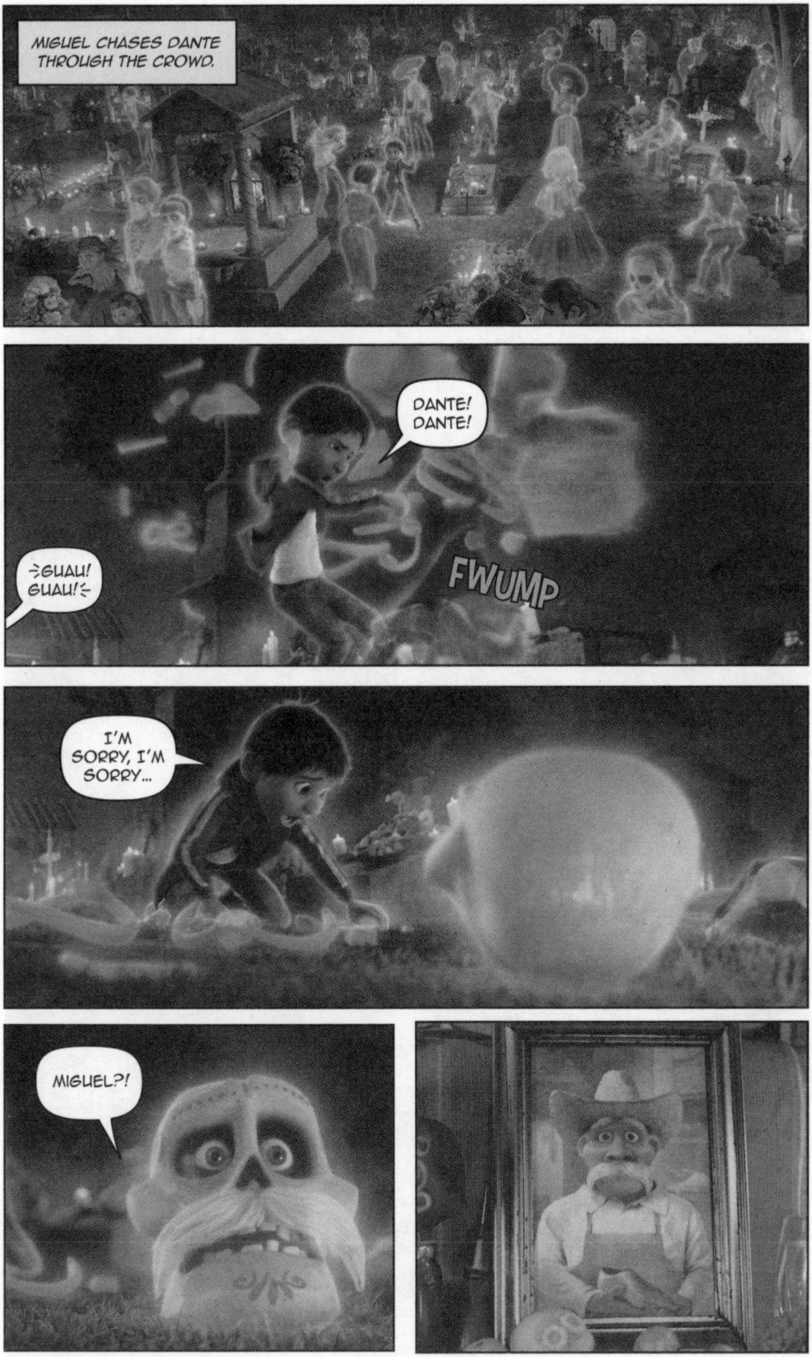
MIGUEL CHASES DANTE THROUGH THE CROWD.
DANTE! DANTE!
¡GUAU! GUAU!
FWUMP
I'M SORRY, I'M SORRY...
MIGUEL?!

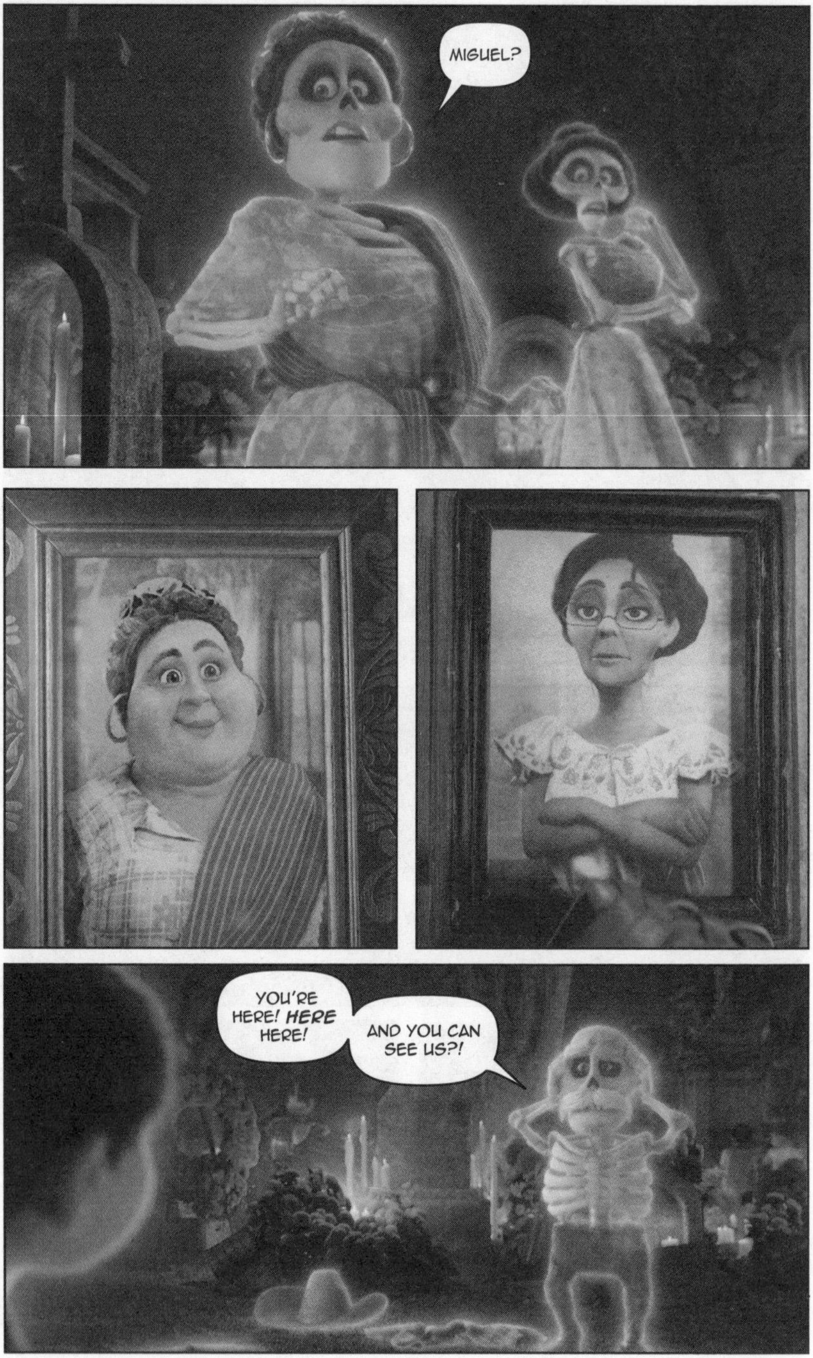
MIGUEL?
YOU'RE HERE! **HERE** HERE!
AND YOU CAN SEE US?!

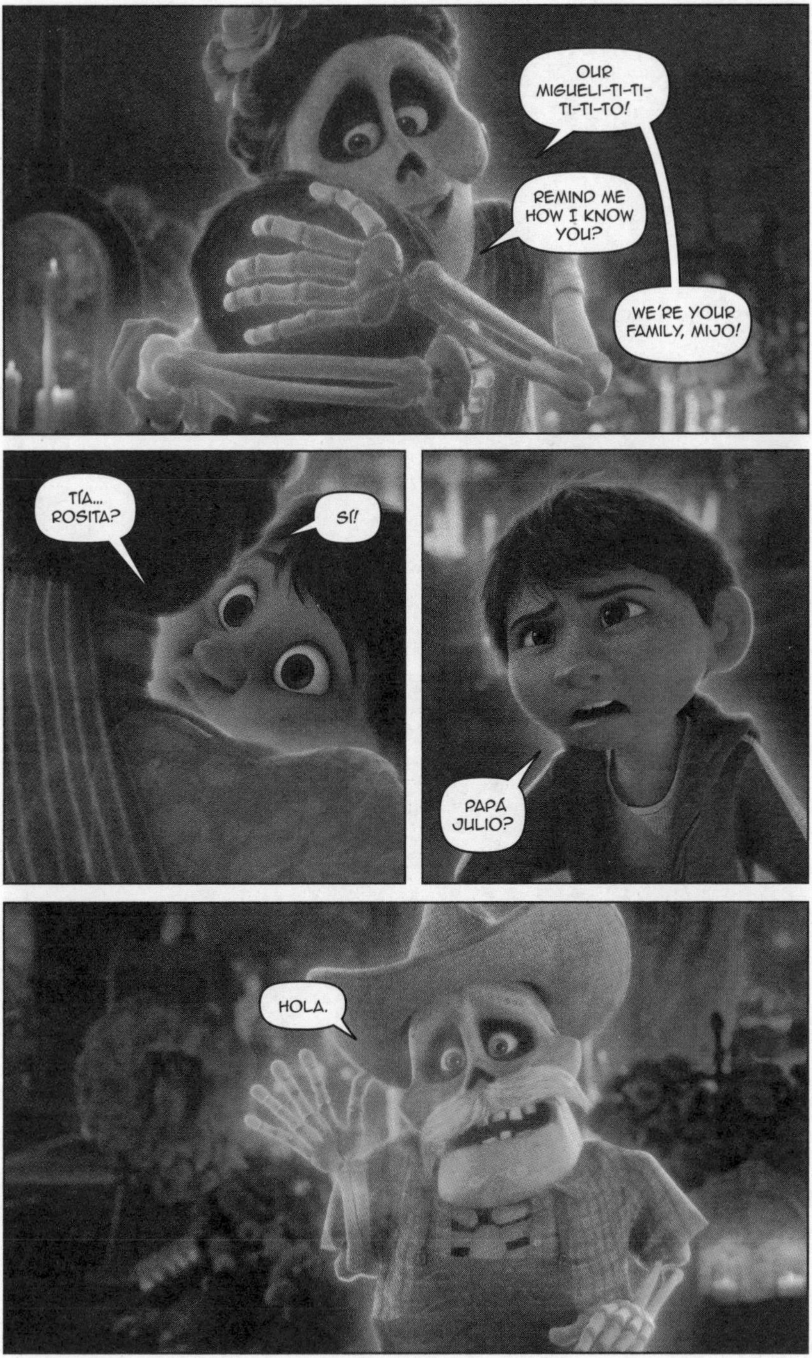
OUR MIGUELI-TI-TI-TI-TI-TO!
REMIND ME HOW I KNOW YOU?
WE'RE YOUR FAMILY, MIJO!
TÍA... ROSITA?
SÍ!
PAPÁ JULIO?
HOLA.

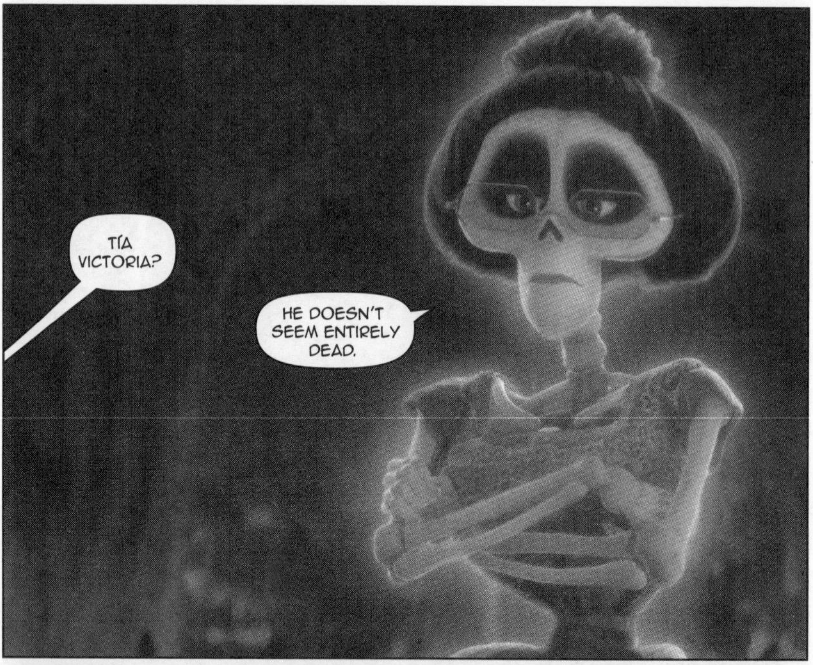
TÍA VICTORIA?
HE DOESN'T SEEM ENTIRELY DEAD.

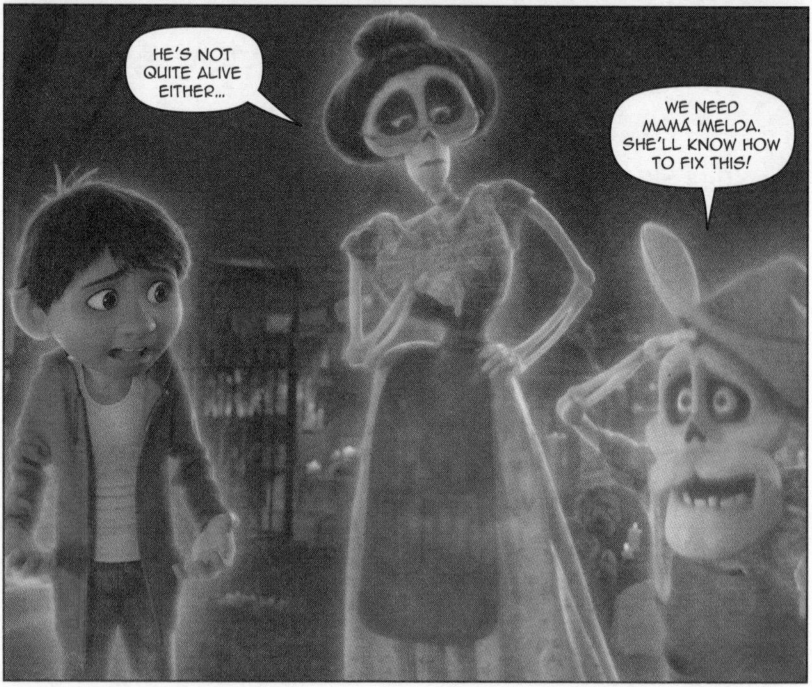
HE'S NOT QUITE ALIVE EITHER...
WE NEED MAMÁ IMELDA. SHE'LL KNOW HOW TO FIX THIS!

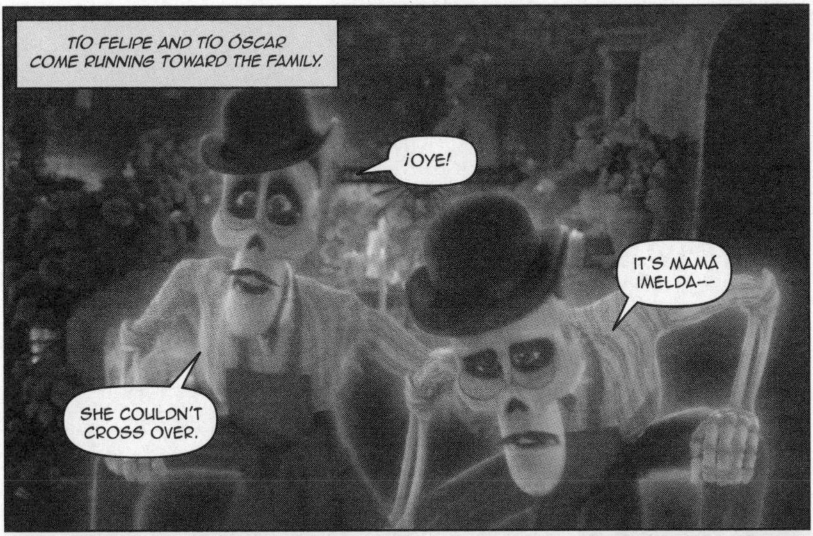
TÍO FELIPE AND TÍO ÓSCAR COME RUNNING TOWARD THE FAMILY.
¡OYE!
IT'S MAMÁ IMELDA--
SHE COULDN'T CROSS OVER.

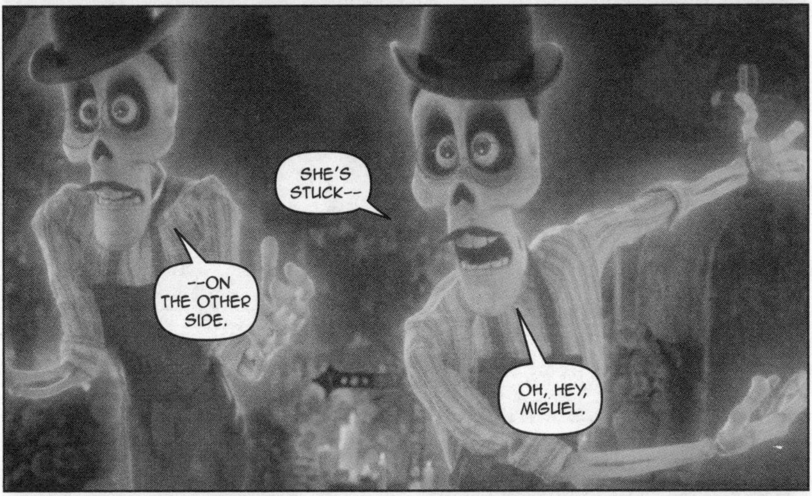
SHE'S STUCK--
--ON THE OTHER SIDE.
OH, HEY, MIGUEL.

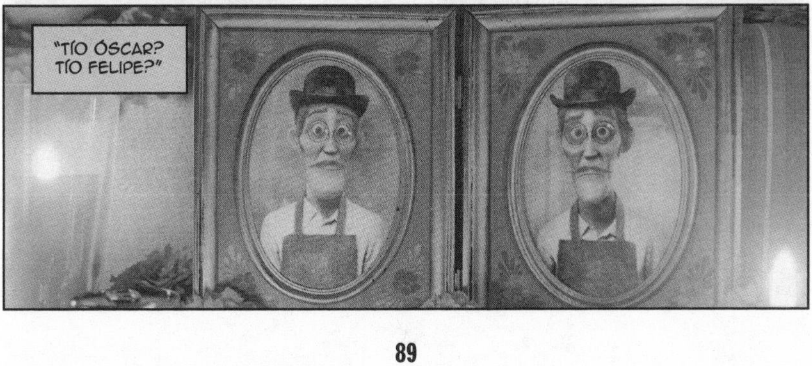
"TÍO ÓSCAR? TÍO FELIPE?"

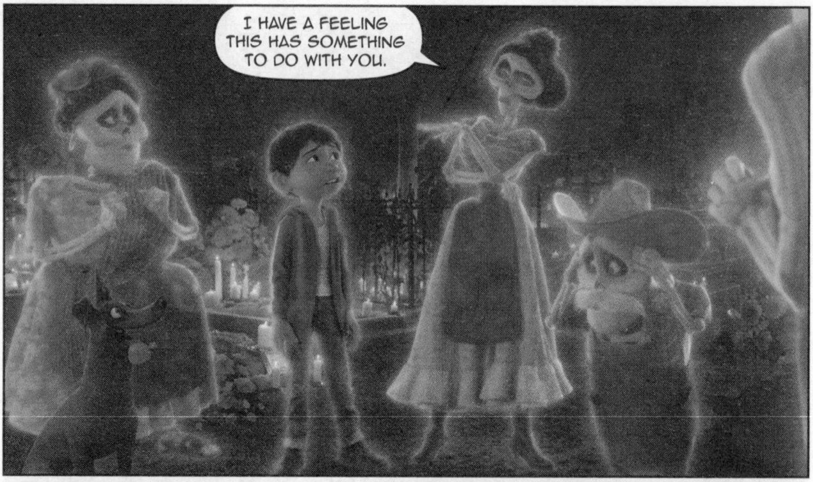
I HAVE A FEELING THIS HAS SOMETHING TO DO WITH YOU.

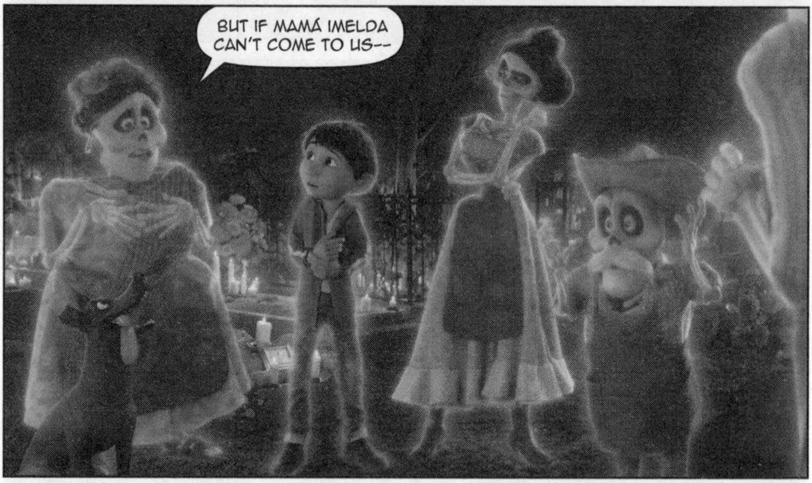
BUT IF MAMÁ IMELDA CAN'T COME TO US--

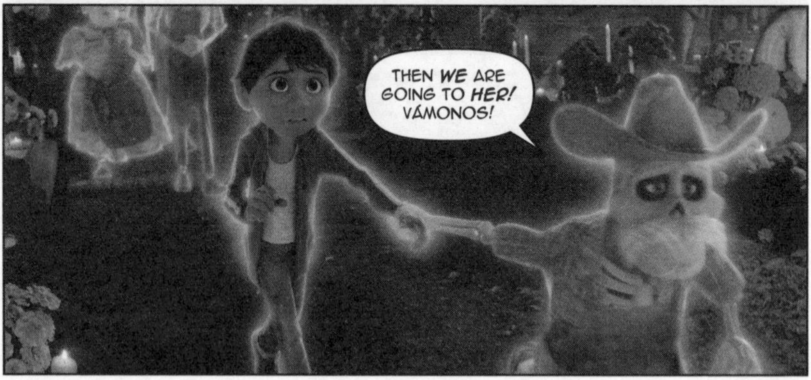
THEN *WE* ARE GOING TO *HER!* VÁMONOS!

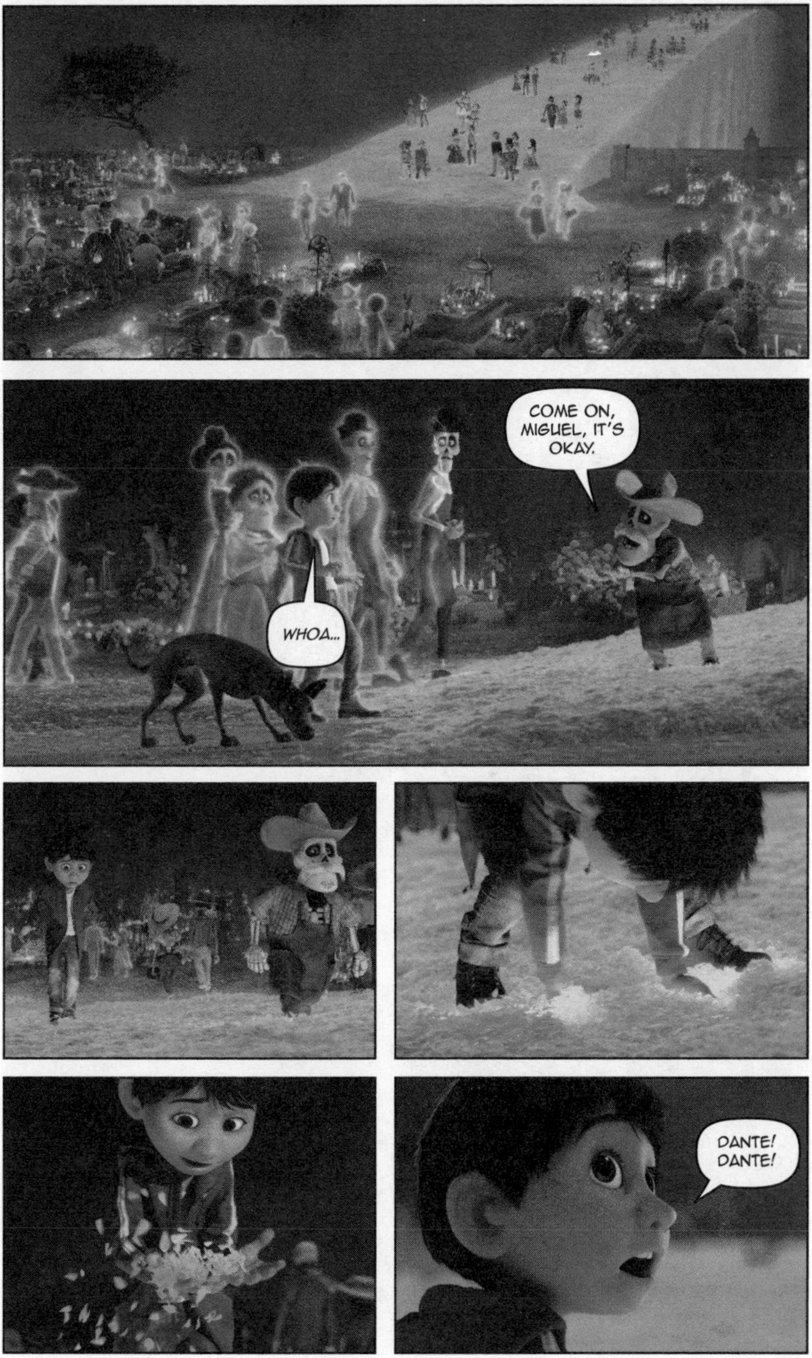
COME ON, MIGUEL, IT'S OKAY.
WHOA...
DANTE! DANTE!

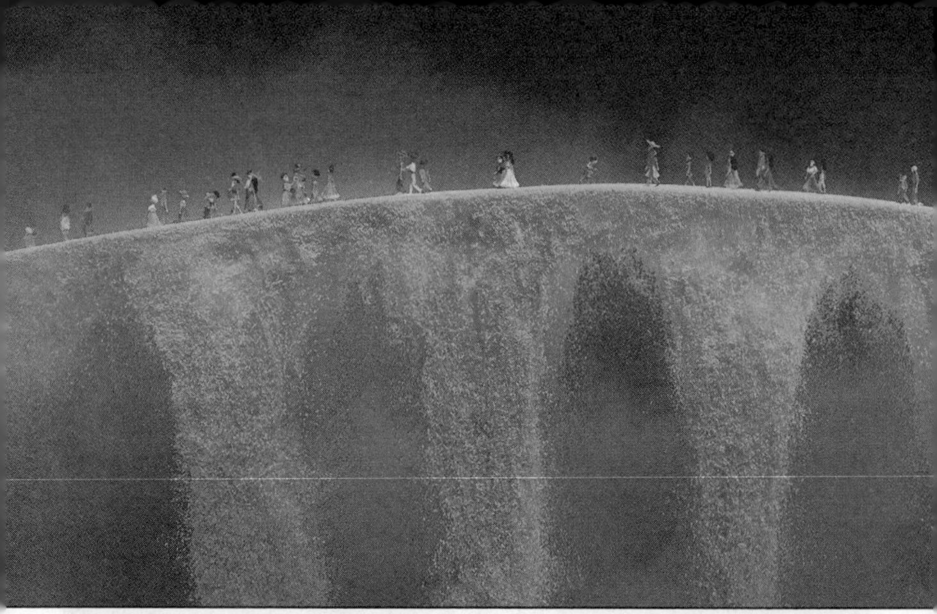

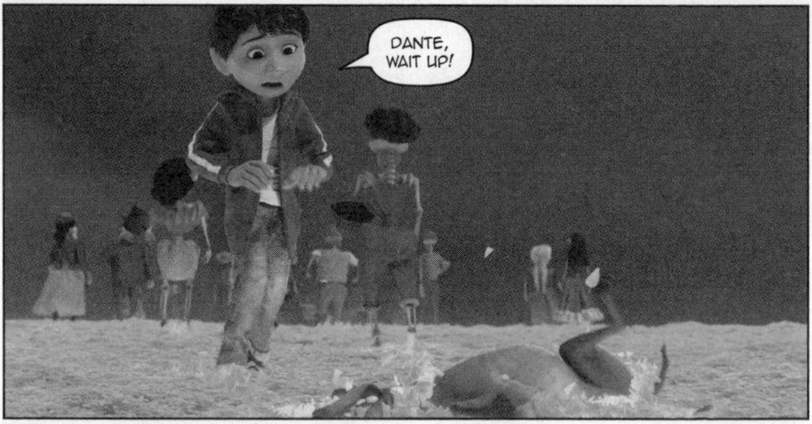
DANTE, WAIT UP!

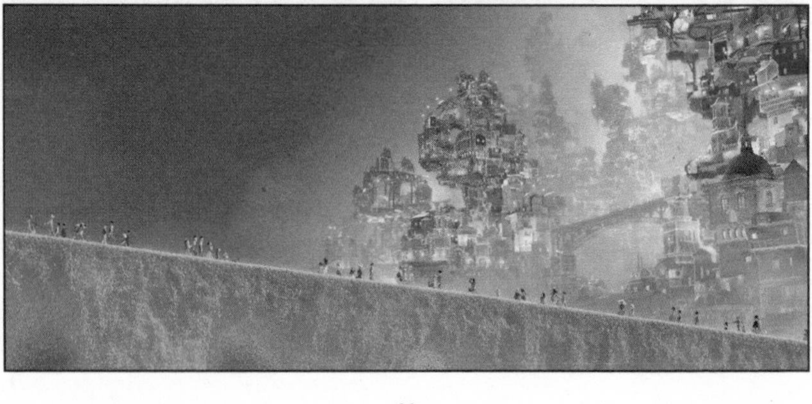

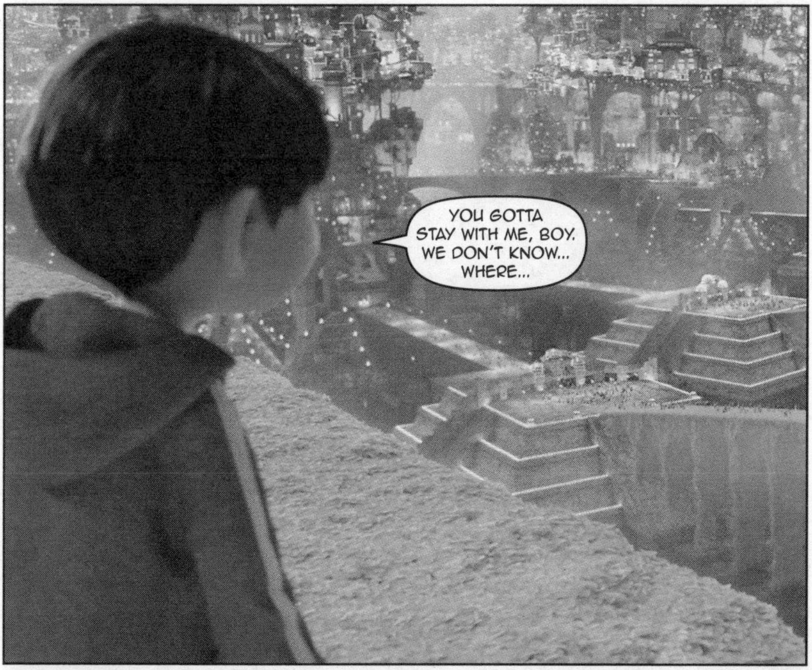
YOU GOTTA STAY WITH ME, BOY. WE DON'T KNOW... WHERE...

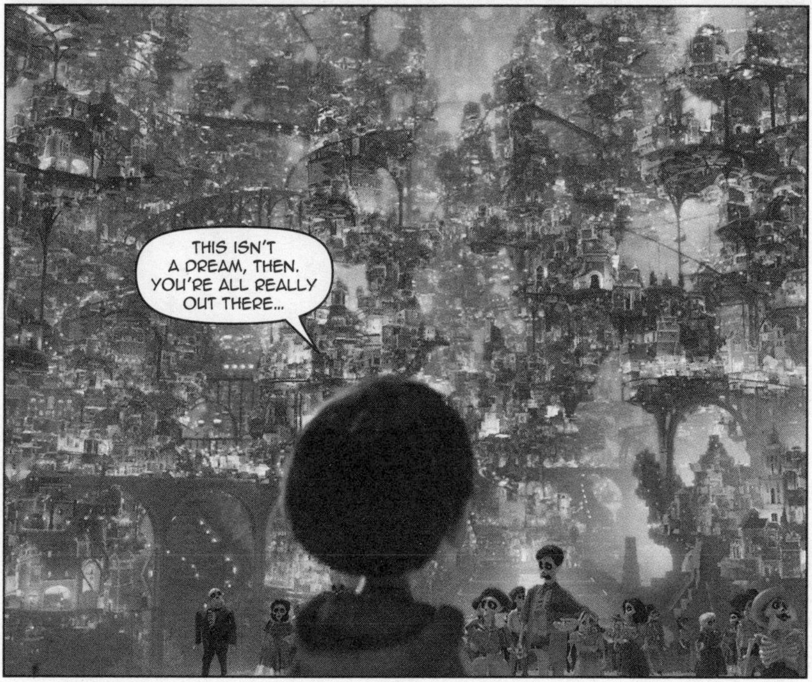
THIS ISN'T A DREAM, THEN. YOU'RE ALL REALLY OUT THERE...

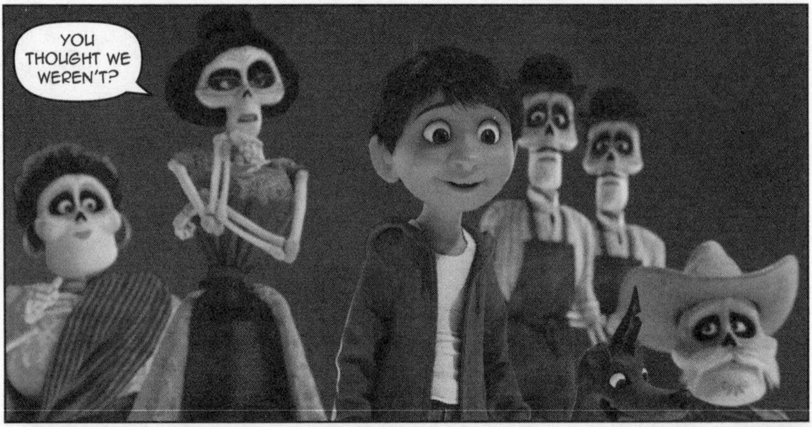
YOU THOUGHT WE WEREN'T?

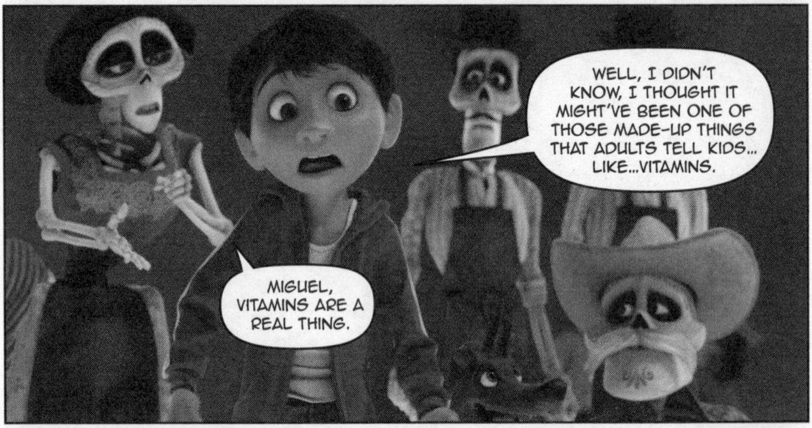
WELL, I DIDN'T KNOW, I THOUGHT IT MIGHT'VE BEEN ONE OF THOSE MADE-UP THINGS THAT ADULTS TELL KIDS... LIKE...VITAMINS.
MIGUEL, VITAMINS ARE A REAL THING.

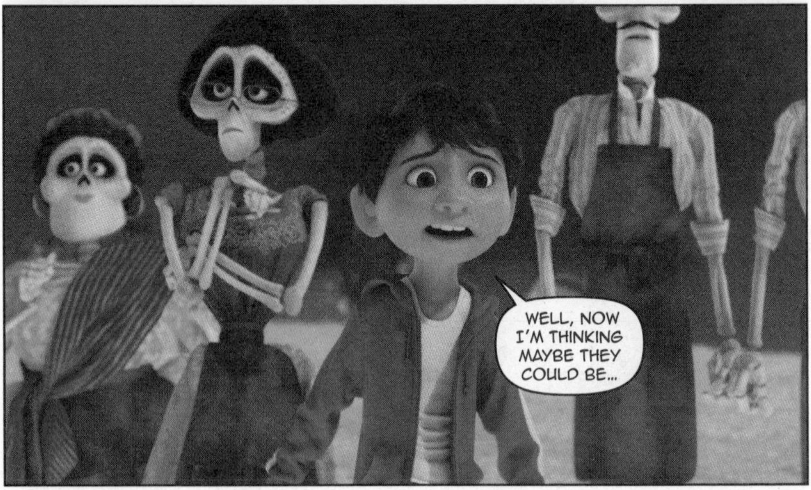
WELL, NOW I'M THINKING MAYBE THEY COULD BE...

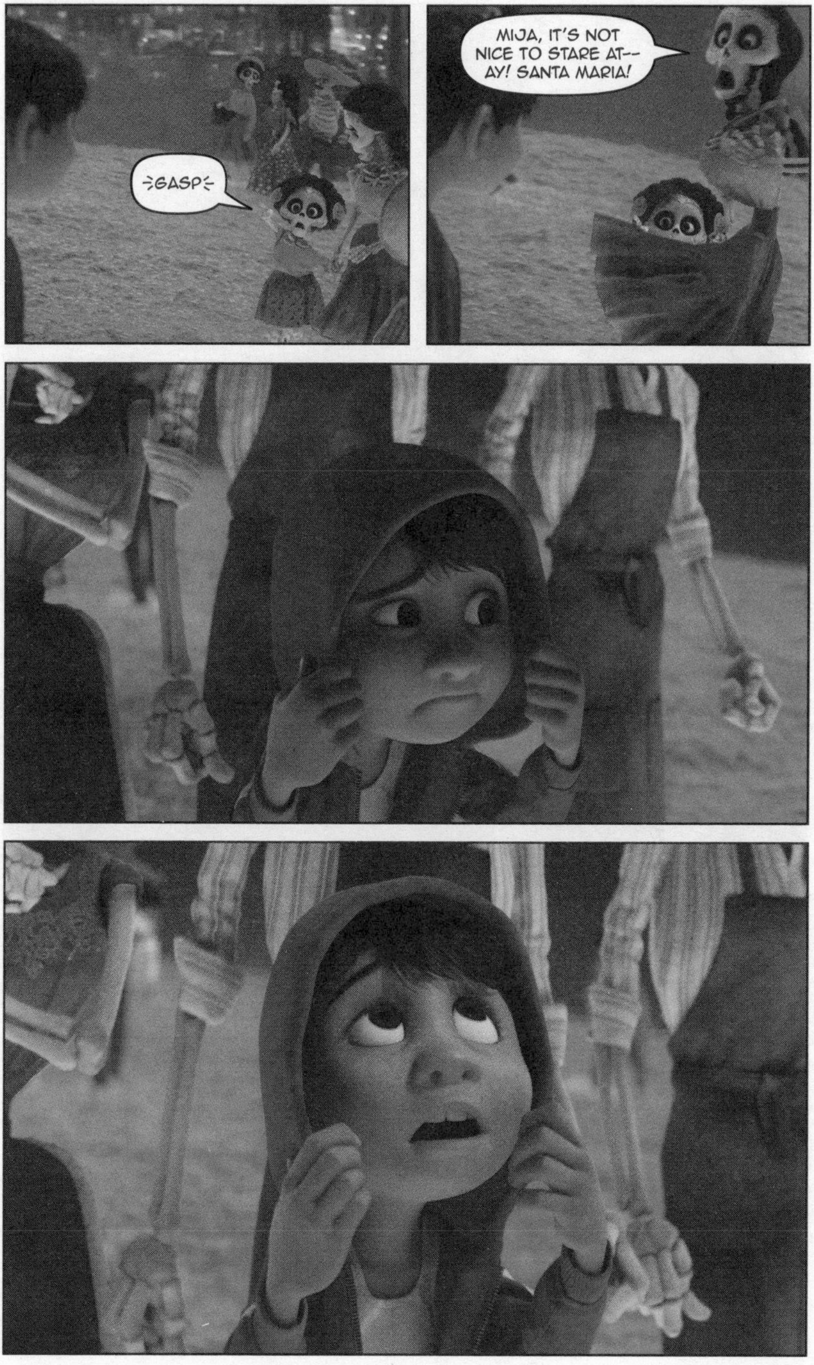

GASP
MIJA, IT'S NOT NICE TO STARE AT-- AY! SANTA MARIA!

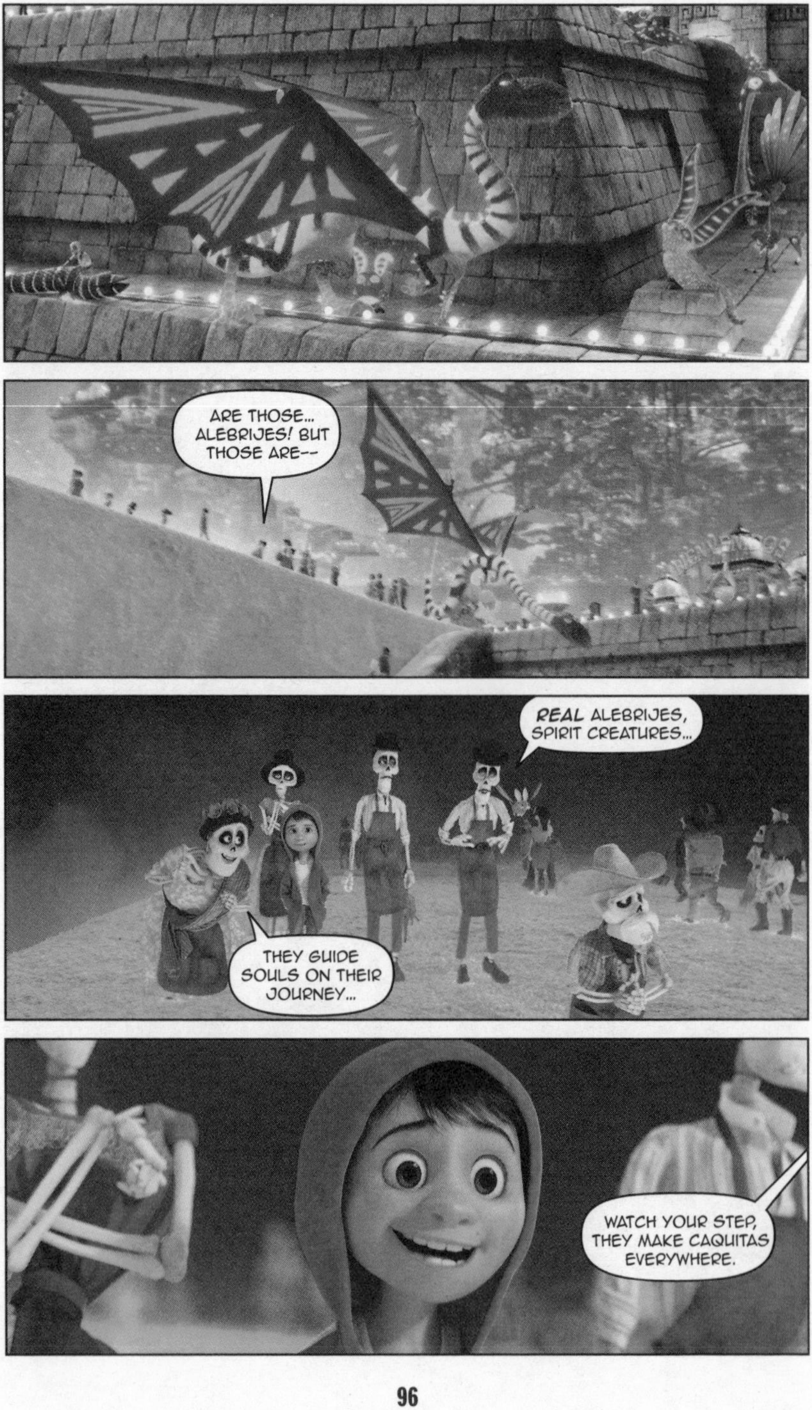
ARE THOSE... ALEBRIJES! BUT THOSE ARE--
REAL ALEBRIJES, SPIRIT CREATURES...
THEY GUIDE SOULS ON THEIR JOURNEY...
WATCH YOUR STEP, THEY MAKE CAQUITAS EVERYWHERE.

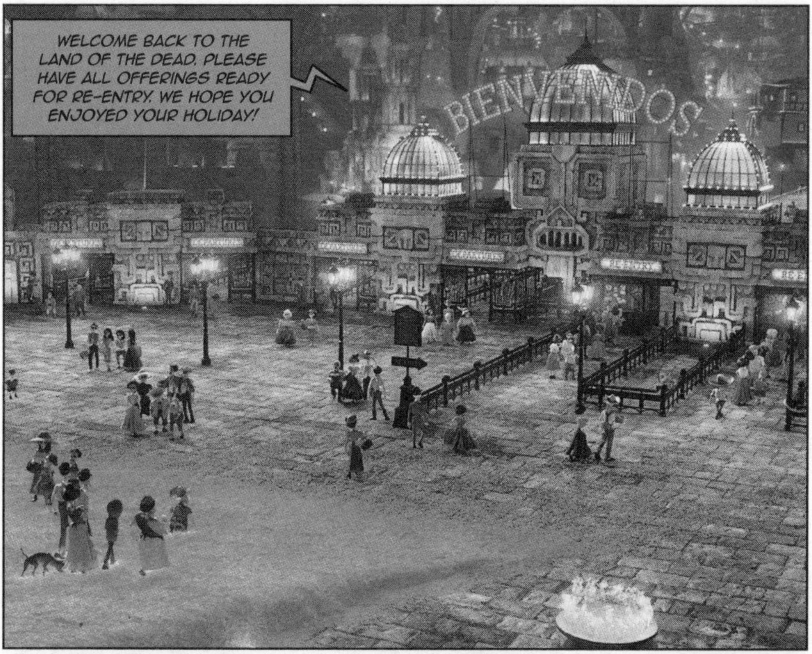
WELCOME BACK TO THE LAND OF THE DEAD. PLEASE HAVE ALL OFFERINGS READY FOR RE-ENTRY. WE HOPE YOU ENJOYED YOUR HOLIDAY!
BIENVENIDOS

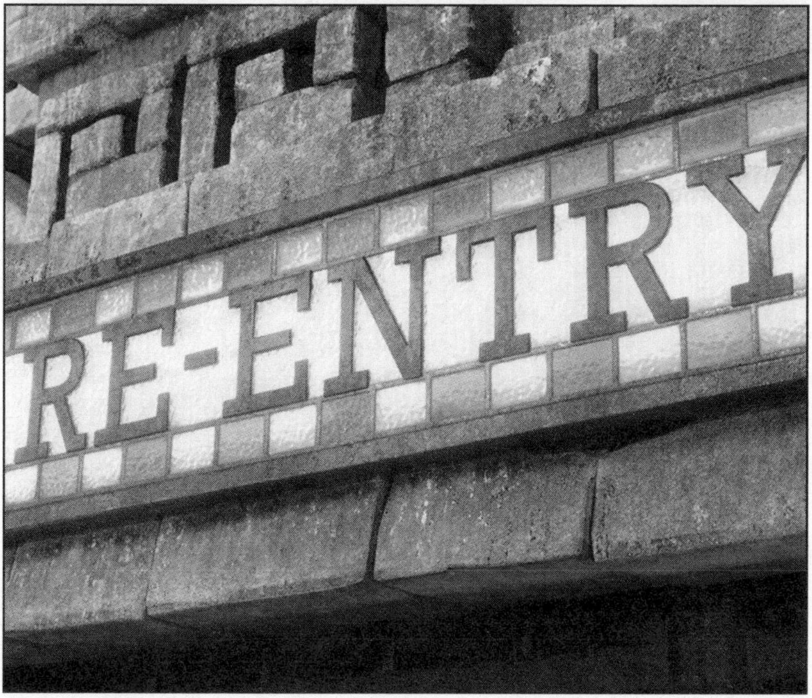
RE-ENTRY

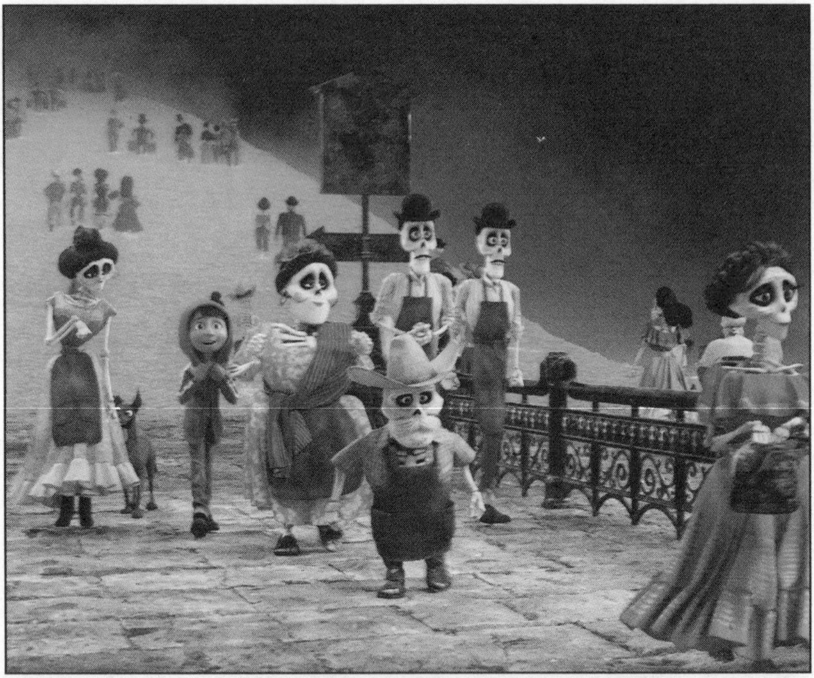

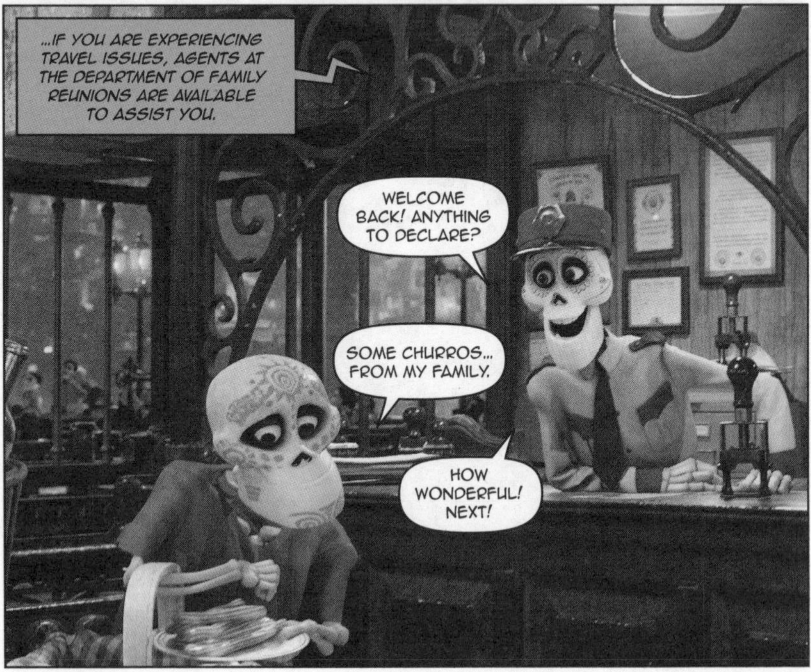
...IF YOU ARE EXPERIENCING TRAVEL ISSUES, AGENTS AT THE DEPARTMENT OF FAMILY REUNIONS ARE AVAILABLE TO ASSIST YOU.
WELCOME BACK! ANYTHING TO DECLARE?
SOME CHURROS... FROM MY FAMILY.
HOW WONDERFUL! NEXT!

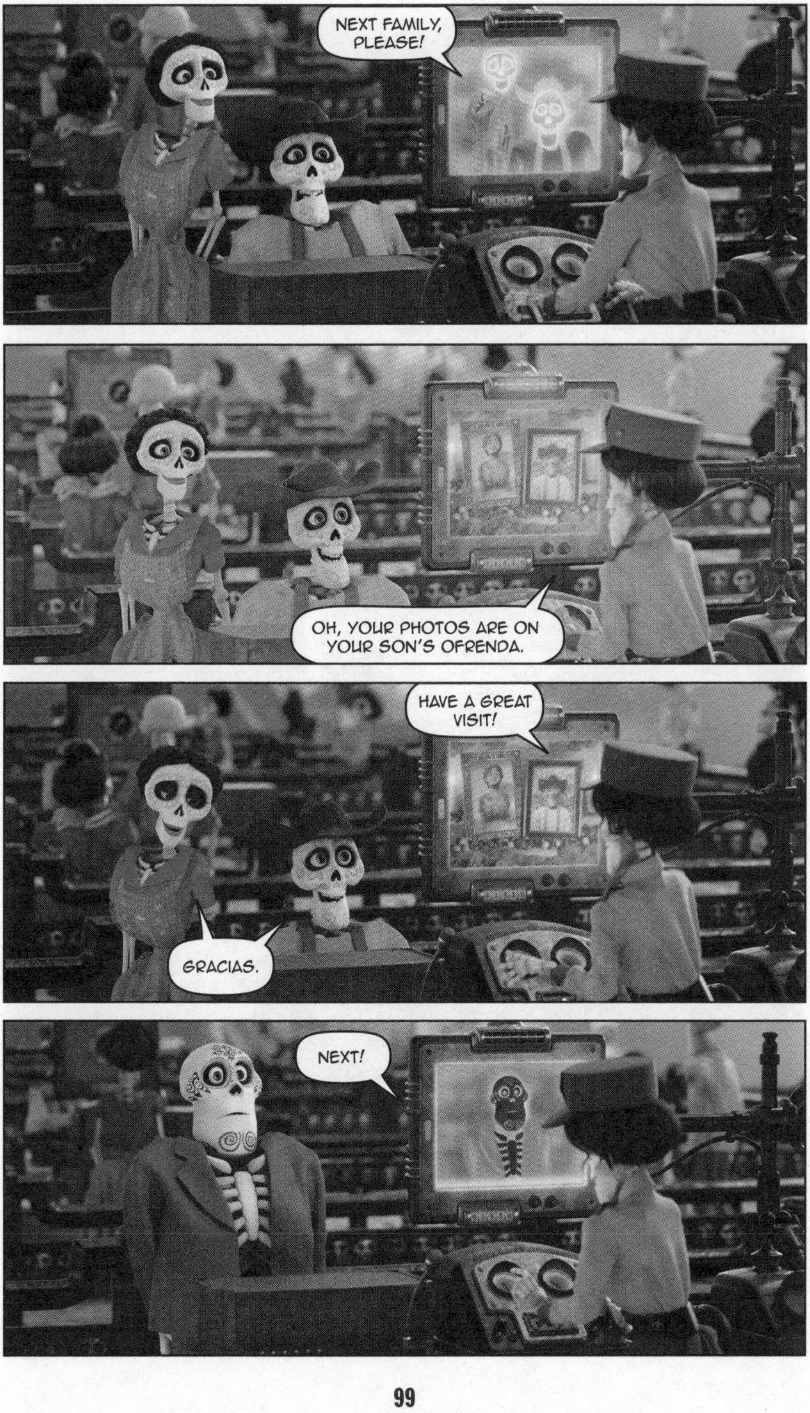
NEXT FAMILY, PLEASE!
OH, YOUR PHOTOS ARE ON YOUR SON'S OFRENDA.
HAVE A GREAT VISIT!
GRACIAS.
NEXT!

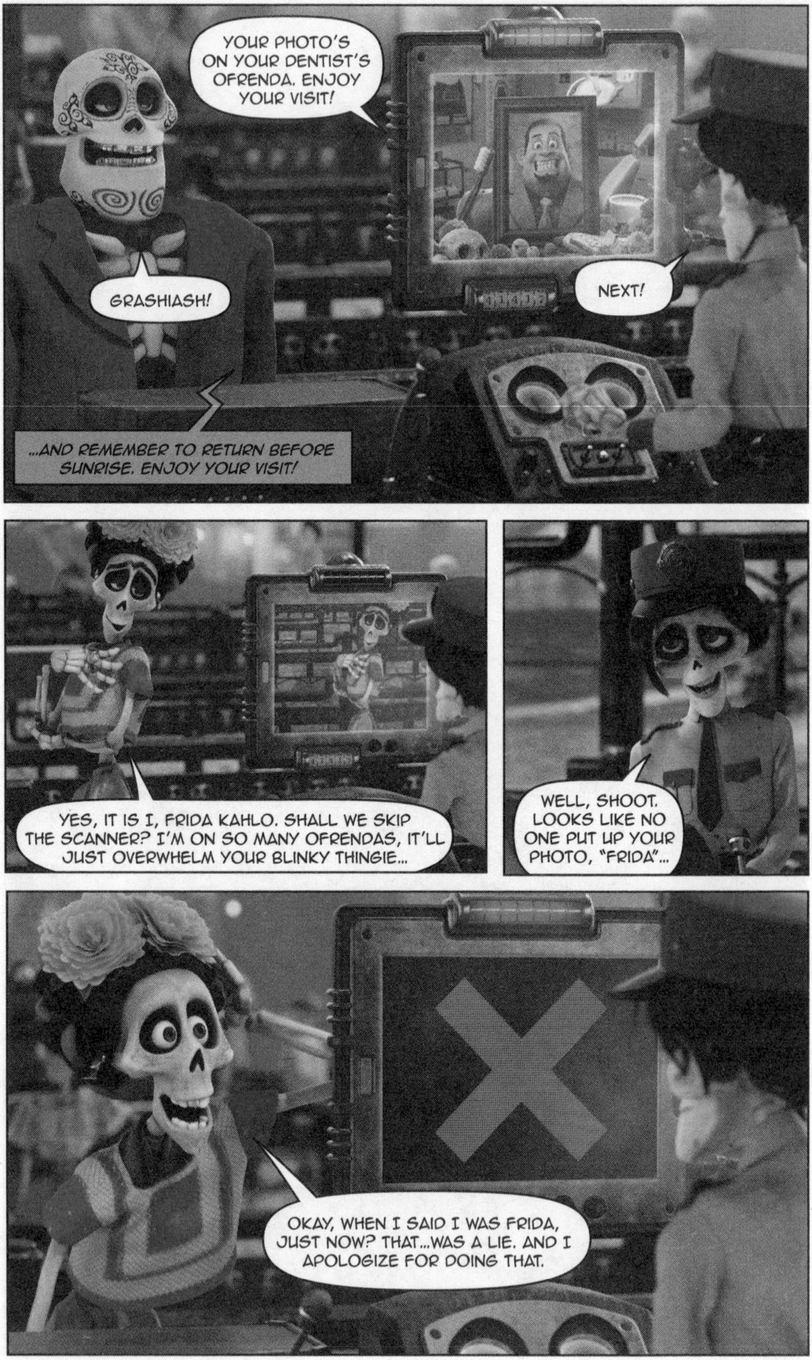
YOUR PHOTO'S ON YOUR DENTIST'S OFRENDA. ENJOY YOUR VISIT!
GRASHIASH!
NEXT!
...AND REMEMBER TO RETURN BEFORE SUNRISE. ENJOY YOUR VISIT!
YES, IT IS I, FRIDA KAHLO. SHALL WE SKIP THE SCANNER? I'M ON SO MANY OFRENDAS, IT'LL JUST OVERWHELM YOUR BLINKY THINGIE...
WELL, SHOOT. LOOKS LIKE NO ONE PUT UP YOUR PHOTO, "FRIDA"...
OKAY, WHEN I SAID I WAS FRIDA, JUST NOW? THAT...WAS A LIE. AND I APOLOGIZE FOR DOING THAT.

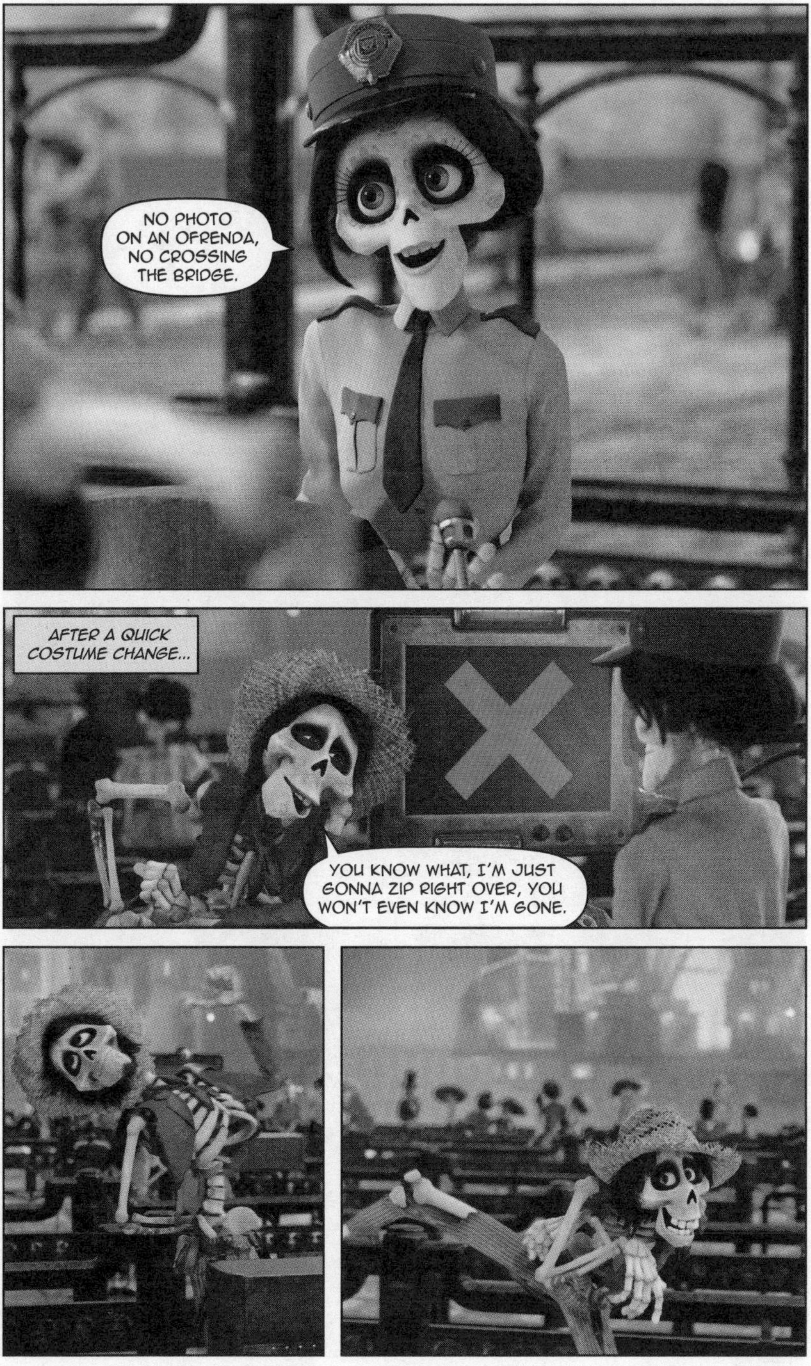
NO PHOTO ON AN OFRENDA, NO CROSSING THE BRIDGE.
AFTER A QUICK COSTUME CHANGE...
YOU KNOW WHAT, I'M JUST GONNA ZIP RIGHT OVER, YOU WON'T EVEN KNOW I'M GONE.

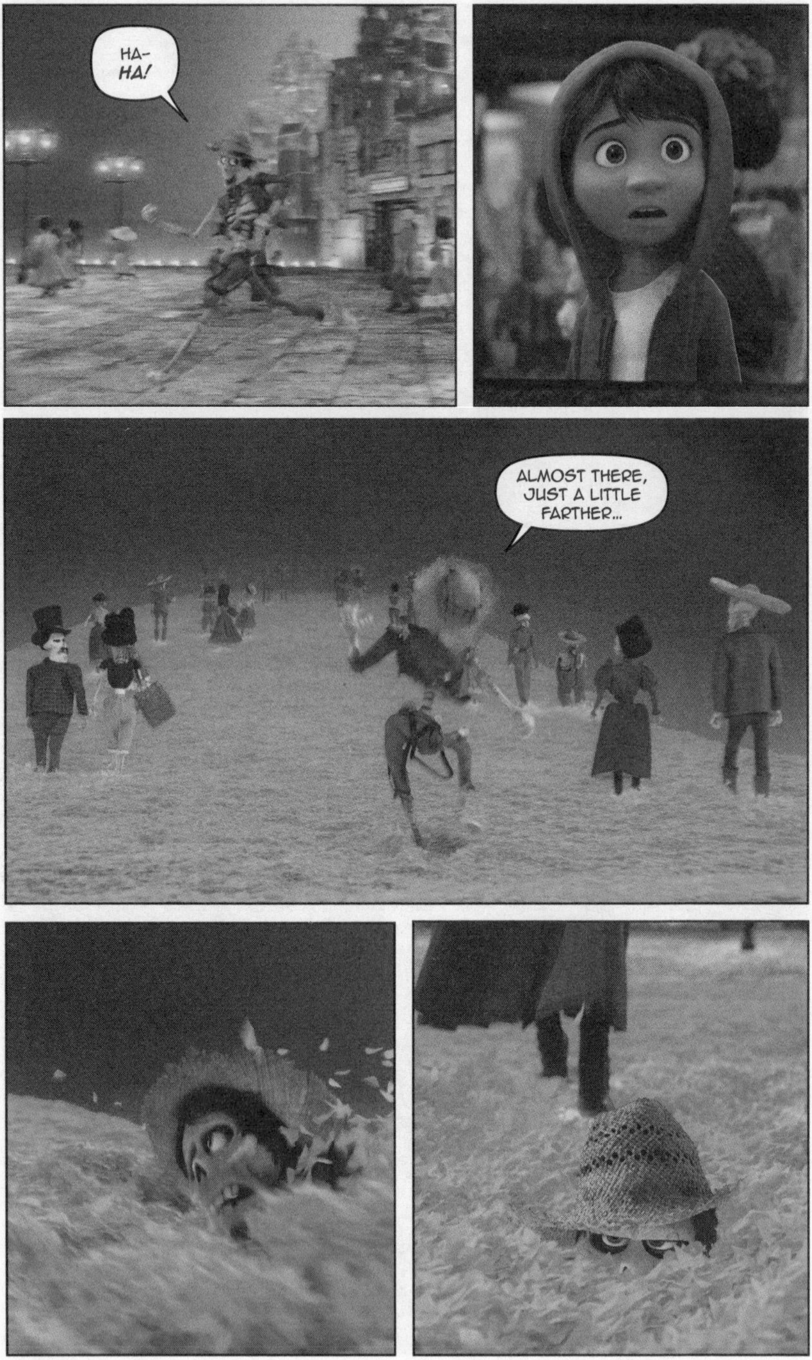
HA-
HA!
ALMOST THERE, JUST A LITTLE FARTHER...

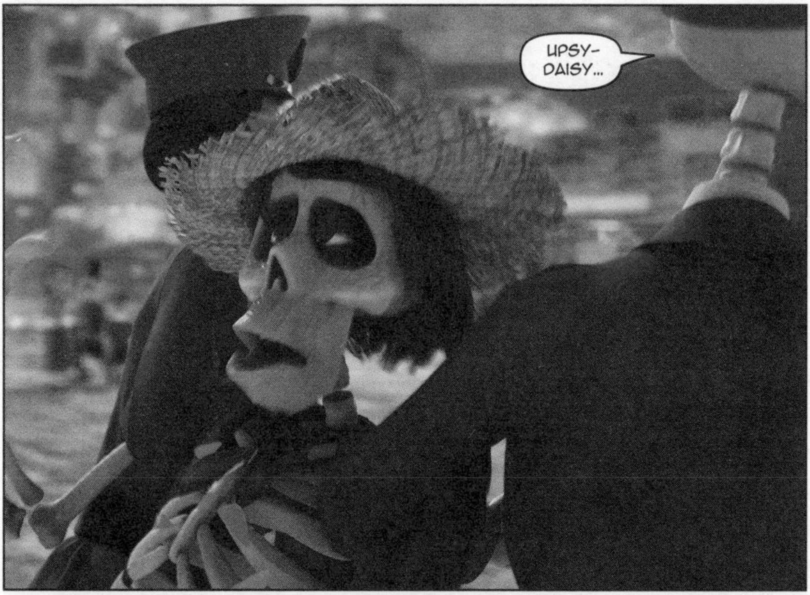
UPSY-DAISY...

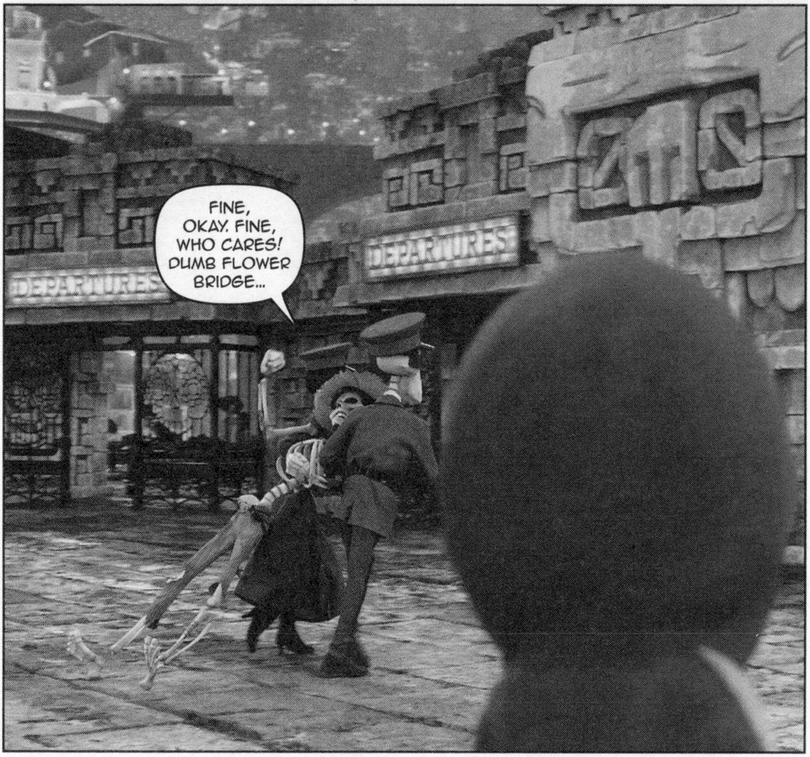
FINE, OKAY. FINE, WHO CARES! DUMB FLOWER BRIDGE...
DEPARTURES
DEPARTURES

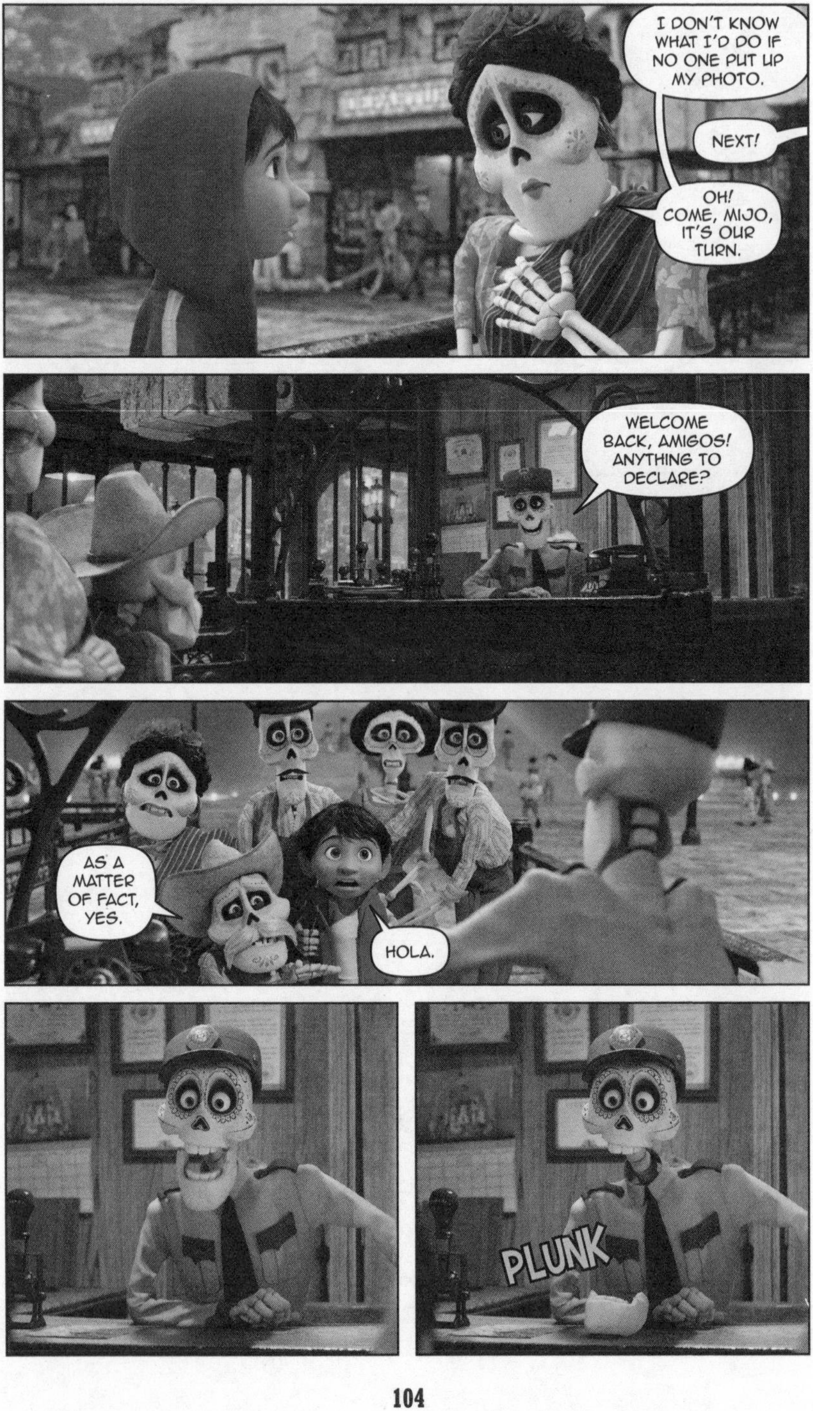
I DON'T KNOW WHAT I'D DO IF NO ONE PUT UP MY PHOTO.
NEXT!
OH! COME, MIJO, IT'S OUR TURN.
WELCOME BACK, AMIGOS! ANYTHING TO DECLARE?
AS A MATTER OF FACT, YES.
HOLA.
PLUNK

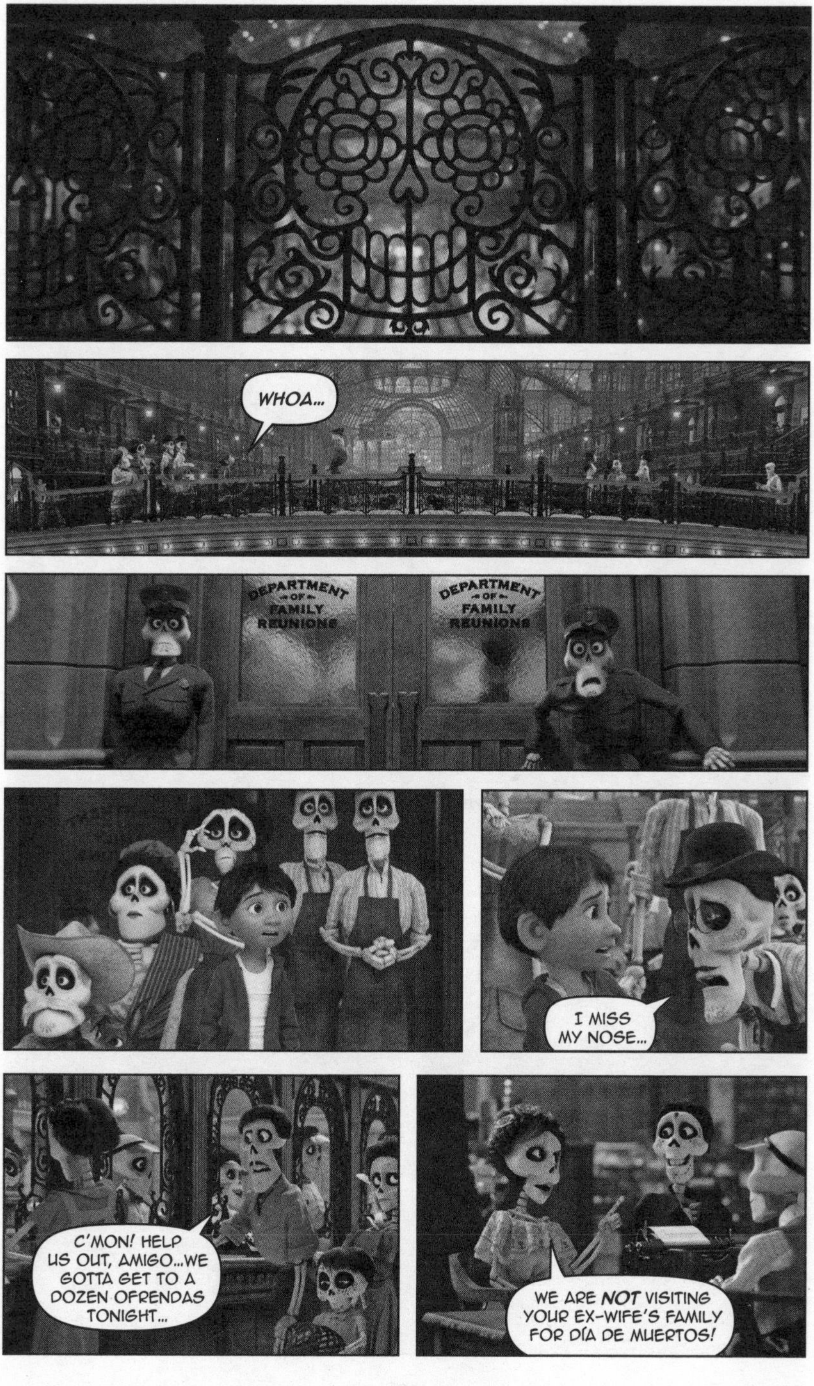
WHOA...
DEPARTMENT OF FAMILY REUNIONS
DEPARTMENT OF FAMILY REUNIONS
I MISS MY NOSE...
C'MON! HELP US OUT, AMIGO...WE GOTTA GET TO A DOZEN OFRENDAS TONIGHT...
WE ARE **NOT** VISITING YOUR EX-WIFE'S FAMILY FOR DÍA DE MUERTOS!

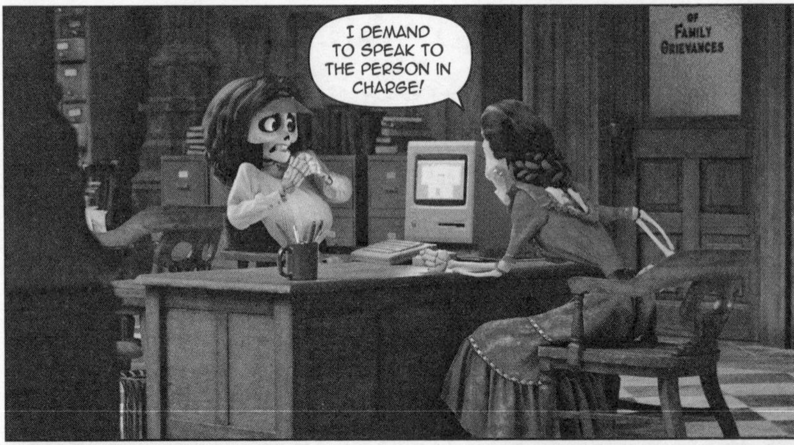
OF
FAMILY
GRIEVANCES
I DEMAND TO SPEAK TO THE PERSON IN CHARGE!

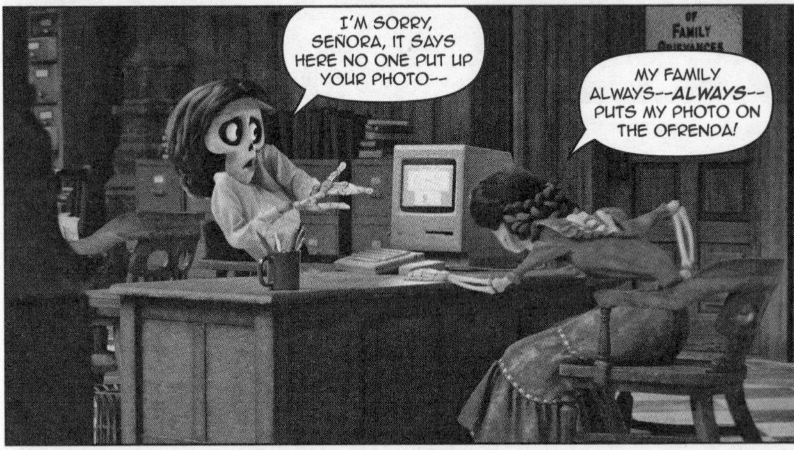
OF
FAMILY
I'M SORRY, SEÑORA, IT SAYS HERE NO ONE PUT UP YOUR PHOTO--
MY FAMILY ALWAYS--*ALWAYS*--PUTS MY PHOTO ON THE OFRENDA!

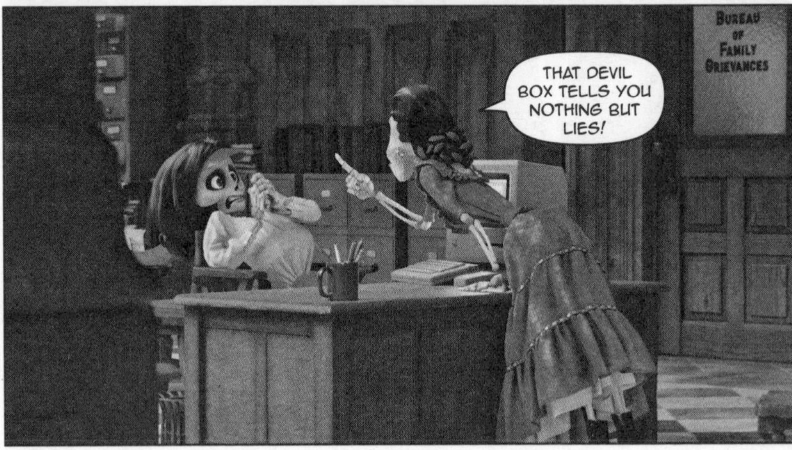
BUREAU
OF
FAMILY
GRIEVANCES
THAT DEVIL BOX TELLS YOU NOTHING BUT LIES!

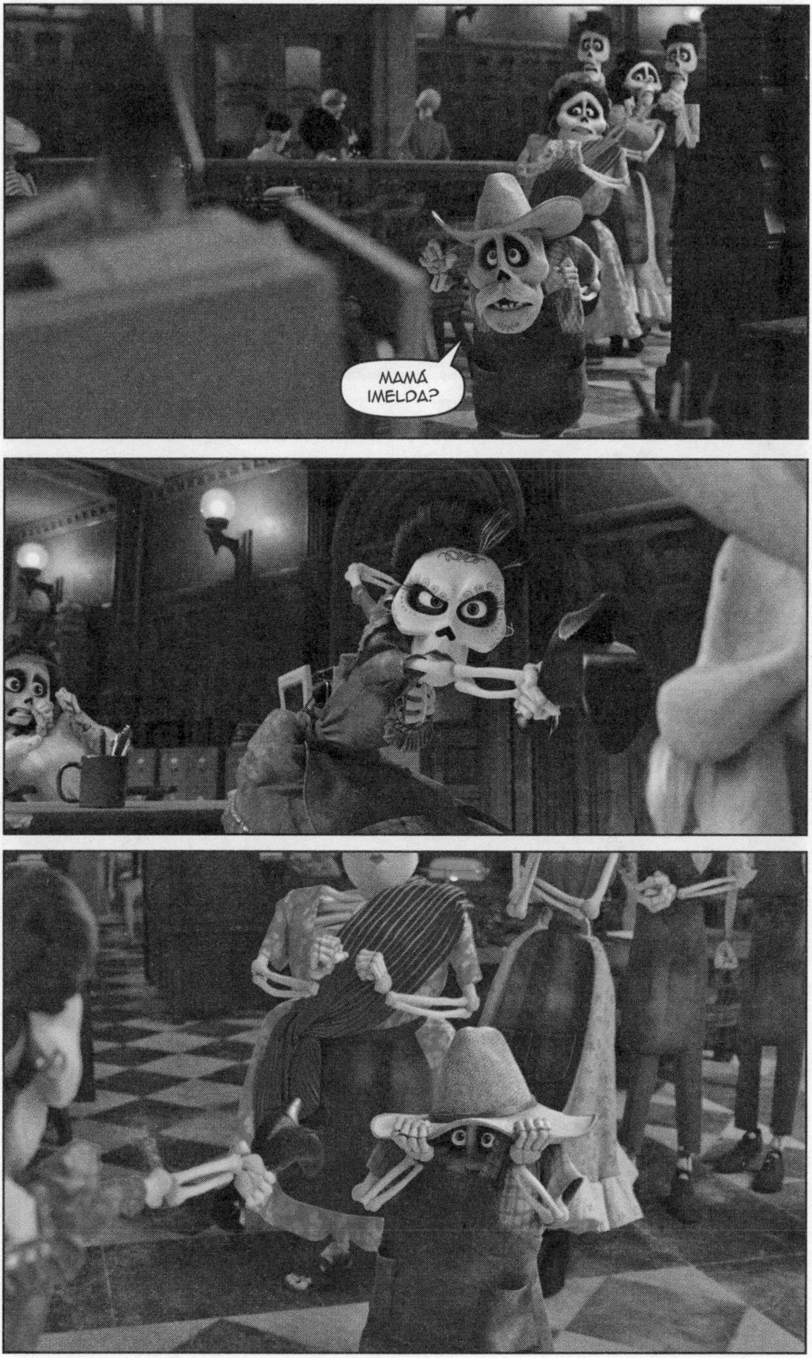
MAMÁ IMELDA?

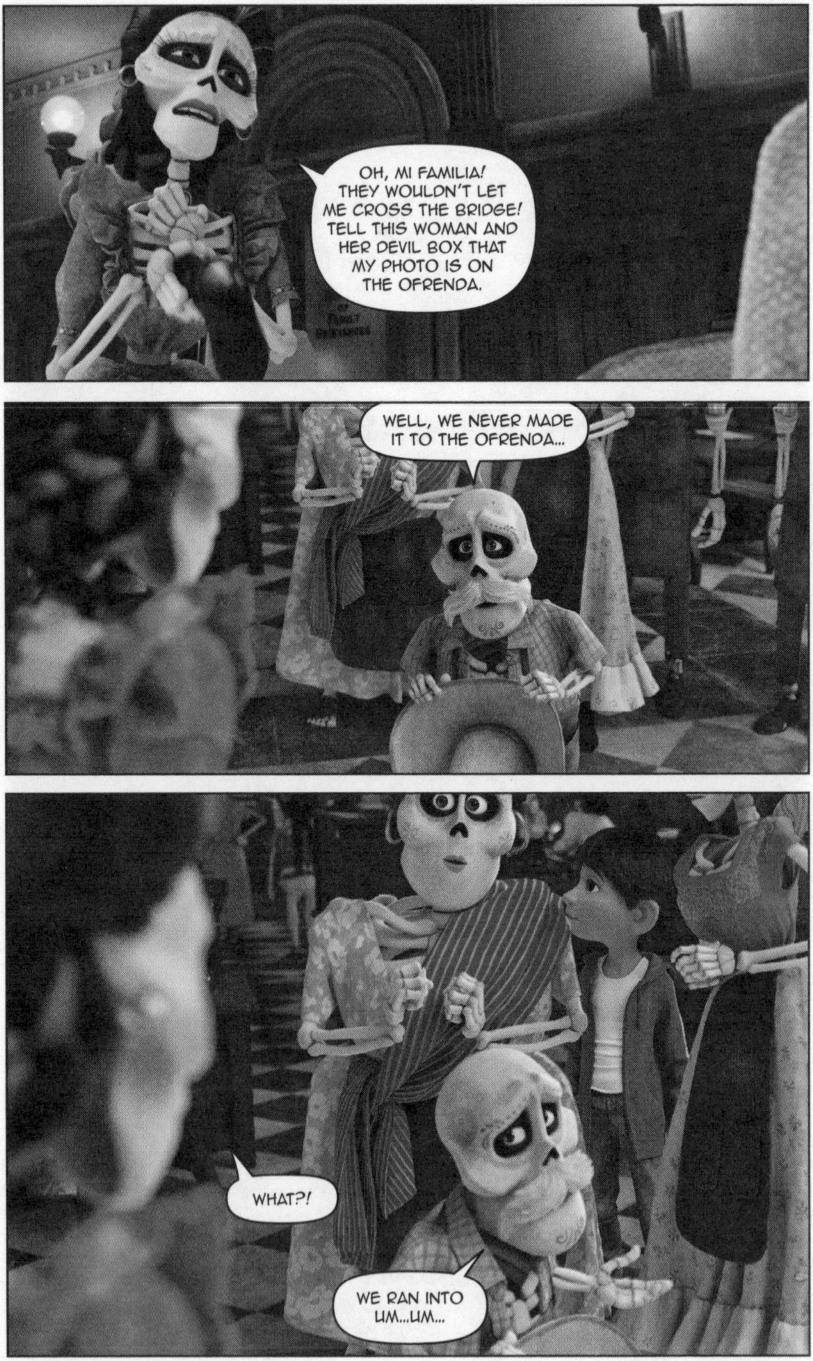
OH, MI FAMILIA! THEY WOULDN'T LET ME CROSS THE BRIDGE! TELL THIS WOMAN AND HER DEVIL BOX THAT MY PHOTO IS ON THE OFRENDA.
WELL, WE NEVER MADE IT TO THE OFRENDA...
WHAT?!
WE RAN INTO UM...UM...

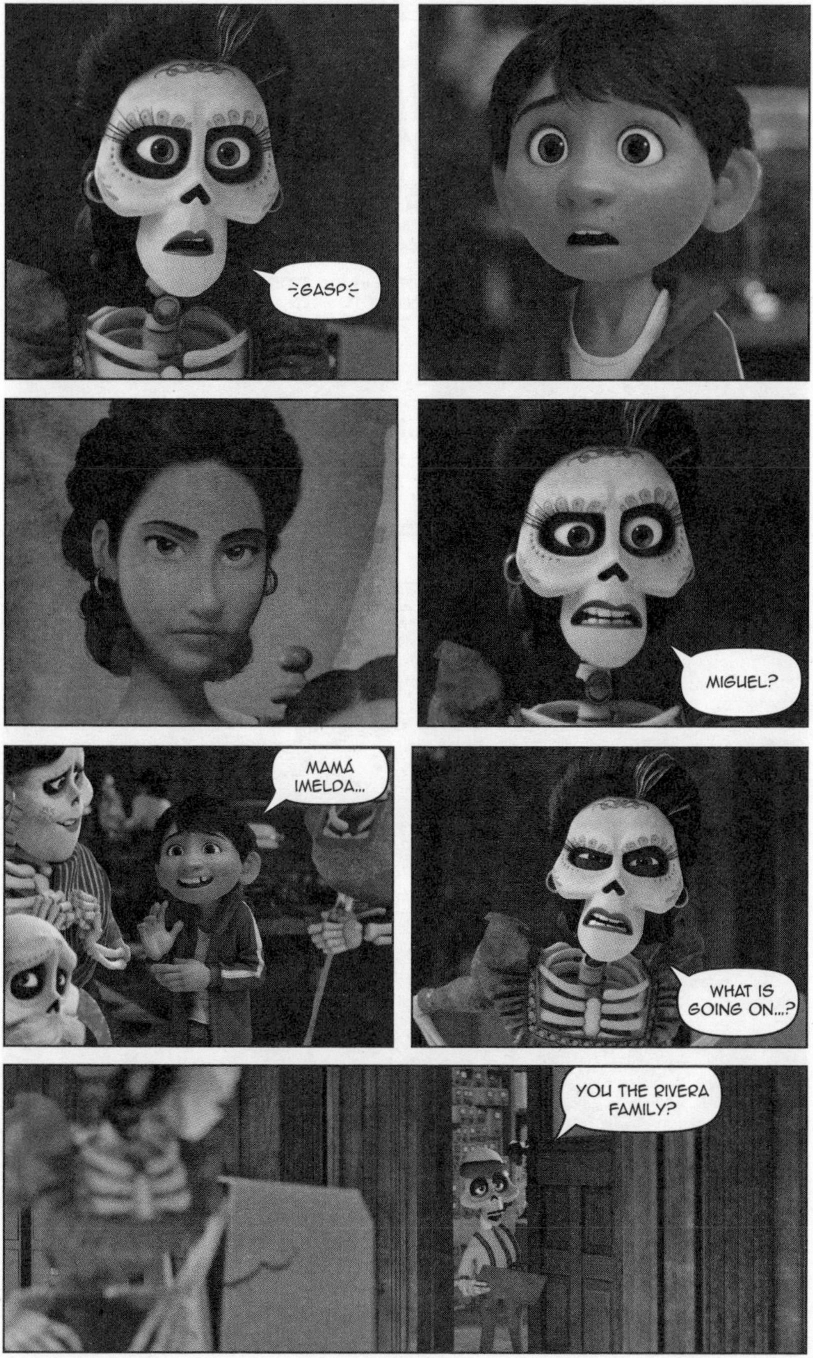

GASP
MIGUEL?
MAMÁ IMELDA...
WHAT IS GOING ON...?
YOU THE RIVERA FAMILY?

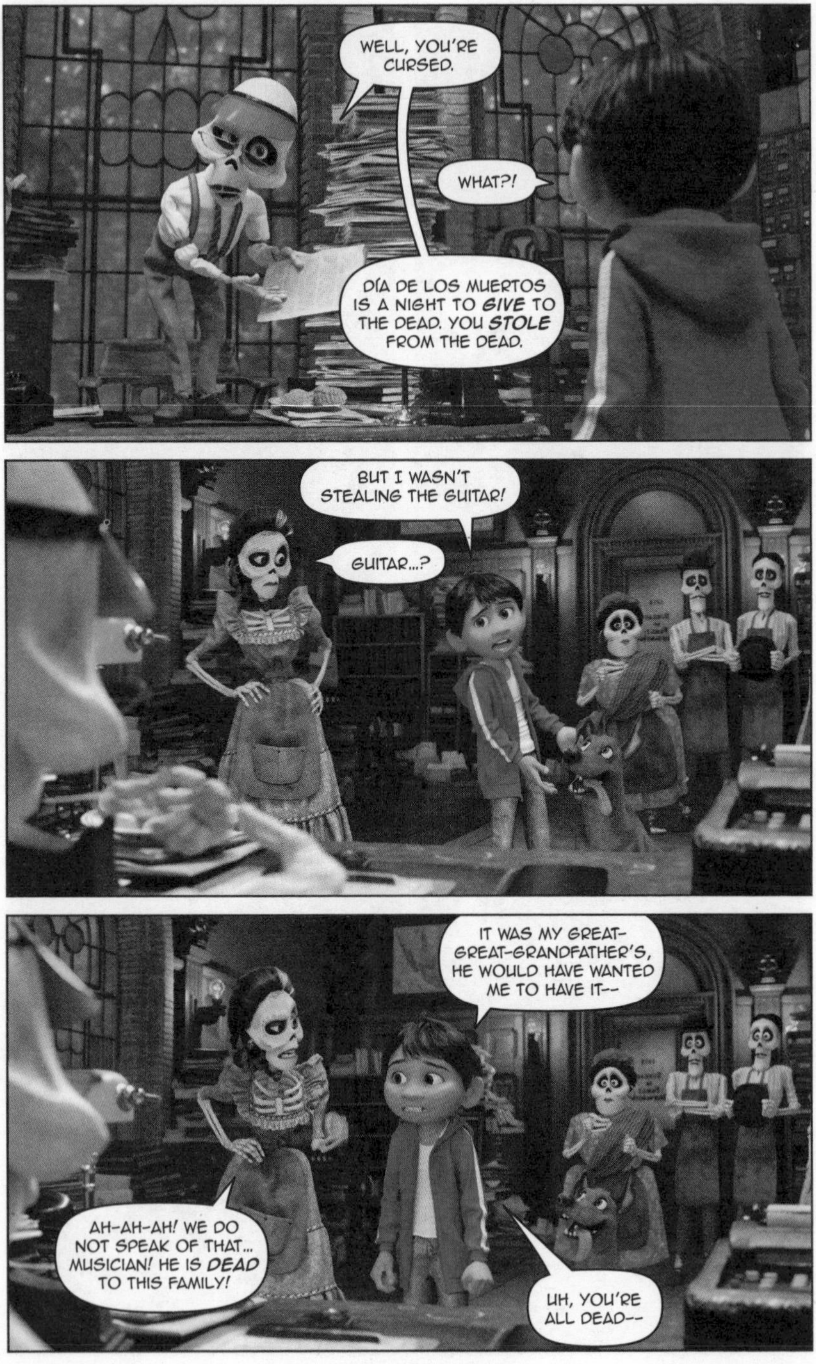
WELL, YOU'RE CURSED.
WHAT?!
DÍA DE LOS MUERTOS IS A NIGHT TO *GIVE* TO THE DEAD. YOU *STOLE* FROM THE DEAD.
BUT I WASN'T STEALING THE GUITAR!
GUITAR...?
IT WAS MY GREAT-GREAT-GRANDFATHER'S, HE WOULD HAVE WANTED ME TO HAVE IT--
AH-AH-AH! WE DO NOT SPEAK OF THAT... MUSICIAN! HE IS *DEAD* TO THIS FAMILY!
UH, YOU'RE ALL DEAD--

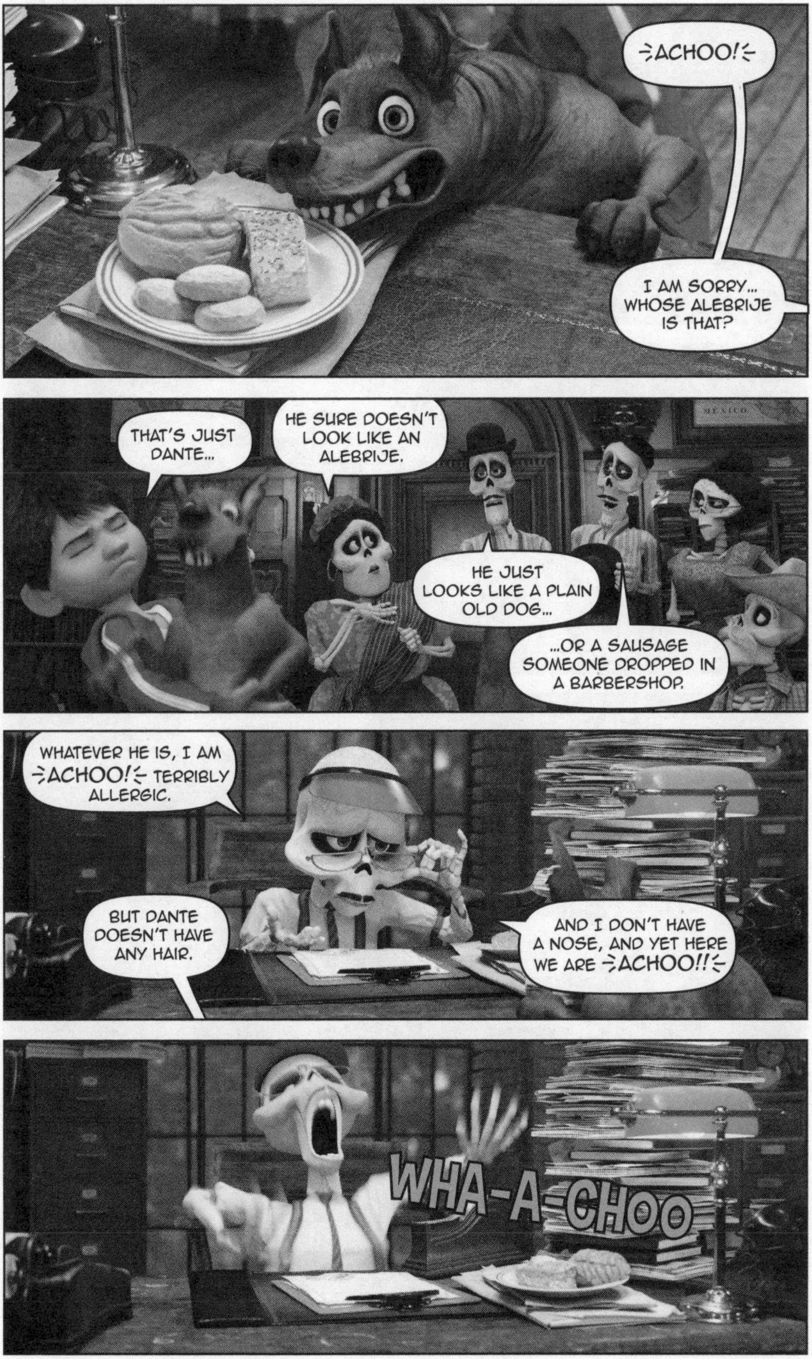
ACHOO!
I AM SORRY... WHOSE ALEBRIJE IS THAT?
THAT'S JUST DANTE...
HE SURE DOESN'T LOOK LIKE AN ALEBRIJE.
HE JUST LOOKS LIKE A PLAIN OLD DOG...
...OR A SAUSAGE SOMEONE DROPPED IN A BARBERSHOP.
WHATEVER HE IS, I AM ACHOO! TERRIBLY ALLERGIC.
BUT DANTE DOESN'T HAVE ANY HAIR.
AND I DON'T HAVE A NOSE, AND YET HERE WE ARE ACHOO!!
WHA-A-CHOO

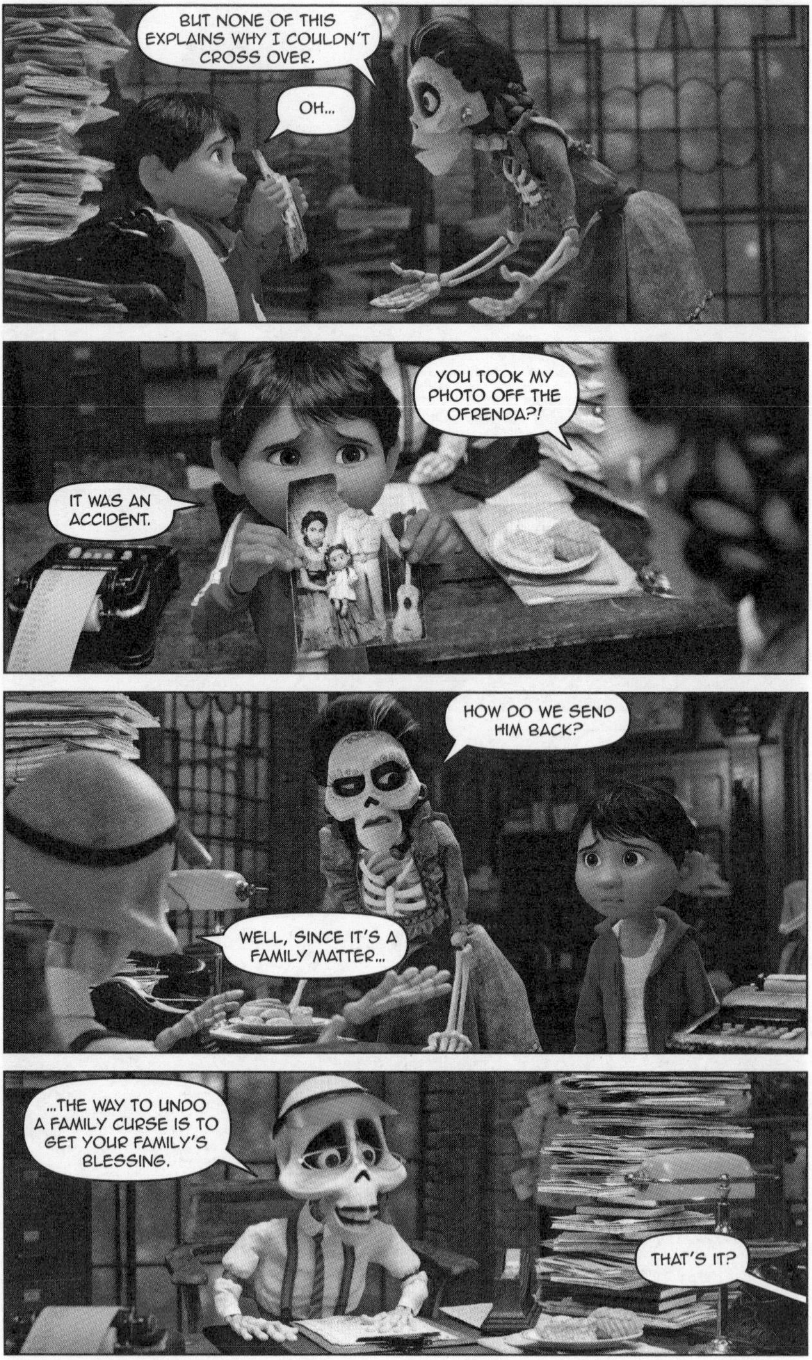
BUT NONE OF THIS EXPLAINS WHY I COULDN'T CROSS OVER.
OH...
YOU TOOK MY PHOTO OFF THE OFRENDA?!
IT WAS AN ACCIDENT.
HOW DO WE SEND HIM BACK?
WELL, SINCE IT'S A FAMILY MATTER...
...THE WAY TO UNDO A FAMILY CURSE IS TO GET YOUR FAMILY'S BLESSING.
THAT'S IT?

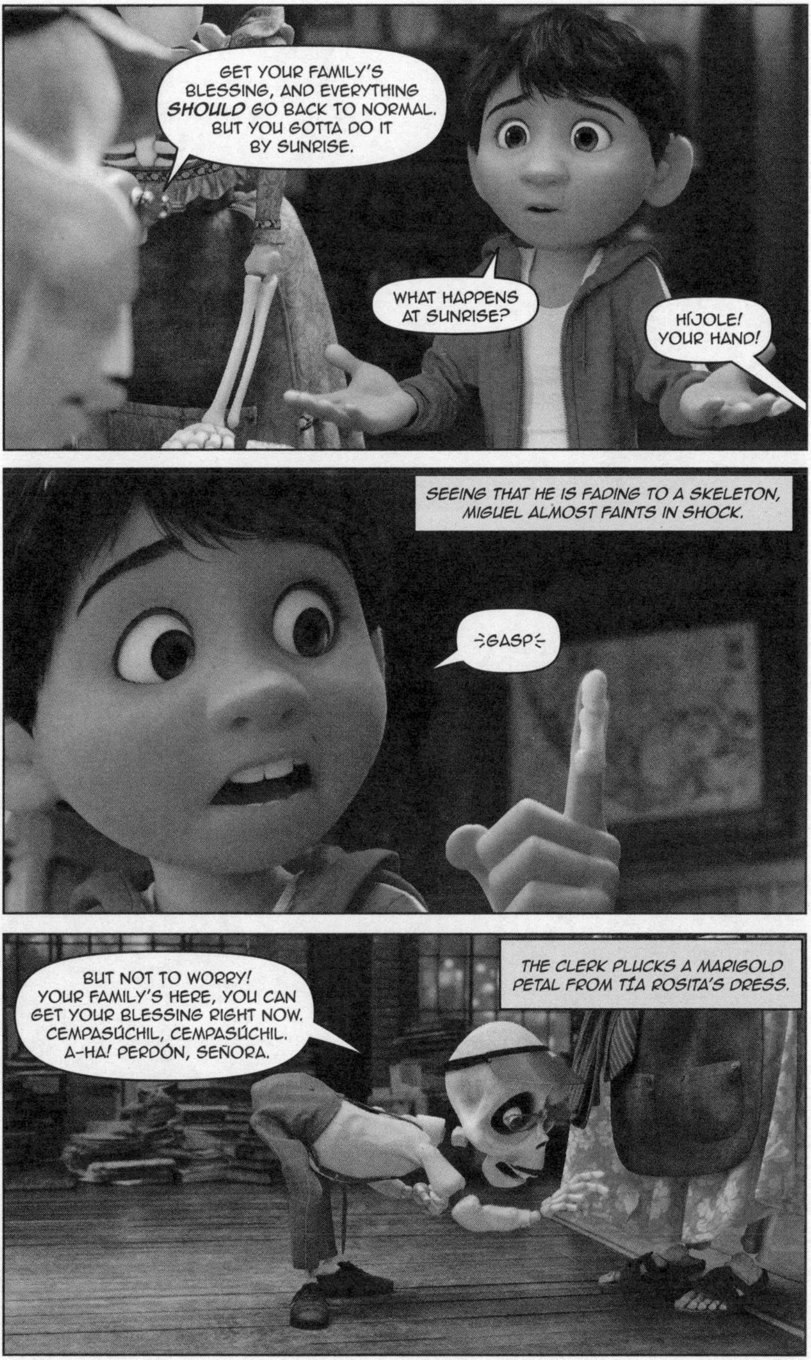
GET YOUR FAMILY'S BLESSING, AND EVERYTHING *SHOULD* GO BACK TO NORMAL. BUT YOU GOTTA DO IT BY SUNRISE.
WHAT HAPPENS AT SUNRISE?
HÍJOLE! YOUR HAND!
SEEING THAT HE IS FADING TO A SKELETON, MIGUEL ALMOST FAINTS IN SHOCK.
GASP
THE CLERK PLUCKS A MARIGOLD PETAL FROM TÍA ROSITA'S DRESS.
BUT NOT TO WORRY! YOUR FAMILY'S HERE, YOU CAN GET YOUR BLESSING RIGHT NOW. CEMPASÚCHIL, CEMPASÚCHIL. A-HA! PERDÓN, SEÑORA.

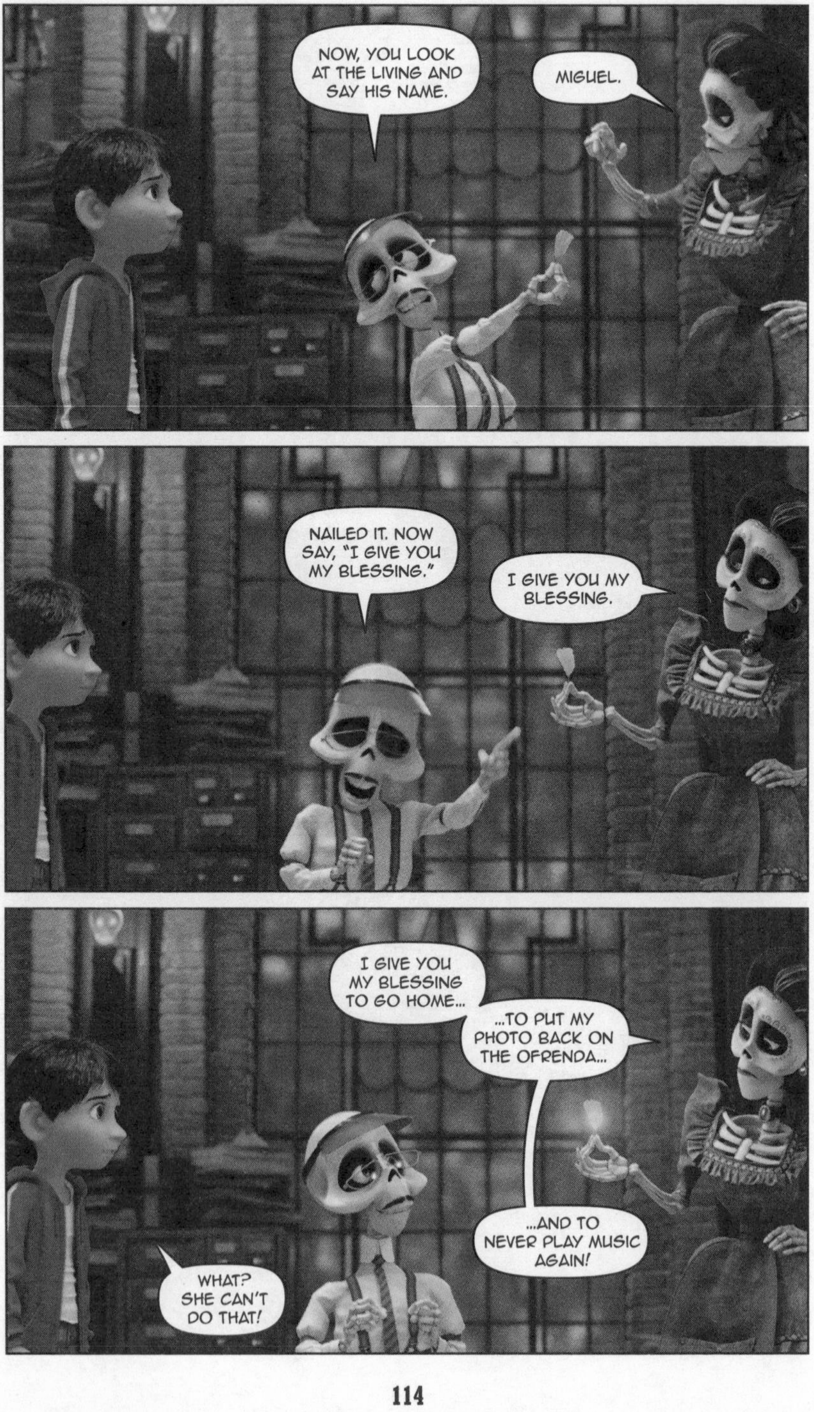
NOW, YOU LOOK AT THE LIVING AND SAY HIS NAME.
MIGUEL.
NAILED IT. NOW SAY, "I GIVE YOU MY BLESSING."
I GIVE YOU MY BLESSING.
I GIVE YOU MY BLESSING TO GO HOME...
...TO PUT MY PHOTO BACK ON THE OFRENDA...
...AND TO NEVER PLAY MUSIC AGAIN!
WHAT? SHE CAN'T DO THAT!

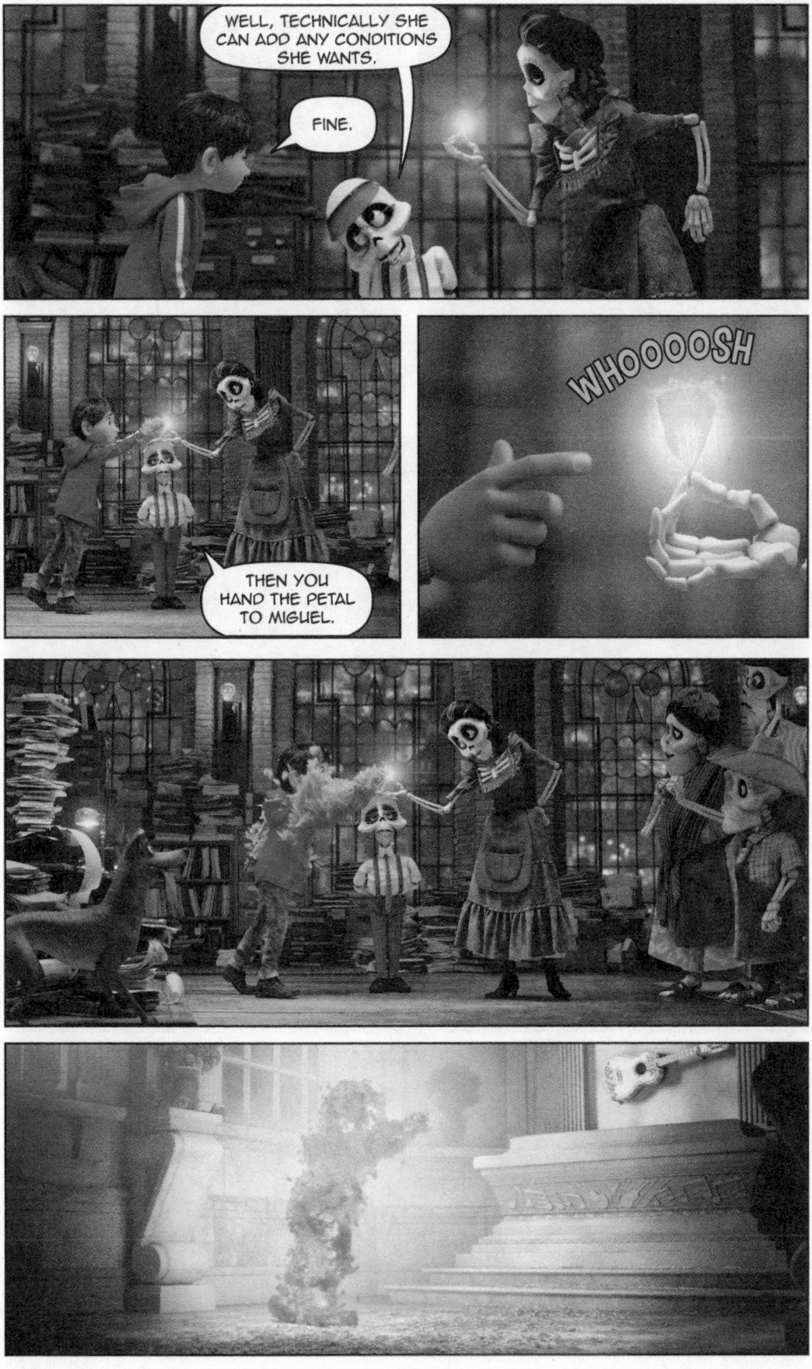
WELL, TECHNICALLY SHE CAN ADD ANY CONDITIONS SHE WANTS.
FINE.
THEN YOU HAND THE PETAL TO MIGUEL.
WHOOOOSH

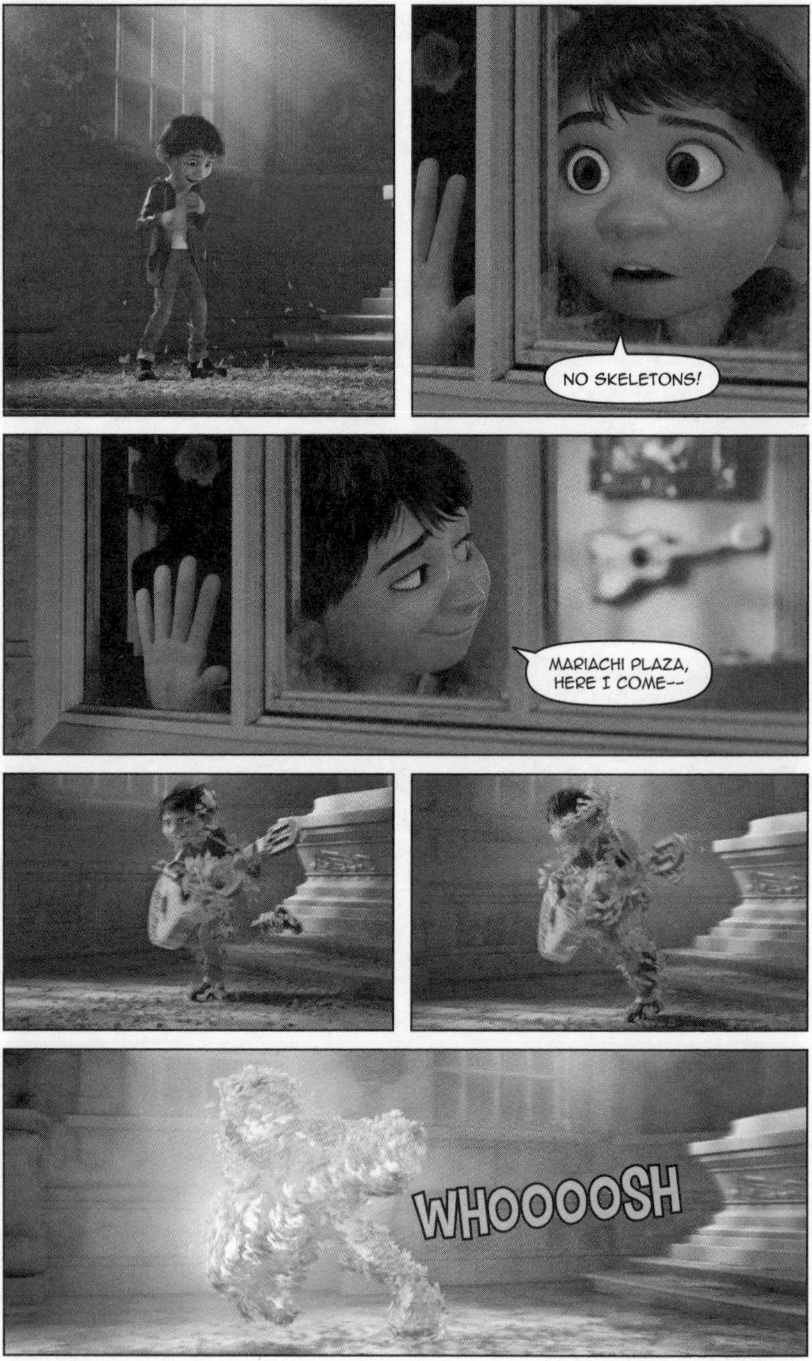
NO SKELETONS!
MARIACHI PLAZA, HERE I COME--
WHOOOOSH

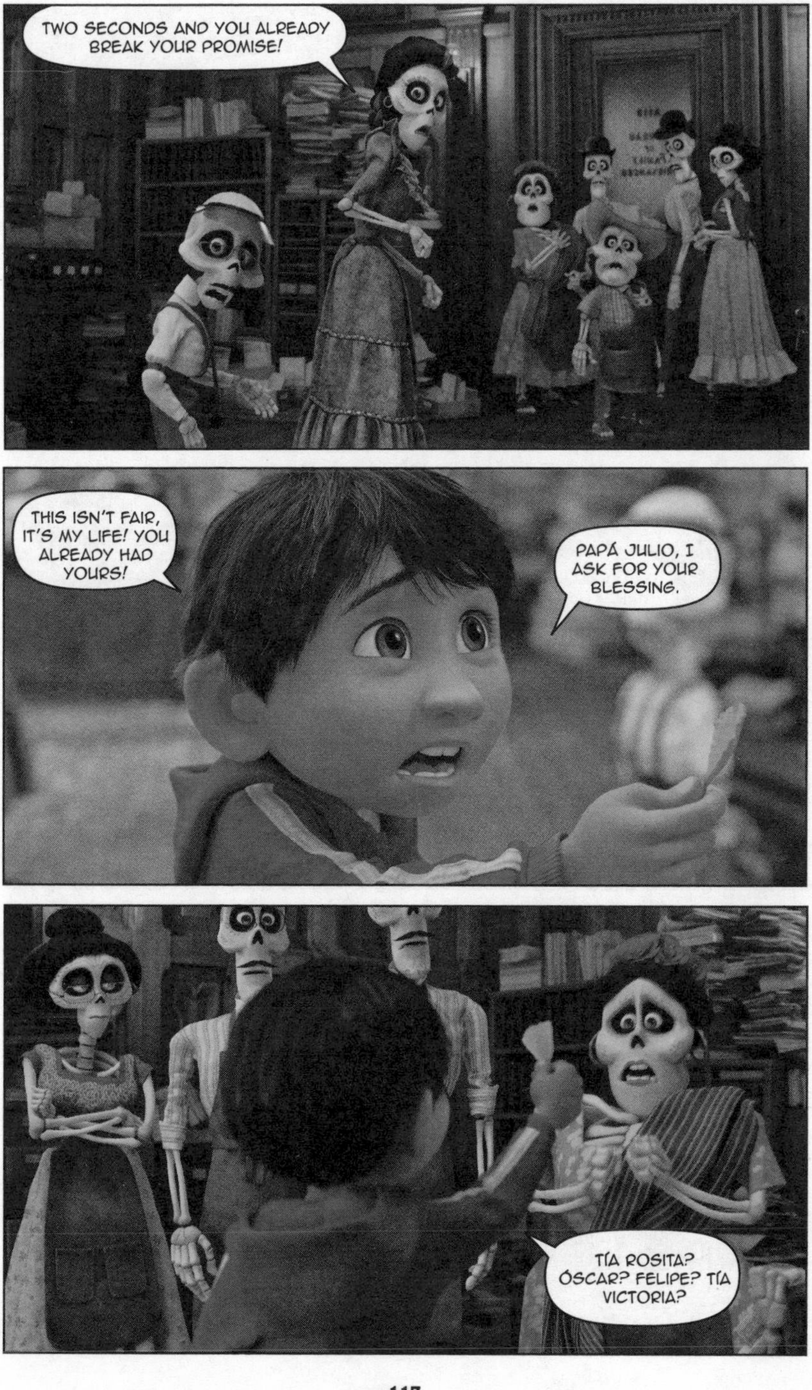
TWO SECONDS AND YOU ALREADY BREAK YOUR PROMISE!
THIS ISN'T FAIR, IT'S MY LIFE! YOU ALREADY HAD YOURS!
PAPÁ JULIO, I ASK FOR YOUR BLESSING.
TÍA ROSITA? ÓSCAR? FELIPE? TÍA VICTORIA?

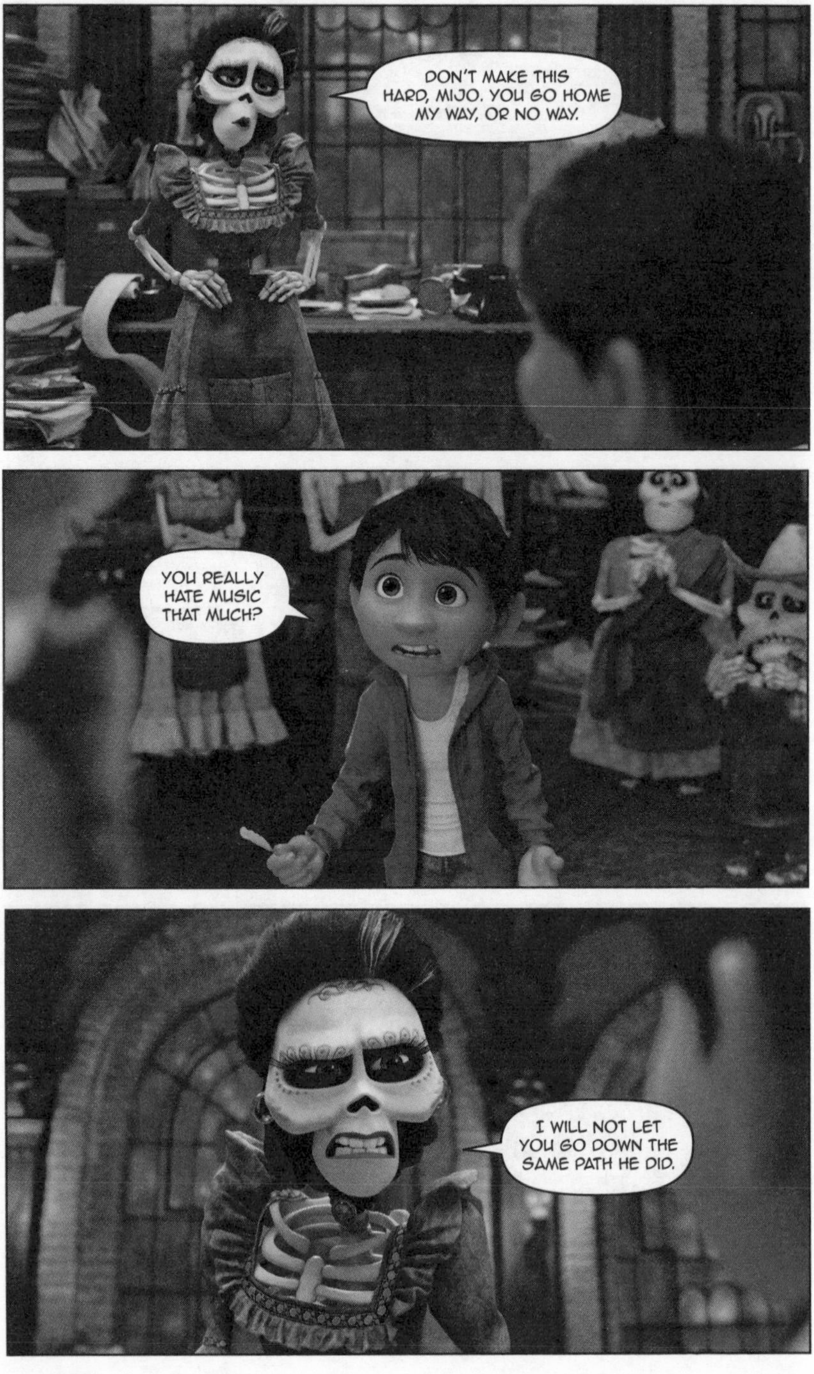
DON'T MAKE THIS HARD, MIJO. YOU GO HOME MY WAY, OR NO WAY.
YOU REALLY HATE MUSIC THAT MUCH?
I WILL NOT LET YOU GO DOWN THE SAME PATH HE DID.

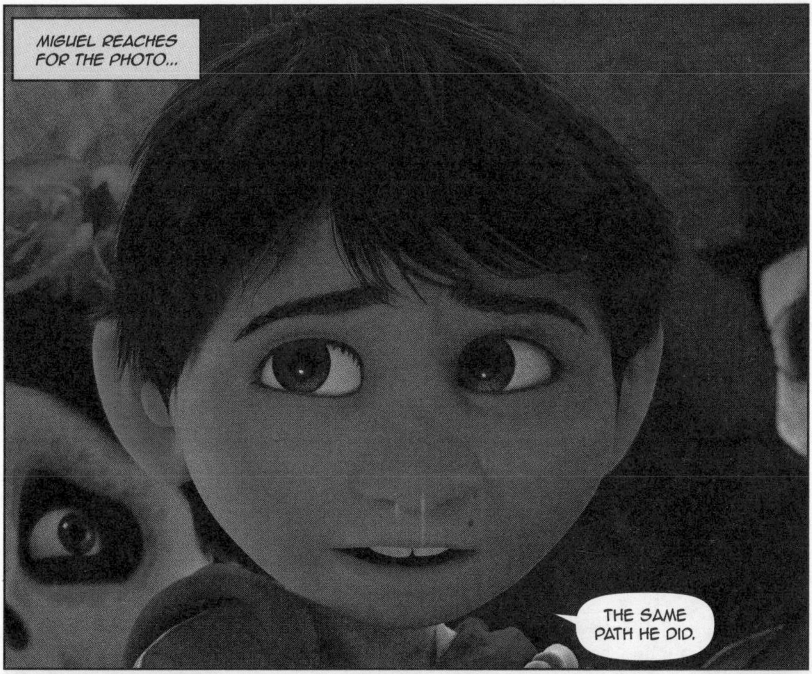
MIGUEL REACHES FOR THE PHOTO...
THE SAME PATH HE DID.

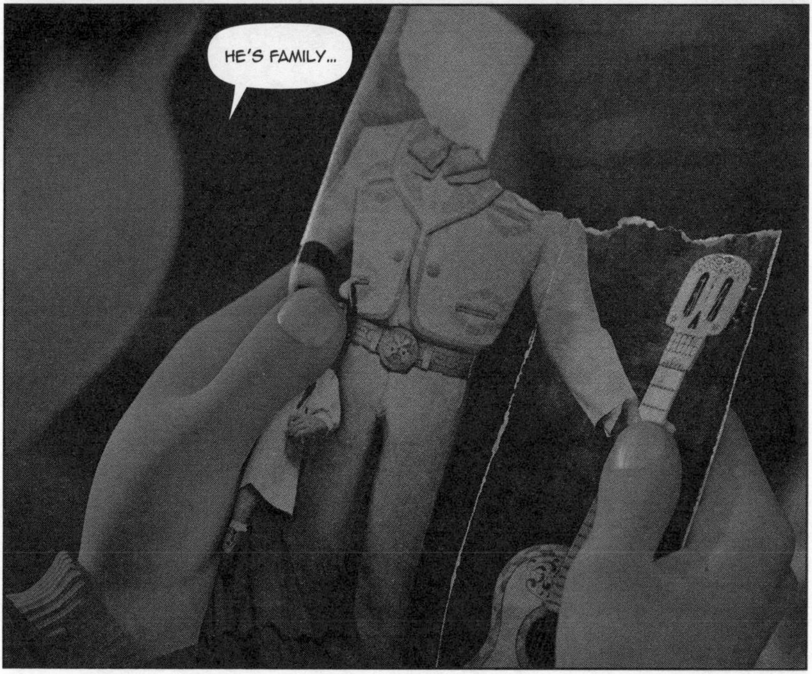
HE'S FAMILY...

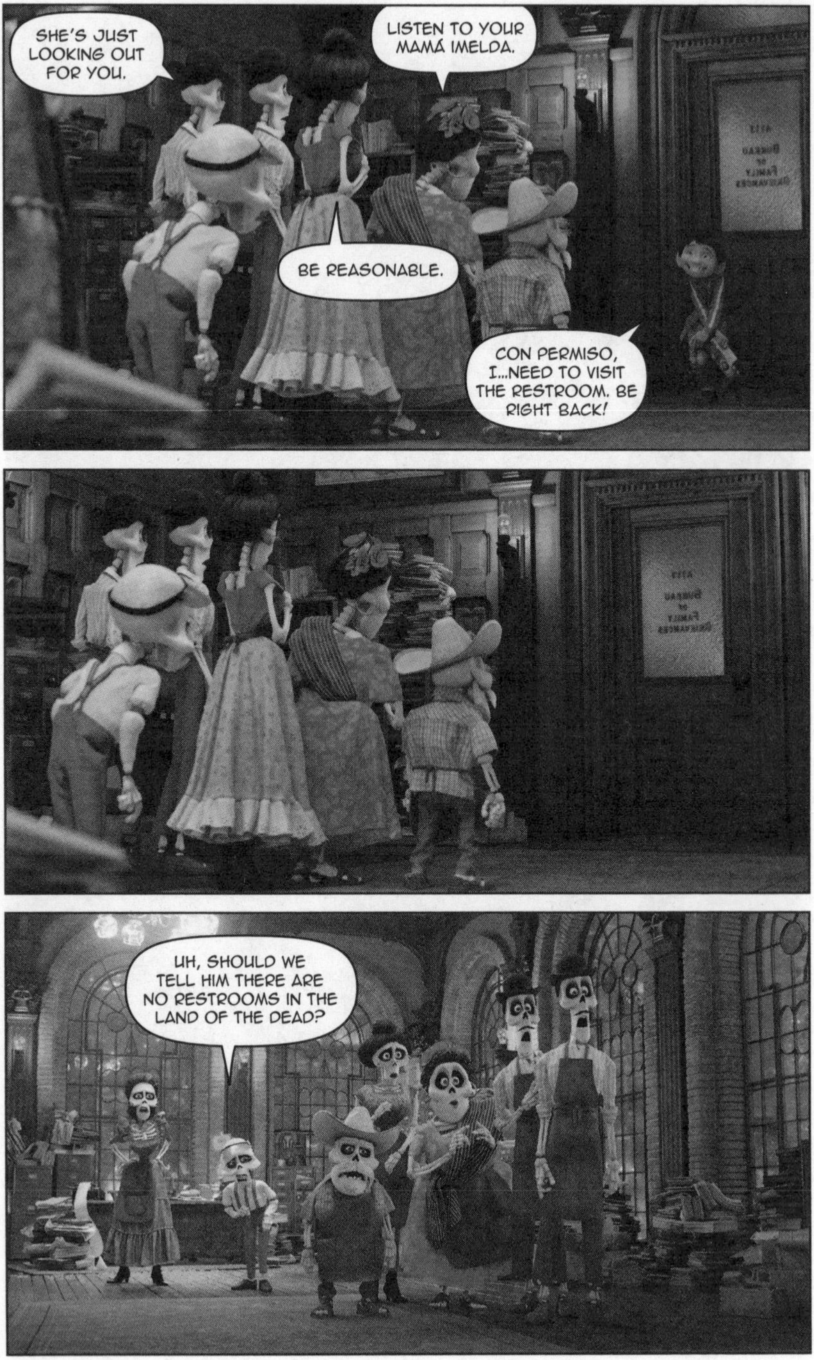
SHE'S JUST LOOKING OUT FOR YOU.
LISTEN TO YOUR MAMÁ IMELDA.
BE REASONABLE.
CON PERMISO, I...NEED TO VISIT THE RESTROOM. BE RIGHT BACK!
UH, SHOULD WE TELL HIM THERE ARE NO RESTROOMS IN THE LAND OF THE DEAD?

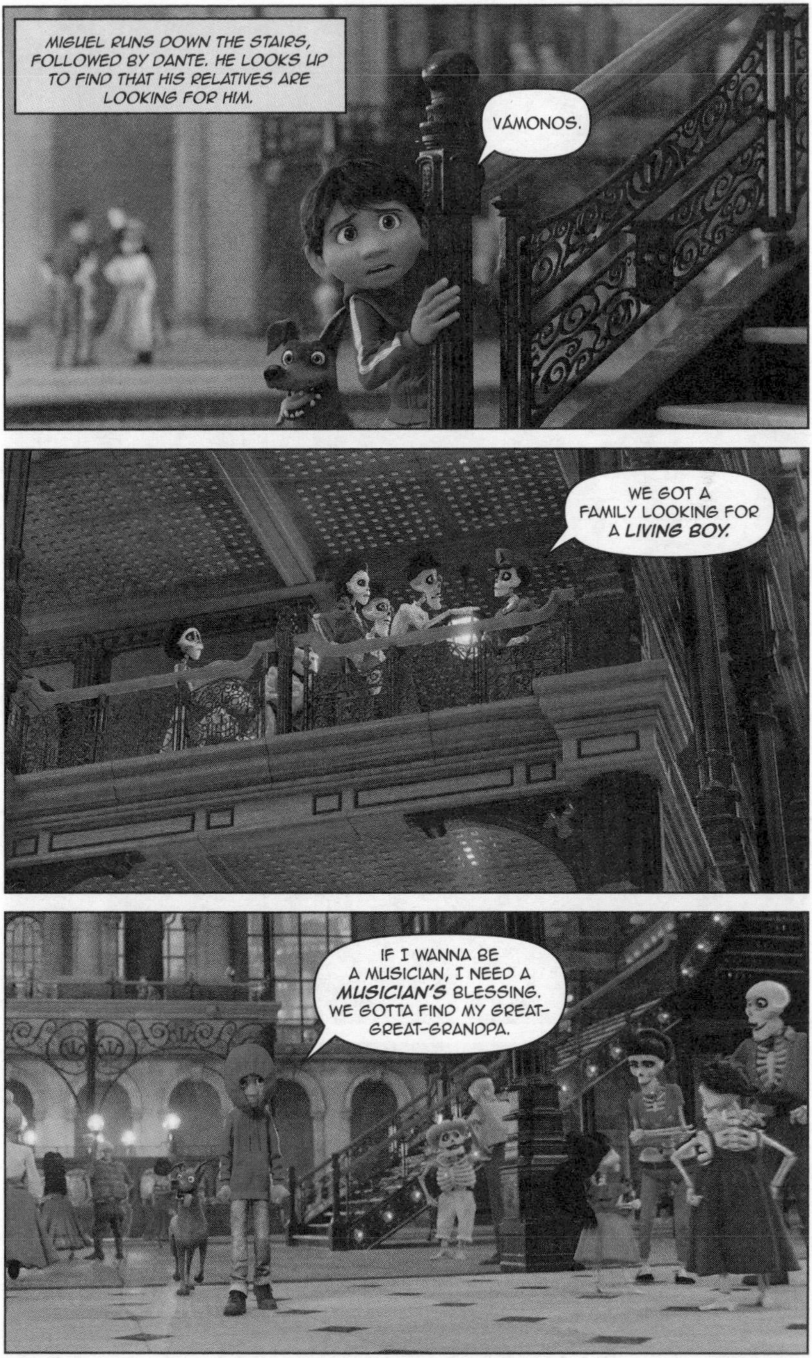
MIGUEL RUNS DOWN THE STAIRS, FOLLOWED BY DANTE. HE LOOKS UP TO FIND THAT HIS RELATIVES ARE LOOKING FOR HIM.
VÁMONOS.
WE GOT A FAMILY LOOKING FOR A *LIVING BOY.*
IF I WANNA BE A MUSICIAN, I NEED A ***MUSICIAN'S*** BLESSING. WE GOTTA FIND MY GREAT-GREAT-GRANDPA.

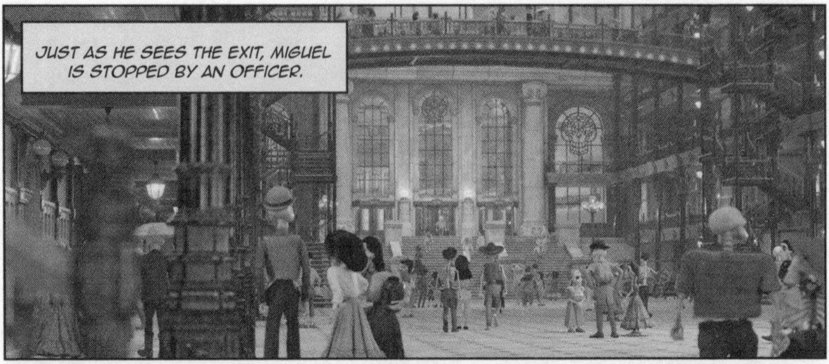
JUST AS HE SEES THE EXIT, MIGUEL IS STOPPED BY AN OFFICER.

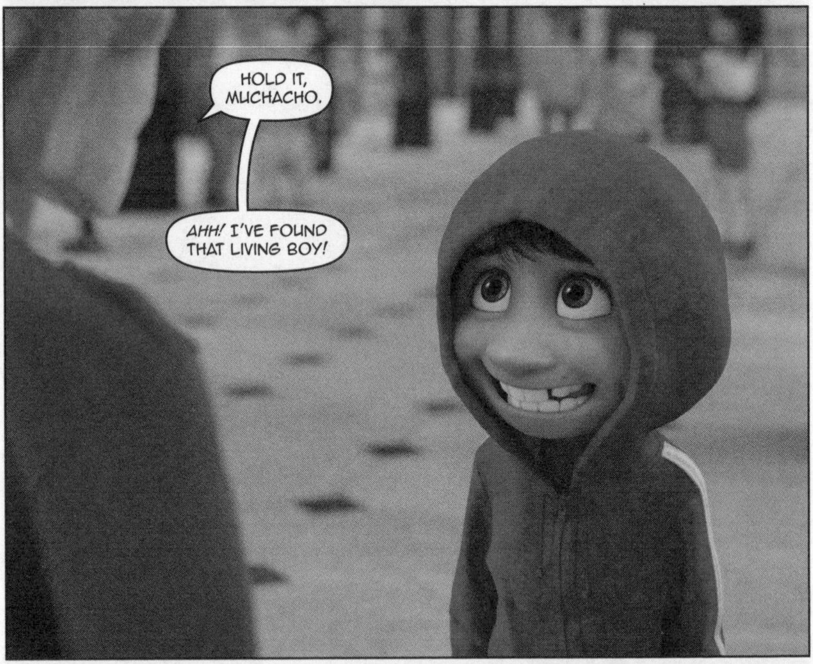
HOLD IT, MUCHACHO.
AHH! I'VE FOUND THAT LIVING BOY!

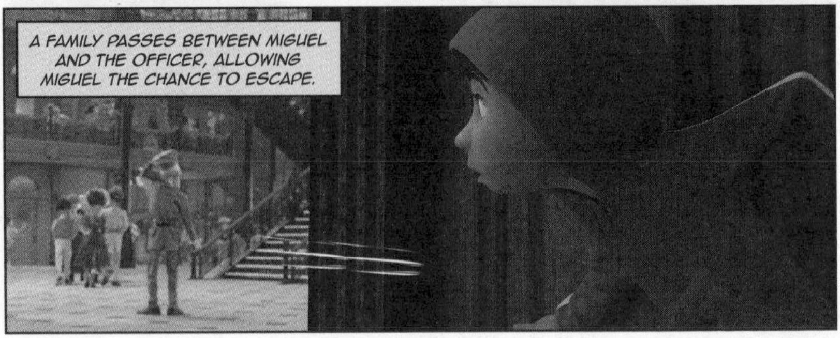
A FAMILY PASSES BETWEEN MIGUEL AND THE OFFICER, ALLOWING MIGUEL THE CHANCE TO ESCAPE.

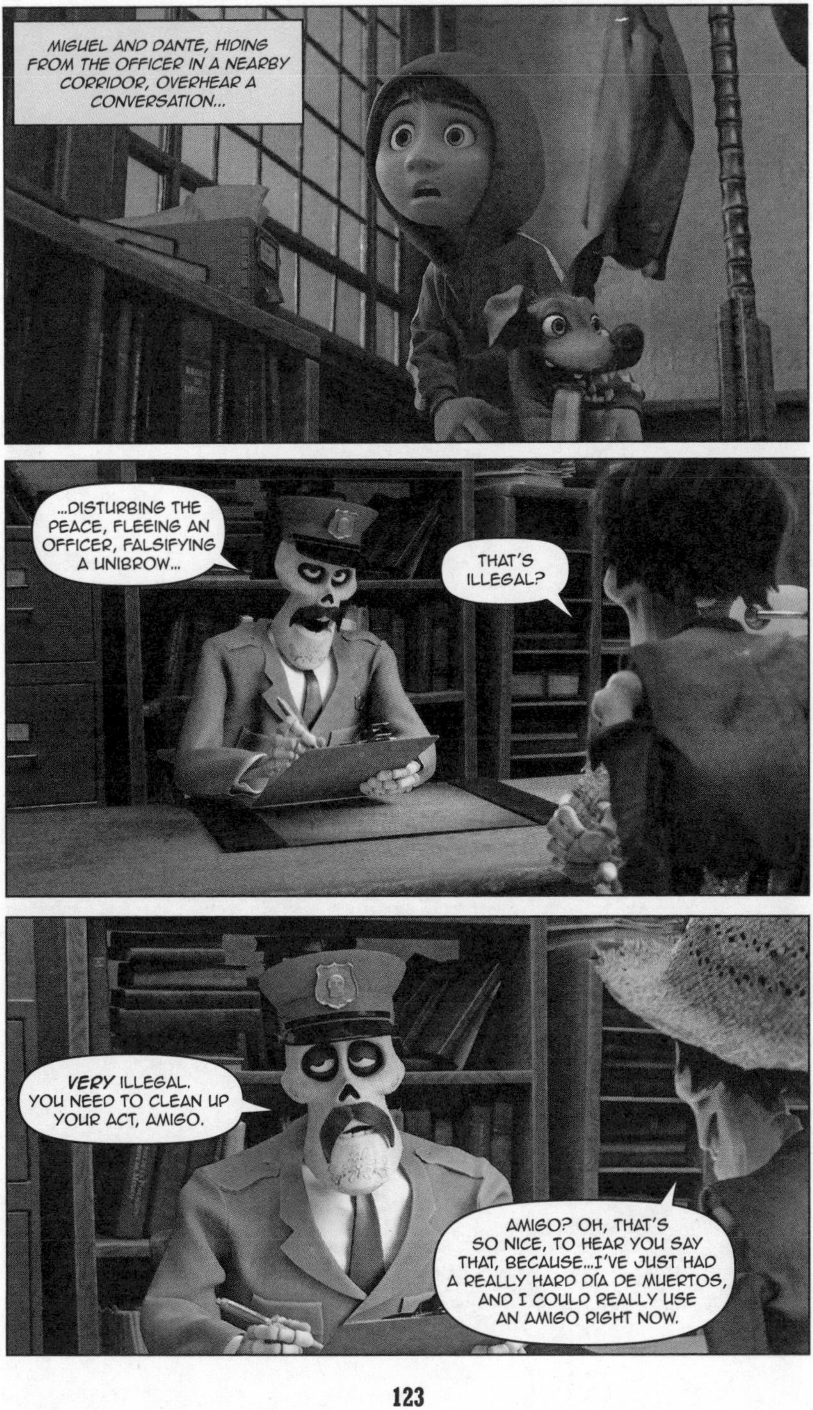
MIGUEL AND DANTE, HIDING FROM THE OFFICER IN A NEARBY CORRIDOR, OVERHEAR A CONVERSATION...
...DISTURBING THE PEACE, FLEEING AN OFFICER, FALSIFYING A UNIBROW...
THAT'S ILLEGAL?
VERY ILLEGAL. YOU NEED TO CLEAN UP YOUR ACT, AMIGO.
AMIGO? OH, THAT'S SO NICE, TO HEAR YOU SAY THAT, BECAUSE...I'VE JUST HAD A REALLY HARD DÍA DE MUERTOS, AND I COULD REALLY USE AN AMIGO RIGHT NOW.

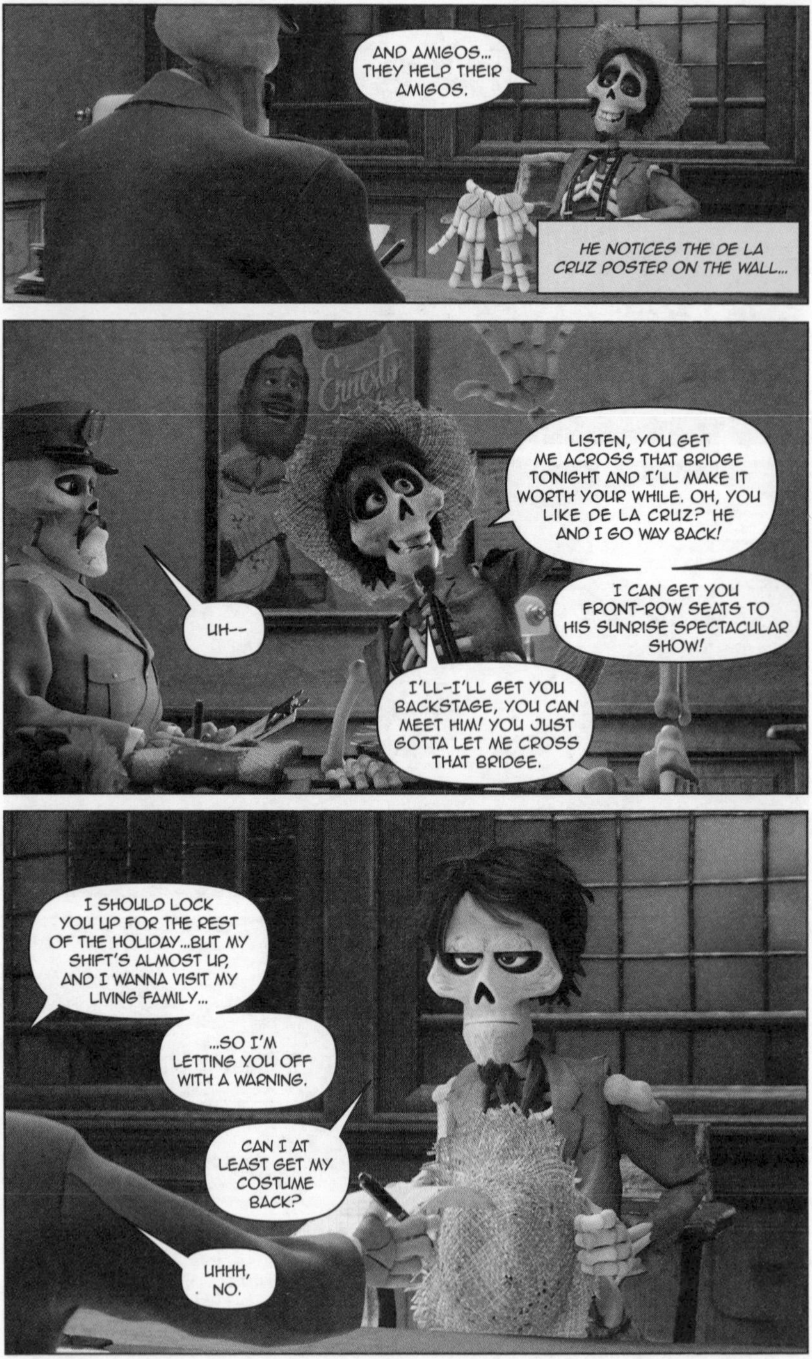
AND AMIGOS... THEY HELP THEIR AMIGOS.
HE NOTICES THE DE LA CRUZ POSTER ON THE WALL...
Ernesto
LISTEN, YOU GET ME ACROSS THAT BRIDGE TONIGHT AND I'LL MAKE IT WORTH YOUR WHILE. OH, YOU LIKE DE LA CRUZ? HE AND I GO WAY BACK!
UH--
I CAN GET YOU FRONT-ROW SEATS TO HIS SUNRISE SPECTACULAR SHOW!
I'LL-I'LL GET YOU BACKSTAGE, YOU CAN MEET HIM! YOU JUST GOTTA LET ME CROSS THAT BRIDGE.
I SHOULD LOCK YOU UP FOR THE REST OF THE HOLIDAY...BUT MY SHIFT'S ALMOST UP, AND I WANNA VISIT MY LIVING FAMILY...
...SO I'M LETTING YOU OFF WITH A WARNING.
CAN I AT LEAST GET MY COSTUME BACK?
UHHH, NO.

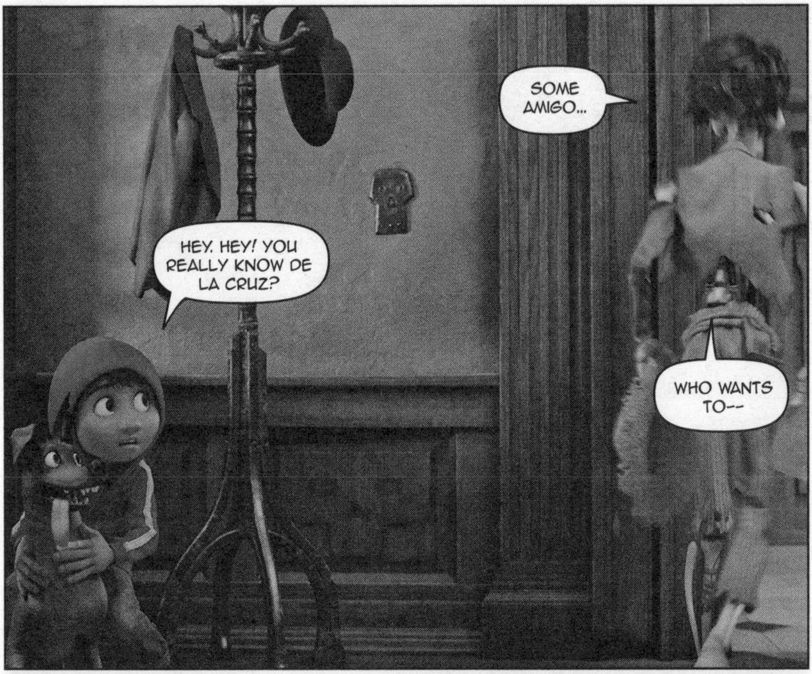
SOME AMIGO...
HEY. HEY! YOU REALLY KNOW DE LA CRUZ?
WHO WANTS TO--

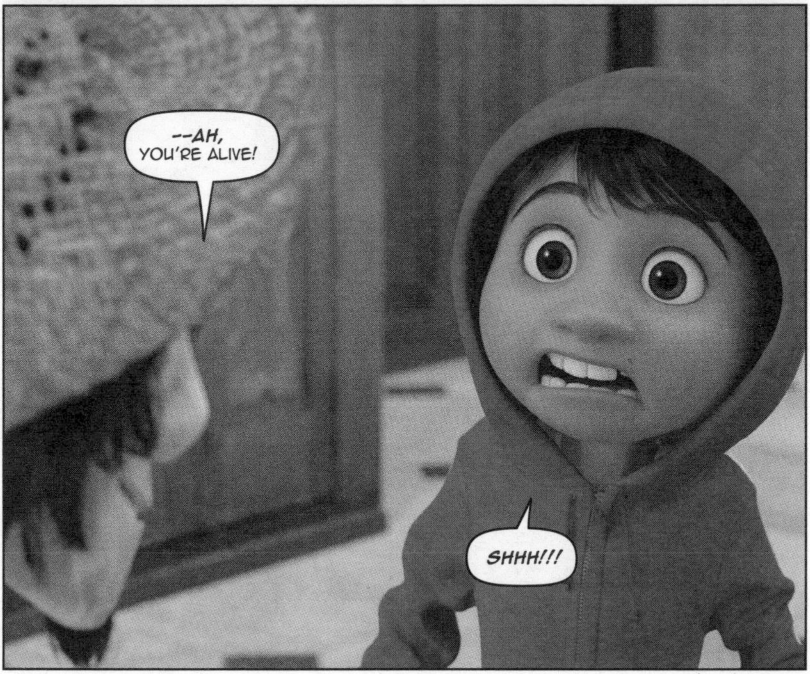
--AH, YOU'RE ALIVE!
SHHH!!!

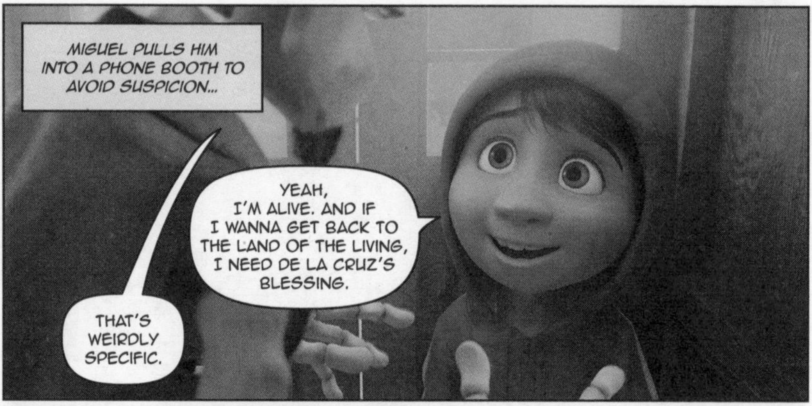
MIGUEL PULLS HIM INTO A PHONE BOOTH TO AVOID SUSPICION...
YEAH, I'M ALIVE. AND IF I WANNA GET BACK TO THE LAND OF THE LIVING, I NEED DE LA CRUZ'S BLESSING.
THAT'S WEIRDLY SPECIFIC.

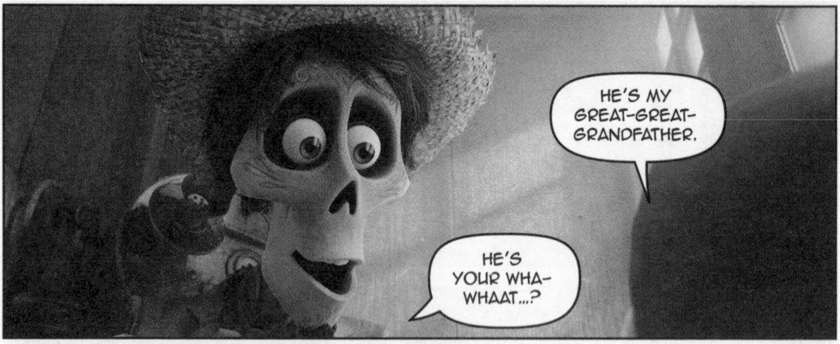
HE'S MY GREAT-GREAT-GRANDFATHER.
HE'S YOUR WHA-WHAAT...?

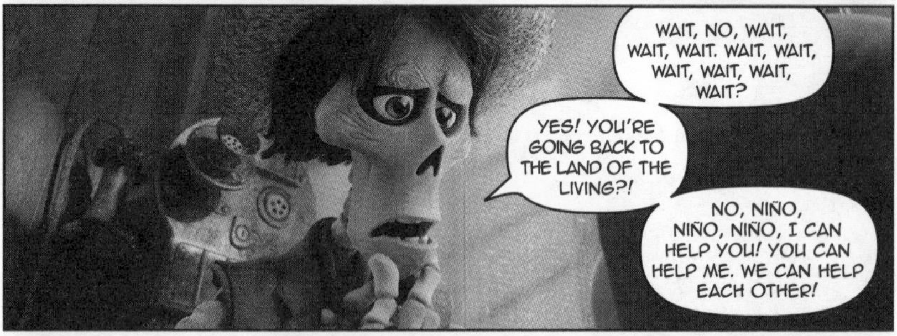
WAIT, NO, WAIT, WAIT, WAIT. WAIT, WAIT, WAIT, WAIT, WAIT, WAIT?
YES! YOU'RE GOING BACK TO THE LAND OF THE LIVING?!
NO, NIÑO, NIÑO, NIÑO, I CAN HELP YOU! YOU CAN HELP ME. WE CAN HELP EACH OTHER!

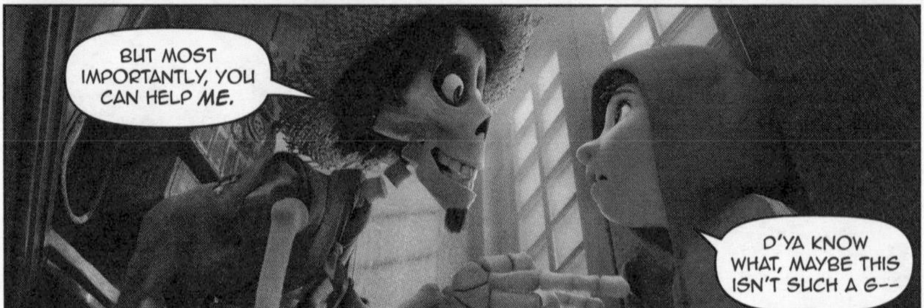
BUT MOST IMPORTANTLY, YOU CAN HELP *ME*.
D'YA KNOW WHAT, MAYBE THIS ISN'T SUCH A G--

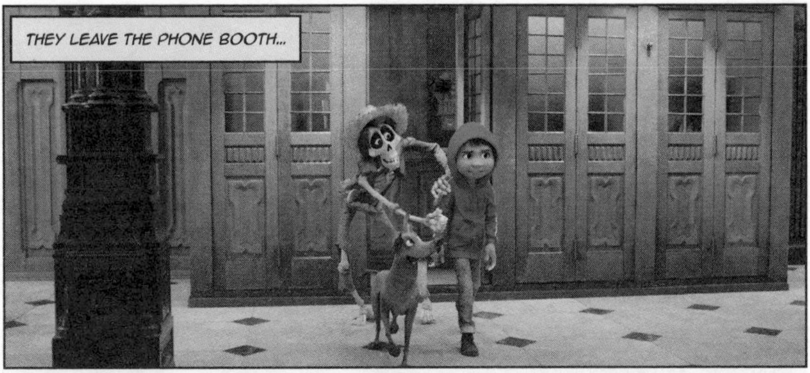
THEY LEAVE THE PHONE BOOTH...

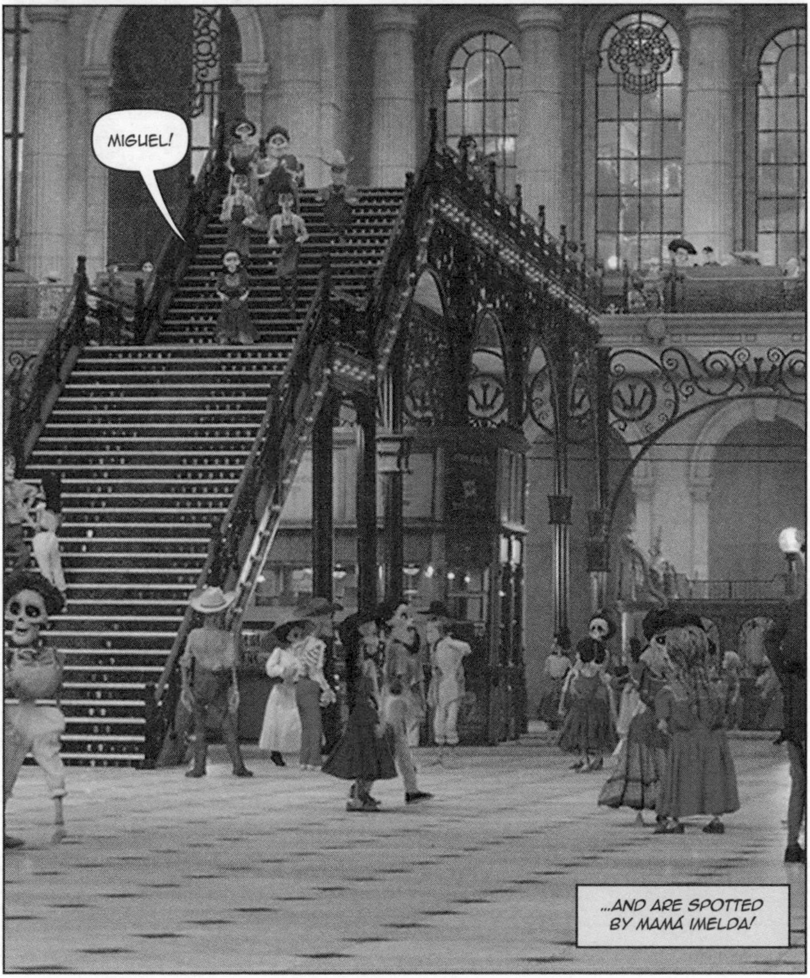
MIGUEL!
...AND ARE SPOTTED BY MAMÁ IMELDA!

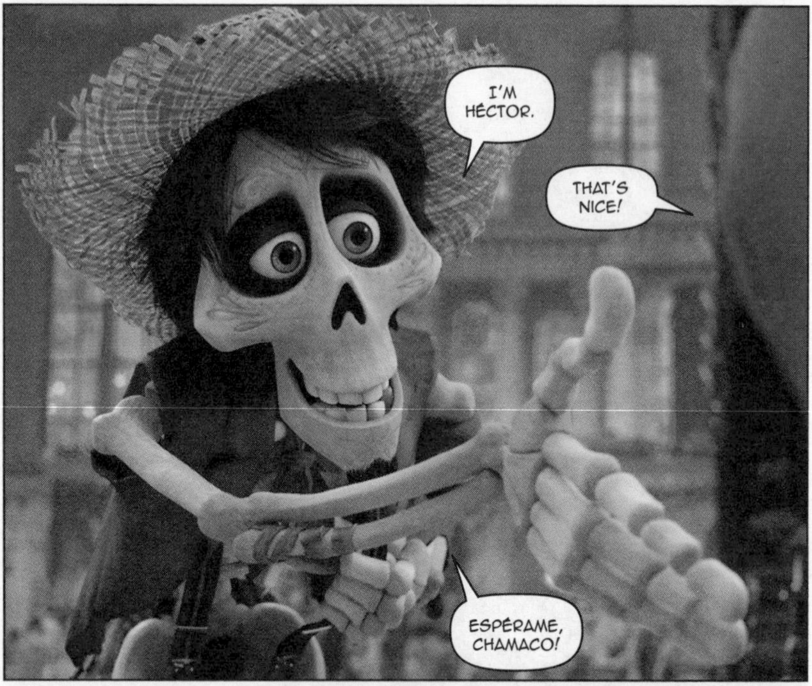
I'M HÉCTOR.
THAT'S NICE!
ESPÉRAME, CHAMACO!

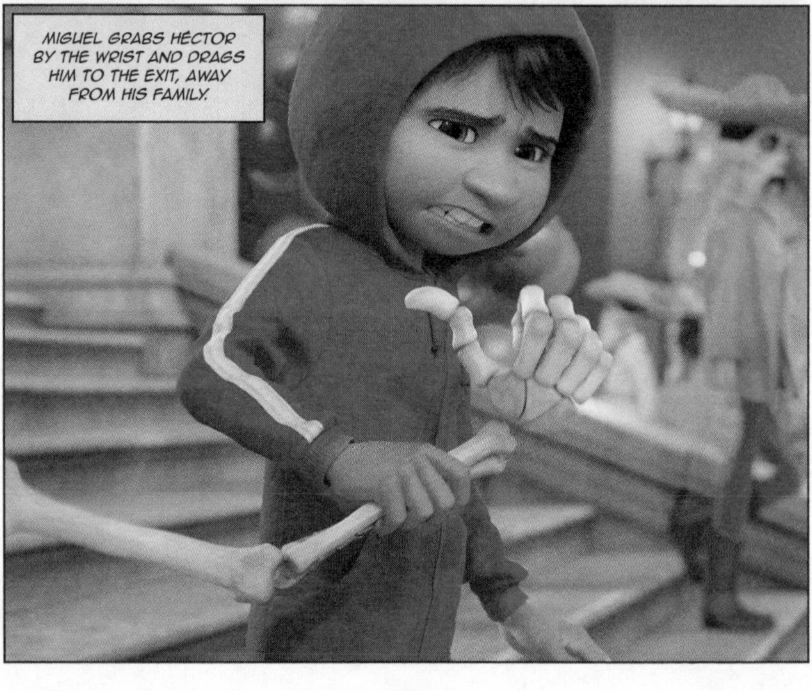
MIGUEL GRABS HÉCTOR BY THE WRIST AND DRAGS HIM TO THE EXIT, AWAY FROM HIS FAMILY.

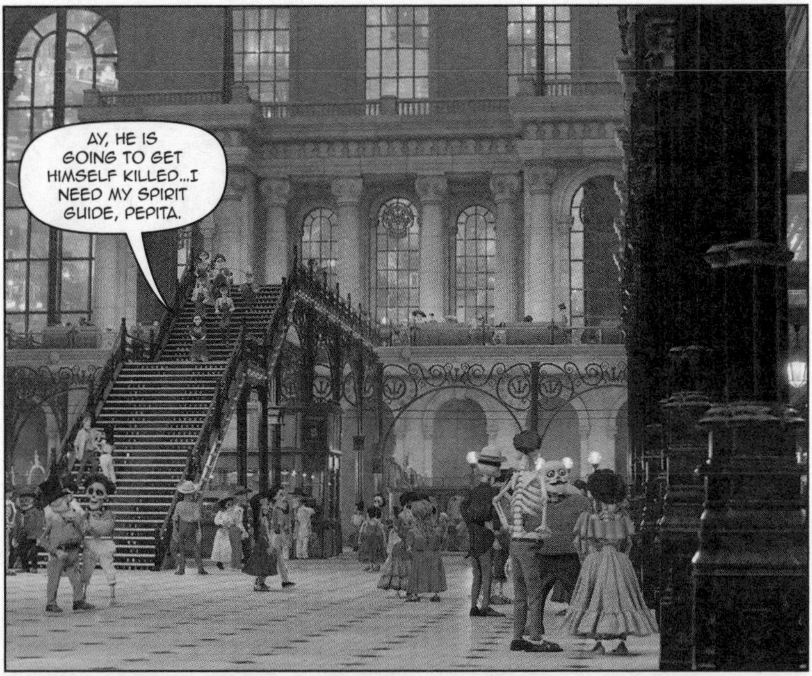
AY, HE IS GOING TO GET HIMSELF KILLED...I NEED MY SPIRIT GUIDE, PEPITA.

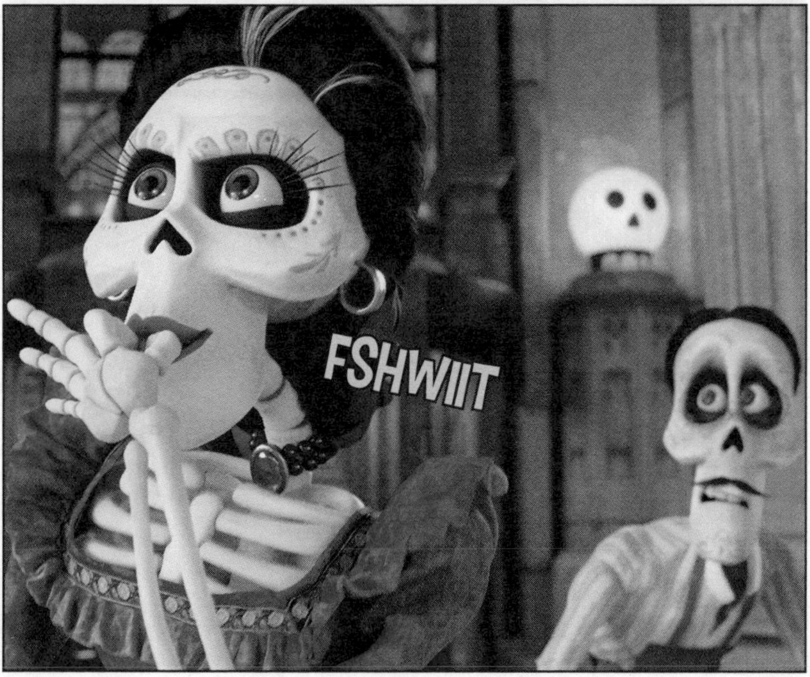
FSHWIIT

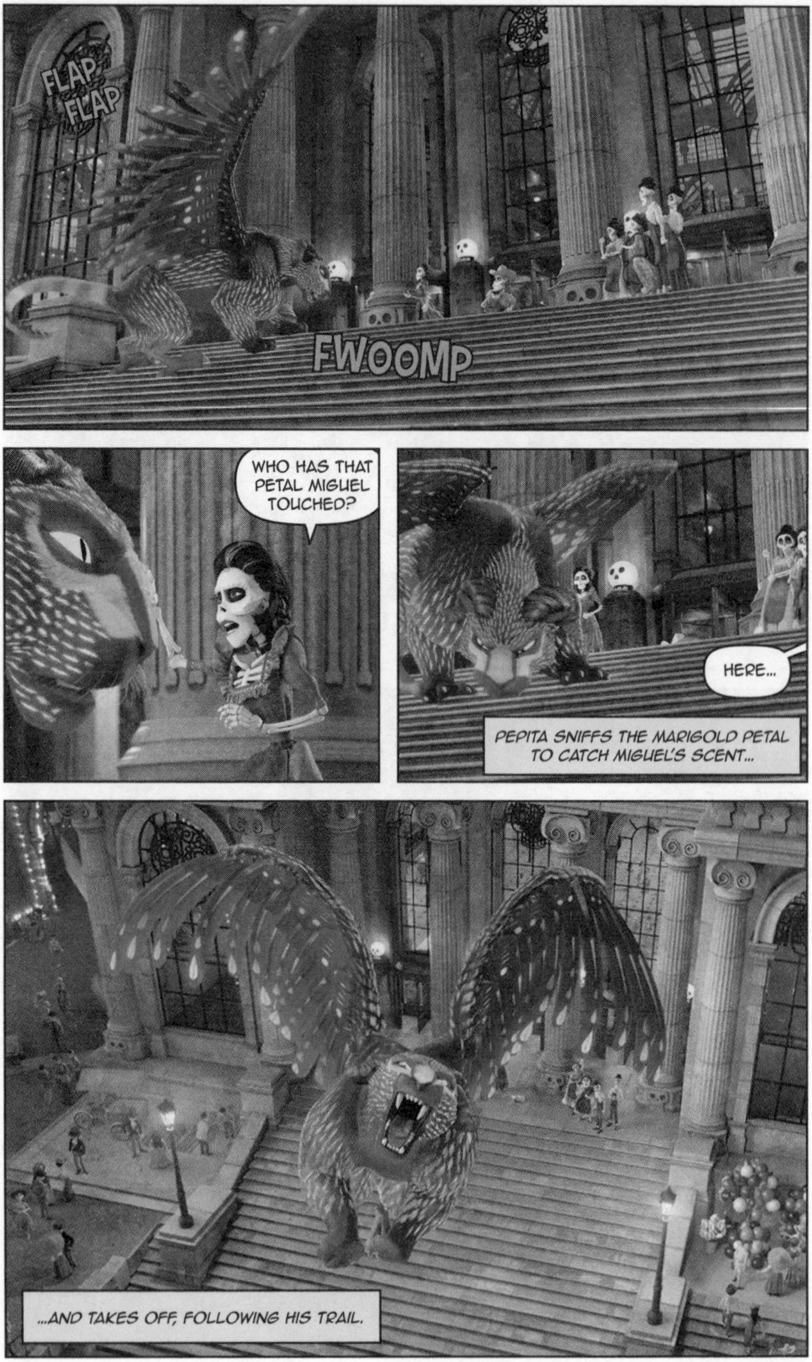
FLAP FLAP
FWOOMP
WHO HAS THAT PETAL MIGUEL TOUCHED?
HERE...
PEPITA SNIFFS THE MARIGOLD PETAL TO CATCH MIGUEL'S SCENT...
...AND TAKES OFF, FOLLOWING HIS TRAIL.

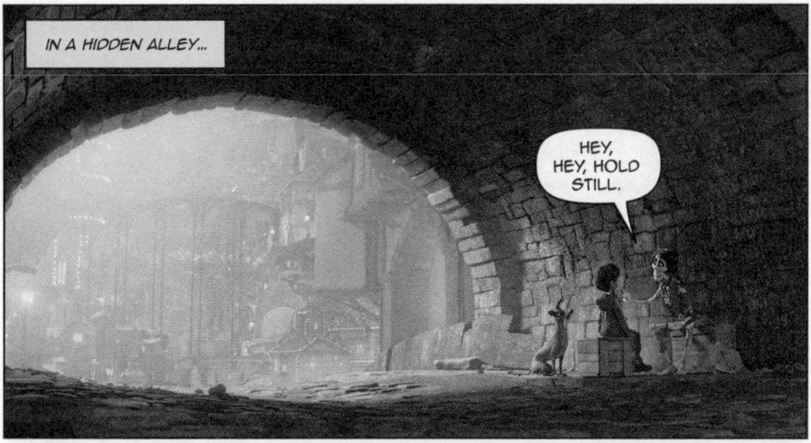
IN A HIDDEN ALLEY...
HEY, HEY, HOLD STILL.

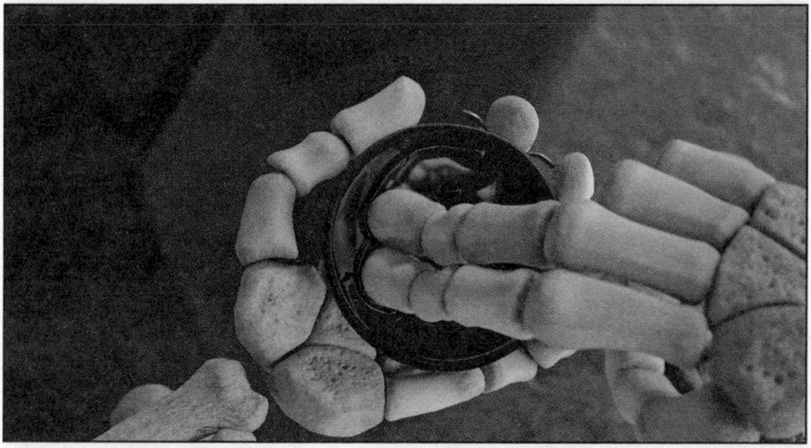

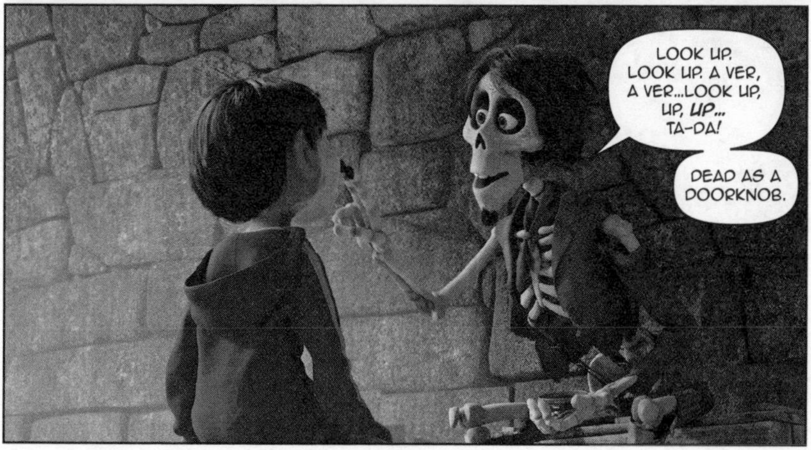
LOOK UP. LOOK UP. A VER, A VER...LOOK UP, UP, *UP*... TA-DA!
DEAD AS A DOORKNOB.

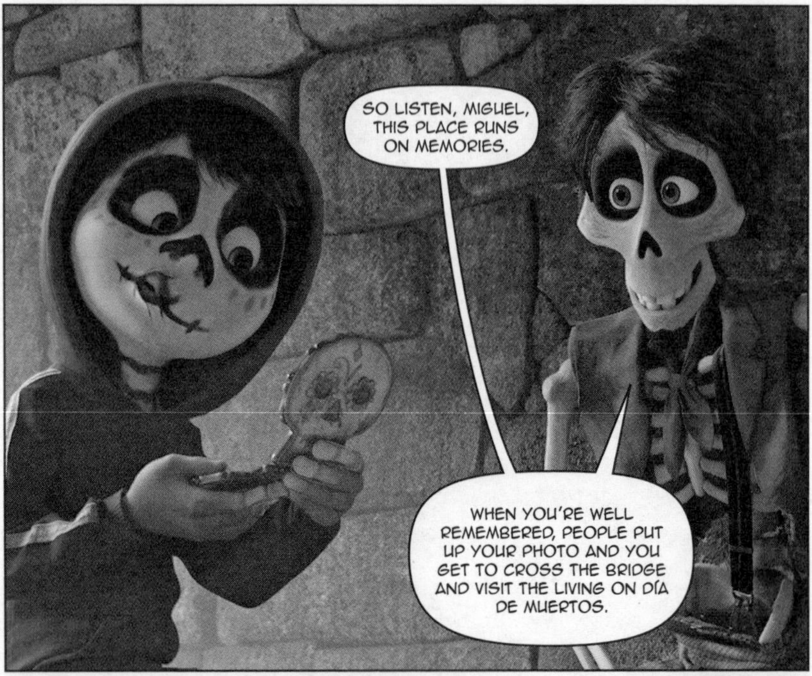
SO LISTEN, MIGUEL, THIS PLACE RUNS ON MEMORIES.
WHEN YOU'RE WELL REMEMBERED, PEOPLE PUT UP YOUR PHOTO AND YOU GET TO CROSS THE BRIDGE AND VISIT THE LIVING ON DÍA DE MUERTOS.

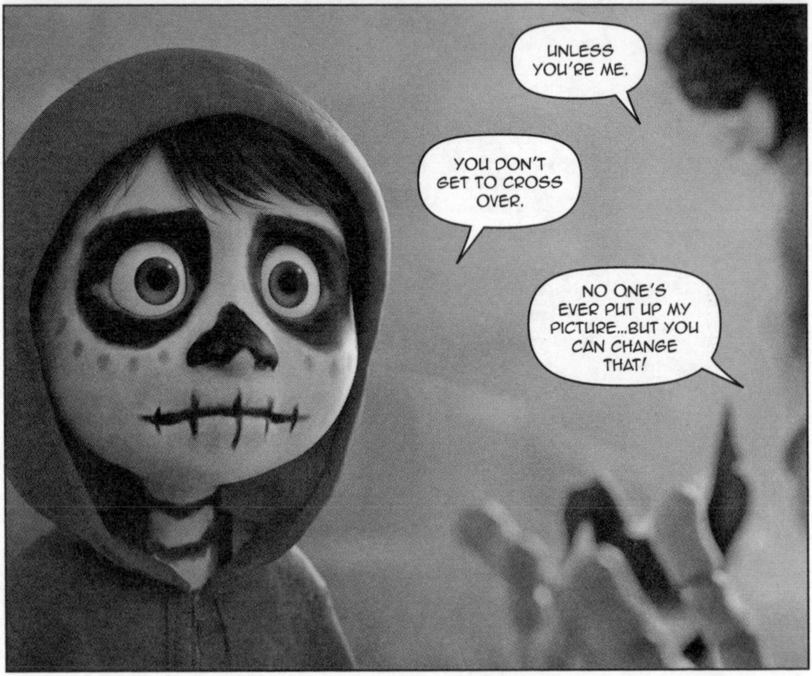
UNLESS YOU'RE ME.
YOU DON'T GET TO CROSS OVER.
NO ONE'S EVER PUT UP MY PICTURE...BUT YOU CAN CHANGE THAT!

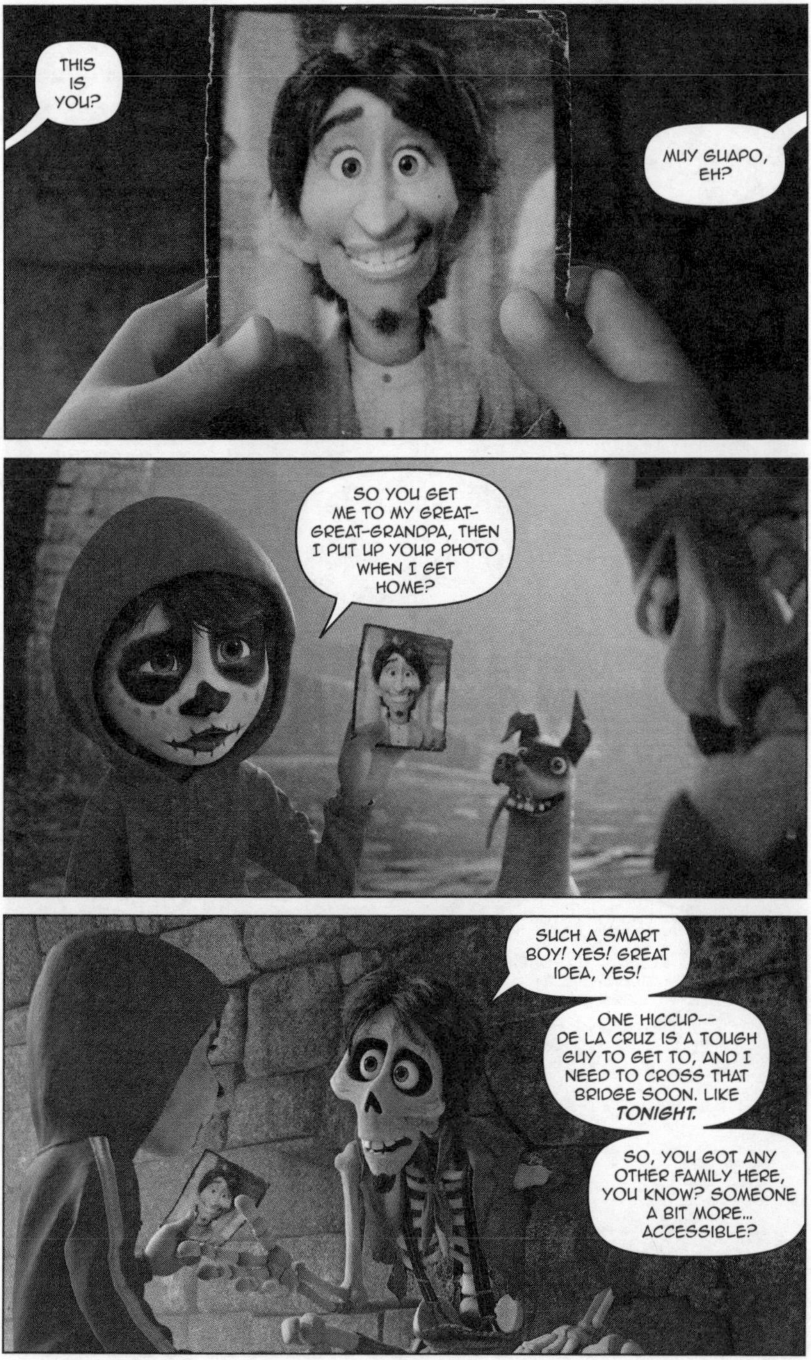
THIS IS YOU?
MUY GUAPO, EH?
SO YOU GET ME TO MY GREAT-GREAT-GRANDPA, THEN I PUT UP YOUR PHOTO WHEN I GET HOME?
SUCH A SMART BOY! YES! GREAT IDEA, YES!
ONE HICCUP-- DE LA CRUZ IS A TOUGH GUY TO GET TO, AND I NEED TO CROSS THAT BRIDGE SOON. LIKE *TONIGHT.*
SO, YOU GOT ANY OTHER FAMILY HERE, YOU KNOW? SOMEONE A BIT MORE... ACCESSIBLE?

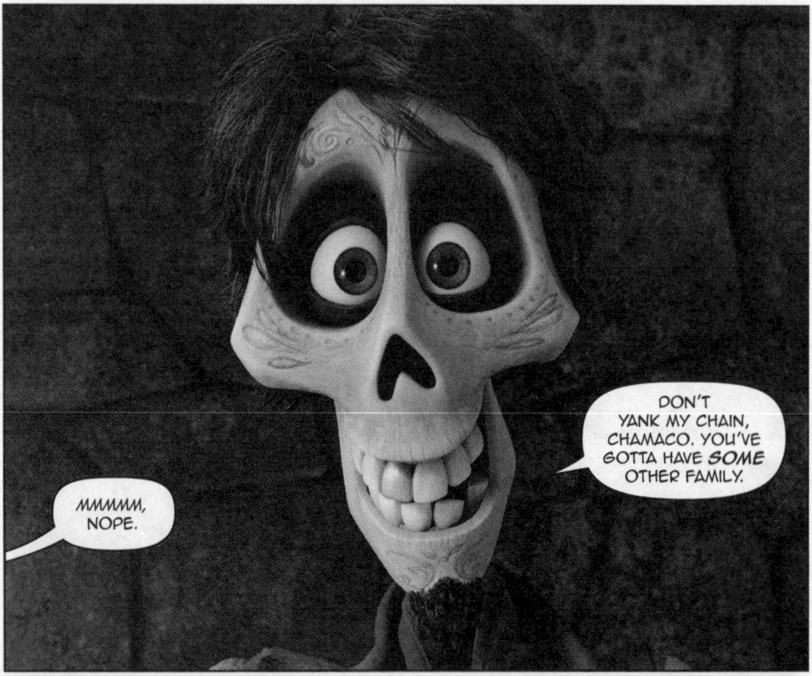
MMMMM, NOPE.
DON'T YANK MY CHAIN, CHAMACO. YOU'VE GOTTA HAVE SOME OTHER FAMILY.

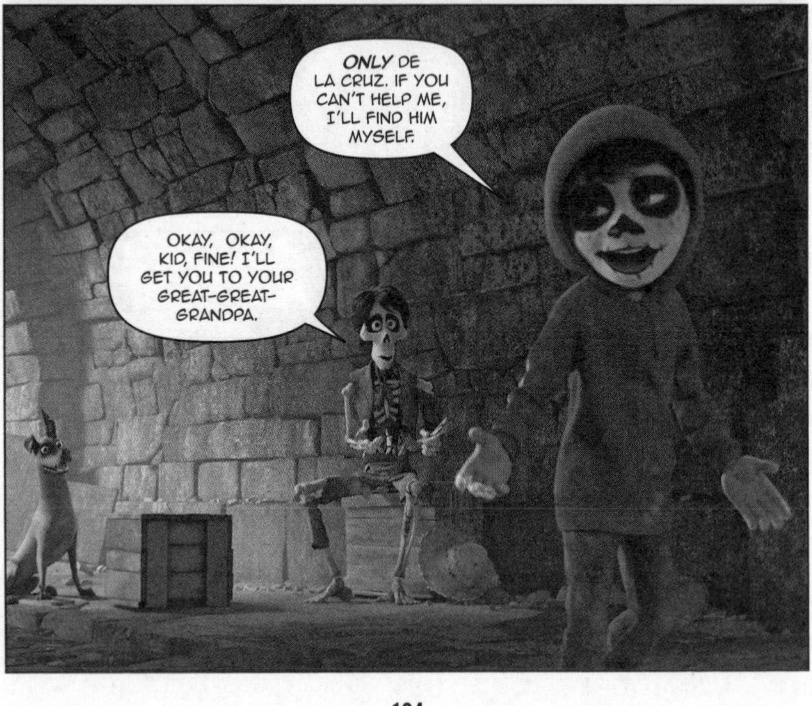
ONLY DE LA CRUZ. IF YOU CAN'T HELP ME, I'LL FIND HIM MYSELF.
OKAY, OKAY, KID, FINE! I'LL GET YOU TO YOUR GREAT-GREAT-GRANDPA.

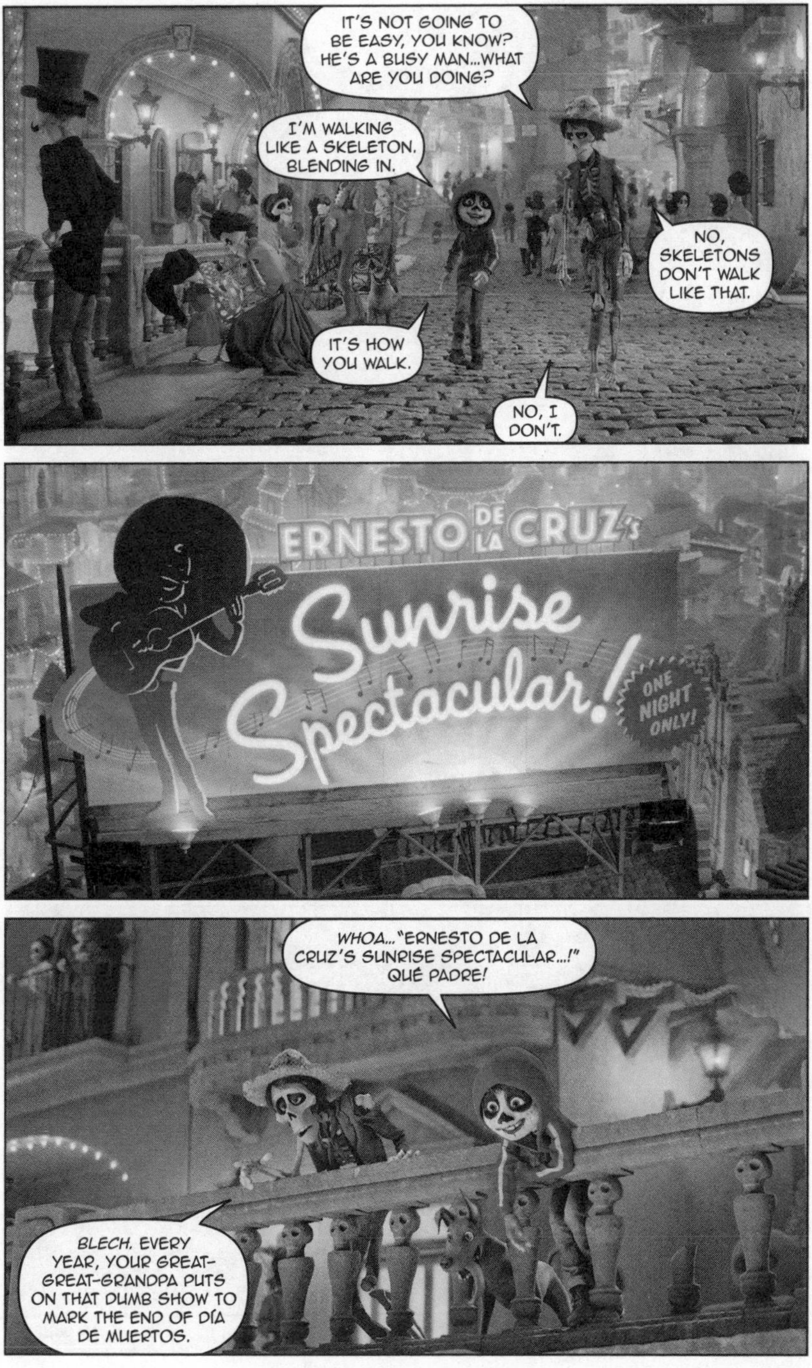
IT'S NOT GOING TO BE EASY, YOU KNOW? HE'S A BUSY MAN...WHAT ARE YOU DOING?
I'M WALKING LIKE A SKELETON. BLENDING IN.
NO, SKELETONS DON'T WALK LIKE THAT.
IT'S HOW YOU WALK.
NO, I DON'T.
ERNESTO DE LA CRUZ'S
Sunrise Spectacular!
ONE NIGHT ONLY!
WHOA... "ERNESTO DE LA CRUZ'S SUNRISE SPECTACULAR...!" QUÉ PADRE!
BLECH. EVERY YEAR, YOUR GREAT-GREAT-GRANDPA PUTS ON THAT DUMB SHOW TO MARK THE END OF DÍA DE MUERTOS.

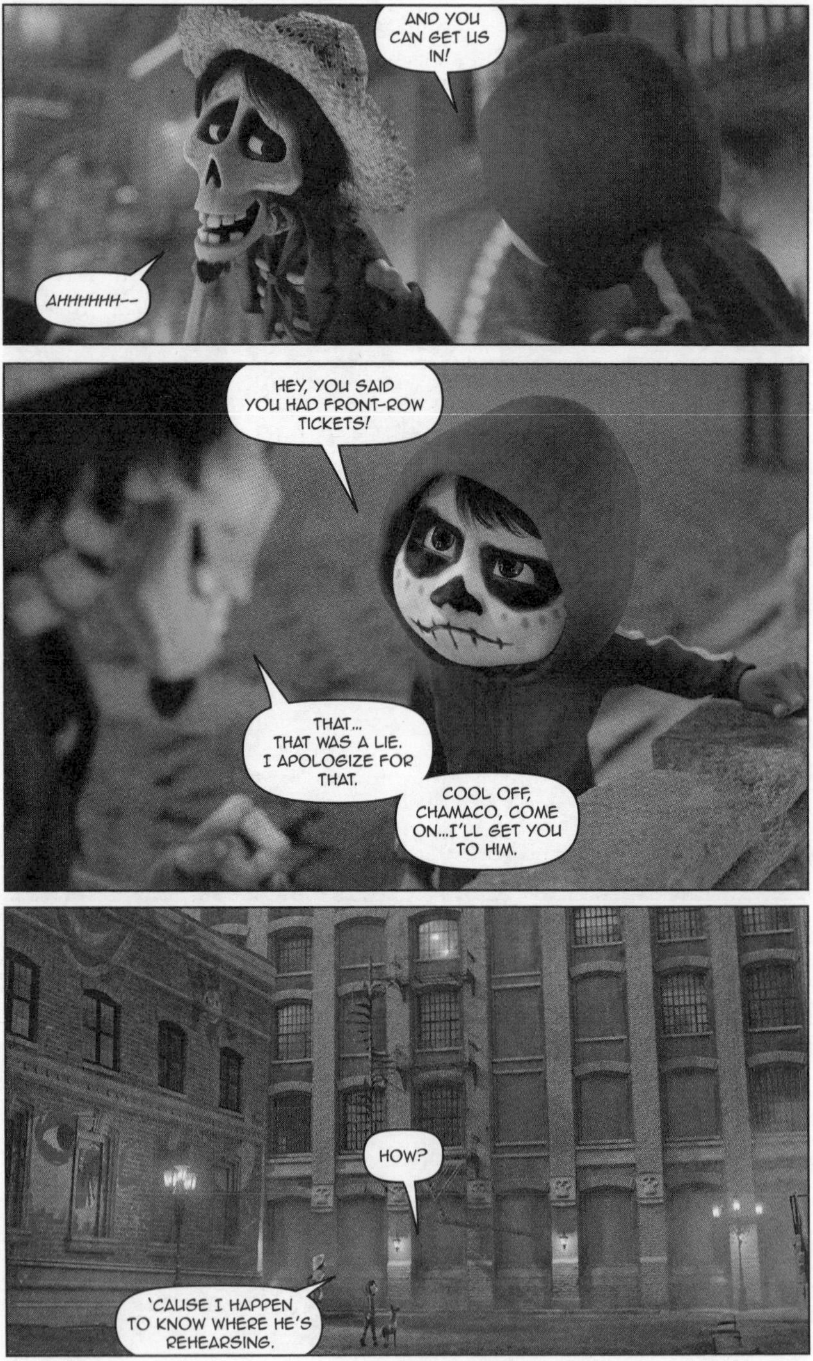
AND YOU CAN GET US IN!
AHHHHHH--
HEY, YOU SAID YOU HAD FRONT-ROW TICKETS!
THAT... THAT WAS A LIE. I APOLOGIZE FOR THAT.
COOL OFF, CHAMACO, COME ON...I'LL GET YOU TO HIM.
HOW?
'CAUSE I HAPPEN TO KNOW WHERE HE'S REHEARSING.

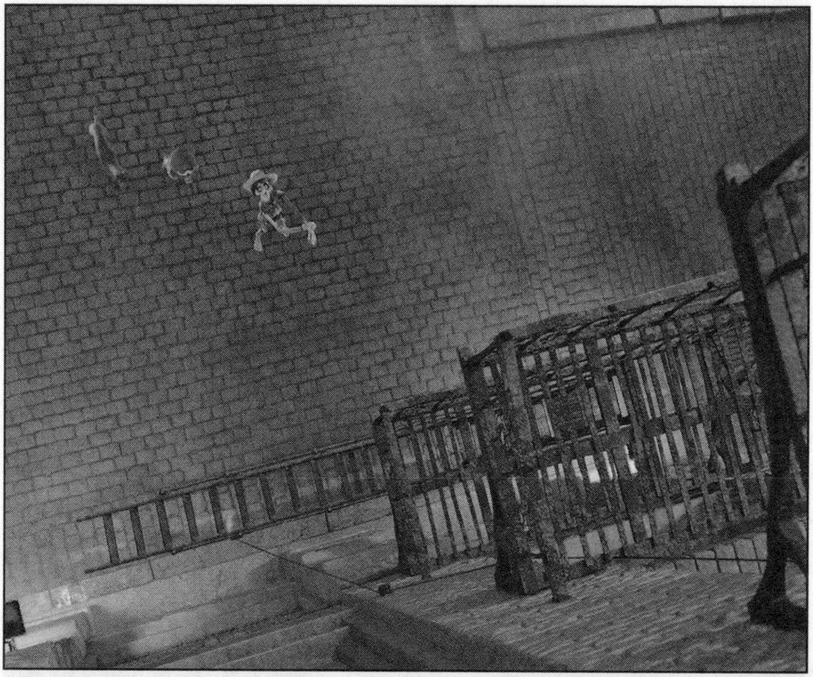

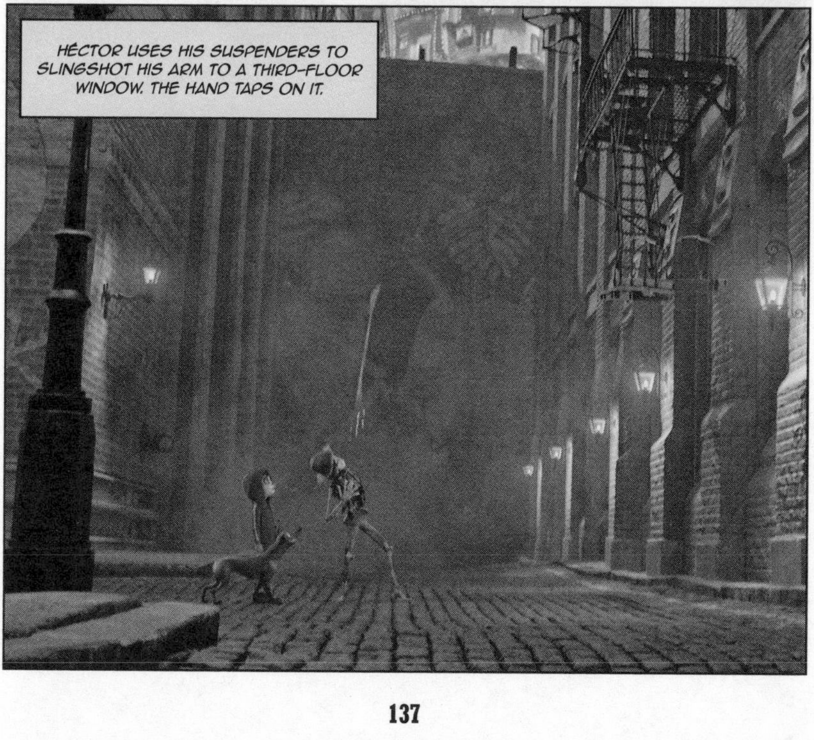
HÉCTOR USES HIS SUSPENDERS TO SLINGSHOT HIS ARM TO A THIRD-FLOOR WINDOW. THE HAND TAPS ON IT.

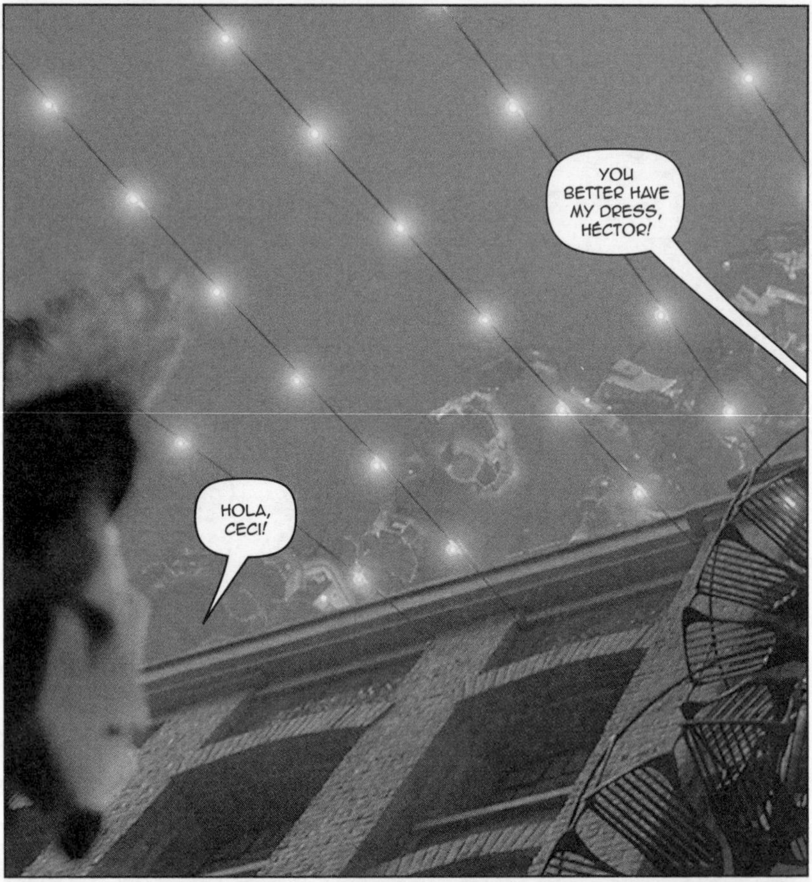
YOU BETTER HAVE MY DRESS, HÉCTOR!
HOLA, CECI!

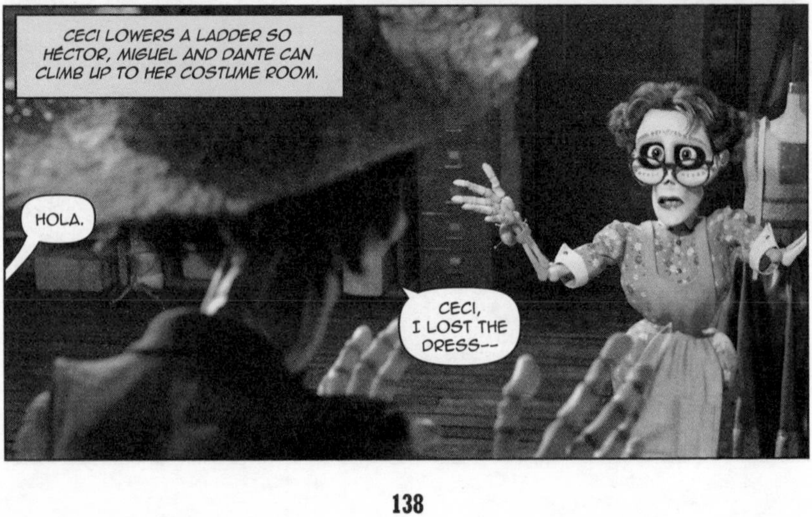
CECI LOWERS A LADDER SO HÉCTOR, MIGUEL AND DANTE CAN CLIMB UP TO HER COSTUME ROOM.
HOLA.
CECI, I LOST THE DRESS--

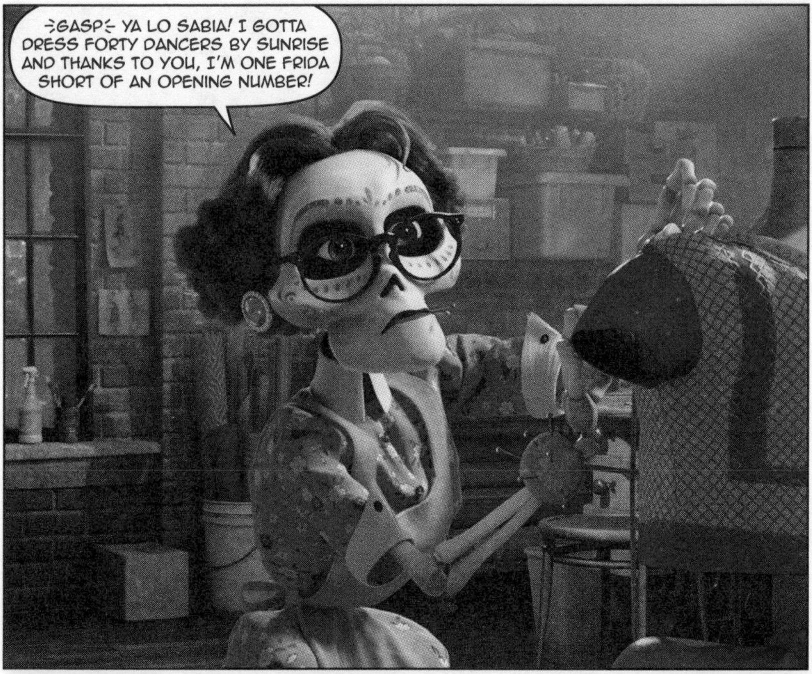
GASP YA LO SABIA! I GOTTA DRESS FORTY DANCERS BY SUNRISE AND THANKS TO YOU, I'M ONE FRIDA SHORT OF AN OPENING NUMBER!

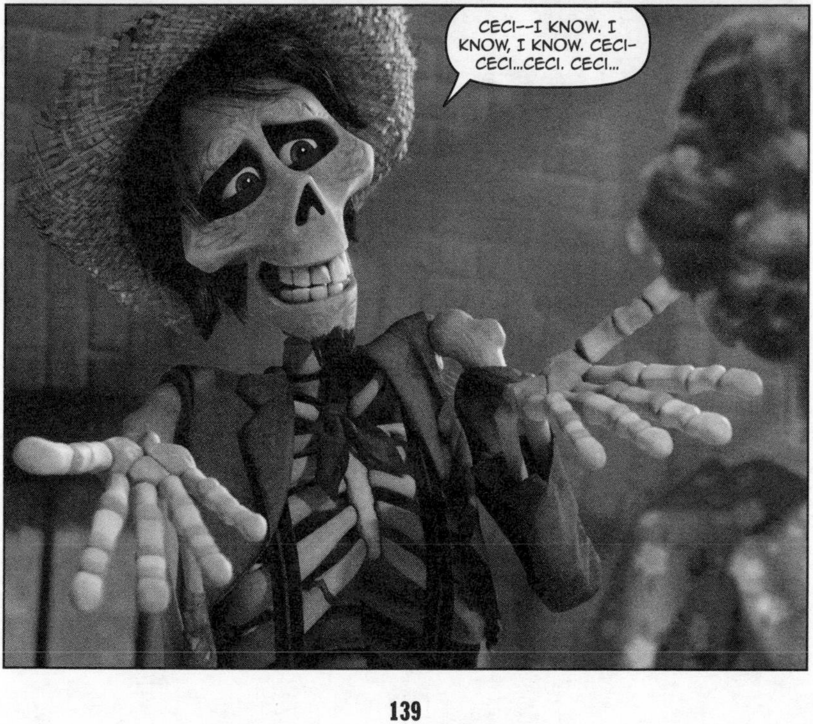
CECI--I KNOW. I KNOW, I KNOW. CECI-CECI...CECI. CECI...

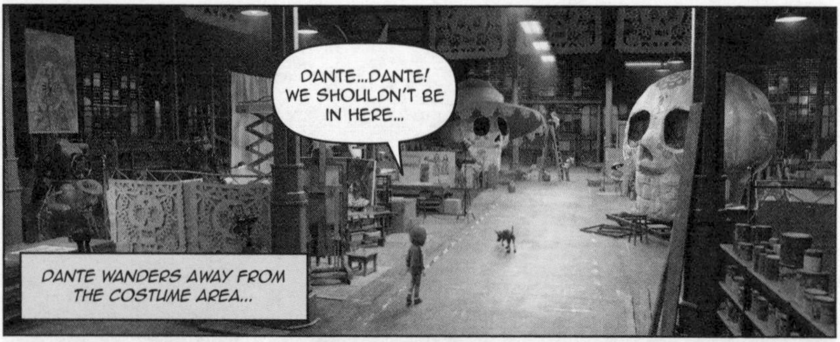
DANTE...DANTE! WE SHOULDN'T BE IN HERE...
DANTE WANDERS AWAY FROM THE COSTUME AREA...

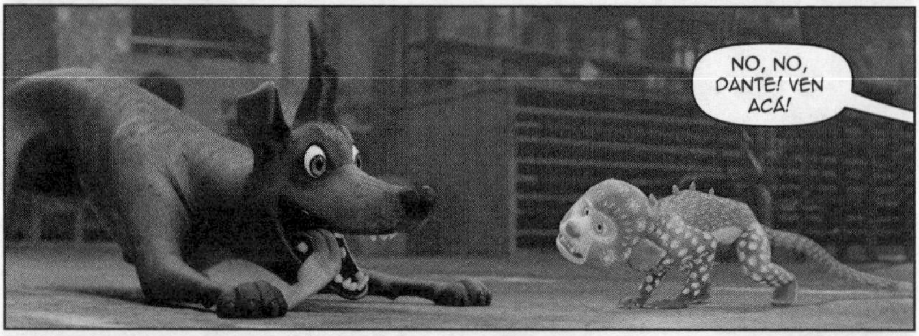
NO, NO, DANTE! VEN ACÁ!

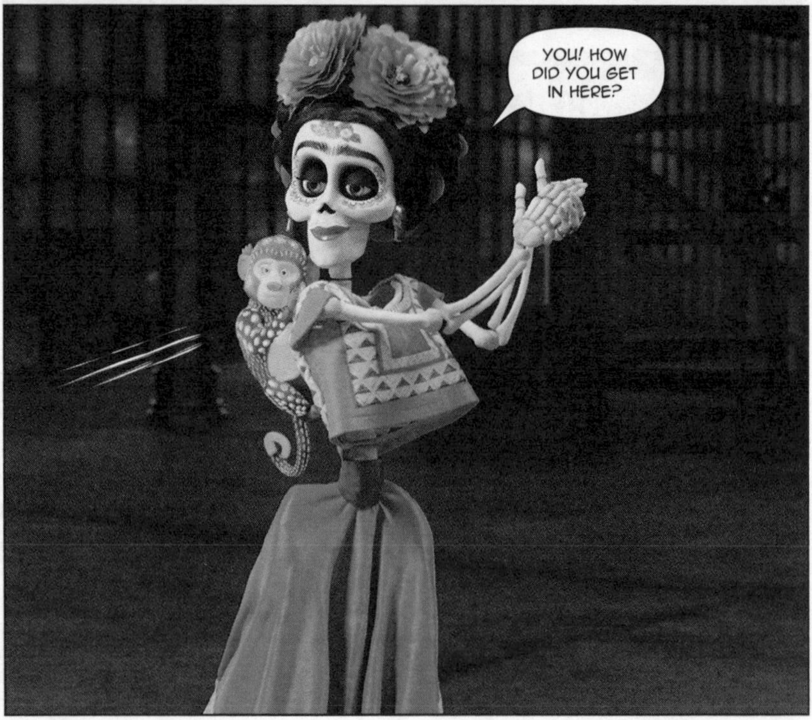
YOU! HOW DID YOU GET IN HERE?

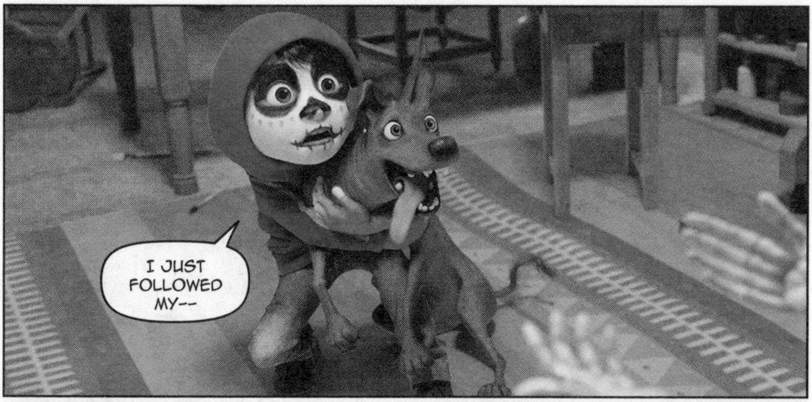
I JUST FOLLOWED MY--

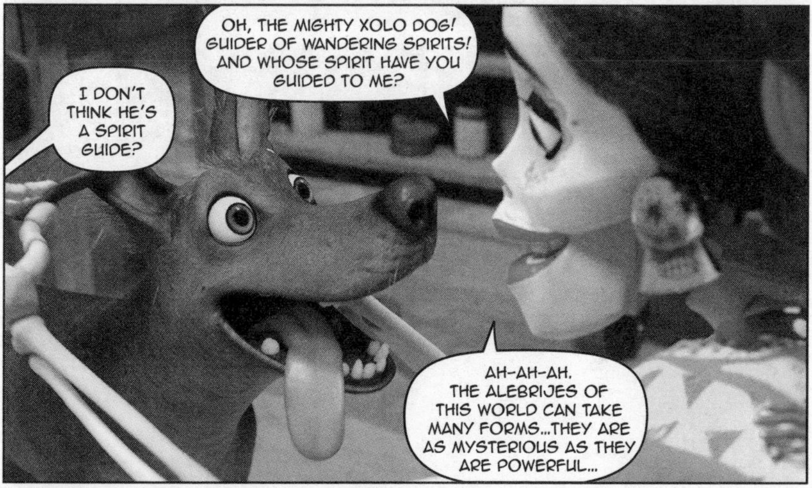
OH, THE MIGHTY XOLO DOG! GUIDER OF WANDERING SPIRITS! AND WHOSE SPIRIT HAVE YOU GUIDED TO ME?
I DON'T THINK HE'S A SPIRIT GUIDE?
AH-AH-AH. THE ALEBRIJES OF THIS WORLD CAN TAKE MANY FORMS...THEY ARE AS MYSTERIOUS AS THEY ARE POWERFUL...

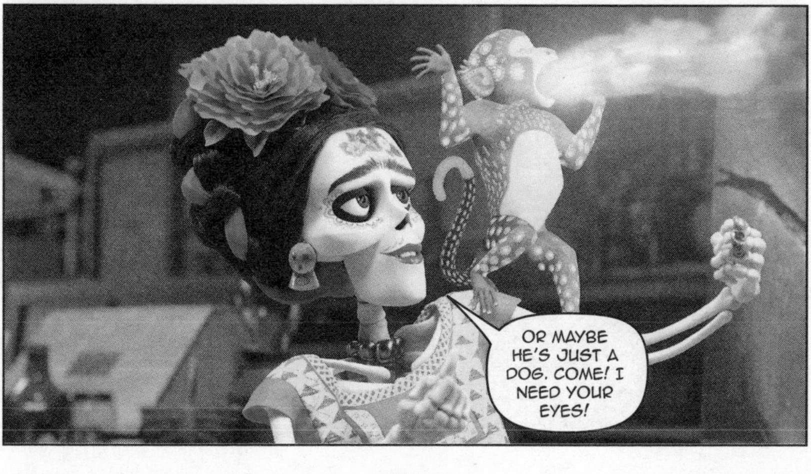
OR MAYBE HE'S JUST A DOG. COME! I NEED YOUR EYES!

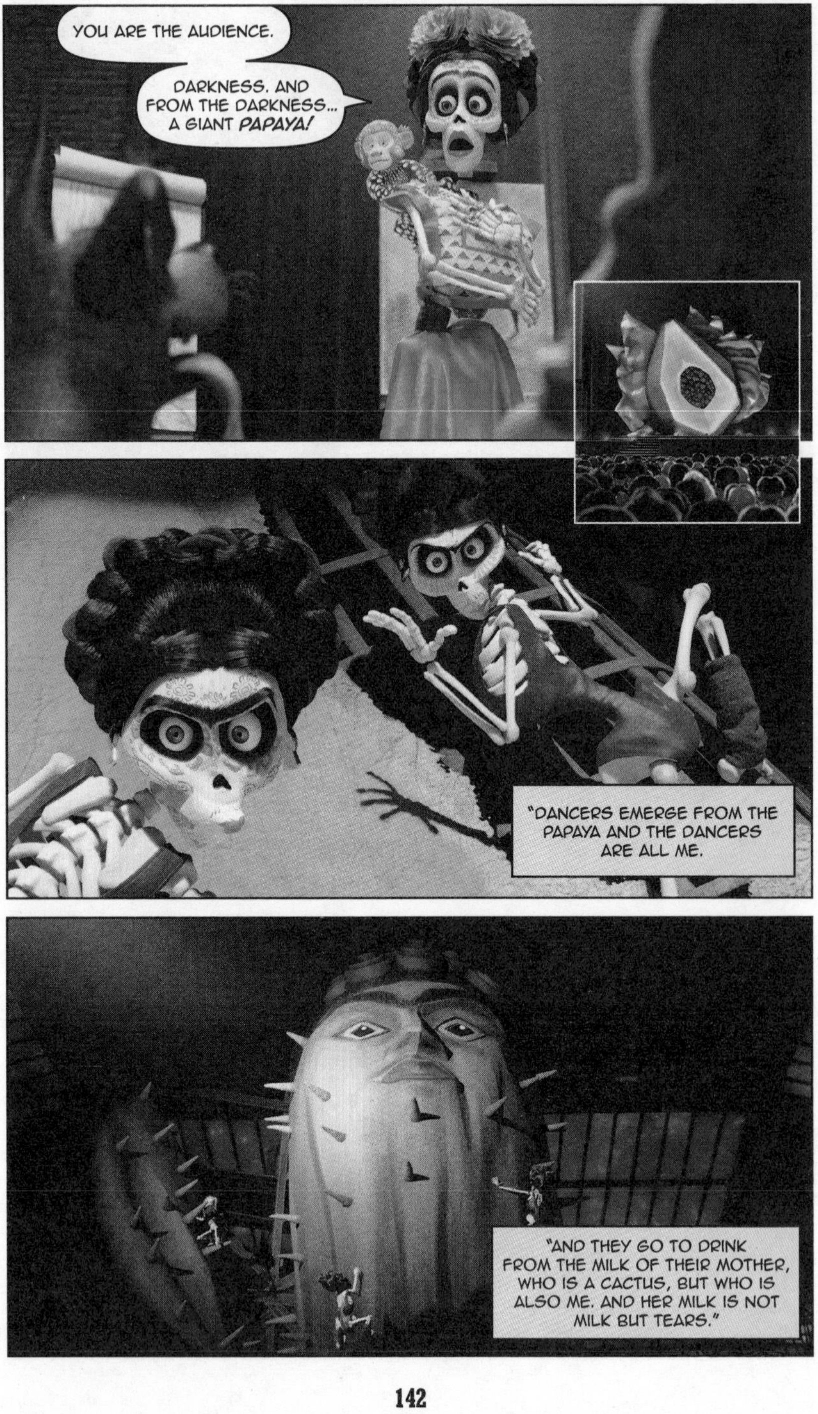
YOU ARE THE AUDIENCE.
DARKNESS. AND FROM THE DARKNESS... A GIANT *PAPAYA!*
"DANCERS EMERGE FROM THE PAPAYA AND THE DANCERS ARE ALL ME.
"AND THEY GO TO DRINK FROM THE MILK OF THEIR MOTHER, WHO IS A CACTUS, BUT WHO IS ALSO ME. AND HER MILK IS NOT MILK BUT TEARS."

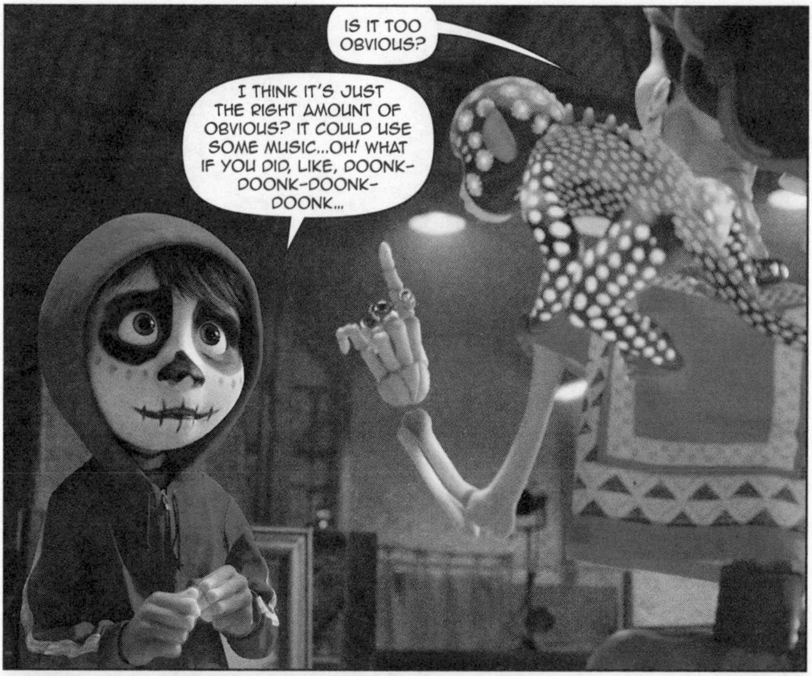
IS IT TOO OBVIOUS?
I THINK IT'S JUST THE RIGHT AMOUNT OF OBVIOUS? IT COULD USE SOME MUSIC...OH! WHAT IF YOU DID, LIKE, DOONK-DOONK-DOONK-DOONK...

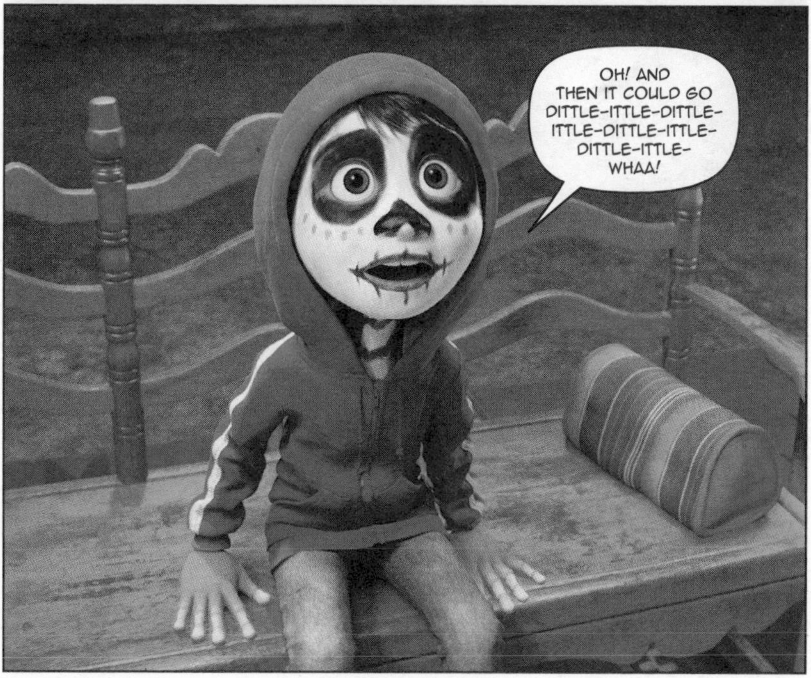
OH! AND THEN IT COULD GO DITTLE-ITTLE-DITTLE-ITTLE-DITTLE-ITTLE-DITTLE-ITTLE-WHAA!

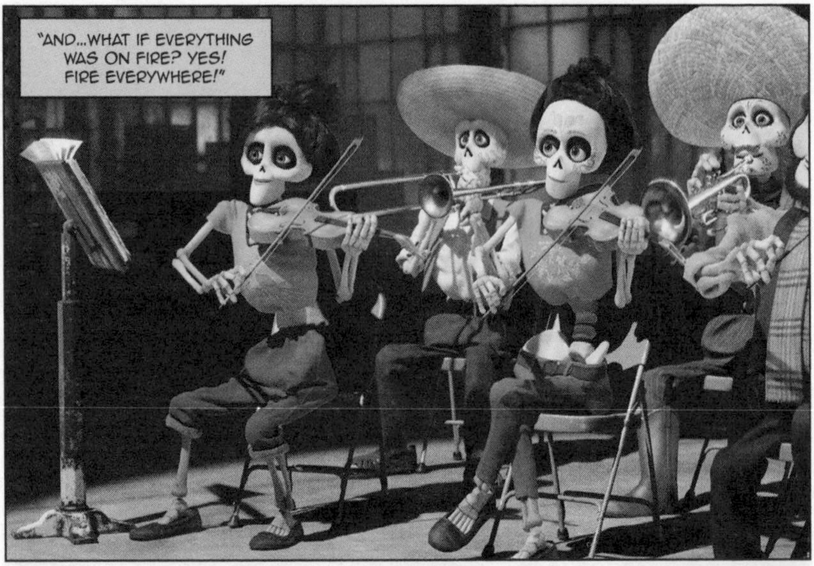
"AND...WHAT IF EVERYTHING WAS ON FIRE? YES! FIRE EVERYWHERE!"

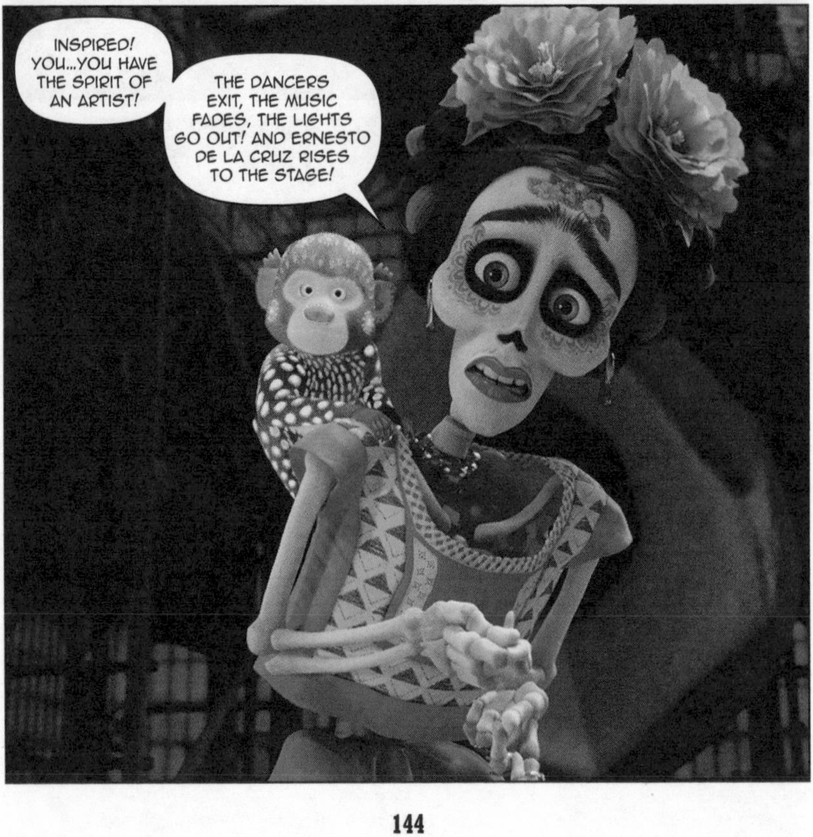
INSPIRED! YOU...YOU HAVE THE SPIRIT OF AN ARTIST!
THE DANCERS EXIT, THE MUSIC FADES, THE LIGHTS GO OUT! AND ERNESTO DE LA CRUZ RISES TO THE STAGE!

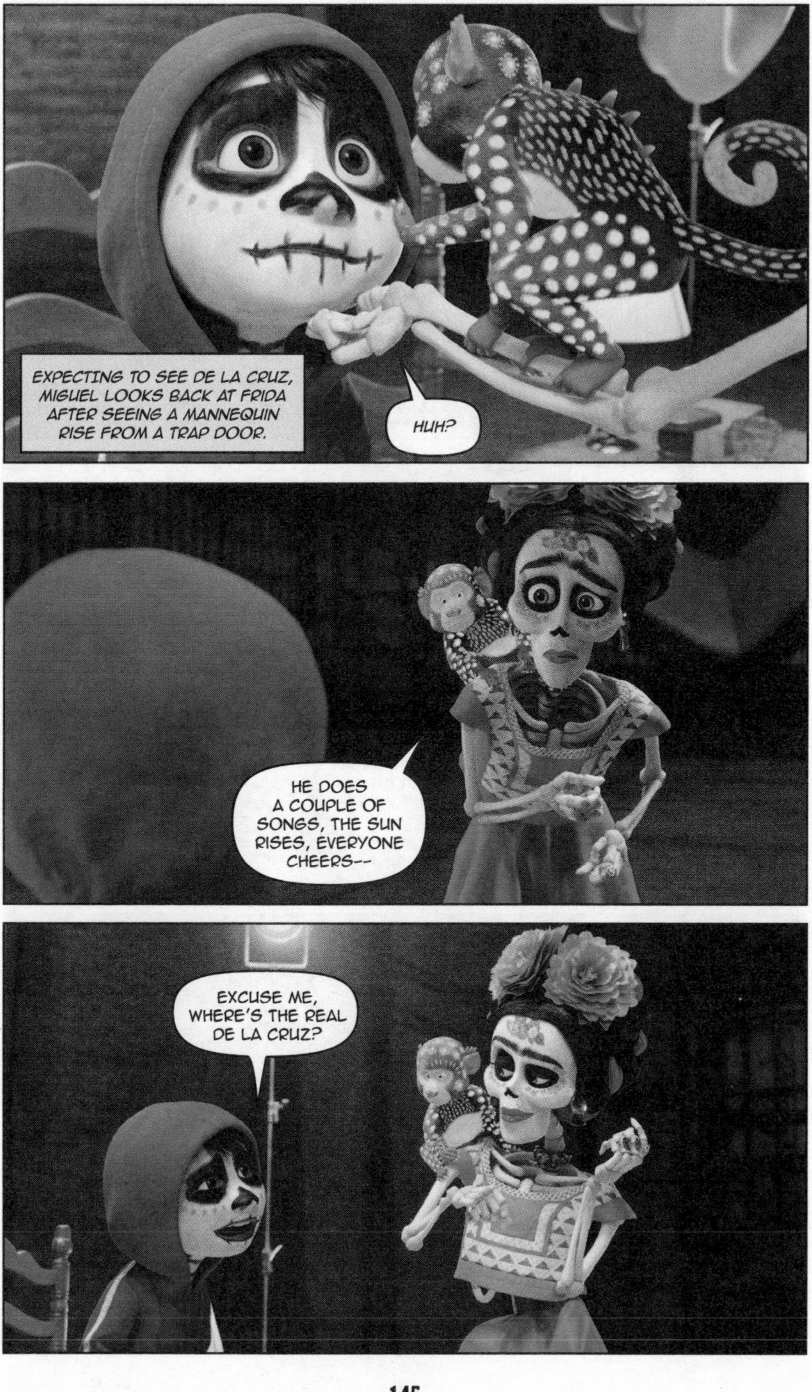
EXPECTING TO SEE DE LA CRUZ, MIGUEL LOOKS BACK AT FRIDA AFTER SEEING A MANNEQUIN RISE FROM A TRAP DOOR.
HUH?
HE DOES A COUPLE OF SONGS, THE SUN RISES, EVERYONE CHEERS--
EXCUSE ME, WHERE'S THE REAL DE LA CRUZ?

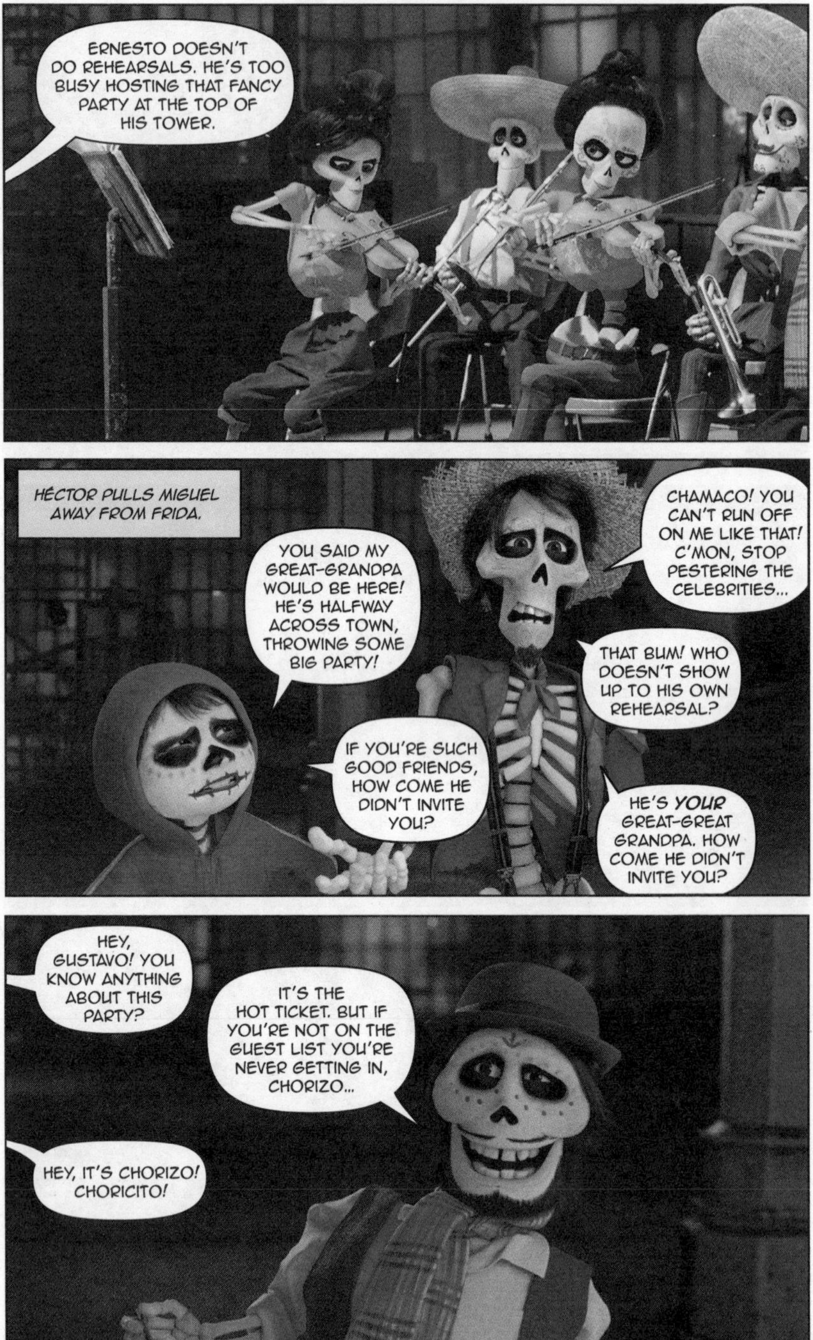
ERNESTO DOESN'T DO REHEARSALS. HE'S TOO BUSY HOSTING THAT FANCY PARTY AT THE TOP OF HIS TOWER.
HÉCTOR PULLS MIGUEL AWAY FROM FRIDA.
CHAMACO! YOU CAN'T RUN OFF ON ME LIKE THAT! C'MON, STOP PESTERING THE CELEBRITIES...
YOU SAID MY GREAT-GRANDPA WOULD BE HERE! HE'S HALFWAY ACROSS TOWN, THROWING SOME BIG PARTY!
THAT BUM! WHO DOESN'T SHOW UP TO HIS OWN REHEARSAL?
IF YOU'RE SUCH GOOD FRIENDS, HOW COME HE DIDN'T INVITE YOU?
HE'S *YOUR* GREAT-GREAT GRANDPA. HOW COME HE DIDN'T INVITE YOU?
HEY, GUSTAVO! YOU KNOW ANYTHING ABOUT THIS PARTY?
IT'S THE HOT TICKET. BUT IF YOU'RE NOT ON THE GUEST LIST YOU'RE NEVER GETTING IN, CHORIZO...
HEY, IT'S CHORIZO! CHORICITO!

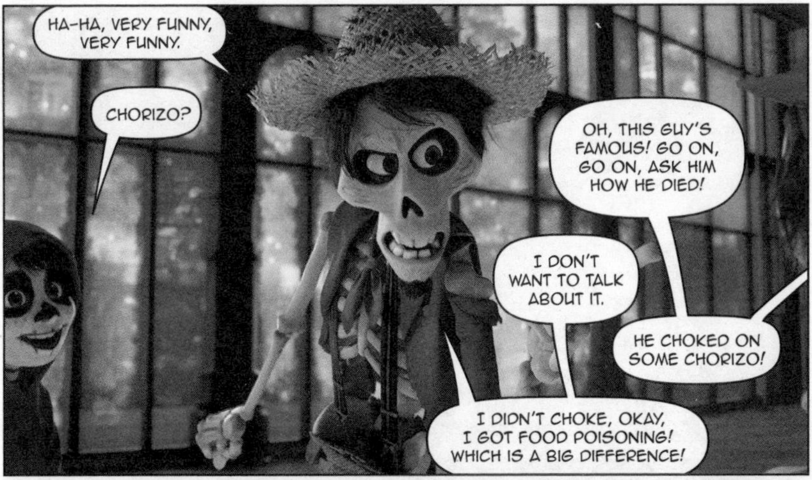
HA-HA, VERY FUNNY, VERY FUNNY.
CHORIZO?
OH, THIS GUY'S FAMOUS! GO ON, GO ON, ASK HIM HOW HE DIED!
I DON'T WANT TO TALK ABOUT IT.
HE CHOKED ON SOME CHORIZO!
I DIDN'T CHOKE, OKAY, I GOT FOOD POISONING! WHICH IS A BIG DIFFERENCE!

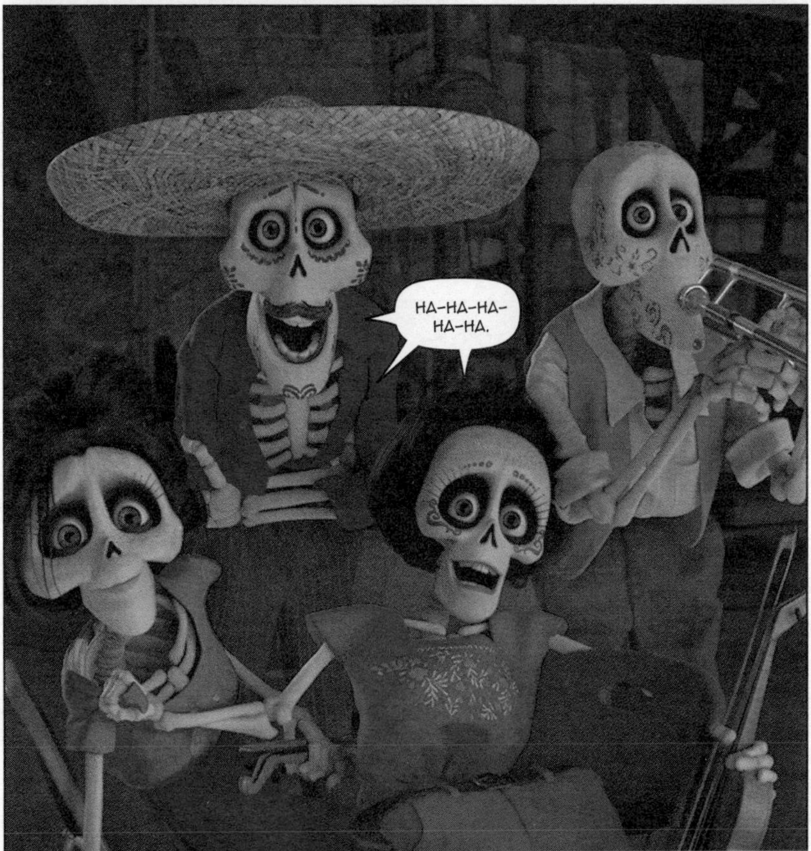
HA-HA-HA-HA-HA.

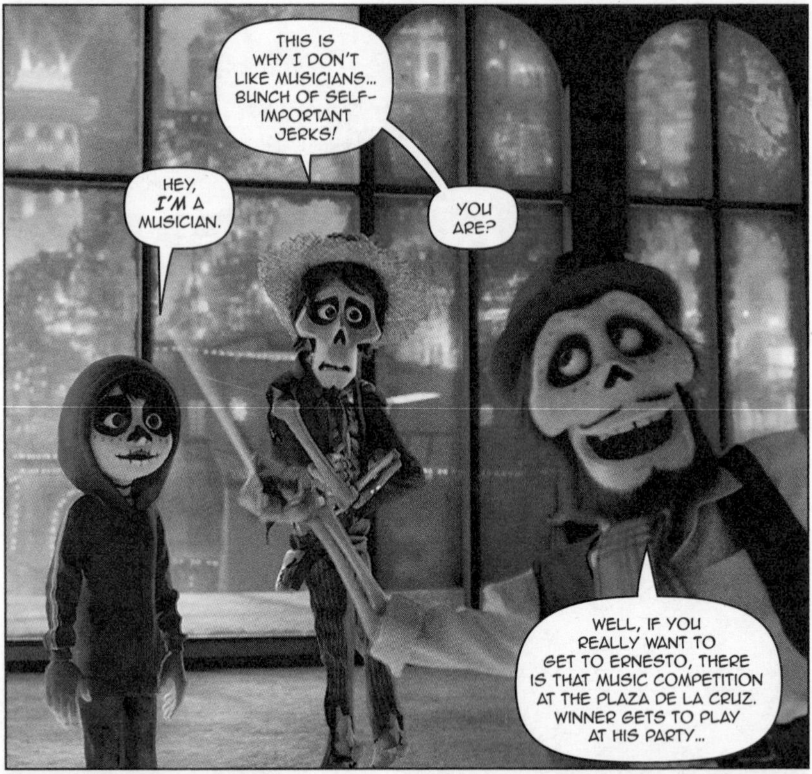
THIS IS WHY I DON'T LIKE MUSICIANS... BUNCH OF SELF-IMPORTANT JERKS!
HEY, I'M A MUSICIAN.
YOU ARE?
WELL, IF YOU REALLY WANT TO GET TO ERNESTO, THERE IS THAT MUSIC COMPETITION AT THE PLAZA DE LA CRUZ. WINNER GETS TO PLAY AT HIS PARTY...

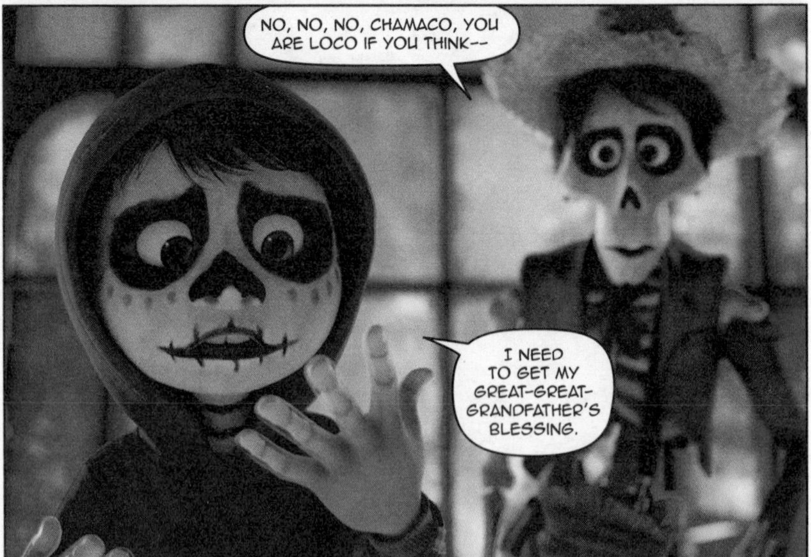
NO, NO, NO, CHAMACO, YOU ARE LOCO IF YOU THINK--
I NEED TO GET MY GREAT-GREAT-GRANDFATHER'S BLESSING.

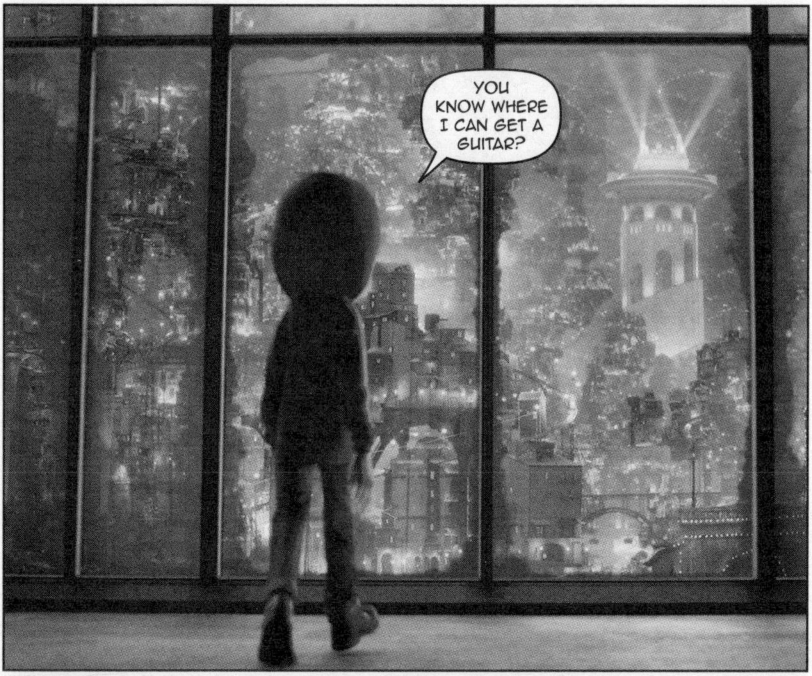
YOU KNOW WHERE I CAN GET A GUITAR?

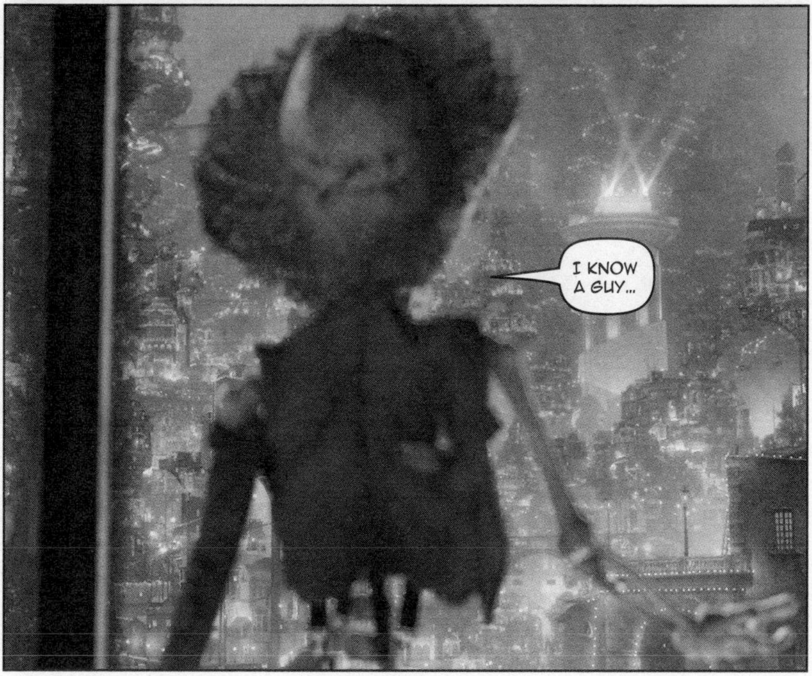
I KNOW A GUY...

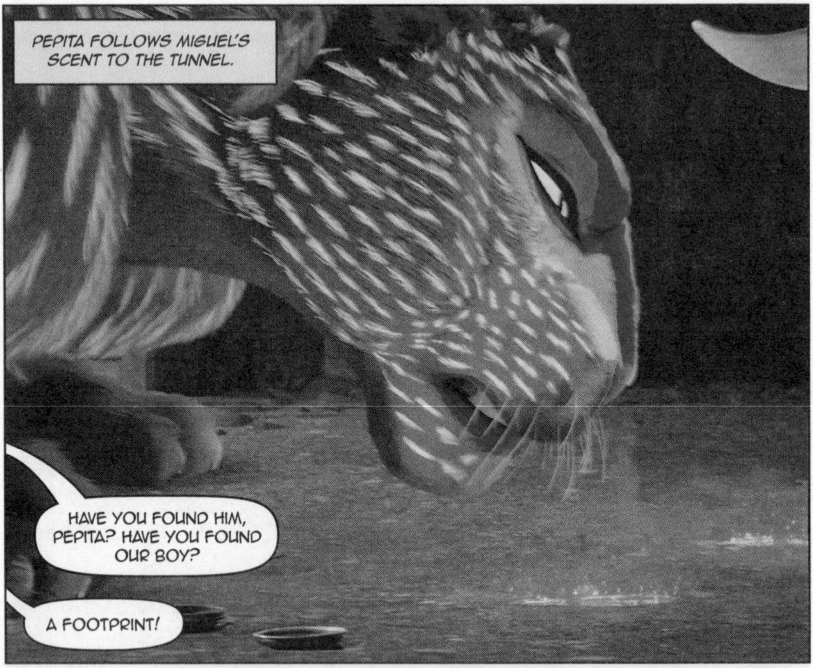
PEPITA FOLLOWS MIGUEL'S SCENT TO THE TUNNEL.
HAVE YOU FOUND HIM, PEPITA? HAVE YOU FOUND OUR BOY?
A FOOTPRINT!

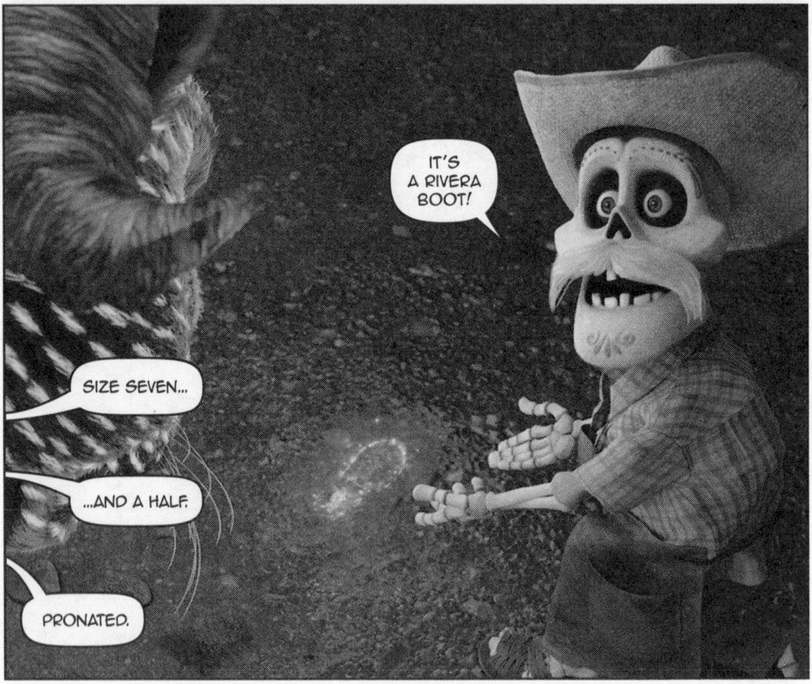
IT'S A RIVERA BOOT!
SIZE SEVEN...
...AND A HALF.
PRONATED.

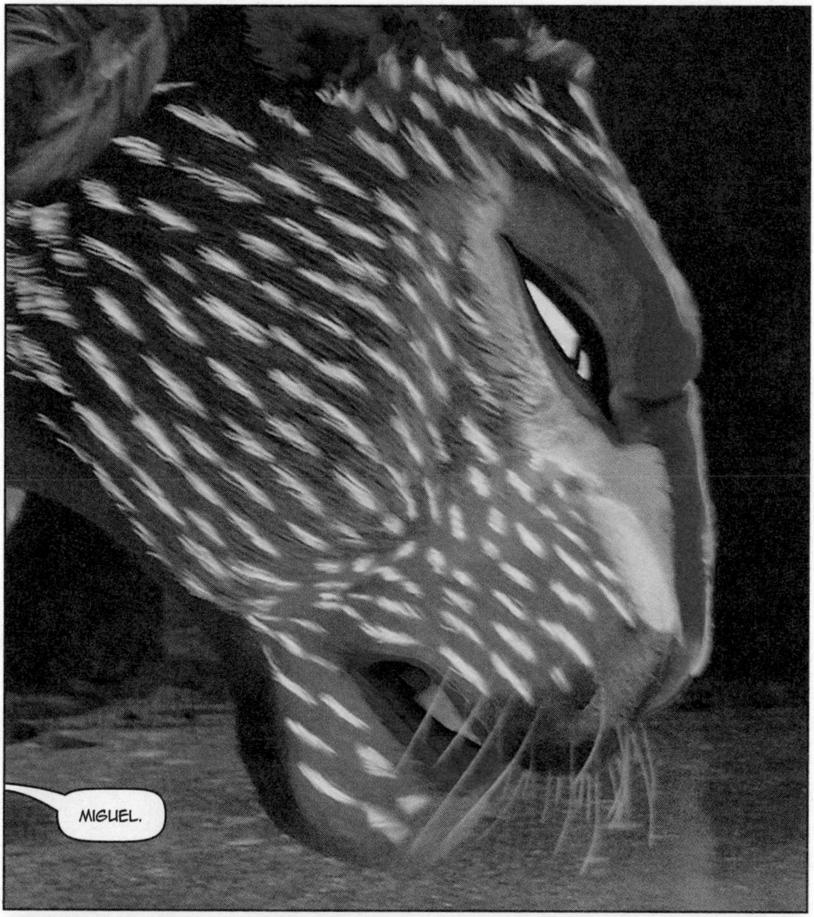
MIGUEL.

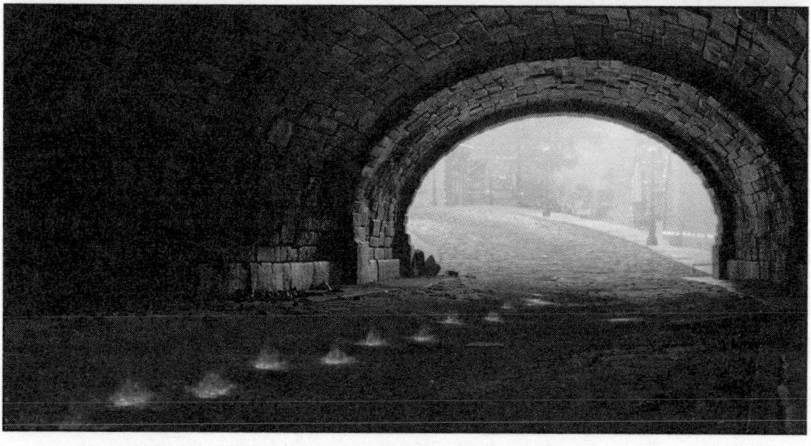

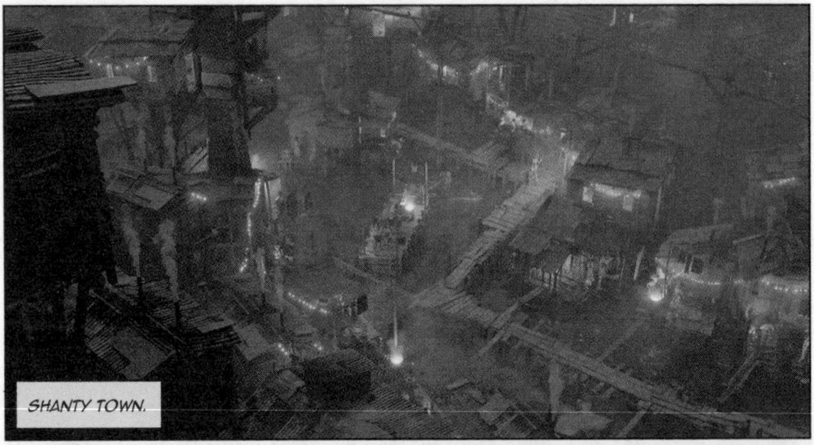
SHANTY TOWN.

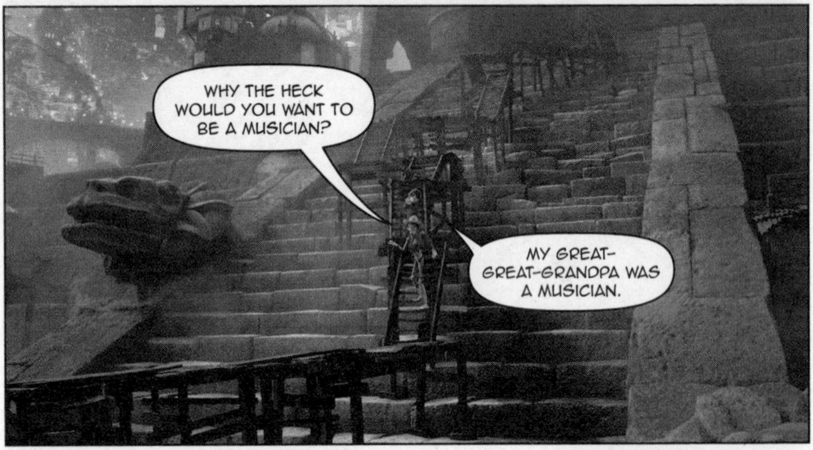
WHY THE HECK WOULD YOU WANT TO BE A MUSICIAN?
MY GREAT-GREAT-GRANDPA WAS A MUSICIAN.

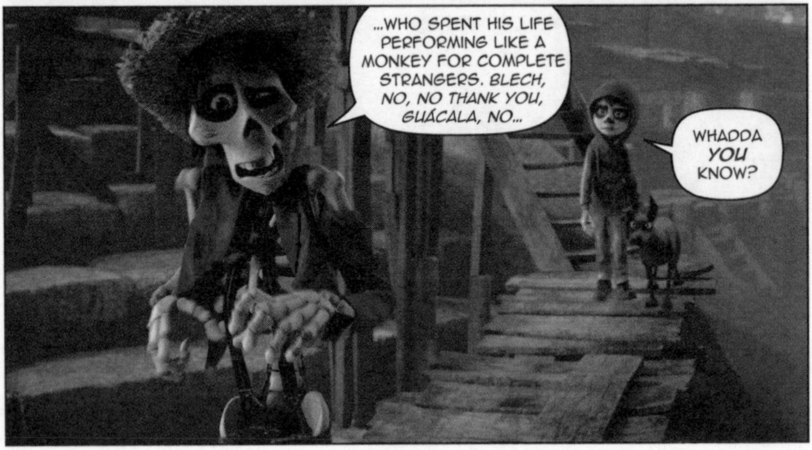
...WHO SPENT HIS LIFE PERFORMING LIKE A MONKEY FOR COMPLETE STRANGERS. *BLECH,* NO, NO THANK YOU, *GUÁCALA,* NO...
WHADDA *YOU* KNOW?

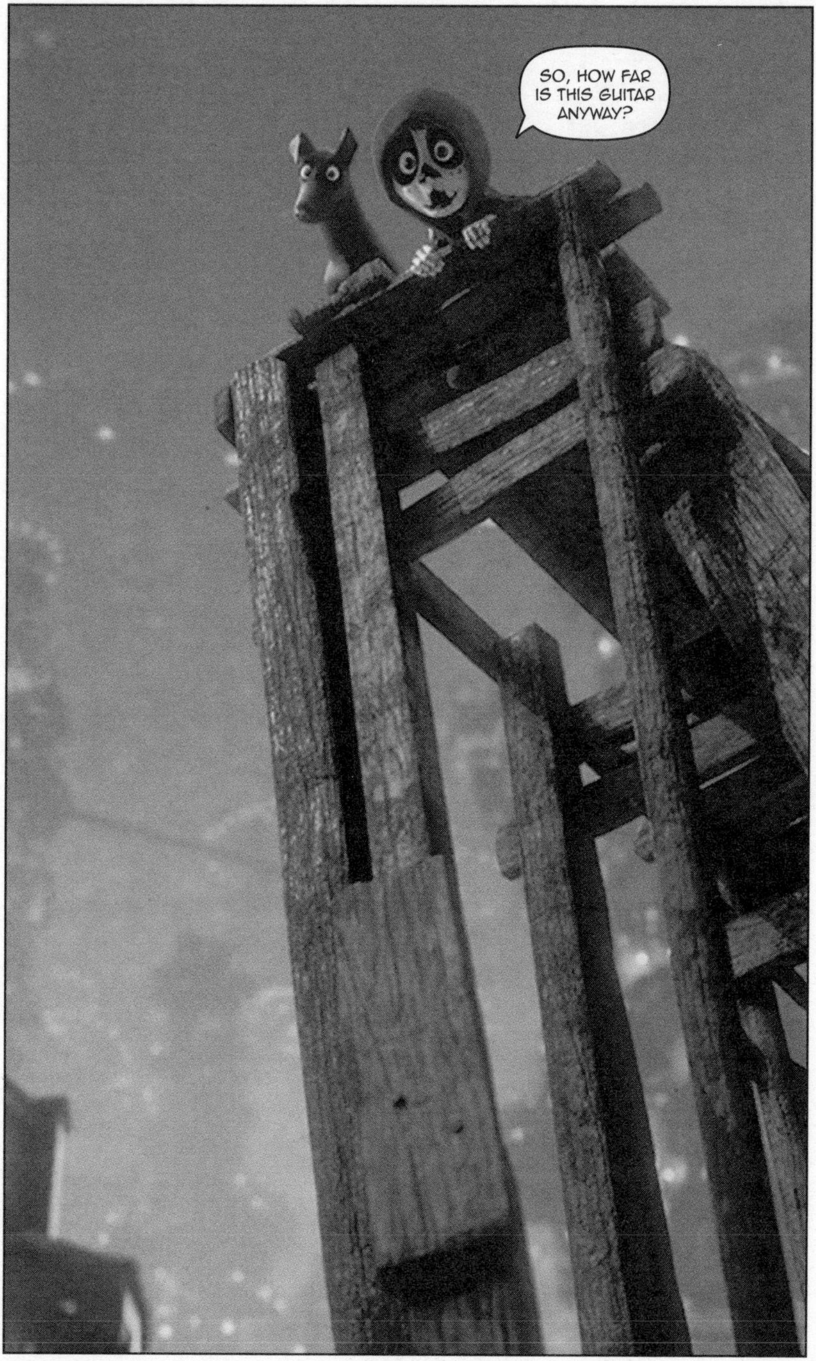
SO, HOW FAR IS THIS GUITAR ANYWAY?

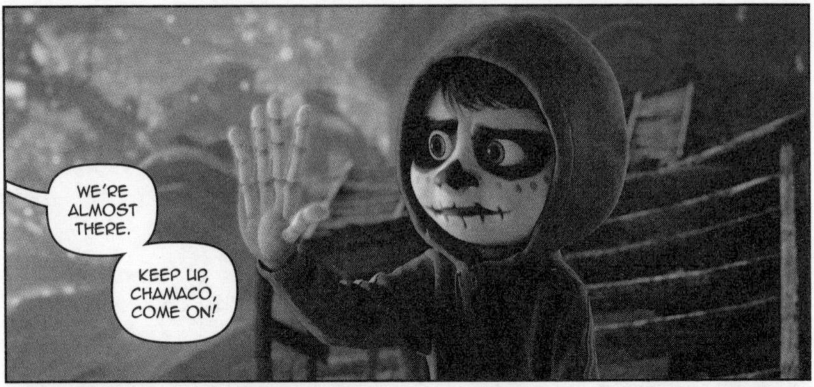
WE'RE ALMOST THERE.
KEEP UP, CHAMACO, COME ON!

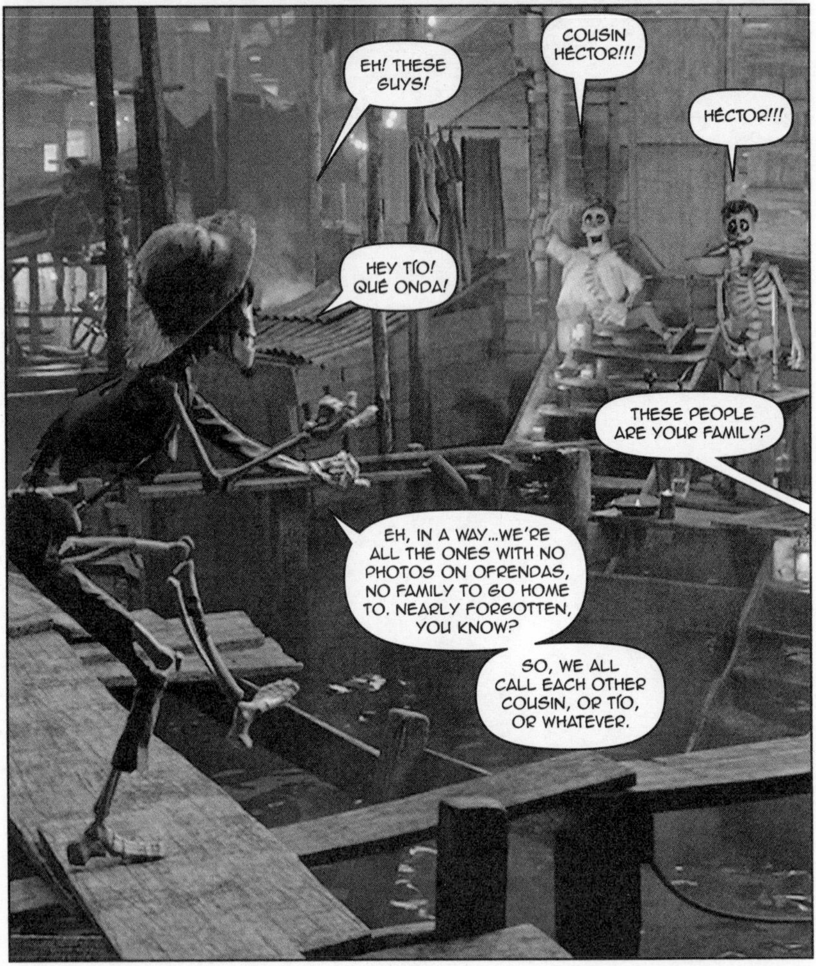
EH! THESE GUYS!
COUSIN HÉCTOR!!!
HÉCTOR!!!
HEY TÍO! QUÉ ONDA!
THESE PEOPLE ARE YOUR FAMILY?
EH, IN A WAY...WE'RE ALL THE ONES WITH NO PHOTOS ON OFRENDAS, NO FAMILY TO GO HOME TO. NEARLY FORGOTTEN, YOU KNOW?
SO, WE ALL CALL EACH OTHER COUSIN, OR TÍO, OR WHATEVER.

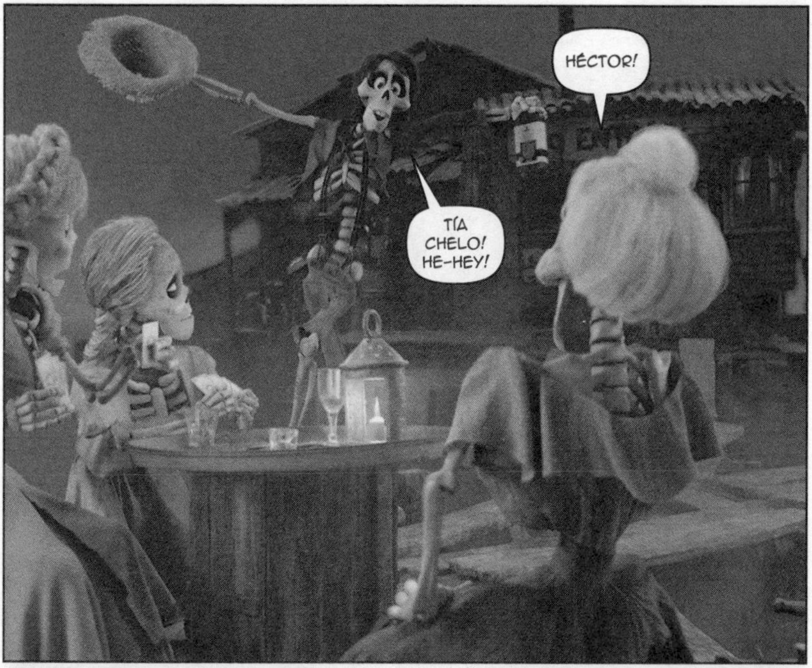
HÉCTOR!
TÍA CHELO! HE-HEY!

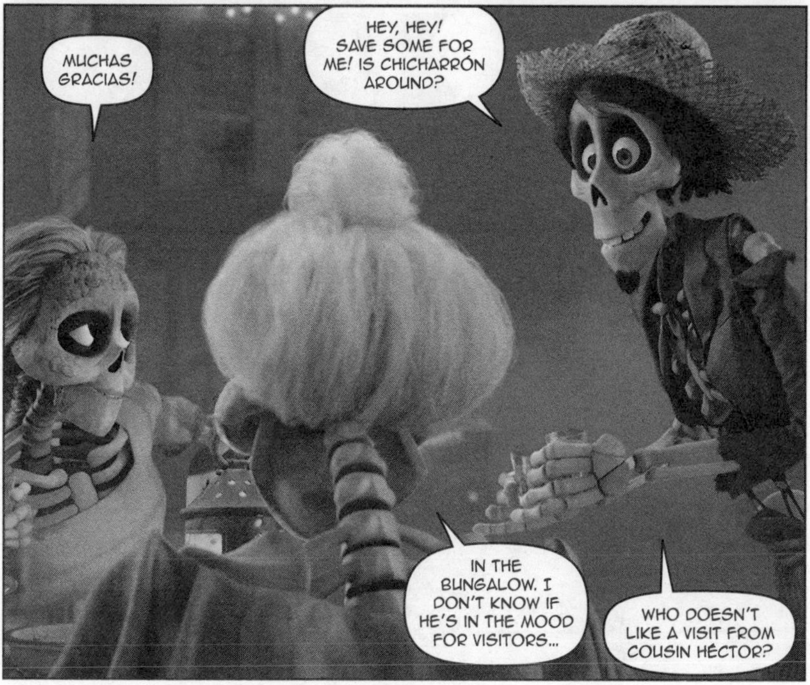
MUCHAS GRACIAS!
HEY, HEY! SAVE SOME FOR ME! IS CHICHARRÓN AROUND?
IN THE BUNGALOW. I DON'T KNOW IF HE'S IN THE MOOD FOR VISITORS...
WHO DOESN'T LIKE A VISIT FROM COUSIN HÉCTOR?

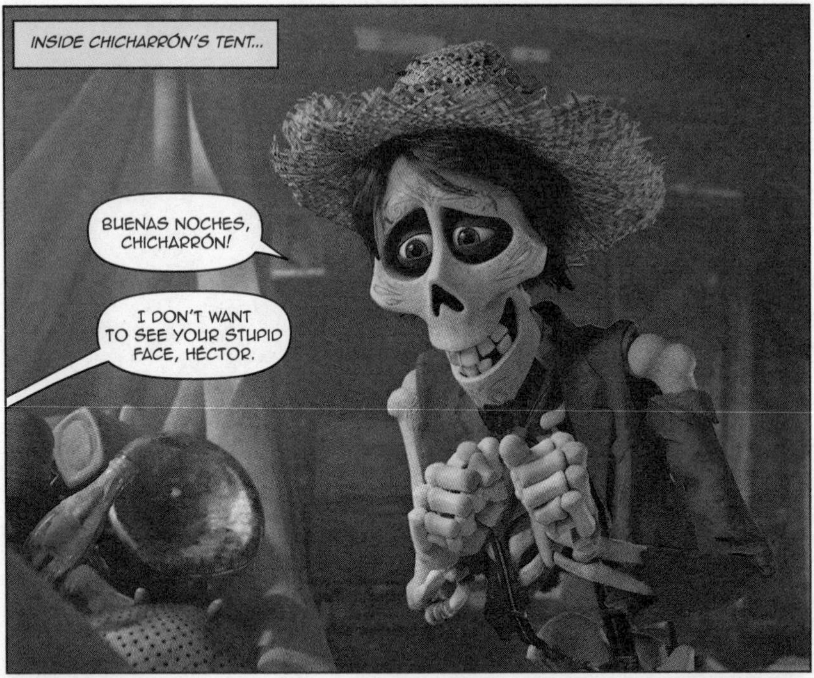
INSIDE CHICHARRÓN'S TENT...
BUENAS NOCHES, CHICHARRÓN!
I DON'T WANT TO SEE YOUR STUPID FACE, HÉCTOR.

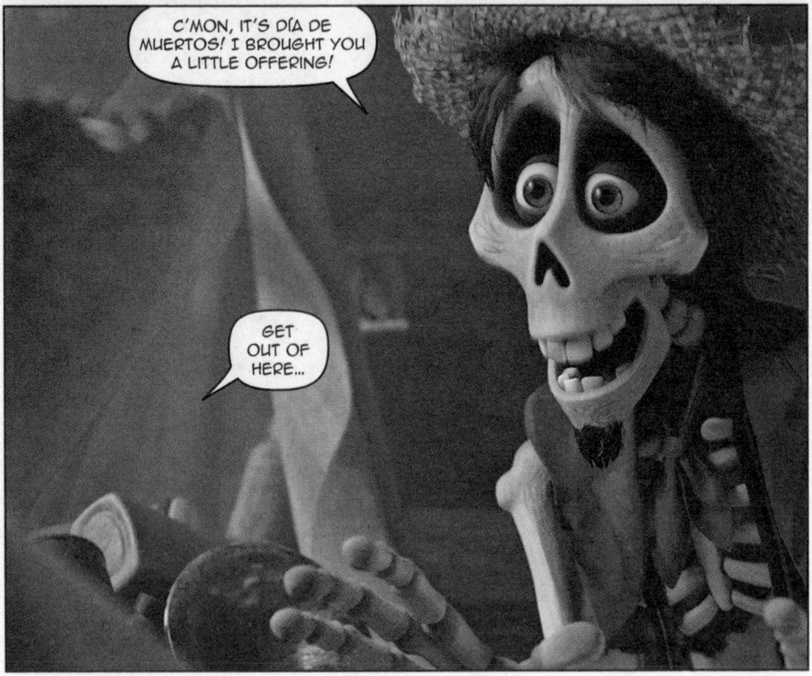
C'MON, IT'S DÍA DE MUERTOS! I BROUGHT YOU A LITTLE OFFERING!
GET OUT OF HERE...

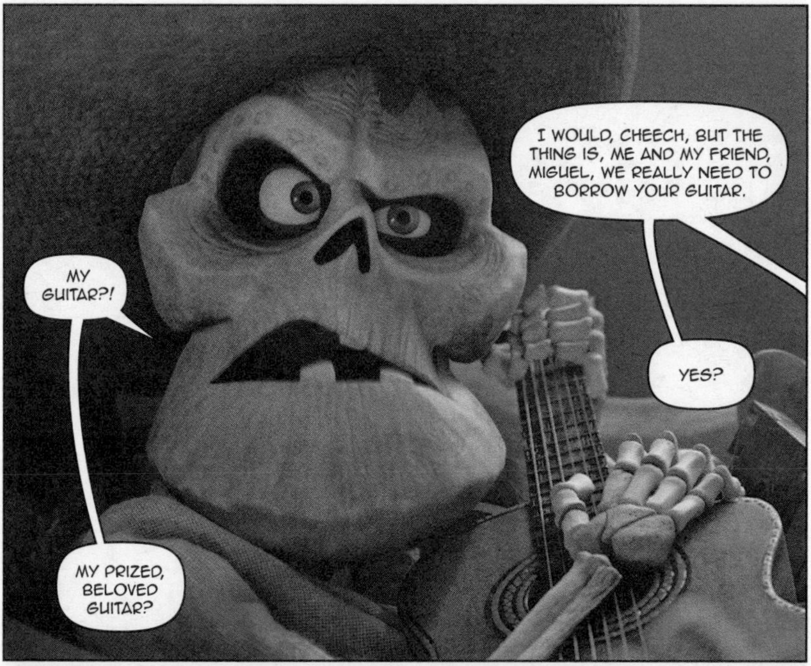
I WOULD, CHEECH, BUT THE THING IS, ME AND MY FRIEND, MIGUEL, WE REALLY NEED TO BORROW YOUR GUITAR.
MY GUITAR?!
YES?
MY PRIZED, BELOVED GUITAR?

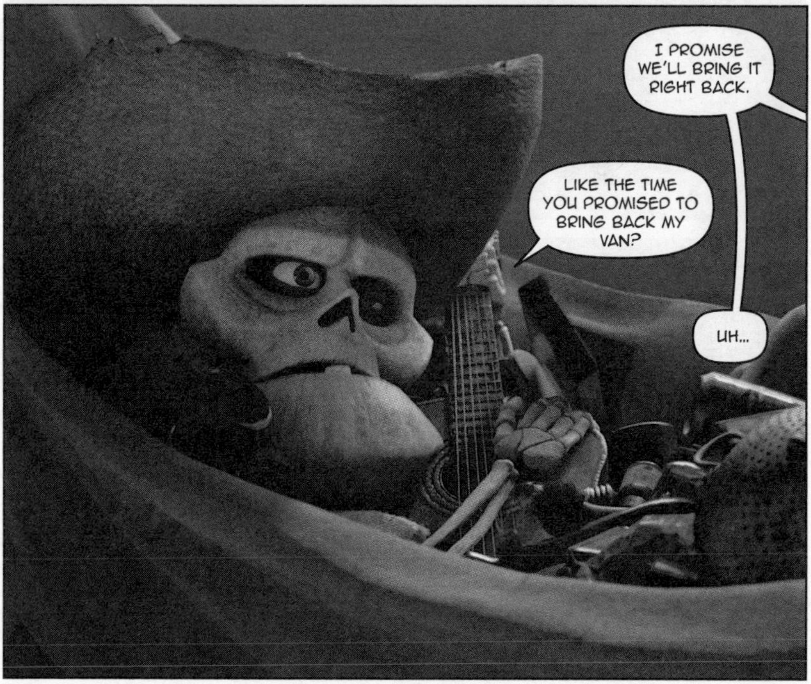
I PROMISE WE'LL BRING IT RIGHT BACK.
LIKE THE TIME YOU PROMISED TO BRING BACK MY VAN?
UH...

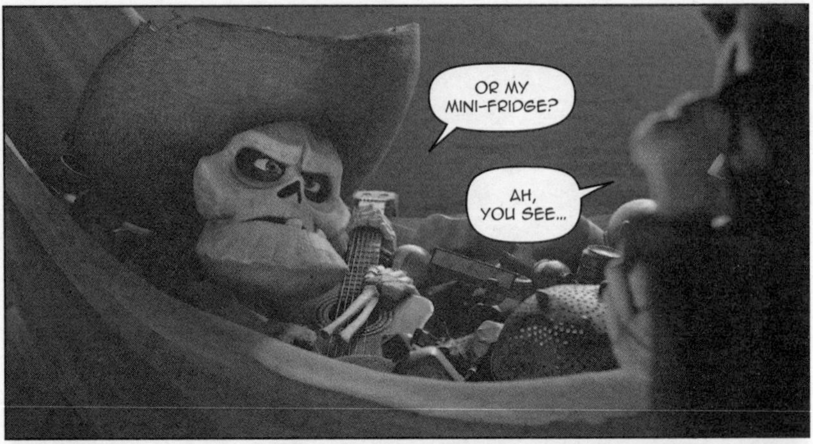
OR MY
MINI-FRIDGE?
AH,
YOU SEE...

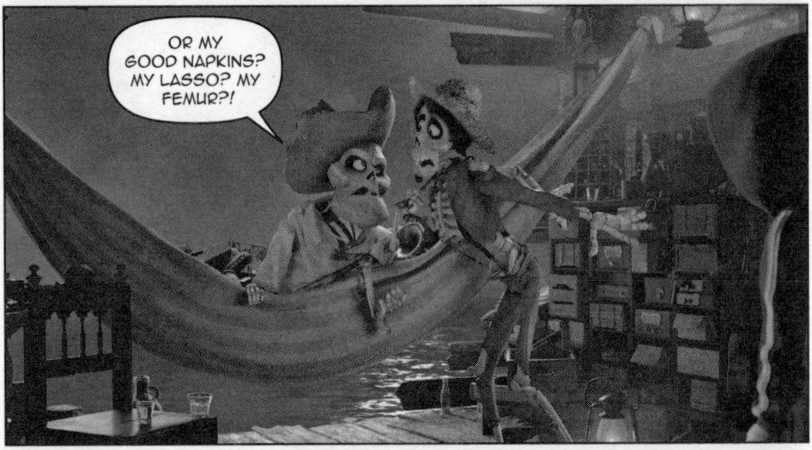
OR MY
GOOD NAPKINS?
MY LASSO? MY
FEMUR?!

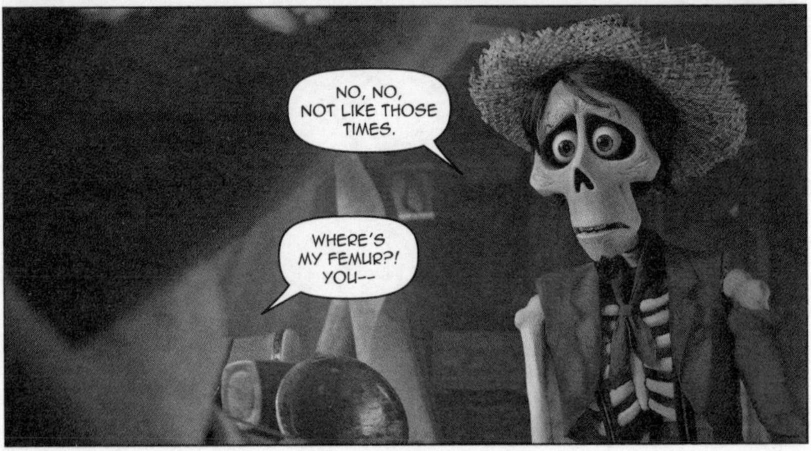
NO, NO,
NOT LIKE THOSE
TIMES.
WHERE'S
MY FEMUR?!
YOU--

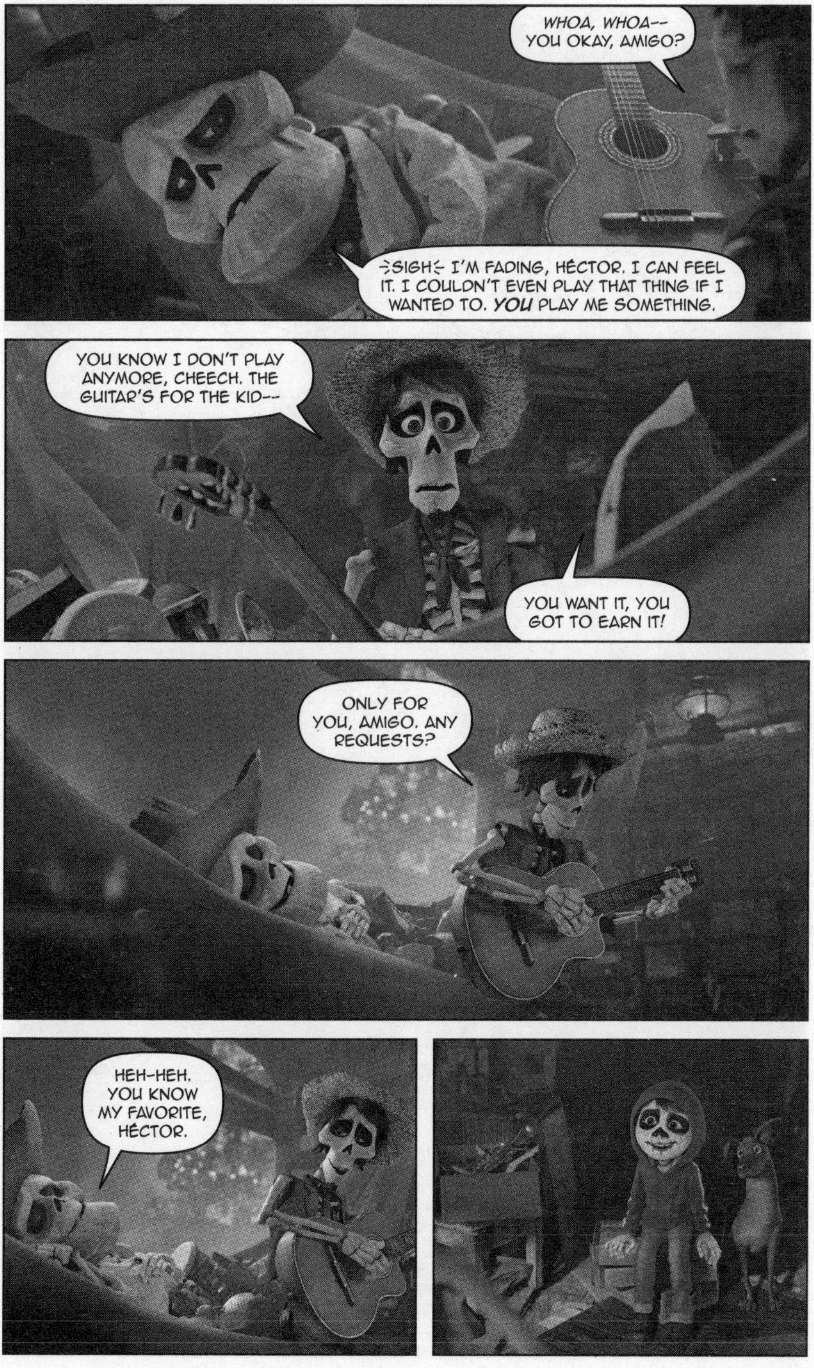
WHOA, WHOA-- YOU OKAY, AMIGO?
≡SIGH≡ I'M FADING, HÉCTOR. I CAN FEEL IT. I COULDN'T EVEN PLAY THAT THING IF I WANTED TO. *YOU* PLAY ME SOMETHING.
YOU KNOW I DON'T PLAY ANYMORE, CHEECH. THE GUITAR'S FOR THE KID--
YOU WANT IT, YOU GOT TO EARN IT!
ONLY FOR YOU, AMIGO. ANY REQUESTS?
HEH-HEH. YOU KNOW MY FAVORITE, HÉCTOR.

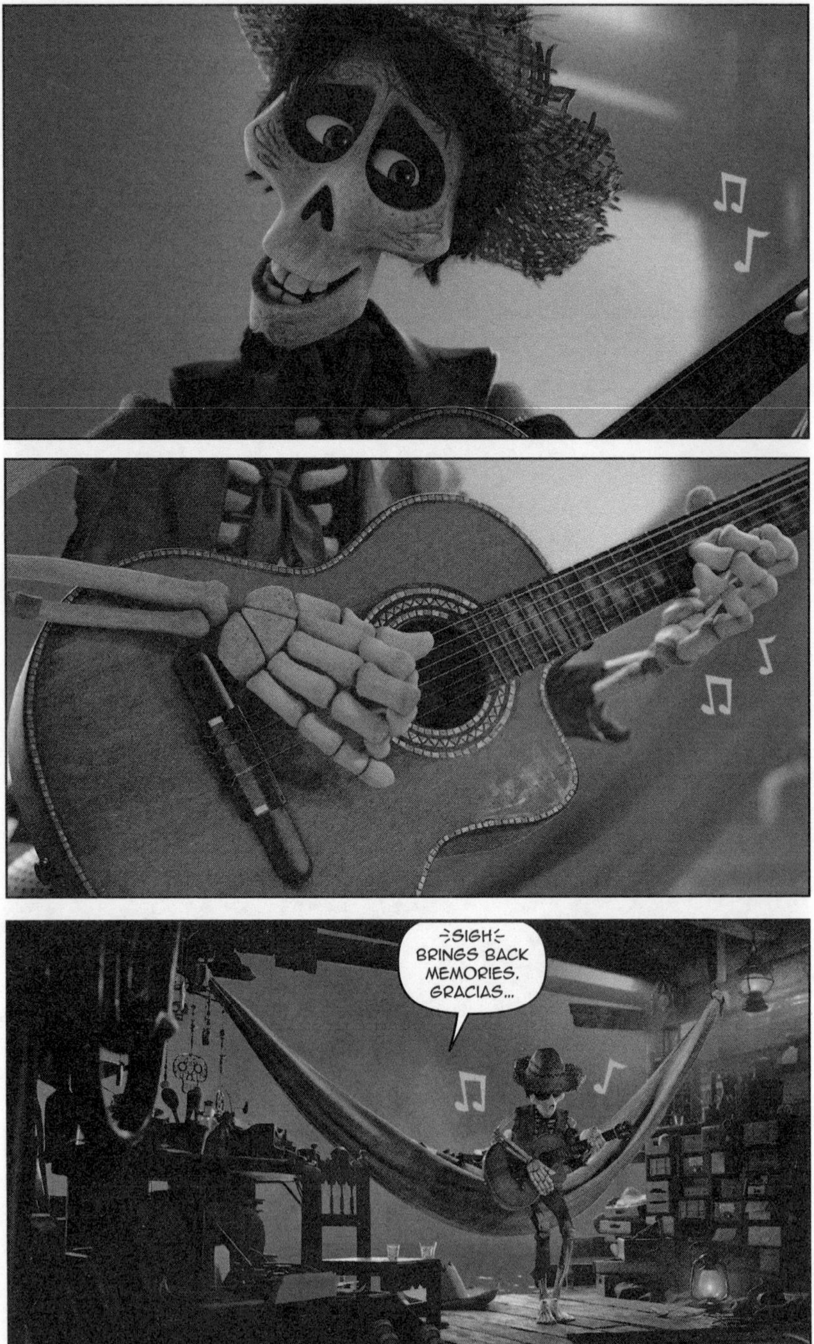

SIGH
BRINGS BACK MEMORIES. GRACIAS...

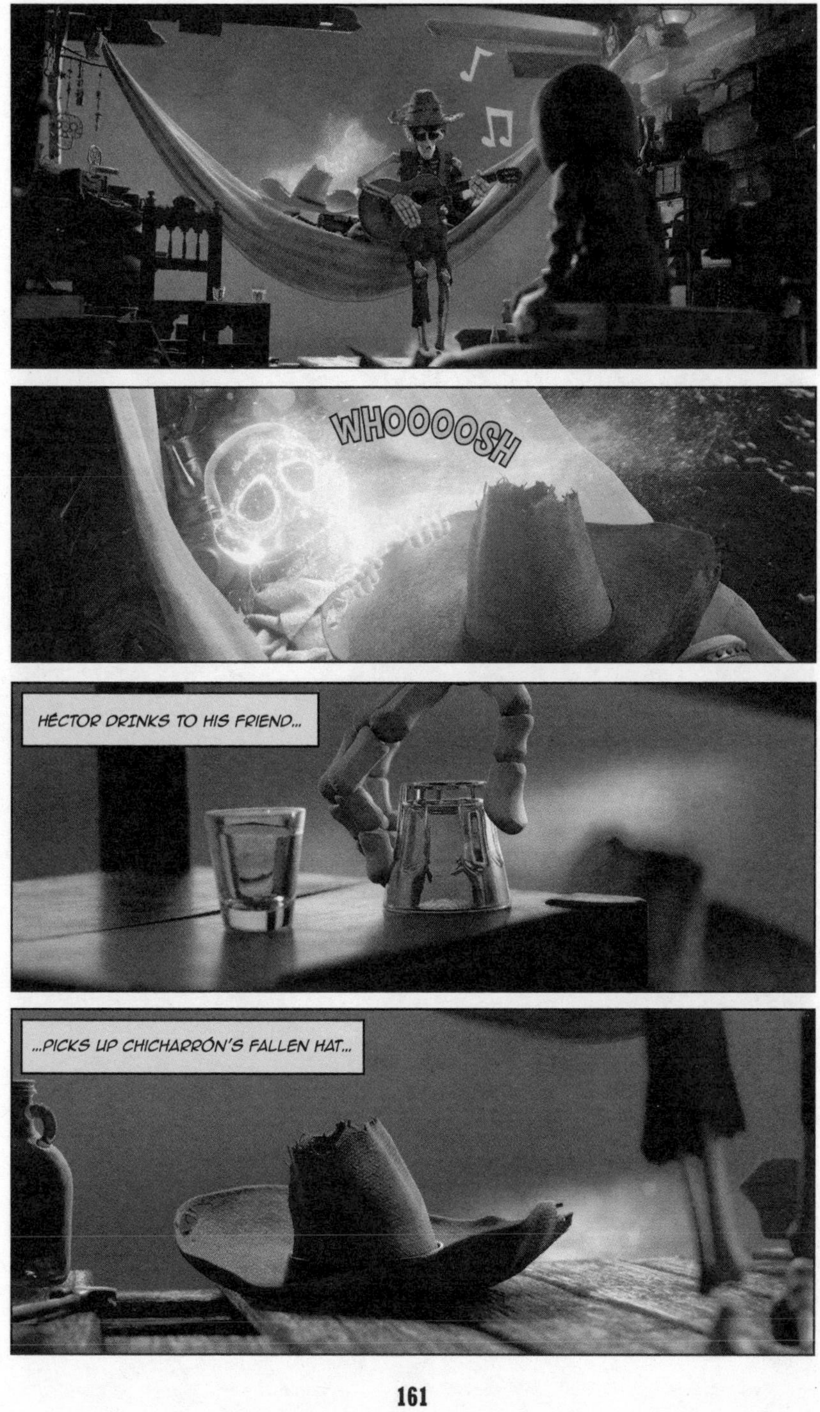
WHOOOOSH
HÉCTOR DRINKS TO HIS FRIEND...
...PICKS UP CHICHARRÓN'S FALLEN HAT...

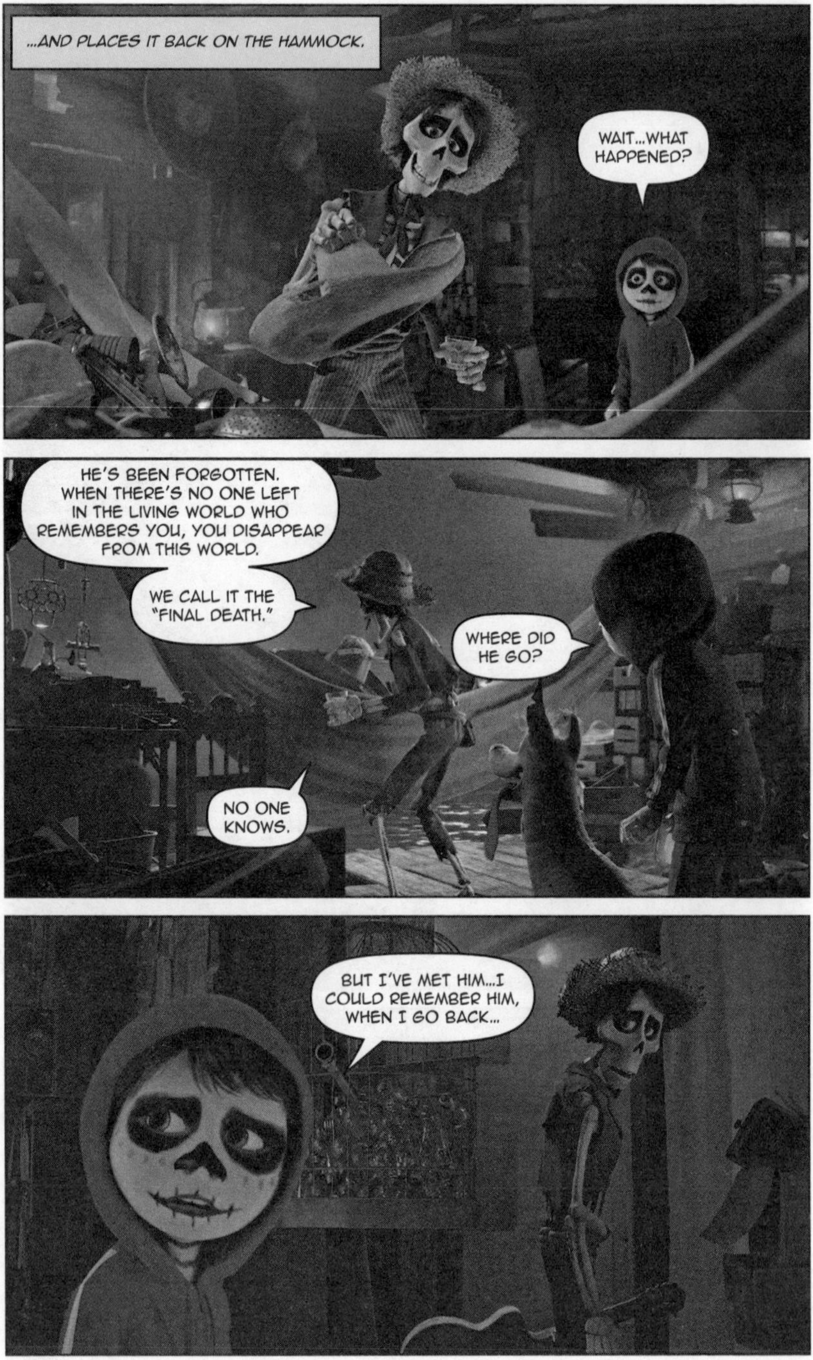
...AND PLACES IT BACK ON THE HAMMOCK.
WAIT...WHAT HAPPENED?
HE'S BEEN FORGOTTEN. WHEN THERE'S NO ONE LEFT IN THE LIVING WORLD WHO REMEMBERS YOU, YOU DISAPPEAR FROM THIS WORLD.
WE CALL IT THE "FINAL DEATH."
WHERE DID HE GO?
NO ONE KNOWS.
BUT I'VE MET HIM...I COULD REMEMBER HIM, WHEN I GO BACK...

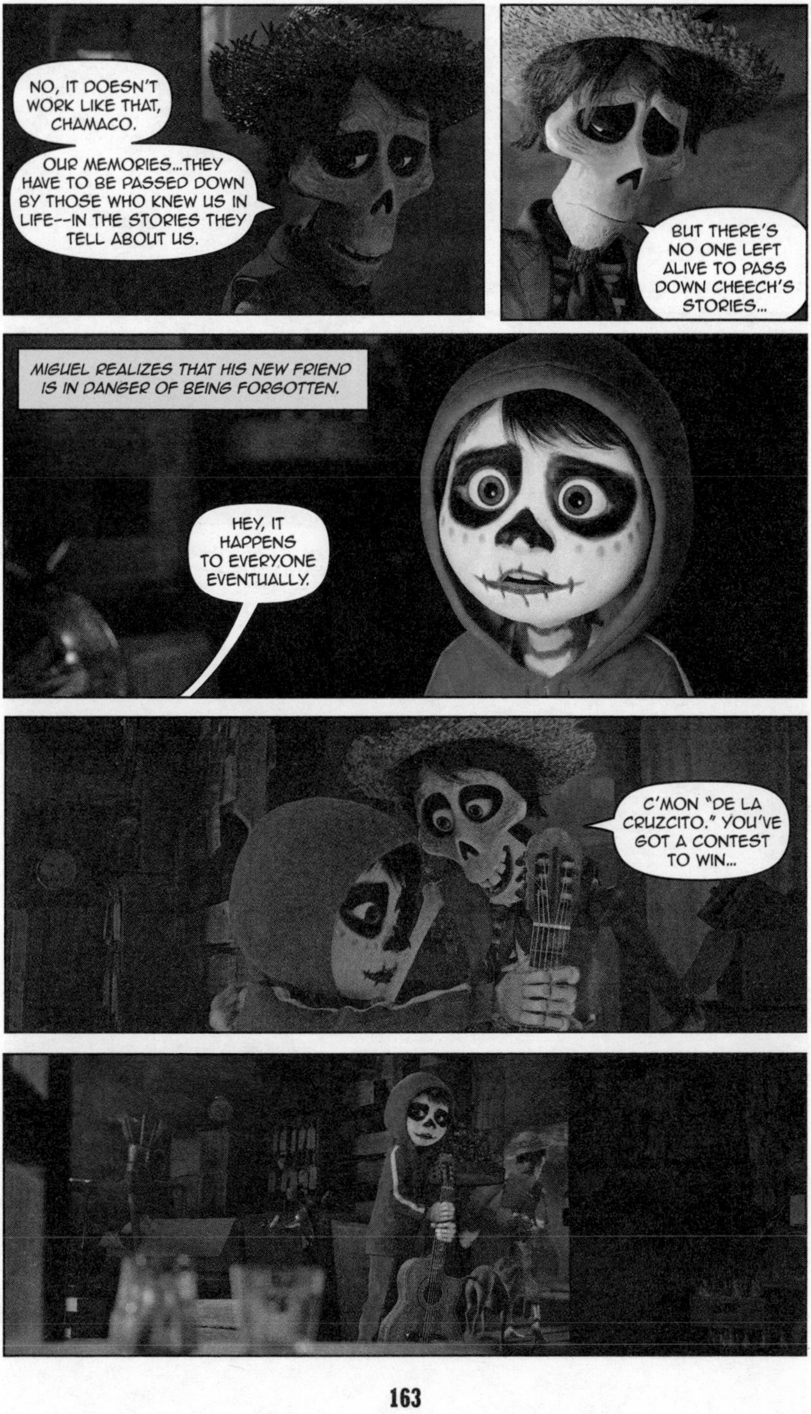
NO, IT DOESN'T WORK LIKE THAT, CHAMACO.
OUR MEMORIES...THEY HAVE TO BE PASSED DOWN BY THOSE WHO KNEW US IN LIFE--IN THE STORIES THEY TELL ABOUT US.
BUT THERE'S NO ONE LEFT ALIVE TO PASS DOWN CHEECH'S STORIES...
MIGUEL REALIZES THAT HIS NEW FRIEND IS IN DANGER OF BEING FORGOTTEN.
HEY, IT HAPPENS TO EVERYONE EVENTUALLY.
C'MON "DE LA CRUZCITO." YOU'VE GOT A CONTEST TO WIN...

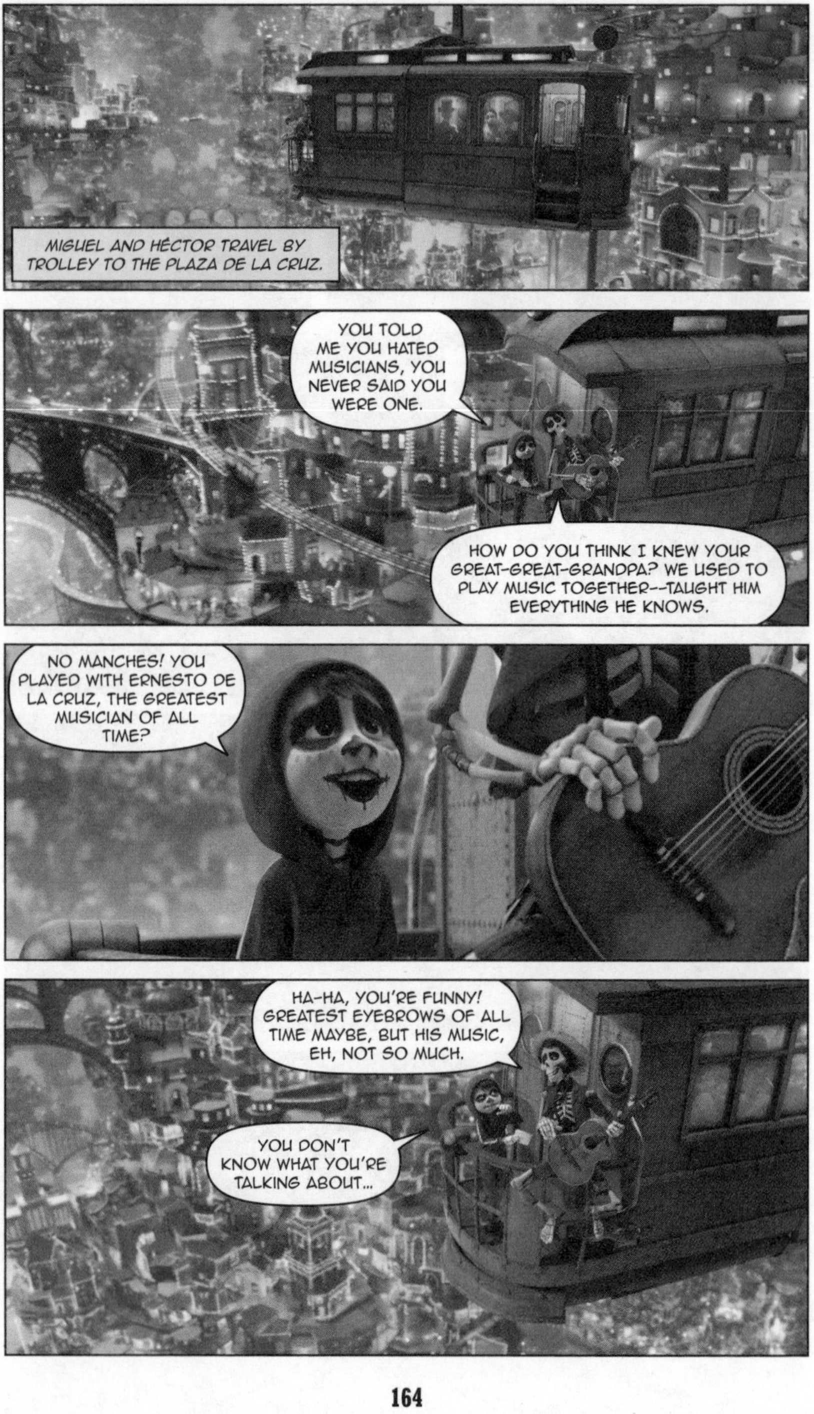
MIGUEL AND HÉCTOR TRAVEL BY TROLLEY TO THE PLAZA DE LA CRUZ.
YOU TOLD ME YOU HATED MUSICIANS, YOU NEVER SAID YOU WERE ONE.
HOW DO YOU THINK I KNEW YOUR GREAT-GREAT-GRANDPA? WE USED TO PLAY MUSIC TOGETHER--TAUGHT HIM EVERYTHING HE KNOWS.
NO MANCHES! YOU PLAYED WITH ERNESTO DE LA CRUZ, THE GREATEST MUSICIAN OF ALL TIME?
HA-HA, YOU'RE FUNNY! GREATEST EYEBROWS OF ALL TIME MAYBE, BUT HIS MUSIC, EH, NOT SO MUCH.
YOU DON'T KNOW WHAT YOU'RE TALKING ABOUT...

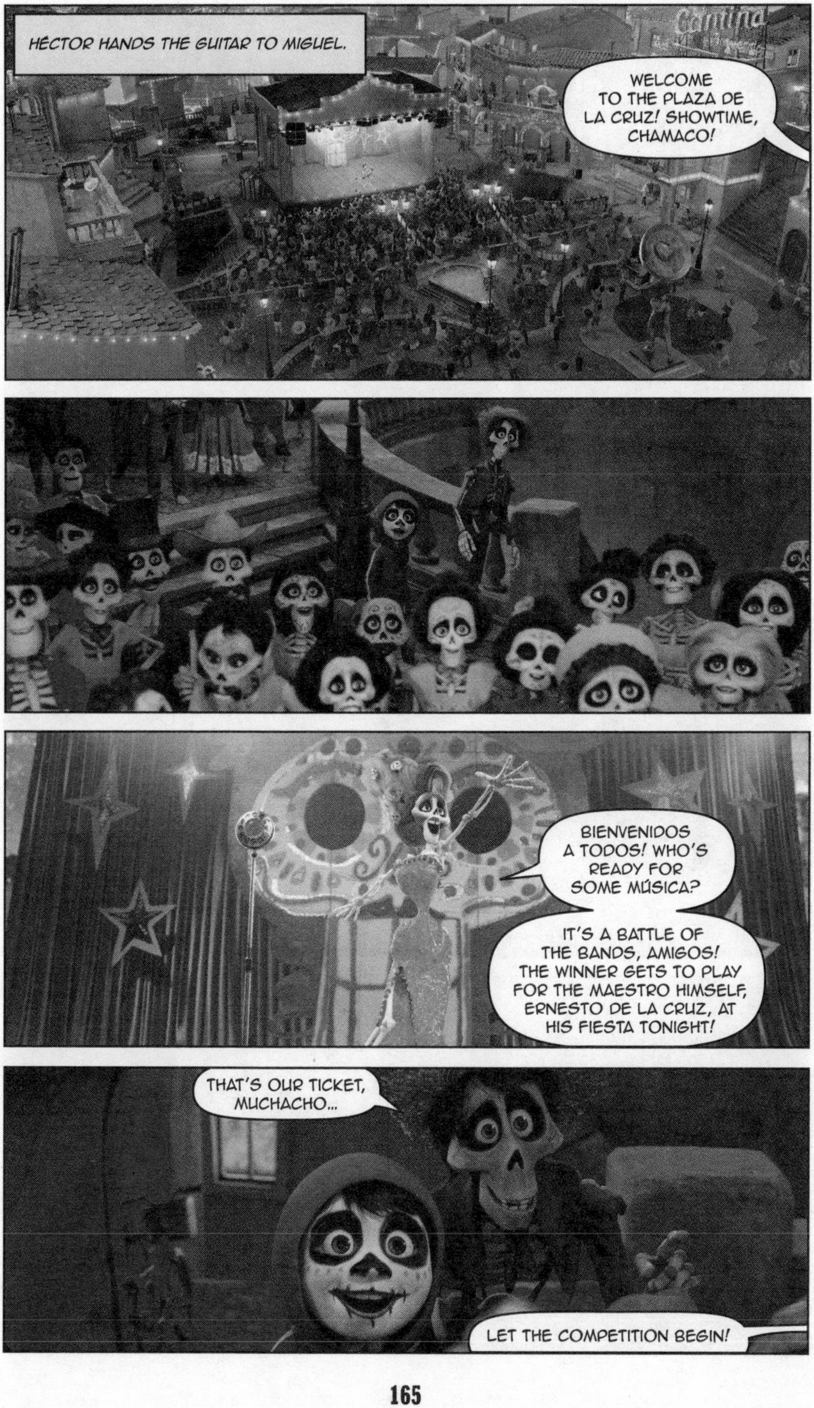
HÉCTOR HANDS THE GUITAR TO MIGUEL.
WELCOME TO THE PLAZA DE LA CRUZ! SHOWTIME, CHAMACO!
BIENVENIDOS A TODOS! WHO'S READY FOR SOME MÚSICA?
IT'S A BATTLE OF THE BANDS, AMIGOS! THE WINNER GETS TO PLAY FOR THE MAESTRO HIMSELF, ERNESTO DE LA CRUZ, AT HIS FIESTA TONIGHT!
THAT'S OUR TICKET, MUCHACHO...
LET THE COMPETITION BEGIN!

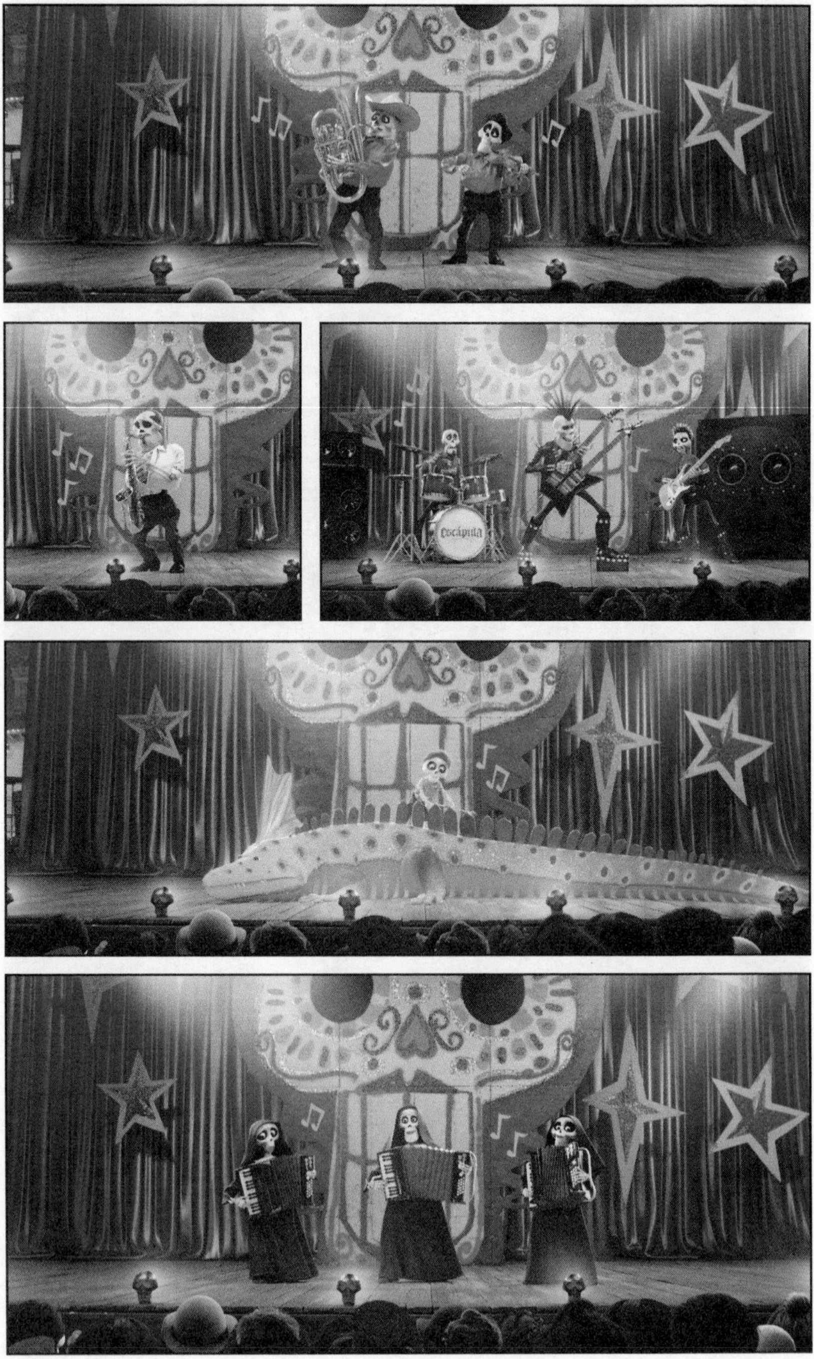

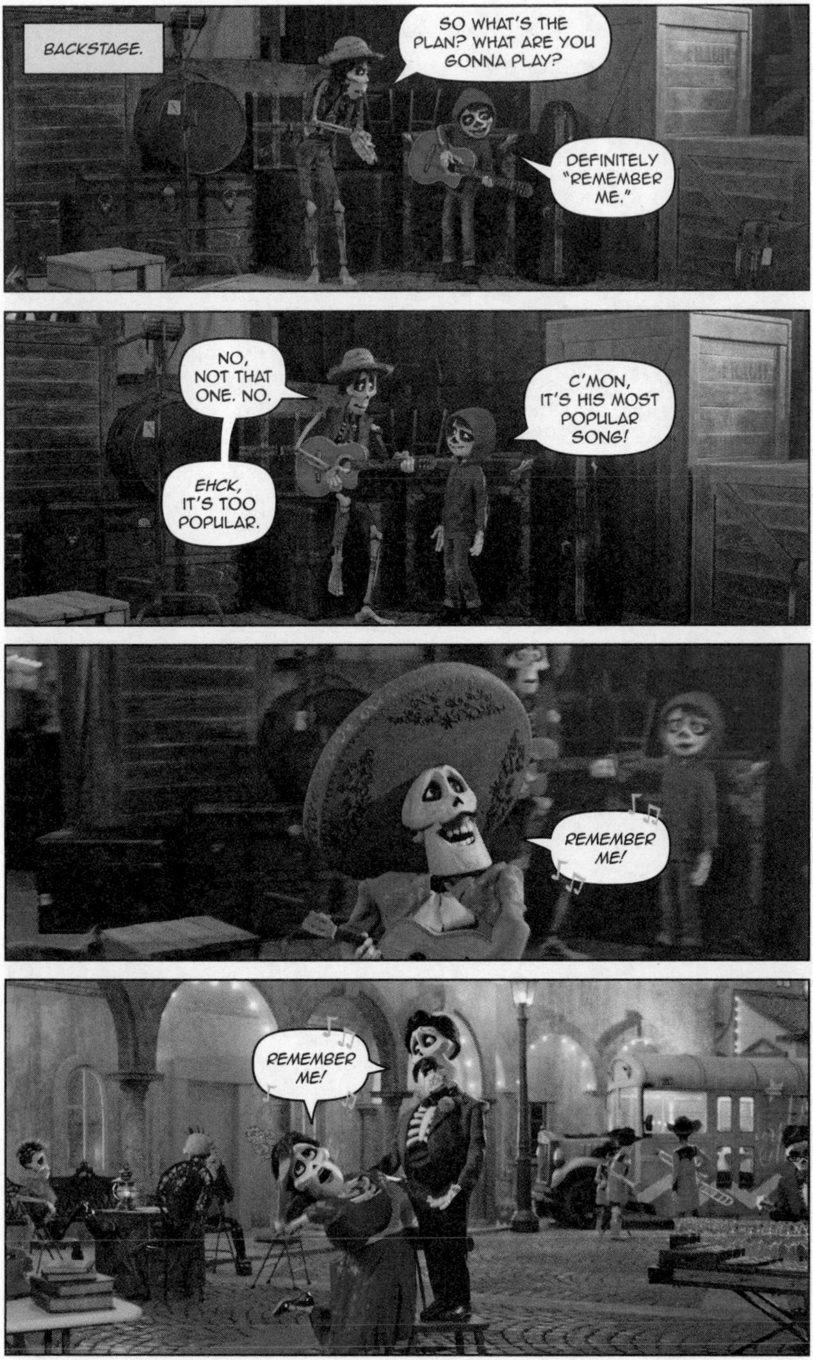
BACKSTAGE.
SO WHAT'S THE PLAN? WHAT ARE YOU GONNA PLAY?
DEFINITELY "REMEMBER ME."
NO, NOT THAT ONE. NO.
EHCK, IT'S TOO POPULAR.
C'MON, IT'S HIS MOST POPULAR SONG!
REMEMBER ME!
REMEMBER ME!

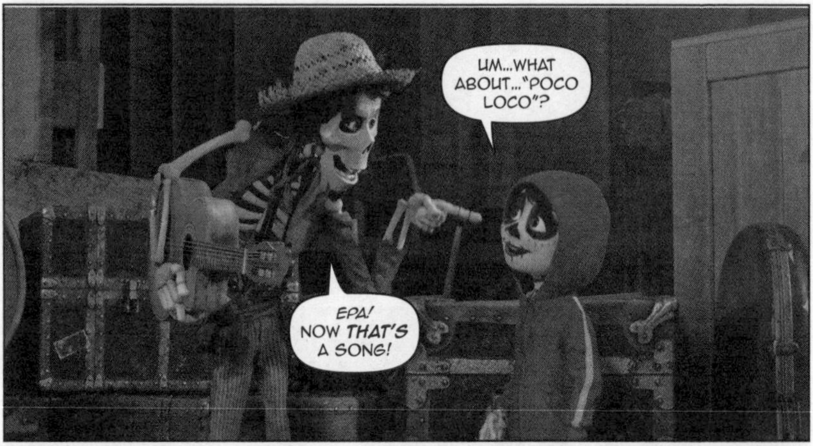
UM...WHAT ABOUT..."POCO LOCO"?
EPA! NOW *THAT'S* A SONG!

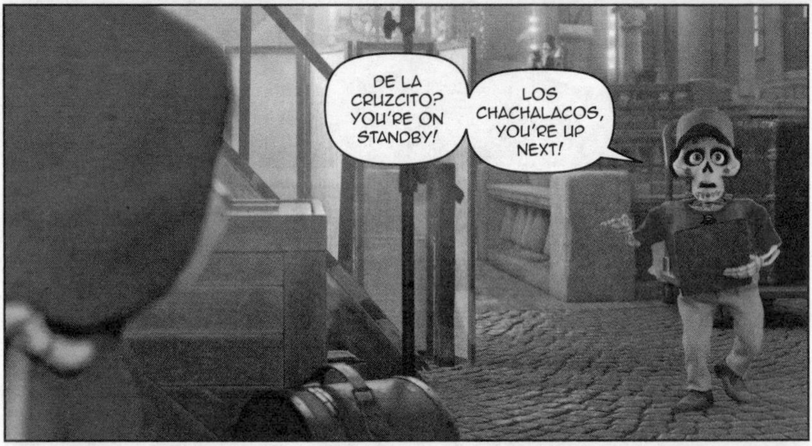
DE LA CRUZCITO? YOU'RE ON STANDBY!
LOS CHACHALACOS, YOU'RE UP NEXT!

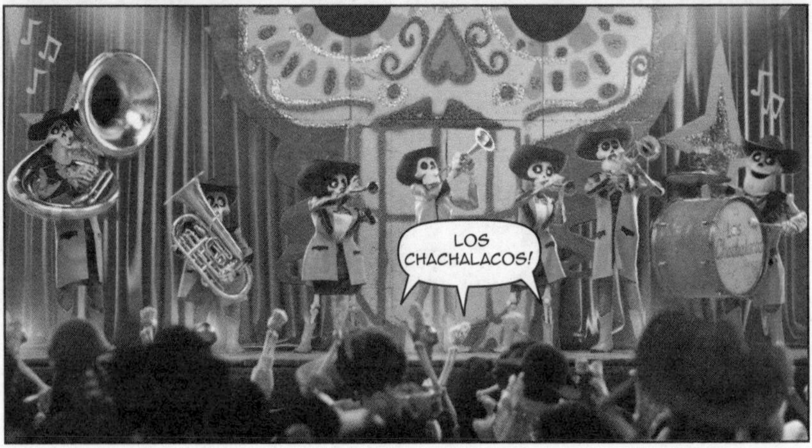
LOS CHACHALACOS!

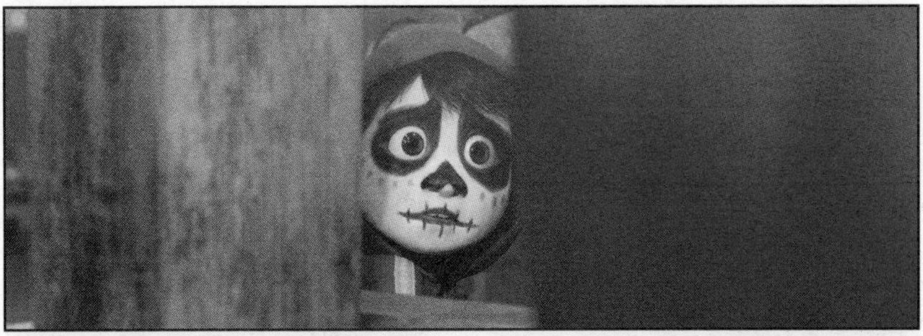

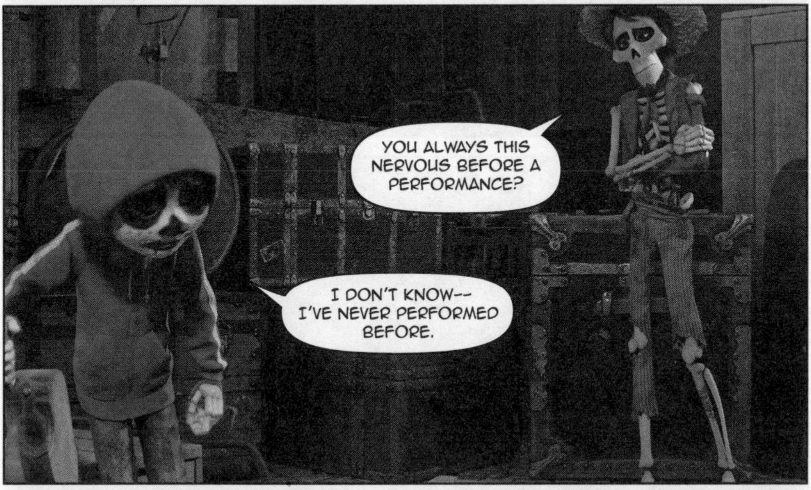
YOU ALWAYS THIS NERVOUS BEFORE A PERFORMANCE?
I DON'T KNOW-- I'VE NEVER PERFORMED BEFORE.

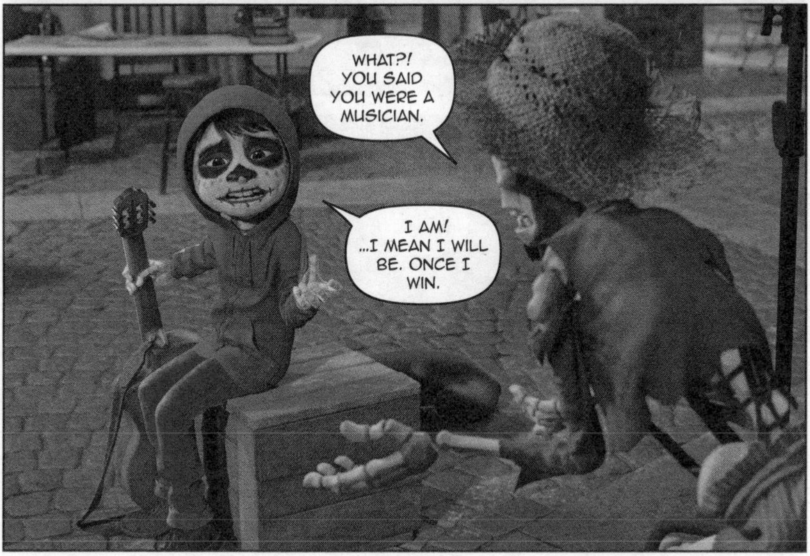
WHAT?! YOU SAID YOU WERE A MUSICIAN.
I AM! ...I MEAN I WILL BE. ONCE I WIN.

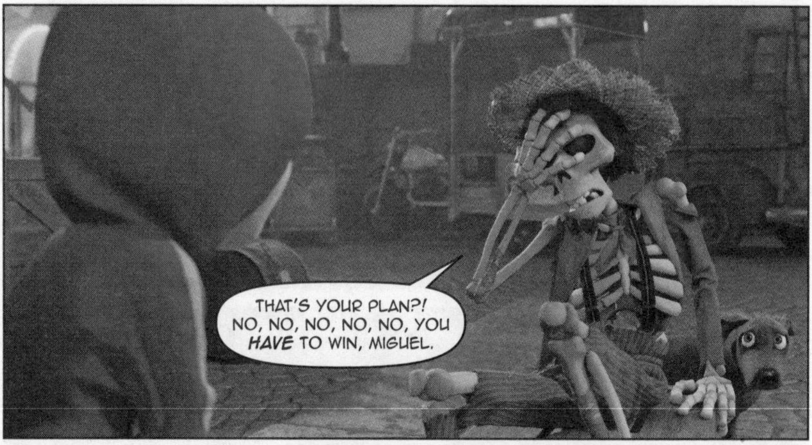
THAT'S YOUR PLAN?! NO, NO, NO, NO, NO, YOU *HAVE* TO WIN, MIGUEL.

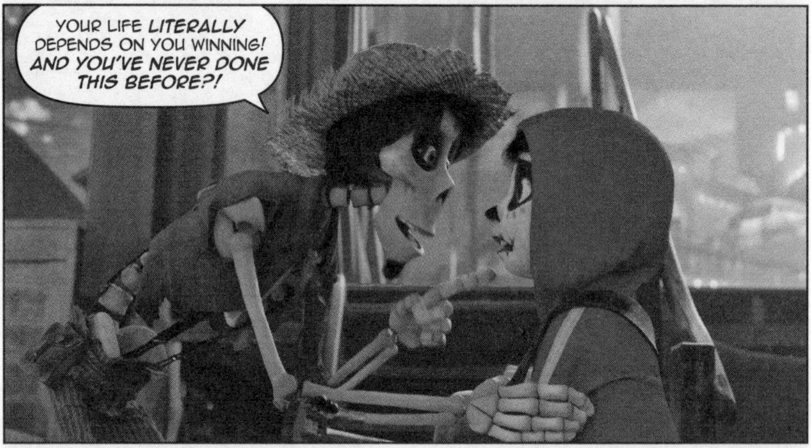
YOUR LIFE *LITERALLY* DEPENDS ON YOU WINNING! *AND YOU'VE NEVER DONE THIS BEFORE?!*

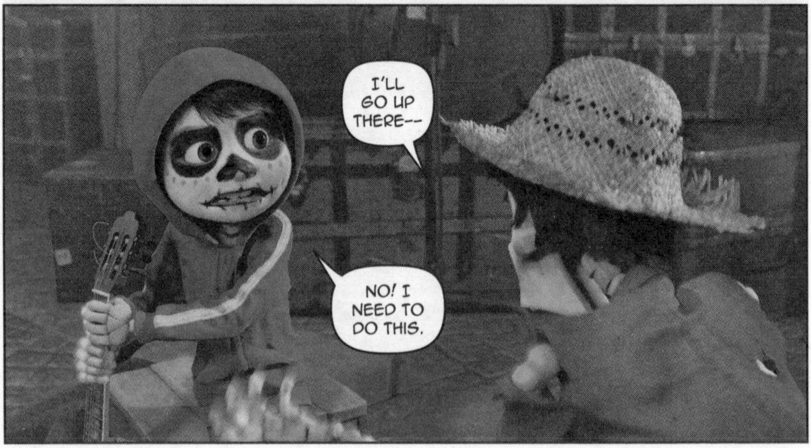
I'LL GO UP THERE--
NO! I NEED TO DO THIS.

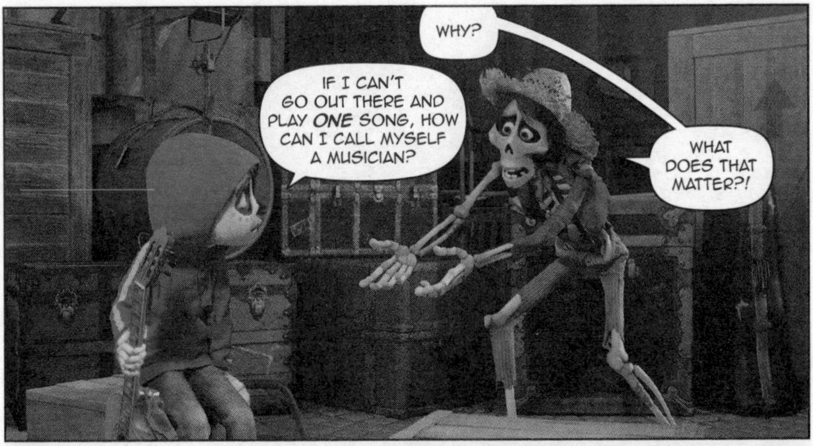
IF I CAN'T GO OUT THERE AND PLAY ONE SONG, HOW CAN I CALL MYSELF A MUSICIAN?
WHY?
WHAT DOES THAT MATTER?!

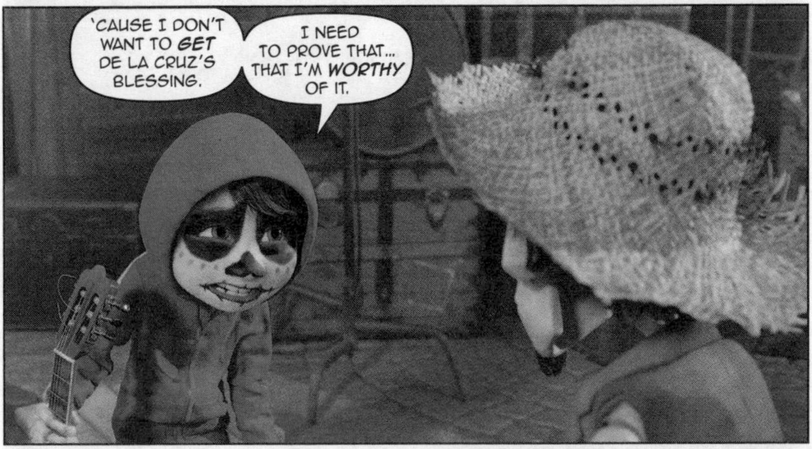
'CAUSE I DON'T WANT TO GET DE LA CRUZ'S BLESSING.
I NEED TO PROVE THAT... THAT I'M WORTHY OF IT.

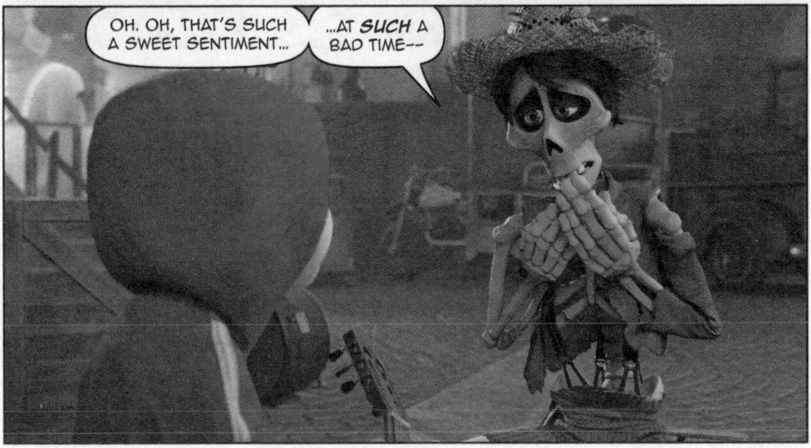
OH. OH, THAT'S SUCH A SWEET SENTIMENT...
...AT SUCH A BAD TIME--

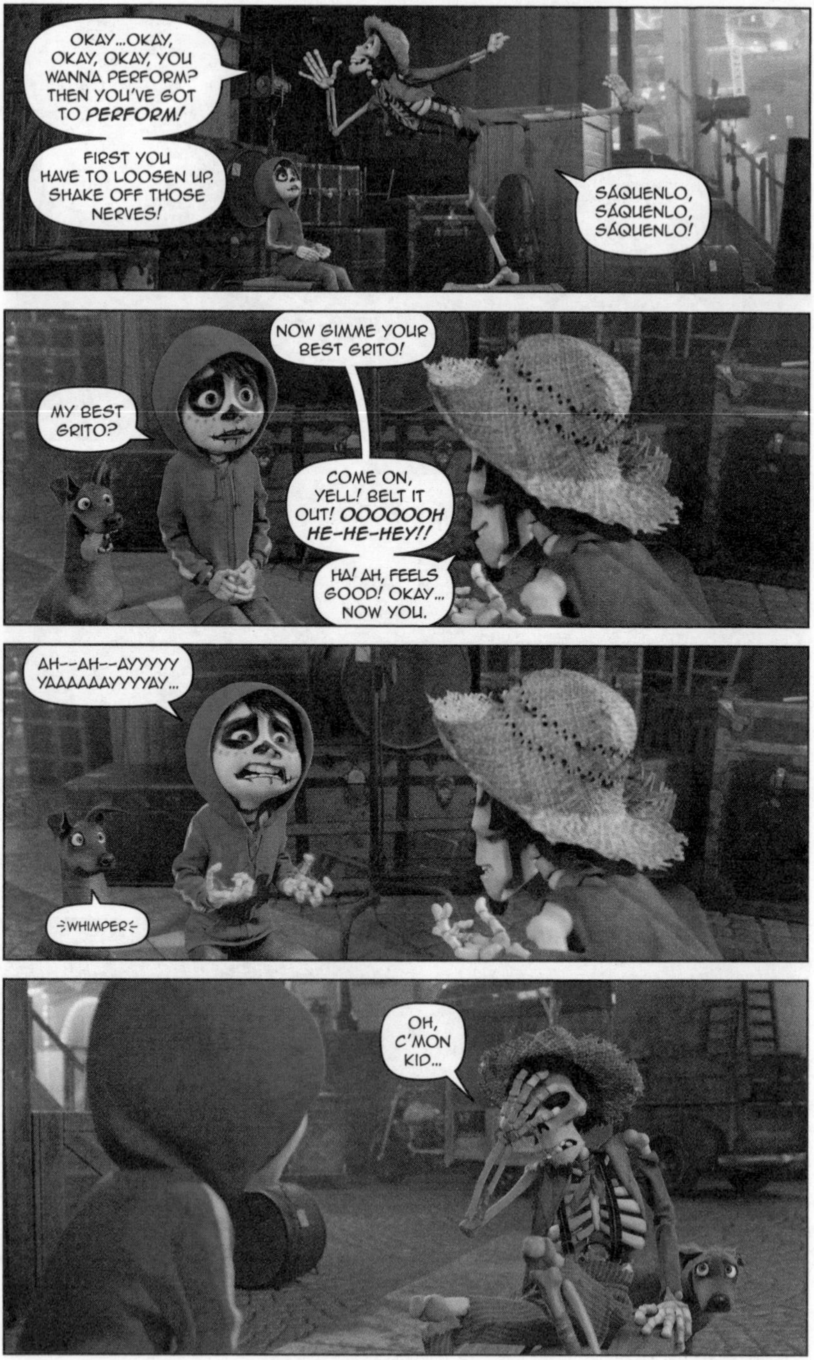
OKAY...OKAY, OKAY, OKAY, YOU WANNA PERFORM? THEN YOU'VE GOT TO *PERFORM!*
FIRST YOU HAVE TO LOOSEN UP. SHAKE OFF THOSE NERVES!
SÁQUENLO, SÁQUENLO, SÁQUENLO!
MY BEST GRITO?
NOW GIMME YOUR BEST GRITO!
COME ON, YELL! BELT IT OUT! *OOOOOOH HE-HE-HEY!!*
HA! AH, FEELS GOOD! OKAY... NOW YOU.
AH--AH--AYYYYY YAAAAAAYYYYAY...
WHIMPER
OH, C'MON KID...

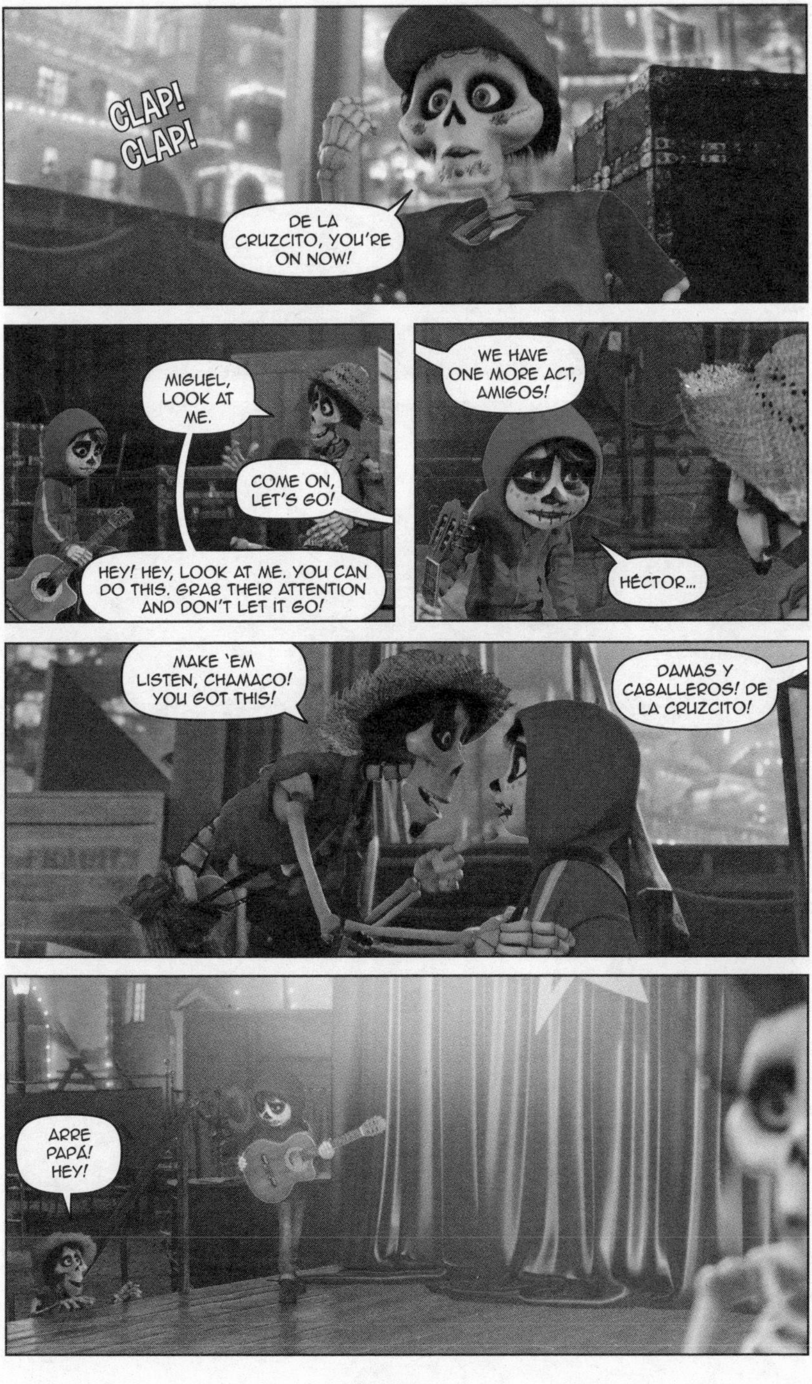
CLAP! CLAP!
DE LA CRUZCITO, YOU'RE ON NOW!
MIGUEL, LOOK AT ME.
COME ON, LET'S GO!
HEY! HEY, LOOK AT ME. YOU CAN DO THIS. GRAB THEIR ATTENTION AND DON'T LET IT GO!
WE HAVE ONE MORE ACT, AMIGOS!
HÉCTOR...
MAKE 'EM LISTEN, CHAMACO! YOU GOT THIS!
DAMAS Y CABALLEROS! DE LA CRUZCITO!
ARRE PAPÁ! HEY!

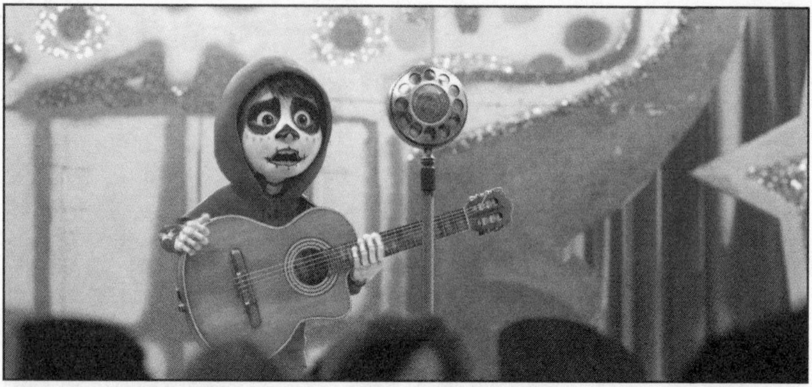

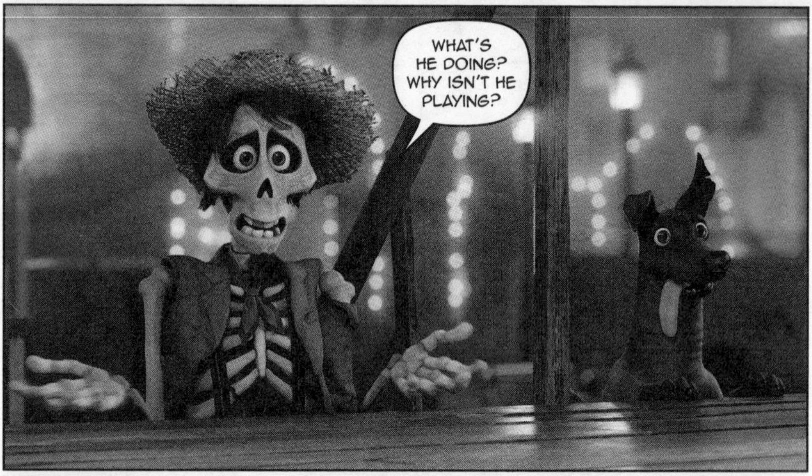
WHAT'S HE DOING? WHY ISN'T HE PLAYING?

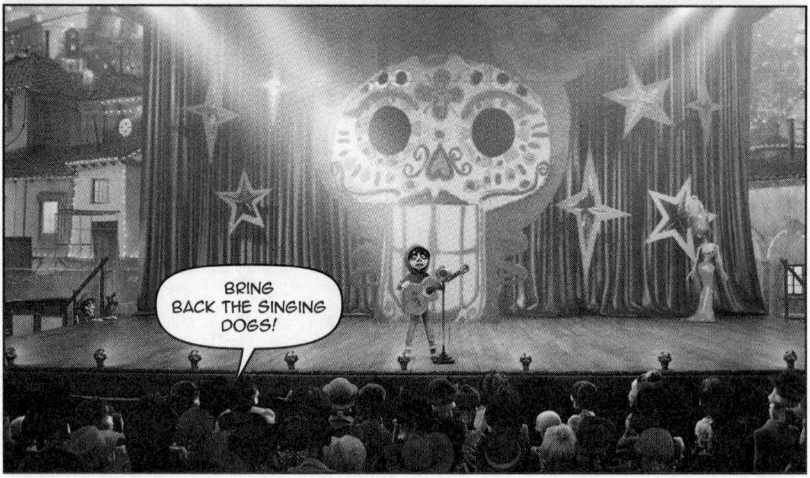
BRING BACK THE SINGING DOGS!

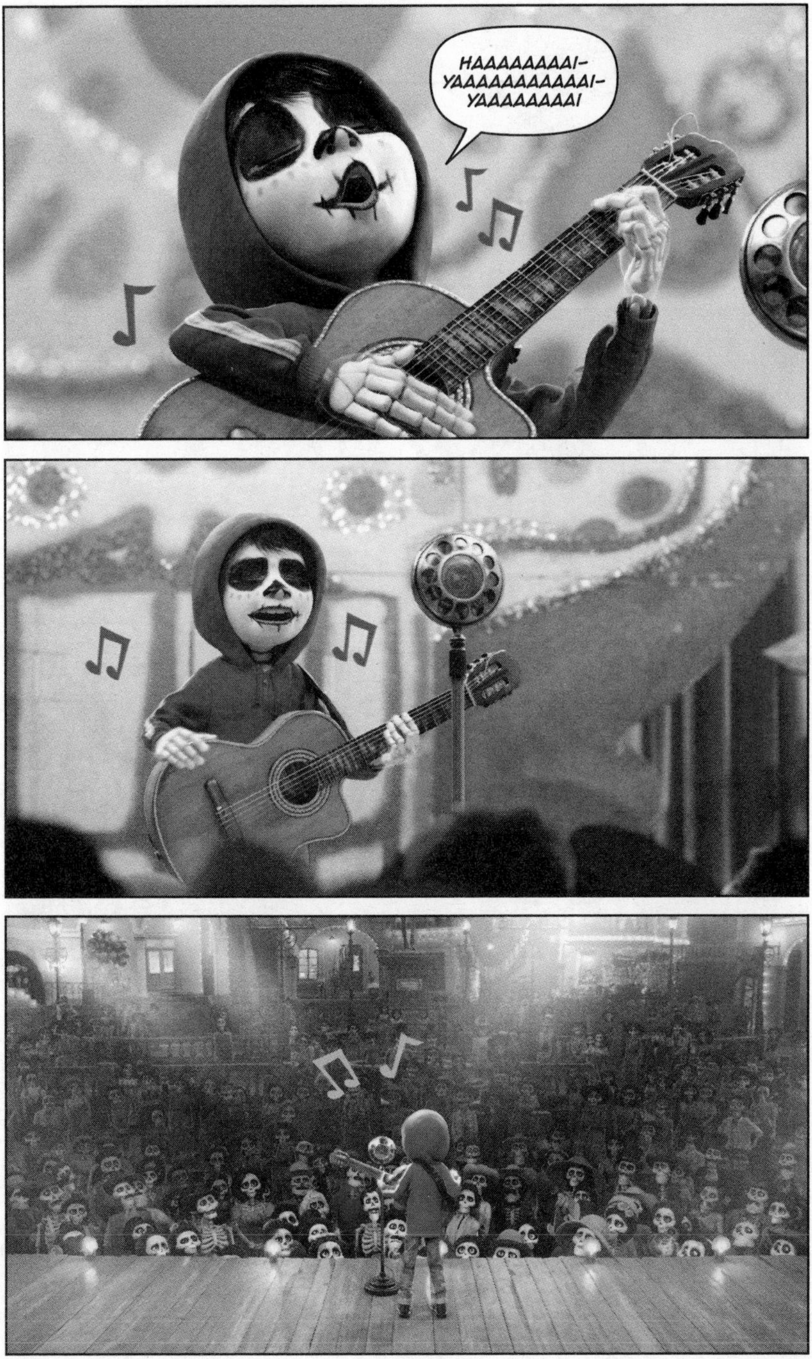
HAAAAAAAAI-
YAAAAAAAAAAAI-
YAAAAAAAAI

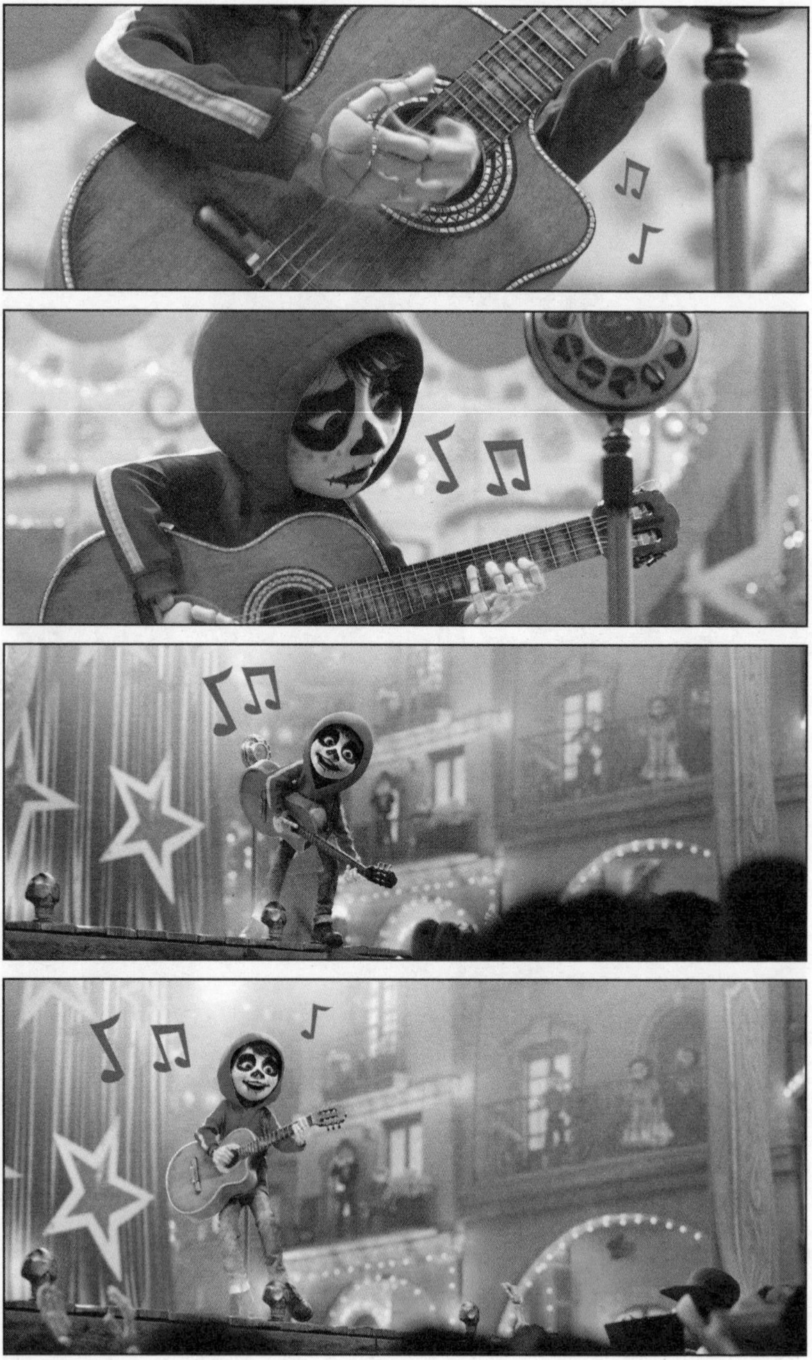

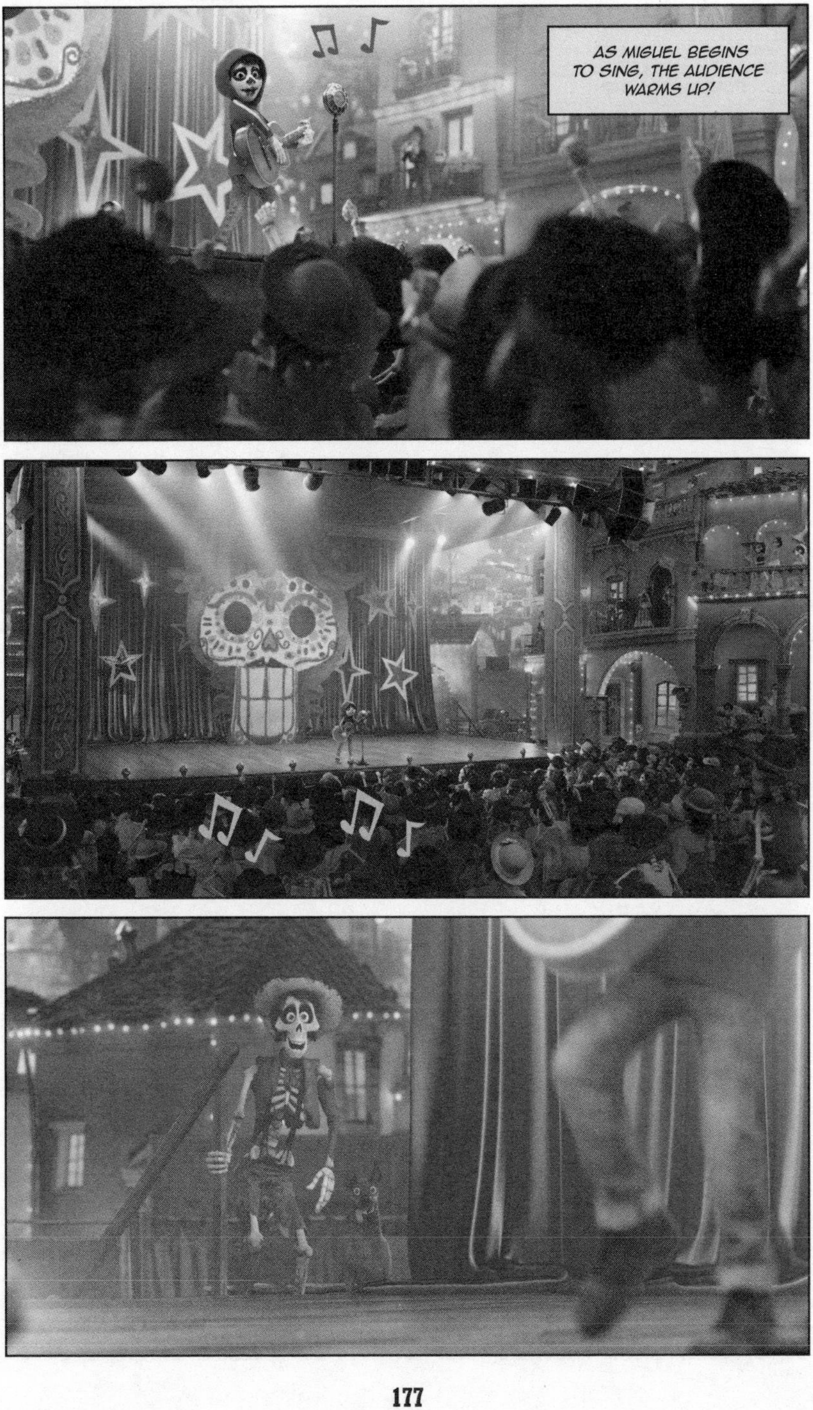
AS MIGUEL BEGINS TO SING, THE AUDIENCE WARMS UP!

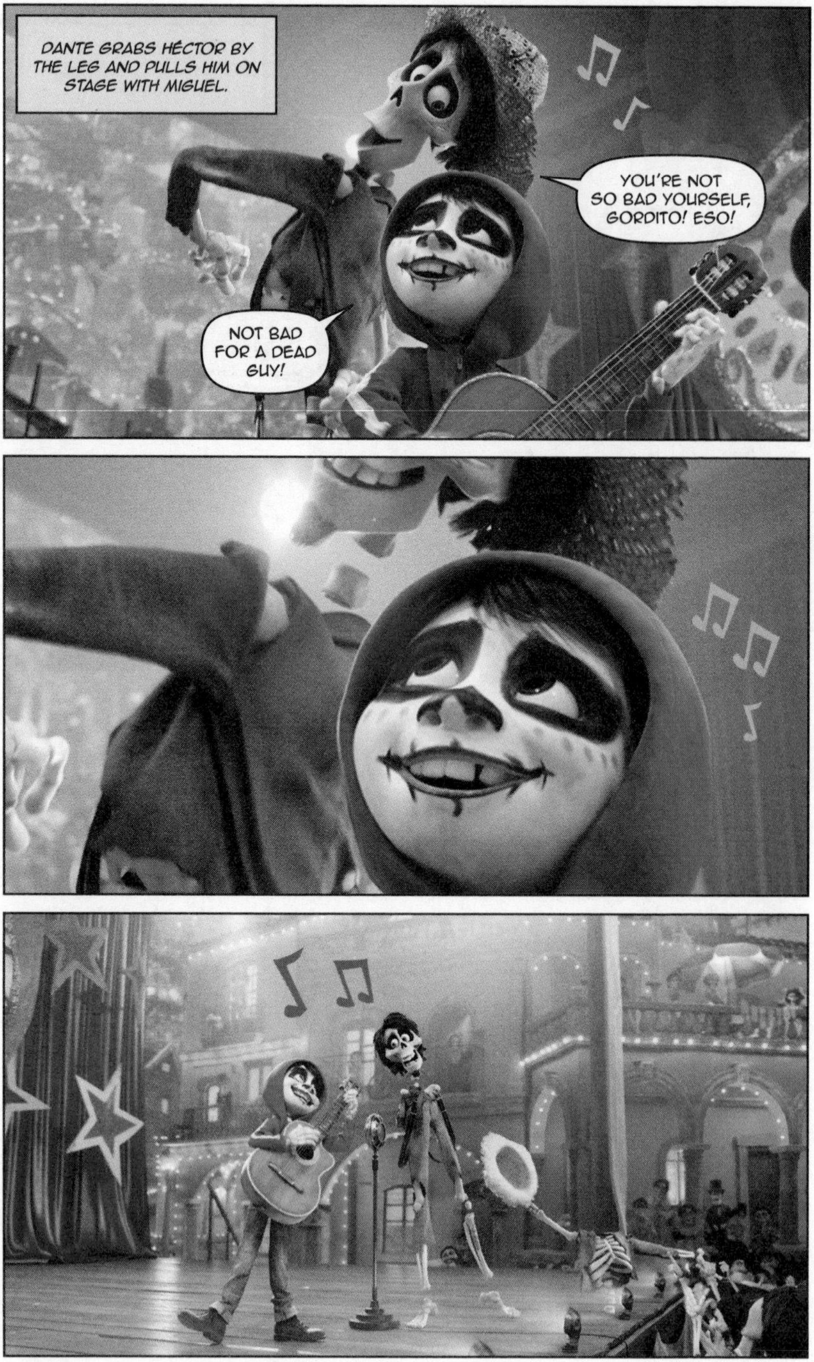
DANTE GRABS HÉCTOR BY THE LEG AND PULLS HIM ON STAGE WITH MIGUEL.
NOT BAD FOR A DEAD GUY!
YOU'RE NOT SO BAD YOURSELF, GORDITO! ESO!

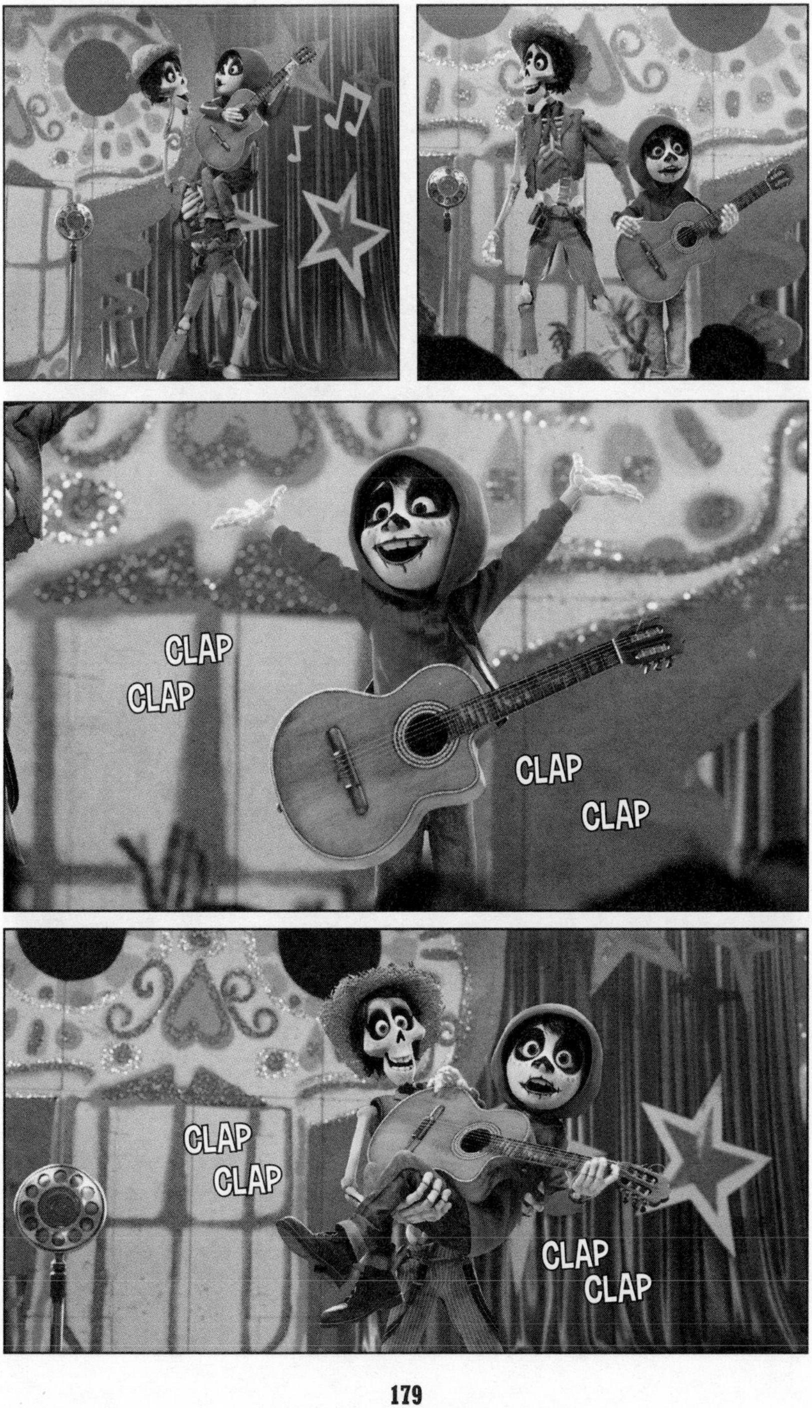
CLAP
CLAP
CLAP
CLAP
CLAP
CLAP
CLAP
CLAP

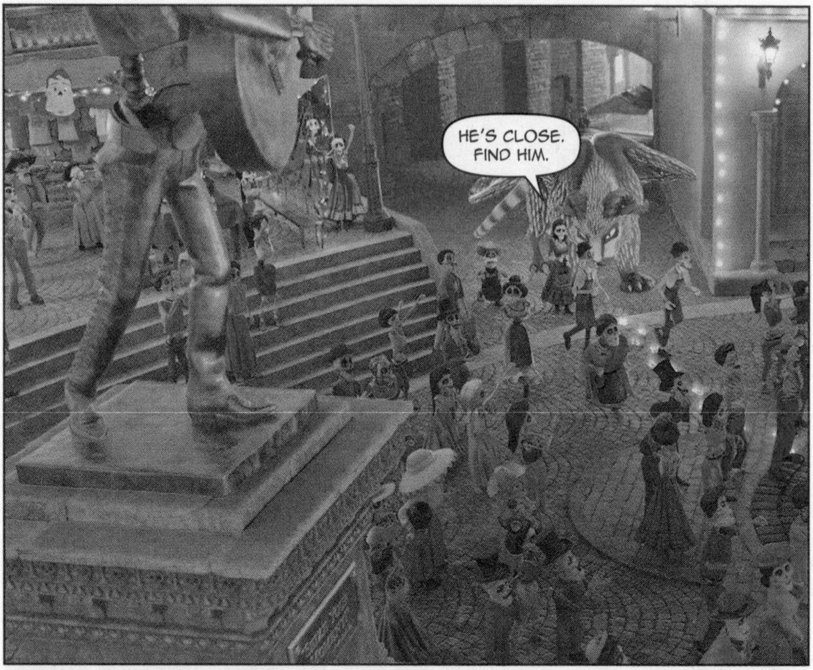
HE'S CLOSE.
FIND HIM.

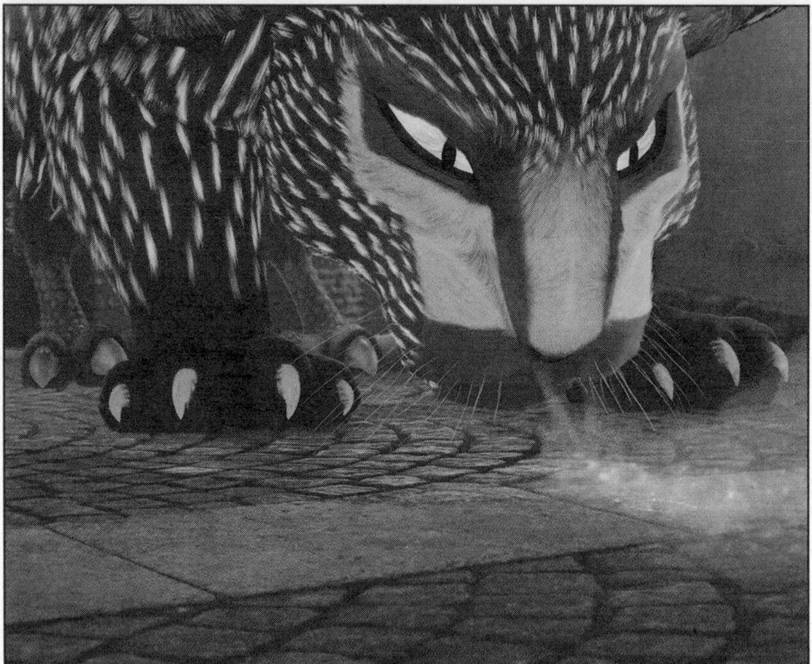

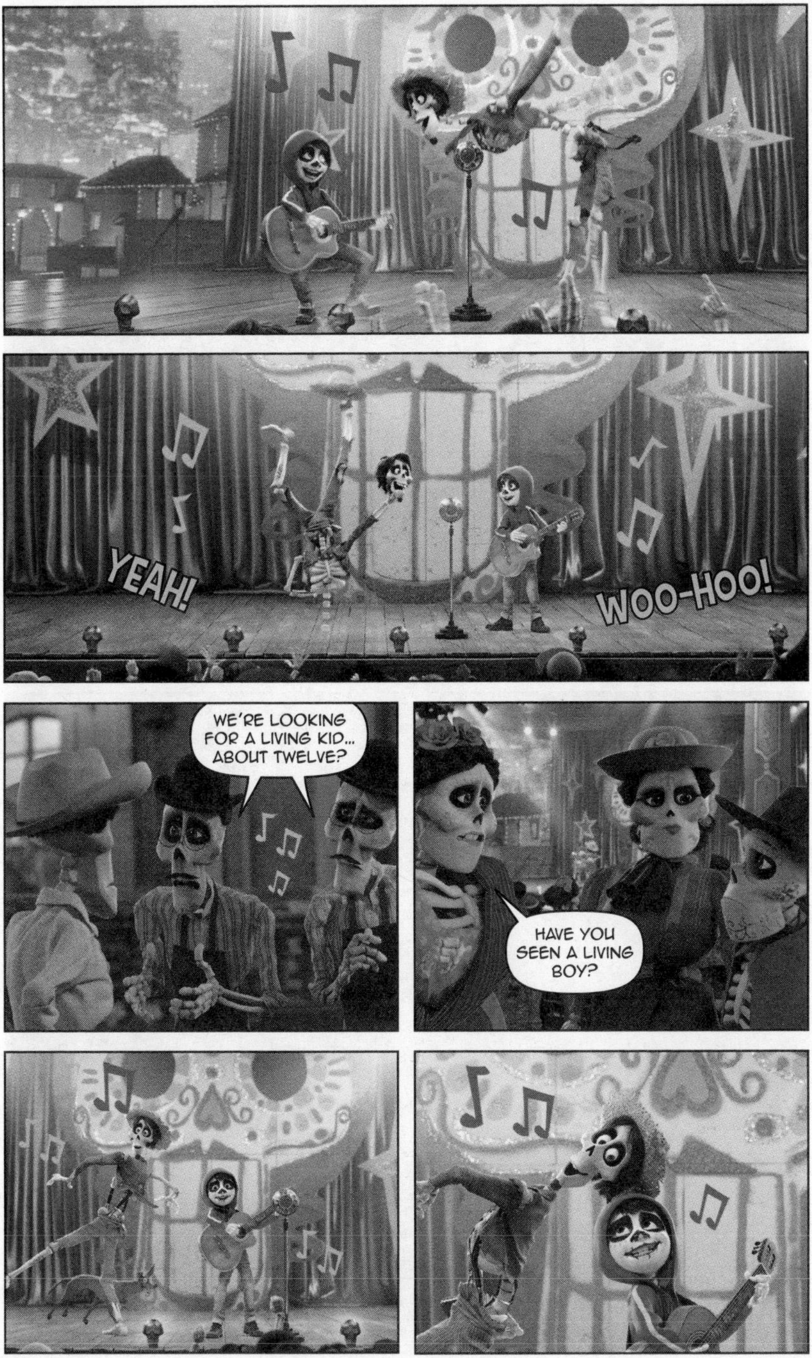
YEAH!
WOO-HOO!
WE'RE LOOKING FOR A LIVING KID... ABOUT TWELVE?
HAVE YOU SEEN A LIVING BOY?

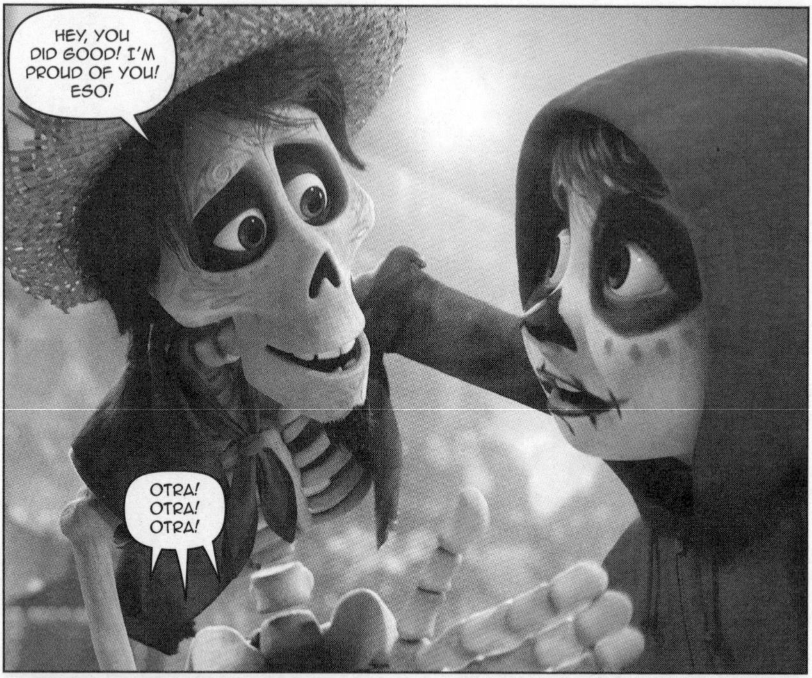
HEY, YOU DID GOOD! I'M PROUD OF YOU! ESO!
OTRA! OTRA! OTRA!

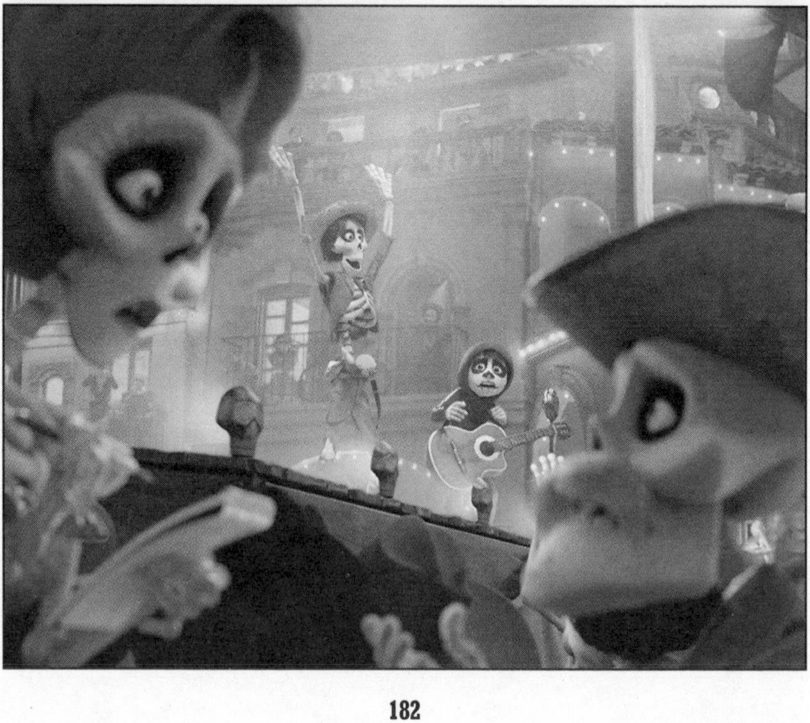

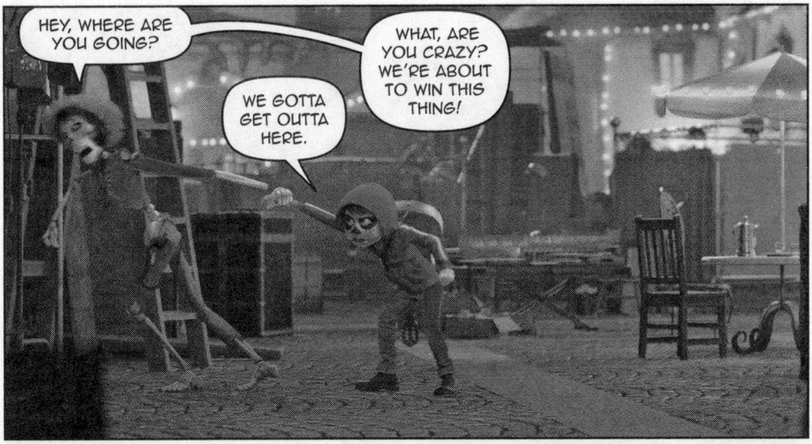
HEY, WHERE ARE YOU GOING?
WE GOTTA GET OUTTA HERE.
WHAT, ARE YOU CRAZY? WE'RE ABOUT TO WIN THIS THING!

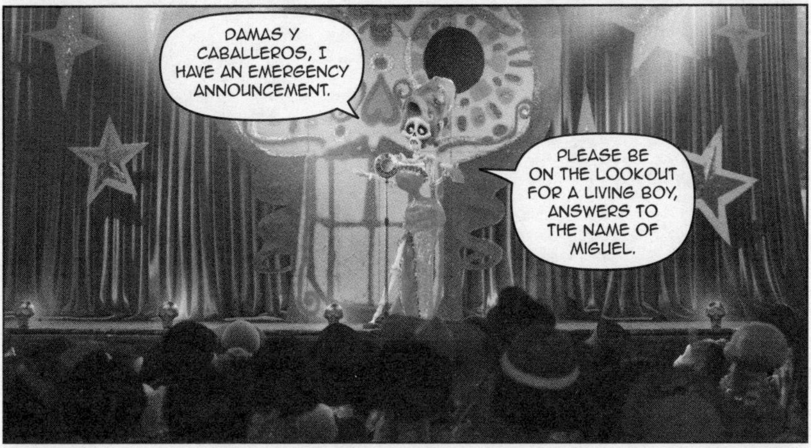
DAMAS Y CABALLEROS, I HAVE AN EMERGENCY ANNOUNCEMENT.
PLEASE BE ON THE LOOKOUT FOR A LIVING BOY, ANSWERS TO THE NAME OF MIGUEL.

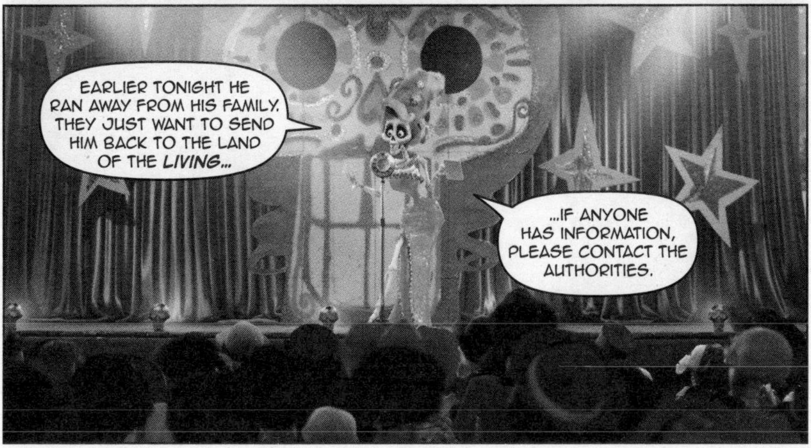
EARLIER TONIGHT HE RAN AWAY FROM HIS FAMILY. THEY JUST WANT TO SEND HIM BACK TO THE LAND OF THE *LIVING*...
...IF ANYONE HAS INFORMATION, PLEASE CONTACT THE AUTHORITIES.

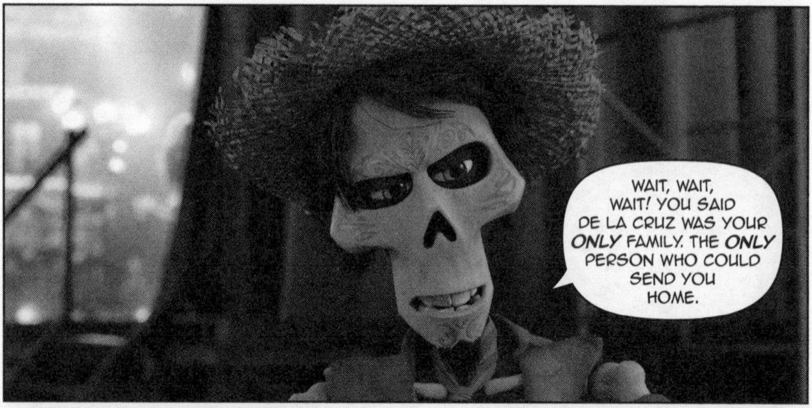
WAIT, WAIT, WAIT! YOU SAID DE LA CRUZ WAS YOUR *ONLY* FAMILY. THE *ONLY* PERSON WHO COULD SEND YOU HOME.

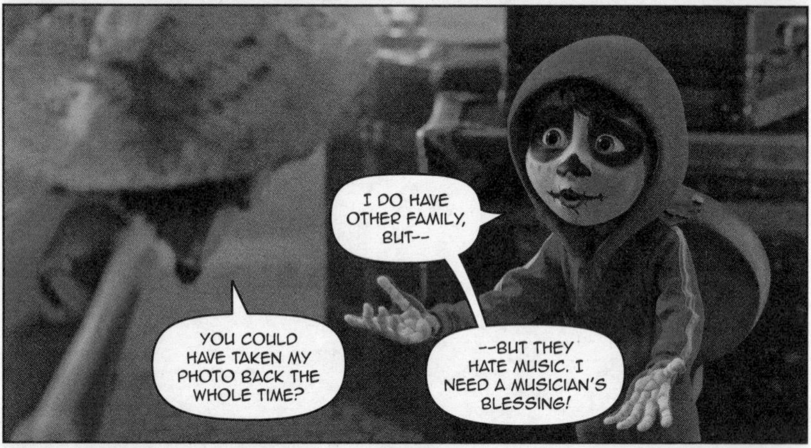
I DO HAVE OTHER FAMILY, BUT--
YOU COULD HAVE TAKEN MY PHOTO BACK THE WHOLE TIME?
--BUT THEY HATE MUSIC. I NEED A MUSICIAN'S BLESSING!

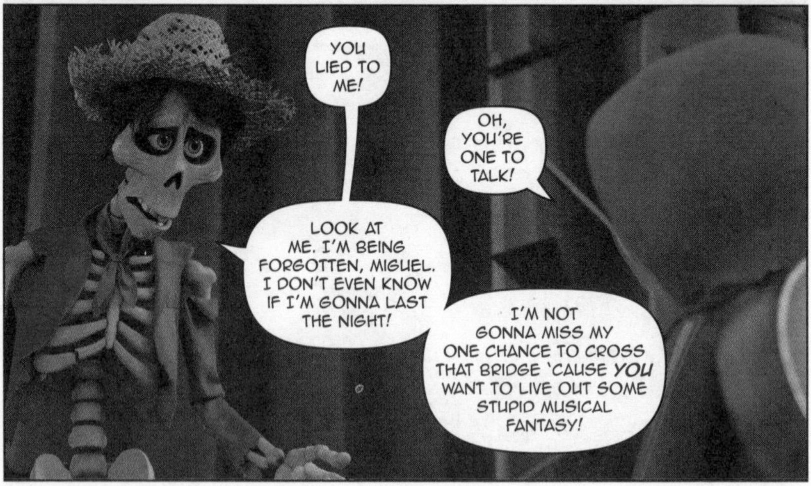
YOU LIED TO ME!
OH, YOU'RE ONE TO TALK!
LOOK AT ME. I'M BEING FORGOTTEN, MIGUEL. I DON'T EVEN KNOW IF I'M GONNA LAST THE NIGHT!
I'M NOT GONNA MISS MY ONE CHANCE TO CROSS THAT BRIDGE 'CAUSE *YOU* WANT TO LIVE OUT SOME STUPID MUSICAL FANTASY!

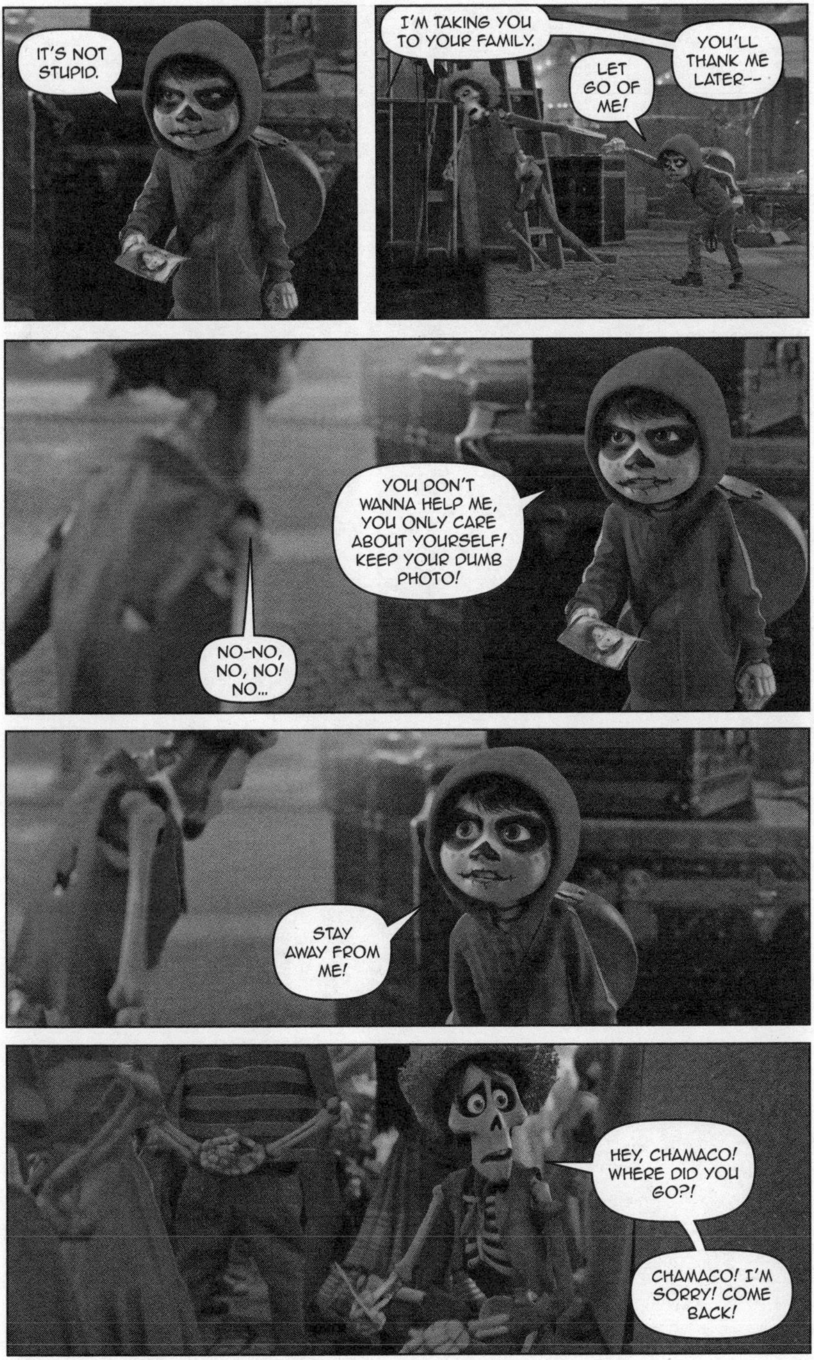
IT'S NOT STUPID.
I'M TAKING YOU TO YOUR FAMILY.
YOU'LL THANK ME LATER--
LET GO OF ME!
YOU DON'T WANNA HELP ME, YOU ONLY CARE ABOUT YOURSELF! KEEP YOUR DUMB PHOTO!
NO-NO, NO, NO! NO...
STAY AWAY FROM ME!
HEY, CHAMACO! WHERE DID YOU GO?!
CHAMACO! I'M SORRY! COME BACK!

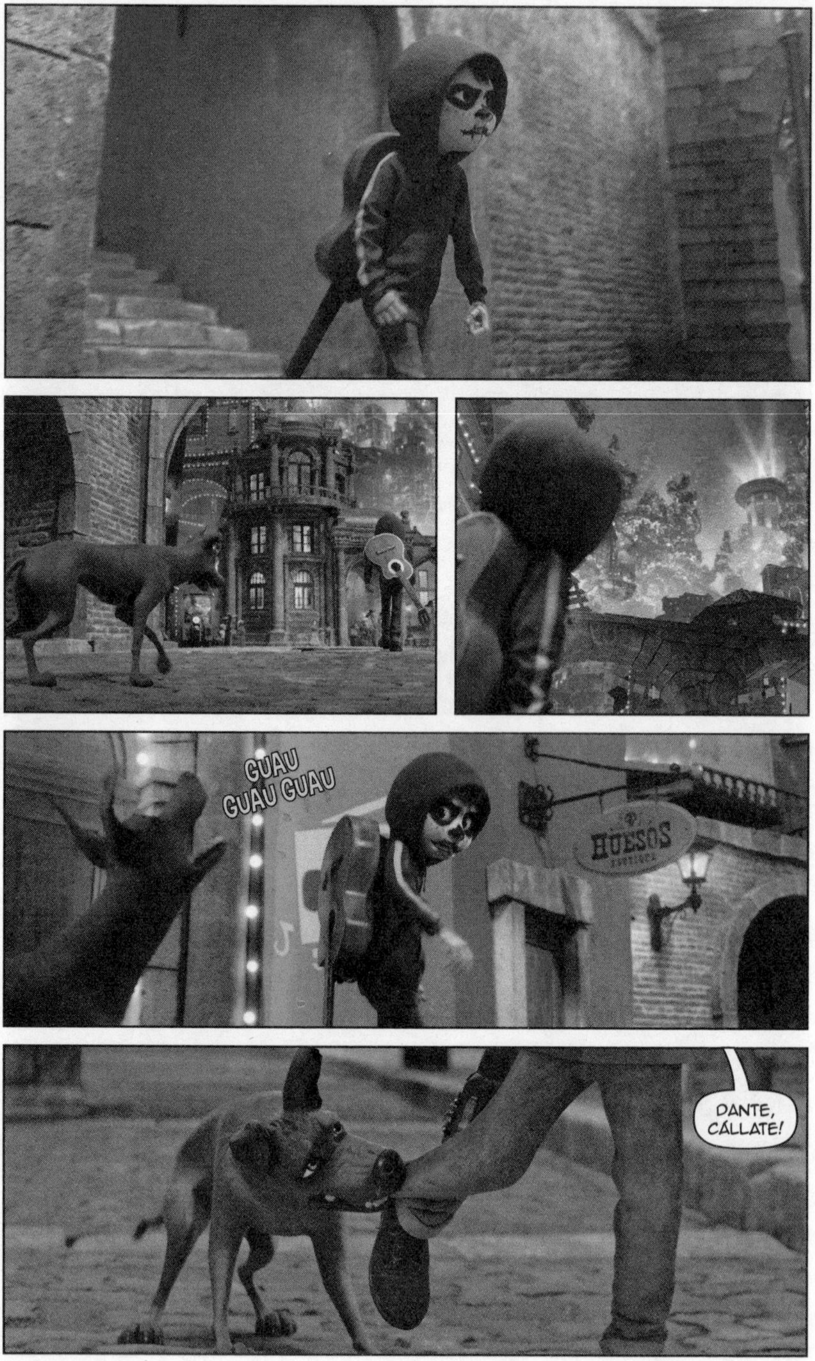
GUAU
GUAU GUAU
HUESOS
DANTE,
CÁLLATE!

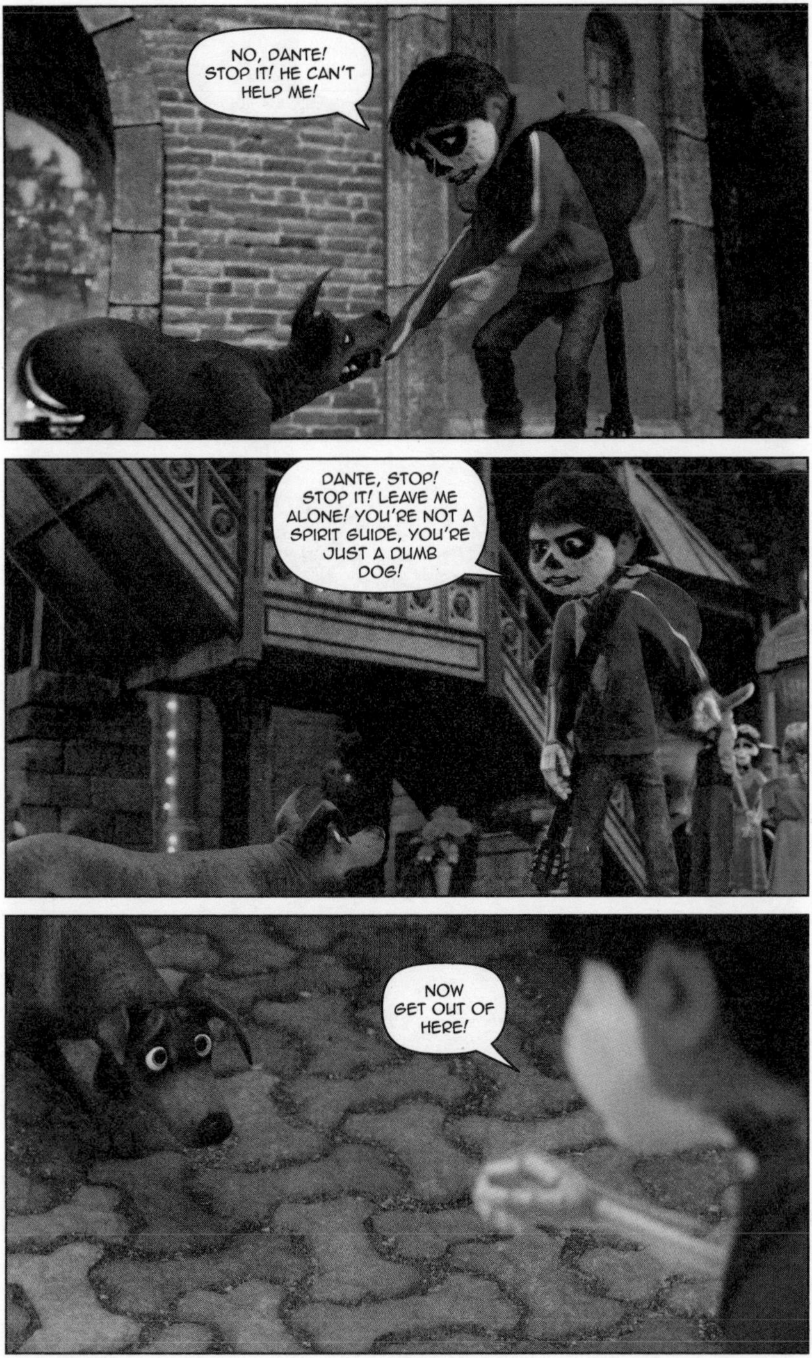
NO, DANTE! STOP IT! HE CAN'T HELP ME!
DANTE, STOP! STOP IT! LEAVE ME ALONE! YOU'RE NOT A SPIRIT GUIDE, YOU'RE JUST A DUMB DOG!
NOW GET OUT OF HERE!

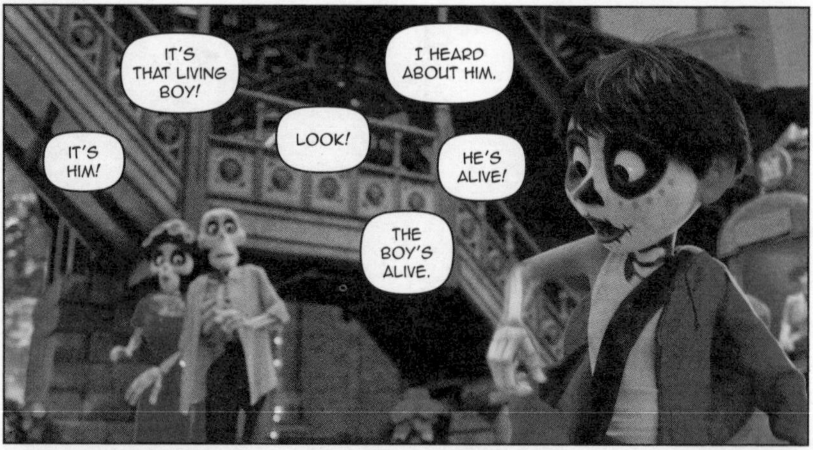
IT'S HIM!
IT'S THAT LIVING BOY!
LOOK!
I HEARD ABOUT HIM.
HE'S ALIVE!
THE BOY'S ALIVE.

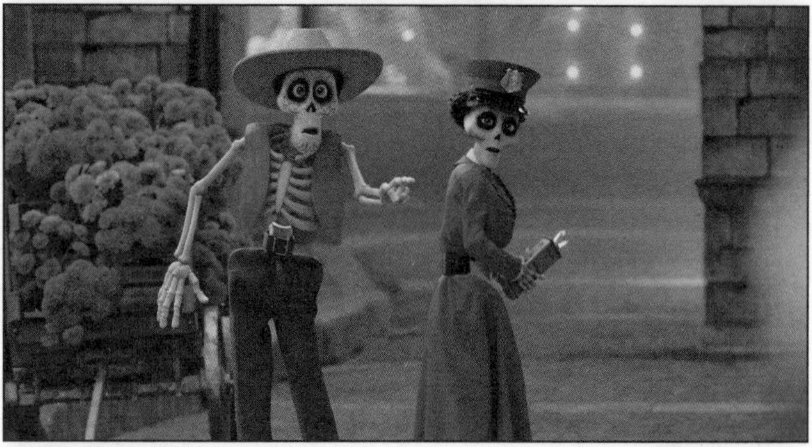

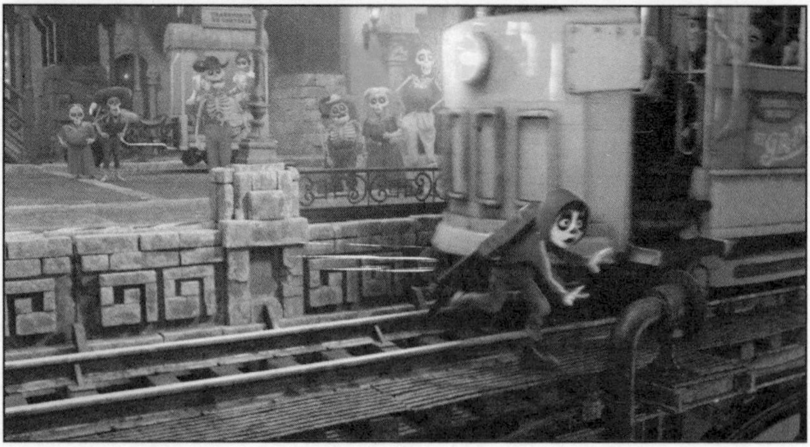

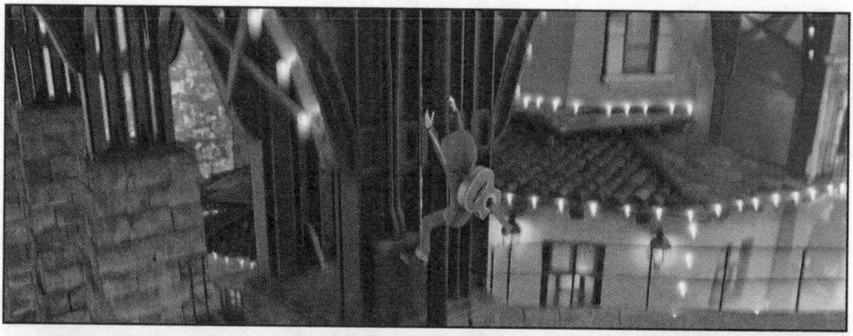

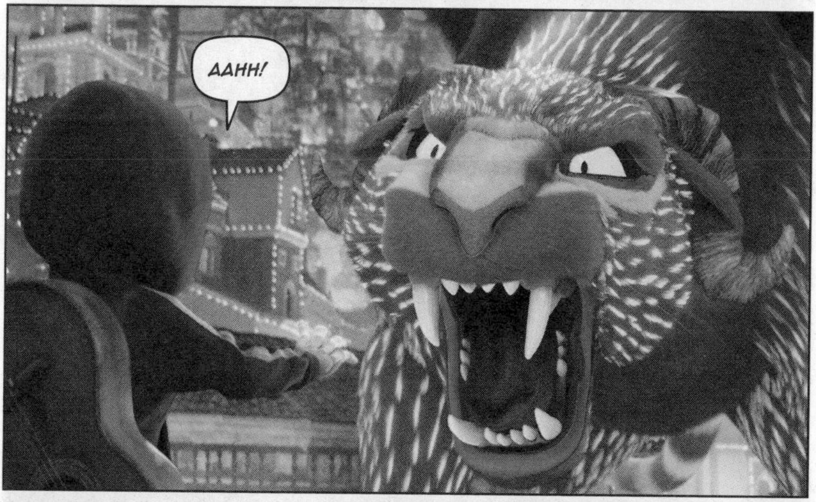
AAHH!

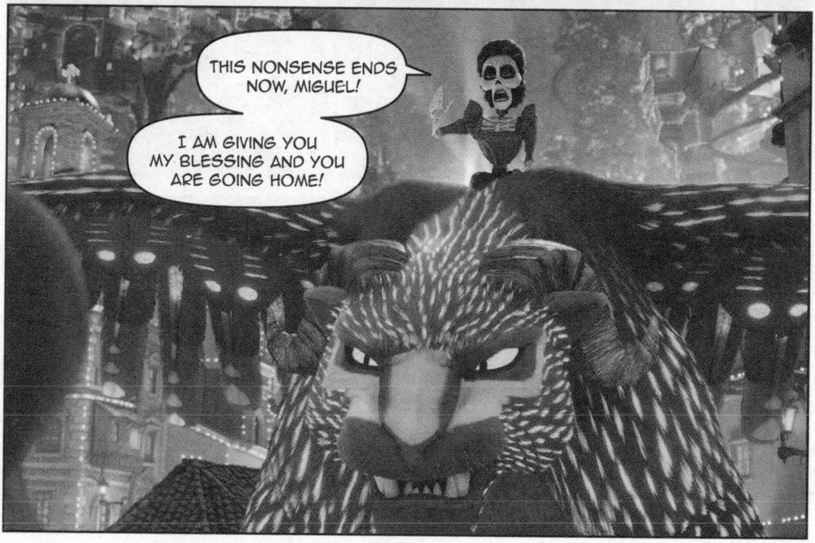
THIS NONSENSE ENDS NOW, MIGUEL!
I AM GIVING YOU MY BLESSING AND YOU ARE GOING HOME!

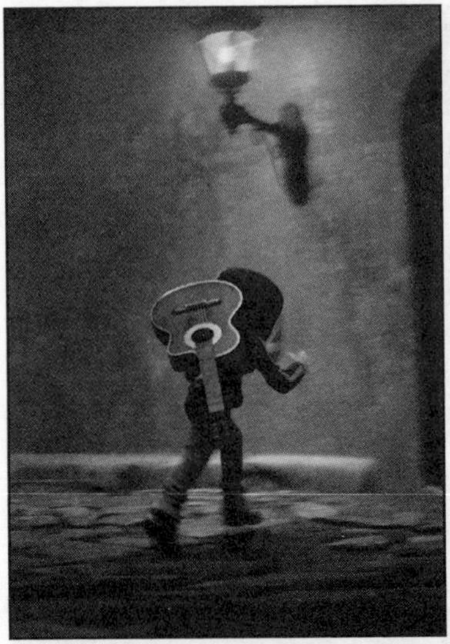

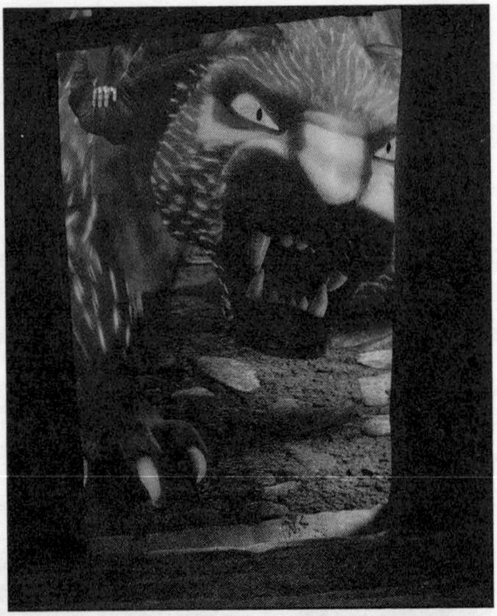

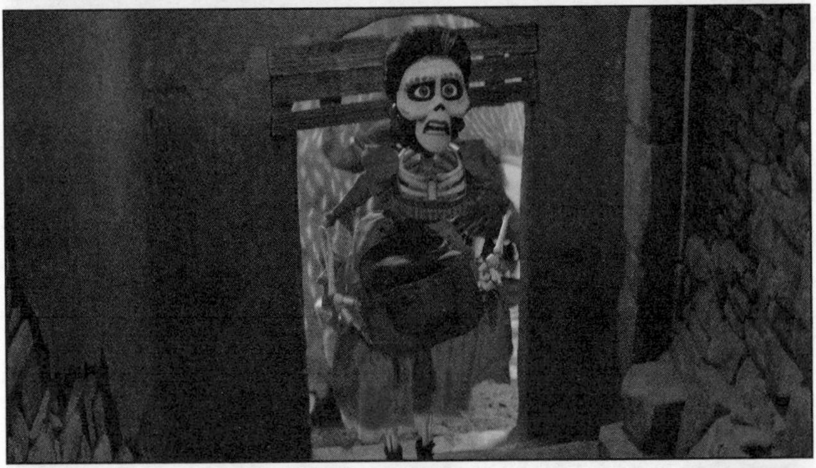

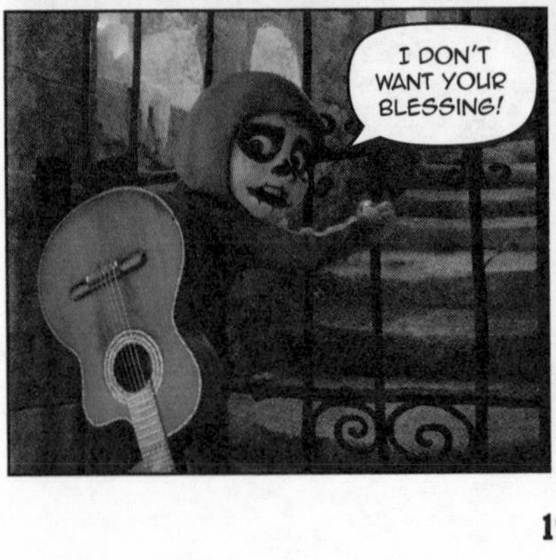
I DON'T WANT YOUR BLESSING!

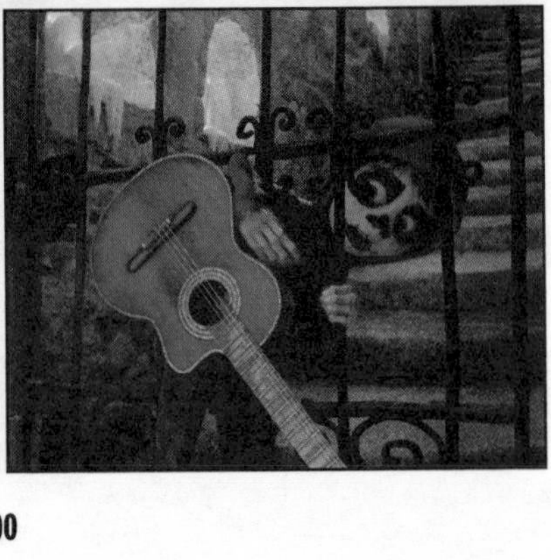

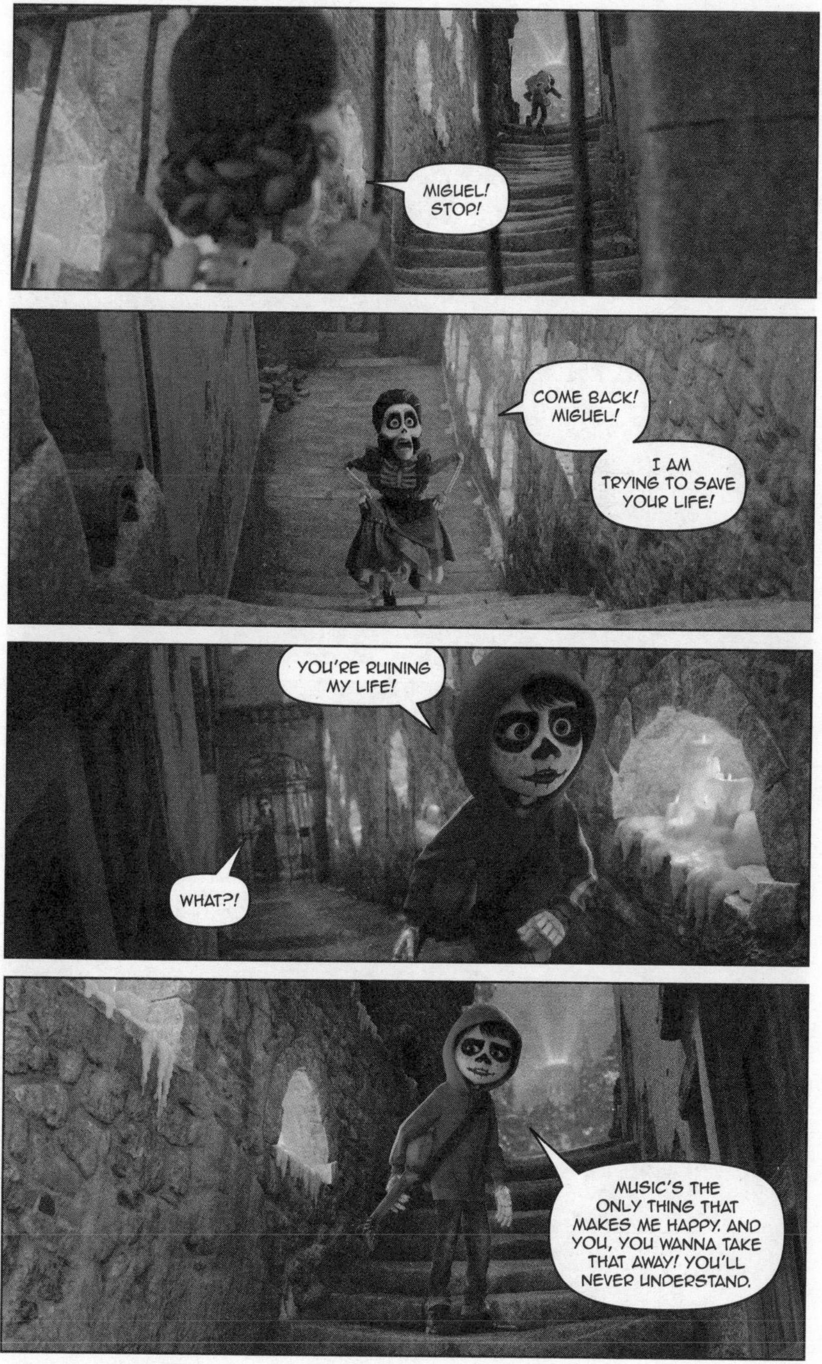
MIGUEL! STOP!
COME BACK! MIGUEL!
I AM TRYING TO SAVE YOUR LIFE!
YOU'RE RUINING MY LIFE!
WHAT?!
MUSIC'S THE ONLY THING THAT MAKES ME HAPPY. AND YOU, YOU WANNA TAKE THAT AWAY! YOU'LL NEVER UNDERSTAND.

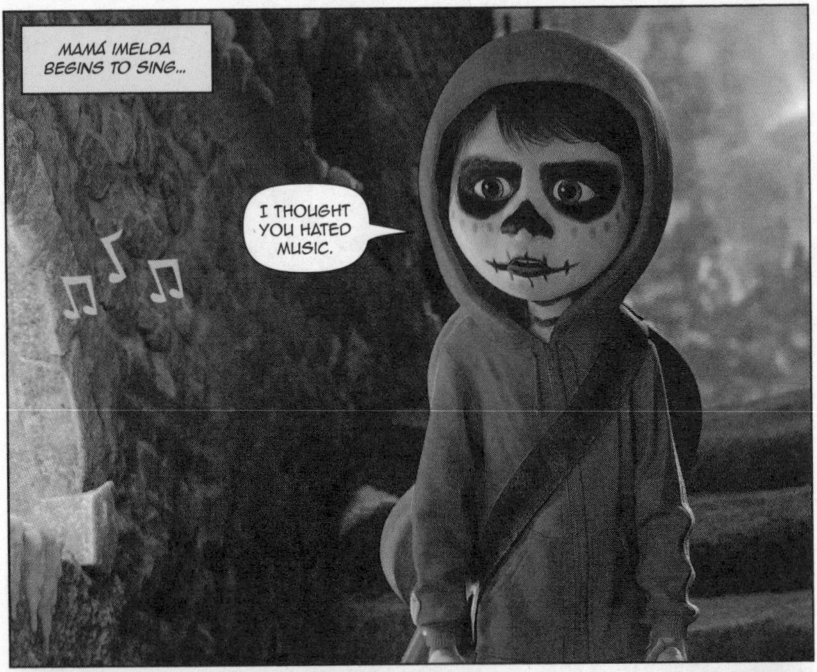
MAMÁ IMELDA BEGINS TO SING...
I THOUGHT YOU HATED MUSIC.

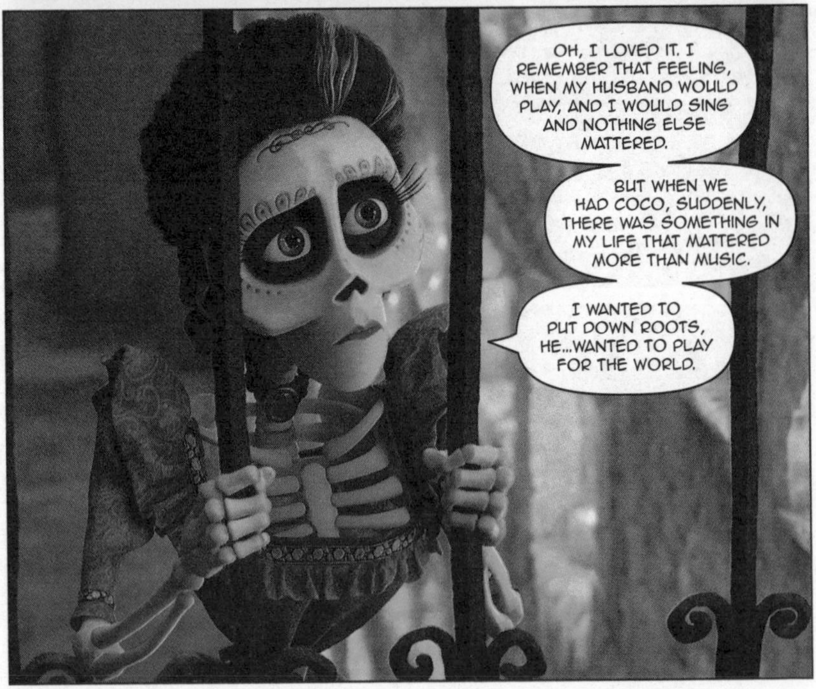
OH, I LOVED IT. I REMEMBER THAT FEELING, WHEN MY HUSBAND WOULD PLAY, AND I WOULD SING AND NOTHING ELSE MATTERED.
BUT WHEN WE HAD COCO, SUDDENLY, THERE WAS SOMETHING IN MY LIFE THAT MATTERED MORE THAN MUSIC.
I WANTED TO PUT DOWN ROOTS, HE...WANTED TO PLAY FOR THE WORLD.

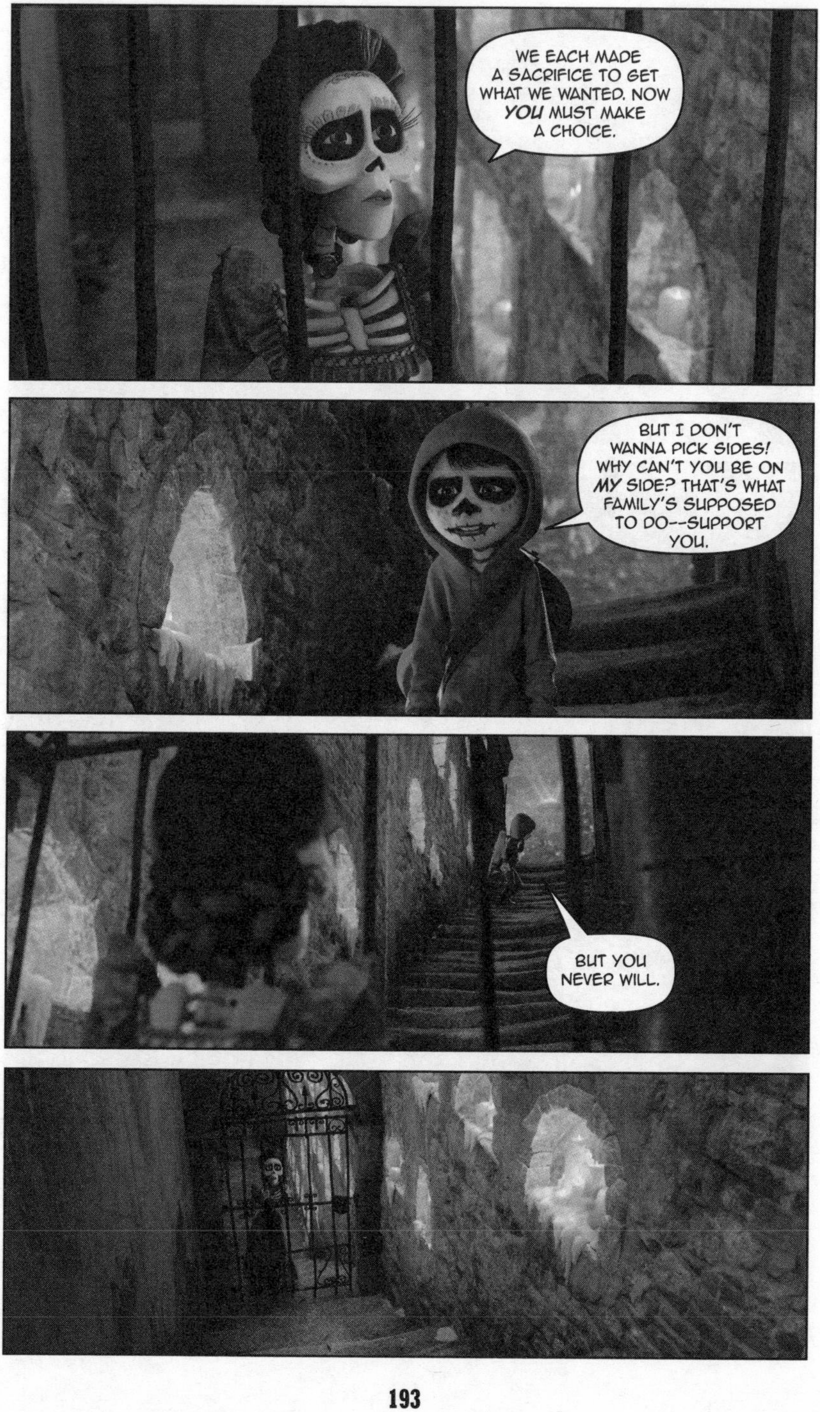
WE EACH MADE A SACRIFICE TO GET WHAT WE WANTED. NOW *YOU* MUST MAKE A CHOICE.
BUT I DON'T WANNA PICK SIDES! WHY CAN'T YOU BE ON *MY* SIDE? THAT'S WHAT FAMILY'S SUPPOSED TO DO--SUPPORT YOU.
BUT YOU NEVER WILL.

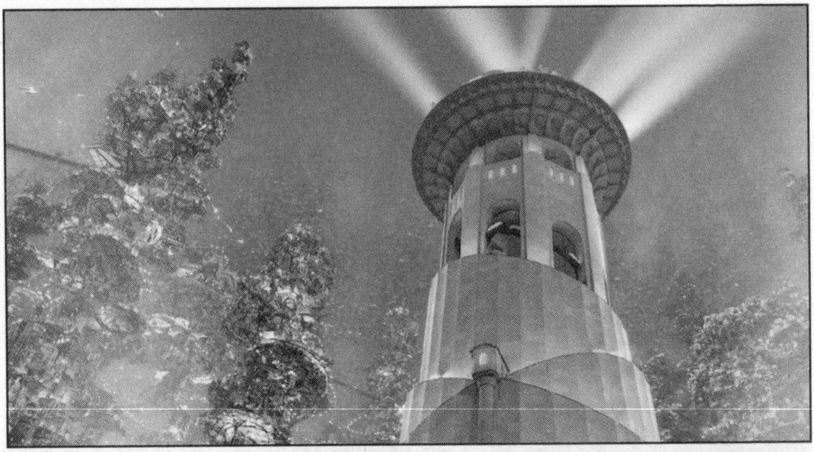

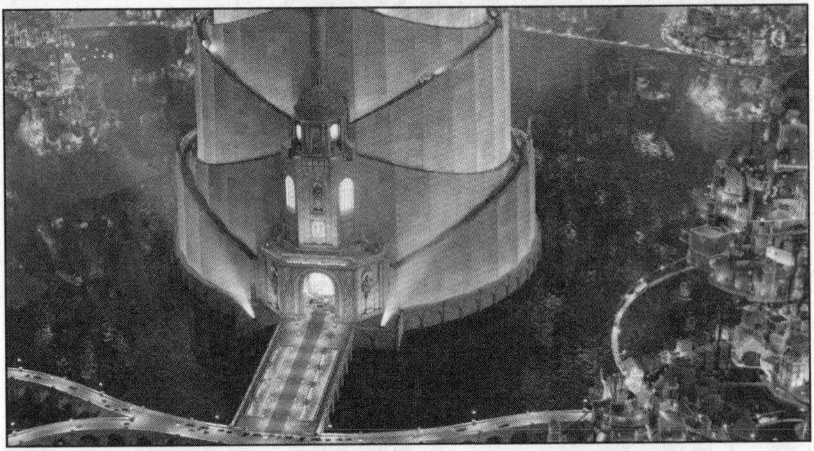

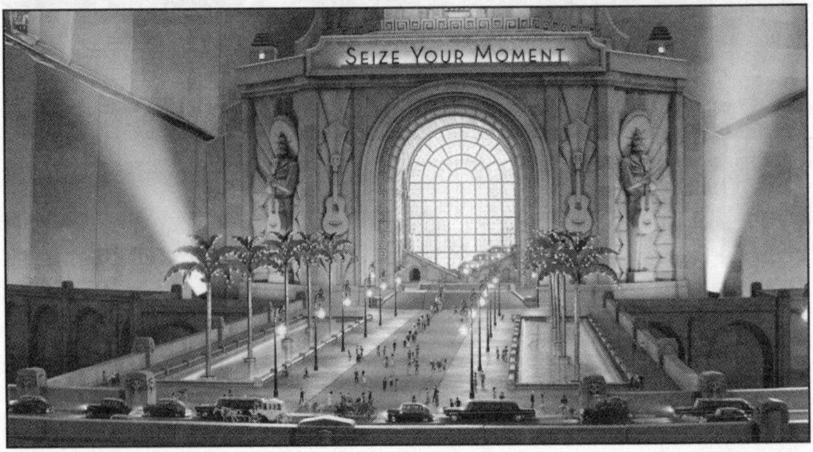
SEIZE YOUR MOMENT

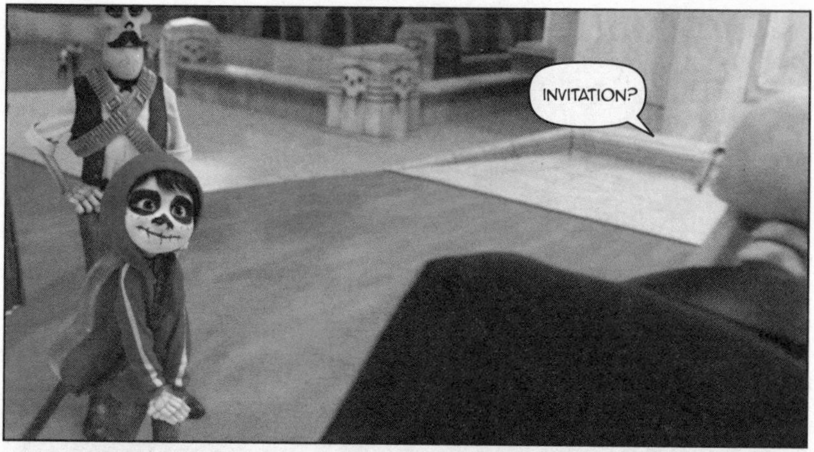
INVITATION?

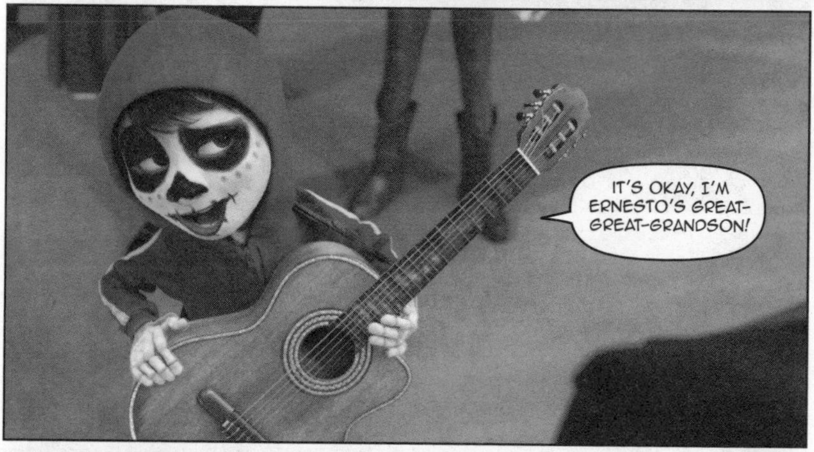
IT'S OKAY, I'M ERNESTO'S GREAT-GREAT-GRANDSON!

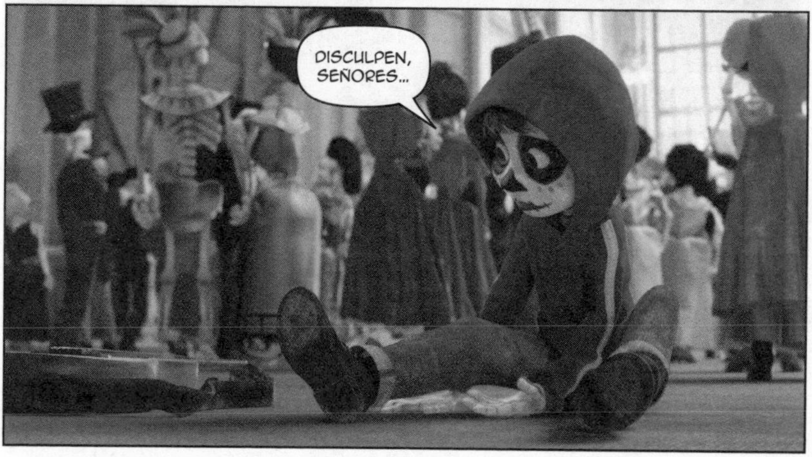
DISCULPEN, SEÑORES...

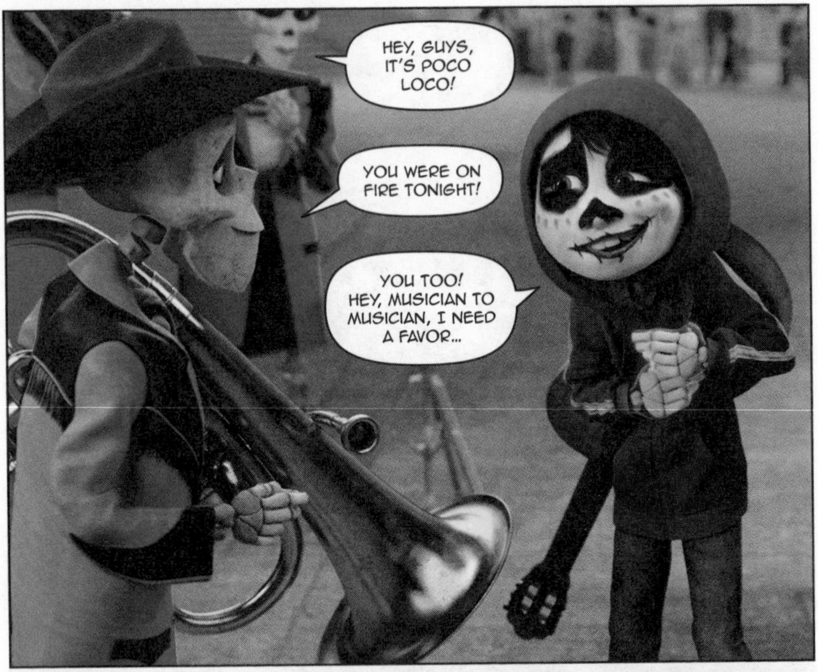
HEY, GUYS, IT'S POCO LOCO!
YOU WERE ON FIRE TONIGHT!
YOU TOO! HEY, MUSICIAN TO MUSICIAN, I NEED A FAVOR...

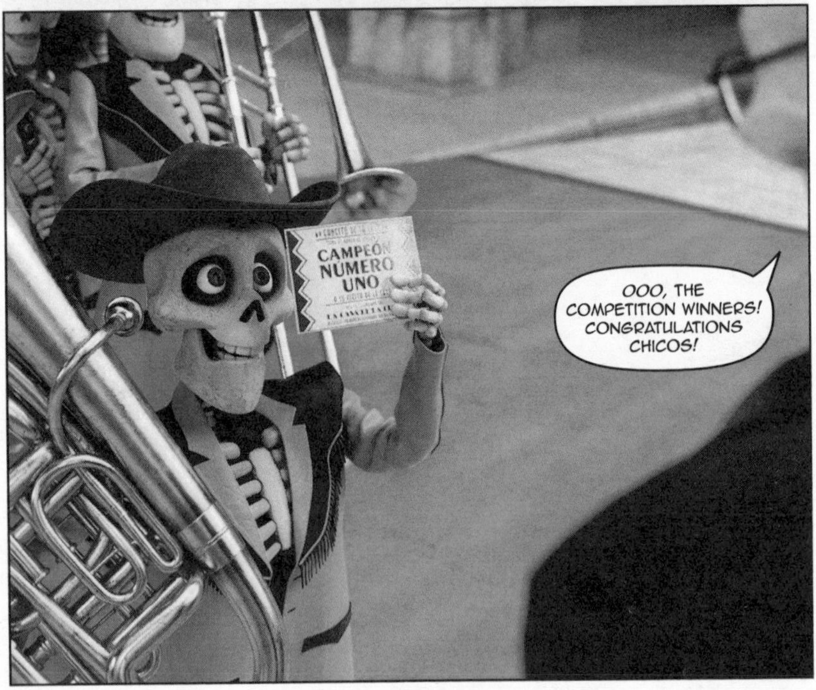
CAMPEÓN NUMERO UNO
OOO, THE COMPETITION WINNERS! CONGRATULATIONS CHICOS!

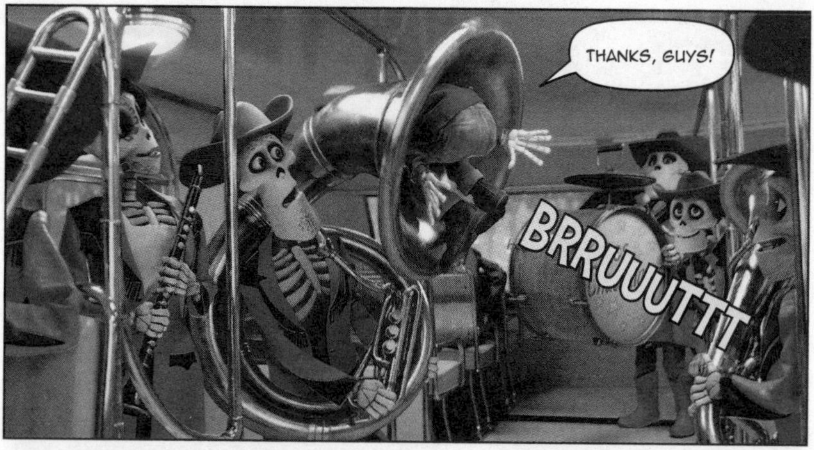
THANKS, GUYS!
BRRUUUTTT

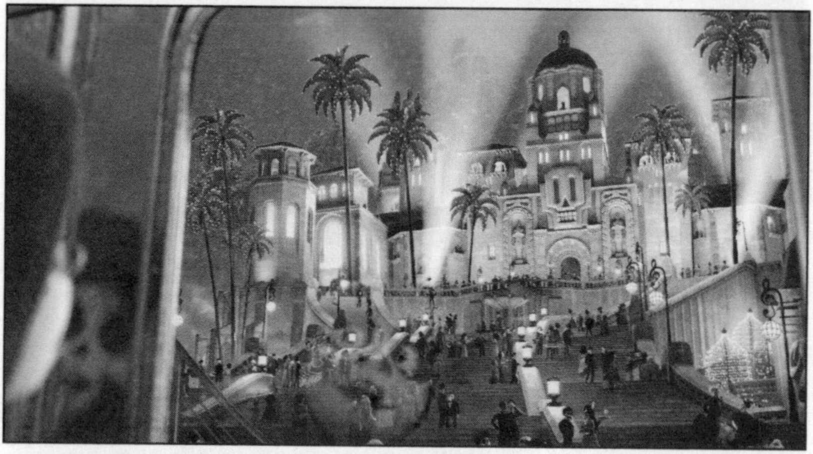

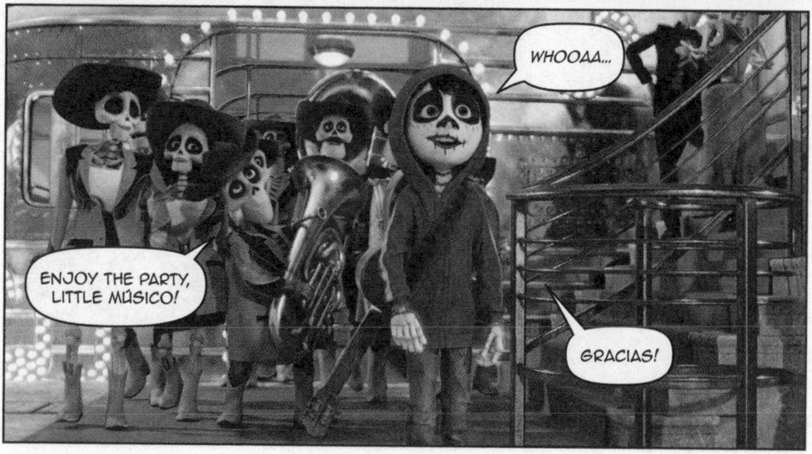
WHOOAA...
ENJOY THE PARTY, LITTLE MÚSICO!
GRACIAS!

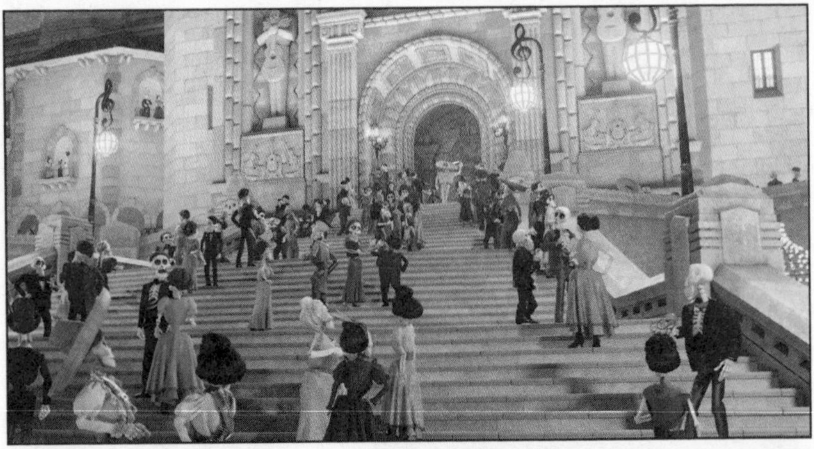

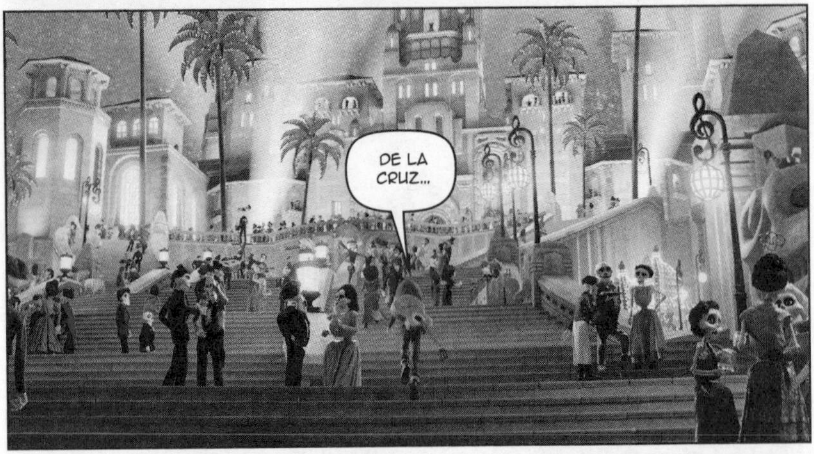
DE LA CRUZ...

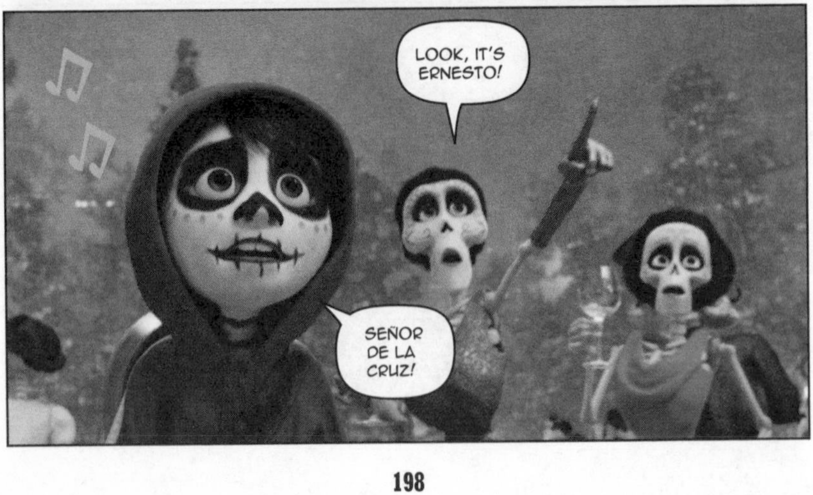
LOOK, IT'S ERNESTO!
SEÑOR DE LA CRUZ!

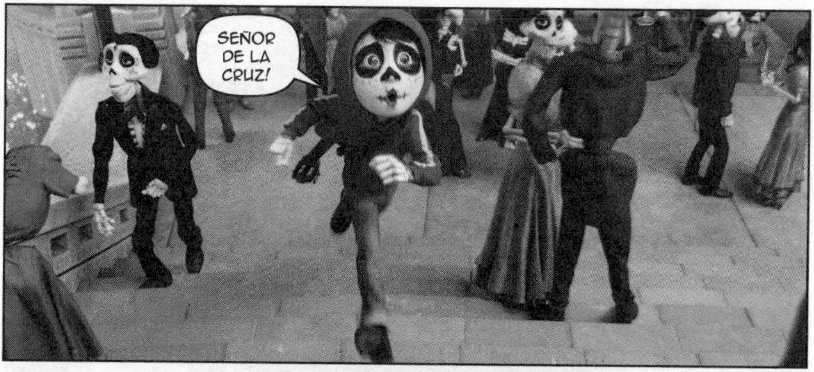
SEÑOR DE LA CRUZ!

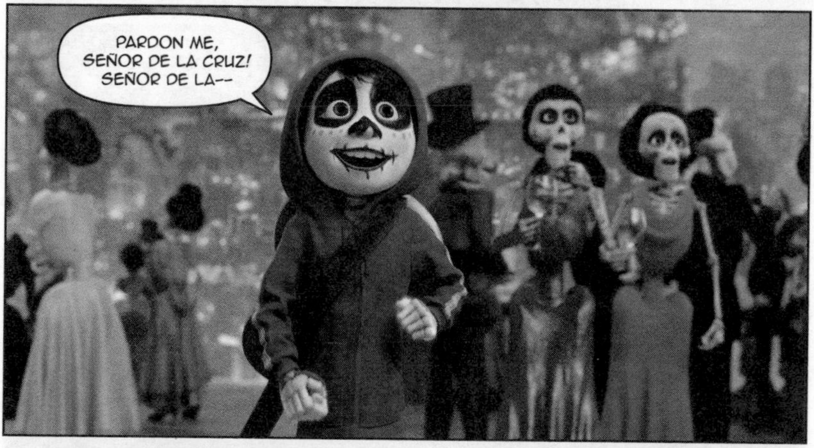
PARDON ME, SEÑOR DE LA CRUZ! SEÑOR DE LA--

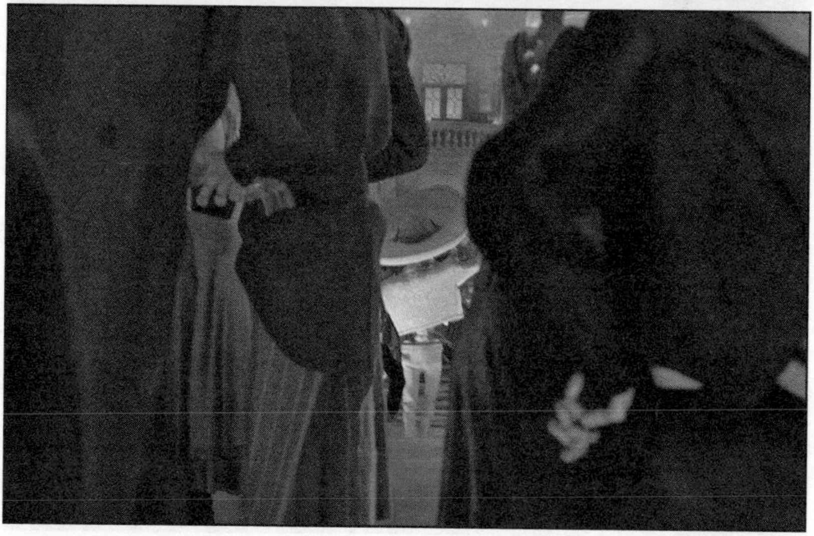

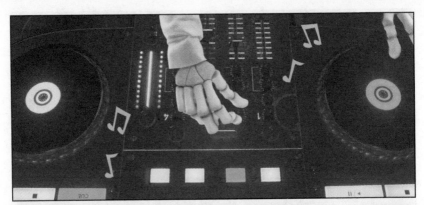

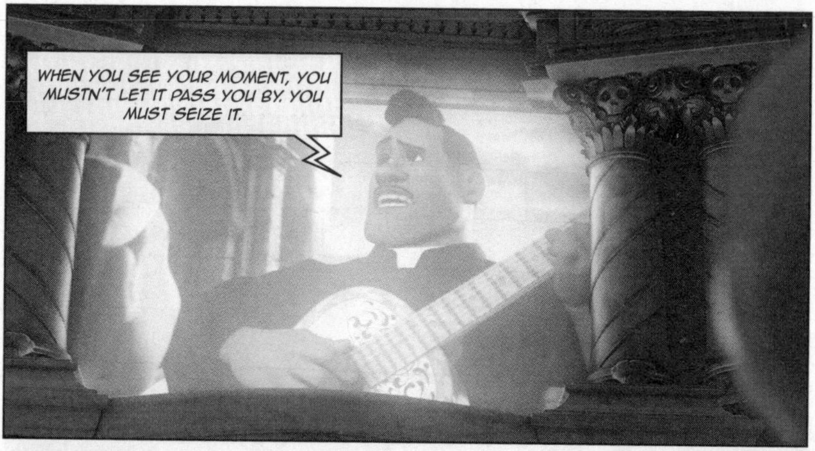
WHEN YOU SEE YOUR MOMENT, YOU MUSTN'T LET IT PASS YOU BY. YOU MUST SEIZE IT.

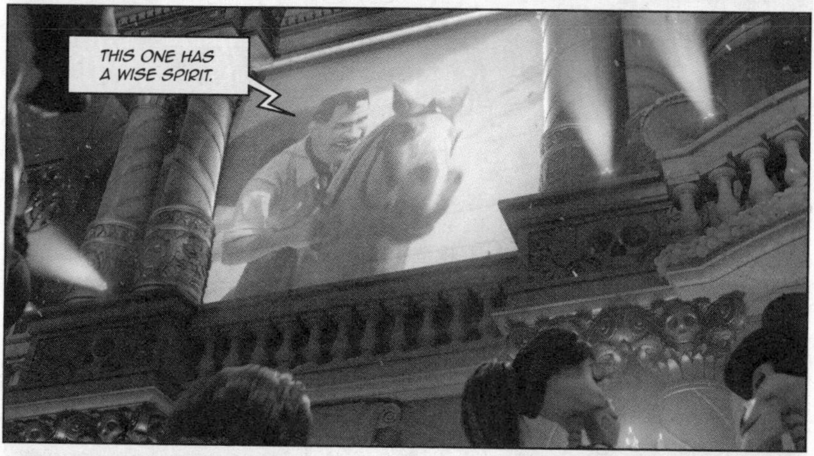
THIS ONE HAS A WISE SPIRIT.

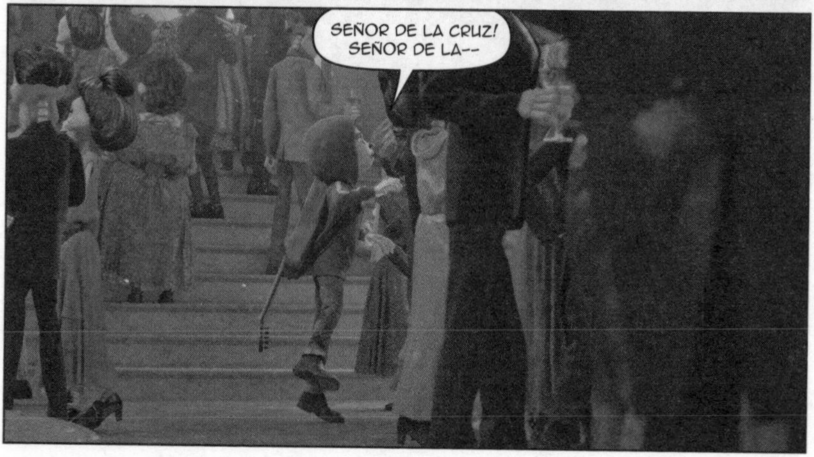
SEÑOR DE LA CRUZ! SEÑOR DE LA--

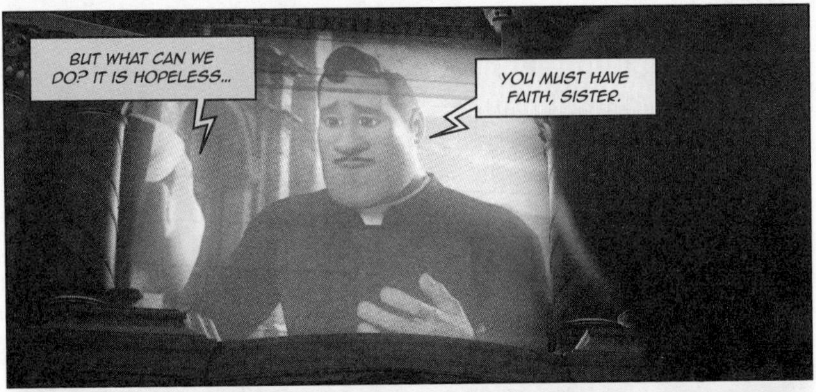
BUT WHAT CAN WE DO? IT IS HOPELESS...
YOU MUST HAVE FAITH, SISTER.

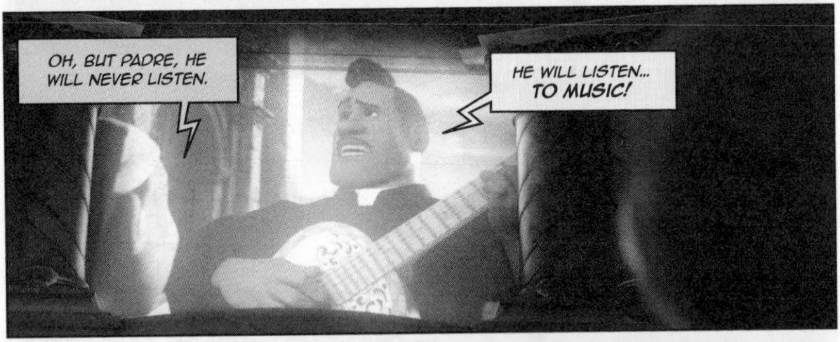
OH, BUT PADRE, HE WILL NEVER LISTEN.
HE WILL LISTEN... TO MUSIC!

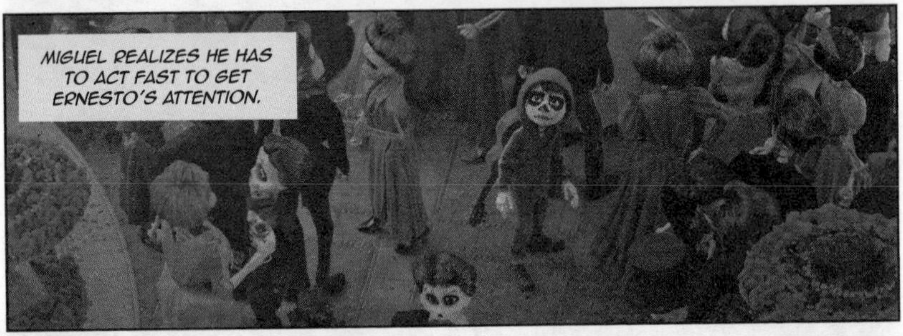
MIGUEL REALIZES HE HAS TO ACT FAST TO GET ERNESTO'S ATTENTION.

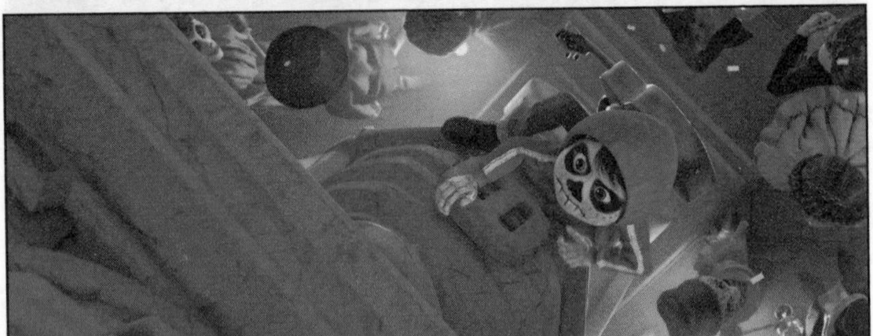

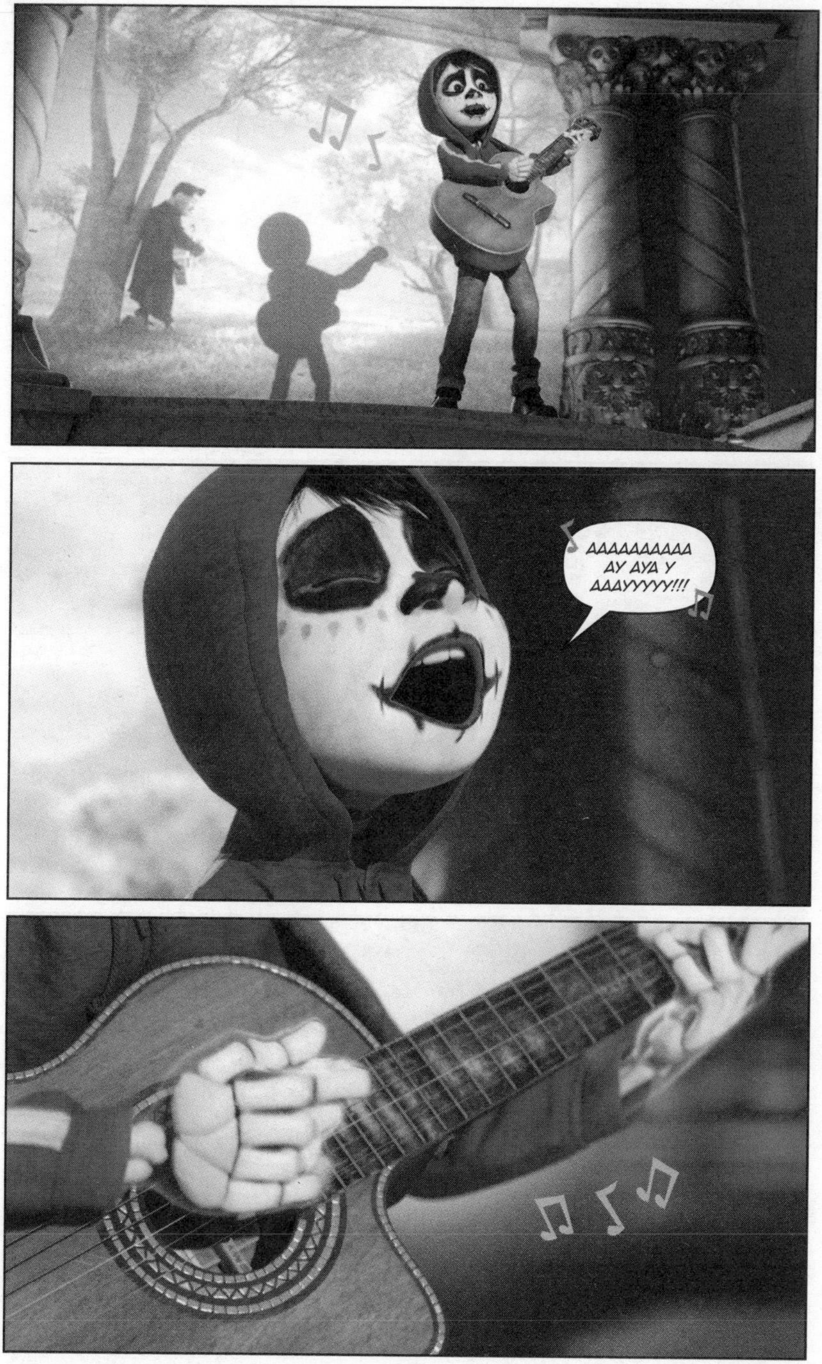
AAAAAAAAAAA
AY AYA Y
AAAAYYYYY!!!

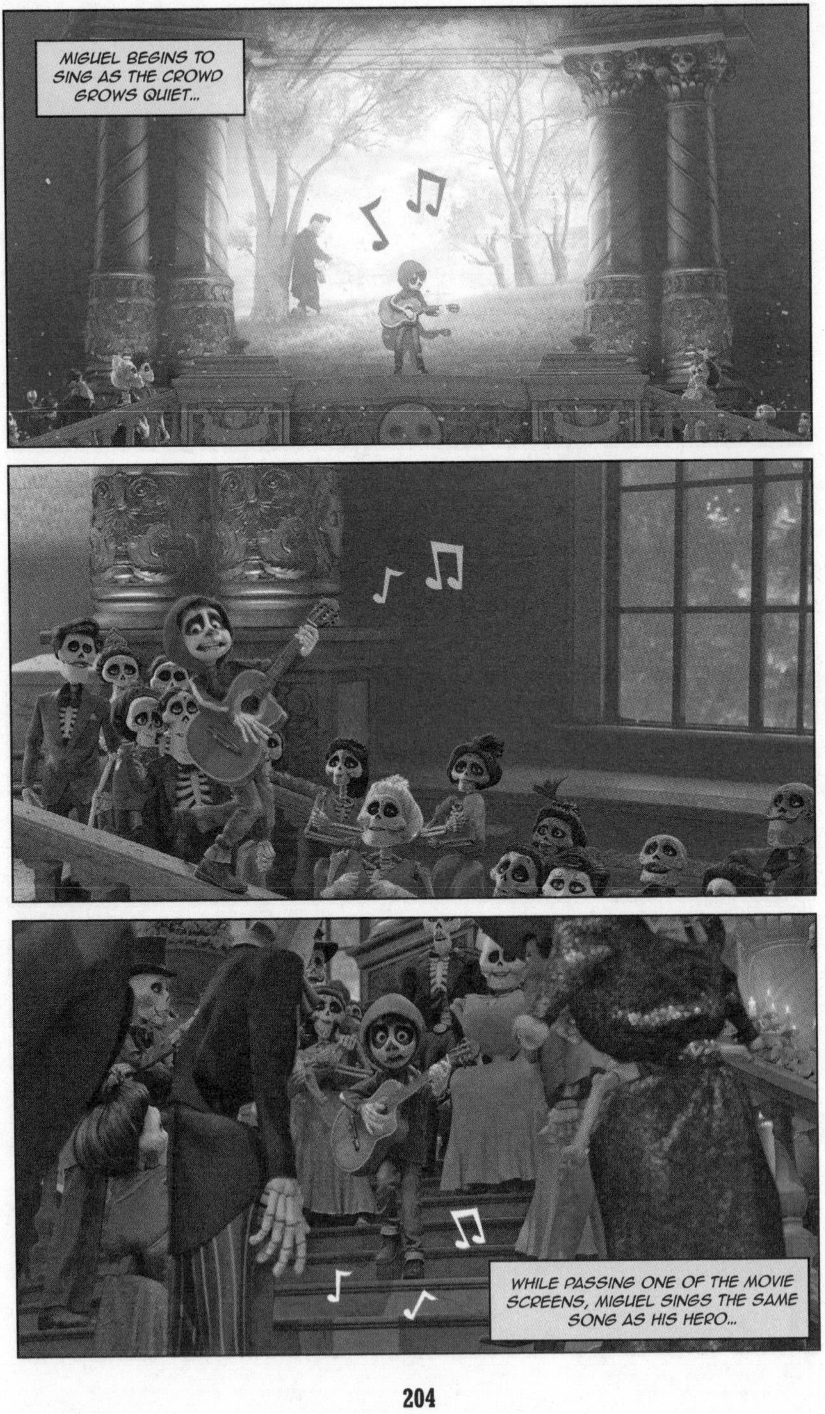
MIGUEL BEGINS TO SING AS THE CROWD GROWS QUIET...
WHILE PASSING ONE OF THE MOVIE SCREENS, MIGUEL SINGS THE SAME SONG AS HIS HERO...

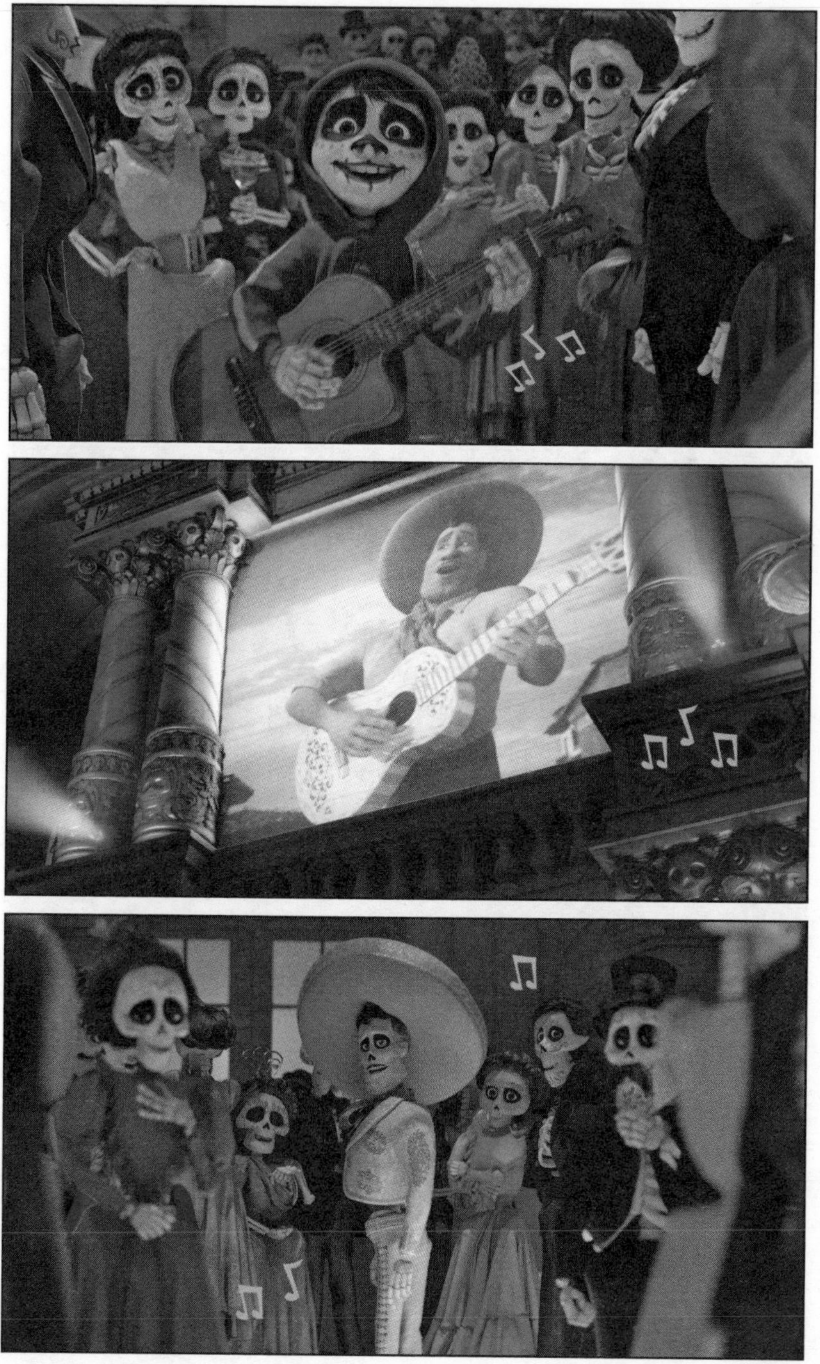

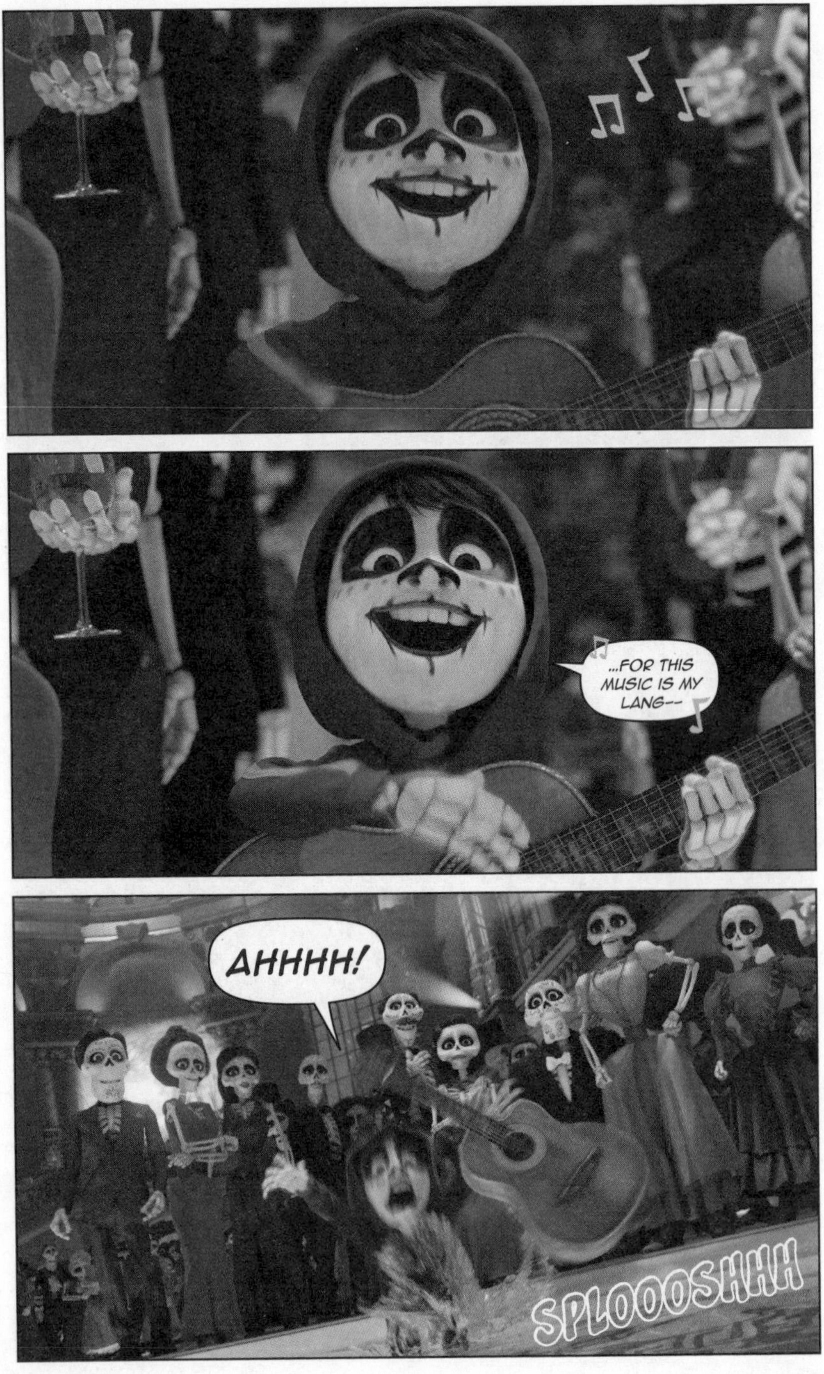
...FOR THIS MUSIC IS MY LANG--
AHHHH!
SPLOOOSHHH

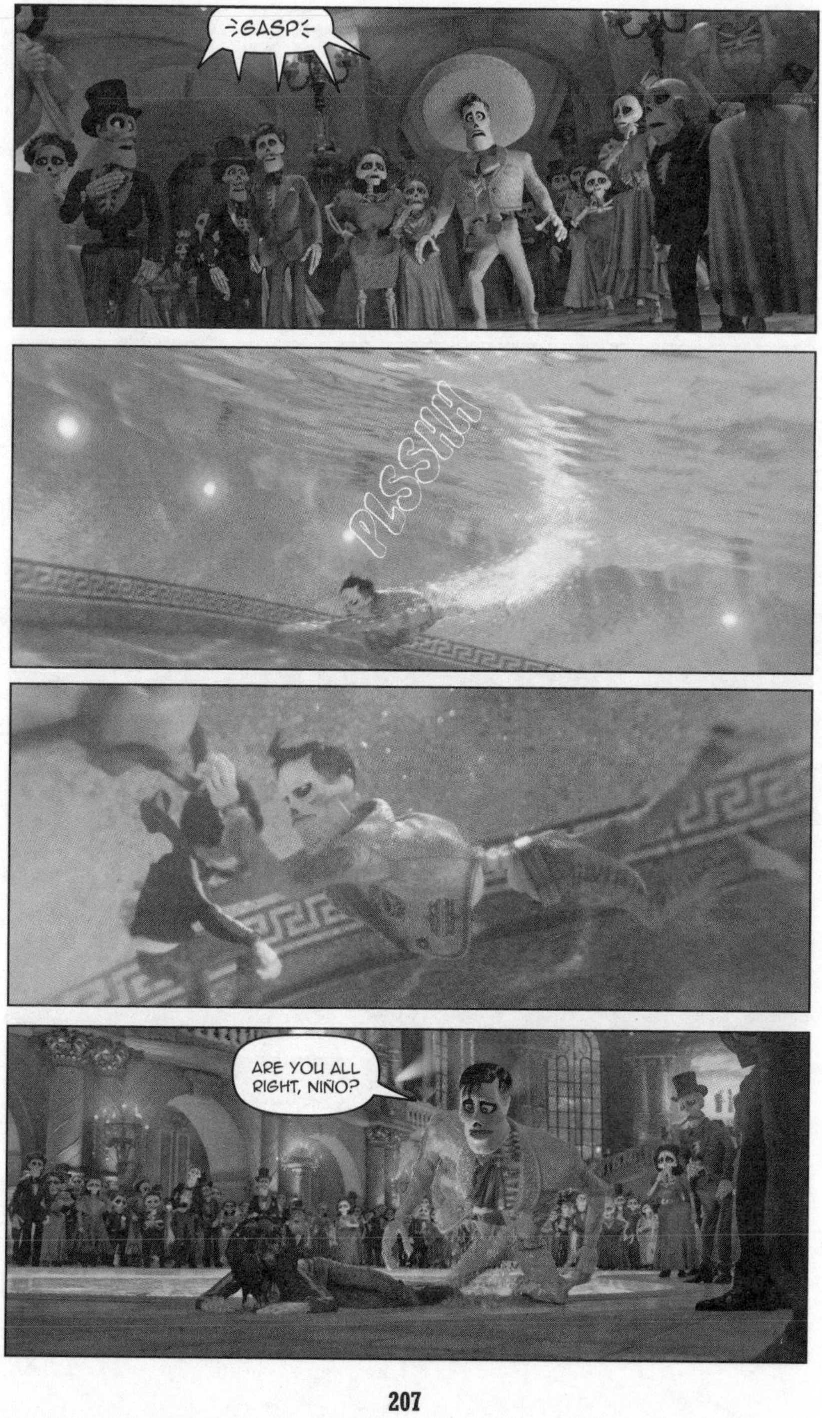
GASP
PLSSHH
ARE YOU ALL RIGHT, NIÑO?

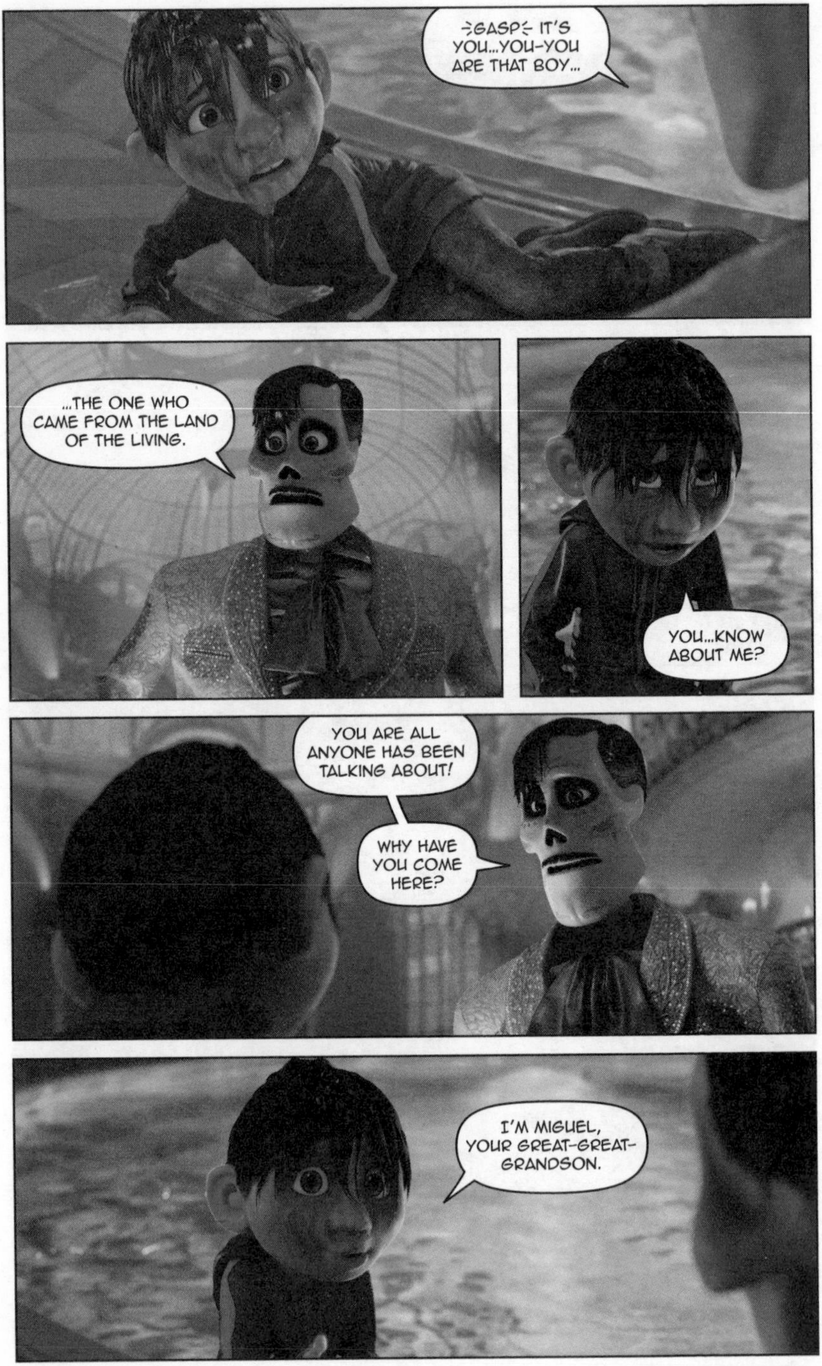

⁼GASP⁼ IT'S YOU...YOU-YOU ARE THAT BOY...
...THE ONE WHO CAME FROM THE LAND OF THE LIVING.
YOU...KNOW ABOUT ME?
YOU ARE ALL ANYONE HAS BEEN TALKING ABOUT!
WHY HAVE YOU COME HERE?
I'M MIGUEL, YOUR GREAT-GREAT-GRANDSON.

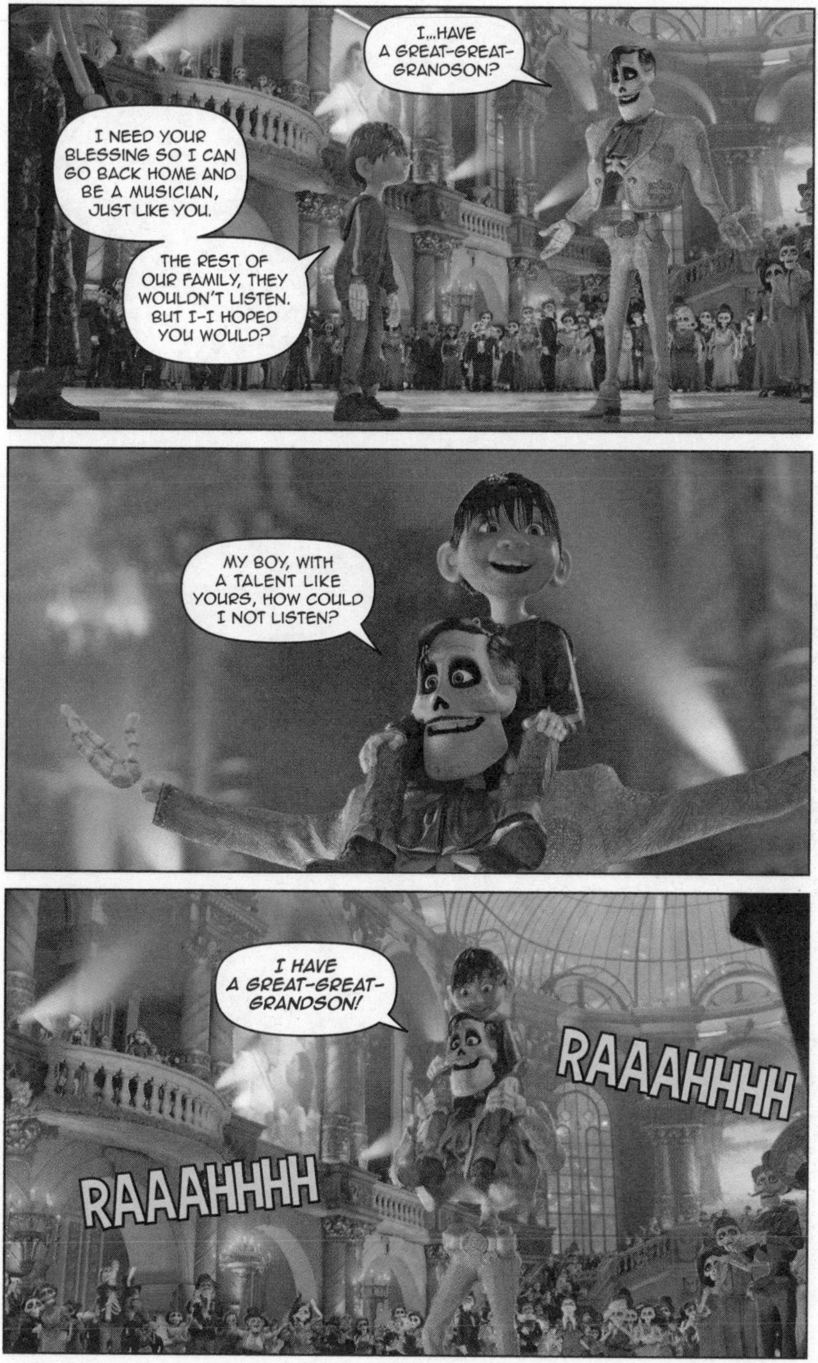
I...HAVE A GREAT-GREAT-GRANDSON?
I NEED YOUR BLESSING SO I CAN GO BACK HOME AND BE A MUSICIAN, JUST LIKE YOU.
THE REST OF OUR FAMILY, THEY WOULDN'T LISTEN. BUT I-I HOPED YOU WOULD?
MY BOY, WITH A TALENT LIKE YOURS, HOW COULD I NOT LISTEN?
I HAVE A GREAT-GREAT-GRANDSON!
RAAAHHHH
RAAAHHHH

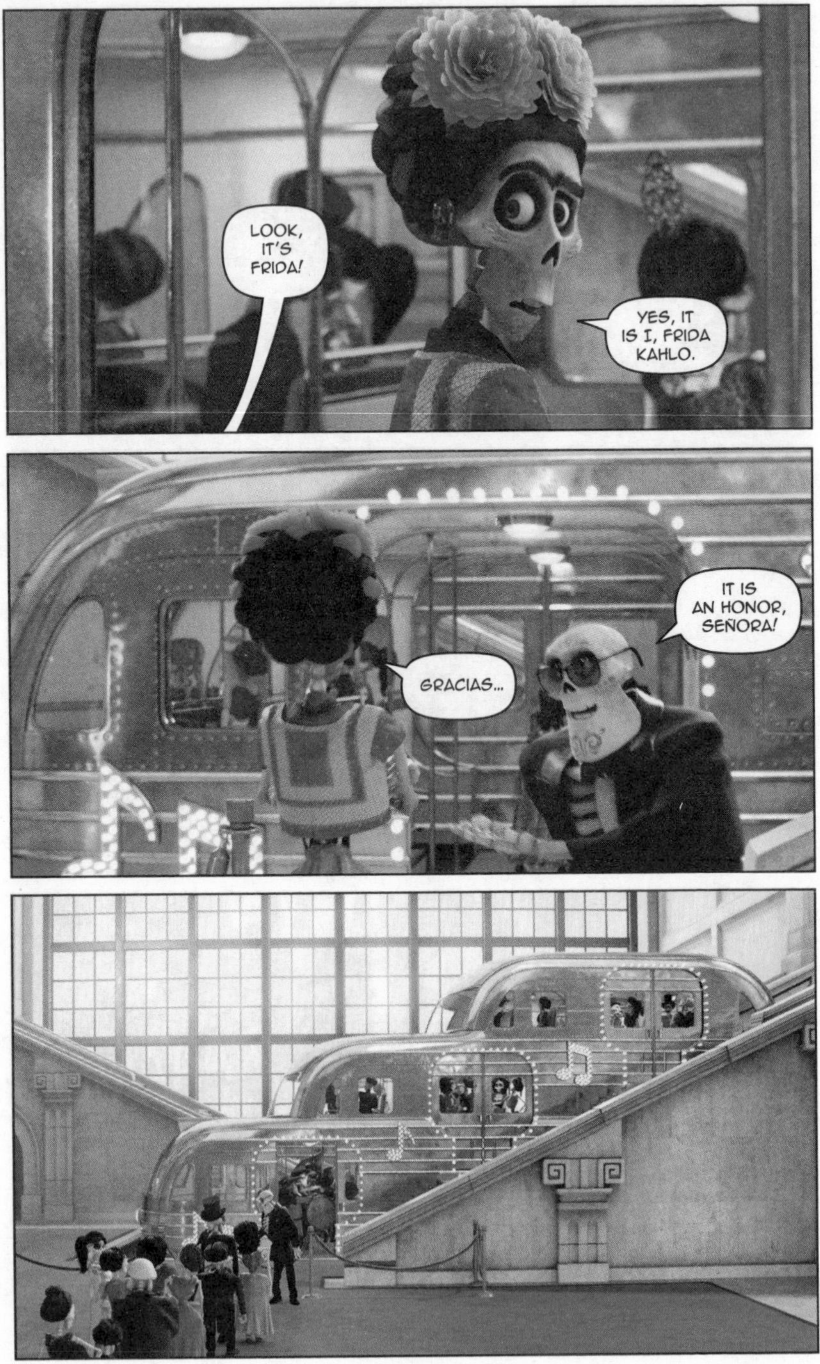
LOOK, IT'S FRIDA!
YES, IT IS I, FRIDA KAHLO.
IT IS AN HONOR, SEÑORA!
GRACIAS...

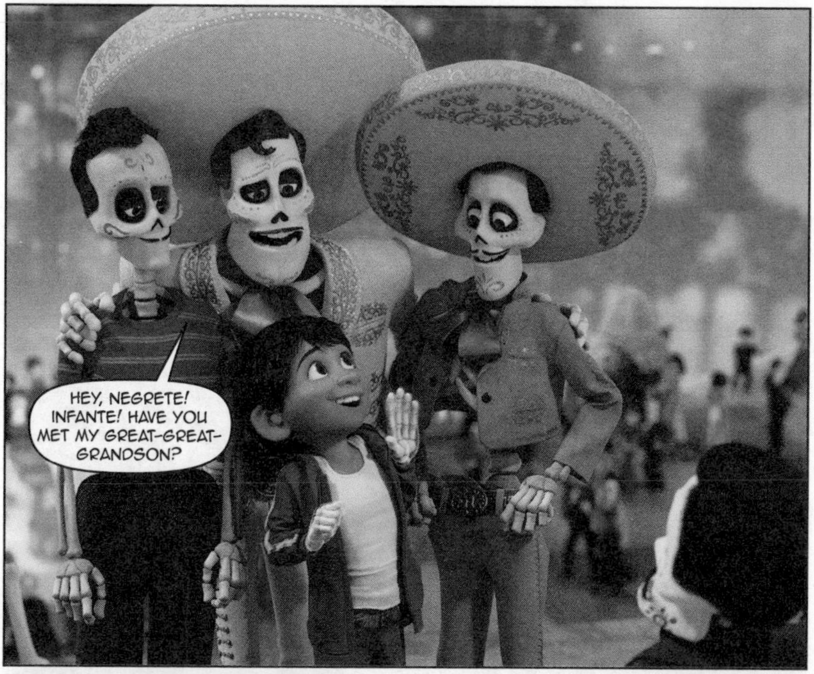
HEY, NEGRETE! INFANTE! HAVE YOU MET MY GREAT-GREAT-GRANDSON?

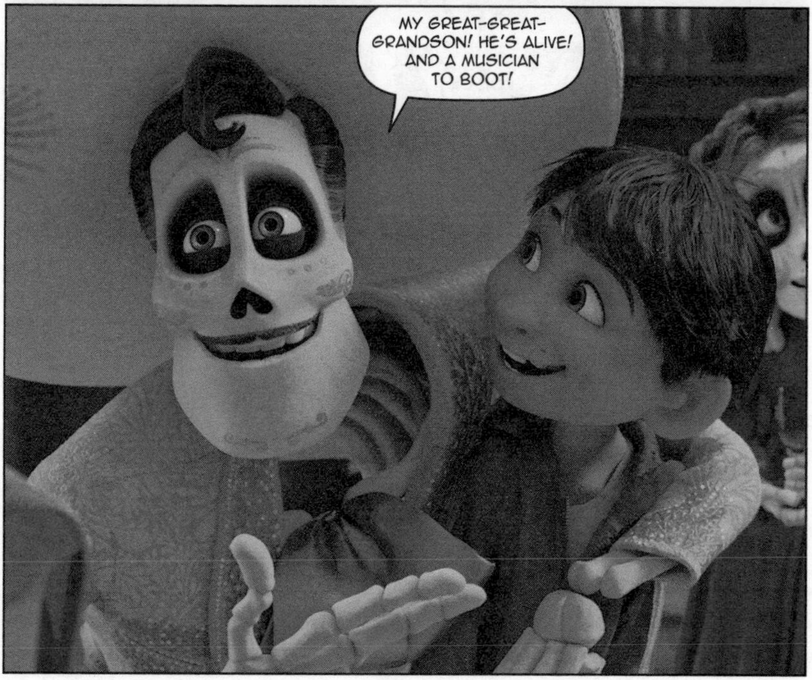
MY GREAT-GREAT-GRANDSON! HE'S ALIVE! AND A MUSICIAN TO BOOT!

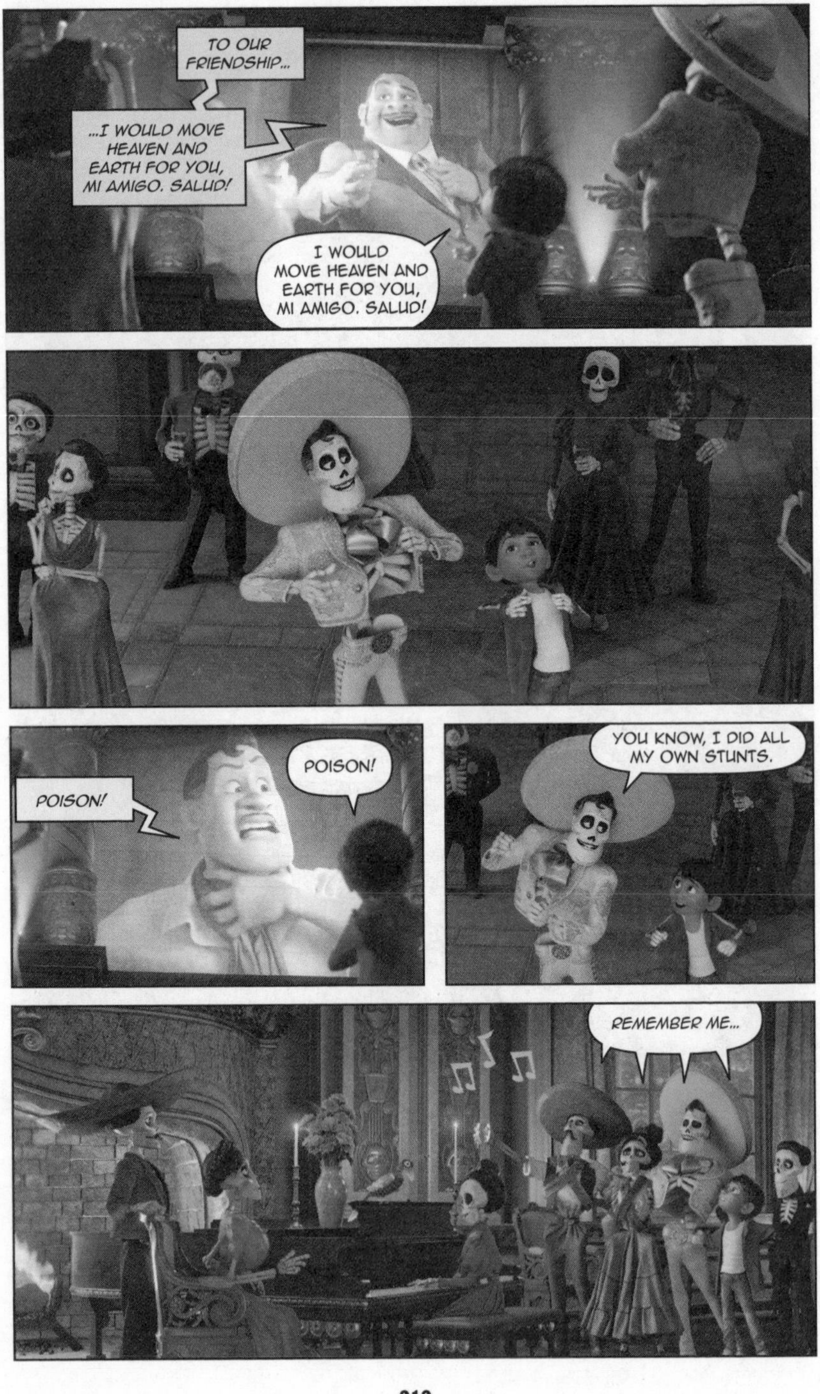
TO OUR FRIENDSHIP...
...I WOULD MOVE HEAVEN AND EARTH FOR YOU, MI AMIGO. SALUD!
I WOULD MOVE HEAVEN AND EARTH FOR YOU, MI AMIGO. SALUD!
POISON!
POISON!
YOU KNOW, I DID ALL MY OWN STUNTS.
REMEMBER ME...

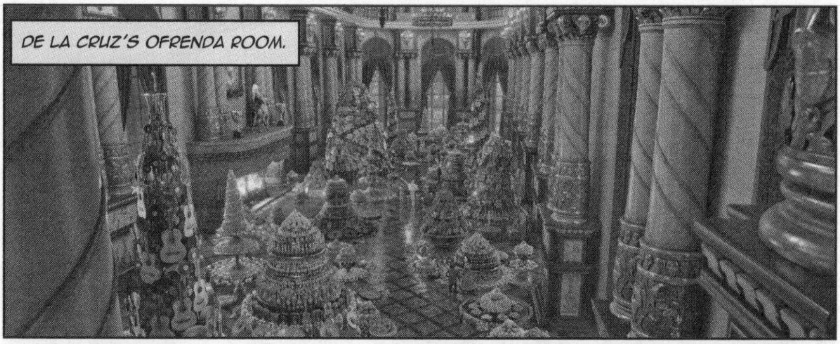
DE LA CRUZ'S OFRENDA ROOM.

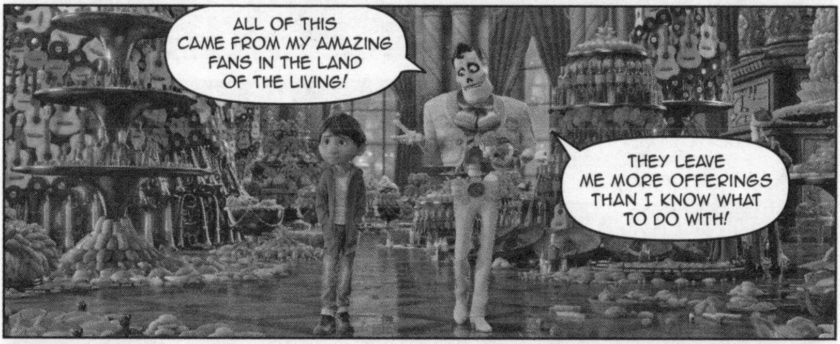
ALL OF THIS CAME FROM MY AMAZING FANS IN THE LAND OF THE LIVING!
THEY LEAVE ME MORE OFFERINGS THAN I KNOW WHAT TO DO WITH!

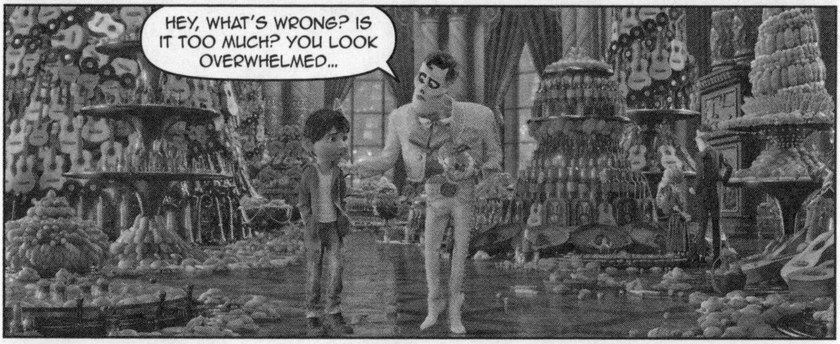
HEY, WHAT'S WRONG? IS IT TOO MUCH? YOU LOOK OVERWHELMED...

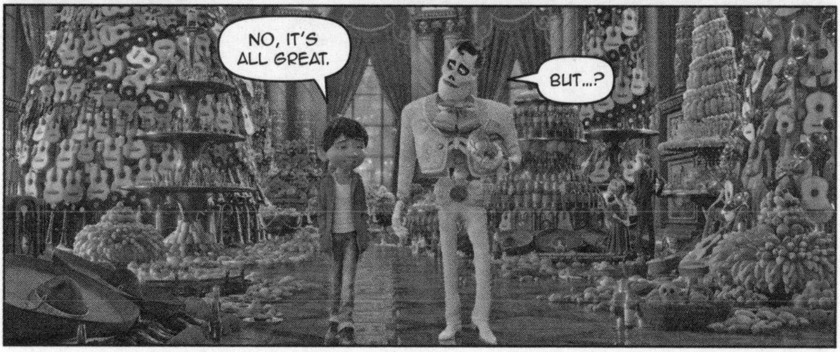
NO, IT'S ALL GREAT.
BUT...?

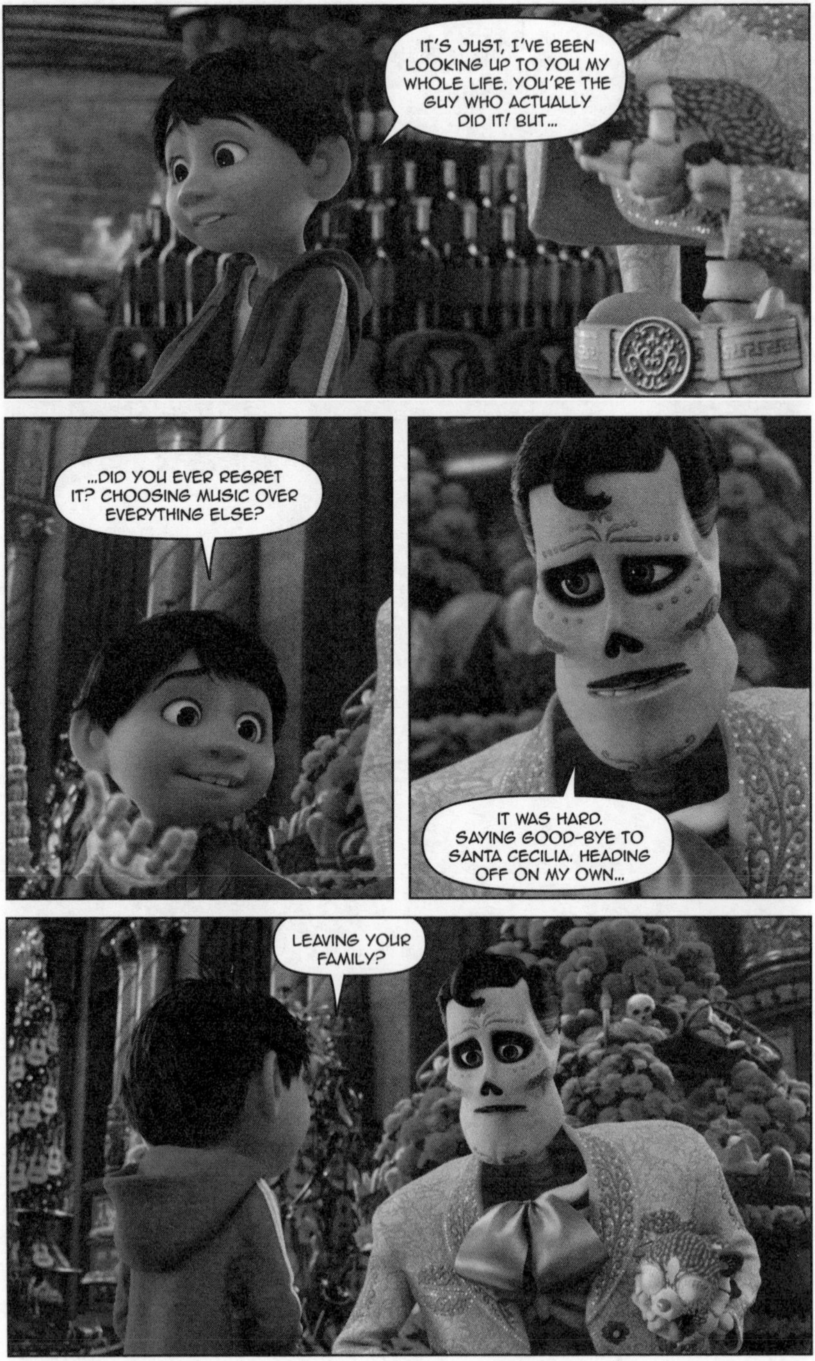
IT'S JUST, I'VE BEEN LOOKING UP TO YOU MY WHOLE LIFE. YOU'RE THE GUY WHO ACTUALLY DID IT! BUT...
...DID YOU EVER REGRET IT? CHOOSING MUSIC OVER EVERYTHING ELSE?
IT WAS HARD. SAYING GOOD-BYE TO SANTA CECILIA. HEADING OFF ON MY OWN...
LEAVING YOUR FAMILY?

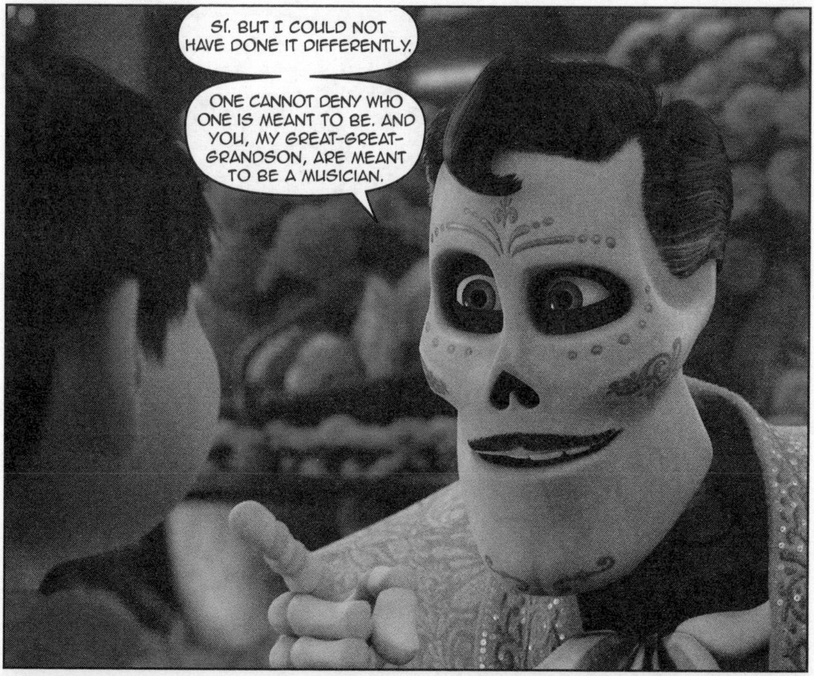
SÍ. BUT I COULD NOT HAVE DONE IT DIFFERENTLY.
ONE CANNOT DENY WHO ONE IS MEANT TO BE. AND YOU, MY GREAT-GREAT-GRANDSON, ARE MEANT TO BE A MUSICIAN.

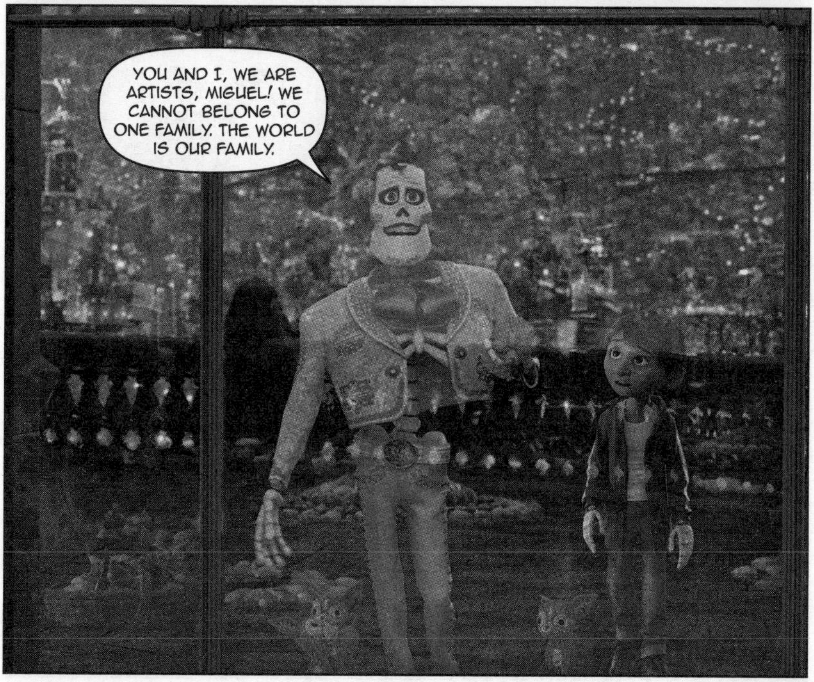
YOU AND I, WE ARE ARTISTS, MIGUEL! WE CANNOT BELONG TO ONE FAMILY. THE WORLD IS OUR FAMILY.

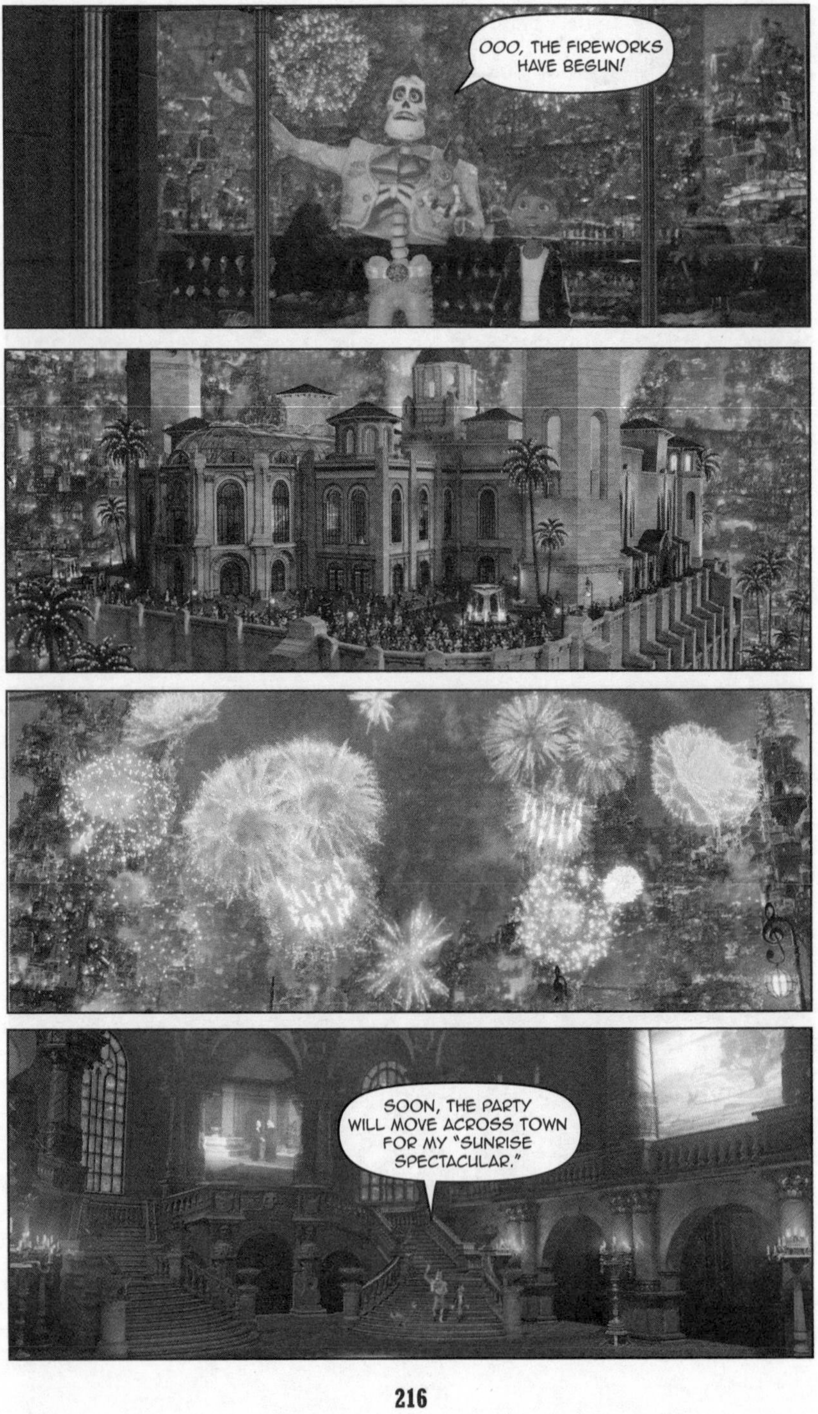
OOO, THE FIREWORKS HAVE BEGUN!
SOON, THE PARTY WILL MOVE ACROSS TOWN FOR MY "SUNRISE SPECTACULAR."

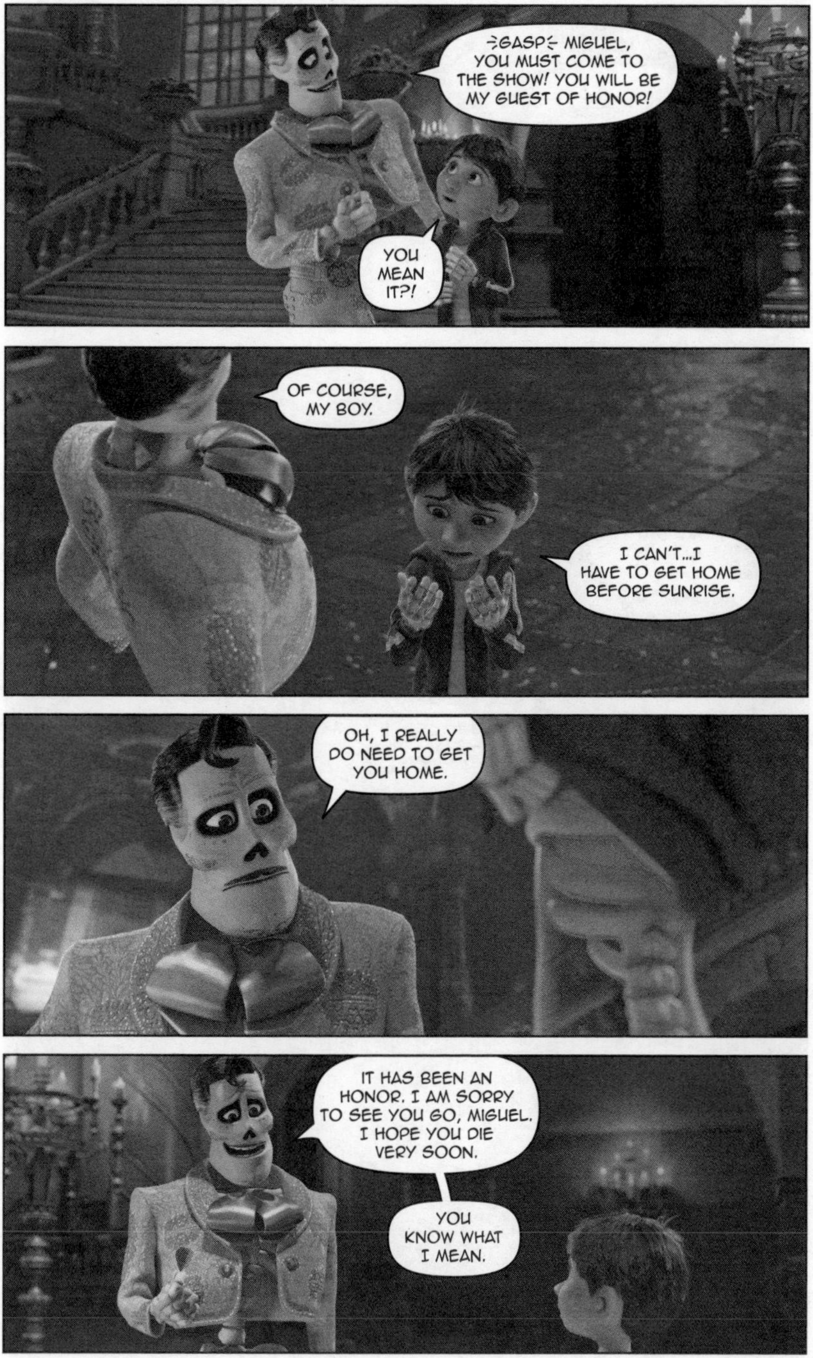

⇁GASP↽ MIGUEL, YOU MUST COME TO THE SHOW! YOU WILL BE MY GUEST OF HONOR!
YOU MEAN IT?!
OF COURSE, MY BOY.
I CAN'T...I HAVE TO GET HOME BEFORE SUNRISE.
OH, I REALLY DO NEED TO GET YOU HOME.
IT HAS BEEN AN HONOR. I AM SORRY TO SEE YOU GO, MIGUEL. I HOPE YOU DIE VERY SOON.
YOU KNOW WHAT I MEAN.

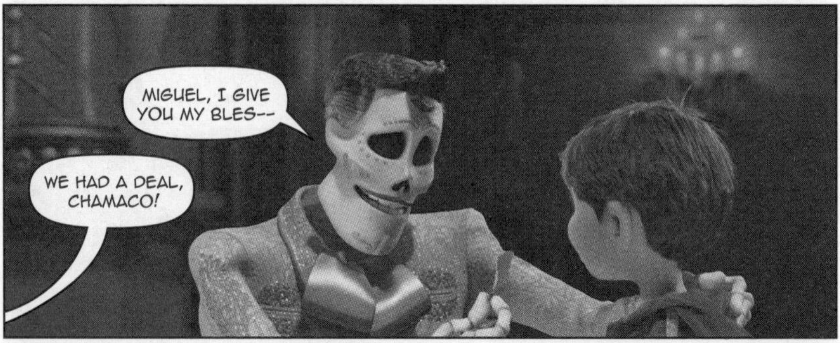
MIGUEL, I GIVE YOU MY BLES--
WE HAD A DEAL, CHAMACO!

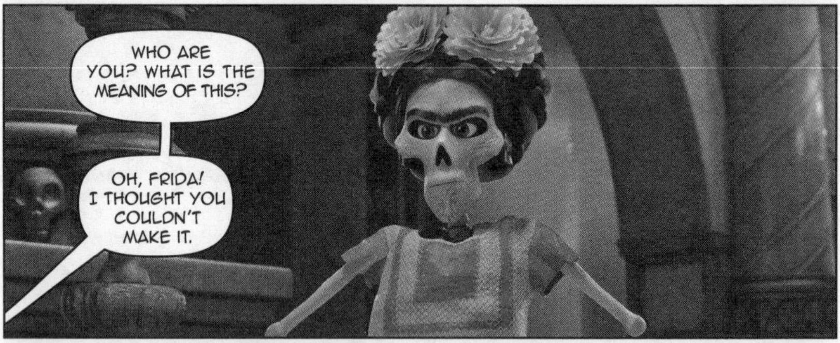
WHO ARE YOU? WHAT IS THE MEANING OF THIS?
OH, FRIDA! I THOUGHT YOU COULDN'T MAKE IT.

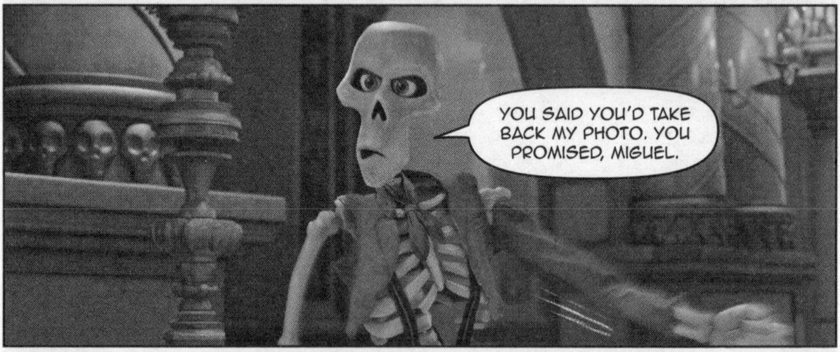
YOU SAID YOU'D TAKE BACK MY PHOTO. YOU PROMISED, MIGUEL.

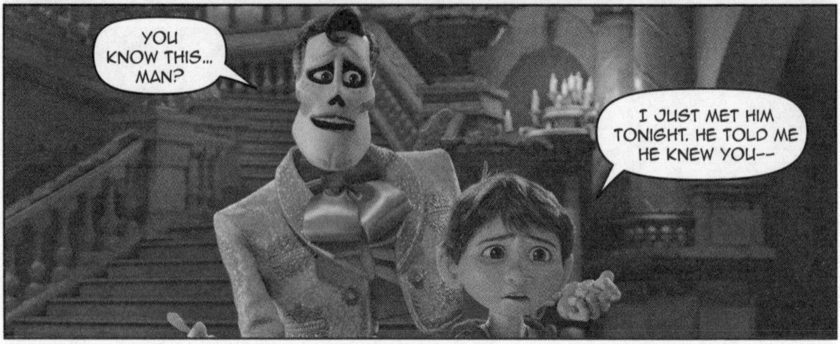
YOU KNOW THIS... MAN?
I JUST MET HIM TONIGHT. HE TOLD ME HE KNEW YOU--

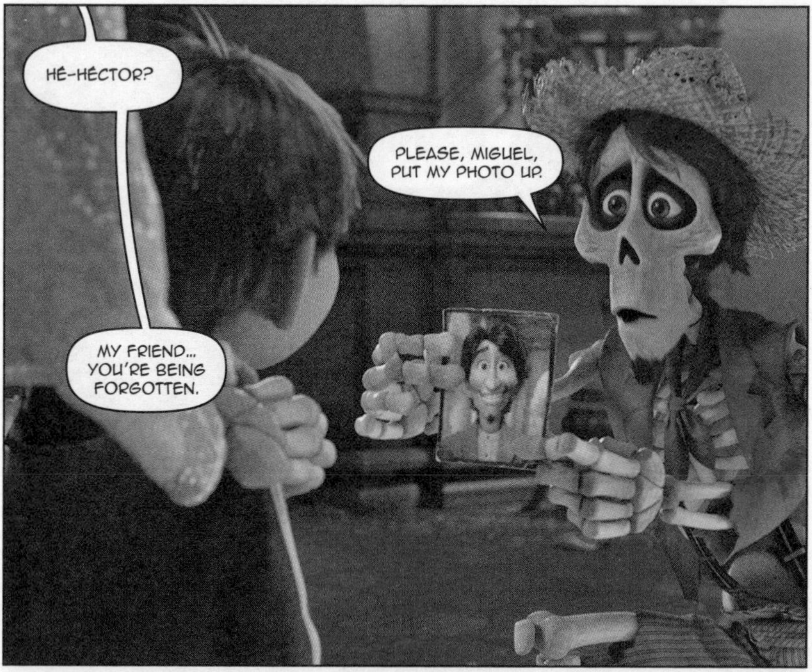
HÉ-HÉCTOR?
PLEASE, MIGUEL, PUT MY PHOTO UP.
MY FRIEND... YOU'RE BEING FORGOTTEN.

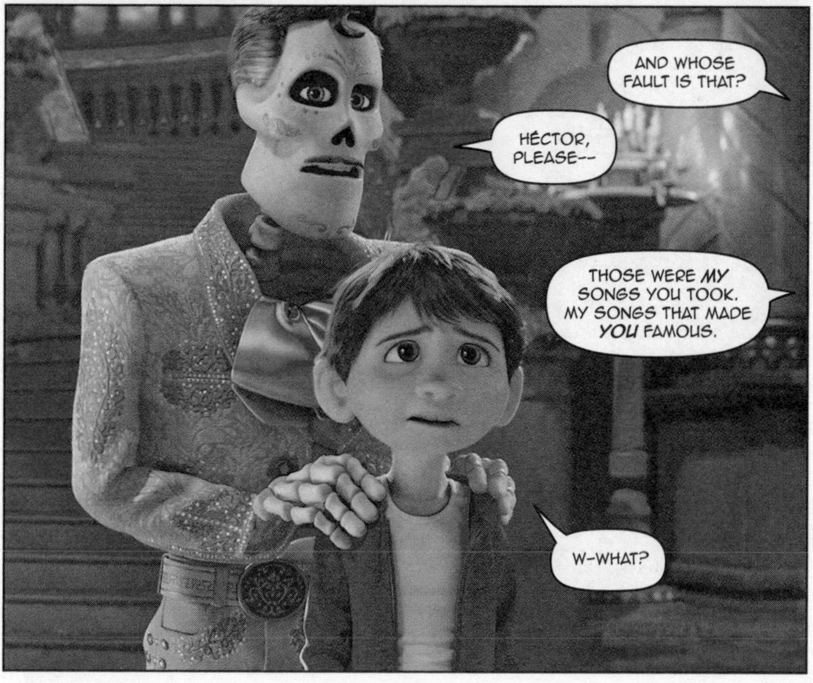
AND WHOSE FAULT IS THAT?
HÉCTOR, PLEASE--
THOSE WERE *MY* SONGS YOU TOOK. MY SONGS THAT MADE *YOU* FAMOUS.
W-WHAT?

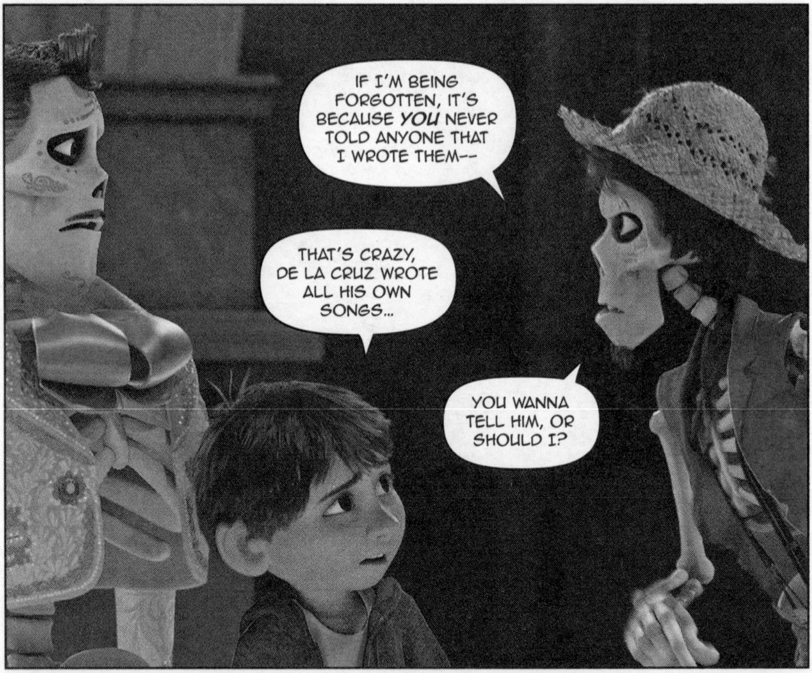
IF I'M BEING FORGOTTEN, IT'S BECAUSE *YOU* NEVER TOLD ANYONE THAT I WROTE THEM--
THAT'S CRAZY, DE LA CRUZ WROTE ALL HIS OWN SONGS...
YOU WANNA TELL HIM, OR SHOULD I?

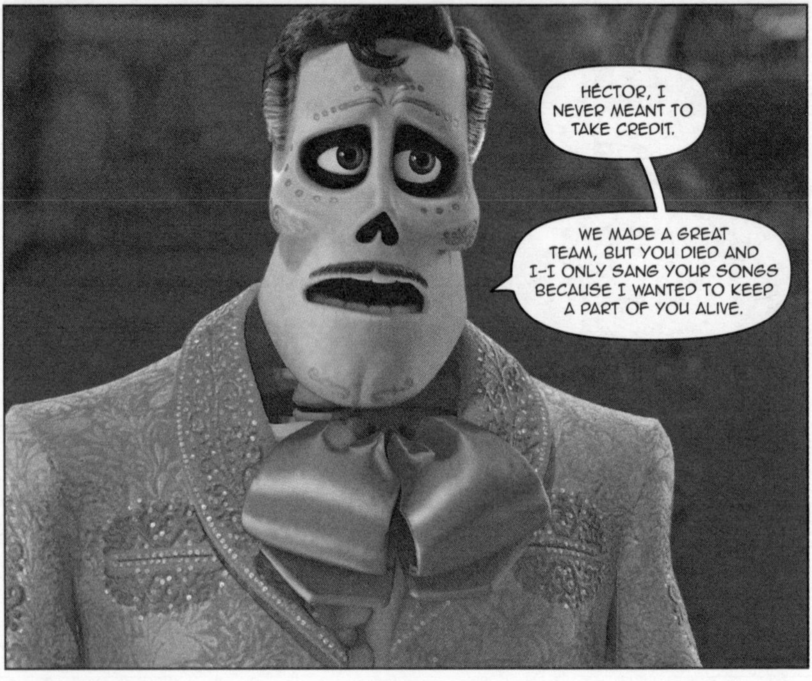
HÉCTOR, I NEVER MEANT TO TAKE CREDIT.
WE MADE A GREAT TEAM, BUT YOU DIED AND I-I ONLY SANG YOUR SONGS BECAUSE I WANTED TO KEEP A PART OF YOU ALIVE.

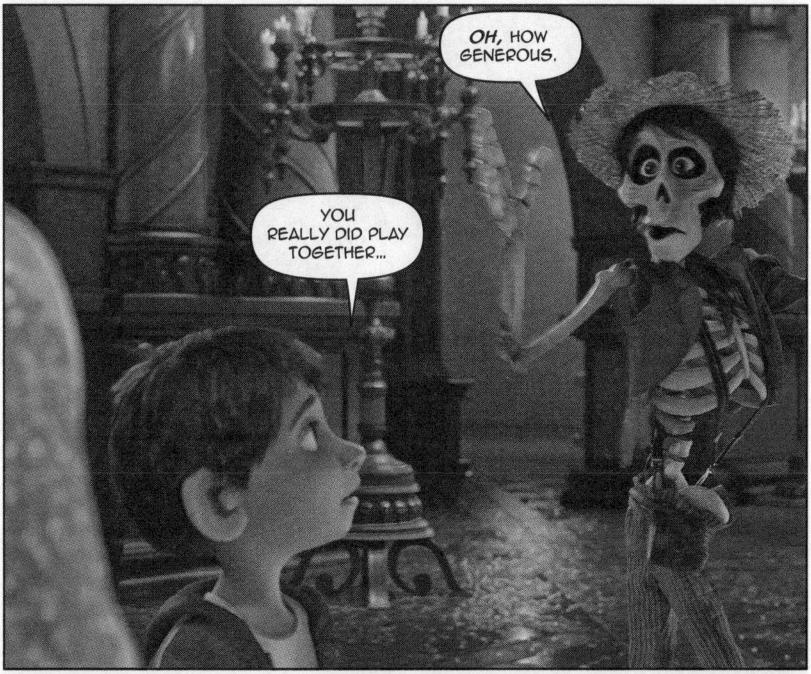
OH, HOW GENEROUS.
YOU REALLY DID PLAY TOGETHER...

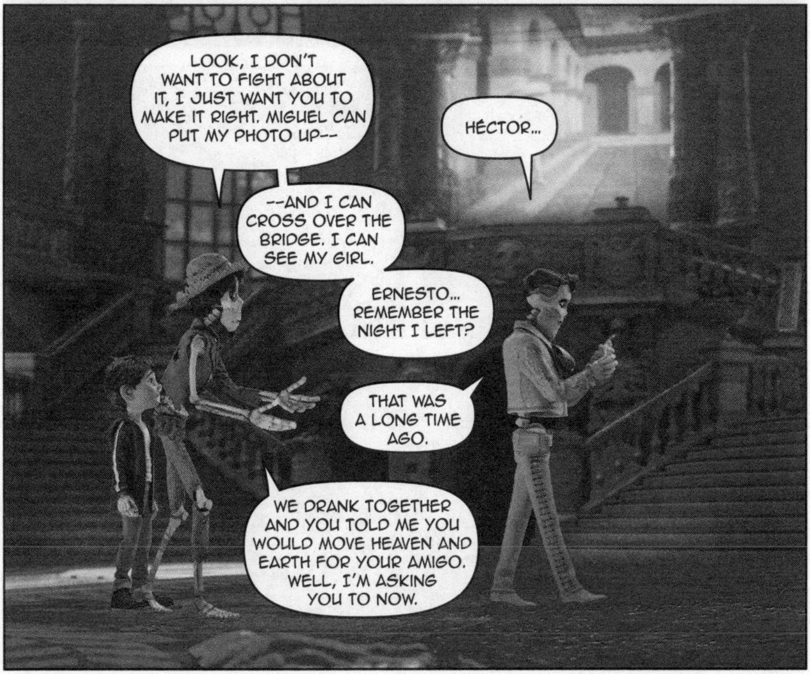
LOOK, I DON'T WANT TO FIGHT ABOUT IT, I JUST WANT YOU TO MAKE IT RIGHT. MIGUEL CAN PUT MY PHOTO UP--
HÉCTOR...
--AND I CAN CROSS OVER THE BRIDGE. I CAN SEE MY GIRL.
ERNESTO... REMEMBER THE NIGHT I LEFT?
THAT WAS A LONG TIME AGO.
WE DRANK TOGETHER AND YOU TOLD ME YOU WOULD MOVE HEAVEN AND EARTH FOR YOUR AMIGO. WELL, I'M ASKING YOU TO NOW.

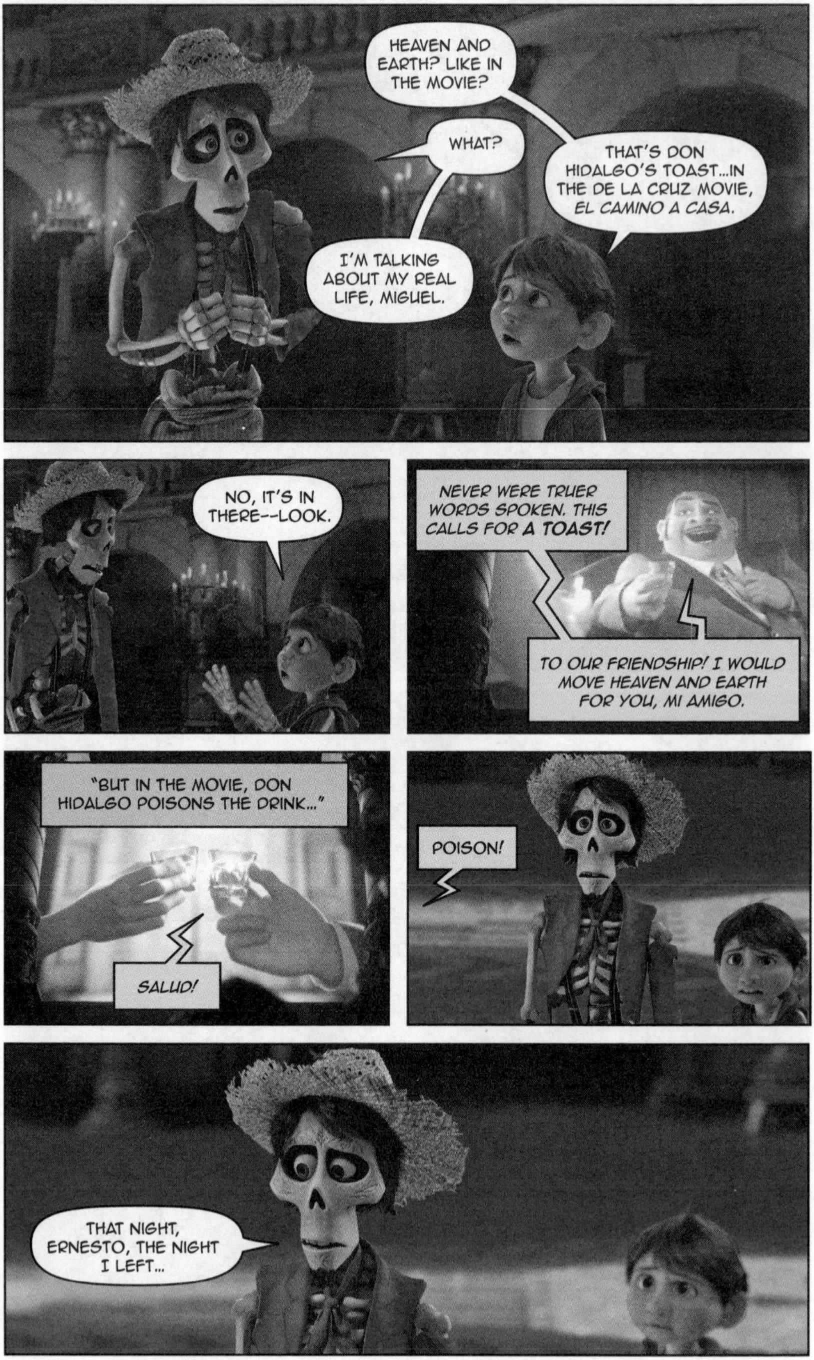
HEAVEN AND EARTH? LIKE IN THE MOVIE?
WHAT?
THAT'S DON HIDALGO'S TOAST...IN THE DE LA CRUZ MOVIE, *EL CAMINO A CASA.*
I'M TALKING ABOUT MY REAL LIFE, MIGUEL.
NO, IT'S IN THERE--LOOK.
*NEVER WERE TRUER WORDS SPOKEN. THIS CALLS FOR **A TOAST!***
TO OUR FRIENDSHIP! I WOULD MOVE HEAVEN AND EARTH FOR YOU, MI AMIGO.
"BUT IN THE MOVIE, DON HIDALGO POISONS THE DRINK..."
SALUD!
POISON!
THAT NIGHT, ERNESTO, THE NIGHT I LEFT...

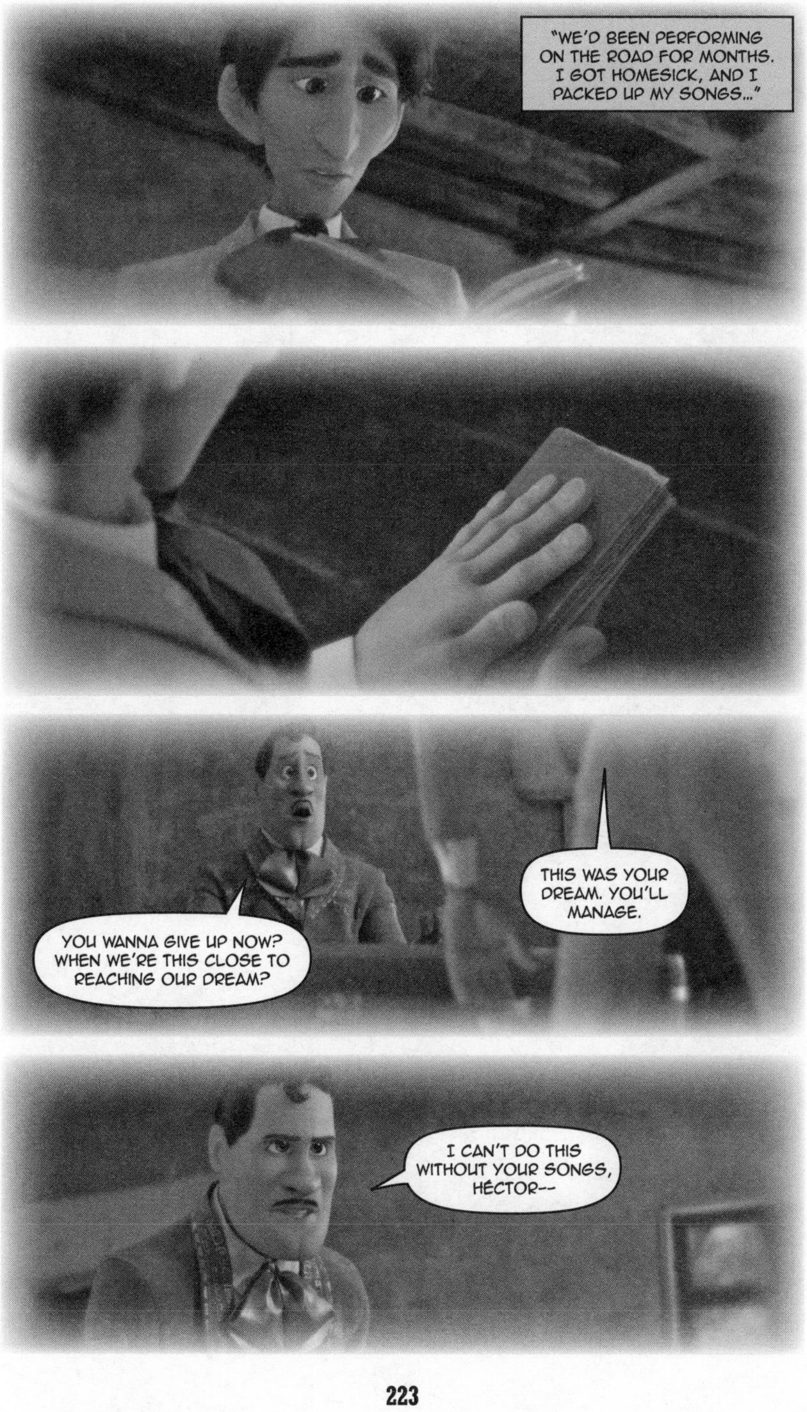
"WE'D BEEN PERFORMING ON THE ROAD FOR MONTHS. I GOT HOMESICK, AND I PACKED UP MY SONGS..."
YOU WANNA GIVE UP NOW? WHEN WE'RE THIS CLOSE TO REACHING OUR DREAM?
THIS WAS YOUR DREAM. YOU'LL MANAGE.
I CAN'T DO THIS WITHOUT YOUR SONGS, HÉCTOR--

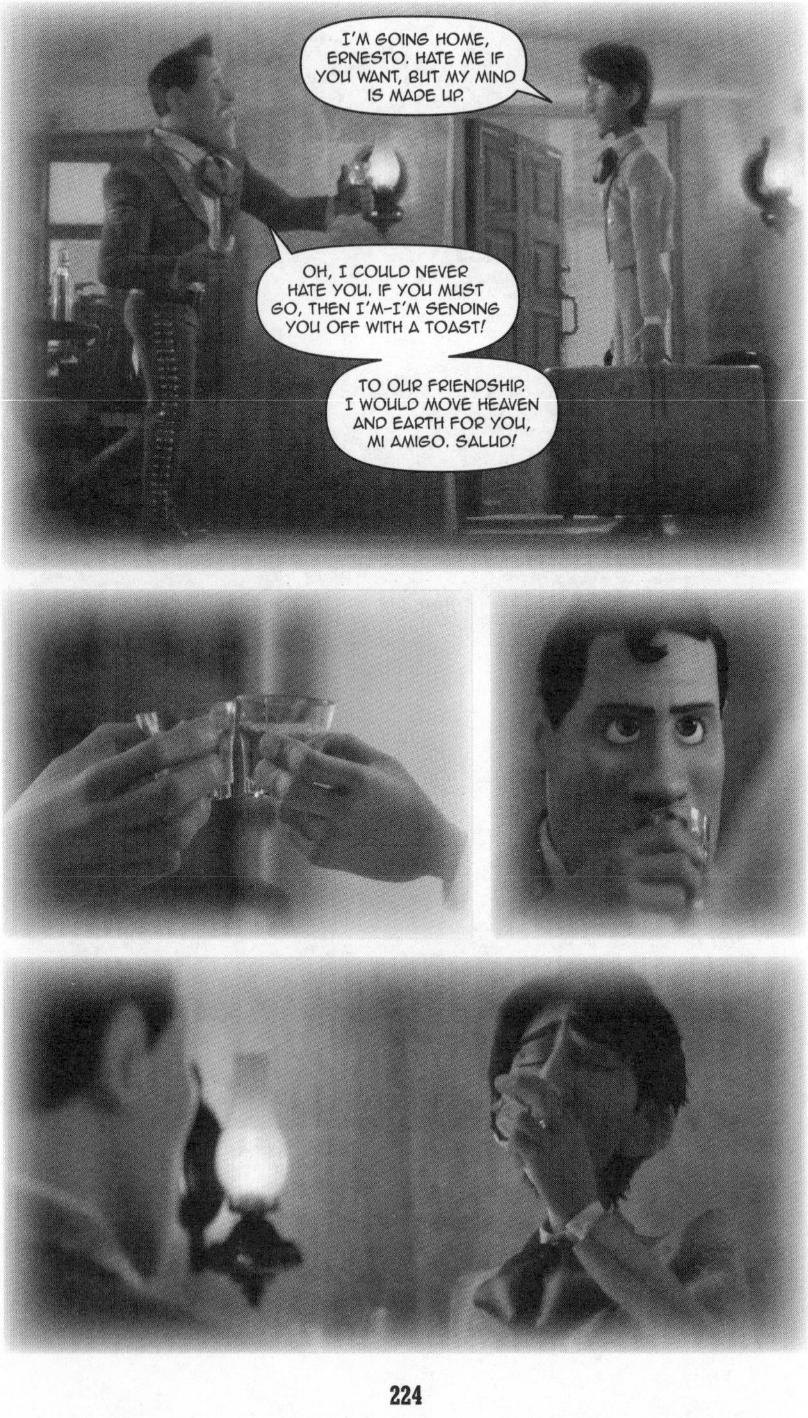
I'M GOING HOME, ERNESTO. HATE ME IF YOU WANT, BUT MY MIND IS MADE UP.
OH, I COULD NEVER HATE YOU. IF YOU MUST GO, THEN I'M-I'M SENDING YOU OFF WITH A TOAST!
TO OUR FRIENDSHIP. I WOULD MOVE HEAVEN AND EARTH FOR YOU, MI AMIGO. SALUD!

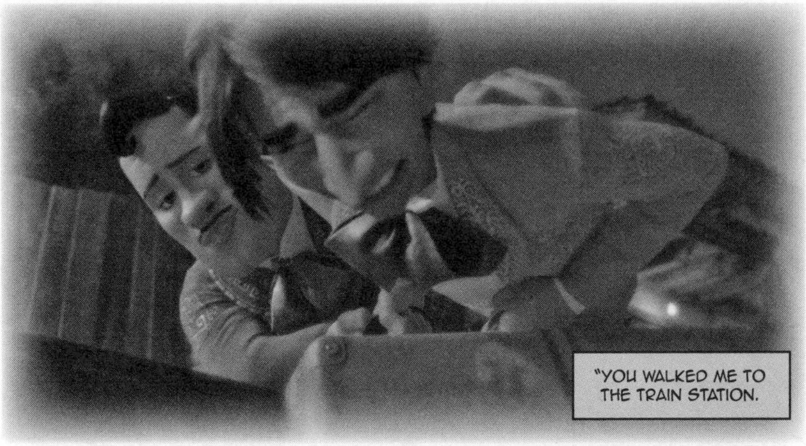
"YOU WALKED ME TO THE TRAIN STATION.

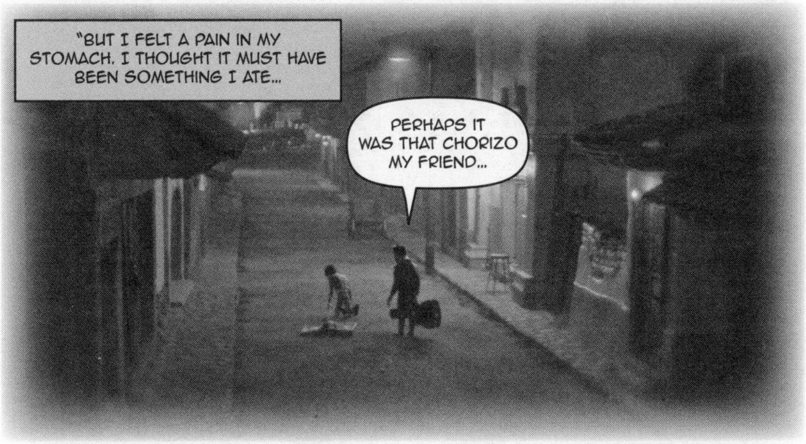
"BUT I FELT A PAIN IN MY STOMACH. I THOUGHT IT MUST HAVE BEEN SOMETHING I ATE...
PERHAPS IT WAS THAT CHORIZO MY FRIEND...

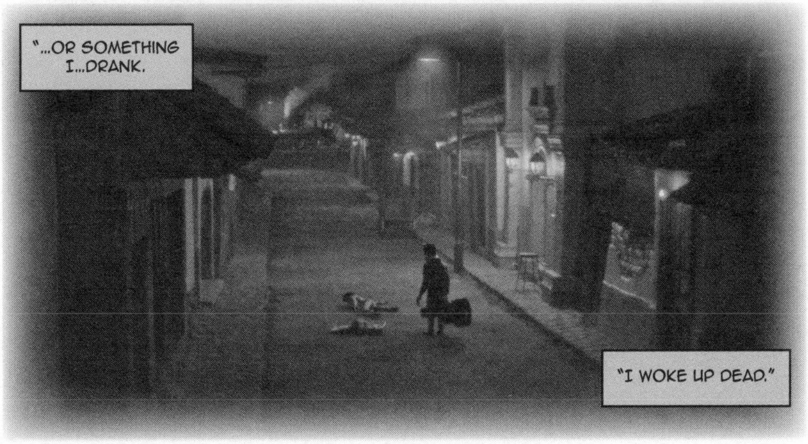
"...OR SOMETHING I...DRANK.
"I WOKE UP DEAD."

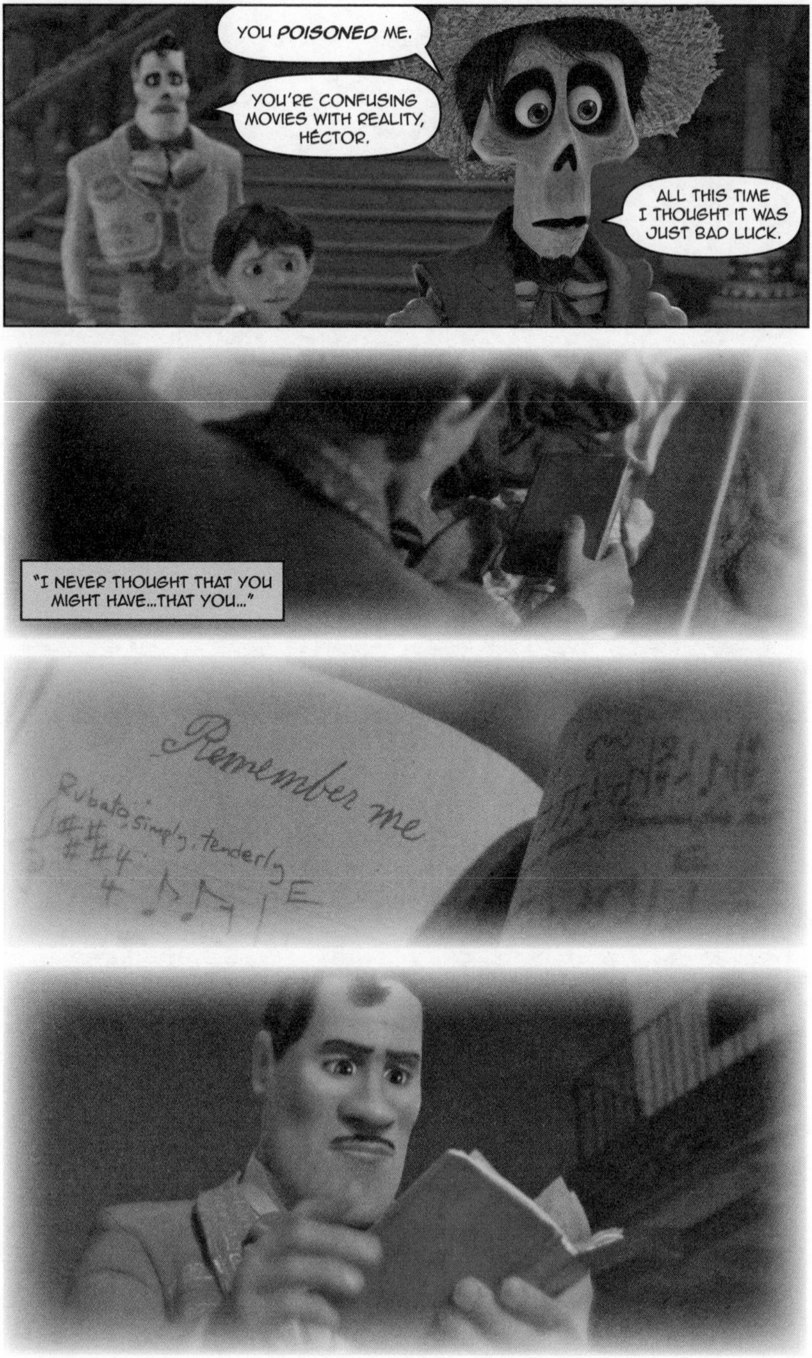
YOU *POISONED* ME.
YOU'RE CONFUSING MOVIES WITH REALITY, HÉCTOR.
ALL THIS TIME I THOUGHT IT WAS JUST BAD LUCK.
"I NEVER THOUGHT THAT YOU MIGHT HAVE...THAT YOU..."
Remember me
Rubato, simply, tenderly

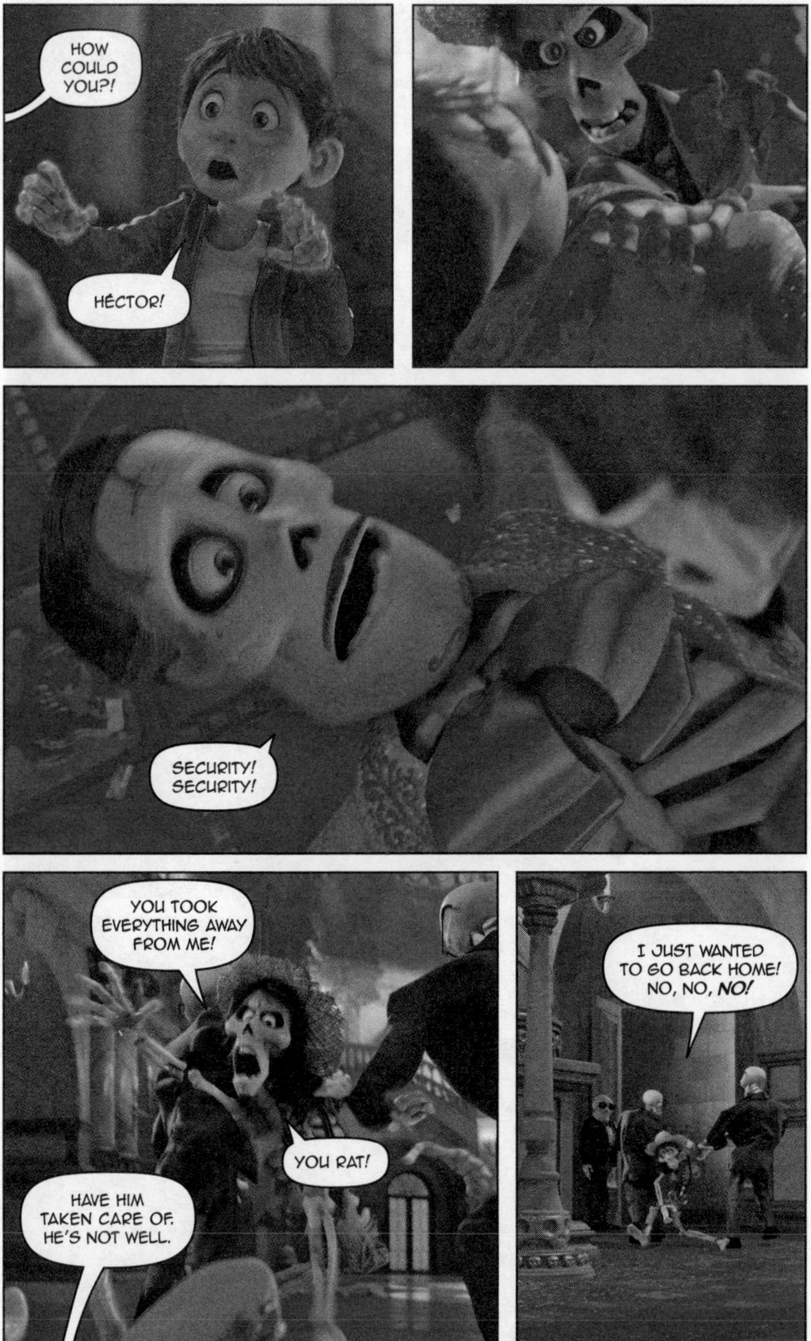
HOW COULD YOU?!
HÉCTOR!
SECURITY! SECURITY!
YOU TOOK EVERYTHING AWAY FROM ME!
YOU RAT!
HAVE HIM TAKEN CARE OF. HE'S NOT WELL.
I JUST WANTED TO GO BACK HOME! NO, NO, ***NO!***

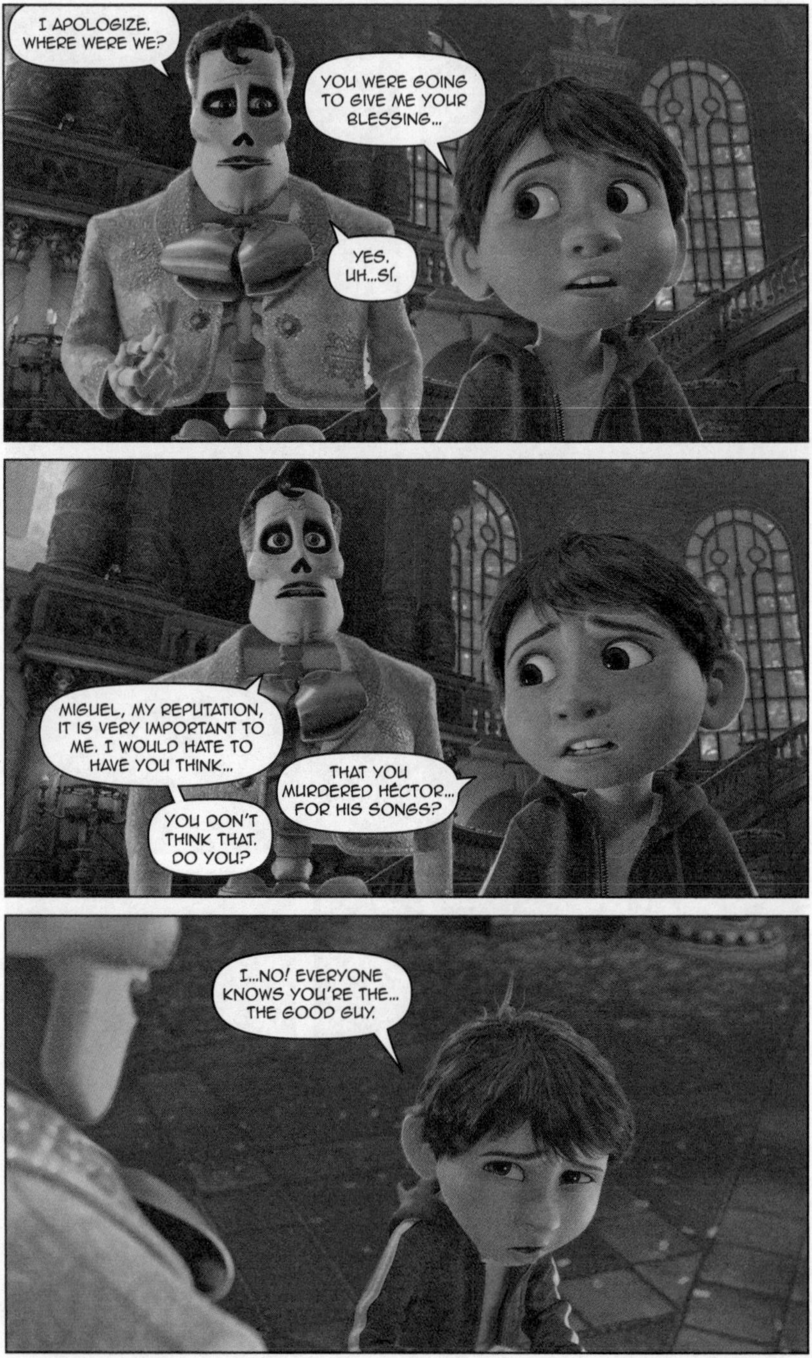
I APOLOGIZE. WHERE WERE WE?
YOU WERE GOING TO GIVE ME YOUR BLESSING...
YES. UH...SÍ.
MIGUEL, MY REPUTATION, IT IS VERY IMPORTANT TO ME. I WOULD HATE TO HAVE YOU THINK...
THAT YOU MURDERED HÉCTOR... FOR HIS SONGS?
YOU DON'T THINK THAT. DO YOU?
I...NO! EVERYONE KNOWS YOU'RE THE... THE GOOD GUY.

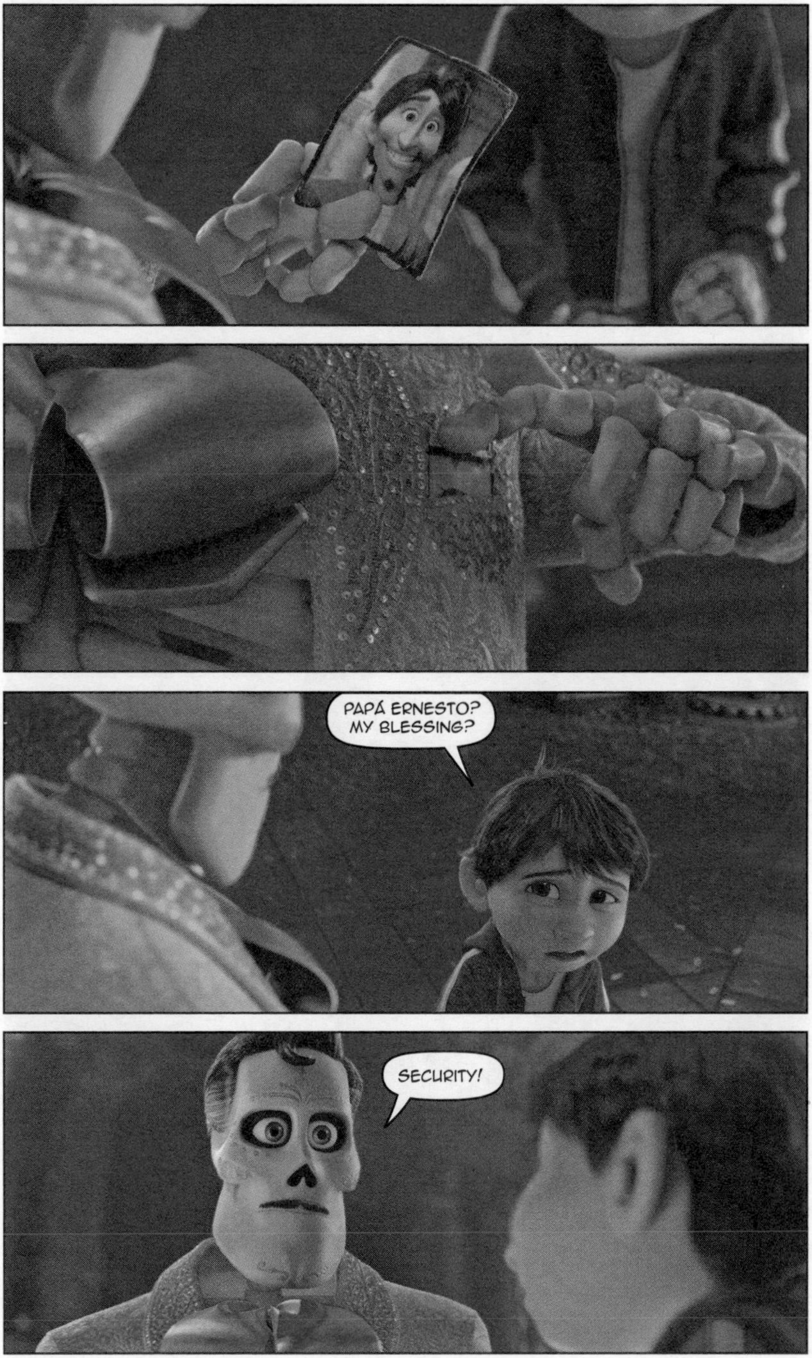
PAPÁ ERNESTO?
MY BLESSING?
SECURITY!

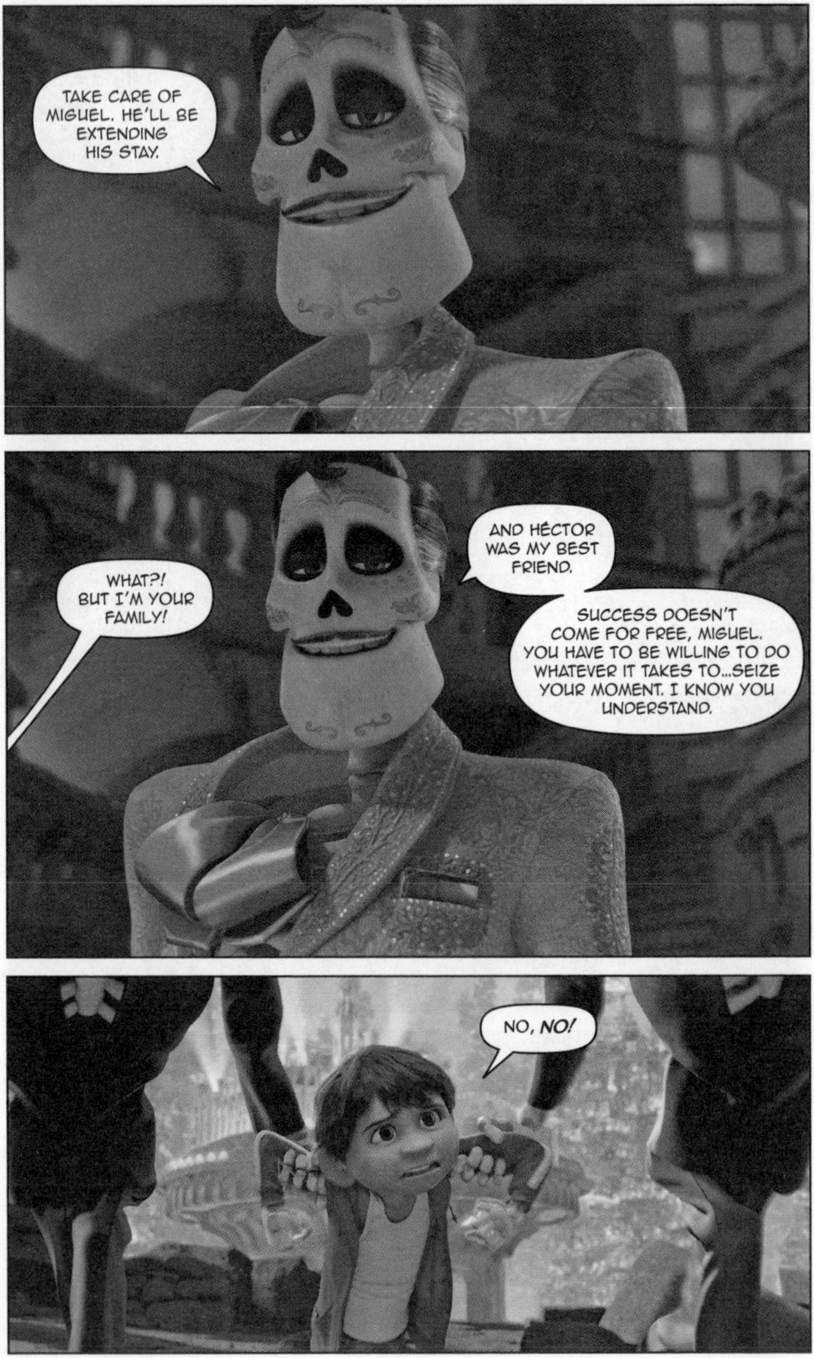

TAKE CARE OF MIGUEL. HE'LL BE EXTENDING HIS STAY.
WHAT?! BUT I'M YOUR FAMILY!
AND HÉCTOR WAS MY BEST FRIEND.
SUCCESS DOESN'T COME FOR FREE, MIGUEL. YOU HAVE TO BE WILLING TO DO WHATEVER IT TAKES TO...SEIZE YOUR MOMENT. I KNOW YOU UNDERSTAND.
NO, *NO!*

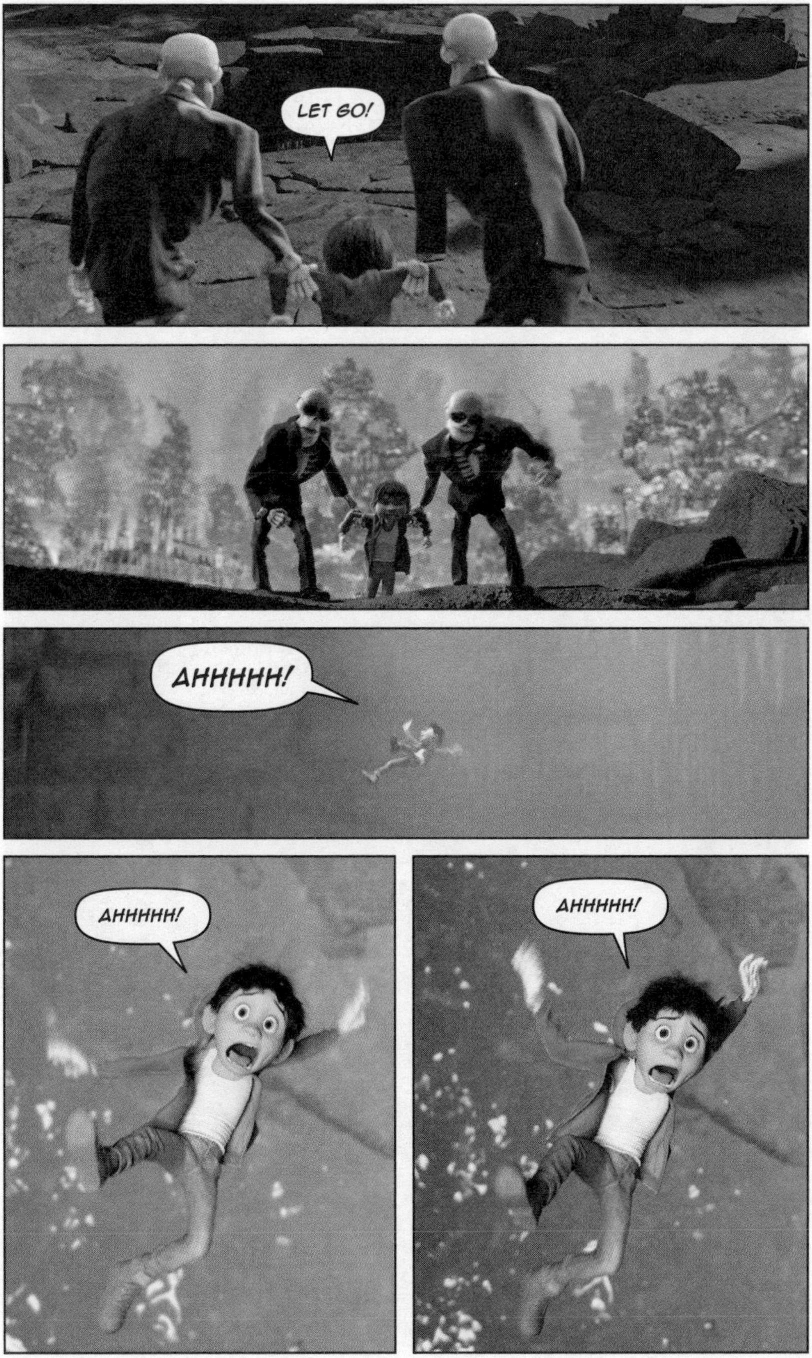
LET GO!
AHHHHH!
AHHHHH!
AHHHHH!

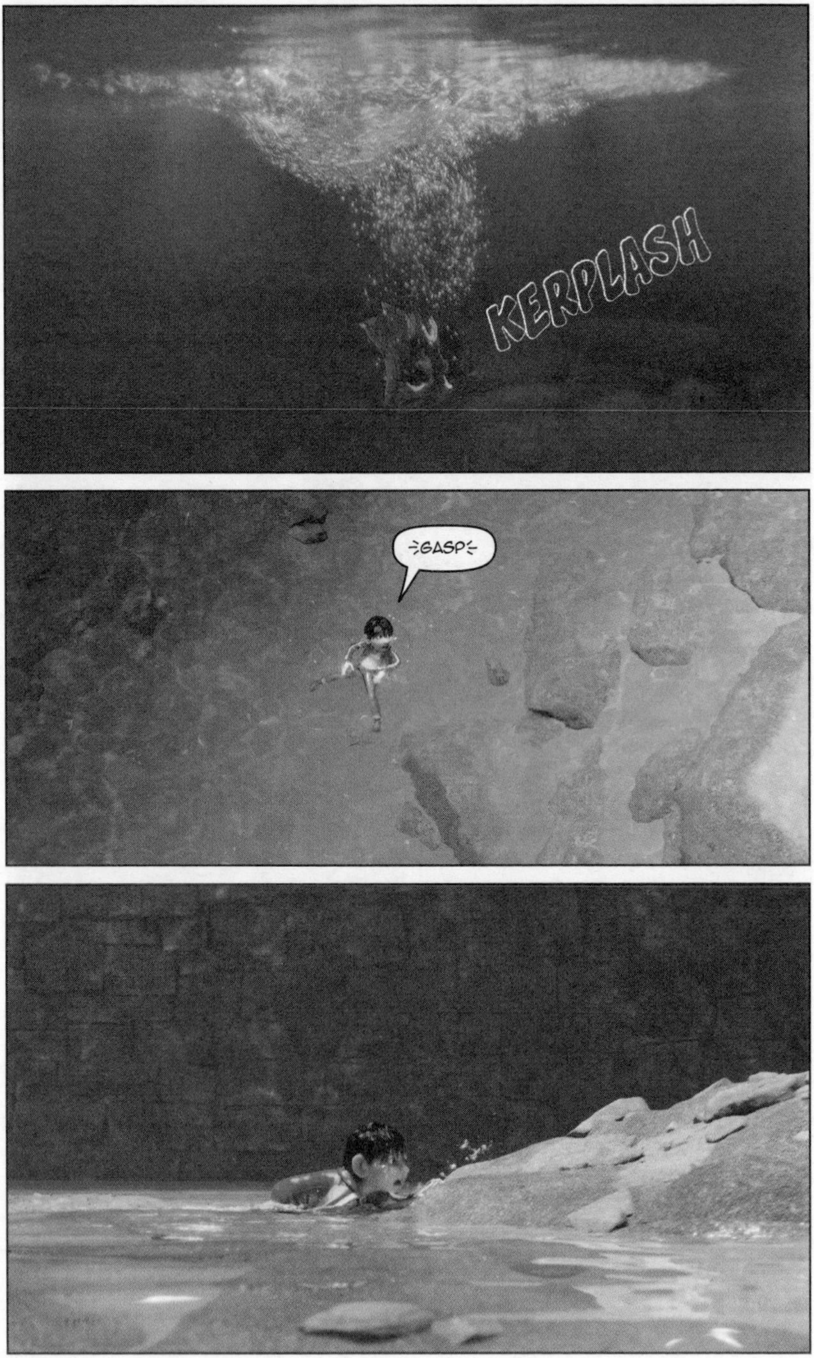
KERPLASH
GASP

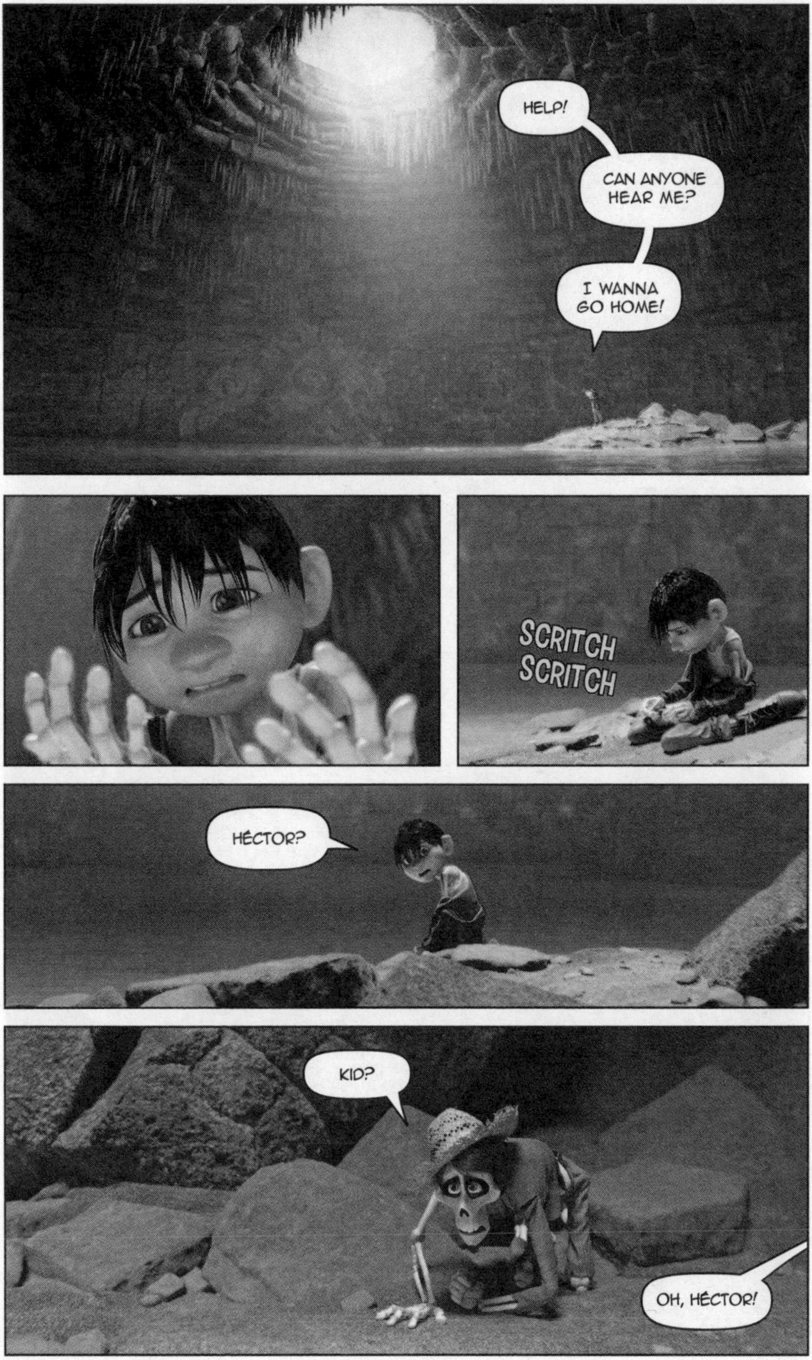
HELP!
CAN ANYONE HEAR ME?
I WANNA GO HOME!
SCRITCH SCRITCH
HÉCTOR?
KID?
OH, HÉCTOR!

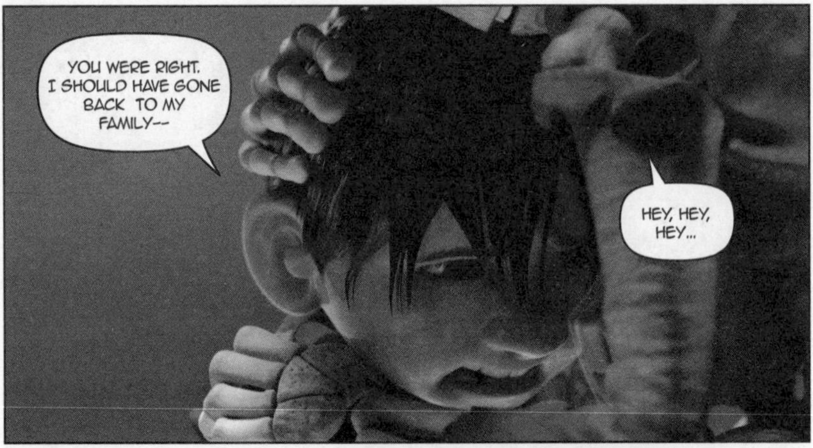
YOU WERE RIGHT. I SHOULD HAVE GONE BACK TO MY FAMILY--
HEY, HEY, HEY...

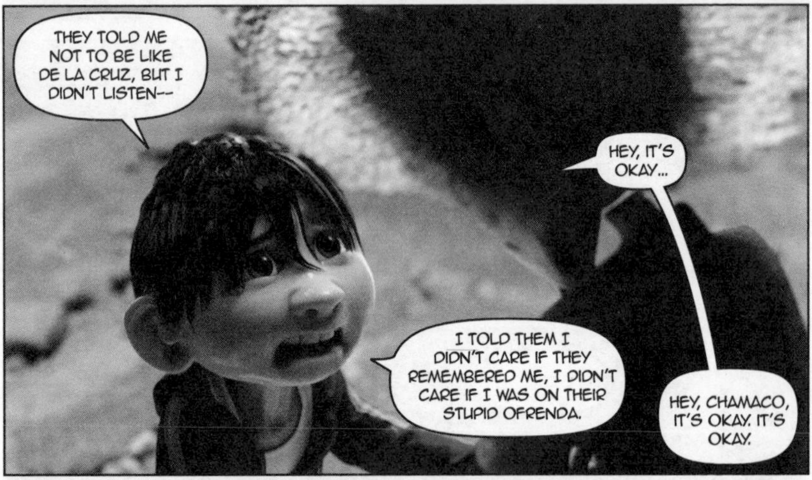
THEY TOLD ME NOT TO BE LIKE DE LA CRUZ, BUT I DIDN'T LISTEN--
HEY, IT'S OKAY...
I TOLD THEM I DIDN'T CARE IF THEY REMEMBERED ME, I DIDN'T CARE IF I WAS ON THEIR STUPID OFRENDA.
HEY, CHAMACO, IT'S OKAY. IT'S OKAY.

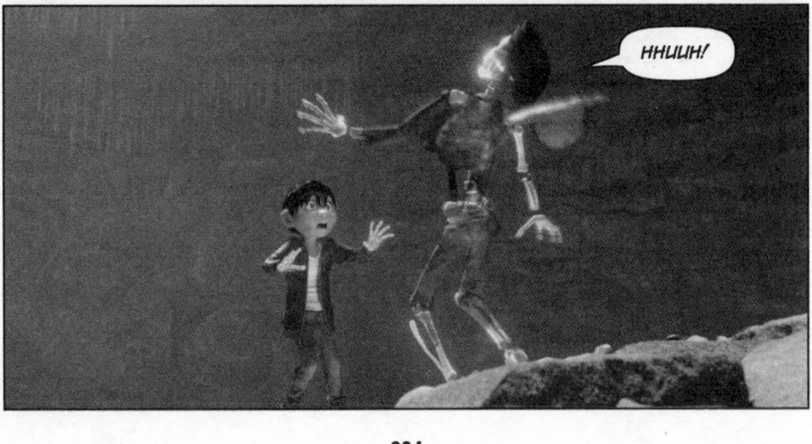
HHUUH!

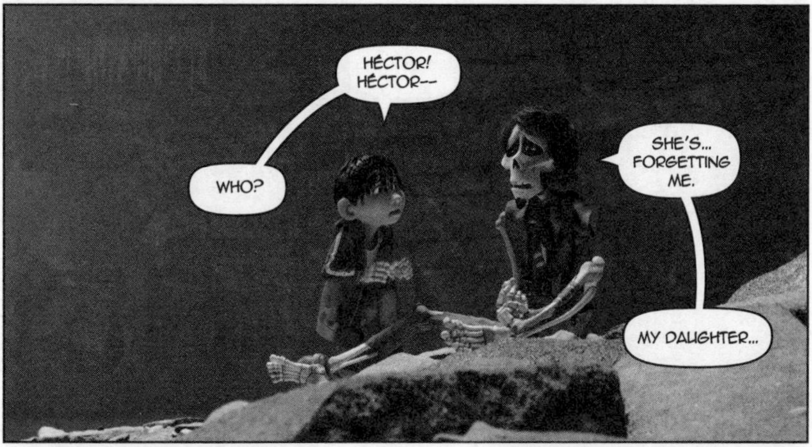
HÉCTOR! HÉCTOR--
WHO?
SHE'S... FORGETTING ME.
MY DAUGHTER...

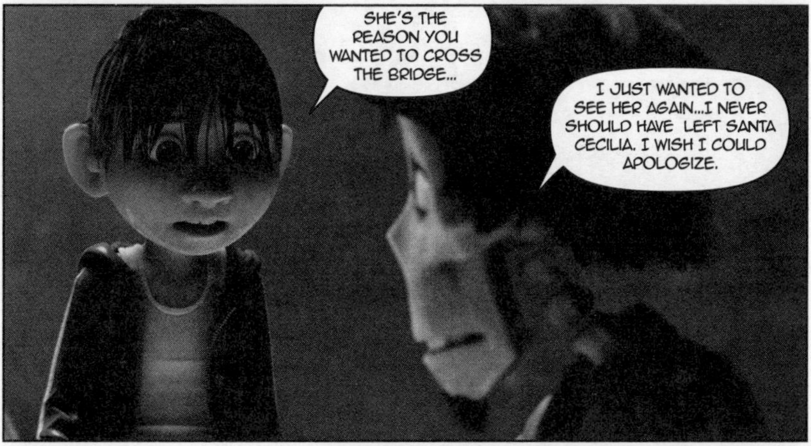
SHE'S THE REASON YOU WANTED TO CROSS THE BRIDGE...
I JUST WANTED TO SEE HER AGAIN...I NEVER SHOULD HAVE LEFT SANTA CECILIA. I WISH I COULD APOLOGIZE.

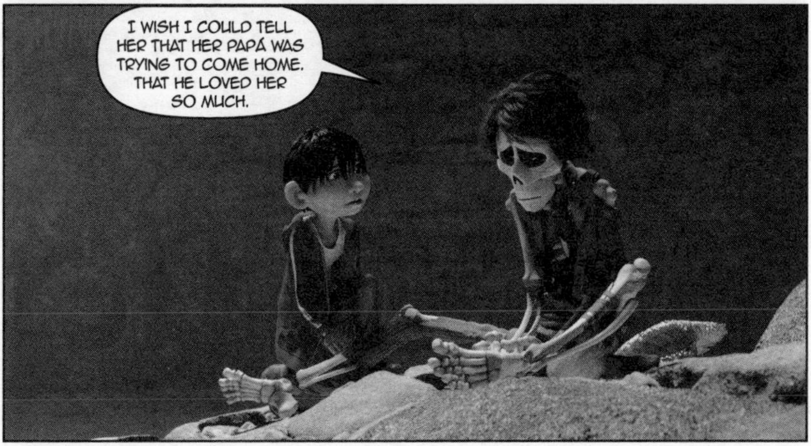
I WISH I COULD TELL HER THAT HER PAPÁ WAS TRYING TO COME HOME. THAT HE LOVED HER SO MUCH.

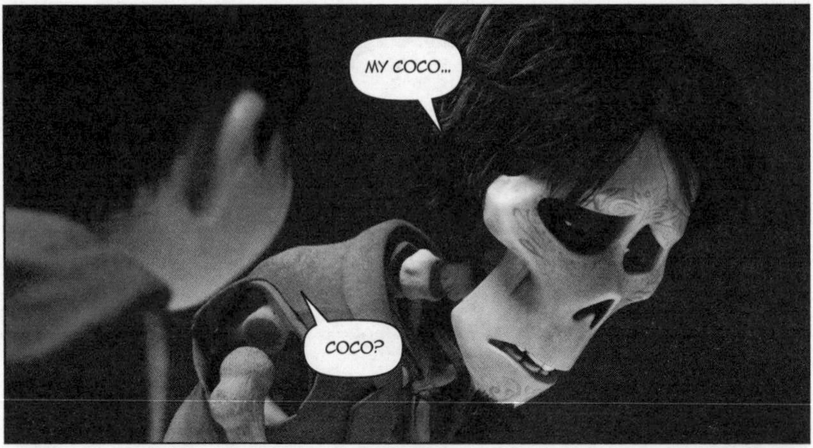
MY COCO...
COCO?

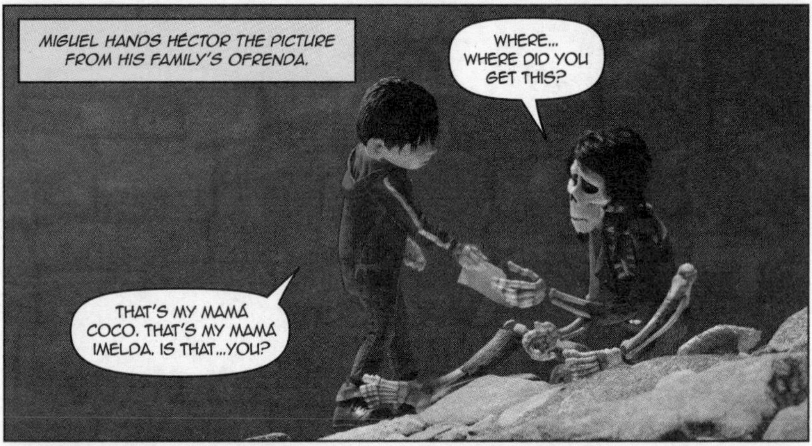
MIGUEL HANDS HÉCTOR THE PICTURE FROM HIS FAMILY'S OFRENDA.
WHERE... WHERE DID YOU GET THIS?
THAT'S MY MAMÁ COCO. THAT'S MY MAMÁ IMELDA. IS THAT...YOU?

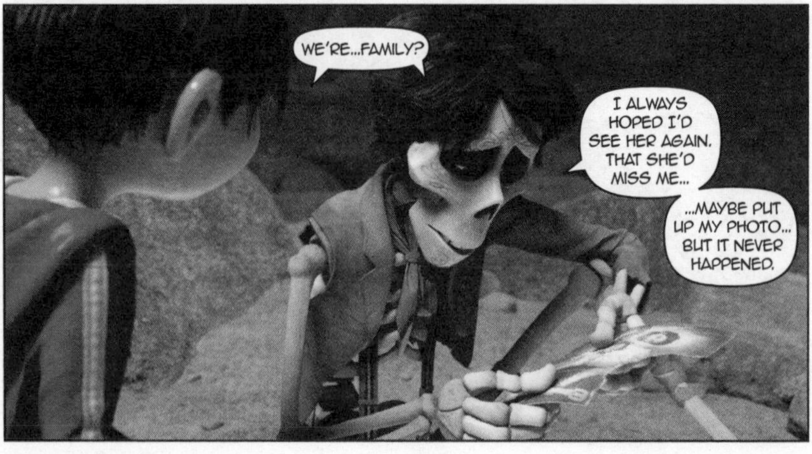
WE'RE...FAMILY?
I ALWAYS HOPED I'D SEE HER AGAIN. THAT SHE'D MISS ME...
...MAYBE PUT UP MY PHOTO... BUT IT NEVER HAPPENED.

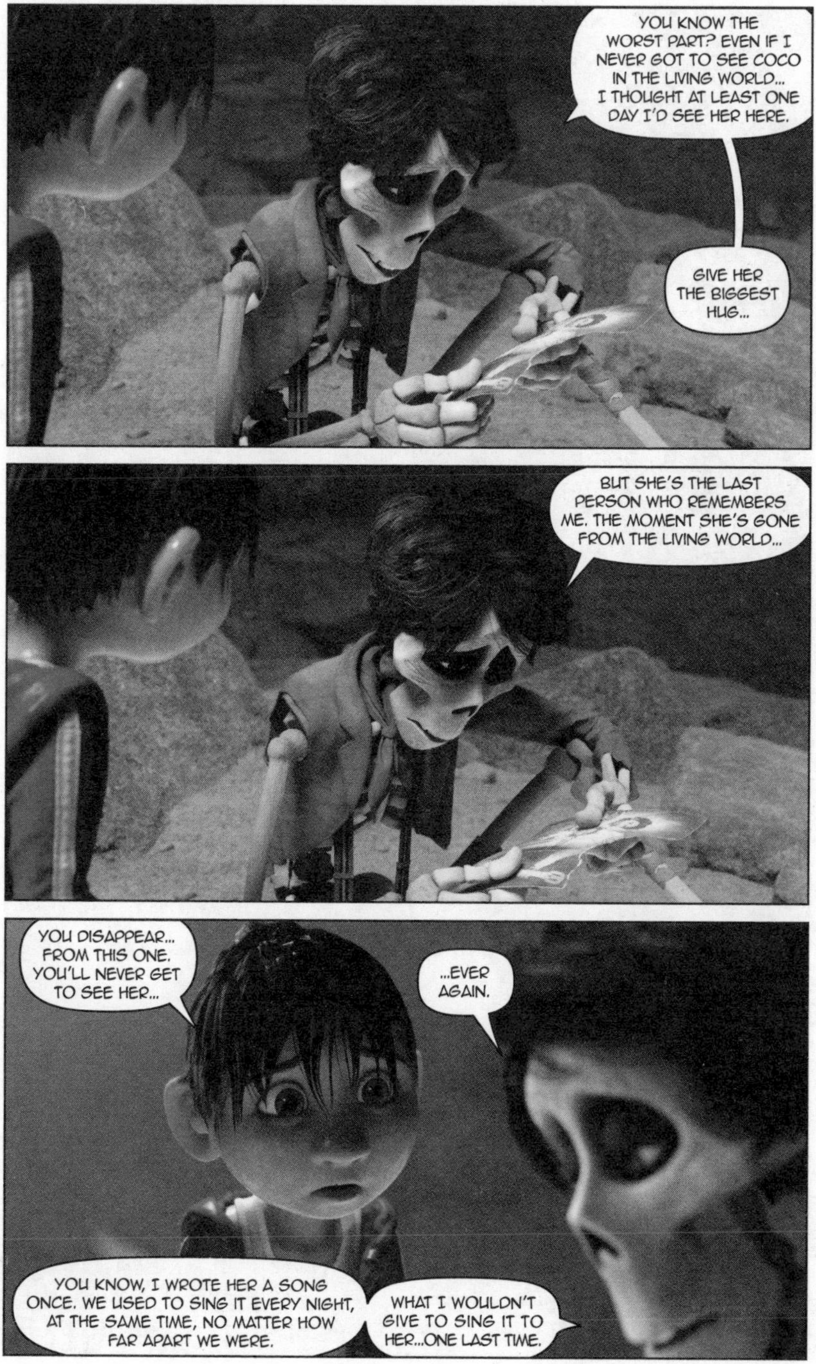
YOU KNOW THE WORST PART? EVEN IF I NEVER GOT TO SEE COCO IN THE LIVING WORLD... I THOUGHT AT LEAST ONE DAY I'D SEE HER HERE.
GIVE HER THE BIGGEST HUG...
BUT SHE'S THE LAST PERSON WHO REMEMBERS ME. THE MOMENT SHE'S GONE FROM THE LIVING WORLD...
YOU DISAPPEAR... FROM THIS ONE. YOU'LL NEVER GET TO SEE HER...
...EVER AGAIN.
YOU KNOW, I WROTE HER A SONG ONCE. WE USED TO SING IT EVERY NIGHT, AT THE SAME TIME, NO MATTER HOW FAR APART WE WERE.
WHAT I WOULDN'T GIVE TO SING IT TO HER...ONE LAST TIME.

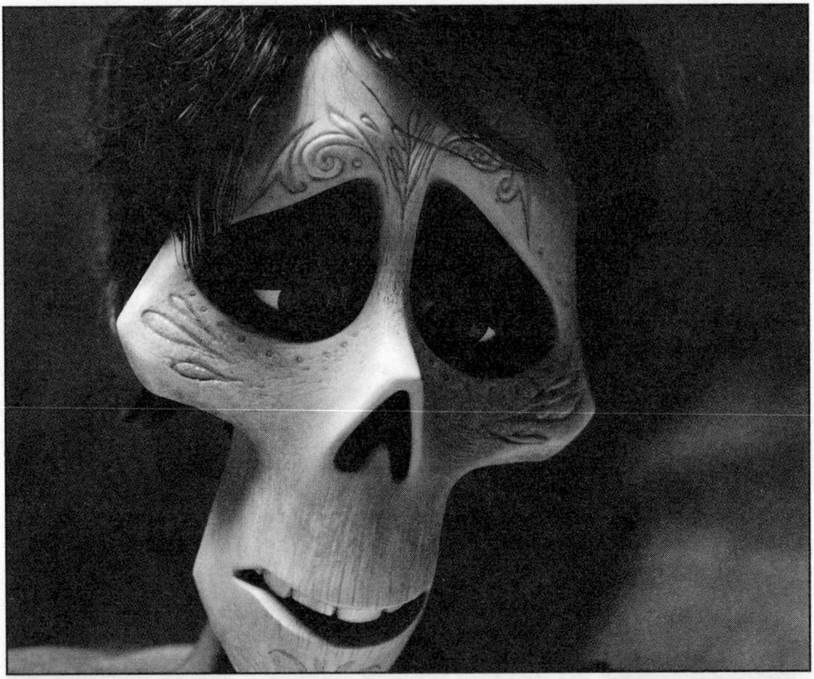

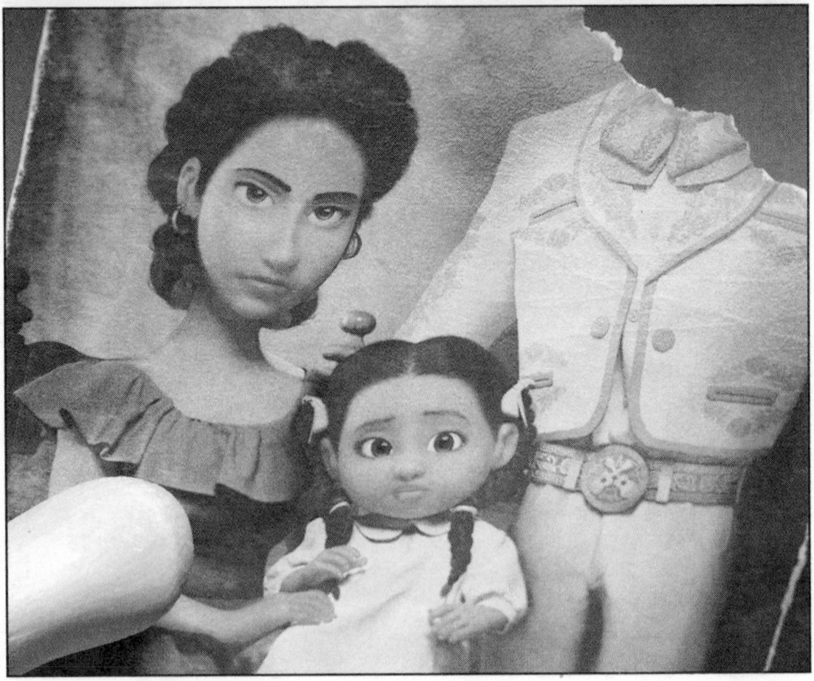

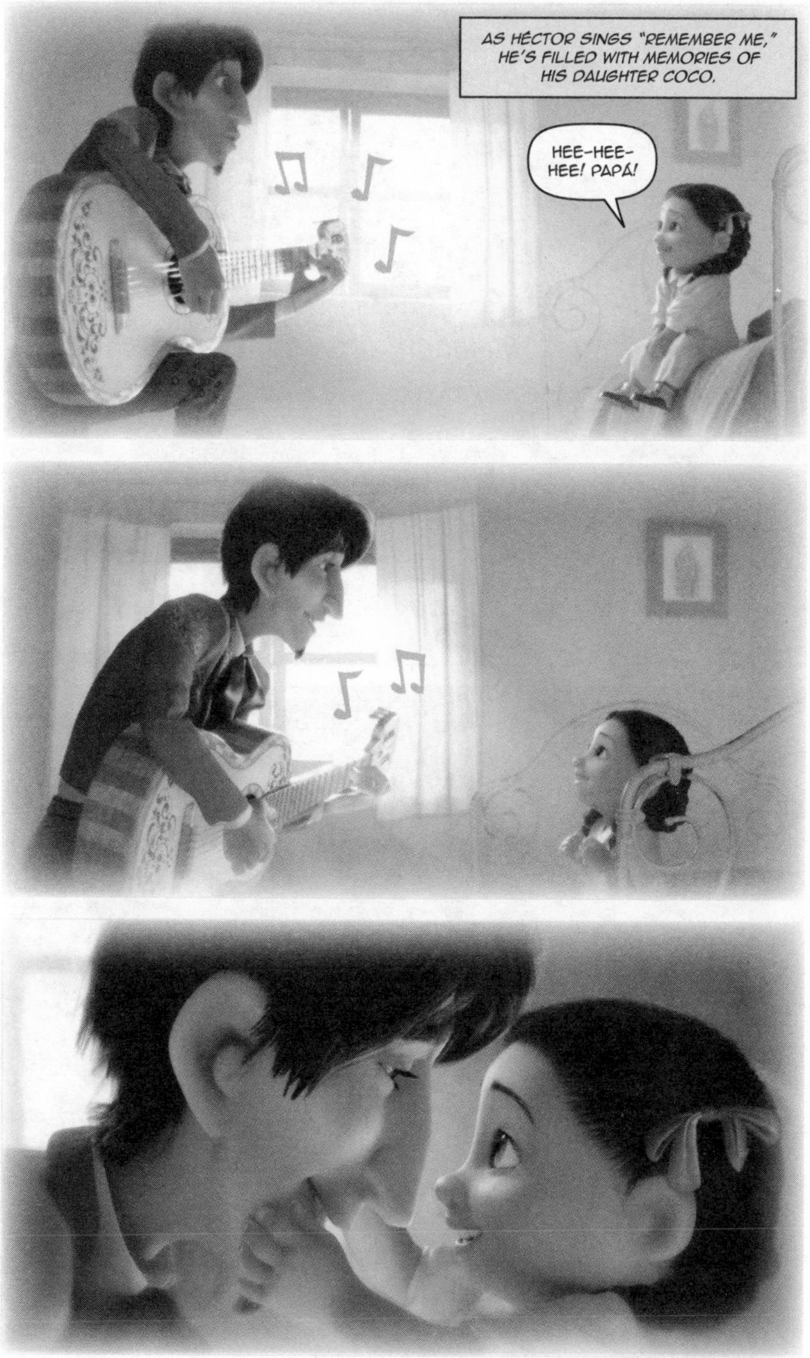
AS HÉCTOR SINGS "REMEMBER ME," HE'S FILLED WITH MEMORIES OF HIS DAUGHTER COCO.
HEE-HEE-HEE! PAPÁ!

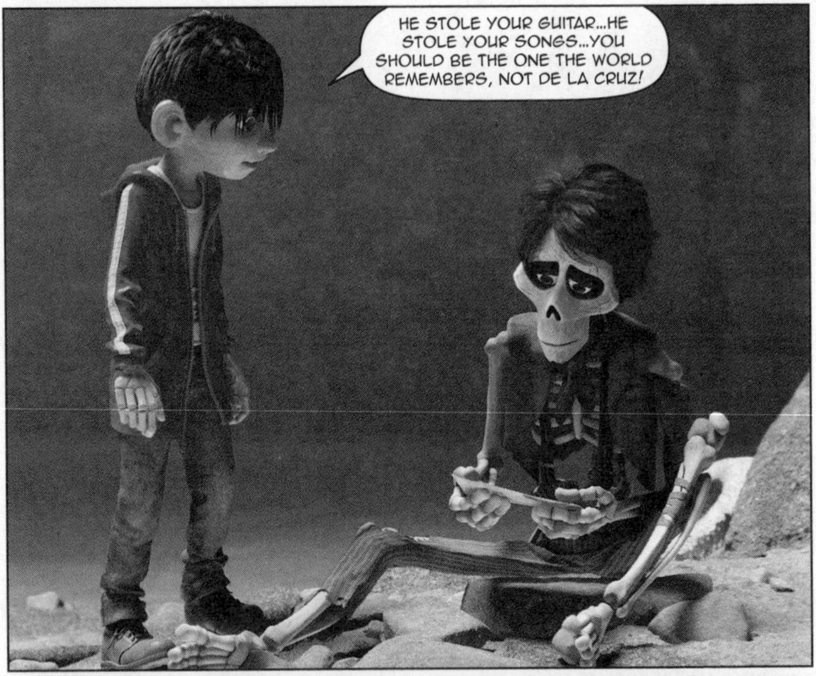
HE STOLE YOUR GUITAR...HE STOLE YOUR SONGS...YOU SHOULD BE THE ONE THE WORLD REMEMBERS, NOT DE LA CRUZ!

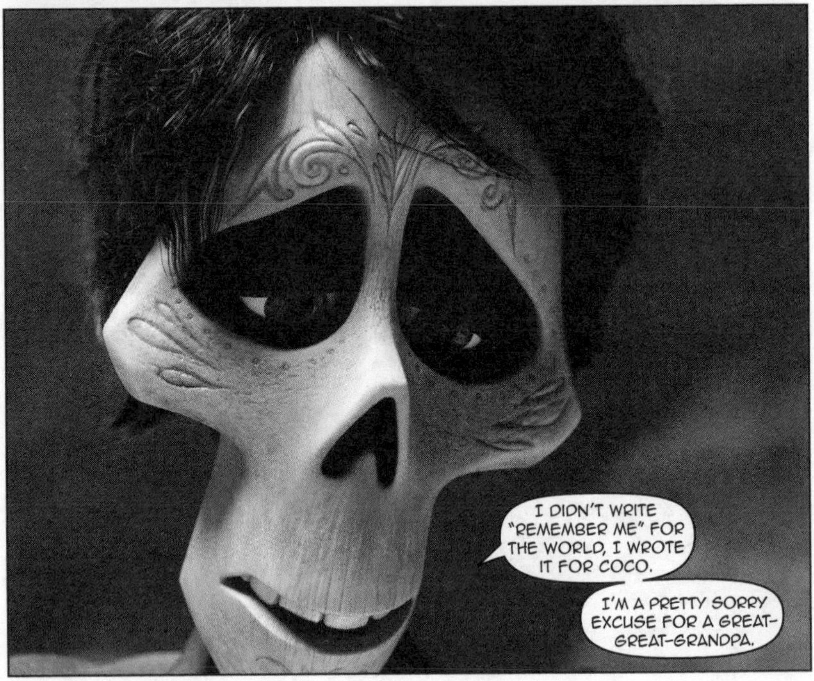
I DIDN'T WRITE "REMEMBER ME" FOR THE WORLD, I WROTE IT FOR COCO.
I'M A PRETTY SORRY EXCUSE FOR A GREAT-GREAT-GRANDPA.

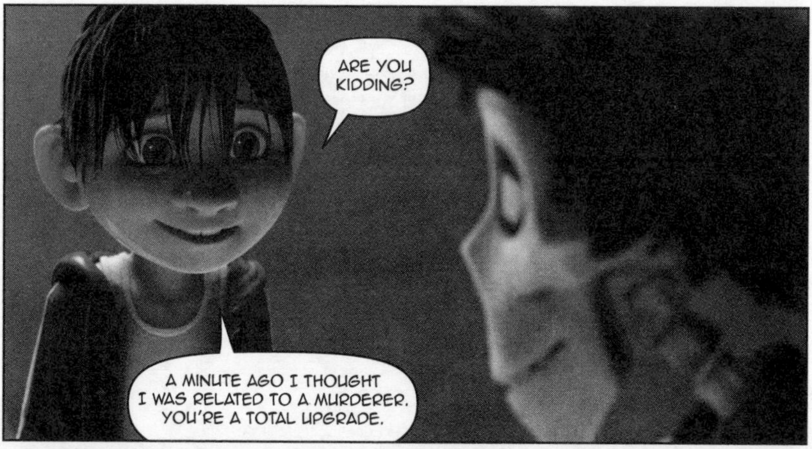
ARE YOU KIDDING?
A MINUTE AGO I THOUGHT I WAS RELATED TO A MURDERER. YOU'RE A TOTAL UPGRADE.

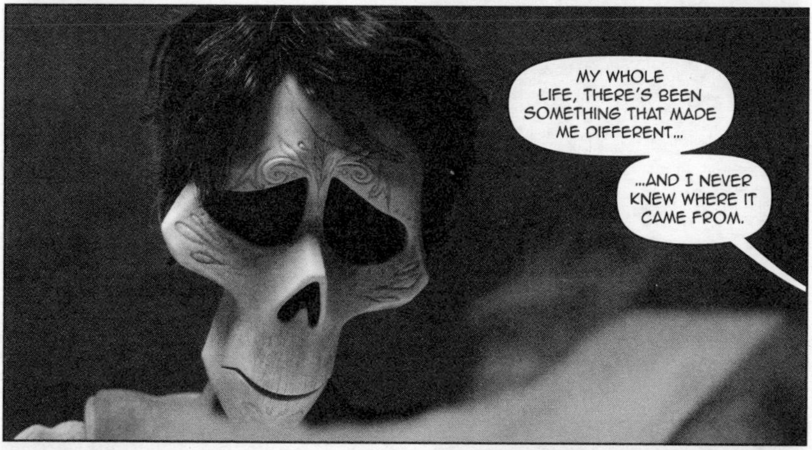
MY WHOLE LIFE, THERE'S BEEN SOMETHING THAT MADE ME DIFFERENT...
...AND I NEVER KNEW WHERE IT CAME FROM.

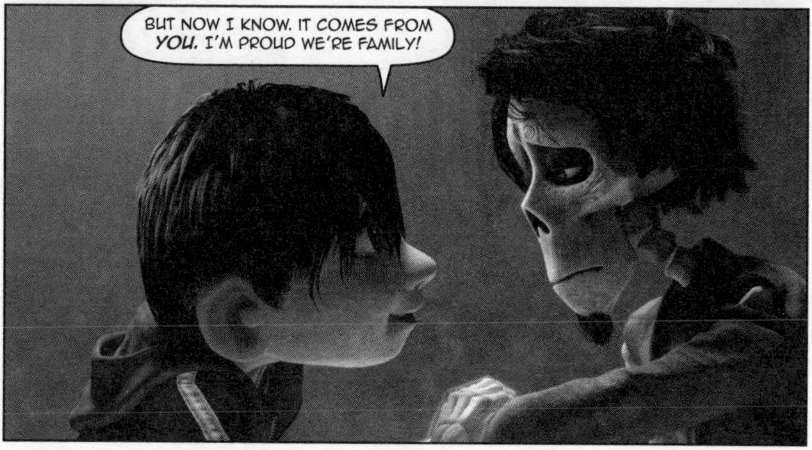
BUT NOW I KNOW. IT COMES FROM *YOU.* I'M PROUD WE'RE FAMILY!

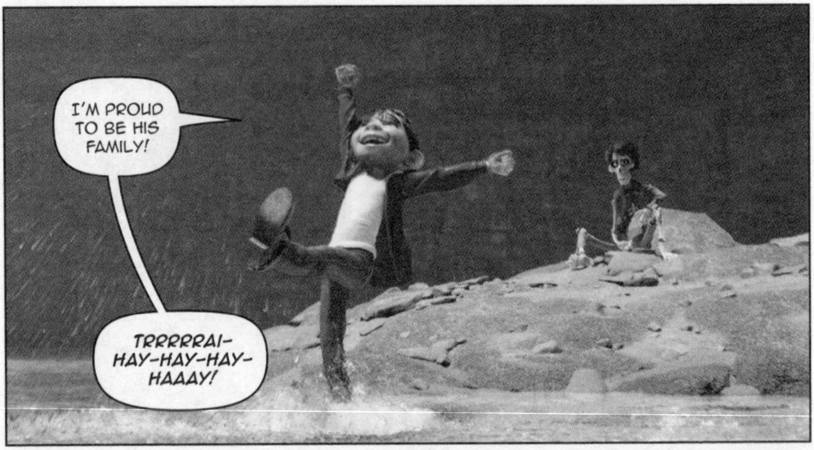
I'M PROUD TO BE HIS FAMILY!
TRRRRRAI-HAY-HAY-HAY-HAAAY!

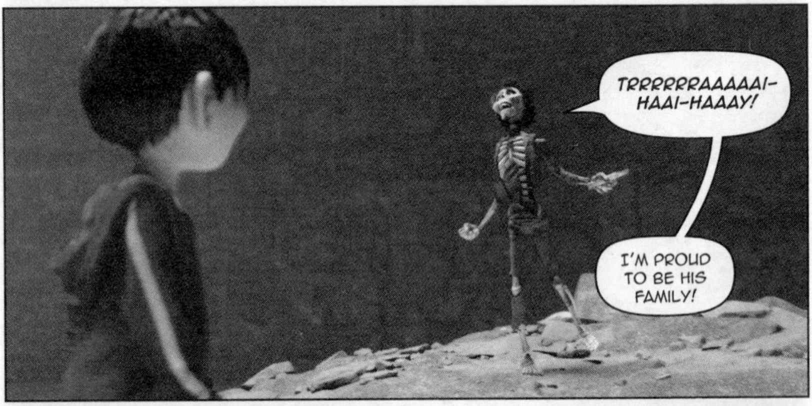
TRRRRRRAAAAAI-HAAI-HAAAY!
I'M PROUD TO BE HIS FAMILY!

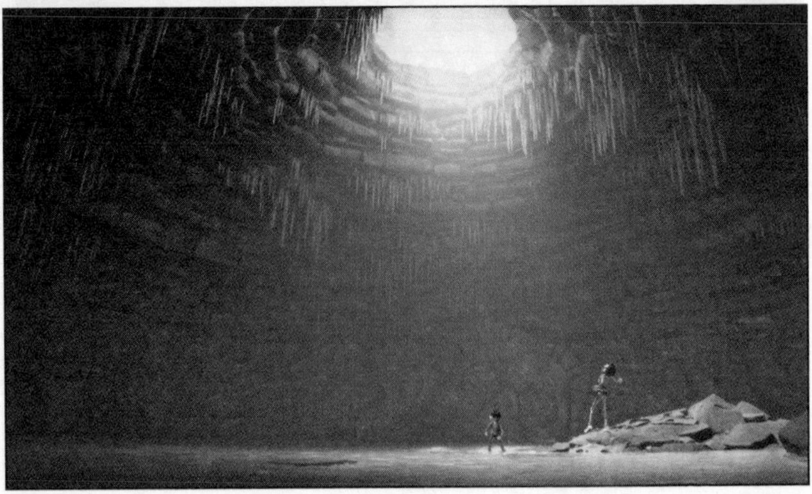

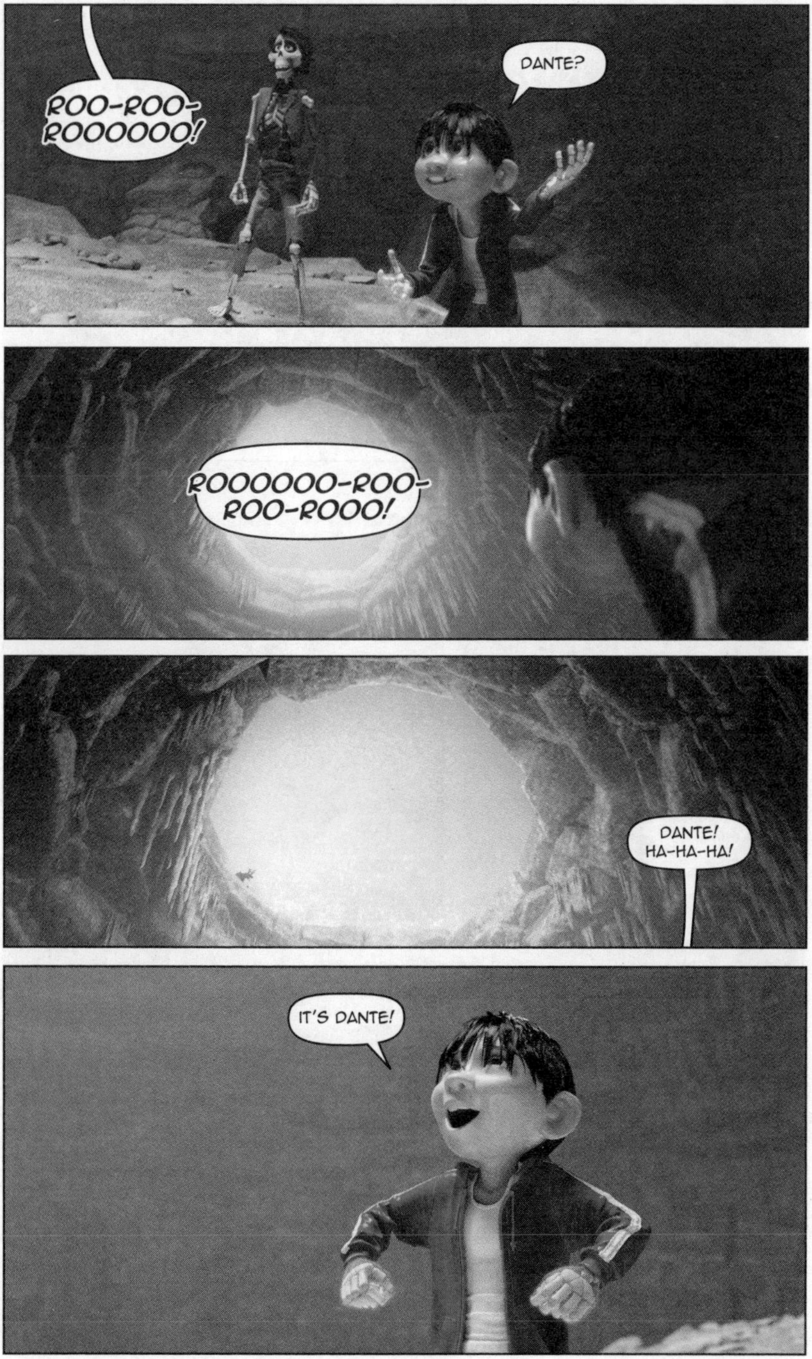
ROO-ROO-ROOOOOO!
DANTE?
ROOOOOO-ROO-ROO-ROOO!
DANTE! HA-HA-HA!
IT'S DANTE!

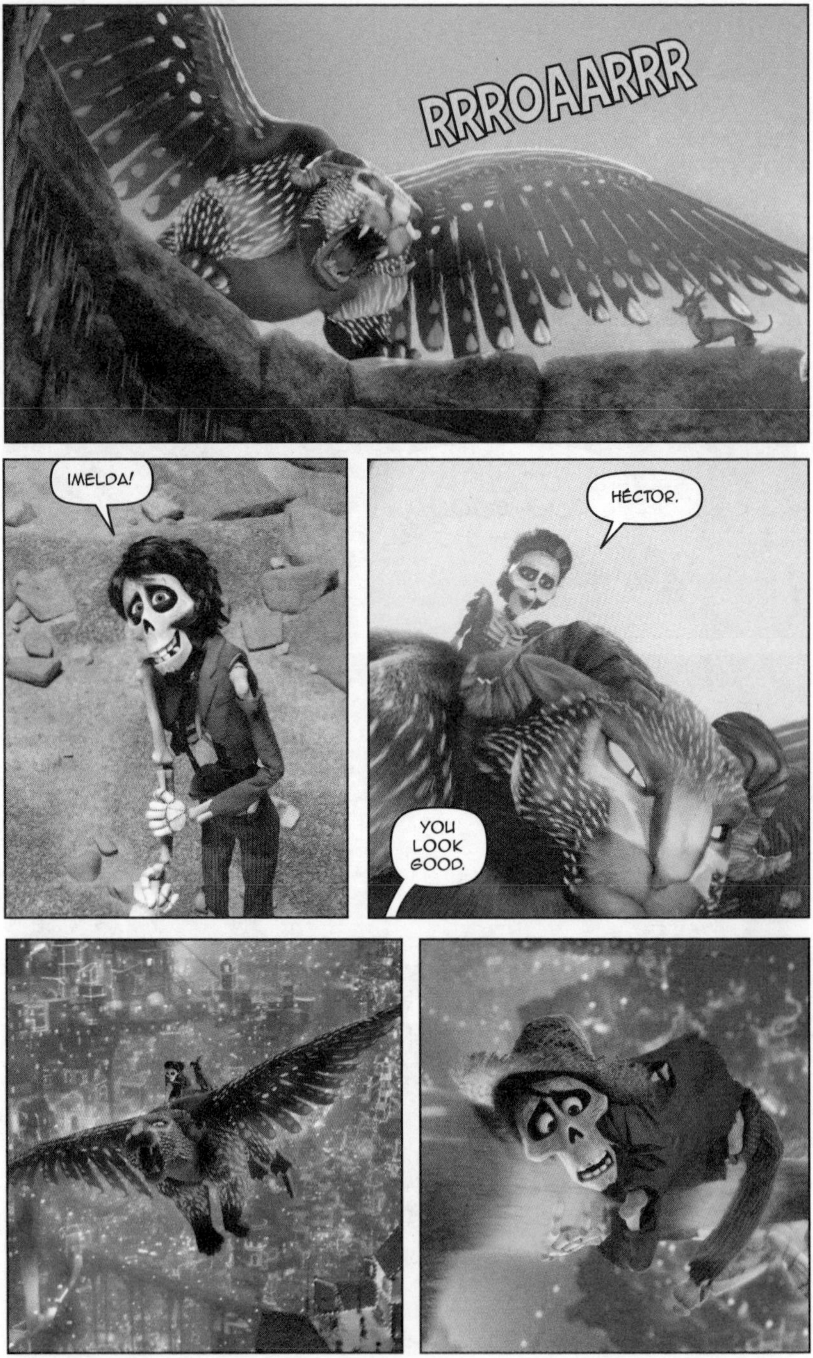
RRROAARRR
IMELDA!
HÉCTOR.
YOU LOOK GOOD.

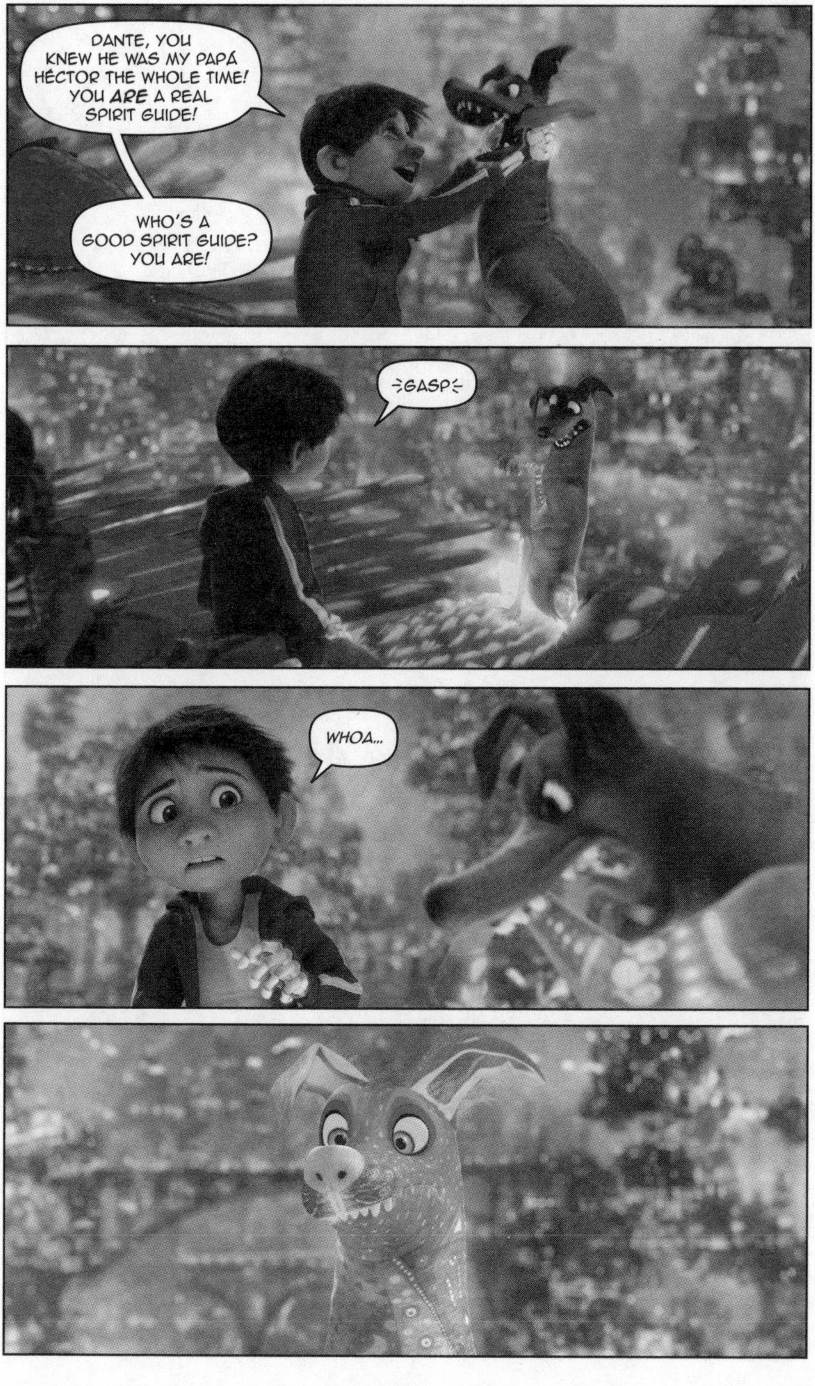

DANTE, YOU KNEW HE WAS MY PAPÁ HÉCTOR THE WHOLE TIME! YOU ARE A REAL SPIRIT GUIDE!
WHO'S A GOOD SPIRIT GUIDE? YOU ARE!
GASP
WHOA...

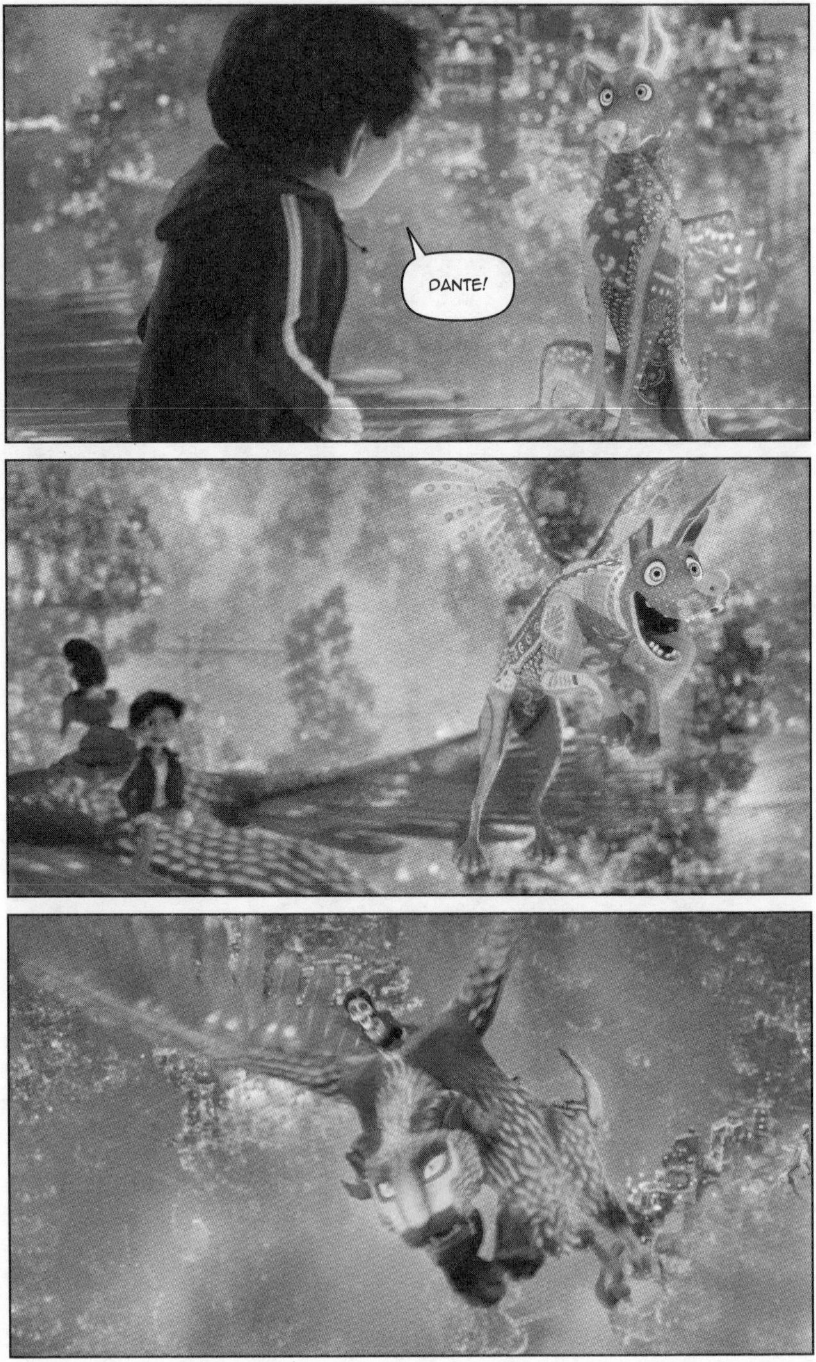
DANTE!

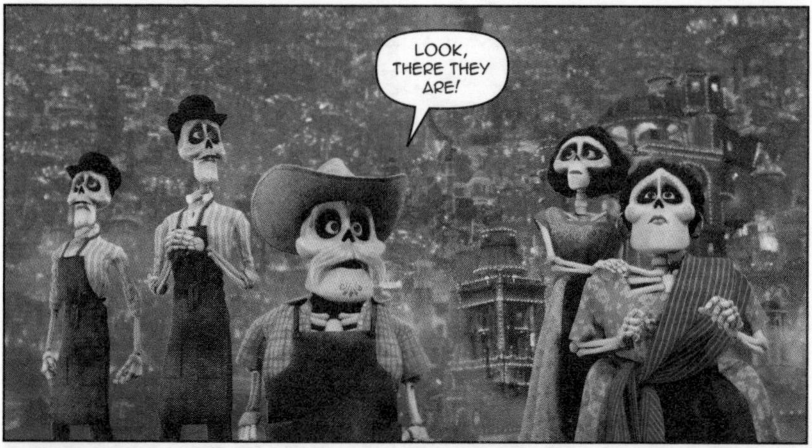
LOOK, THERE THEY ARE!

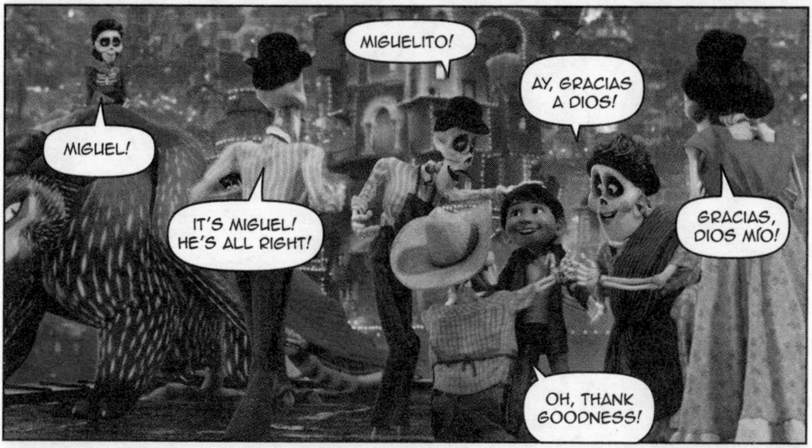
MIGUEL!
IT'S MIGUEL! HE'S ALL RIGHT!
MIGUELITO!
AY, GRACIAS A DIOS!
GRACIAS, DIOS MÍO!
OH, THANK GOODNESS!

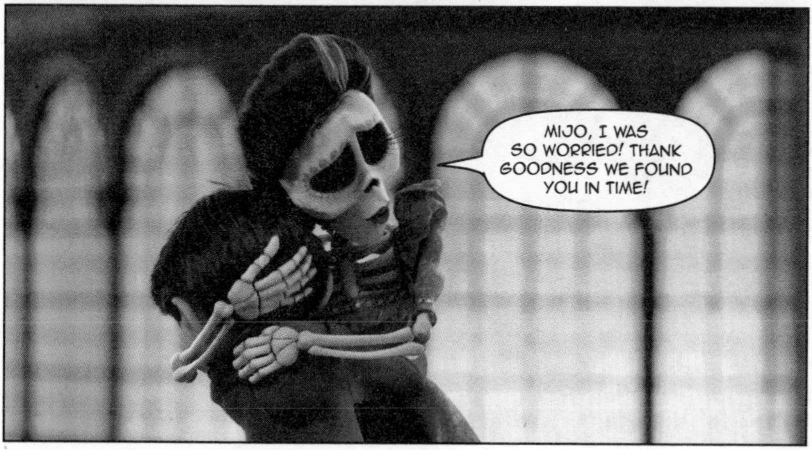
MIJO, I WAS SO WORRIED! THANK GOODNESS WE FOUND YOU IN TIME!

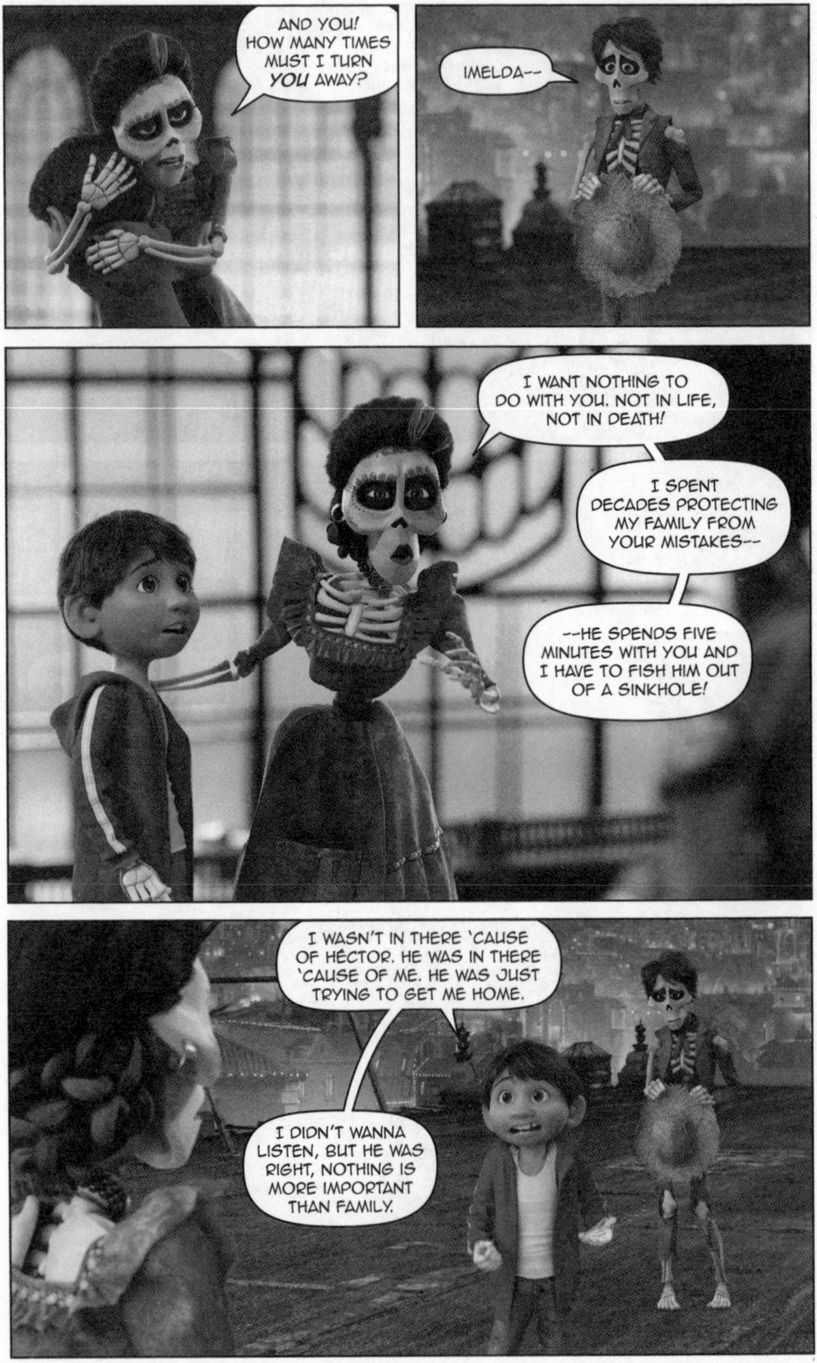
AND YOU! HOW MANY TIMES MUST I TURN *YOU* AWAY?
IMELDA--
I WANT NOTHING TO DO WITH YOU. NOT IN LIFE, NOT IN DEATH!
I SPENT DECADES PROTECTING MY FAMILY FROM YOUR MISTAKES--
--HE SPENDS FIVE MINUTES WITH YOU AND I HAVE TO FISH HIM OUT OF A SINKHOLE!
I WASN'T IN THERE 'CAUSE OF HÉCTOR. HE WAS IN THERE 'CAUSE OF ME. HE WAS JUST TRYING TO GET ME HOME.
I DIDN'T WANNA LISTEN, BUT HE WAS RIGHT, NOTHING IS MORE IMPORTANT THAN FAMILY.

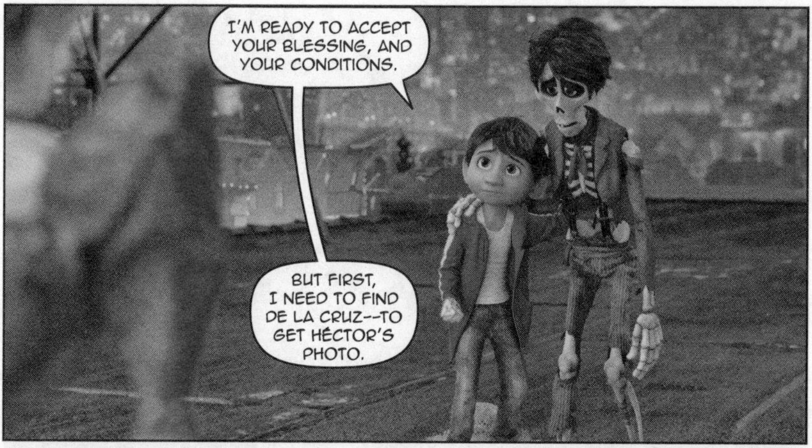
I'M READY TO ACCEPT YOUR BLESSING, AND YOUR CONDITIONS.
BUT FIRST, I NEED TO FIND DE LA CRUZ--TO GET HÉCTOR'S PHOTO.

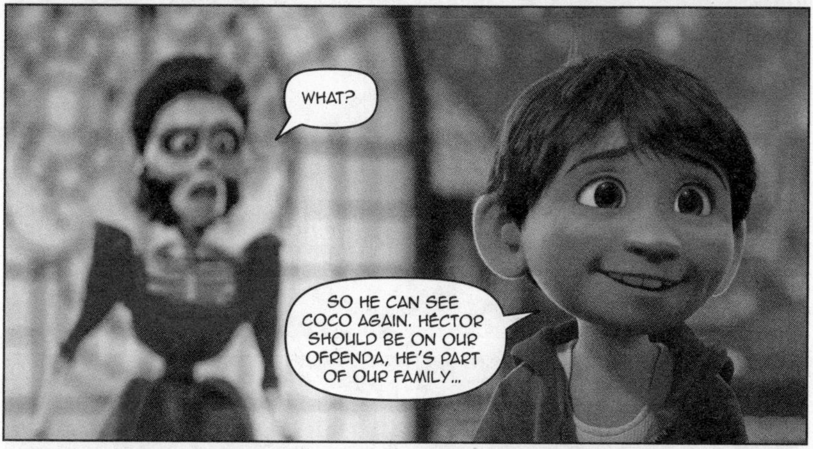
WHAT?
SO HE CAN SEE COCO AGAIN. HÉCTOR SHOULD BE ON OUR OFRENDA, HE'S PART OF OUR FAMILY...

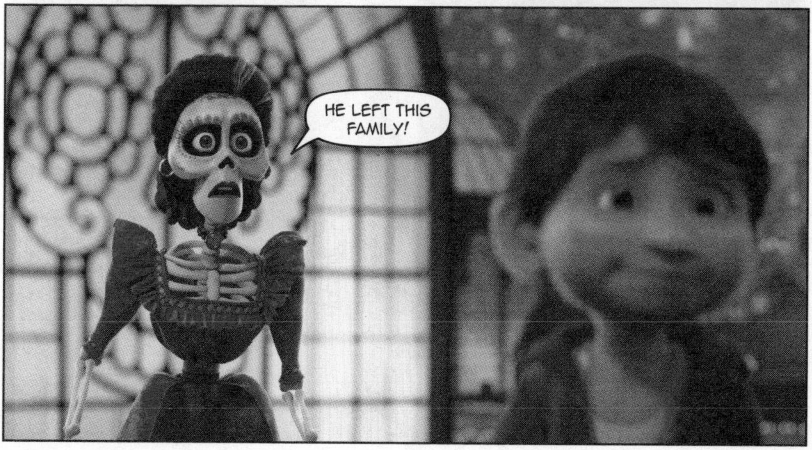
HE LEFT THIS FAMILY!

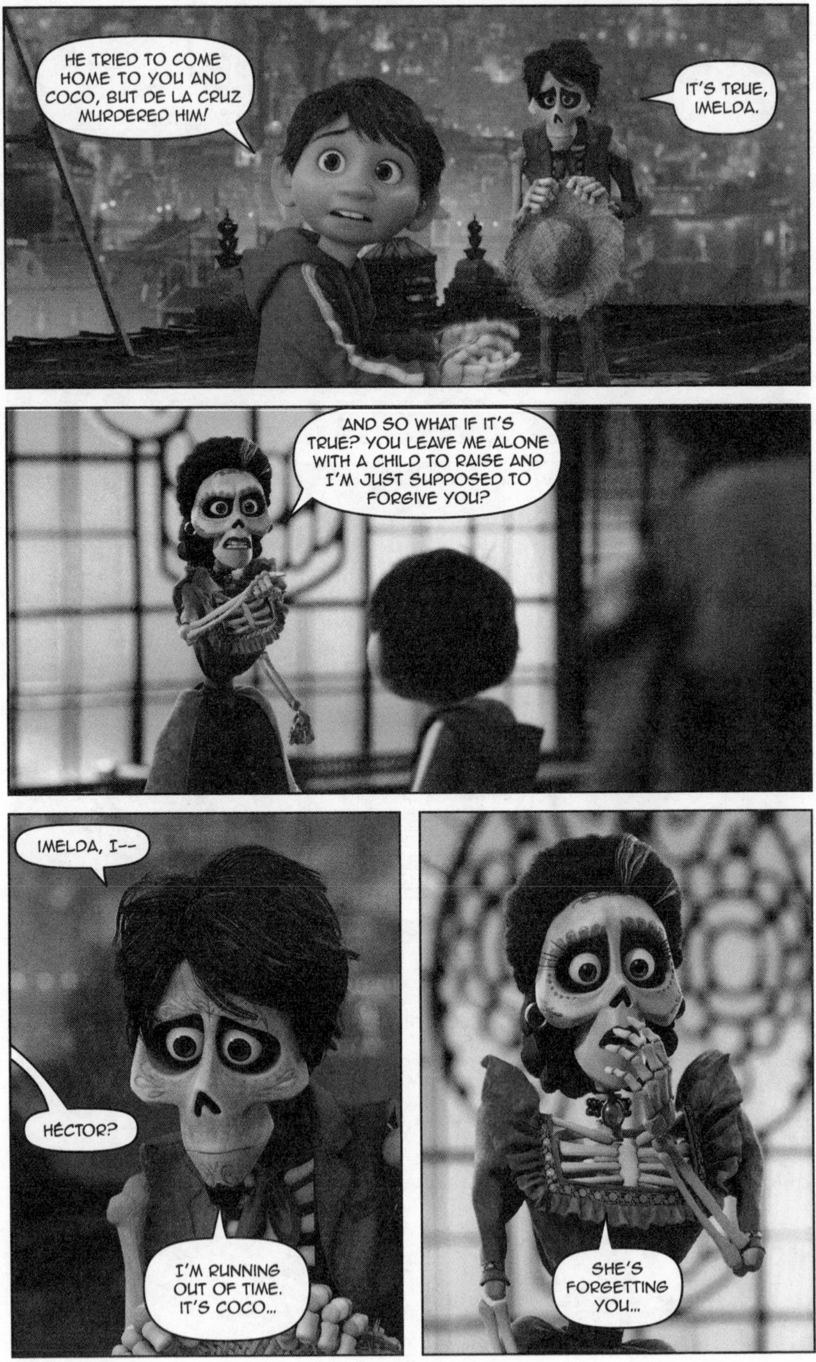
HE TRIED TO COME HOME TO YOU AND COCO, BUT DE LA CRUZ MURDERED HIM!
IT'S TRUE, IMELDA.
AND SO WHAT IF IT'S TRUE? YOU LEAVE ME ALONE WITH A CHILD TO RAISE AND I'M JUST SUPPOSED TO FORGIVE YOU?
IMELDA, I--
HÉCTOR?
I'M RUNNING OUT OF TIME. IT'S COCO...
SHE'S FORGETTING YOU...

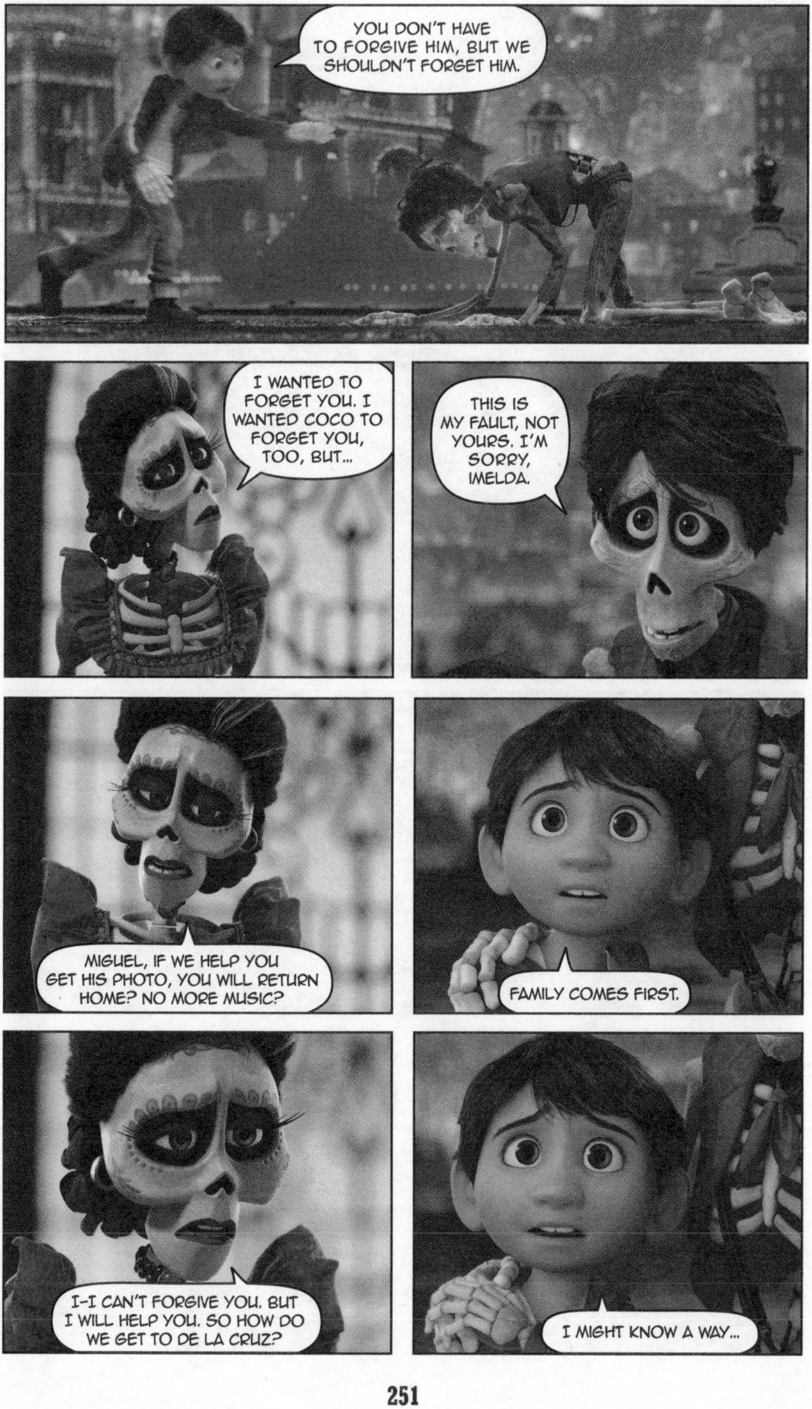
YOU DON'T HAVE TO FORGIVE HIM, BUT WE SHOULDN'T FORGET HIM.
I WANTED TO FORGET YOU. I WANTED COCO TO FORGET YOU, TOO, BUT...
THIS IS MY FAULT, NOT YOURS. I'M SORRY, IMELDA.
MIGUEL, IF WE HELP YOU GET HIS PHOTO, YOU WILL RETURN HOME? NO MORE MUSIC?
FAMILY COMES FIRST.
I-I CAN'T FORGIVE YOU. BUT I WILL HELP YOU. SO HOW DO WE GET TO DE LA CRUZ?
I MIGHT KNOW A WAY...

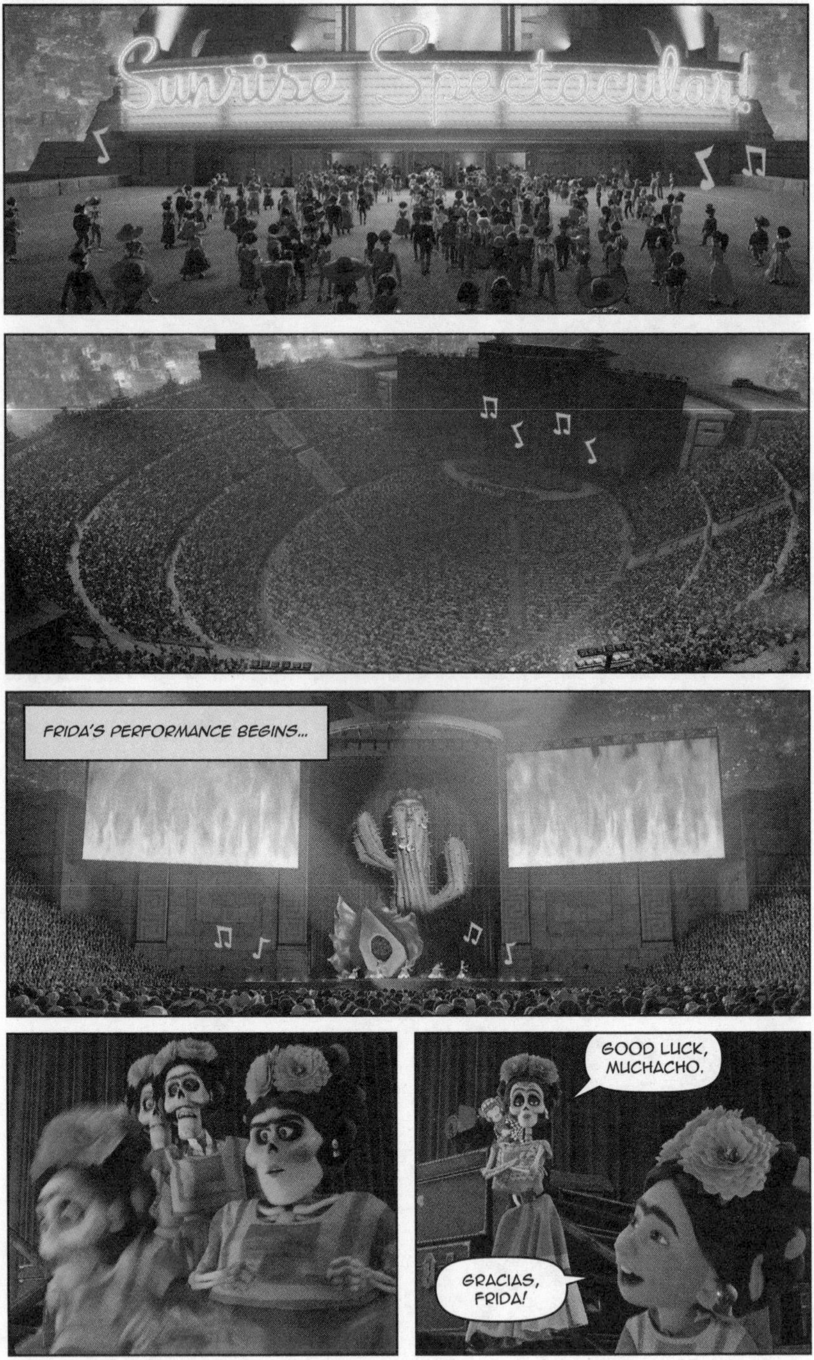
Sunrise Spectacular!
FRIDA'S PERFORMANCE BEGINS...
GOOD LUCK, MUCHACHO.
GRACIAS, FRIDA!

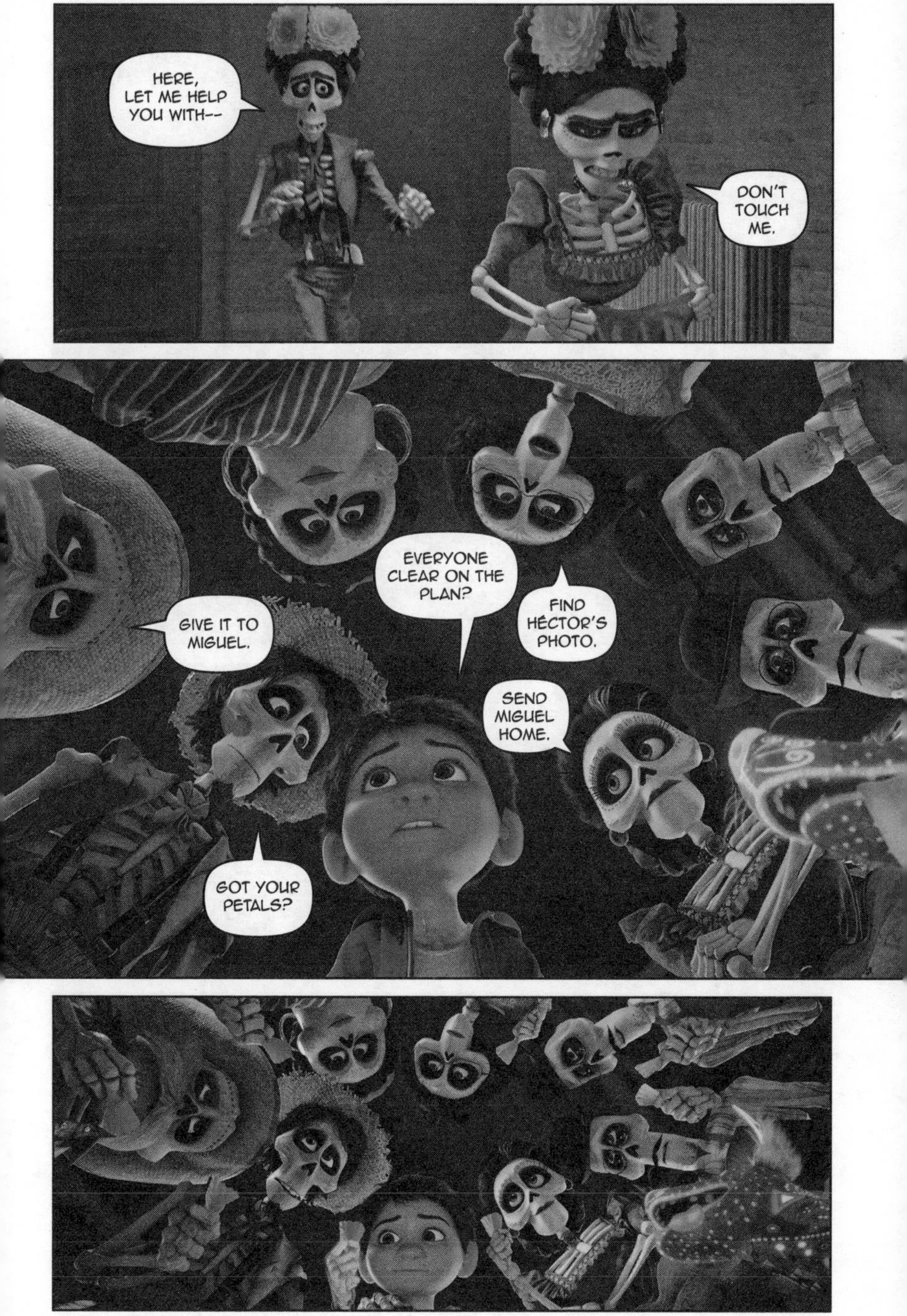
HERE, LET ME HELP YOU WITH--
DON'T TOUCH ME.
EVERYONE CLEAR ON THE PLAN?
FIND HÉCTOR'S PHOTO.
GIVE IT TO MIGUEL.
SEND MIGUEL HOME.
GOT YOUR PETALS?

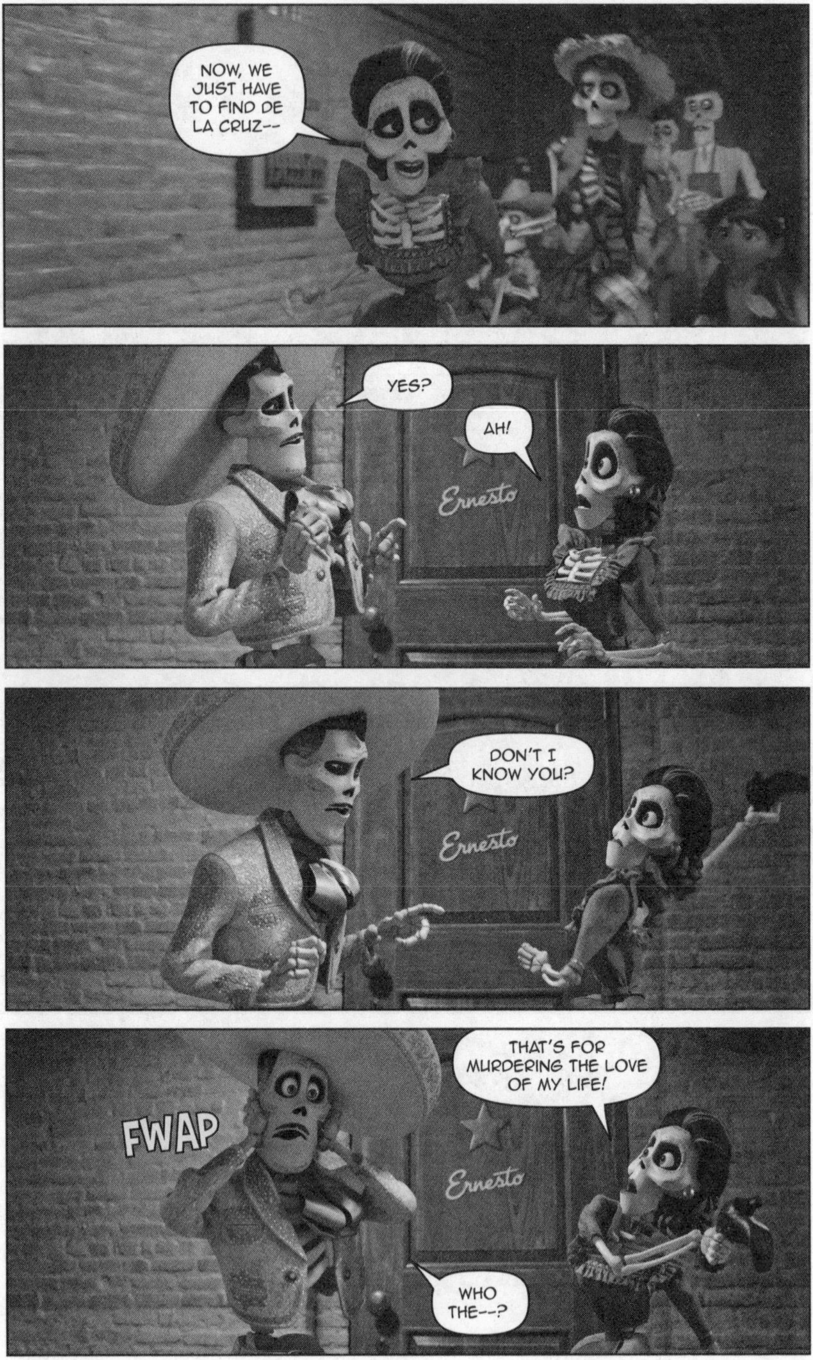
NOW, WE JUST HAVE TO FIND DE LA CRUZ--
YES?
AH!
Ernesto
DON'T I KNOW YOU?
Ernesto
FWAP
THAT'S FOR MURDERING THE LOVE OF MY LIFE!
Ernesto
WHO THE--?

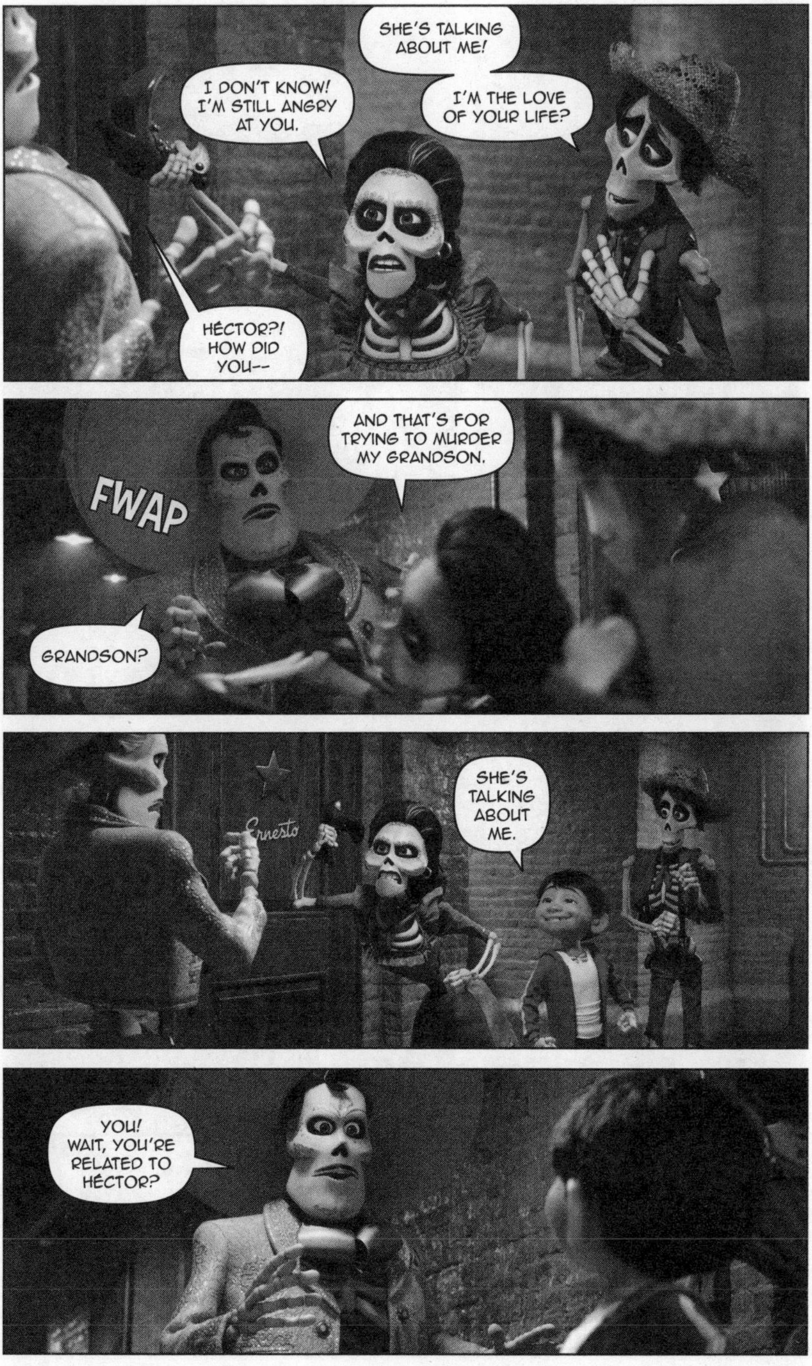
HÉCTOR?! HOW DID YOU--
SHE'S TALKING ABOUT ME!
I'M THE LOVE OF YOUR LIFE?
I DON'T KNOW! I'M STILL ANGRY AT YOU.
FWAP
AND THAT'S FOR TRYING TO MURDER MY GRANDSON.
GRANDSON?
Ernesto
SHE'S TALKING ABOUT ME.
YOU! WAIT, YOU'RE RELATED TO HÉCTOR?

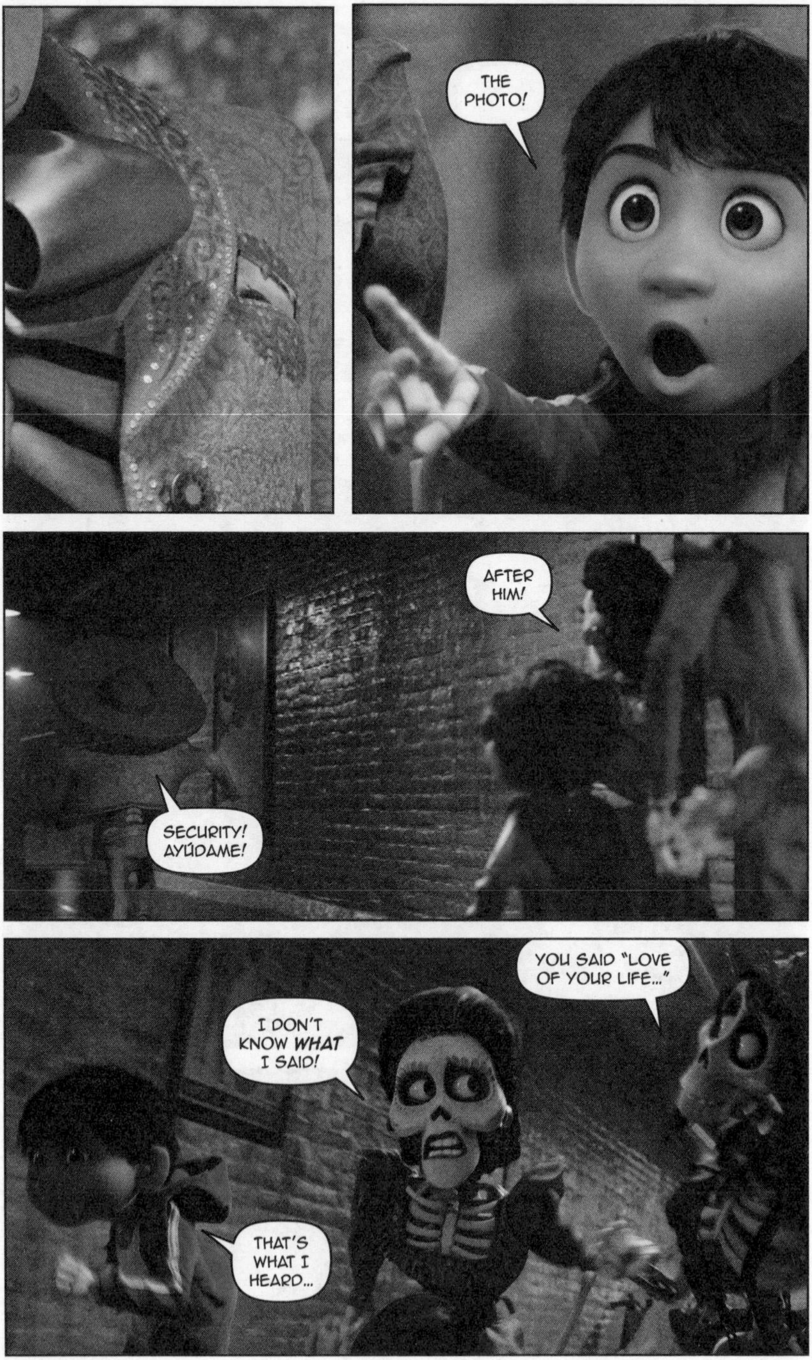
THE PHOTO!
AFTER HIM!
SECURITY! AYÚDAME!
YOU SAID "LOVE OF YOUR LIFE..."
I DON'T KNOW *WHAT* I SAID!
THAT'S WHAT I HEARD...

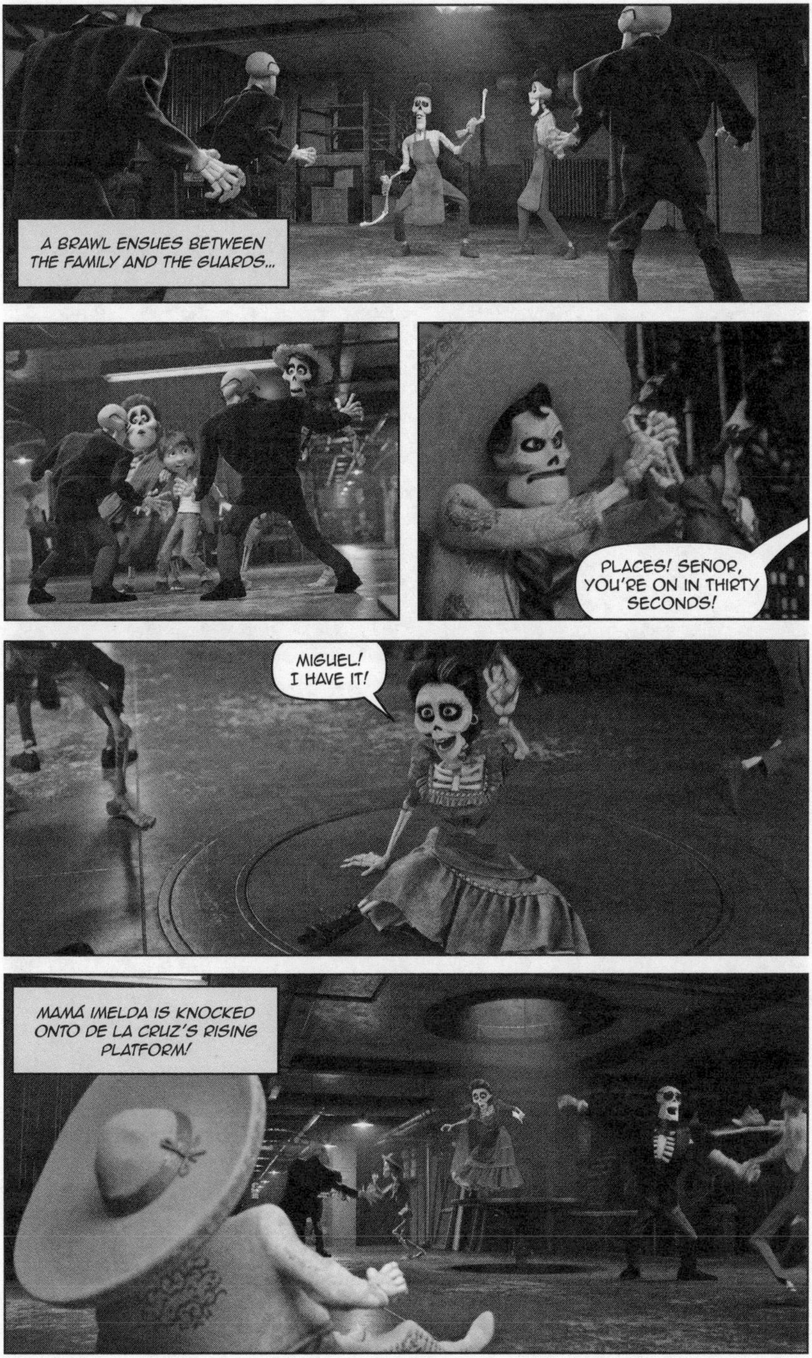
A BRAWL ENSUES BETWEEN THE FAMILY AND THE GUARDS...
PLACES! SEÑOR, YOU'RE ON IN THIRTY SECONDS!
MIGUEL! I HAVE IT!
MAMÁ IMELDA IS KNOCKED ONTO DE LA CRUZ'S RISING PLATFORM!

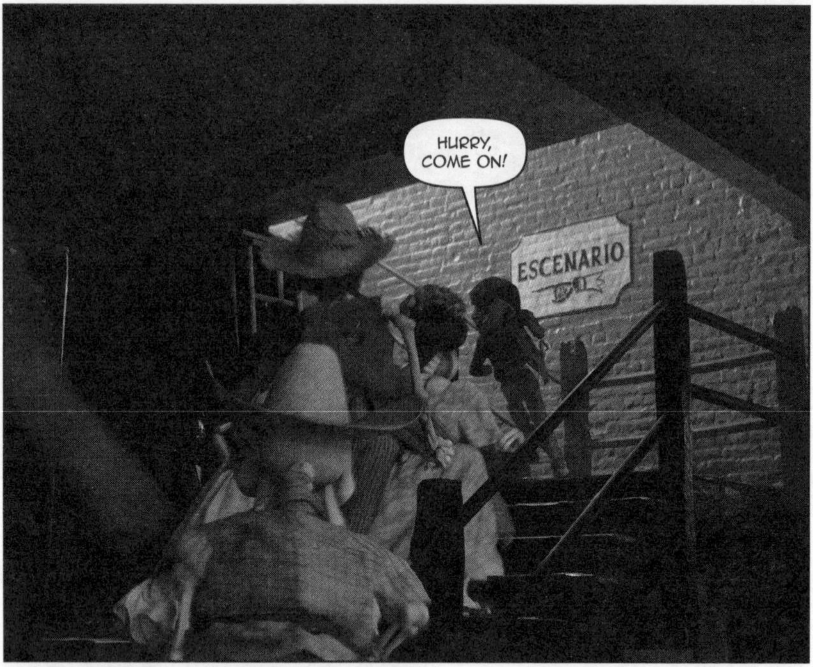
HURRY, COME ON!
ESCENARIO

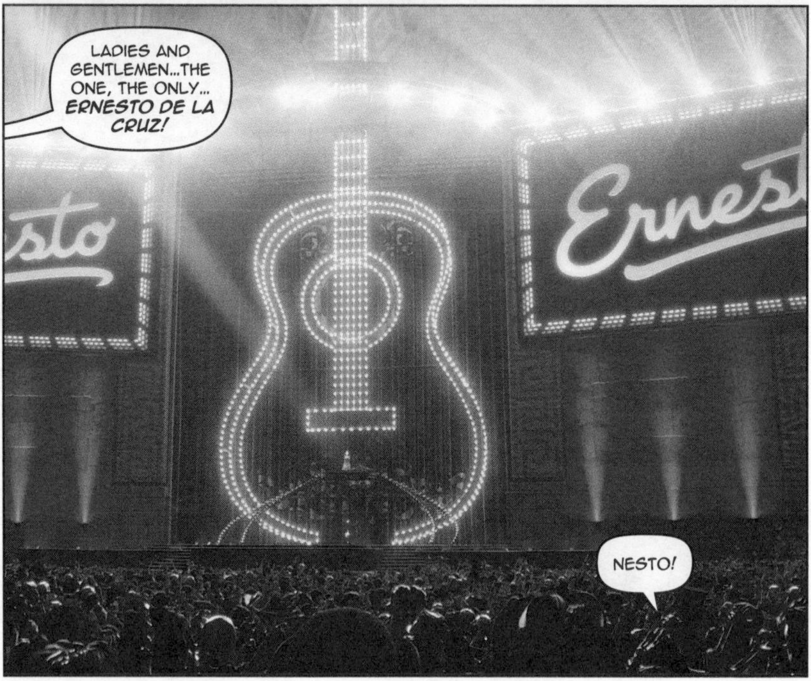
LADIES AND GENTLEMEN...THE ONE, THE ONLY... ***ERNESTO DE LA CRUZ!***
Ernesto
Ernesto
NESTO!

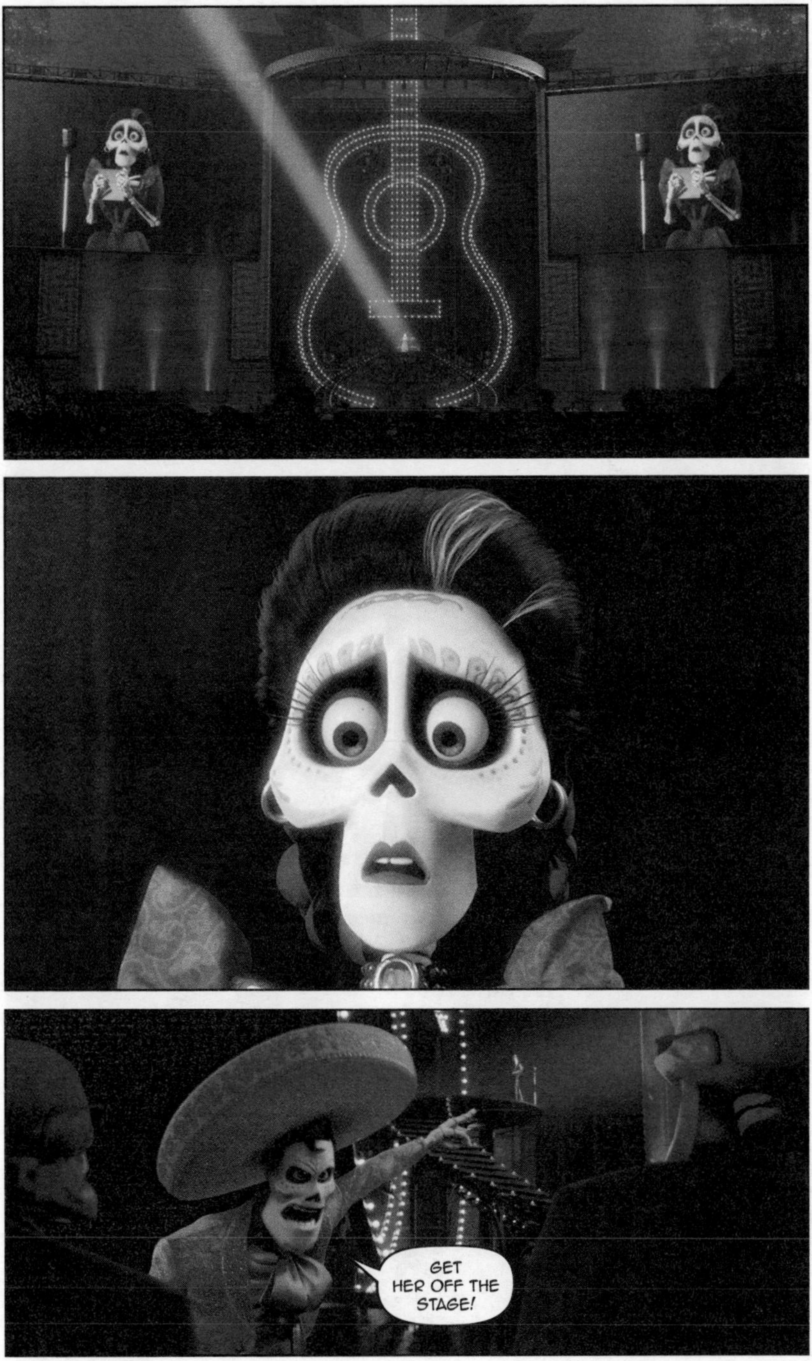
GET HER OFF THE STAGE!

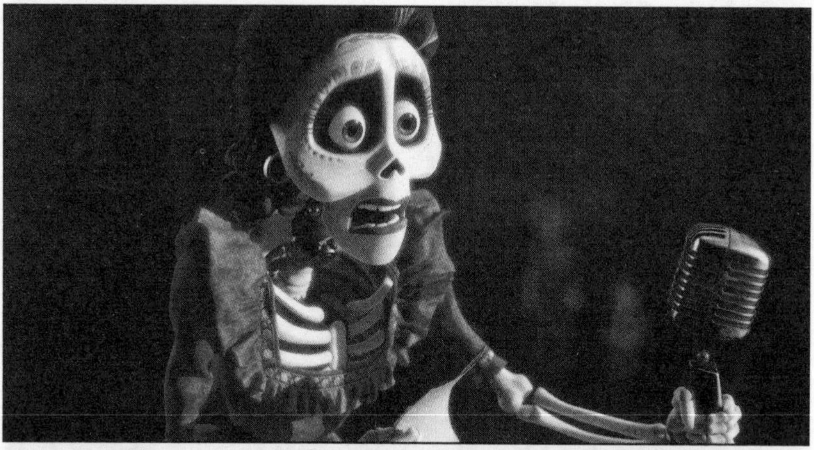

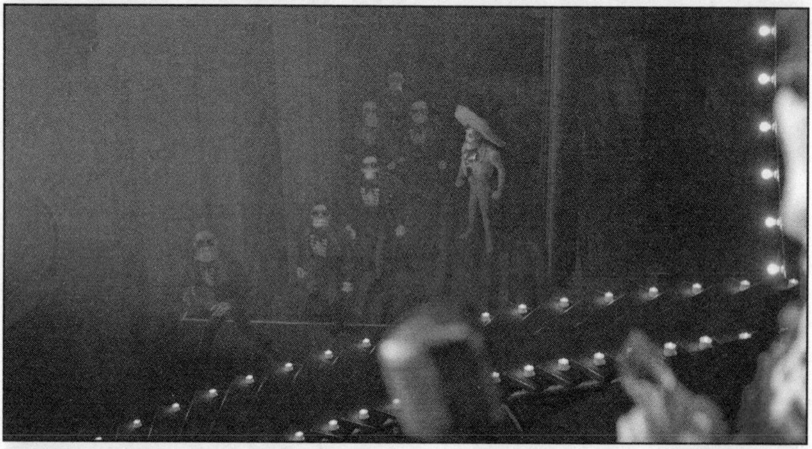

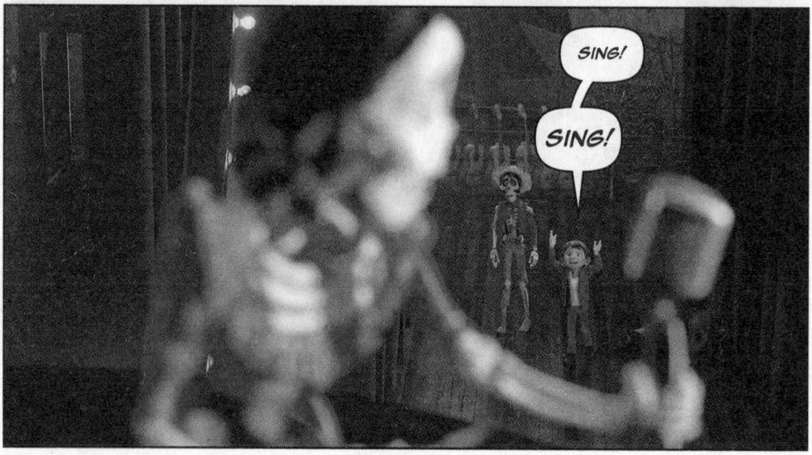
SING!
SING!

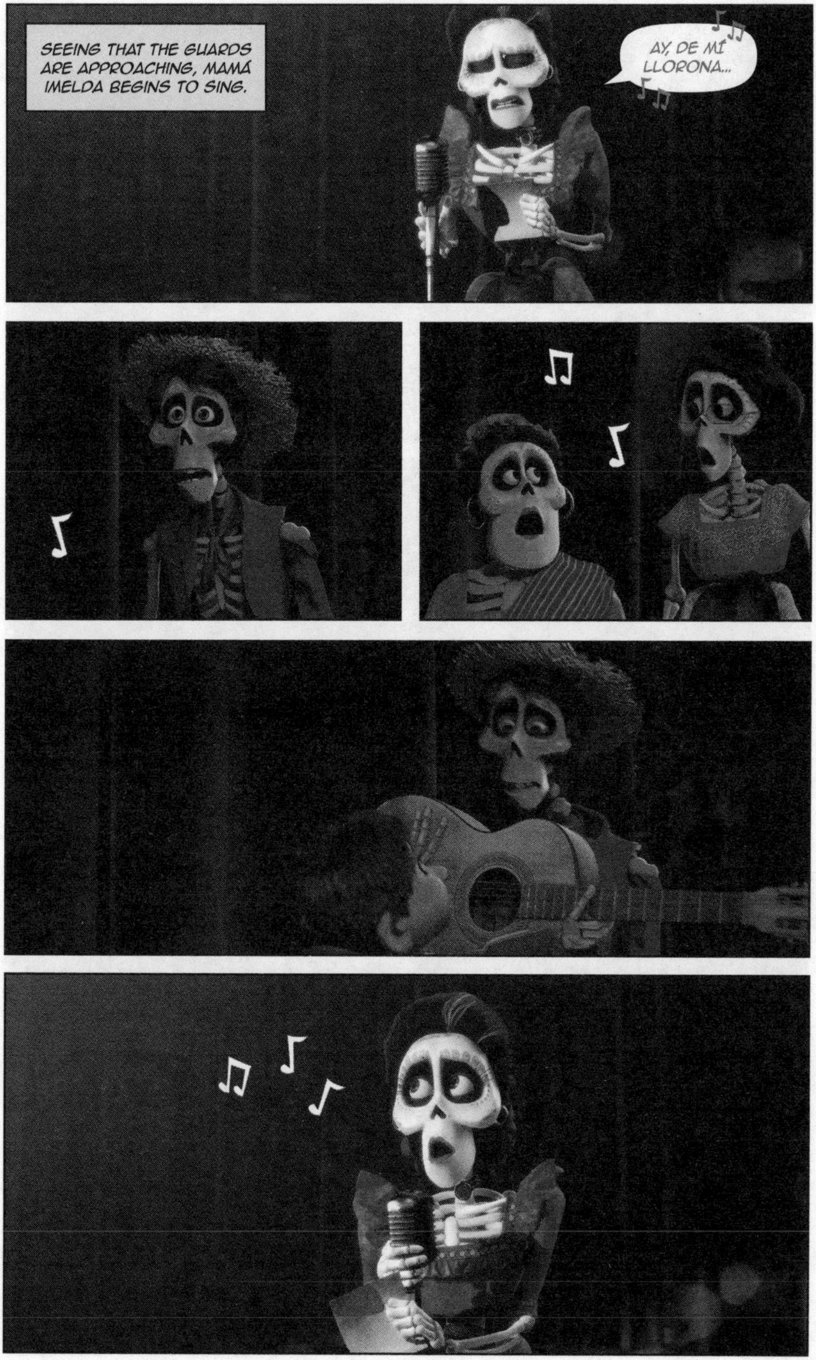
SEEING THAT THE GUARDS ARE APPROACHING, MAMÁ IMELDA BEGINS TO SING.
AY, DE MÍ LLORONA...

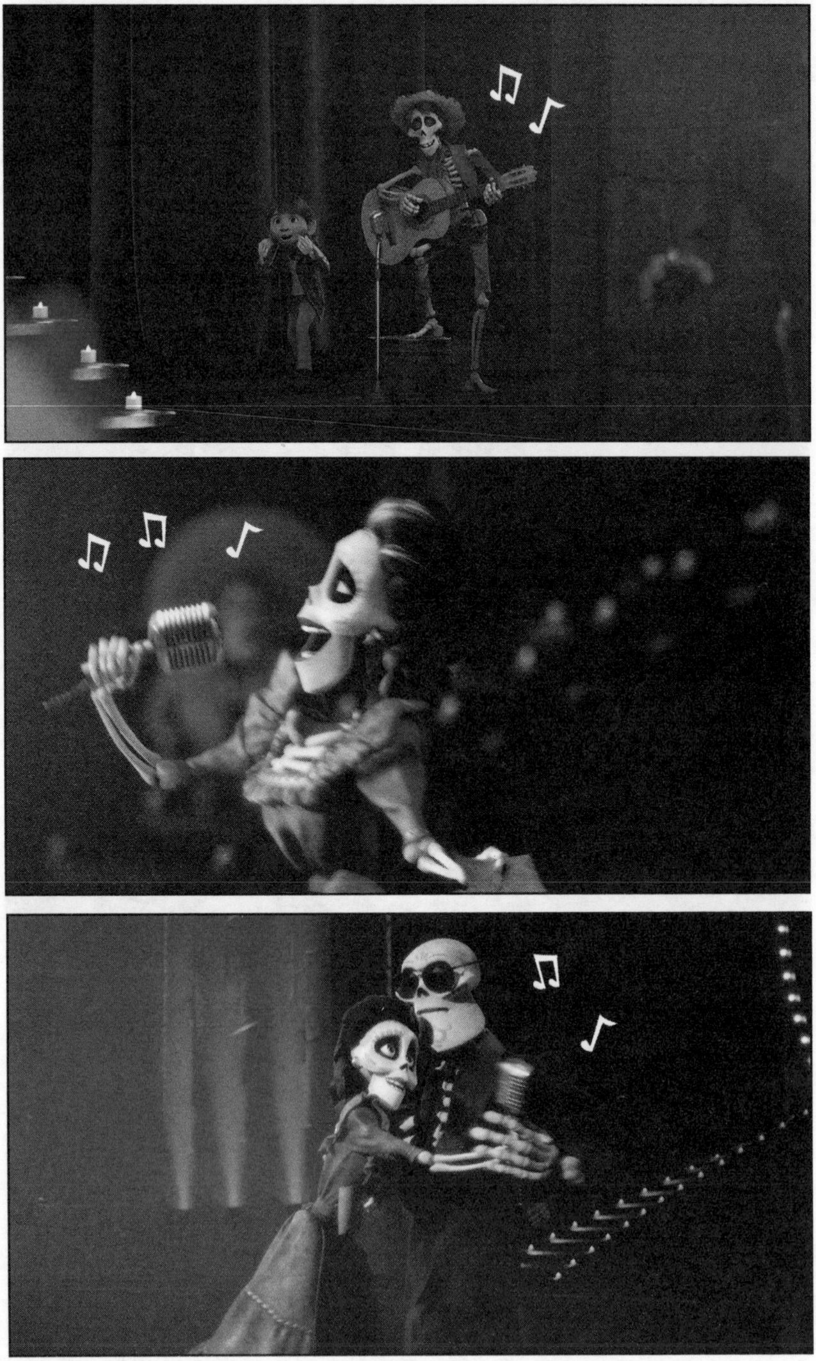

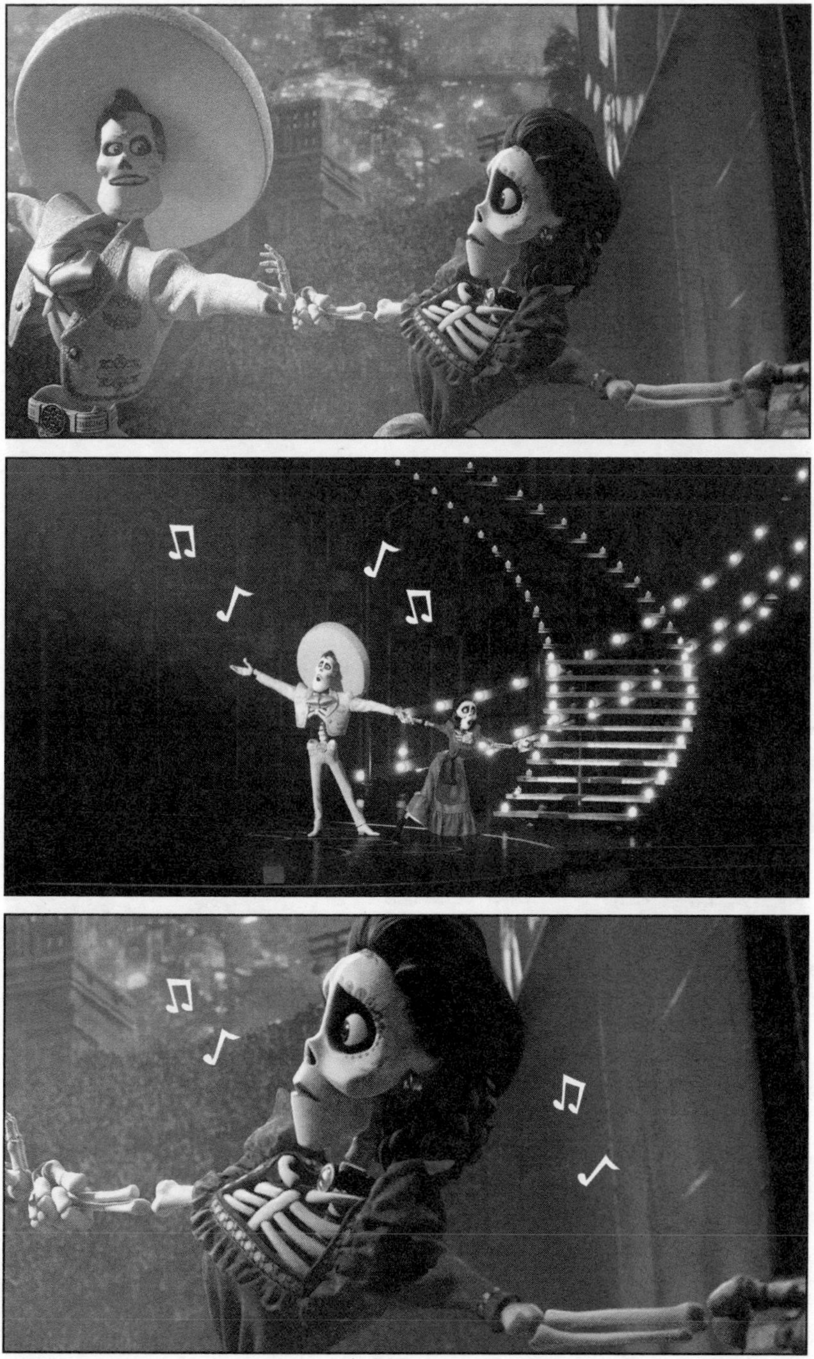

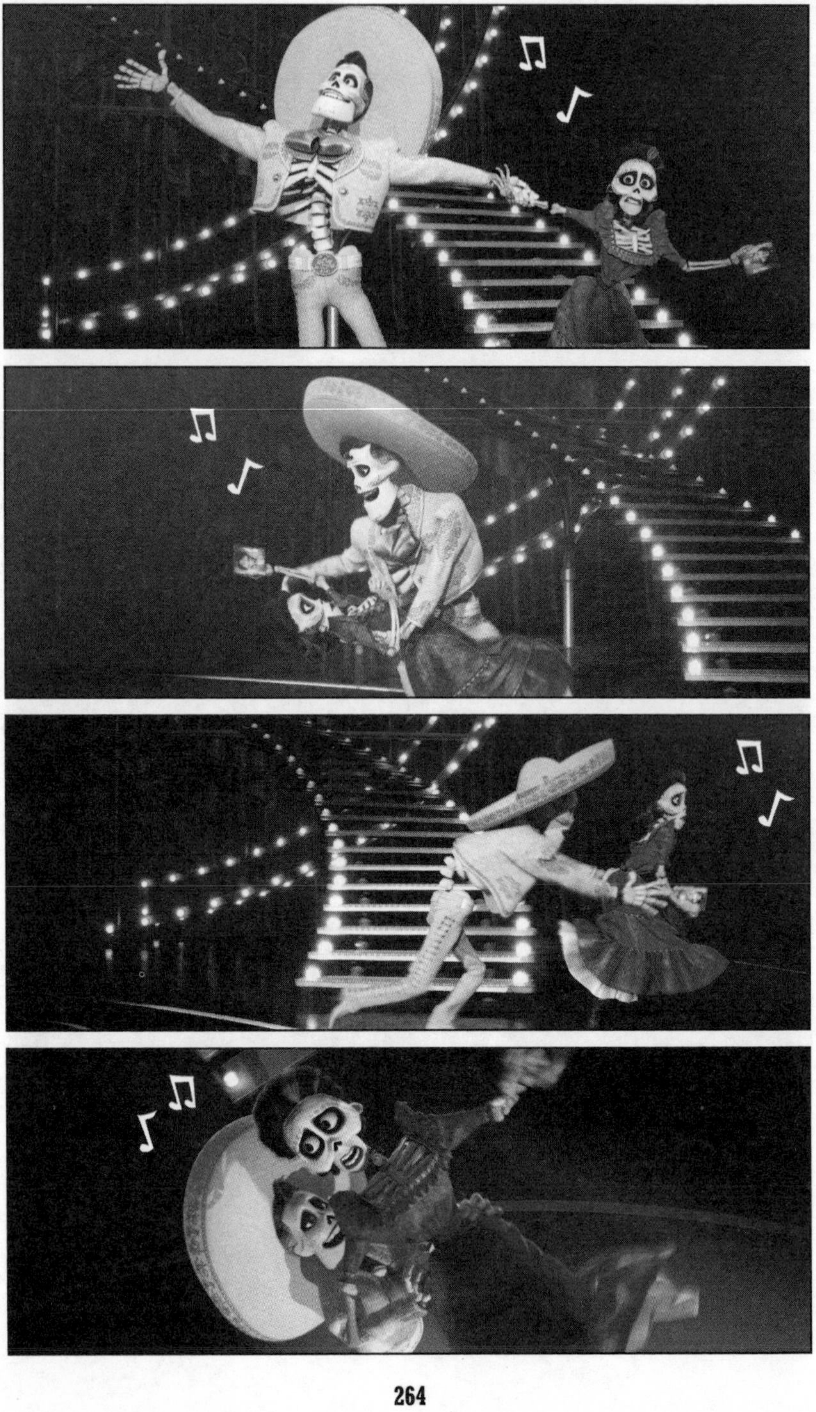

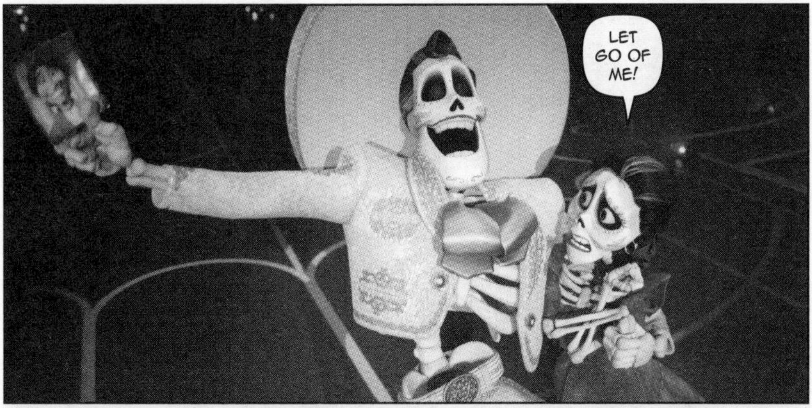
LET GO OF ME!

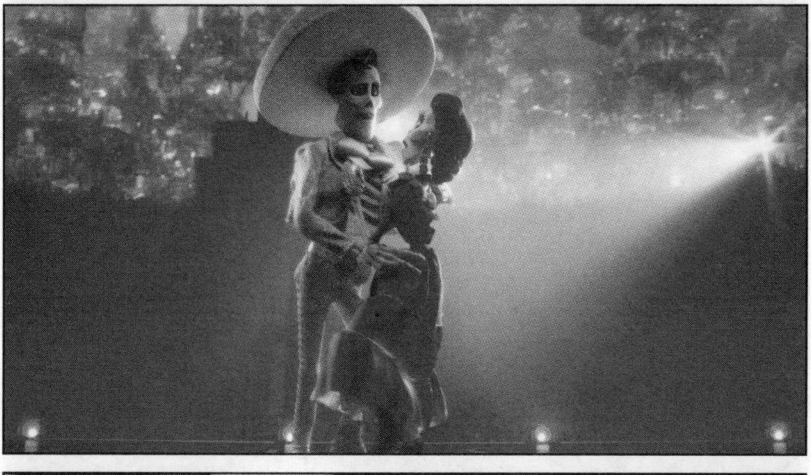

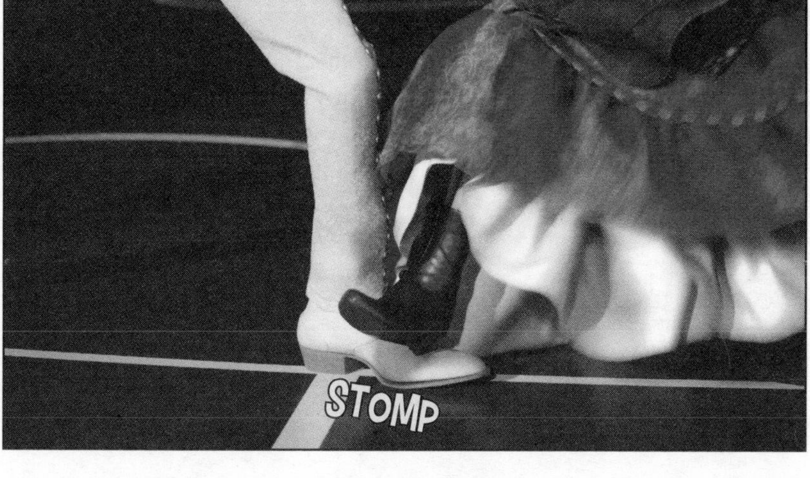
STOMP

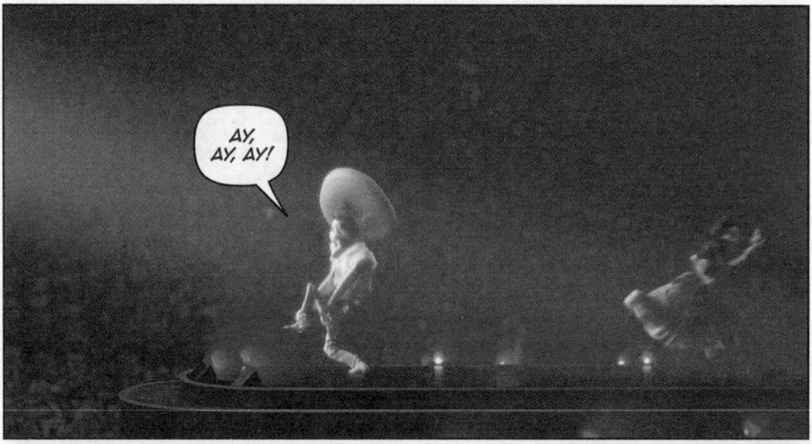
AY, AY, AY!

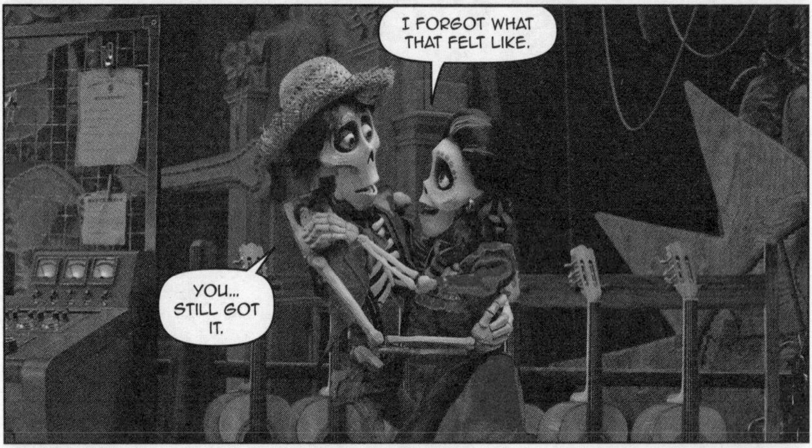
I FORGOT WHAT THAT FELT LIKE.
YOU... STILL GOT IT.

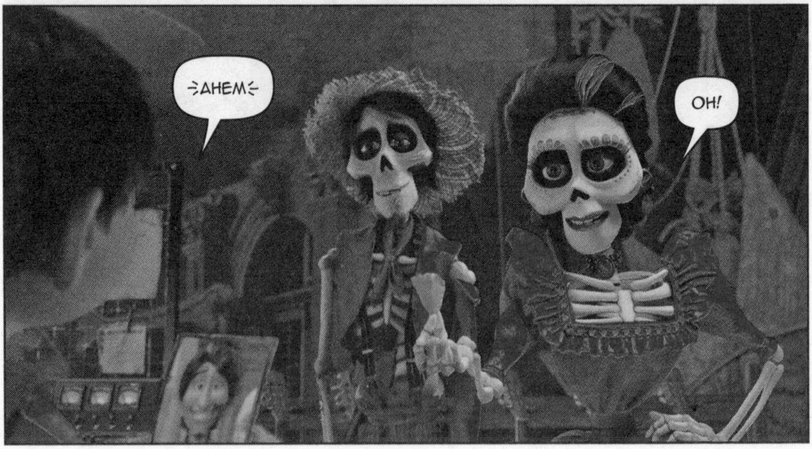
AHEM
OH!

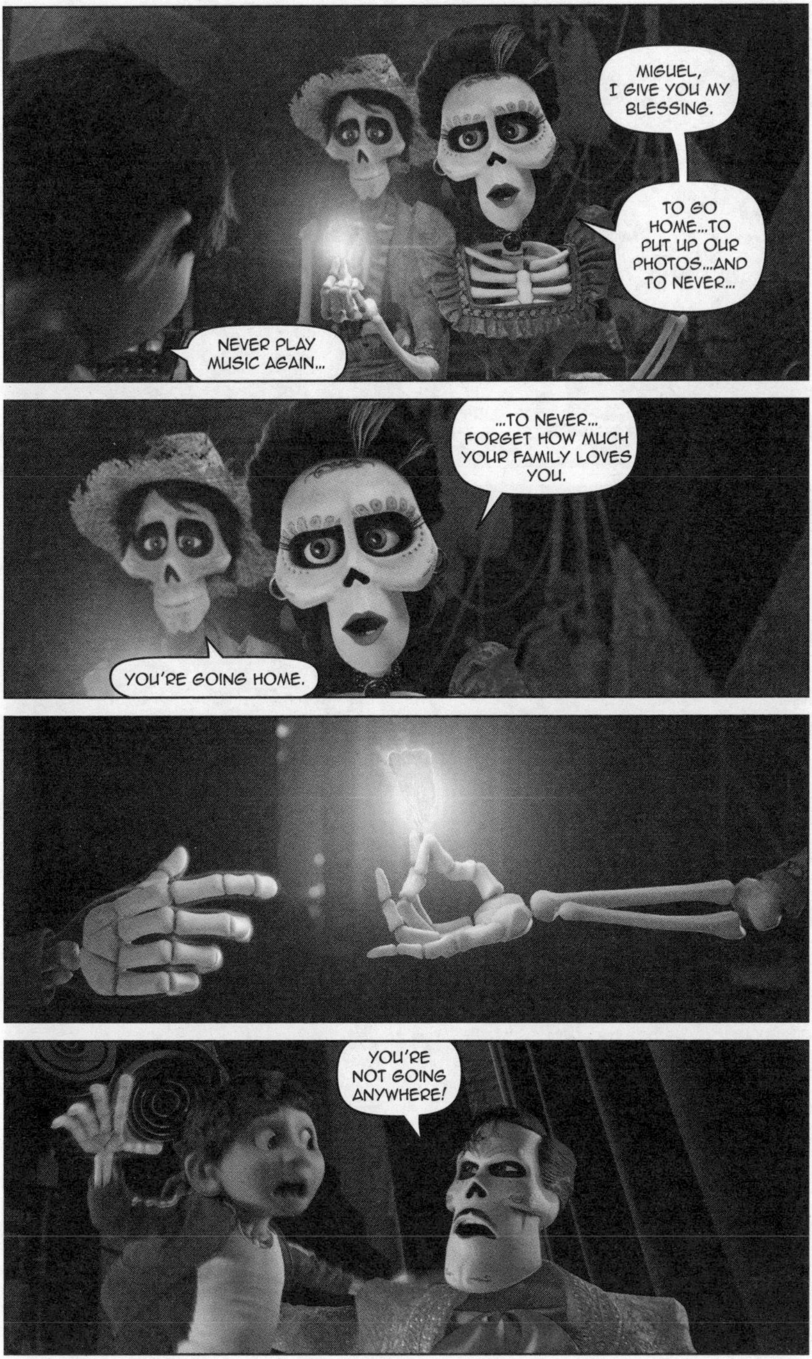
MIGUEL, I GIVE YOU MY BLESSING.
TO GO HOME...TO PUT UP OUR PHOTOS...AND TO NEVER...
NEVER PLAY MUSIC AGAIN...
...TO NEVER... FORGET HOW MUCH YOUR FAMILY LOVES YOU.
YOU'RE GOING HOME.
YOU'RE NOT GOING ANYWHERE!

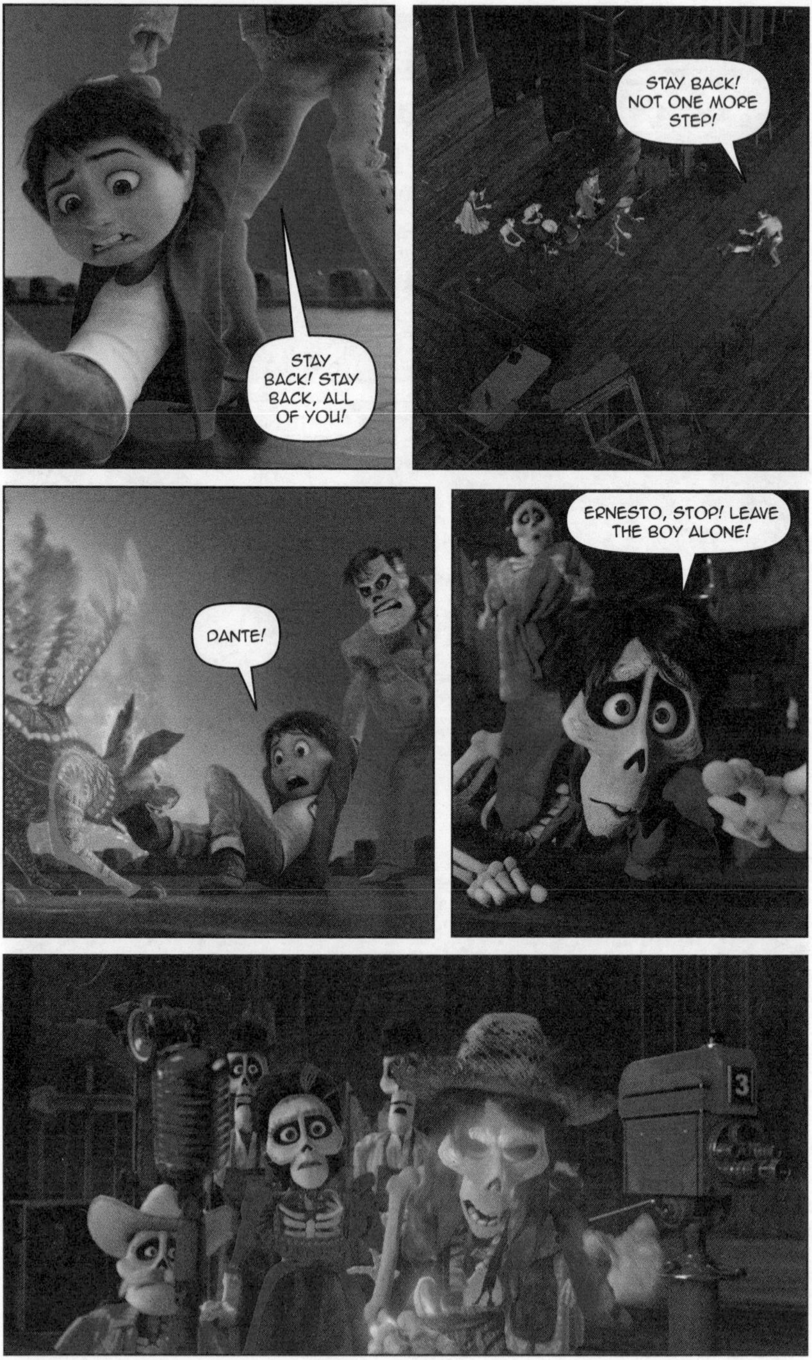
STAY BACK! STAY BACK, ALL OF YOU!
STAY BACK! NOT ONE MORE STEP!
DANTE!
ERNESTO, STOP! LEAVE THE BOY ALONE!
3

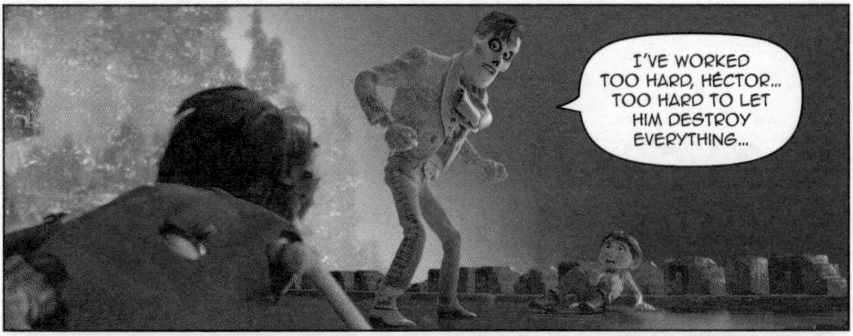
I'VE WORKED TOO HARD, HÉCTOR... TOO HARD TO LET HIM DESTROY EVERYTHING...

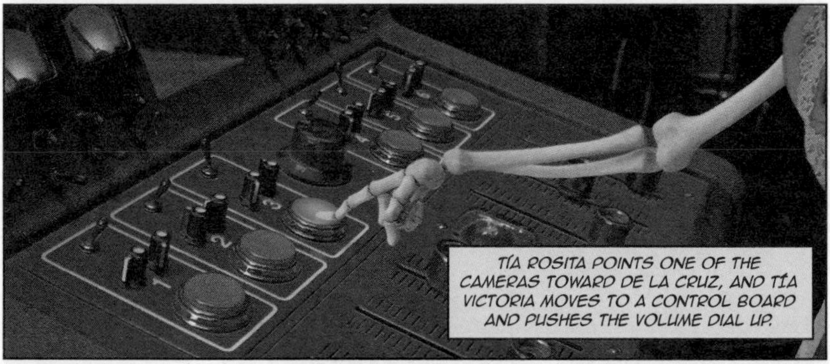
TÍA ROSITA POINTS ONE OF THE CAMERAS TOWARD DE LA CRUZ, AND TÍA VICTORIA MOVES TO A CONTROL BOARD AND PUSHES THE VOLUME DIAL UP.

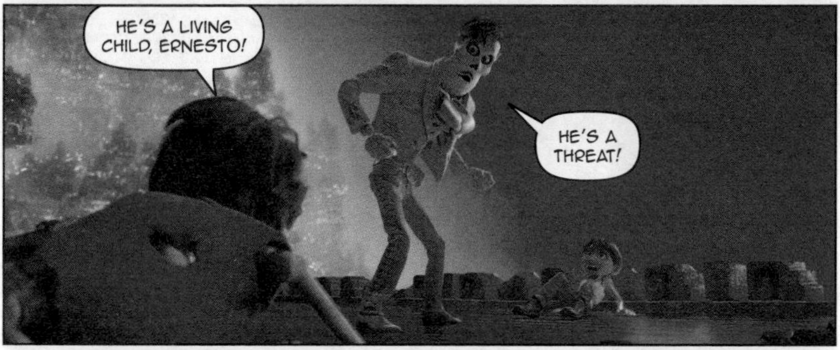
HE'S A LIVING CHILD, ERNESTO!
HE'S A THREAT!

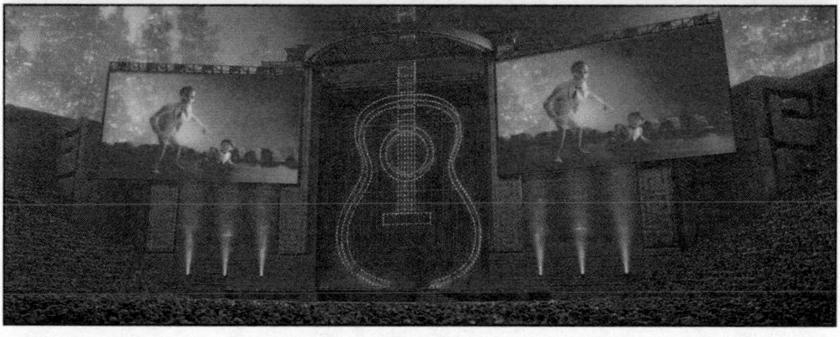

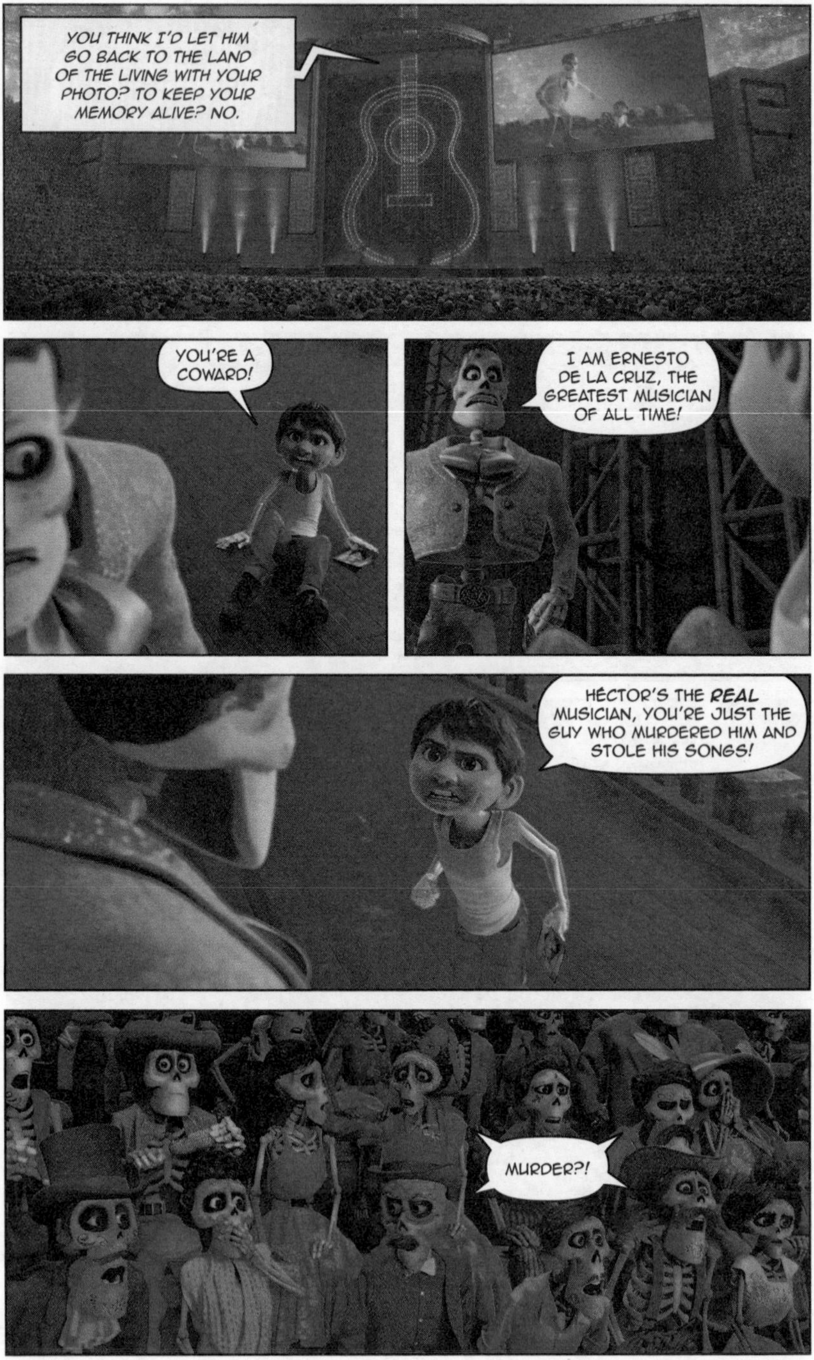
YOU THINK I'D LET HIM GO BACK TO THE LAND OF THE LIVING WITH YOUR PHOTO? TO KEEP YOUR MEMORY ALIVE? NO.
YOU'RE A COWARD!
I AM ERNESTO DE LA CRUZ, THE GREATEST MUSICIAN OF ALL TIME!
HÉCTOR'S THE REAL MUSICIAN, YOU'RE JUST THE GUY WHO MURDERED HIM AND STOLE HIS SONGS!
MURDER?!

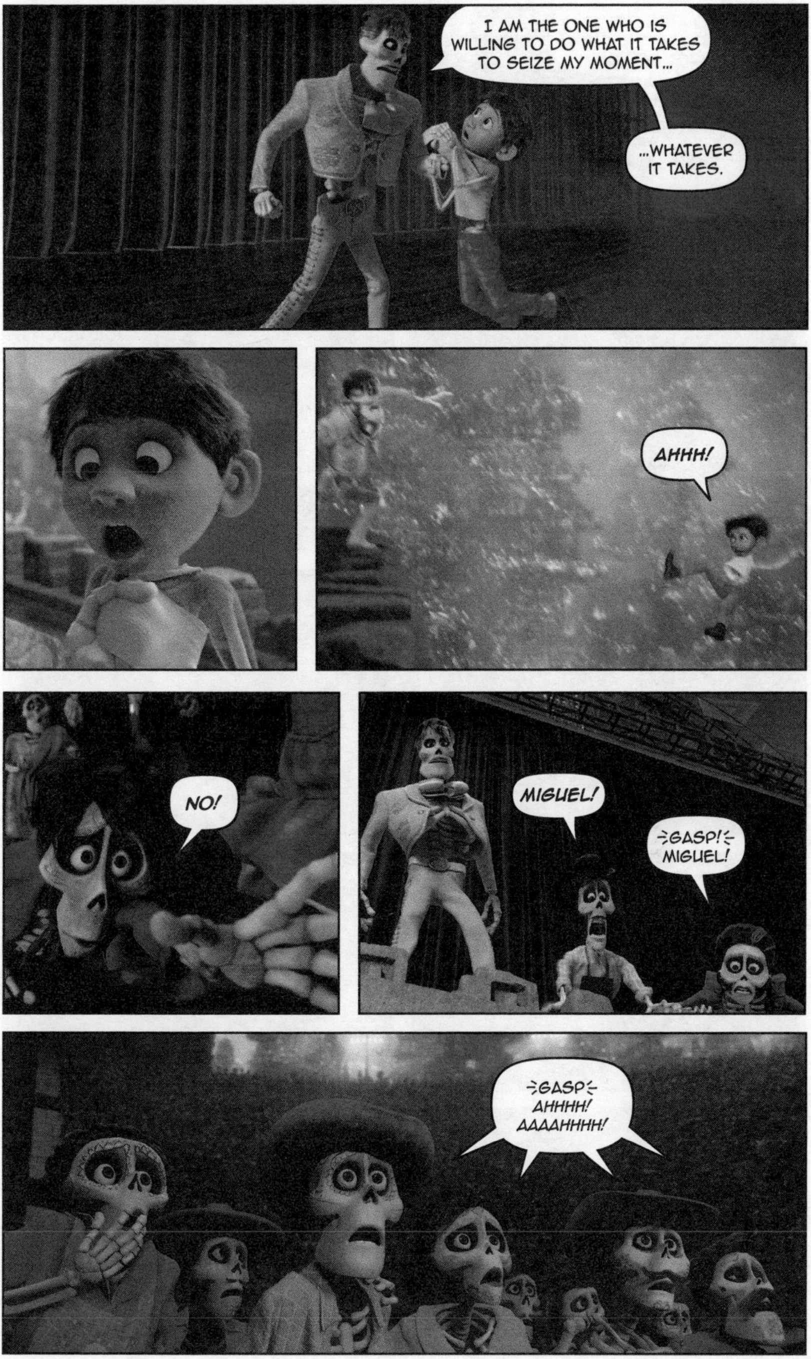
I AM THE ONE WHO IS WILLING TO DO WHAT IT TAKES TO SEIZE MY MOMENT...
...WHATEVER IT TAKES.
AHHH!
NO!
MIGUEL!
GASP! MIGUEL!
GASP AHHHH! AAAAHHHH!

APOLOGIES, OLD FRIEND, BUT THE SHOW MUST GO ON.

ROO-ROO-ROOOOOO!

AHHHHH!

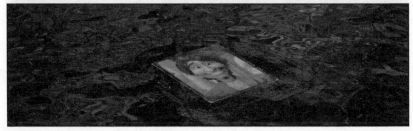

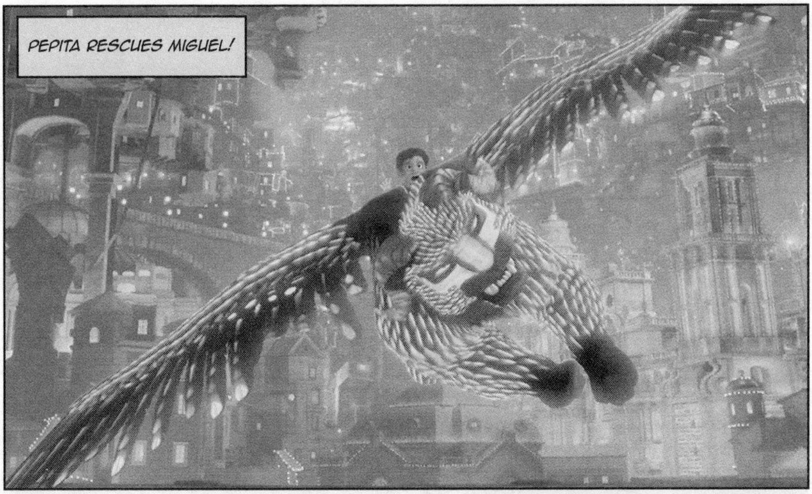
PEPITA RESCUES MIGUEL!

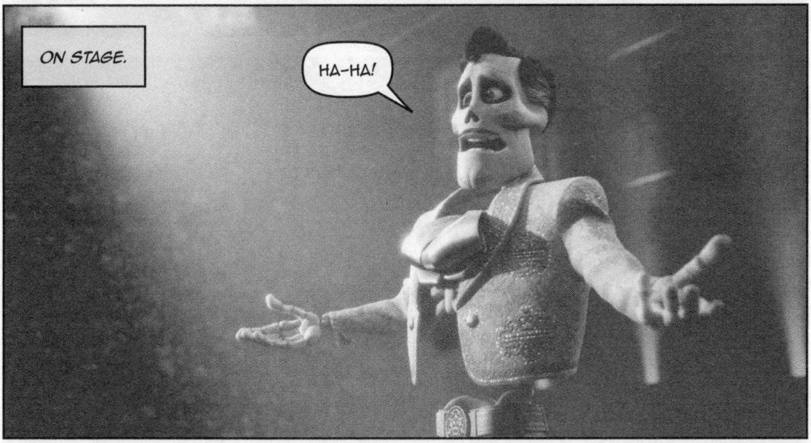
ON STAGE.
HA-HA!

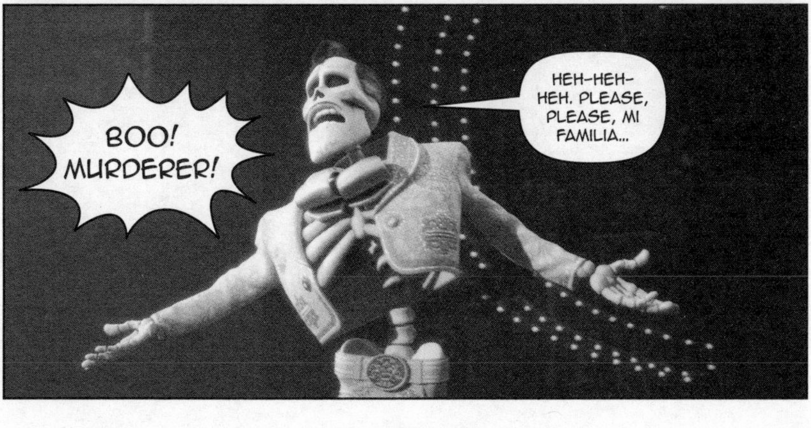
HEH-HEH-HEH. PLEASE, PLEASE, MI FAMILIA...
BOO! MURDERER!

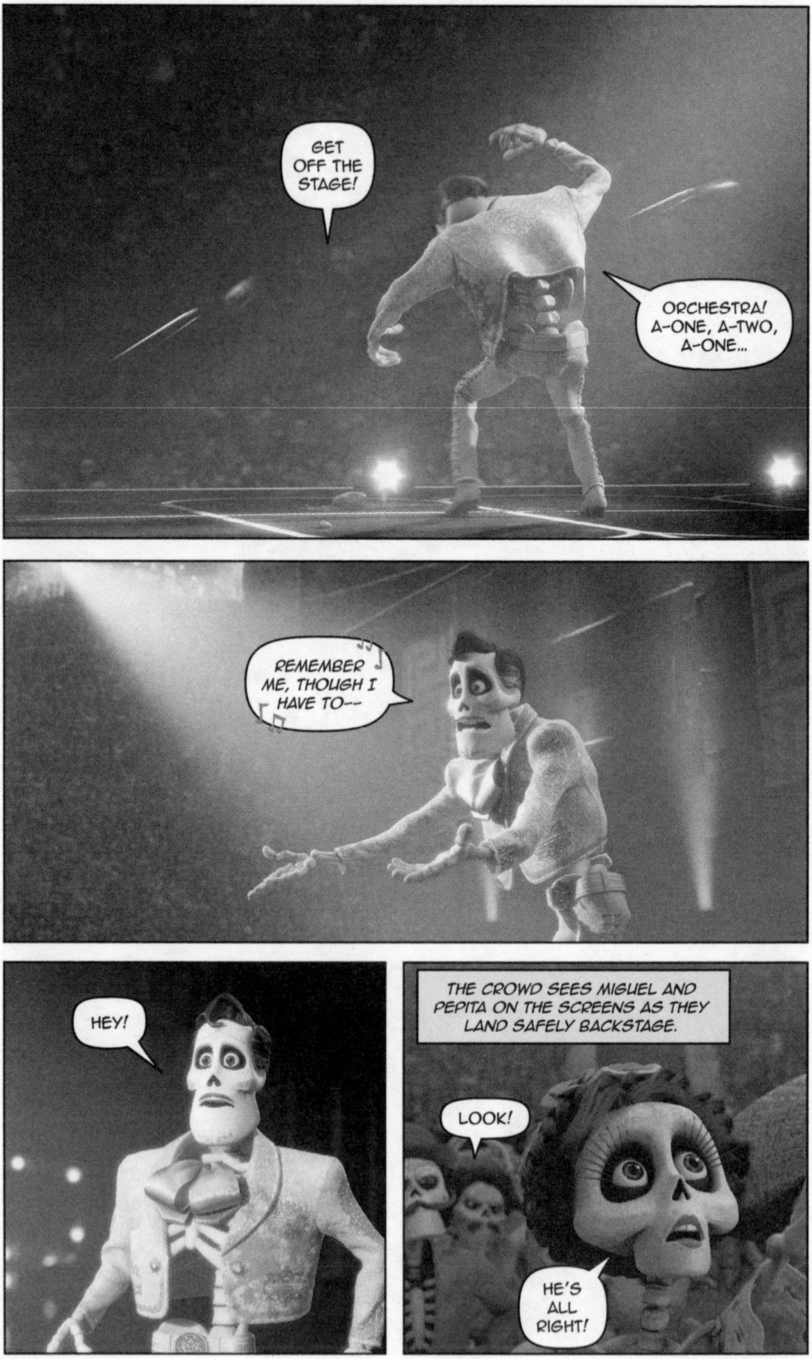
GET OFF THE STAGE!
ORCHESTRA! A-ONE, A-TWO, A-ONE...
REMEMBER ME, THOUGH I HAVE TO--
HEY!
THE CROWD SEES MIGUEL AND PEPITA ON THE SCREENS AS THEY LAND SAFELY BACKSTAGE.
LOOK!
HE'S ALL RIGHT!

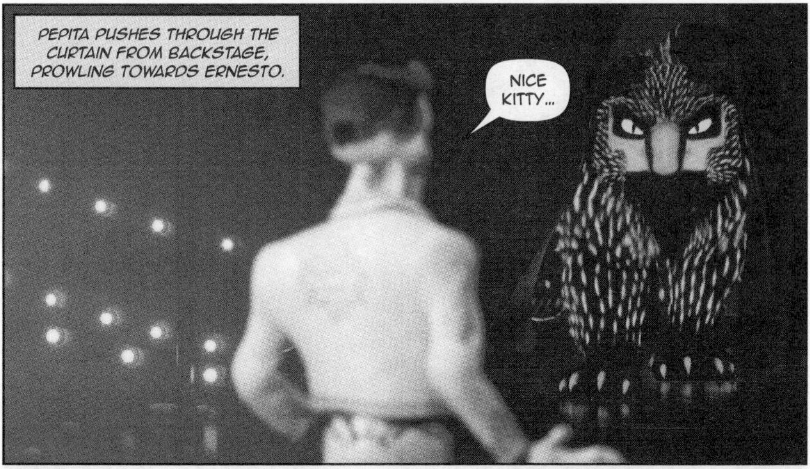
PEPITA PUSHES THROUGH THE CURTAIN FROM BACKSTAGE, PROWLING TOWARDS ERNESTO.
NICE KITTY...

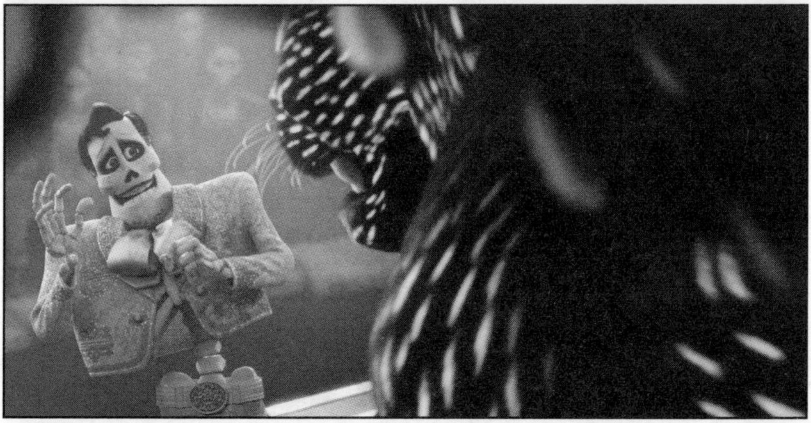

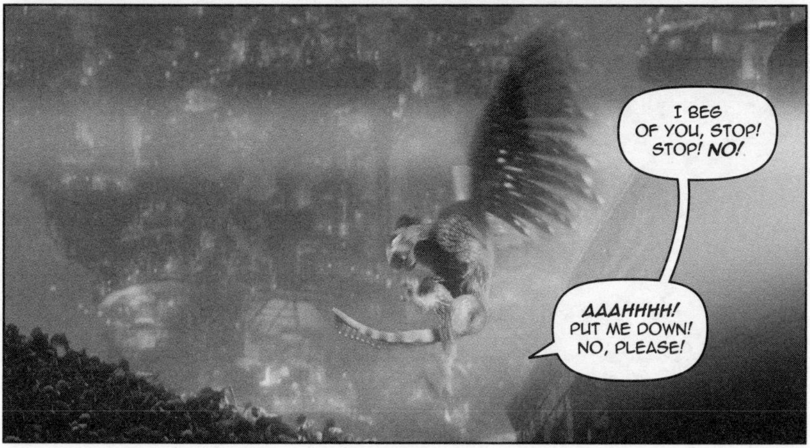
I BEG OF YOU, STOP! STOP! NO!
AAAHHHH! PUT ME DOWN! NO, PLEASE!

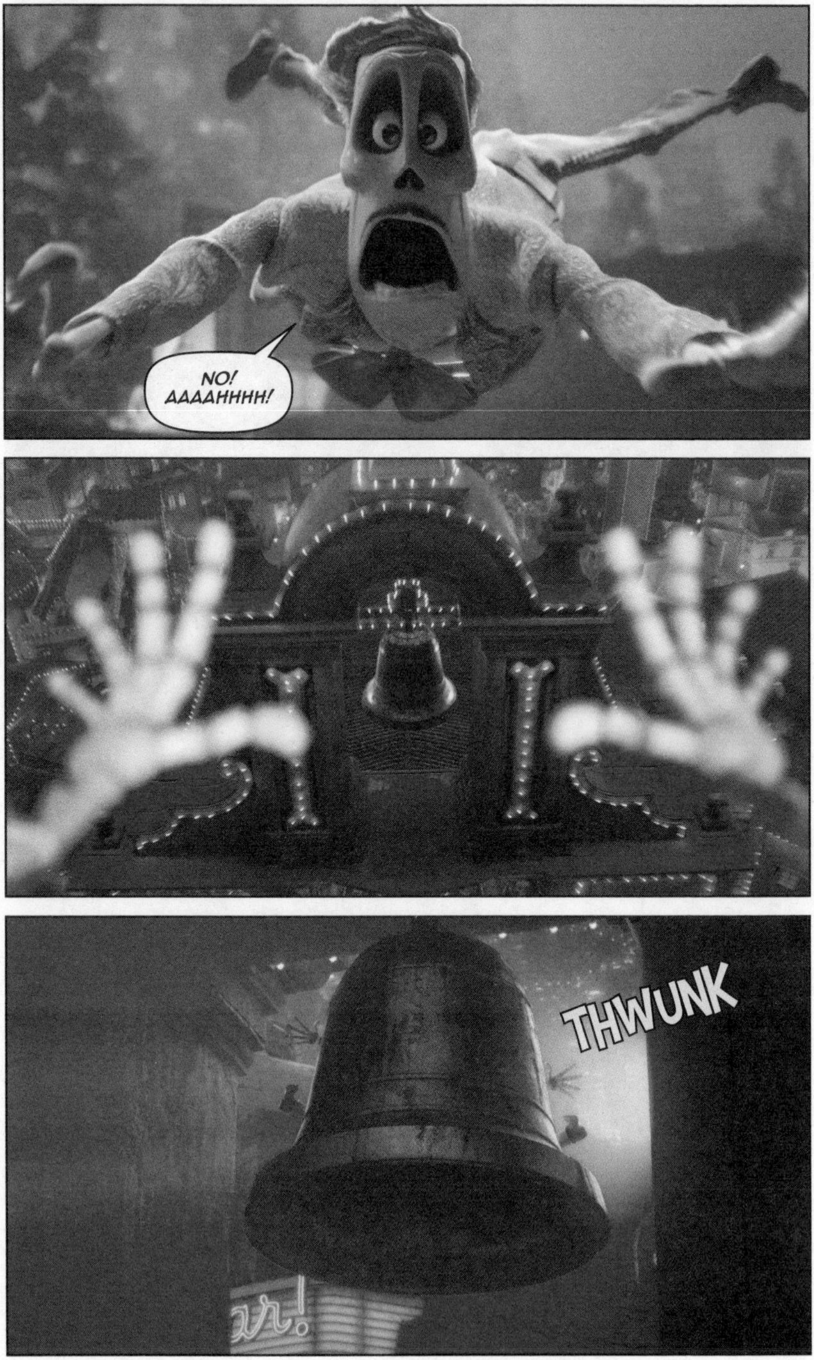
NO! AAAAHHHH!
THWUNK

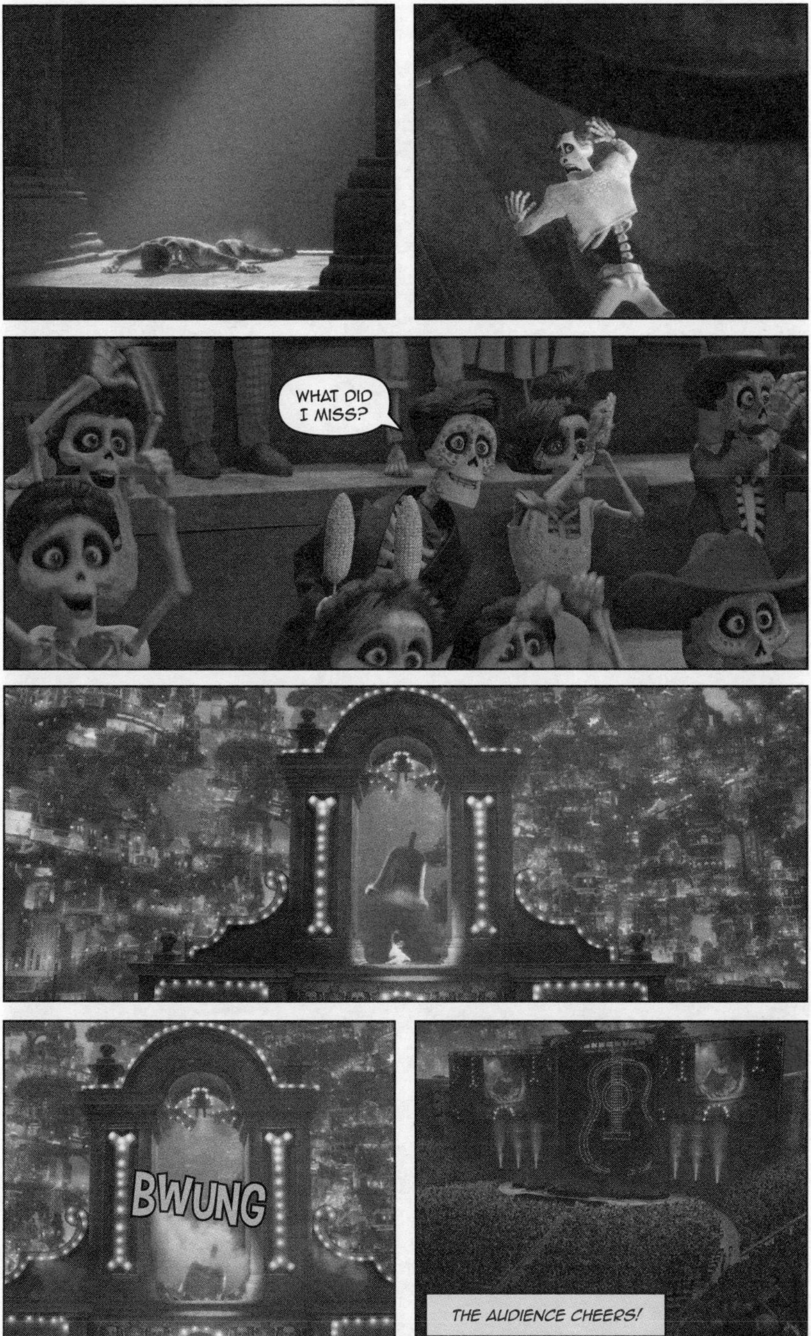
WHAT DID I MISS?
BWUNG
THE AUDIENCE CHEERS!

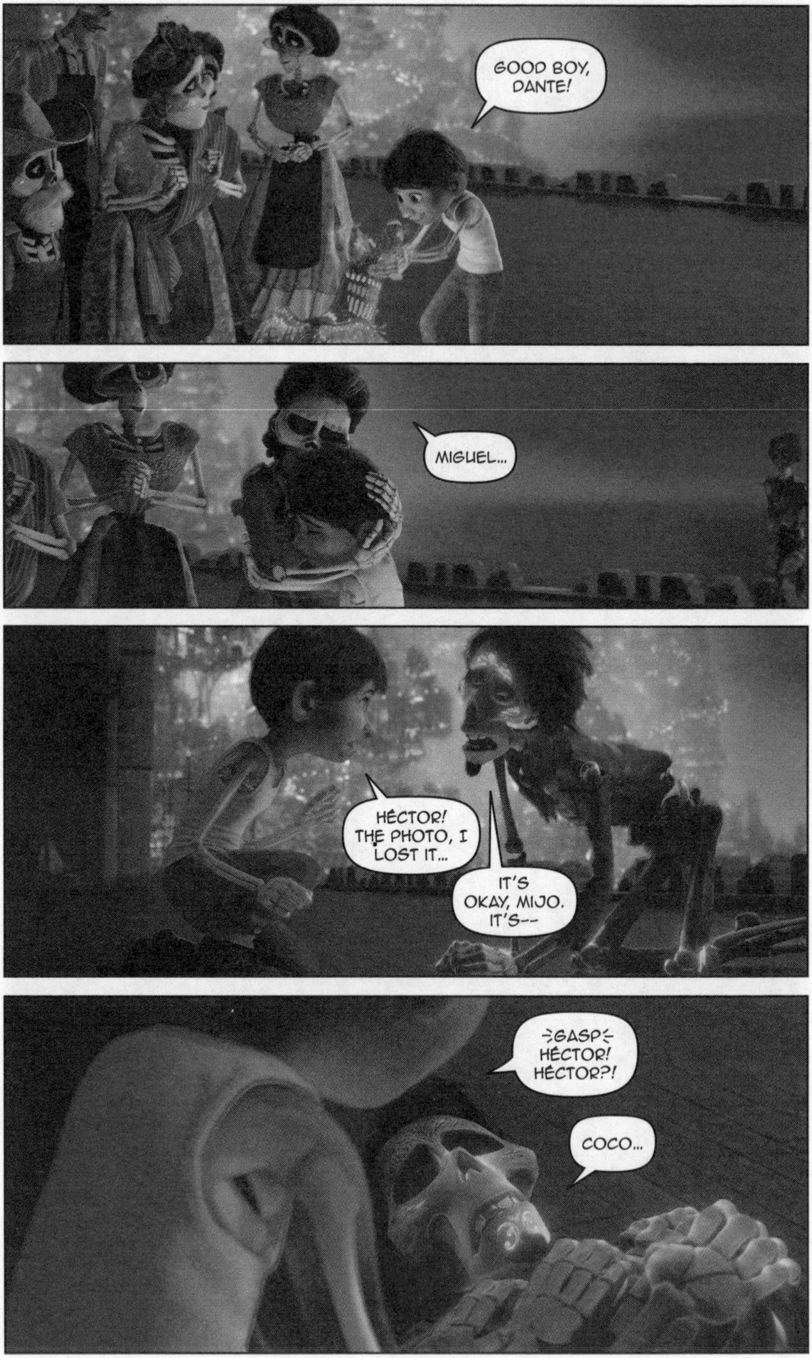
GOOD BOY, DANTE!
MIGUEL...
HÉCTOR! THE PHOTO, I LOST IT...
IT'S OKAY, MIJO. IT'S--
⸗GASP⸗ HÉCTOR! HÉCTOR?!
COCO...

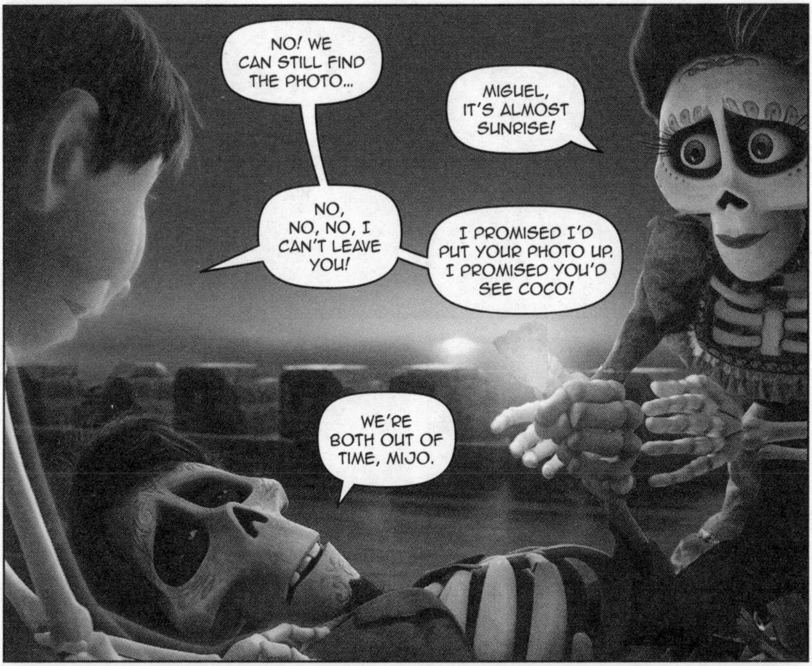
NO! WE CAN STILL FIND THE PHOTO...
MIGUEL, IT'S ALMOST SUNRISE!
NO, NO, NO, I CAN'T LEAVE YOU!
I PROMISED I'D PUT YOUR PHOTO UP. I PROMISED YOU'D SEE COCO!
WE'RE BOTH OUT OF TIME, MIJO.

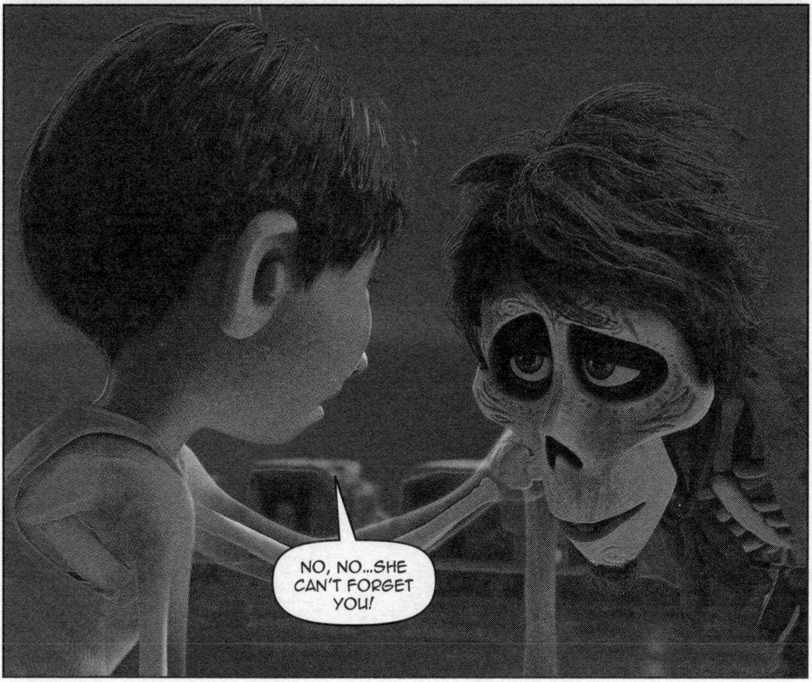
NO, NO...SHE CAN'T FORGET YOU!

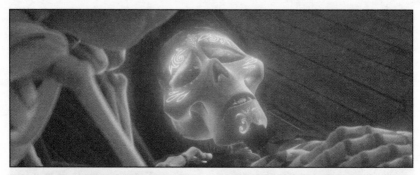

I JUST WANTED HER TO KNOW THAT I LOVED HER.

HÉCTOR--

YOU HAVE OUR BLESSING, MIGUEL.

NO CONDITIONS.

NO, PAPÁ HÉCTOR, PLEASE! NO...

GO HOME.

I PROMISE I WON'T LET COCO FORGET YOU.

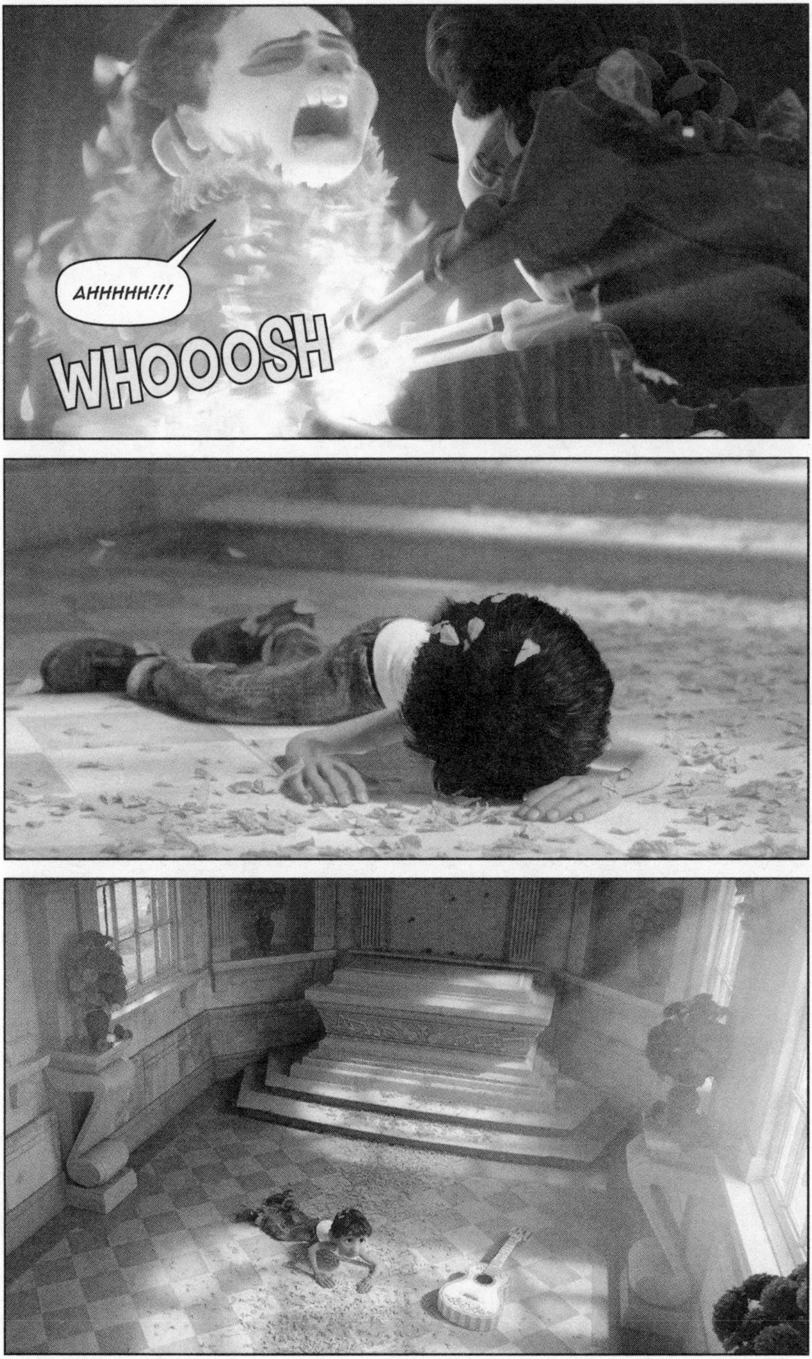
AHHHHH!!!
WHOOOSH

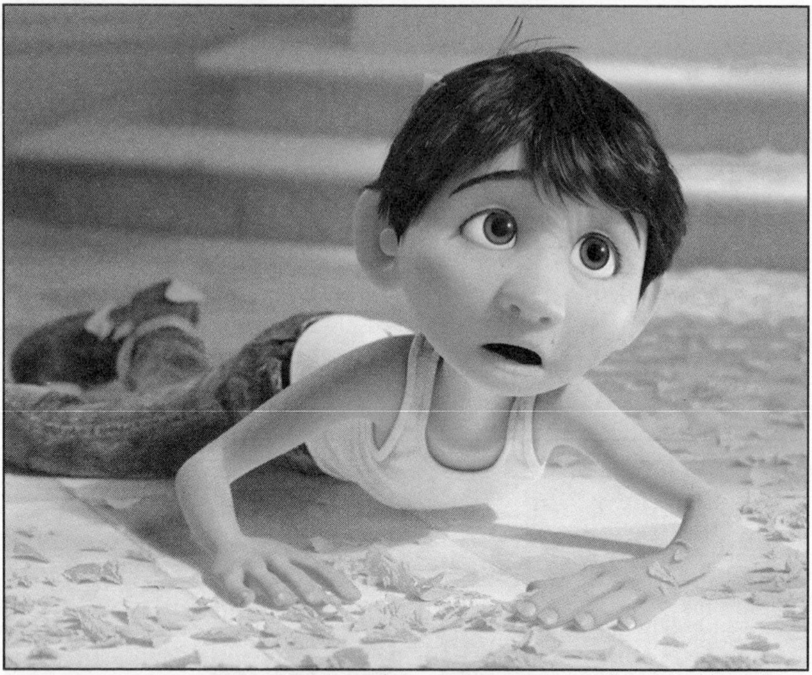

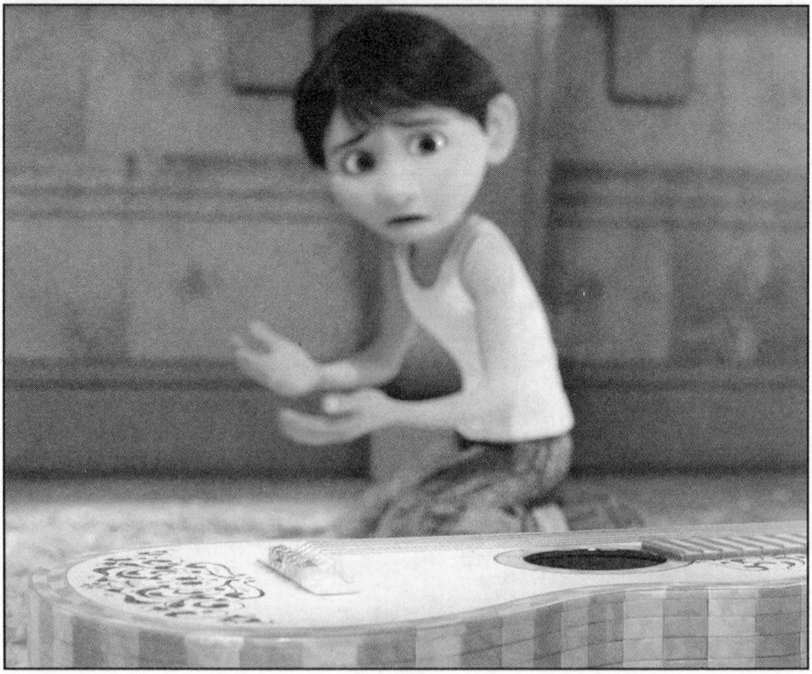

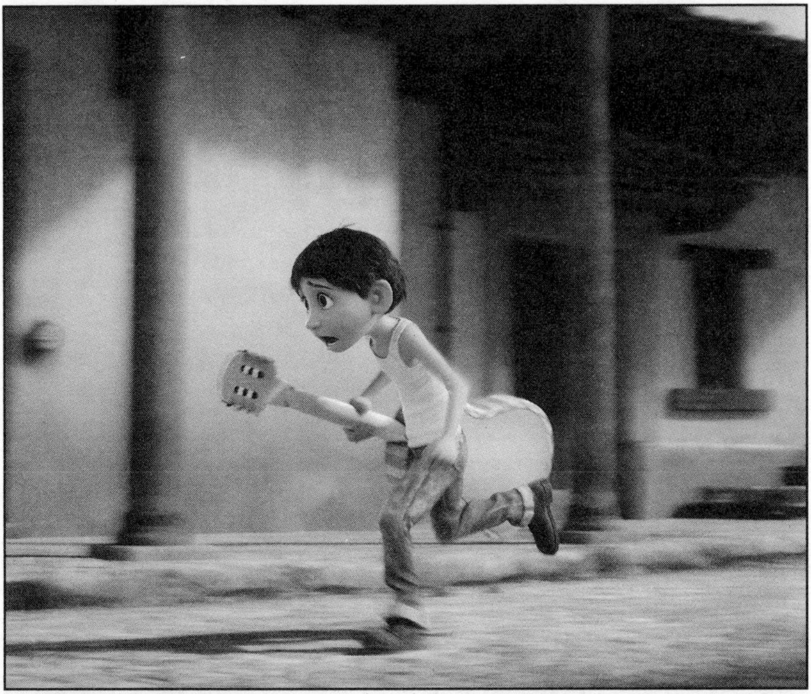

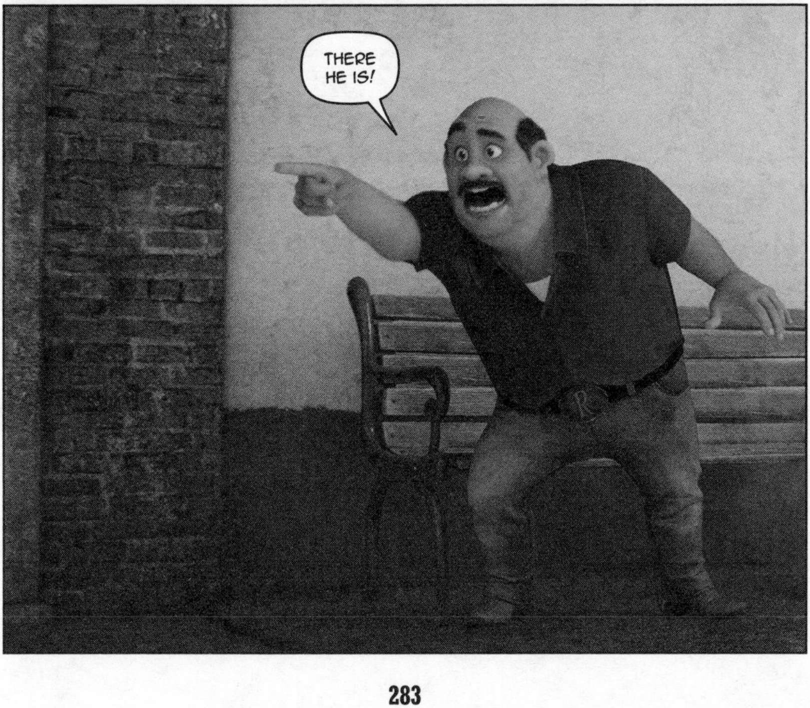
THERE HE IS!

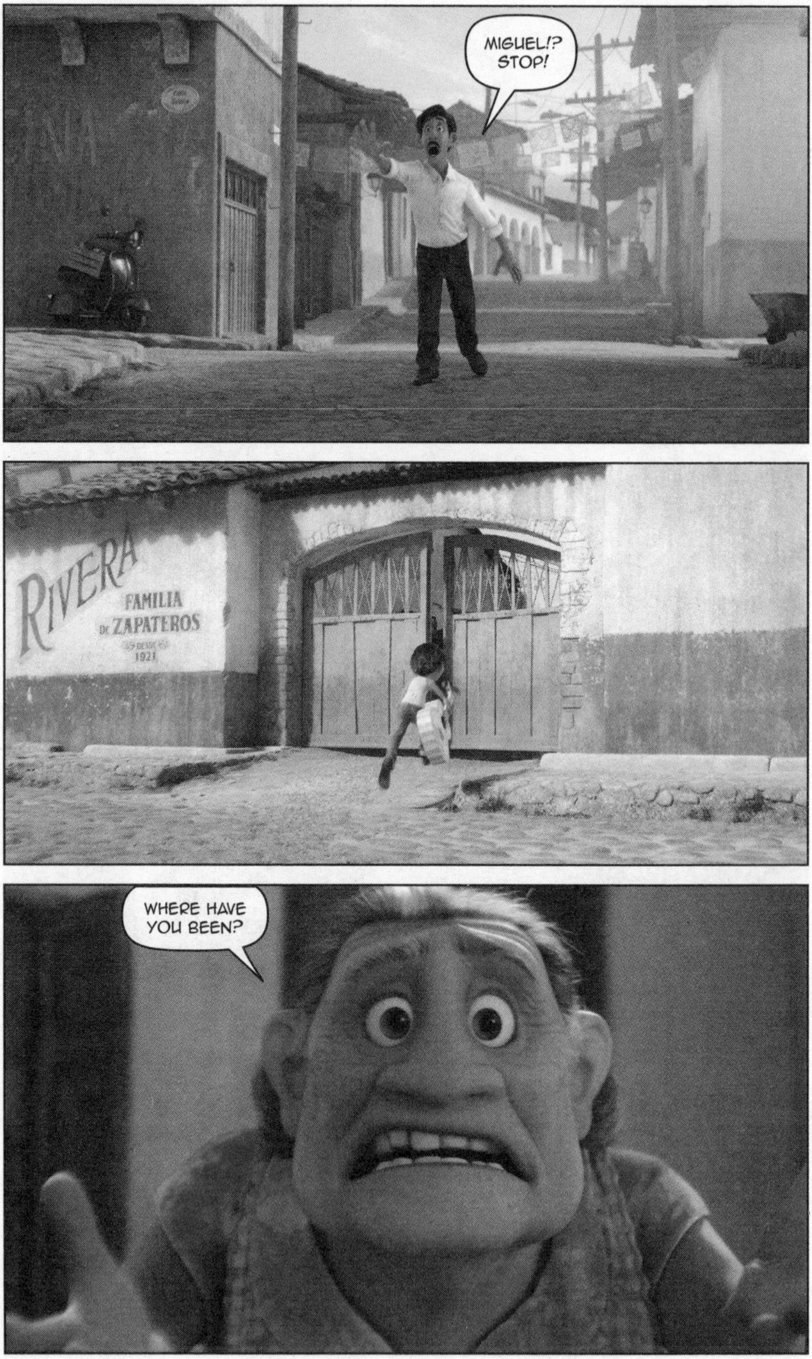
MIGUEL!? STOP!
RIVERA
FAMILIA
DE ZAPATEROS
1921
WHERE HAVE YOU BEEN?

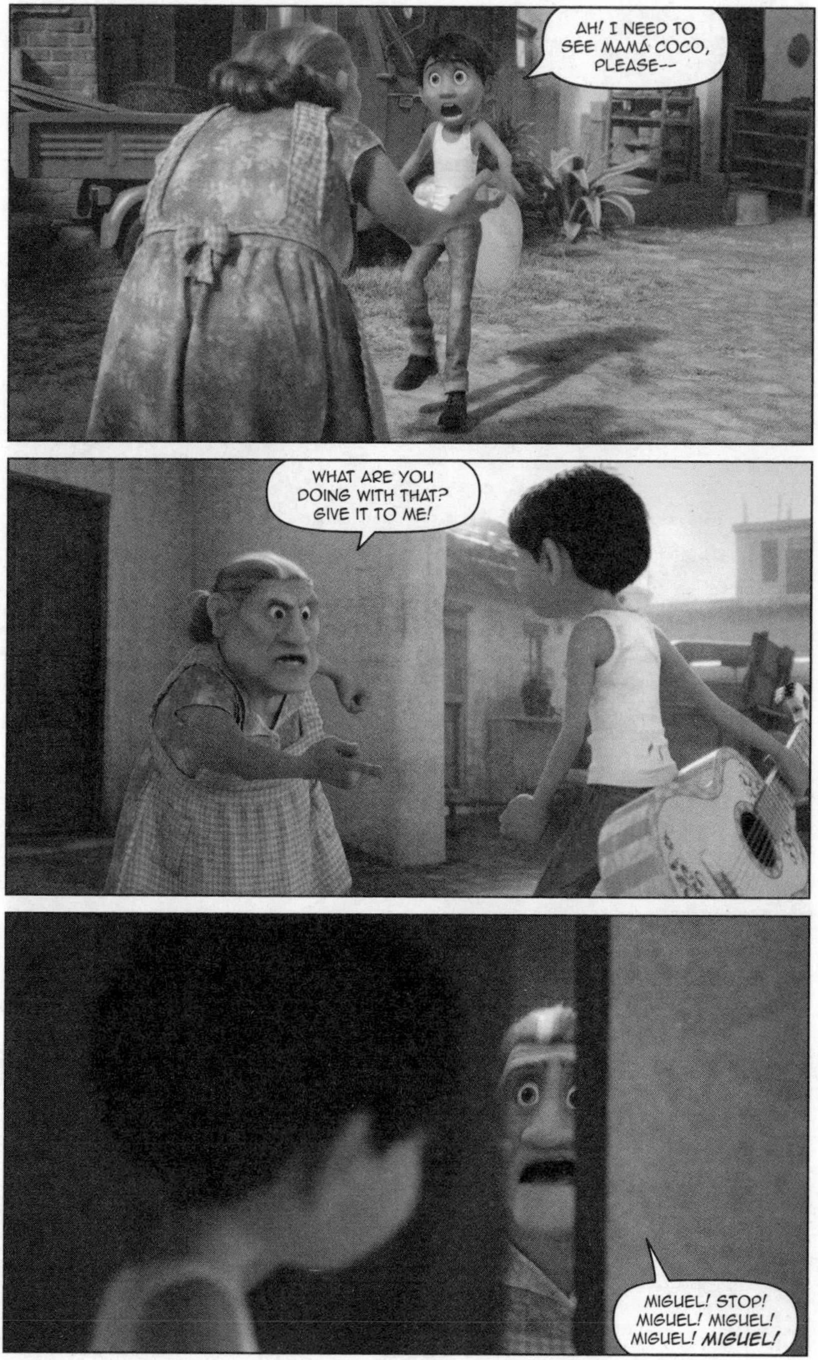
AH! I NEED TO SEE MAMÁ COCO, PLEASE--
WHAT ARE YOU DOING WITH THAT? GIVE IT TO ME!
MIGUEL! STOP! MIGUEL! MIGUEL! MIGUEL! MIGUEL!

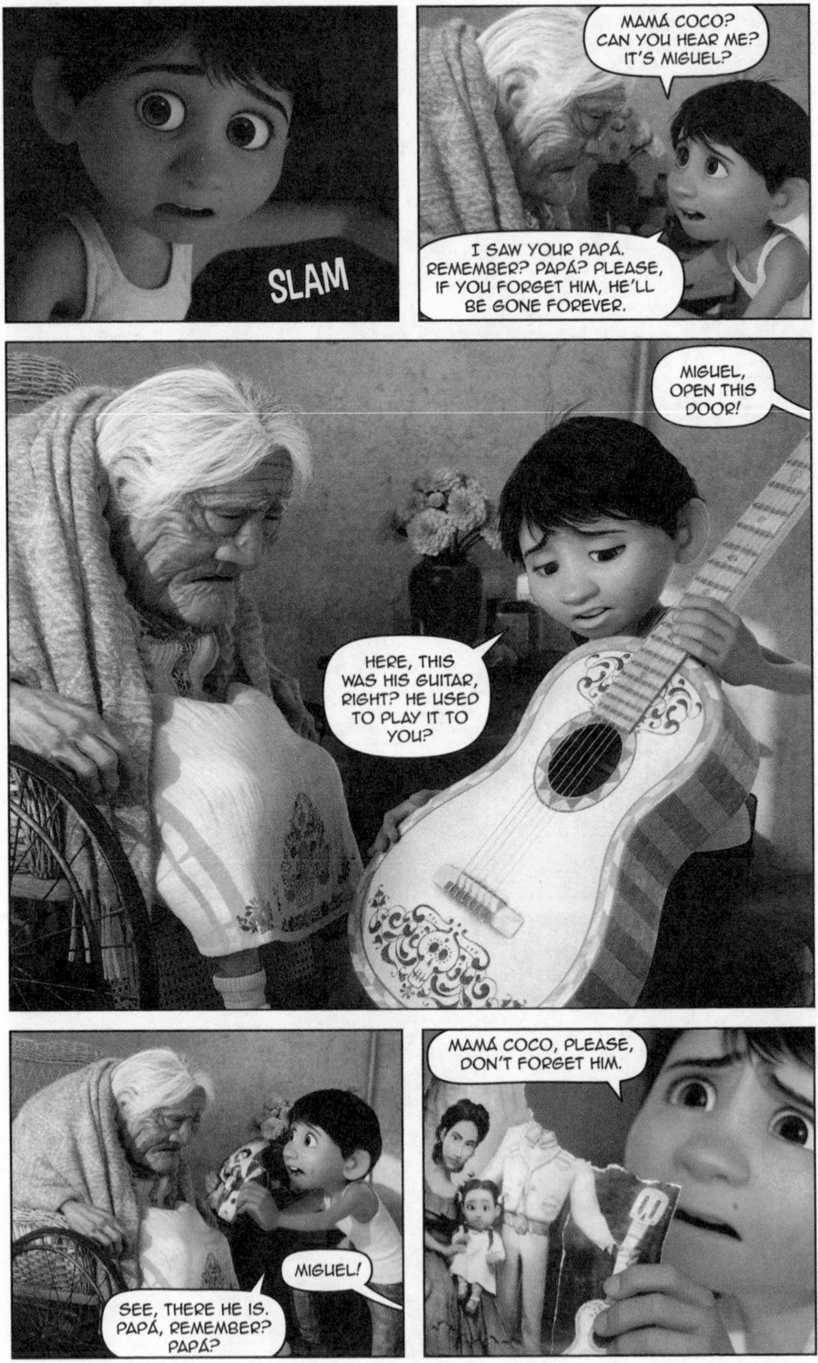
SLAM
MAMÁ COCO? CAN YOU HEAR ME? IT'S MIGUEL?
I SAW YOUR PAPÁ. REMEMBER? PAPÁ? PLEASE, IF YOU FORGET HIM, HE'LL BE GONE FOREVER.
MIGUEL, OPEN THIS DOOR!
HERE, THIS WAS HIS GUITAR, RIGHT? HE USED TO PLAY IT TO YOU?
MIGUEL!
SEE, THERE HE IS. PAPÁ, REMEMBER? PAPÁ?
MAMÁ COCO, PLEASE, DON'T FORGET HIM.

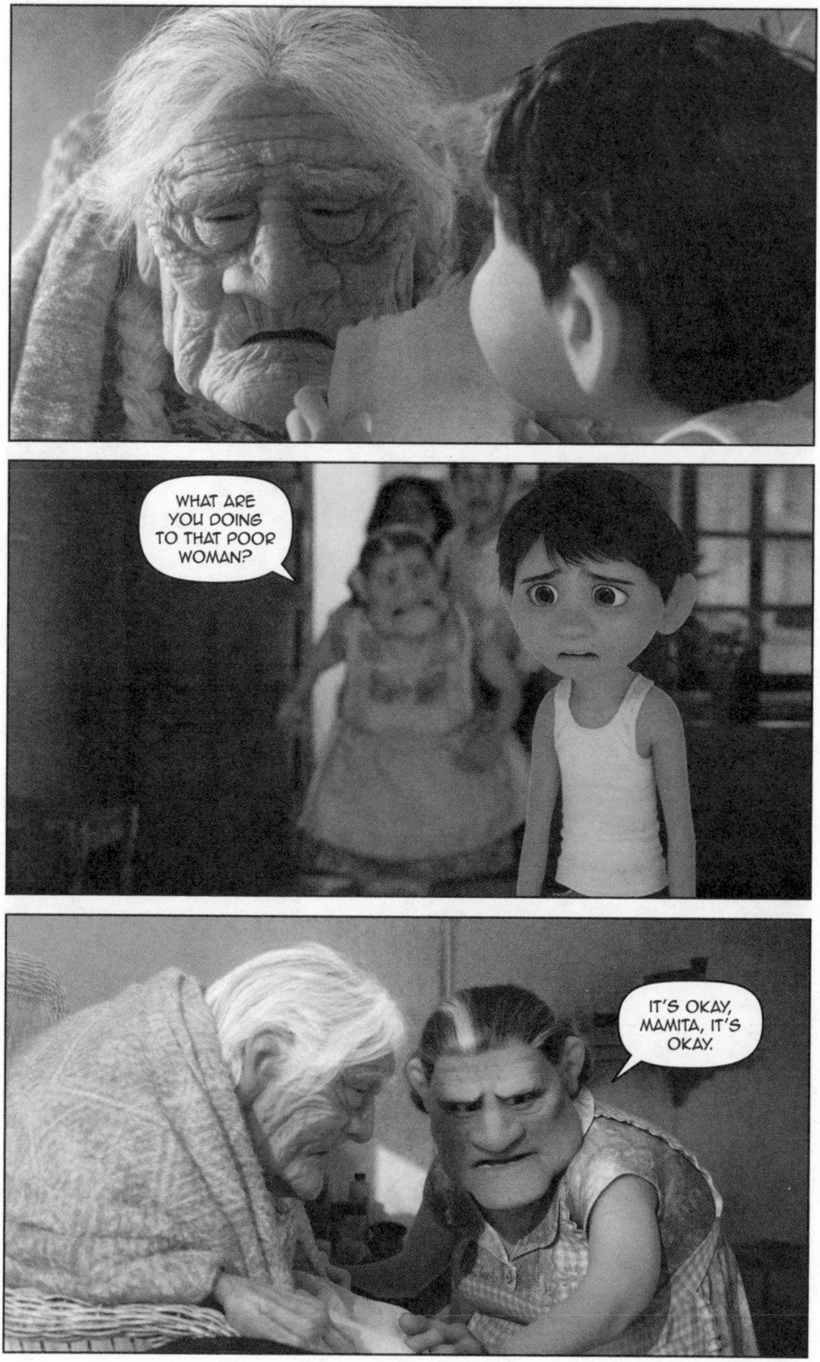
WHAT ARE YOU DOING TO THAT POOR WOMAN?
IT'S OKAY, MAMITA, IT'S OKAY.

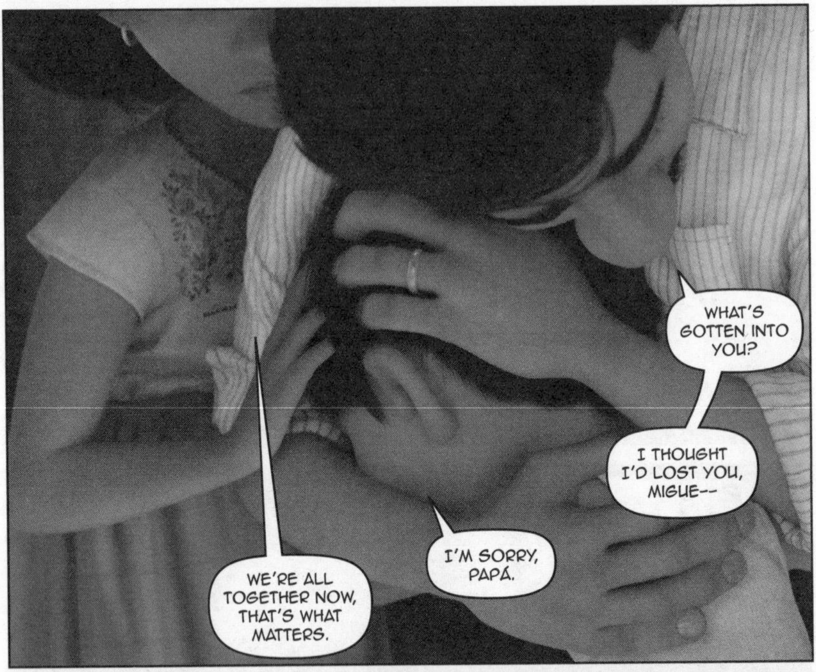
WHAT'S GOTTEN INTO YOU?
I THOUGHT I'D LOST YOU, MIGUE--
I'M SORRY, PAPÁ.
WE'RE ALL TOGETHER NOW, THAT'S WHAT MATTERS.

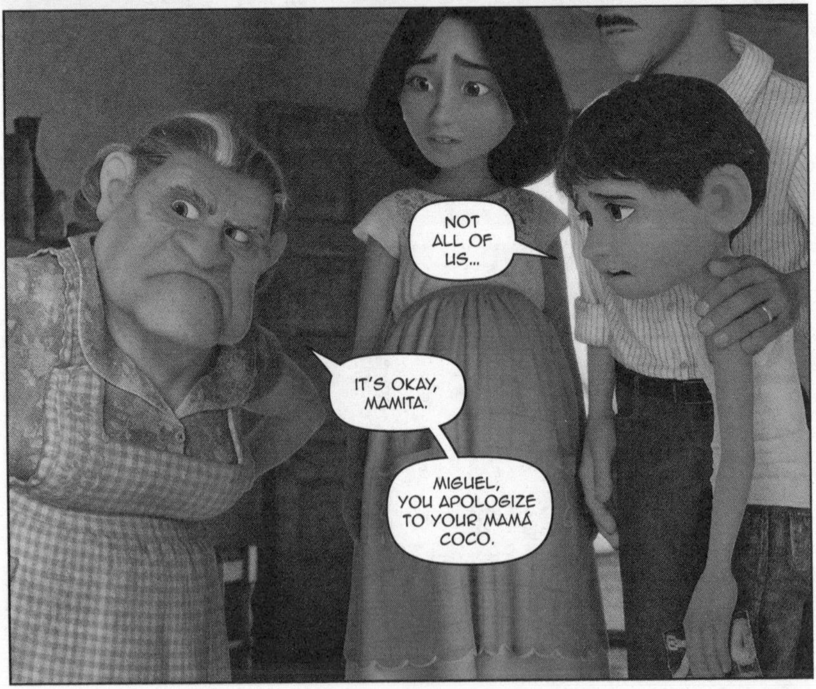
NOT ALL OF US...
IT'S OKAY, MAMITA.
MIGUEL, YOU APOLOGIZE TO YOUR MAMÁ COCO.

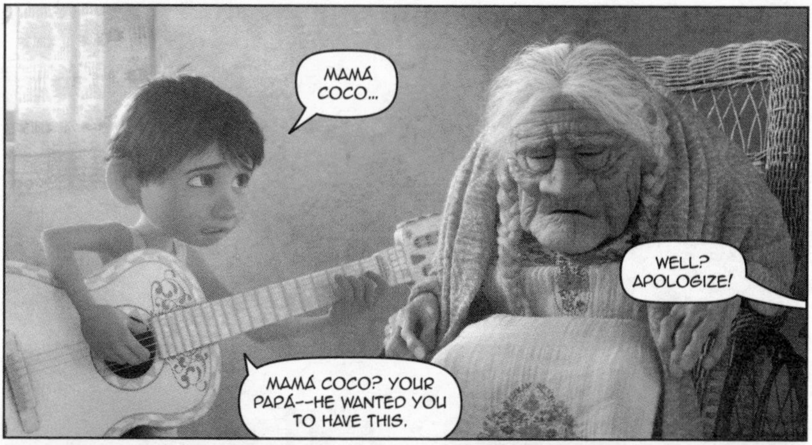
MAMÁ COCO...
WELL? APOLOGIZE!
MAMÁ COCO? YOUR PAPÁ--HE WANTED YOU TO HAVE THIS.

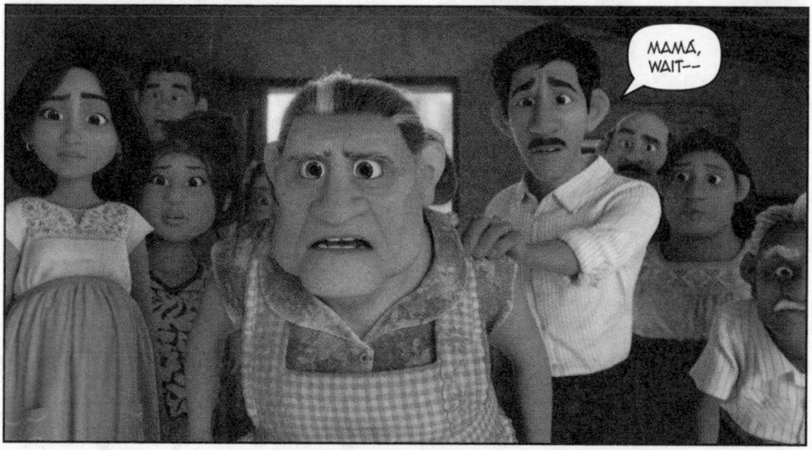
MAMÁ, WAIT--

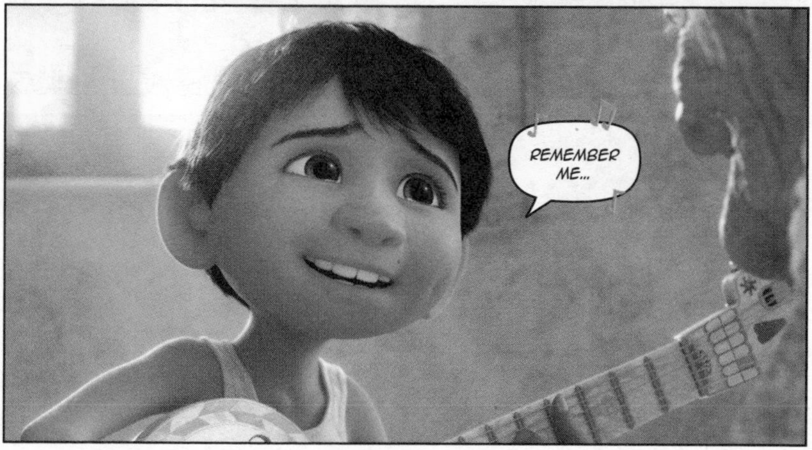
REMEMBER ME...

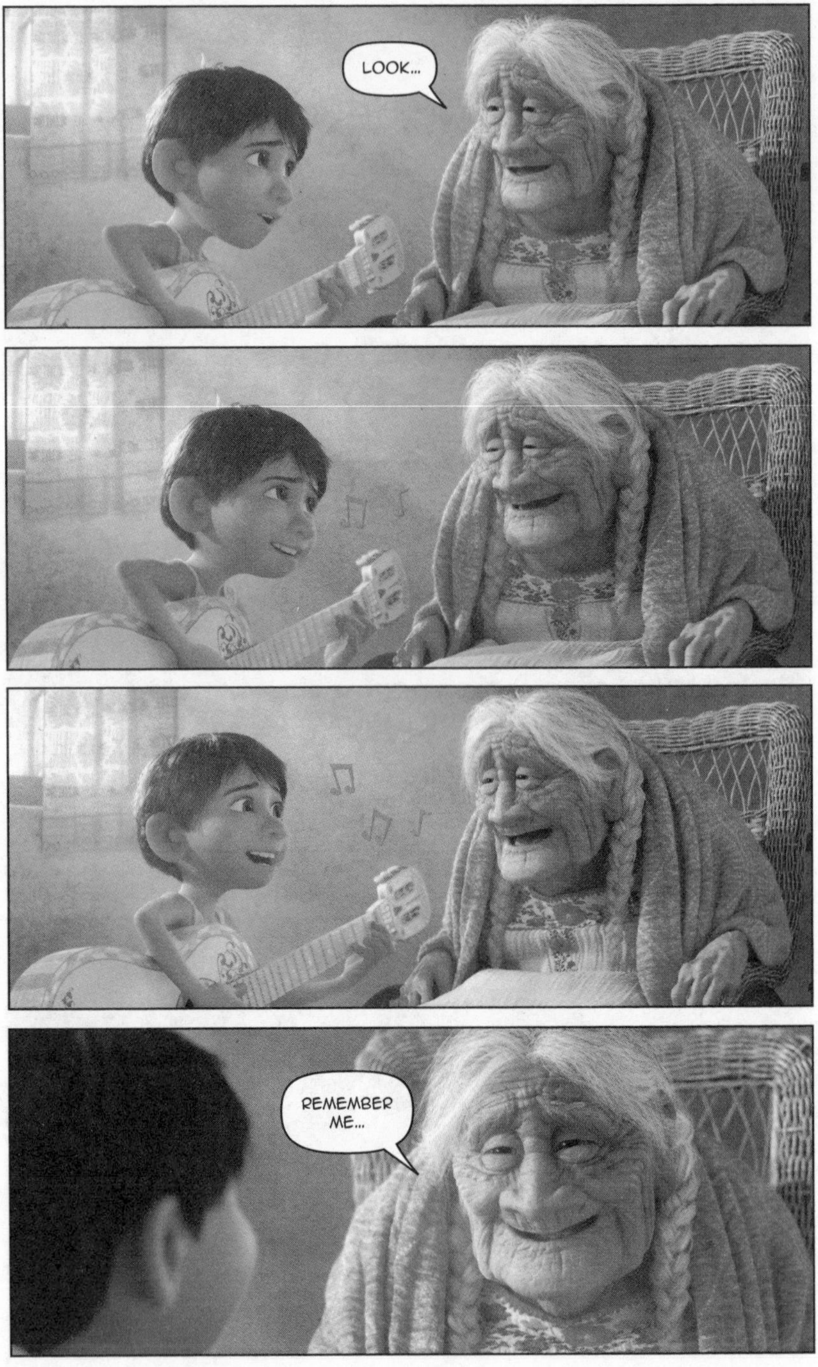
LOOK...
REMEMBER ME...

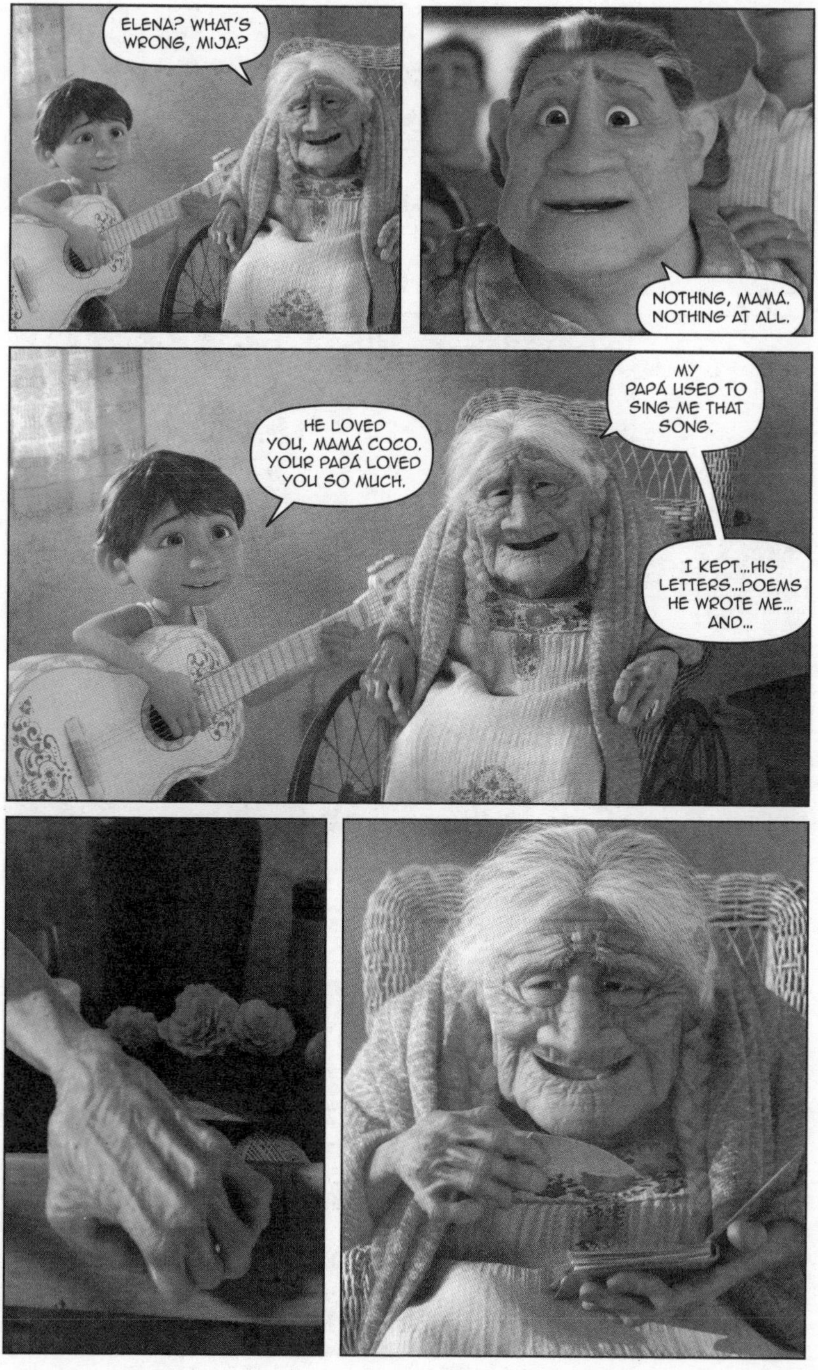
ELENA? WHAT'S WRONG, MIJA?
NOTHING, MAMÁ. NOTHING AT ALL.
MY PAPÁ USED TO SING ME THAT SONG.
HE LOVED YOU, MAMÁ COCO. YOUR PAPÁ LOVED YOU SO MUCH.
I KEPT...HIS LETTERS...POEMS HE WROTE ME... AND...

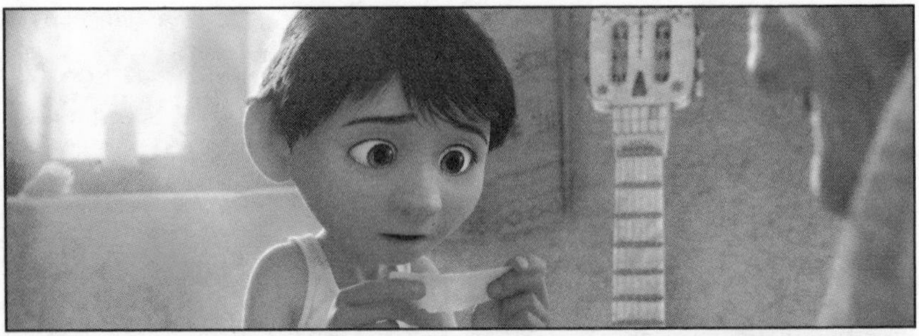

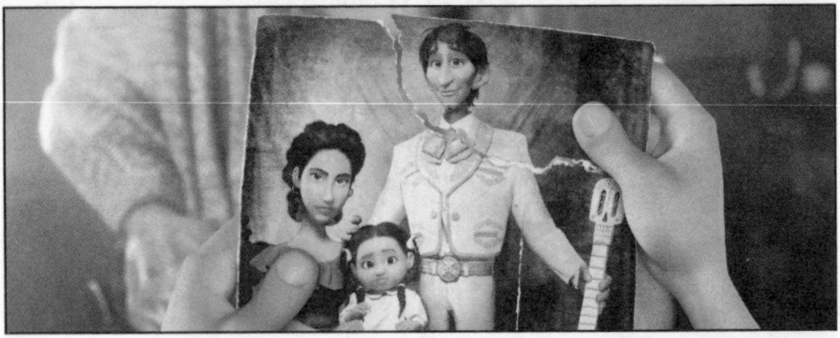

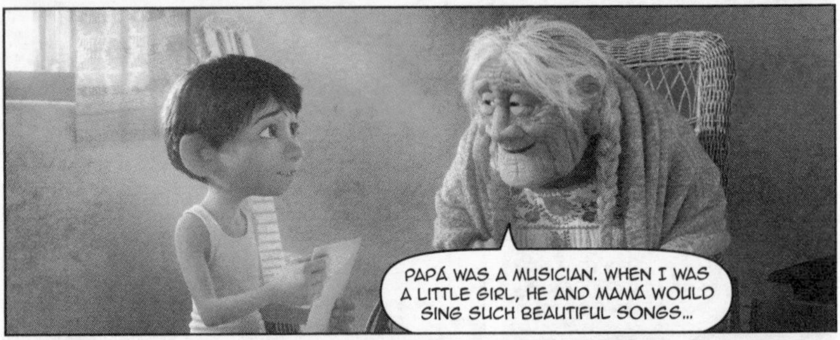
PAPÁ WAS A MUSICIAN. WHEN I WAS A LITTLE GIRL, HE AND MAMÁ WOULD SING SUCH BEAUTIFUL SONGS...

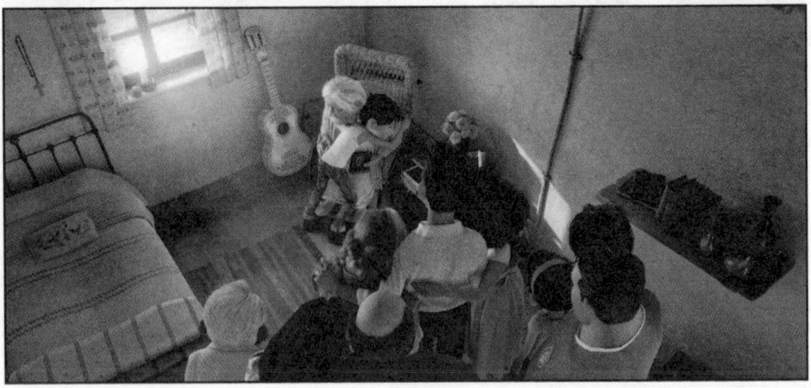

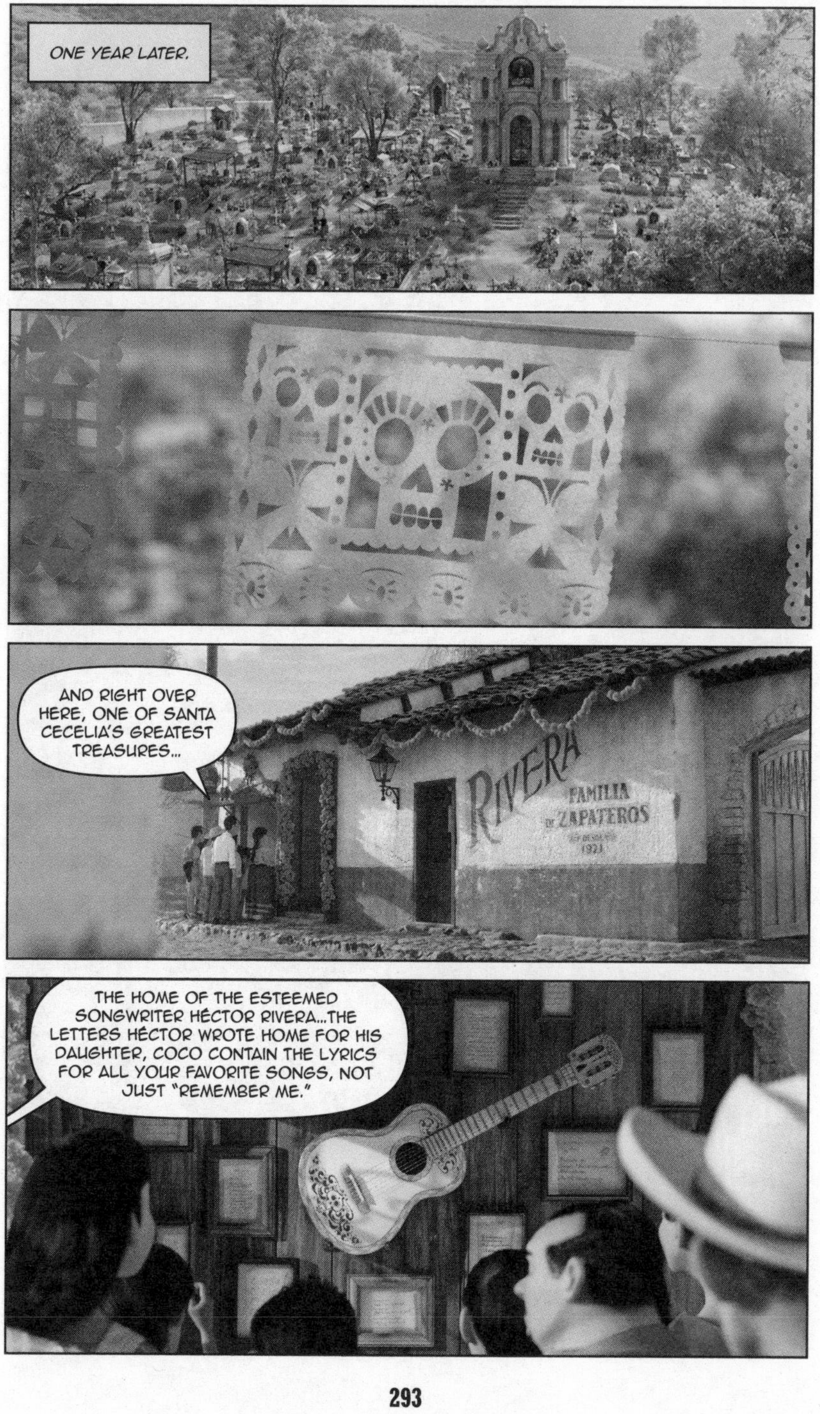
ONE YEAR LATER.
AND RIGHT OVER HERE, ONE OF SANTA CECELIA'S GREATEST TREASURES...
RIVERA
FAMILIA
ZAPATEROS
THE HOME OF THE ESTEEMED SONGWRITER HÉCTOR RIVERA...THE LETTERS HÉCTOR WROTE HOME FOR HIS DAUGHTER, COCO CONTAIN THE LYRICS FOR ALL YOUR FAVORITE SONGS, NOT JUST "REMEMBER ME."

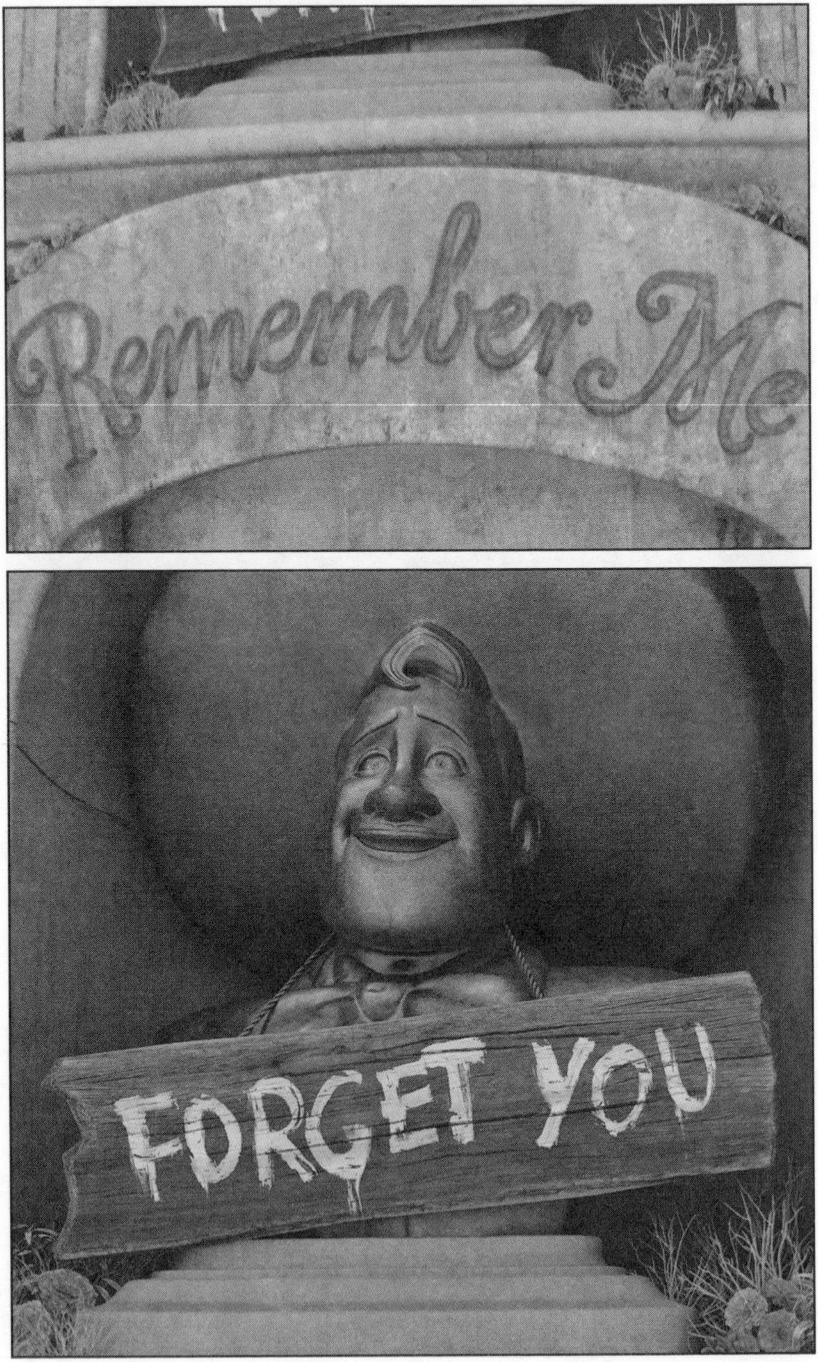
Remember Me
FORGET YOU

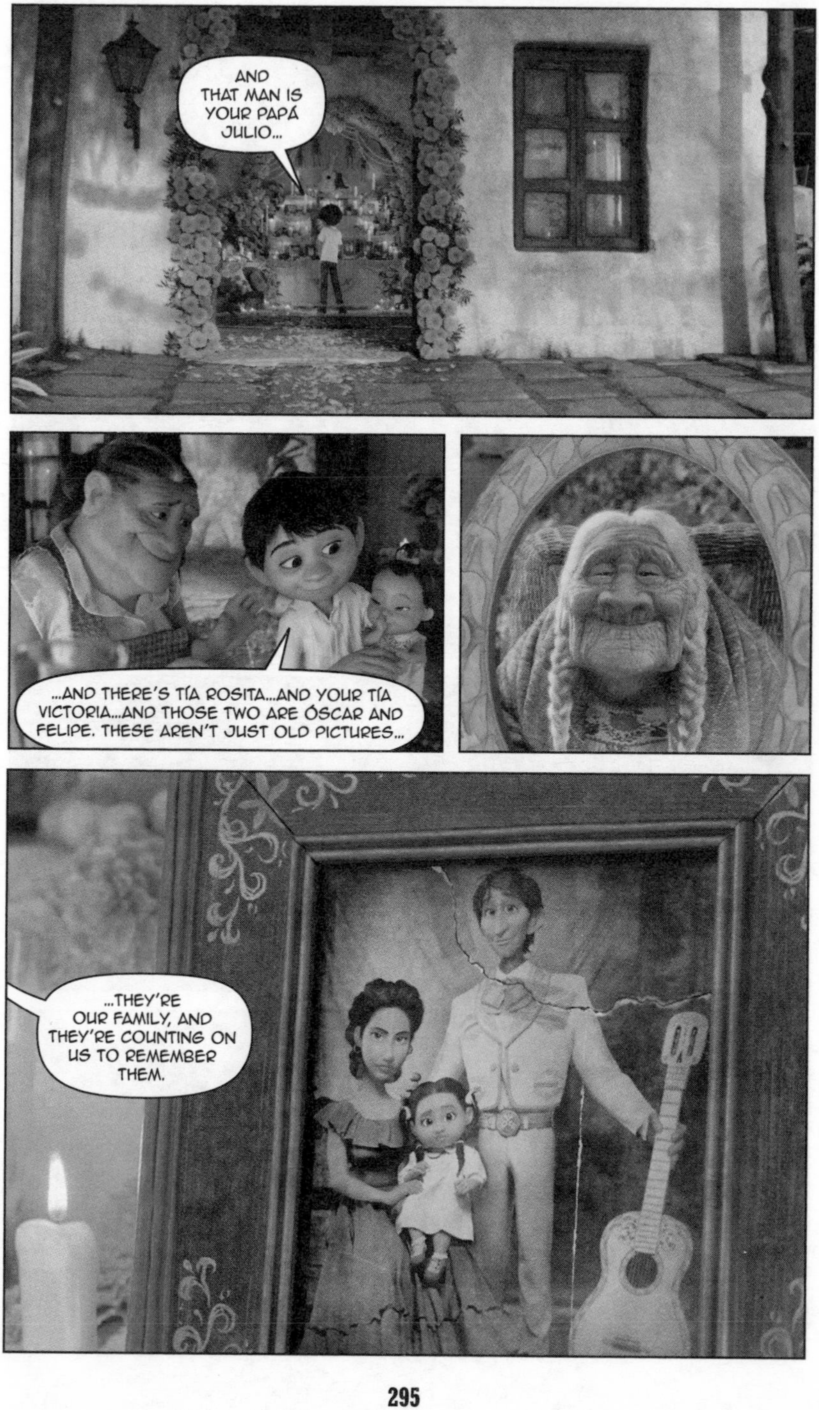
AND THAT MAN IS YOUR PAPÁ JULIO...
...AND THERE'S TÍA ROSITA...AND YOUR TÍA VICTORIA...AND THOSE TWO ARE ÓSCAR AND FELIPE. THESE AREN'T JUST OLD PICTURES...
...THEY'RE OUR FAMILY, AND THEY'RE COUNTING ON US TO REMEMBER THEM.

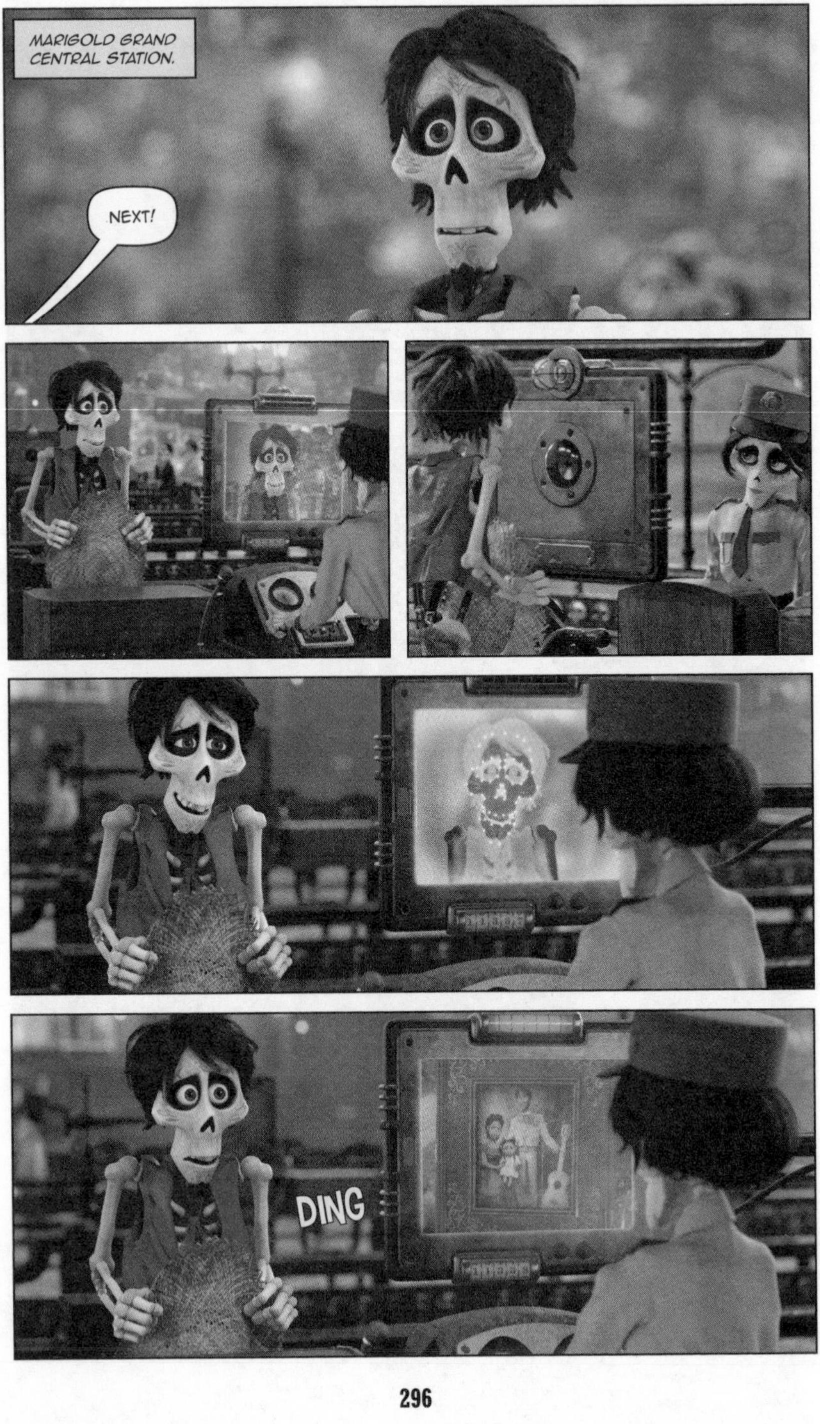
MARIGOLD GRAND CENTRAL STATION.
NEXT!
DING

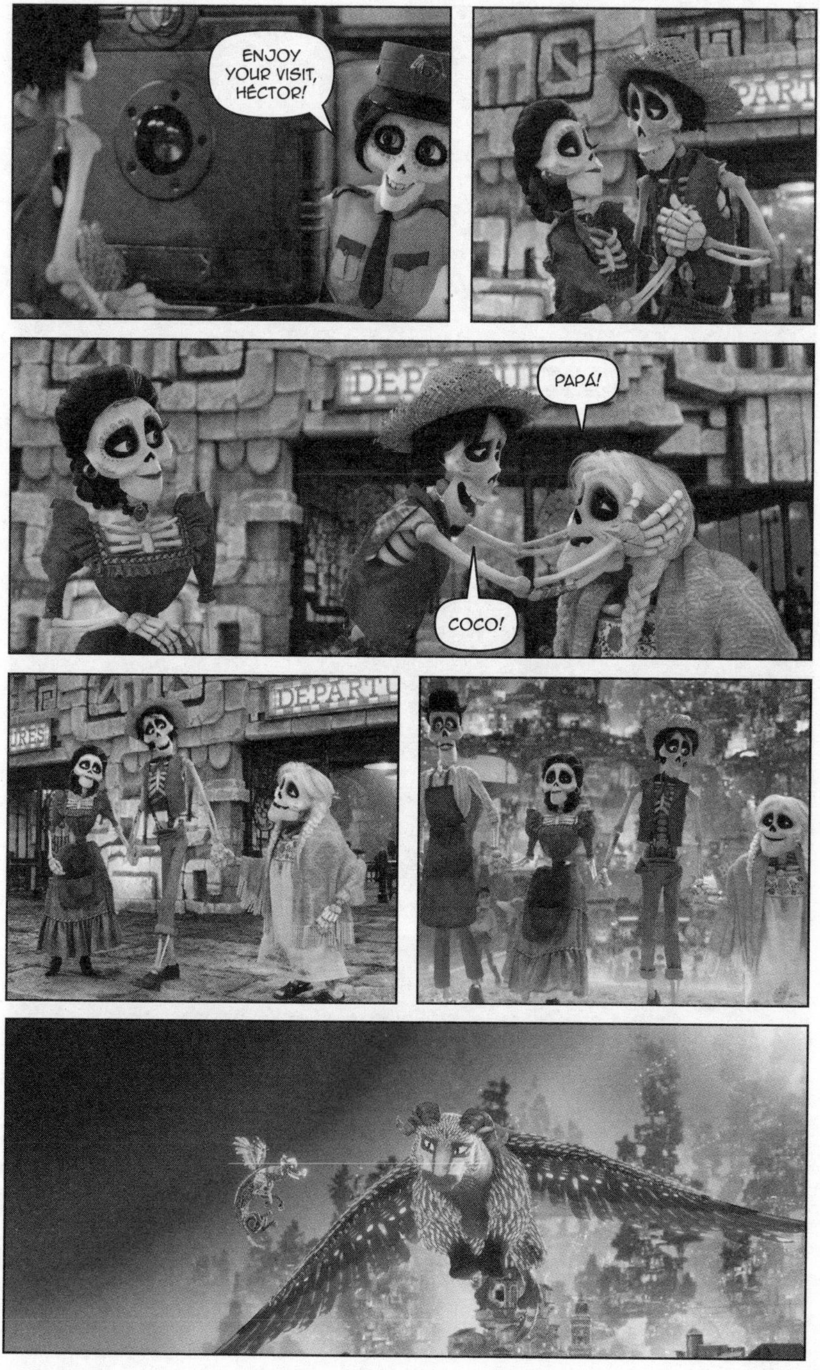
ENJOY YOUR VISIT, HÉCTOR!
PAPÁ!
COCO!

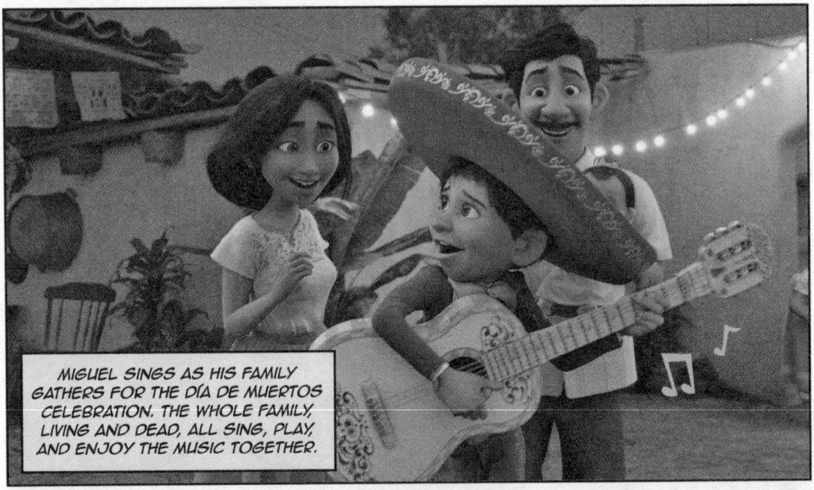
MIGUEL SINGS AS HIS FAMILY GATHERS FOR THE DÍA DE MUERTOS CELEBRATION. THE WHOLE FAMILY, LIVING AND DEAD, ALL SING, PLAY, AND ENJOY THE MUSIC TOGETHER.

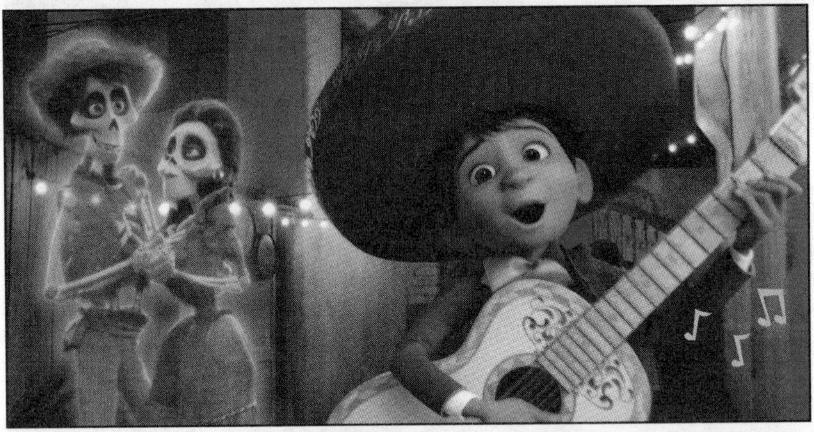

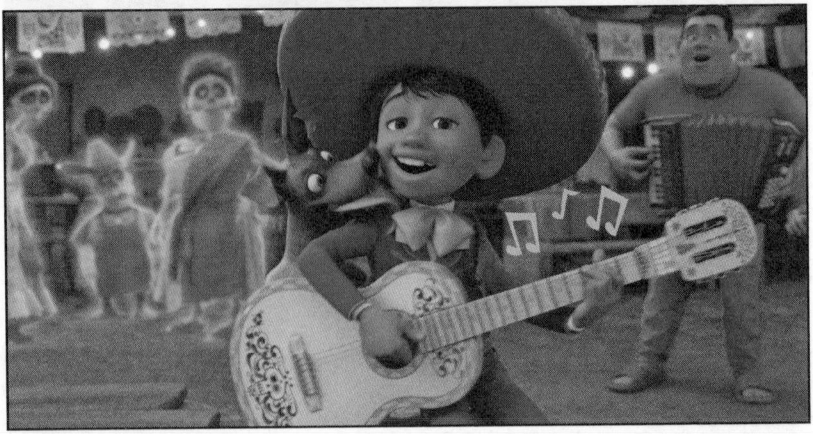

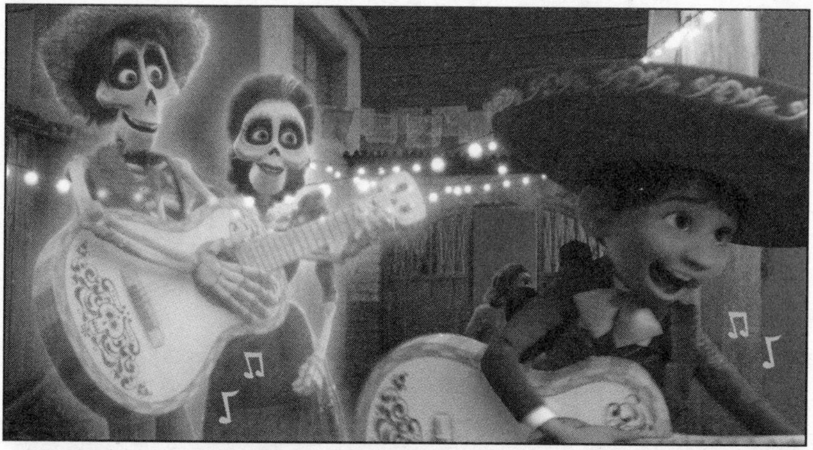

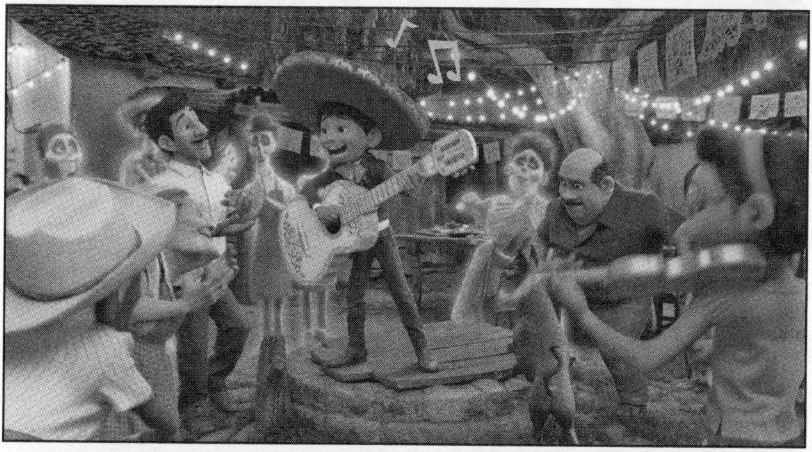

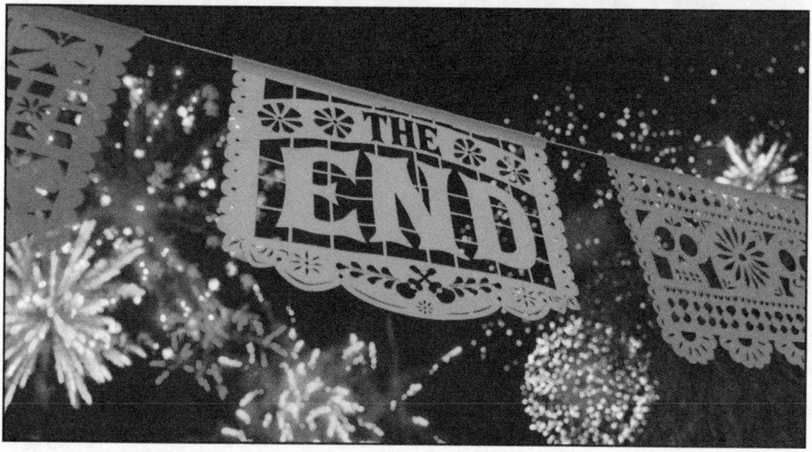
THE
END

DANTE'S LUNCH

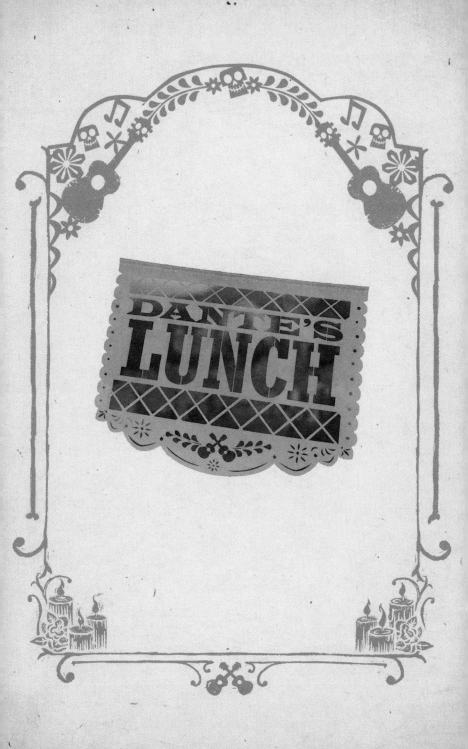

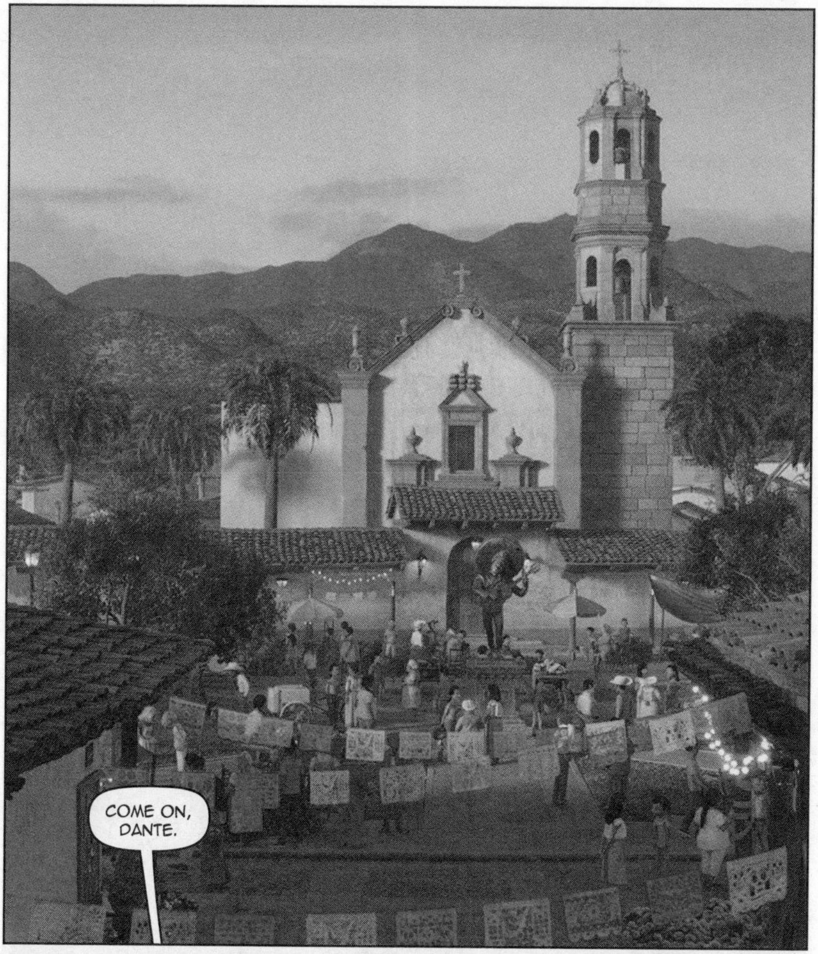
COME ON, DANTE.

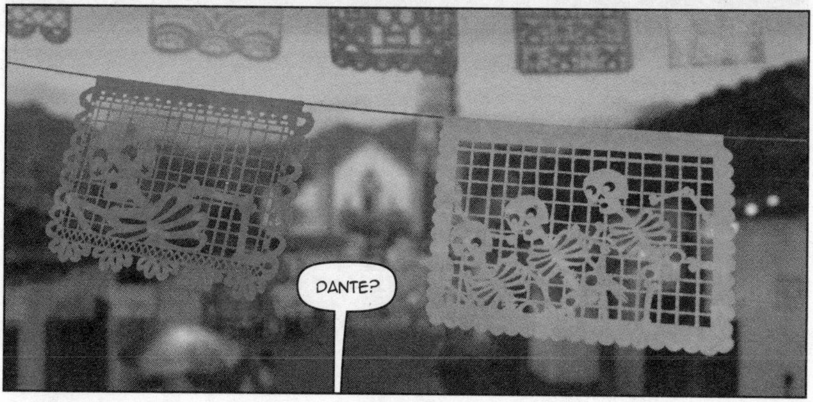
DANTE?

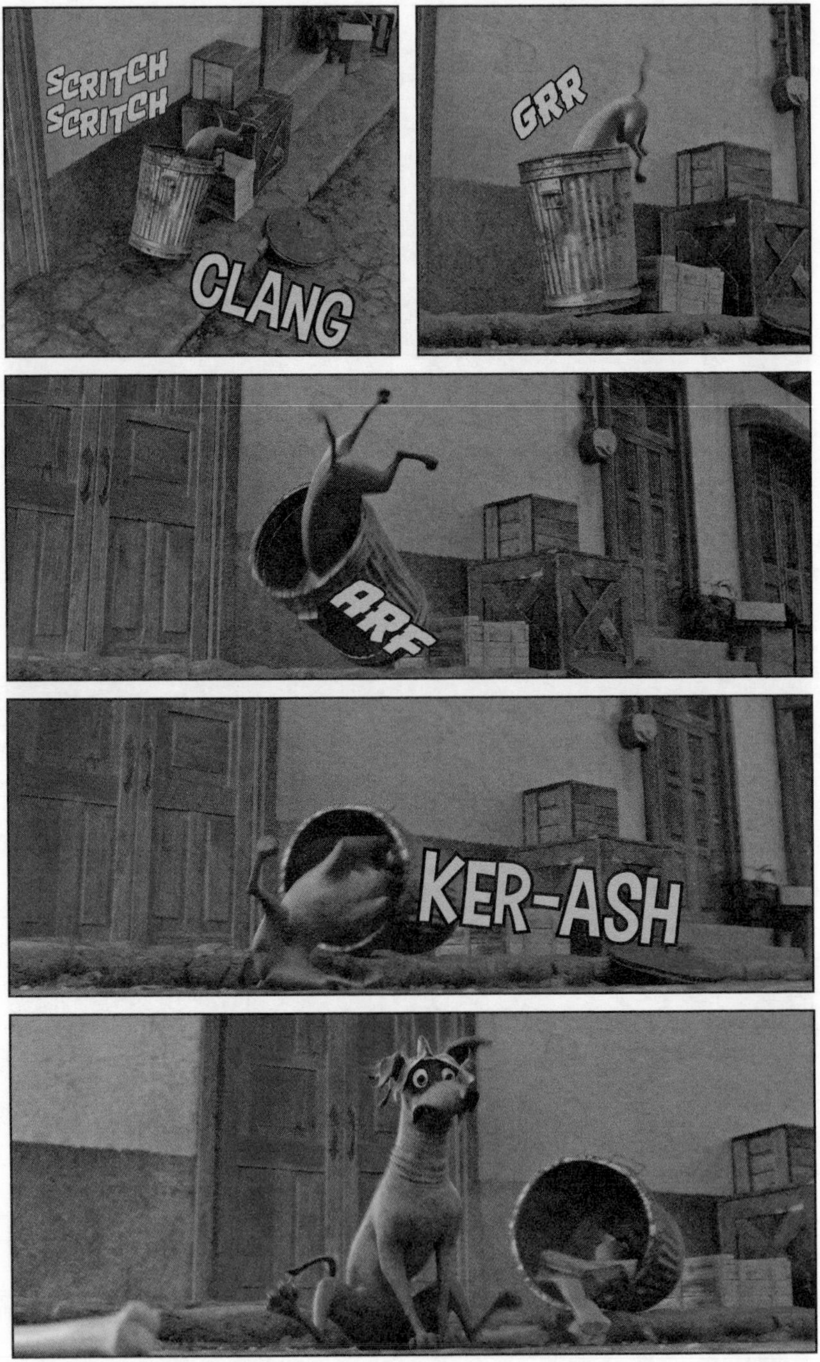
SCRITCH
SCRITCH
CLANG
GRR
ARF
KER-ASH

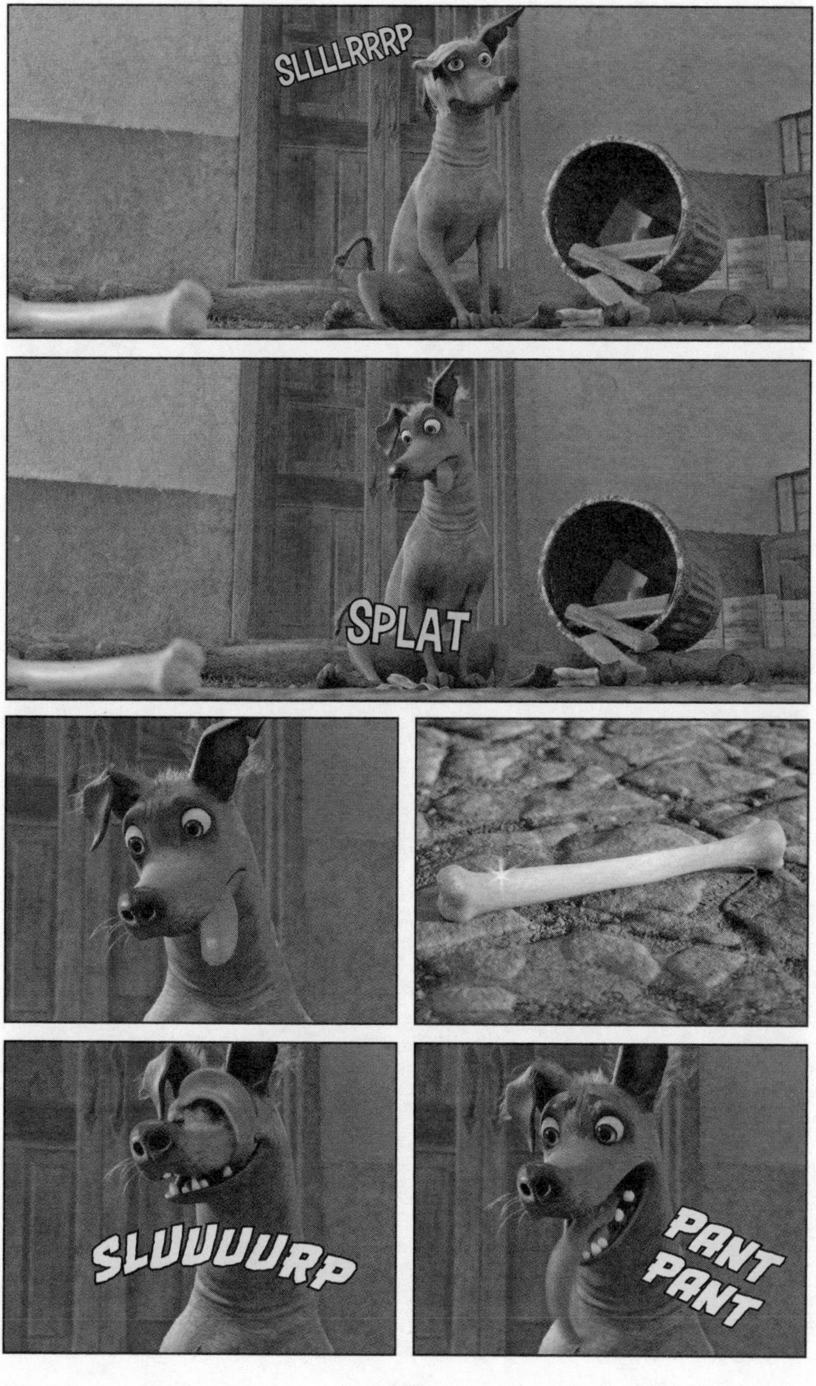
SLLLLRRRP
SPLAT
SLUUUURP
PANT
PANT

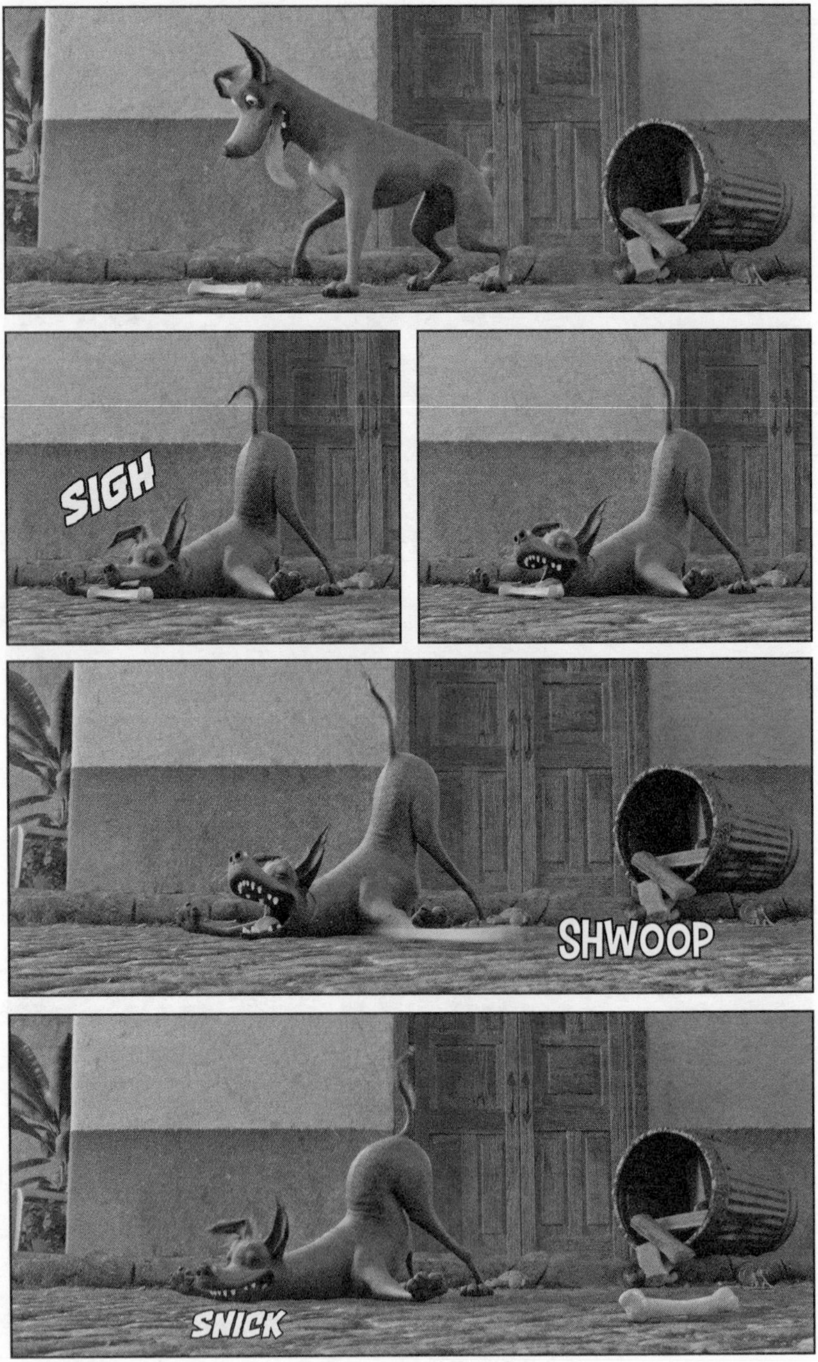
SIGH
SHWOOP
SNICK

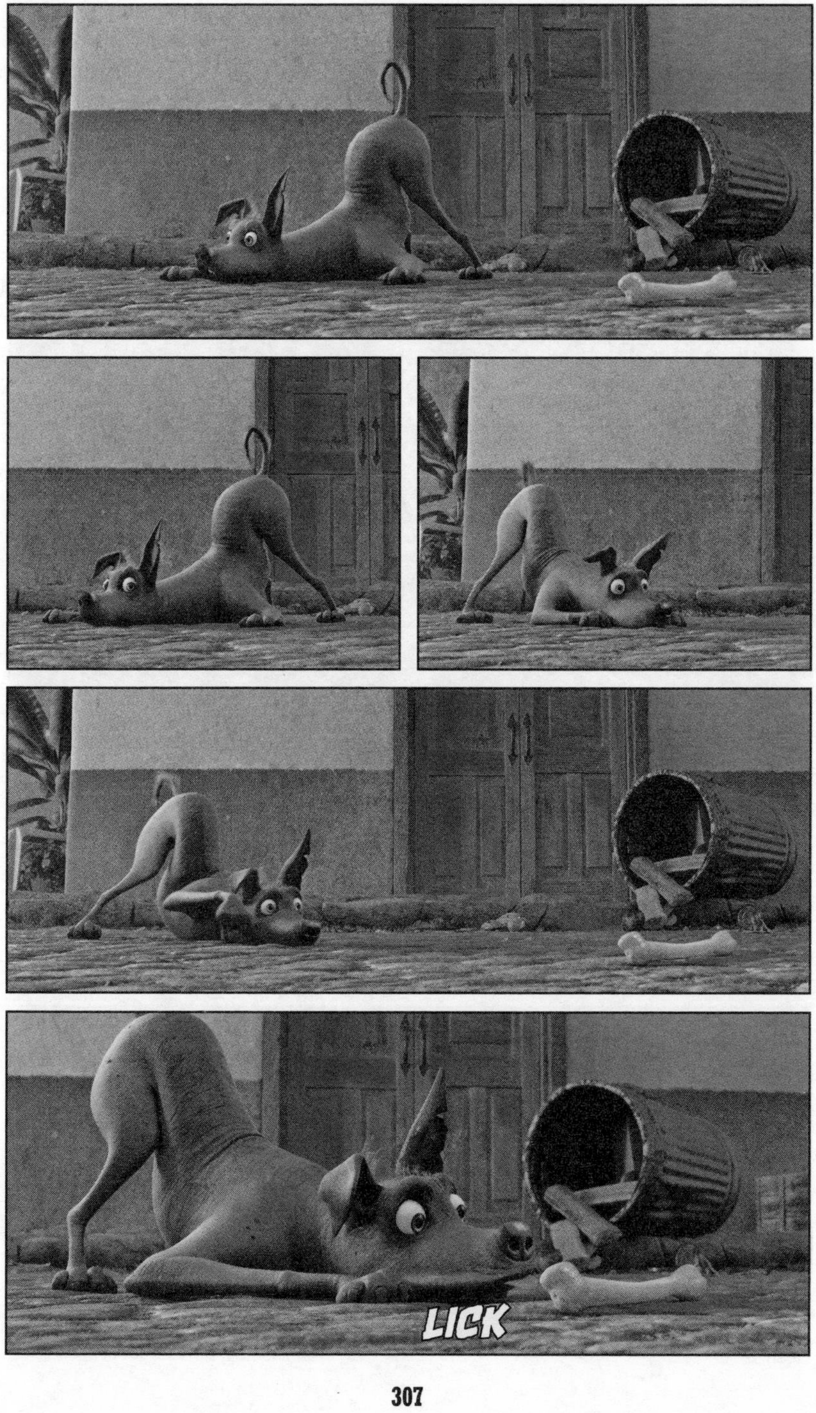
LICK

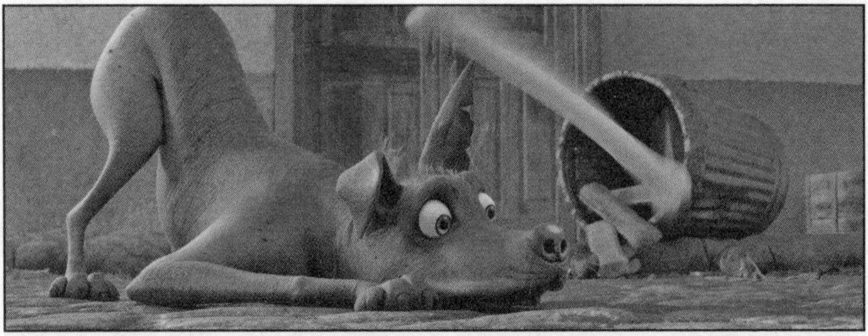
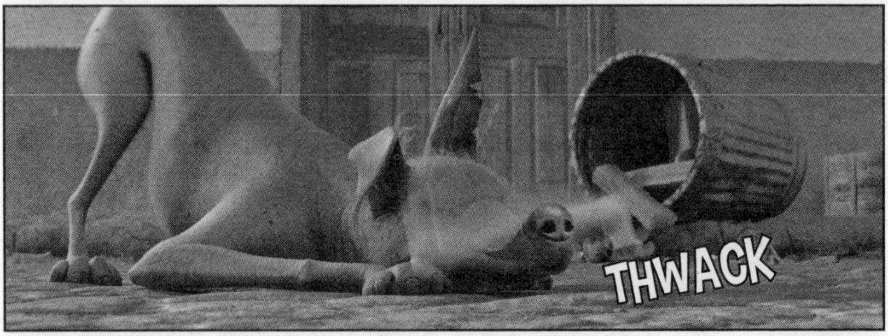
THWACK
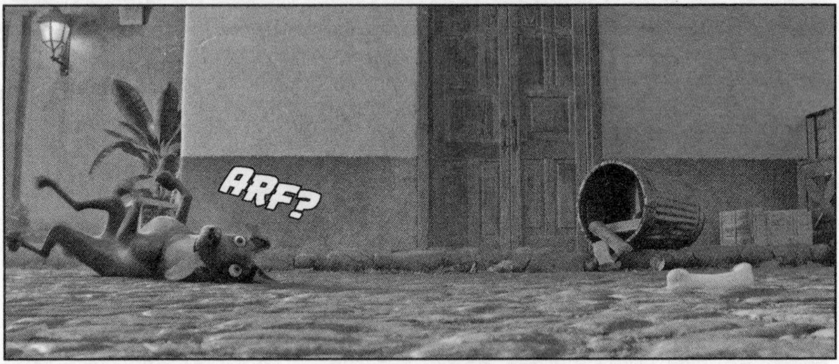
ARF?
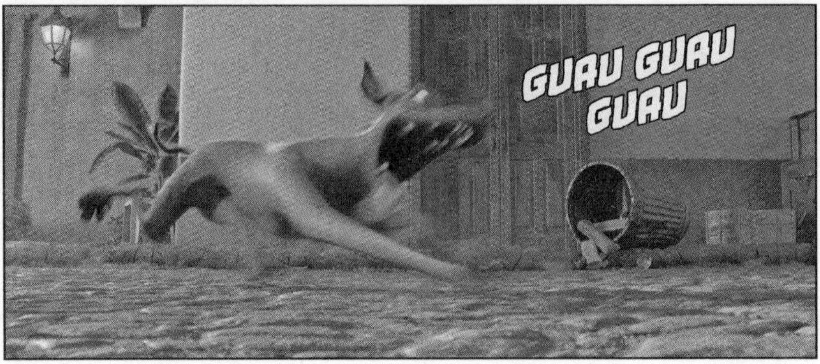
GUAU GUAU
GUAU

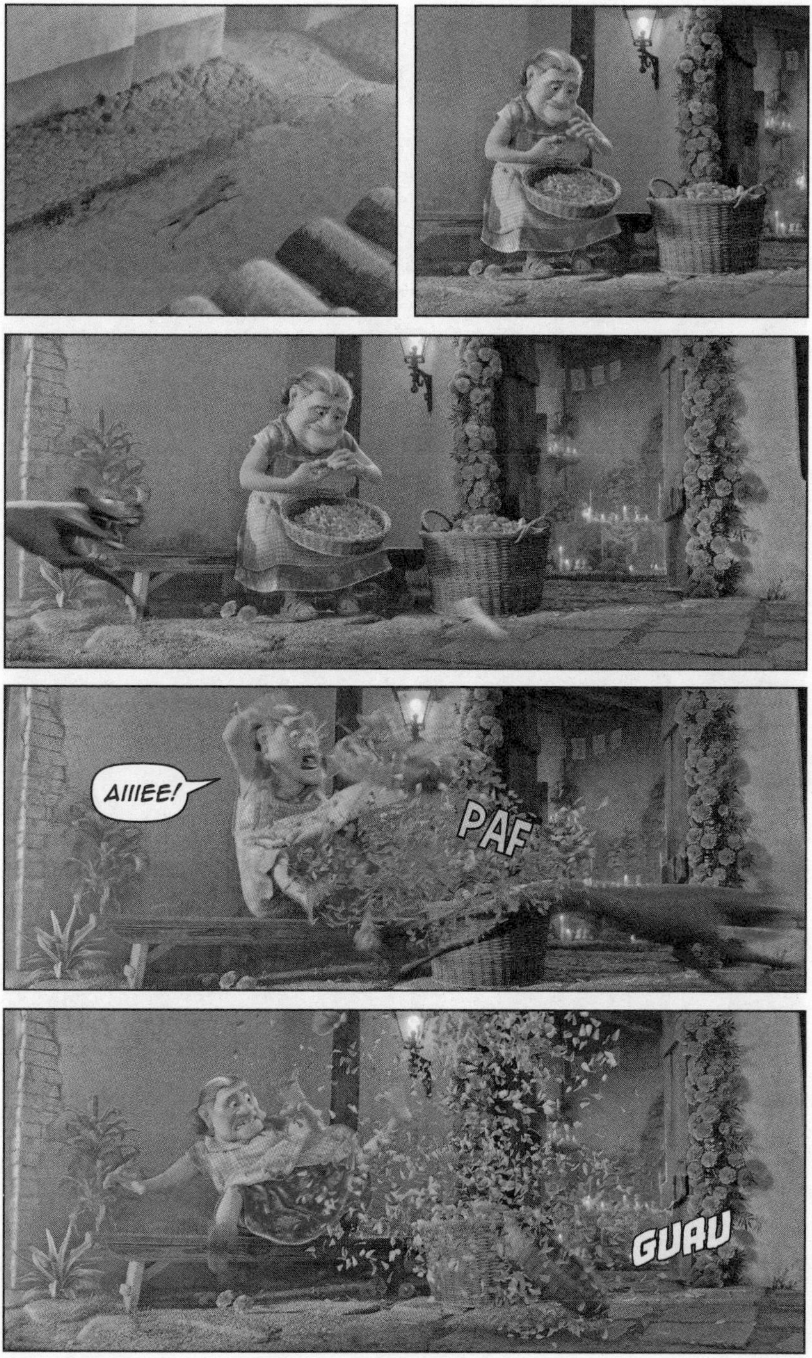
AIIIEE!
PAF
GUAU

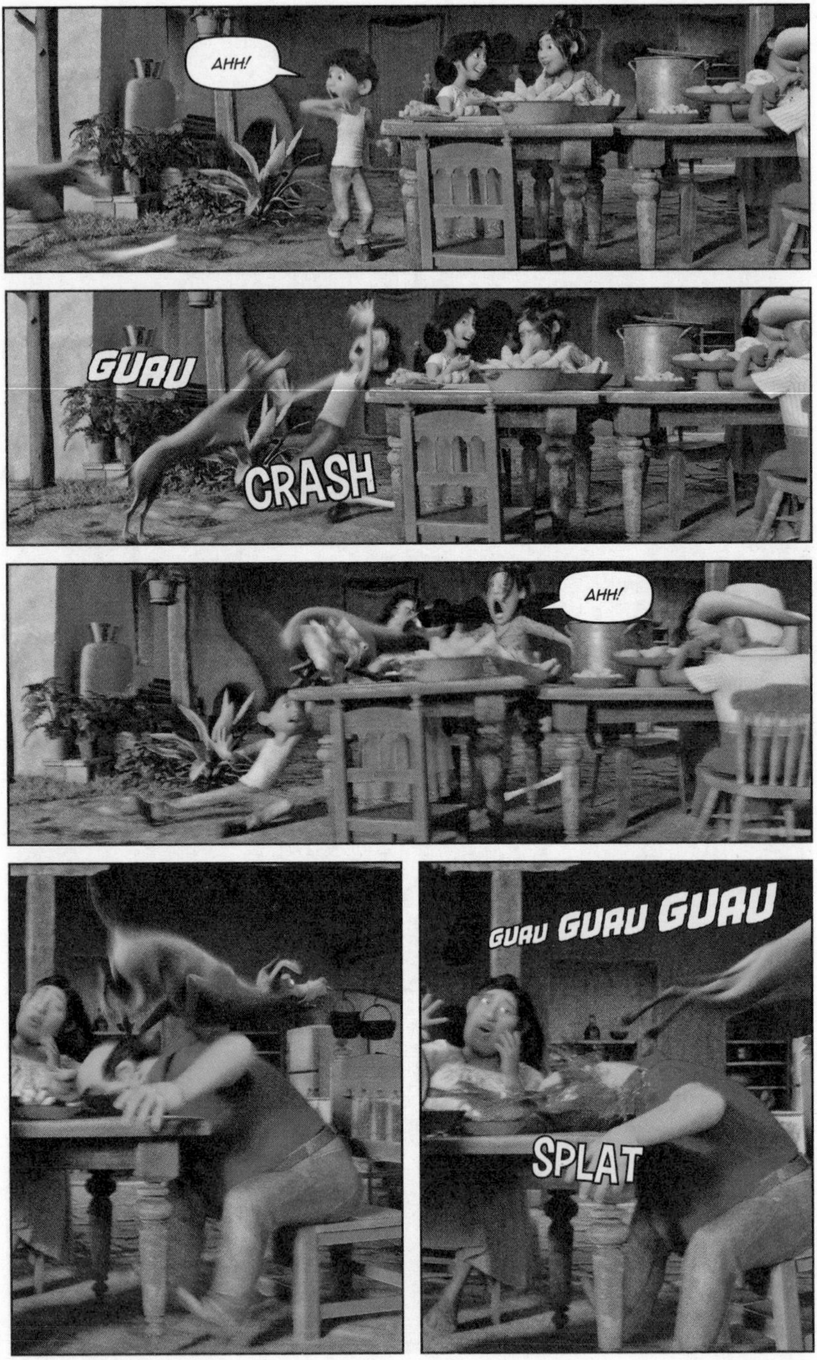
AHH!
GUAU
CRASH
AHH!
GUAU GUAU GUAU
SPLAT

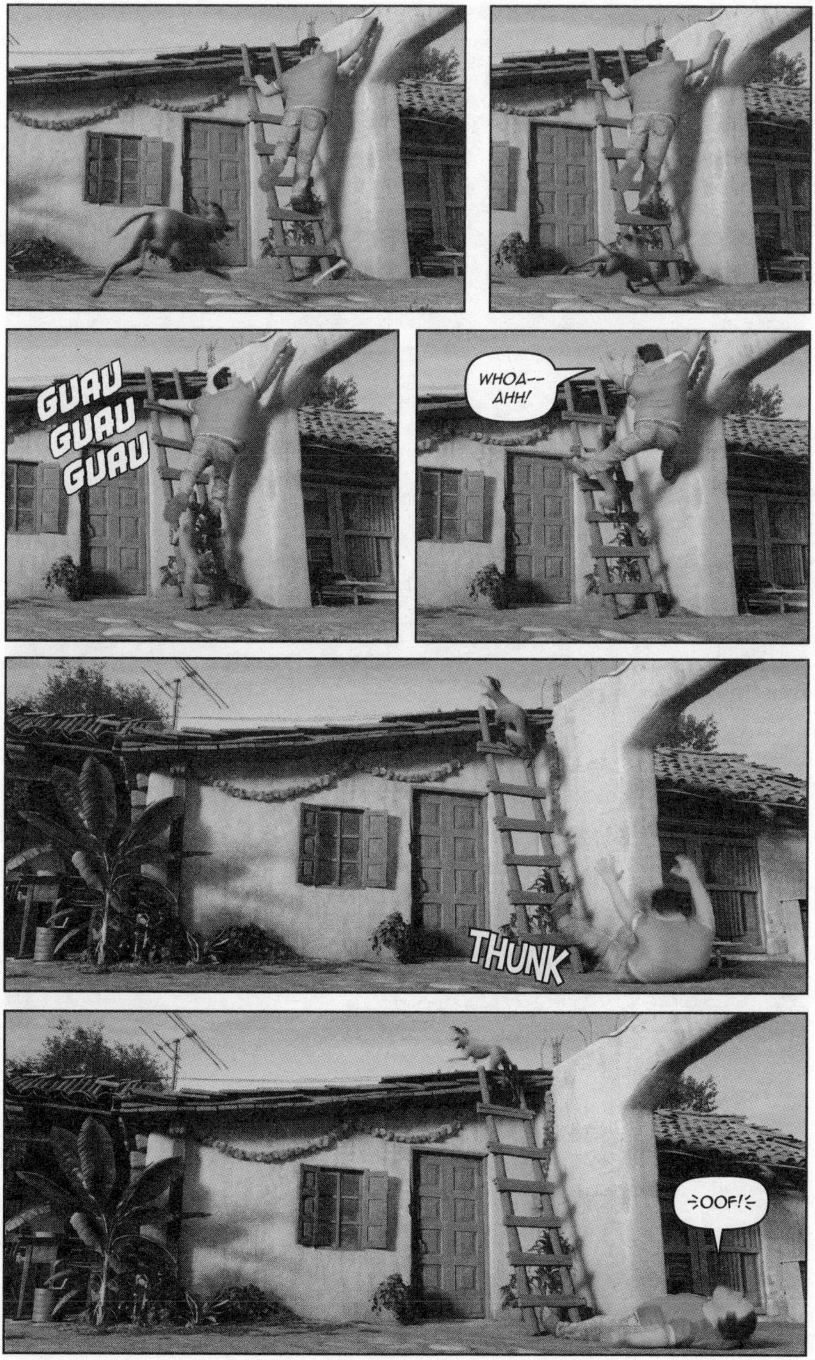
GUAU
GUAU
GUAU
WHOA--
AHH!
THUNK
OOF!

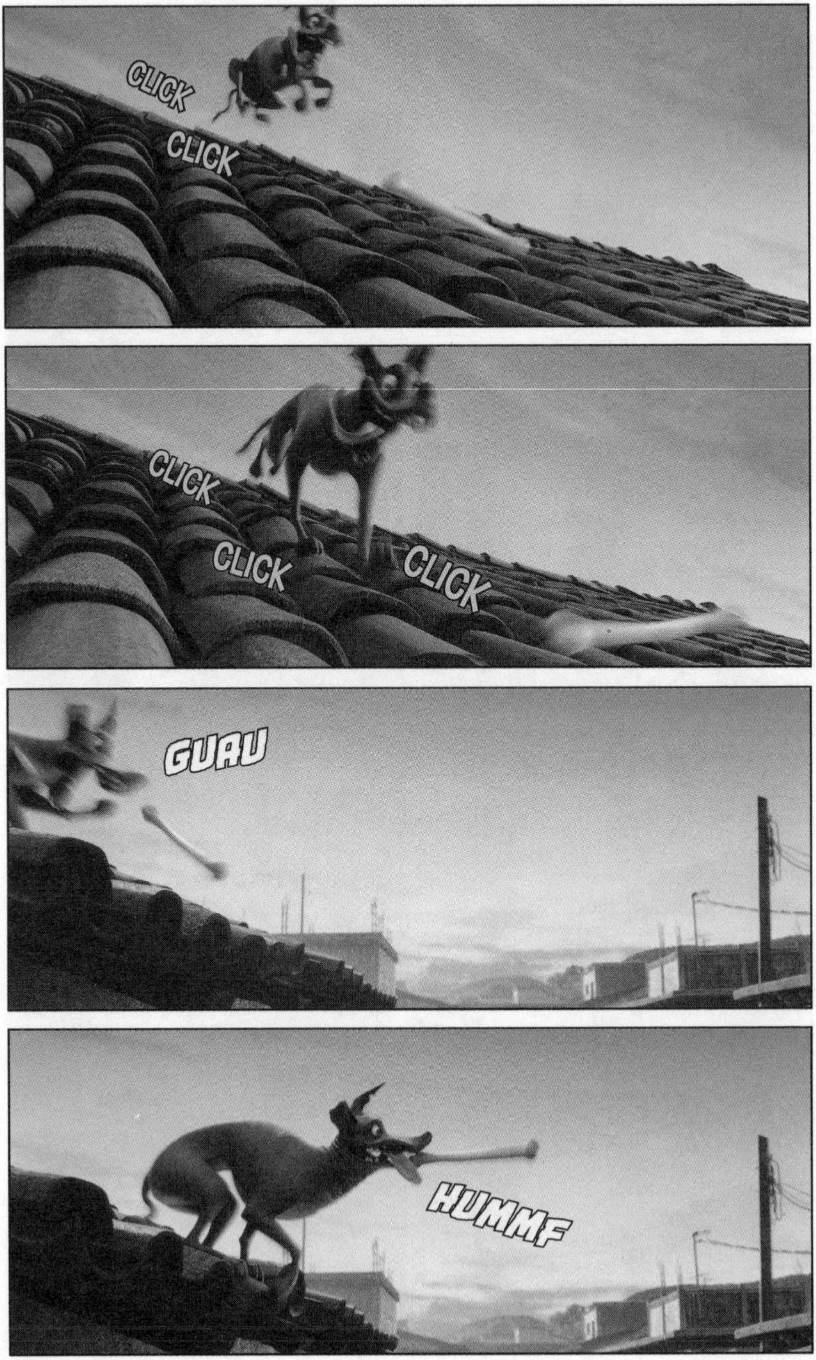
CLICK
CLICK
CLICK
CLICK
CLICK
GUAU
HUMMF

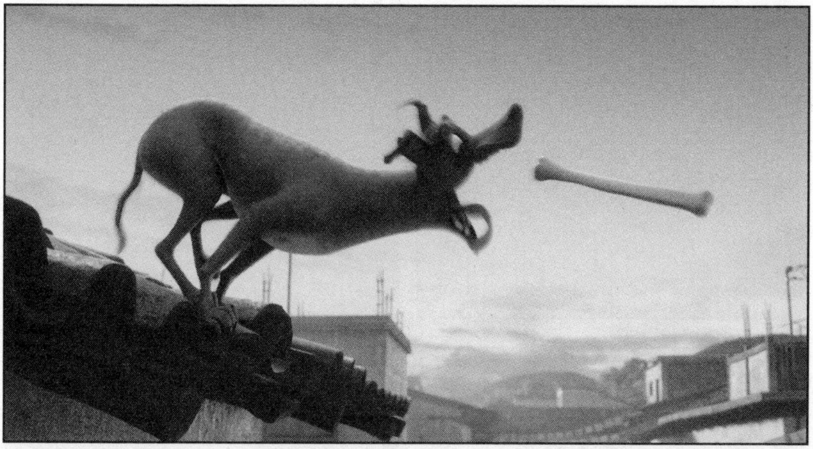

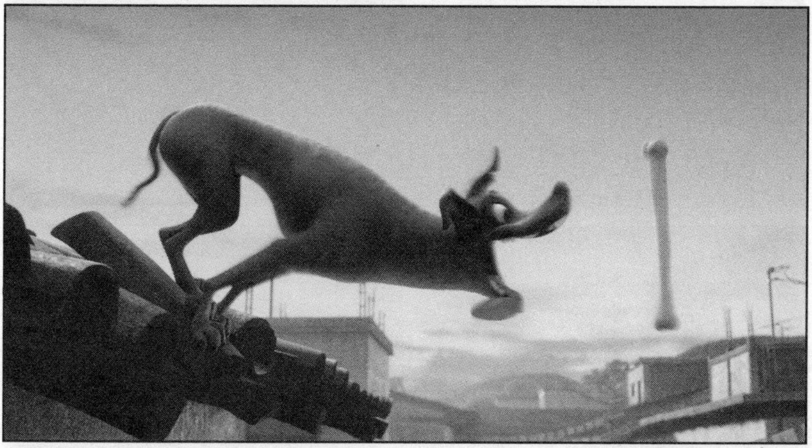

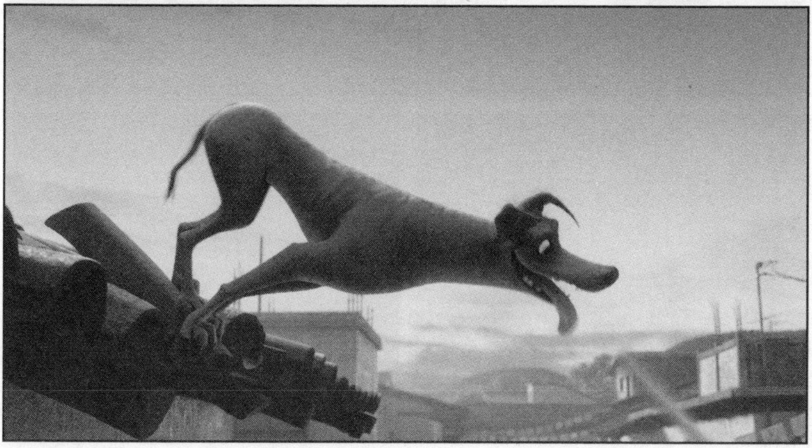

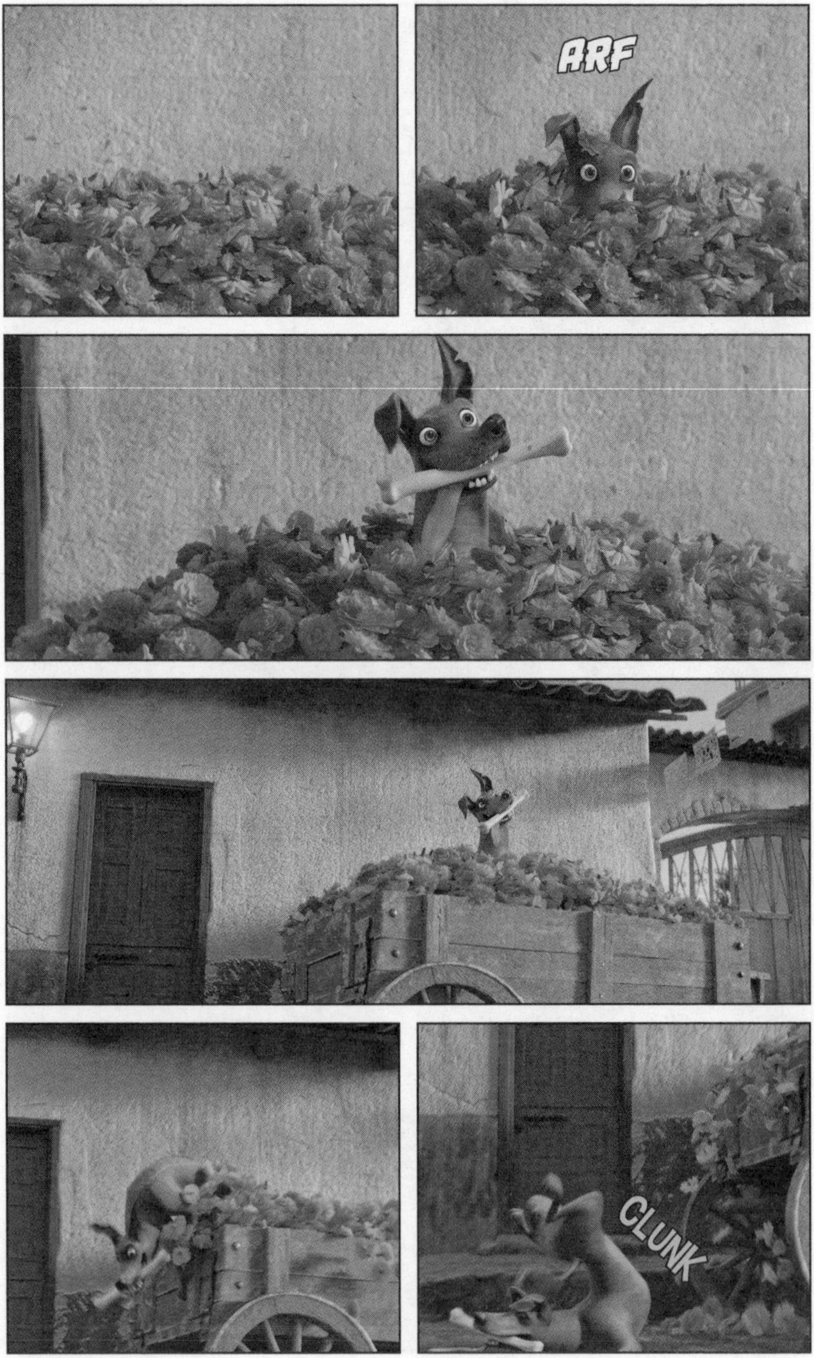
ARF
CLUNK

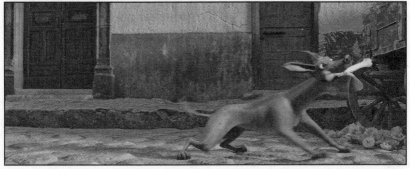

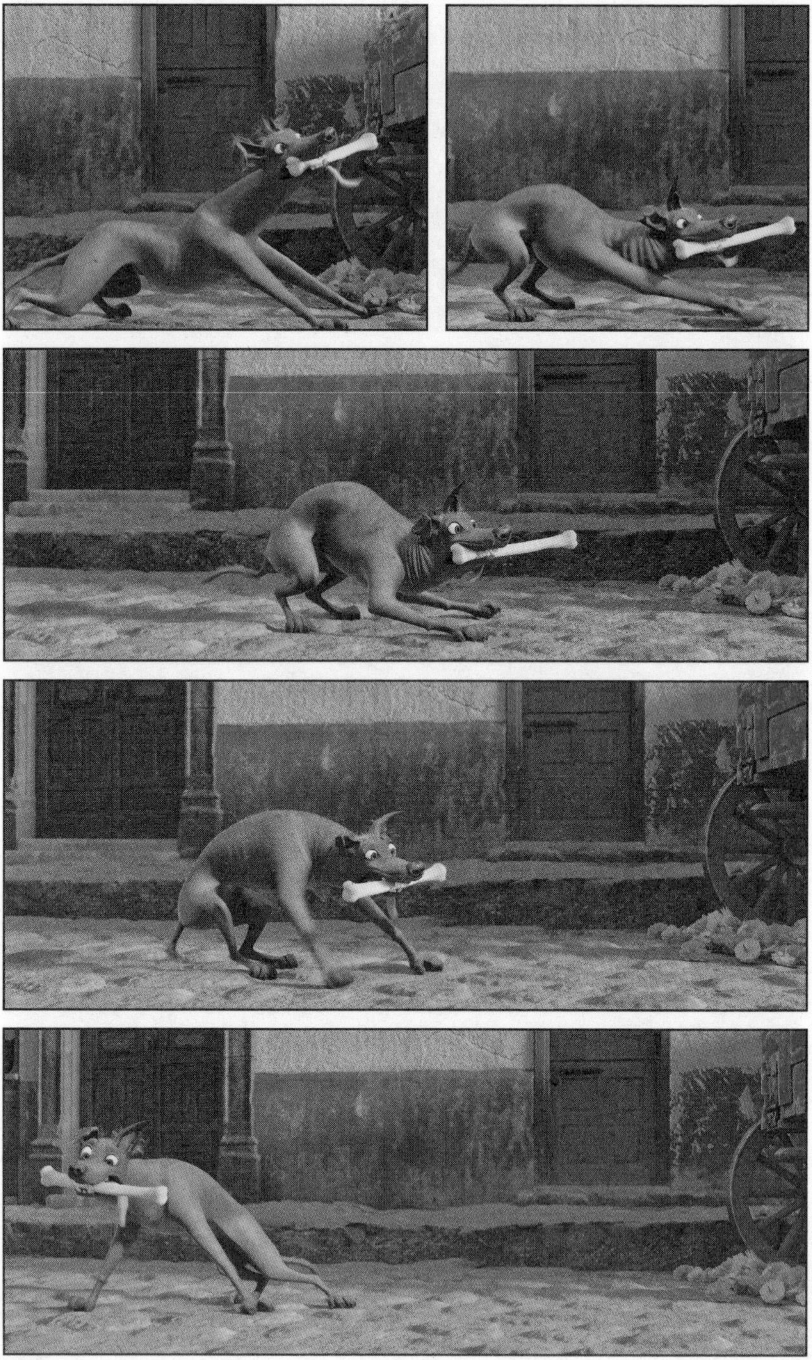

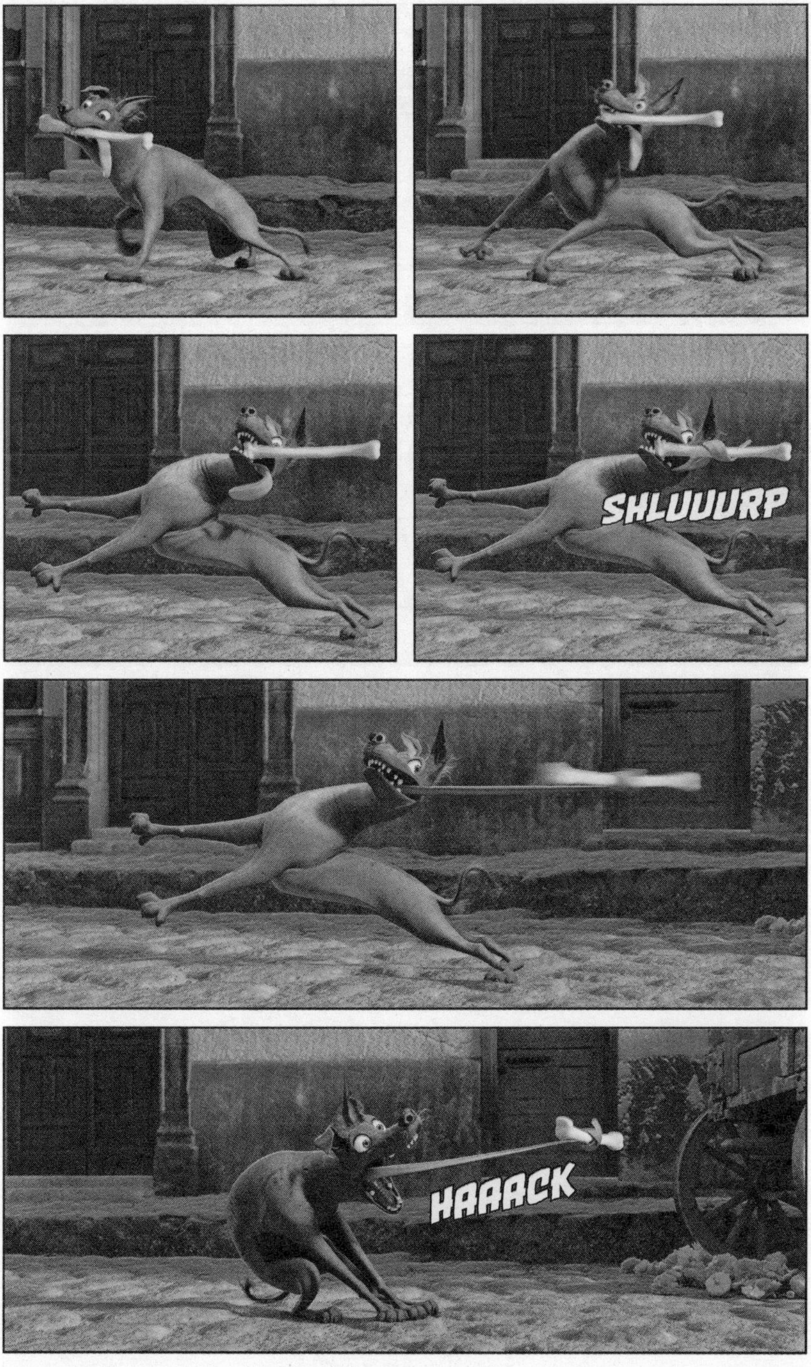
SHLUUURP
HAAACK

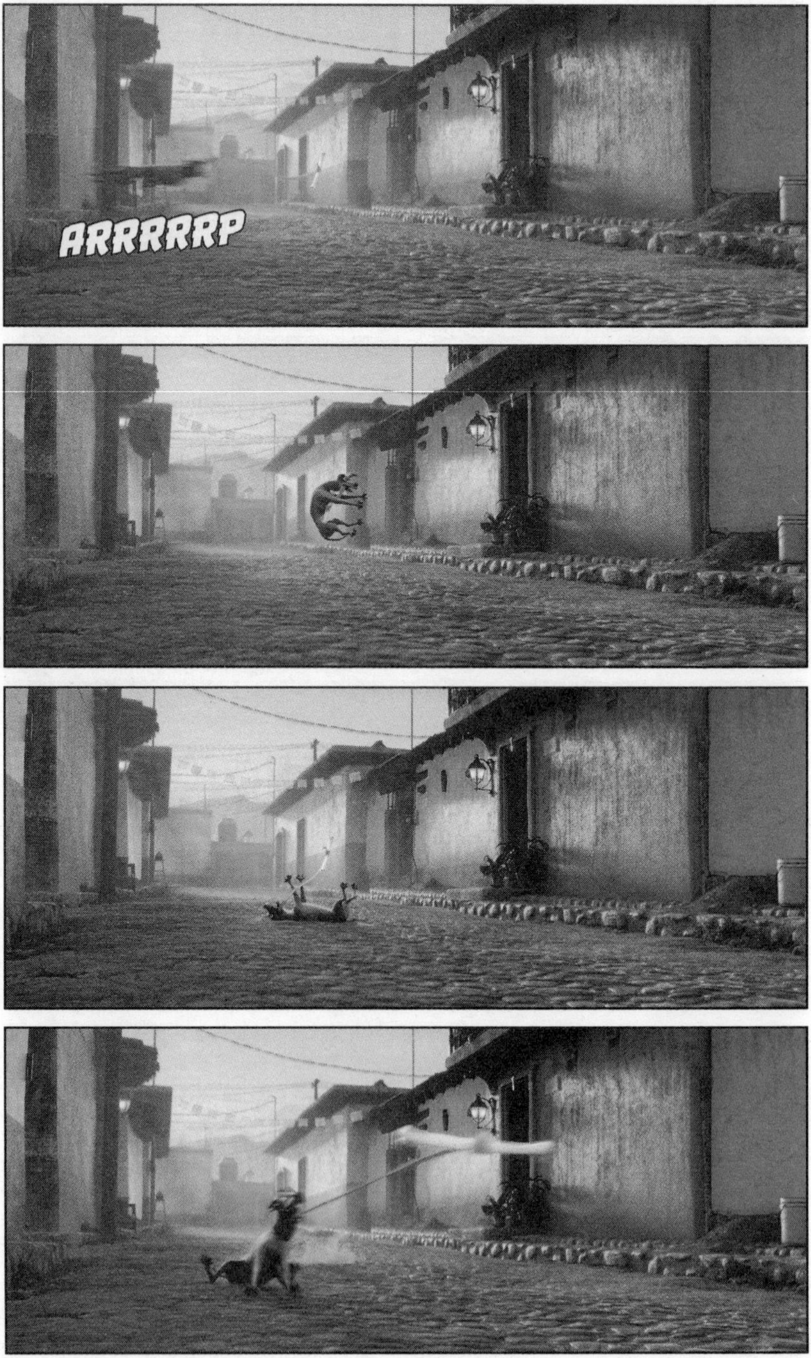
ARRRRRRP

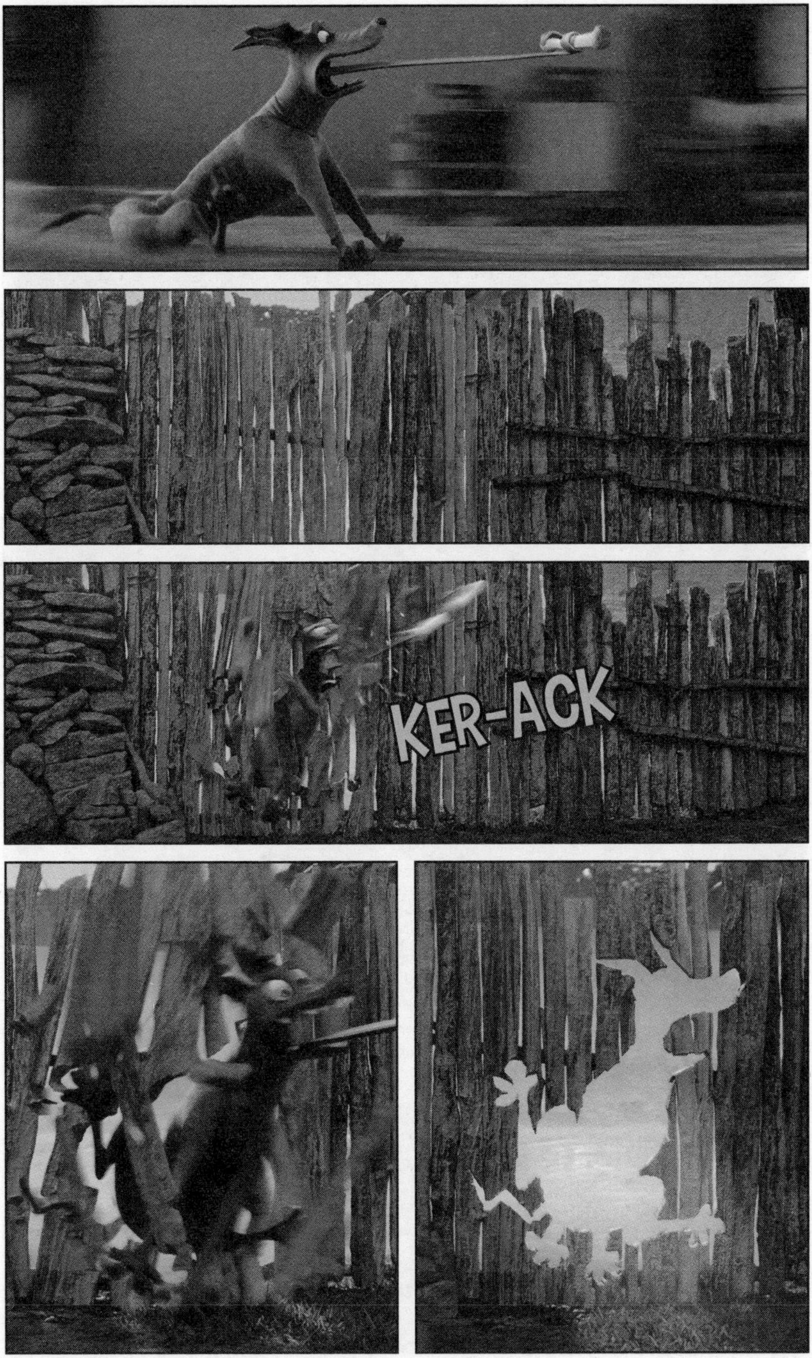
KER-ACK

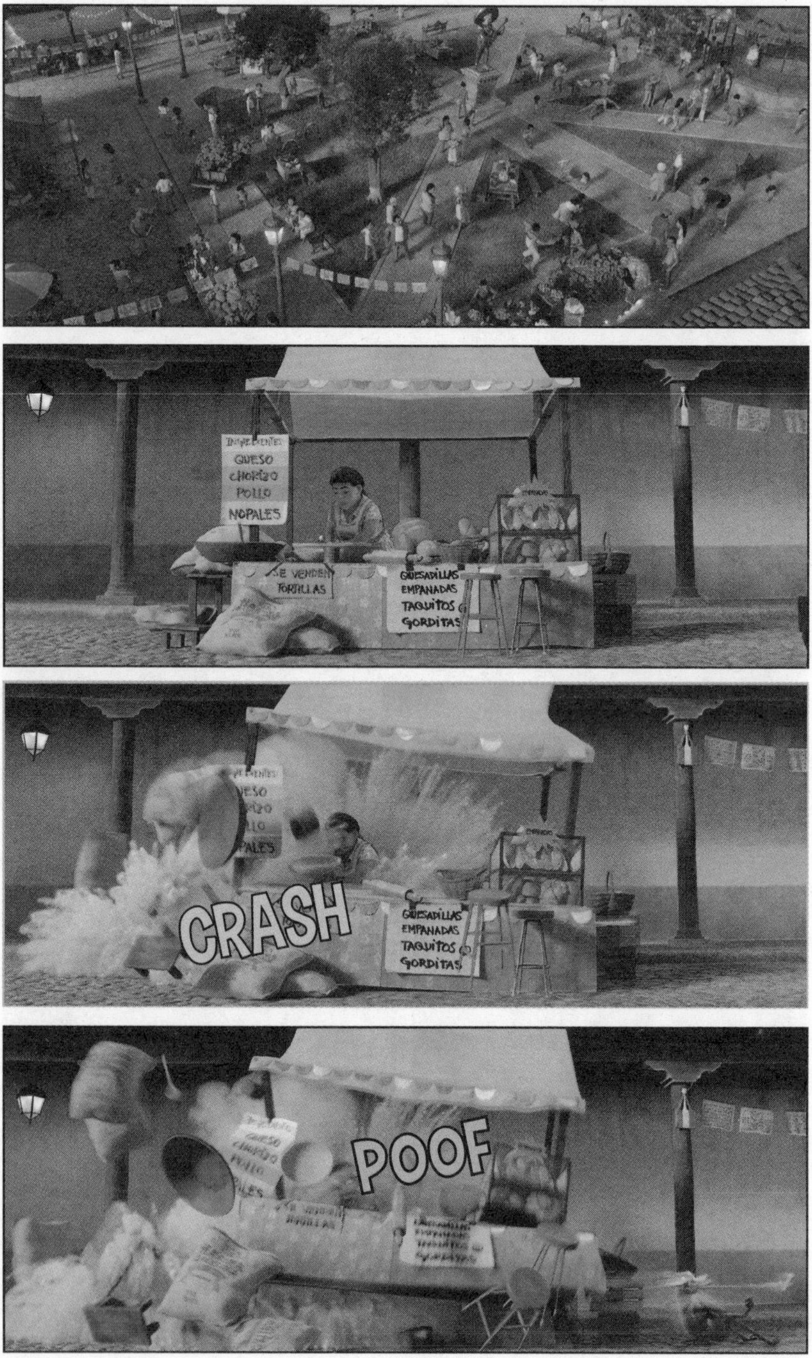
QUESO
CHORIZO
POLLO
NOPALES
SE VENDEN TORTILLAS
QUESADILLAS
EMPANADAS
TAQUITOS
GORDITAS
CRASH
POOF

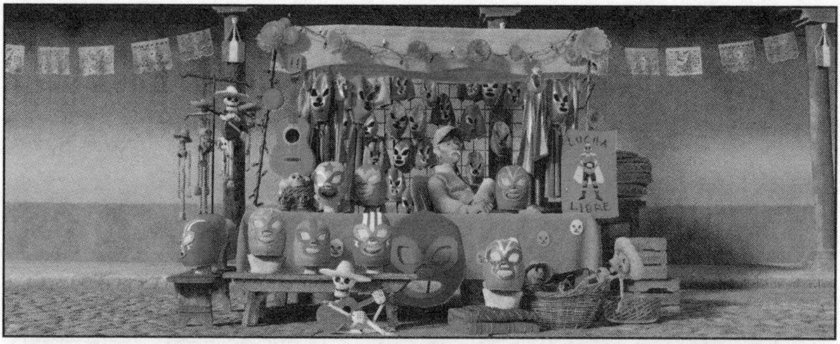
LUCHA
LIBRE

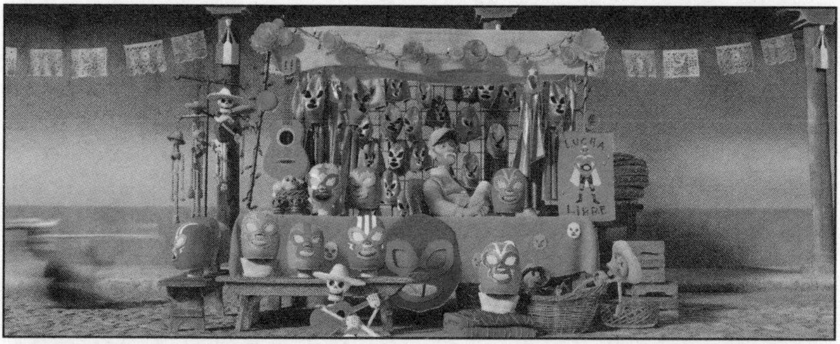
LUCHA
LIBRE

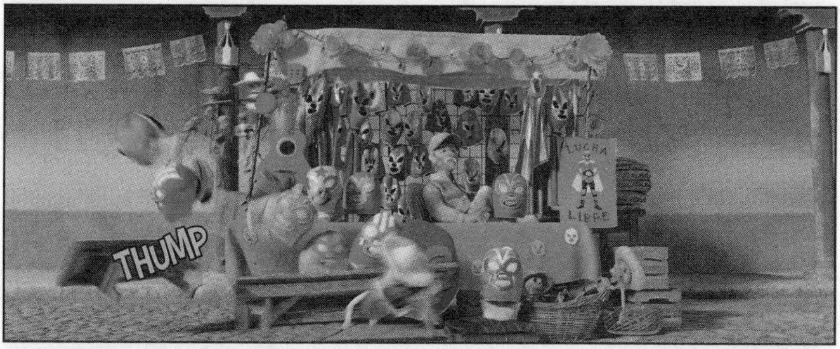
LUCHA
LIBRE
THUMP

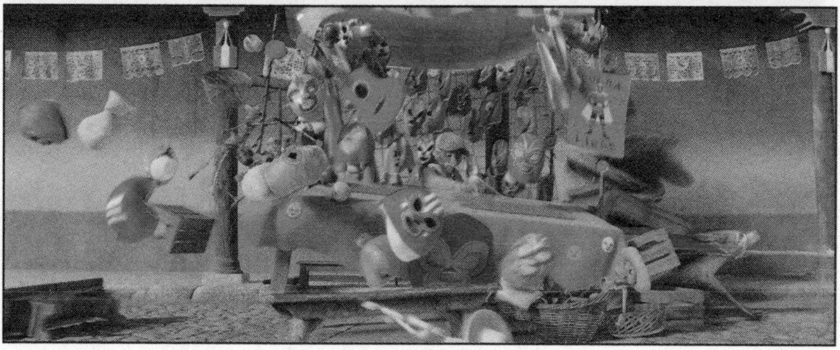

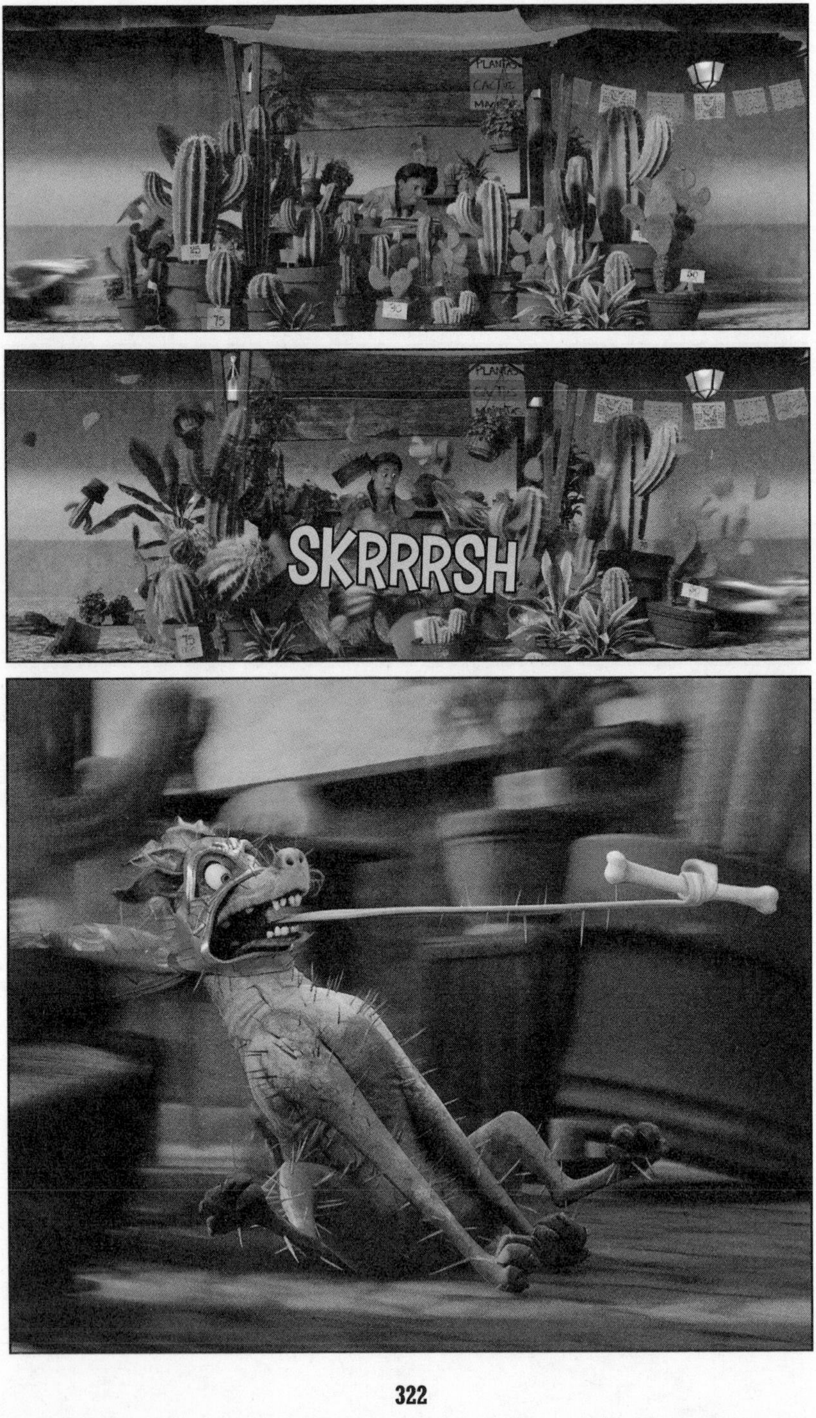
SKRRRSH

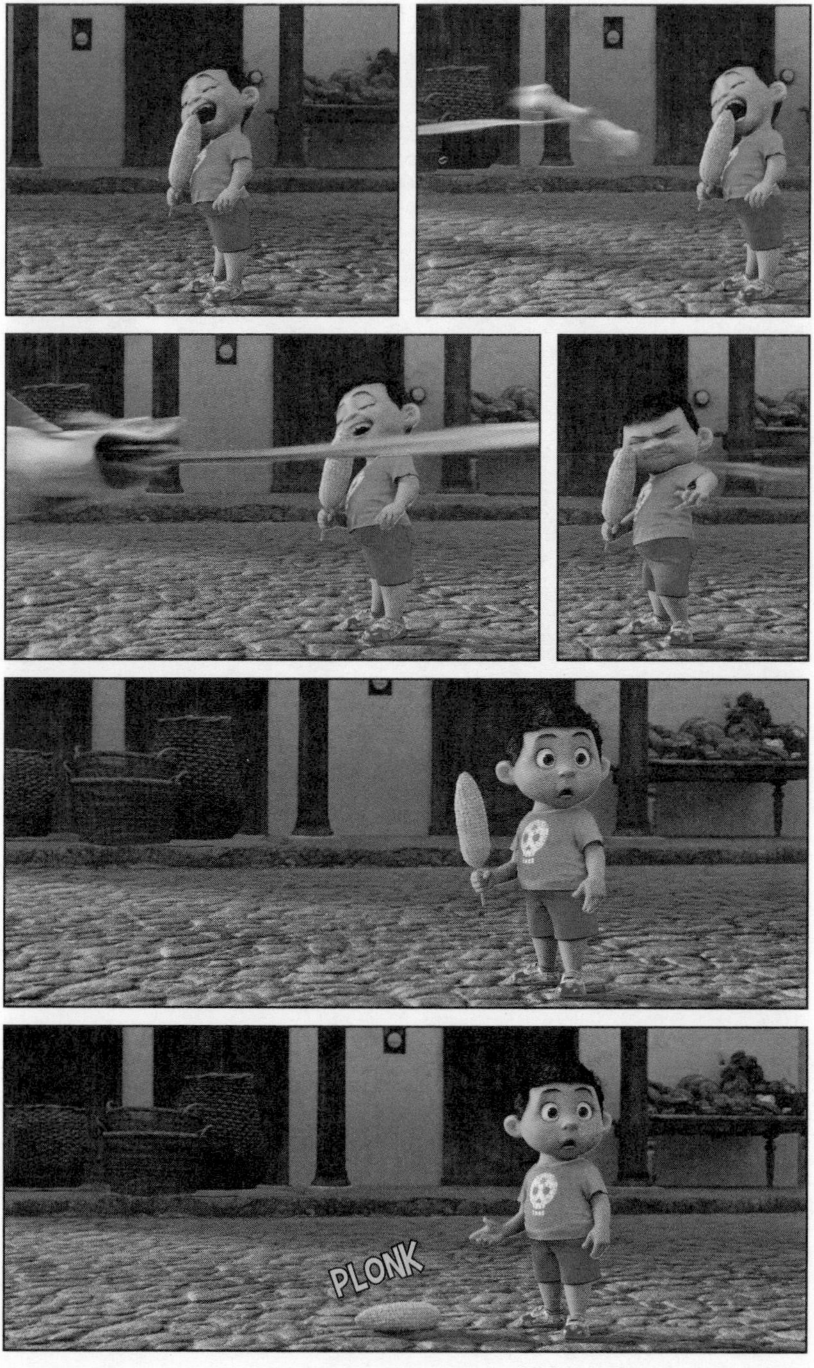
PLONK

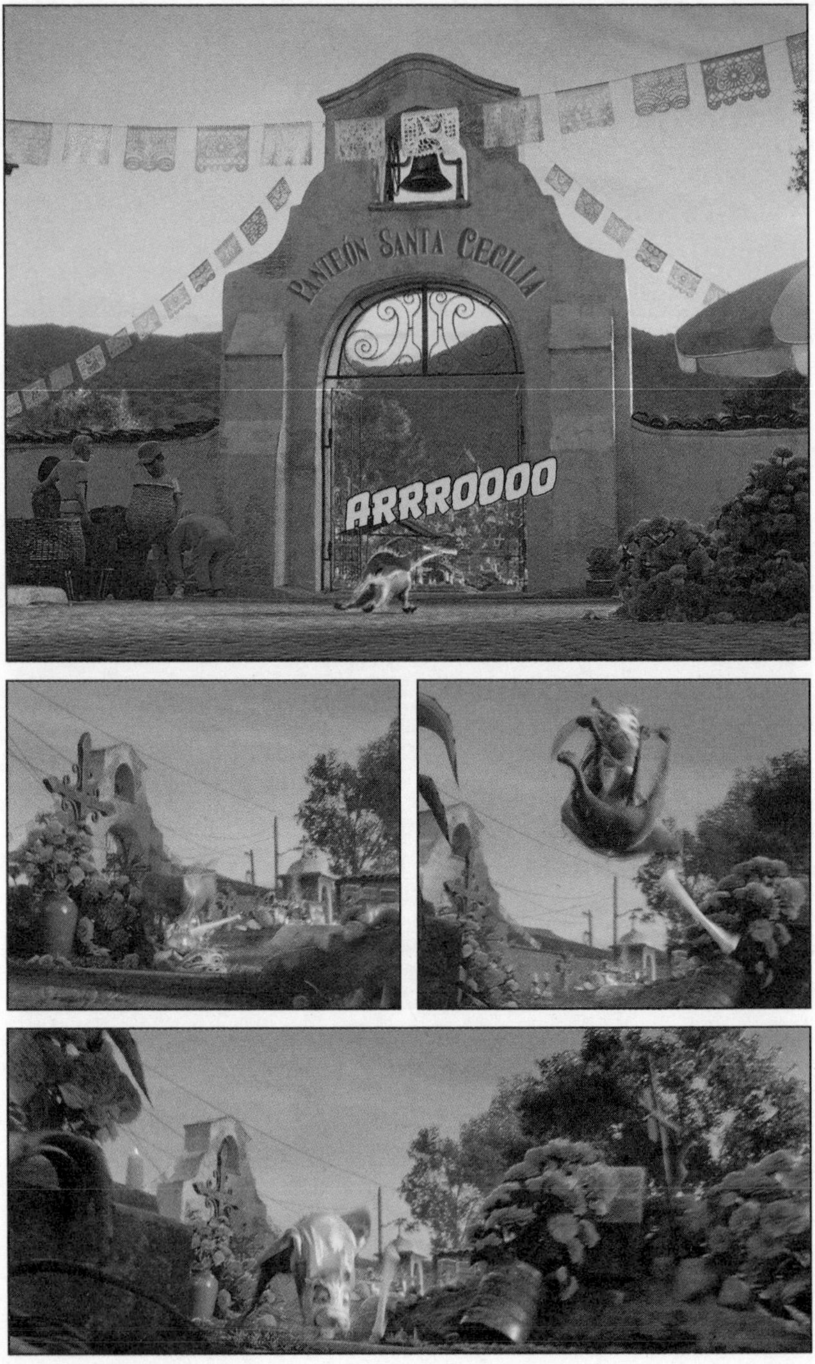
PANTEÓN SANTA CECILIA
ARRROOOO

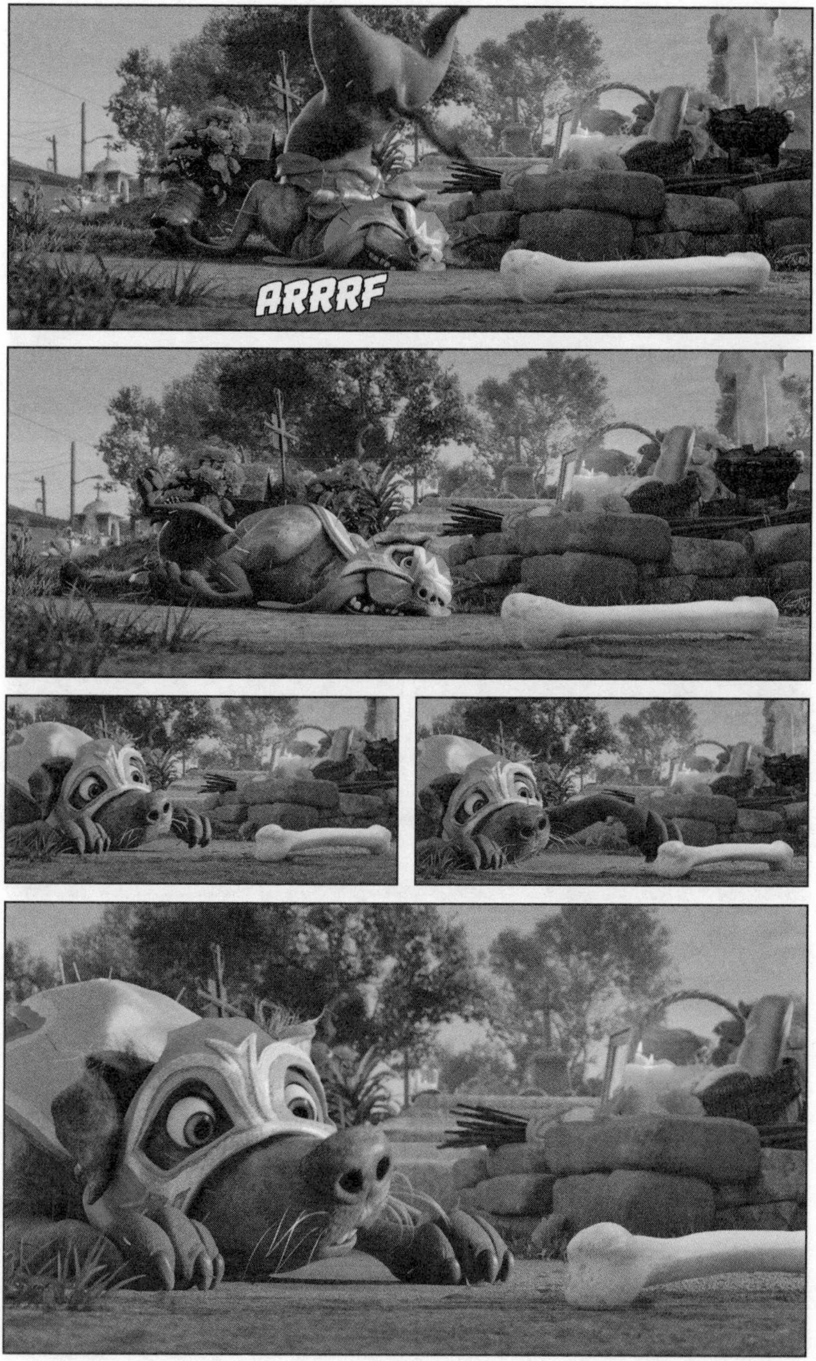
ARRRF

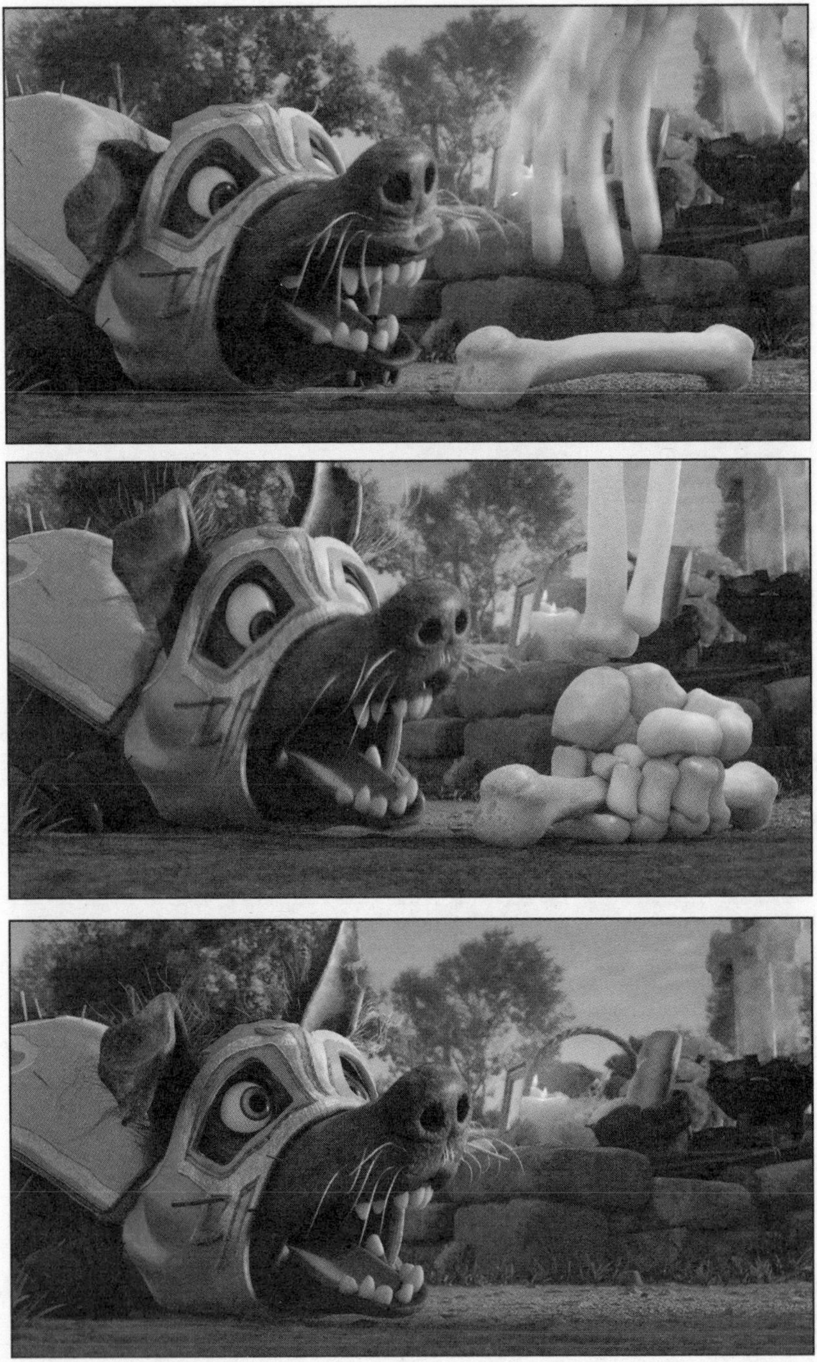

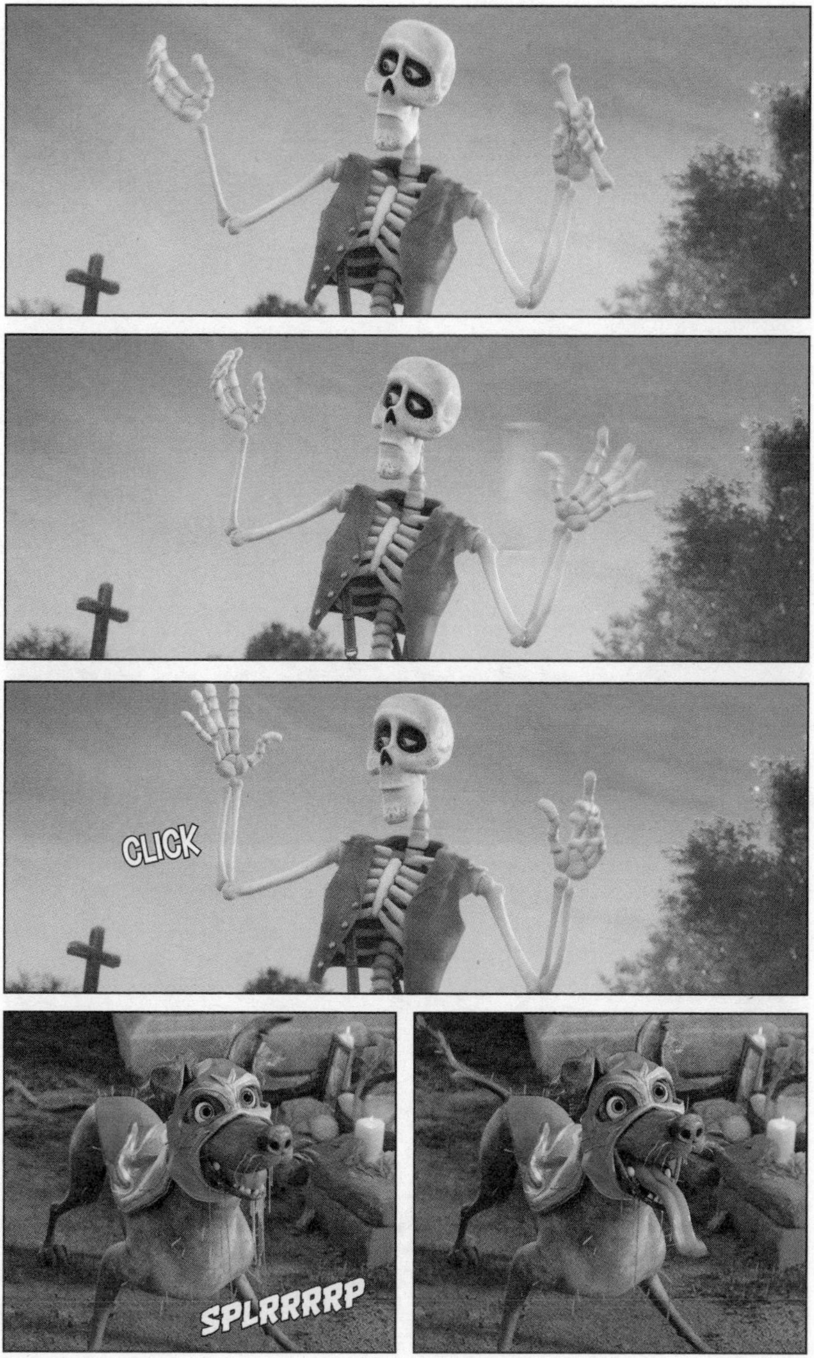
CLICK
SPLRRRRP

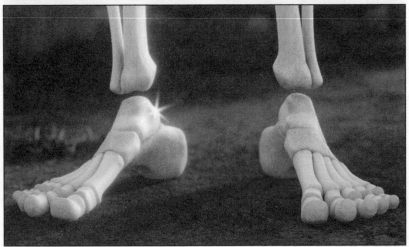

SHHLURP

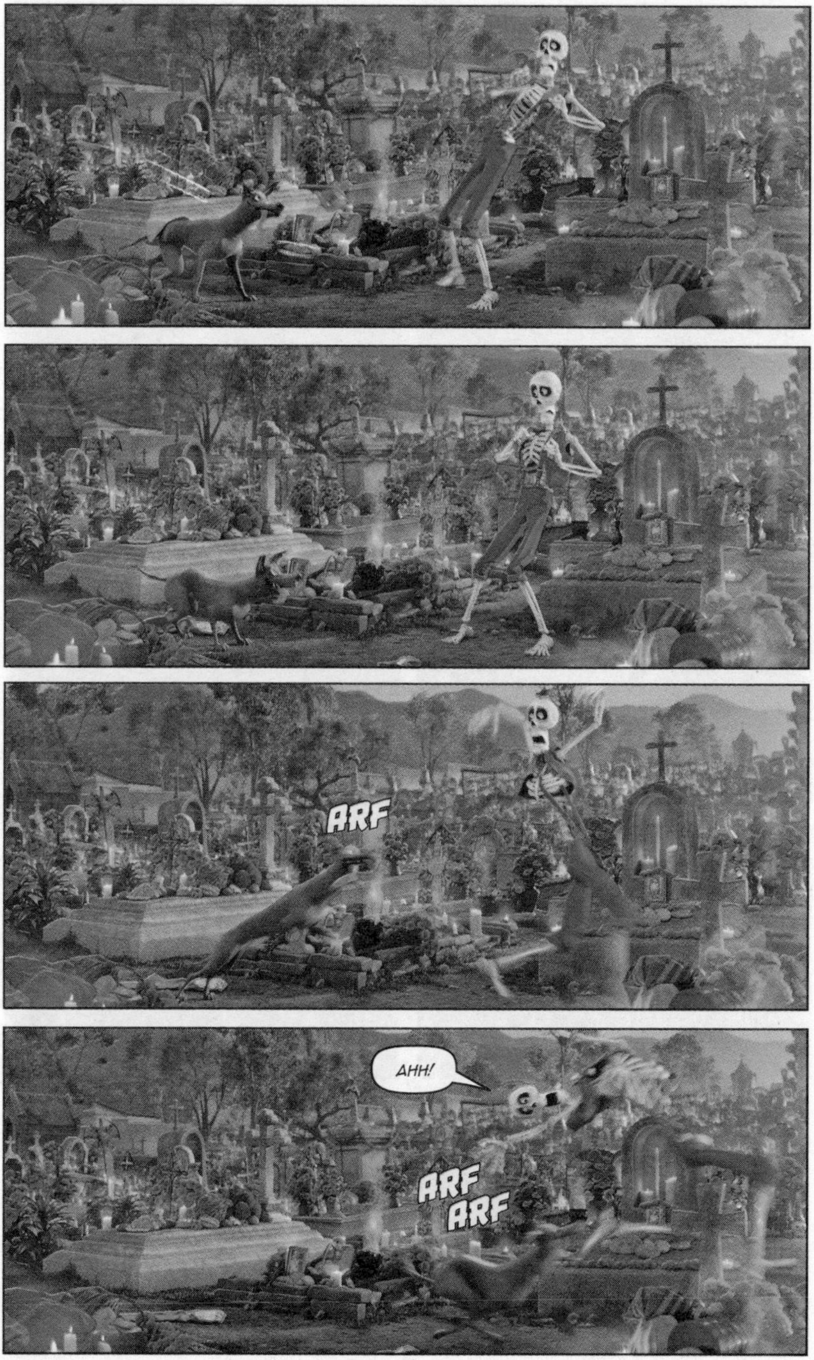
ARF
AHH!
ARF
ARF

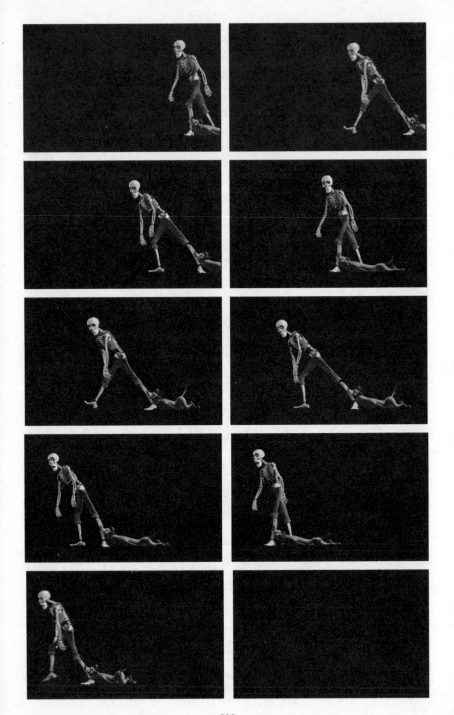